LISBON

LISBON

a novel by

VALERIE SHERWOOD

NAL BOOKS

NEW AMERICAN LIBRARY

A DIVISION OF PENGUIN BOOKS USA INC., NEW YORK

PUBLISHED IN CANADA BY
PENGUIN BOOKS CANADA LIMITED, MARKHAM, ONTARIO

Published simultaneously in Canada by Penguin Books Canada Limited

 NAL BOOKS TRADEMARK REG. U.S. PAT. OFF. AND FOREIGN COUNTRIES
REGISTERED TRADEMARK—MARCA REGISTRADA
HECHO EN DRESDEN, TN, U.S.A.

SIGNET, SIGNET CLASSIC, MENTOR, ONYX, PLUME, MERIDIAN and
NAL BOOKS are published in the United States by New American Library,
a division of Penguin Books USA Inc.,
1633 Broadway, New York, New York 10019,
in Canada by Penguin Books Canada Limited,
2801 John Street, Markham, Ontario L3R 1B4

Library of Congress Cataloging-in-Publication Data

Sherwood, Valerie.
    Lisbon : a novel / by Valerie Sherwood.
    p. cm.
    ISBN 0-453-00614-0
    I. Title.
    PS3569.H455L5   1989
    813'.54—dc20   89-3426
                                                               CIP

Designed by Leonard Telesca

First Printing, September, 1989

1 2 3 4 5 6 7 8 9

PRINTED IN THE UNITED STATES OF AMERICA

DEDICATION

To glamorous Fluffy, my beautiful long-haired Persian cat, Fluffy who came to us as a half-grown kitten, just fur and bone, so near starvation I feared the kitten would drop dead before managing to consume that first bowl of milk I proffered, Fluffy of the big green wondering eyes and enormous ruff and short white gloves and high white boots, with a snowy white waistcoat and an enormous burst of frosty white fur at the throat, the whole effect made more formal by a satiny black coat and big sweeping plumelike black tail, Fluffy the "sleeping beauty" who loves to dream the days away and play madly at night, affectionate Fluffy of the high sweet treble meow and soft gentle purr, to Fluffy who—for all that obviously aristocratic lineage—was set on a path of despair when first we met and who has won through to the lordly position of premier pet in our household, to Fluffy so obviously suited for a wandering life of "castle to castle," this book is affectionately dedicated.

Foreword

In the dim reaches of the past when thick ice sheets crept down over Europe and cold northern mists obscured the continent, there was facing the broad Atlantic a land of sunshine and flowers. And from time immemorial there was human habitation near the mouth of the great river that flowed down from the Pyrenees, striking southwestward to the sea.

From the cave dwellings of Stone Age peoples to the hilltop fortresses of the Lusitanians, men had lusted for this land and for this port. Warriors from many lands claimed it, fought for it, died for it. Phoenician traders took the port and sailed from it until the Romans drove them out. The Romans left their blood here—and their children. Here they imposed their Pax Romana until the land was wrested from them. Vandals, Visigoths, Iberians all held sway here. The invading Moors from Africa held it for almost half a thousand years and left behind their water wheels and their mosques. Then the crusaders swept through on their way elsewhere, and Christian rule returned to the ancient city.

When new lands were discovered beyond the western ocean, daring Portuguese traders developed a far-flung empire and built a glittering capital near the mouth of the river.

That river was the Tagus and the city was Lisbon, an opulent paradise of Western civilization.

But there was a snake in their Eden.

Offshore from this earthly paradise the ocean's blue depths concealed a sleeping monster that those who had sailed these waters on the black lateen-sailed Phoenician ships or the long Roman galleys or the magnificent vessels of the East India trade never knew existed.

Deep down offshore, concealed from view, lay the Gorringe Bank, a massive fault line, a deep rip in the earth's crust that stretched its licking tongue along the dark sea floor from the mouth of the Mediterranean out into the wild Atlantic. Along this fault gigantic submarine mountains had been pushed up where the colliding continental plates of Africa and Europe ground together, locked in a titanic struggle hidden from man's eyes by the blue depths of the Atlantic Ocean. Indeed had the Gorringe Bank risen from sea level instead of through mud and sediment from the deep sea floor, from its roots it would have reared up seven miles—more than a mile higher than Mount Everest.

And yet this awesome escarpment lay unseen beneath the waters, and the wooden sailing ships rode over it unsuspecting, never dreaming that forces that could trigger the destruction of the port from which they sailed lurked far below.

Looming before the city, offshore, slumbering, these submerged mountainous cliffs—for all their giant bulk—rested uneasily along the treacherous line of the fault. Inevitably, powered by the overwhelming pressure of colliding continents, one day a portion of that fault would move—and when it did, it would bring the city of Lisbon tumbling down.

Nothing lasts forever.

This is the story of Lisbon in the gallant last days of her Golden Era when she stood unmatched for wealth and beauty—and it is the story of the beautiful English girl whose fate was so strangely intertwined with the fate of the doomed city.

Her story began among the crags and fells and mists in the north of England, but we find her in Lisbon, where she has been for less than a fortnight. . . .

—Valerie Sherwood

BOOK I

Charlotte

1

Lisbon, Portugal, Summer 1739

In a little while the morning sunlight would pour down in a shower of gold upon Lisbon's pink palaces and tile-roofed mansions and magnificent churches—a golden shower even more extravagant and sparkling than the recent rain of gold and diamonds that had poured in from the Portuguese colony of Brazil, to fill Lisbon's coffers and make this gleaming city of light, set like a jewel into Europe's western coast, rich beyond the dreams of avarice.

But dawn was yet to break over the expensive houses of the fashionable Portas del Sol, high above the city. At the front door of one of the newer ones, a flat-fronted mansion of stone, a sleepy servant held a torch, and into its glow two horses came out of the darkness, led by another servant.

"But I thought you said there would be a coach?" came a warm female voice from just inside; then the striking young woman who was speaking came through the tall oak door. Charlotte would have been considered an exceptional beauty in any country—and especially in Portugal, where so many dark-skinned invaders over the centuries had left an olive tone imprinted upon the complexions of the people—with her bright golden hair, flaming red in the wavering light of the torch, and her fair peach-bloom complexion that spoke of English skies. She was four and twenty, of medium height, and there was spirit and poise in every line of her slender body. As she walked, she was pulling on a pair of peach kid gloves whose color blended with the handsome, tight-bodiced, full-skirted gown of apricot silk that swayed about her lissome small-boned figure.

"I have changed my mind," said the tall dark man who now brushed by her. He was booted and dressed for travel in a dark suit heavily ornamented with gold buttons and braid.

"But, Rowan, you know I do not ride!" A desperate note had crept into her voice.

Silhouetted against the light of the torch, he turned and swung around to face her. "Yes, I am aware that you are afraid of horses, Charlotte," he drawled. "And also of the reason," he added lazily.

A tremor went through Charlotte's slight frame. How unkind of Rowan to remind her that as a tiny child she had seen her father trampled to death by a pair of careening runaway horses! It was true enough that she had never since been able to rid herself of her fear of them.

"Then since you *are* aware of that, Rowan—" she began.

"Spare me the details," he cut in. "I have decided not to take you with me after all."

Charlotte stared up at the tall figure of her husband in disbelief. "But . . . but you woke me from a sound sleep not an hour ago and told me to dress, that we were leaving at once for Evora! You said—"

"Never mind what I said." His tone was crisp. "I have changed my mind. I will take João with me and leave Vasco to look after you." He frowned. "This mission is too important to drag a woman along."

As he moved toward the saddled horse, the torchlight flickered over his dark face as she stared at him, trying to understand. His moods had been always mercurial, but it seemed to her that ever since their arrival in Lisbon, Rowan had behaved like a madman, changing his mind abruptly with every wind that blew, out at all hours himself, yet insisting that she keep to the house. She was aware—for he had told her so less than an hour ago when he had shaken her awake in the darkness of her bed-chamber—of the urgency of his projected meeting. As she was pulling on her clothes, she had surmised that this must be the reason behind Rowan's wildly shifting moods—and indeed the reason for their hurried trip to Portugal. Rowan was in London so much, away from her. How could she know what intrigues he might be mixed up in?

Behind her now in the wide doorway a new face loomed, round and indignant and wearing a servant's ruffled cap. She was grumbling audibly and her muttered words came over Charlotte's shoulder. "Why did you wake Mistress Charlotte if you wasn't taking her with you?"

Charlotte averted a clash between Rowan and the servant girl with a swift, "Be silent, Wend." And turned again to face her husband, who had been eager enough to "drag a woman along" an hour ago. "I am wondering the same thing, Rowan. Why *did* you change your mind about taking me with you?"

The tall man studied her for a few moments before he spoke. Then abruptly he laughed.

"Perhaps I decided that I did not desire your company after all, Charlotte. But at least you shall have the privilege of watching me ride away." He vaulted to the saddle, moving with the easy grace of the born horseman. "I leave you to imagine why."

Bright spots of color flamed Charlotte's cheeks.

"No, I do *not* know why!" she flashed. "And I pray that before you leave you will be good enough to tell me!"

But the heavy lids had closed halfway down like shutters over those consuming dark eyes. "We will not quarrel before the servants, Charlotte," he warned her silkily. "And now that you have been so amiable as to dress to see me off in the dawn, you may tell me good-bye."

"Good-bye, Rowan." Charlotte's voice was wooden. He had moments of great tenderness, this man she had married, but they were overshadowed by moments like these. And worse.

"Oh, just one more thing." He had signaled to João but now reined up in the very act of riding away. "You are not to roam around Lisbon, Charlotte. I expect you to stay in the house until I return."

Charlotte felt her teeth clench. "And when will that be?"

He shrugged. "At least a week. Do not expect me before that—I may be longer." Without waiting for a response from his wife, who had gone pale with anger, he rode away, clattering over the cobbles. João, now mounted, followed him.

Charlotte would have been amazed at what her husband was thinking:

The lying wench! Smiling at me guilelessly with those melting violet eyes that always shake my resolve. How do I know what she has heard, what she may already be planning? Well, she will find me ready!

And then he thought of how tempting she had looked in bed when he had roused her but an hour ago, of how he had almost postponed this venture just so that he might join her in that big square bed and feel her wondrous softness against his hard body and savor her sweetness. He was lost in a vision of satin thighs and lacy ruffles and passion that always overcame him at her touch.

She was a witch, she held him in thrall!

He groaned into the darkness, and behind him, riding silently, João, who spoke no English, wondered what the altercation had been about.

From the doorway Charlotte watched the two of them disappear into the darkness. She waited until the sound of their hoofbeats faded away. Then she turned to Wend, who was tugging at her sleeve, entreating her to come back inside and get some sleep.

"I do not know whether to laugh or cry!" Charlotte exploded in exasperation. "Apparently Rowan got me up only to insult me!"

"He does act strange, sure enough," agreed Wend with an apprehensive look back over her shoulder as she pulled her mistress inside and shut the front door firmly behind her. And when Charlotte made no comment, "I mean, worse that usual." She sighed.

In the darkness, Charlotte was biting her lips, her mind swirling with rebellious thoughts.

"Wend, I will not be ruled by him any longer!" she burst out. "He left me alone for months on end, and then suddenly appeared, and the moment he arrived, told me to pack, that we were off to Portugal!"

"I well remember." Wend's rueful voice carried the memory of how, having packed with dizzying speed and leaving behind half the things they would need, they had departed at once for the coast and embarked on the first ship bound for Lisbon.

This was not Charlotte's first visit to Portugal. But it had been a long time since the dark domineering man she had married had deigned to take her with him anywhere. And of late he had left her alone to endure the rigors of winter in the north of England.

"I do not understand why Rowan brought me along at all," she wailed. "We have been here almost a fortnight, and yesterday was the first time he has let me out of the house!"

Wend gave a commiserating nod that set her cap askew on the other side. She was of the firm opinion that the master was entirely mad. Kind, considerate Mistress Charlotte didn't deserve such a husband! Wend had always been fiercely loyal to her young mistress.

"And yesterday at dinner!" Charlotte's voice trailed off. She supposed she should not be discussing her husband with Wend, even though she and Wend were so close. But what had happened at dinner had alarmed her.

When they had first arrived in Lisbon, Rowan had found them accommodations at an inn on the outskirts. Charlotte had been impatient to go down into the town, but Rowan had been adamant and she had not wanted to cross him. And after all, suppose she *did* go into the town alone and someone insulted her? Like as not, Rowan would seek the fellow out and run him through—and if he did, the authorities might remember the last time Rowan Keynes and his young bride had visited Lisbon and what had happened then. . . . No, she could not chance it.

But a week later, when Rowan had moved her to this handsome house in the Portas del Sol, Charlotte had walked through the large high-ceilinged rooms with a springy step. And today, when he had taken her out in style in a hired coach, visiting her favorite places, buying her things, making a point of being charming, she had cherished hopes that Lisbon had worked its magic and things could be all right between them again.

But then in the main square Rowan had run across a friend from London—one of his gaming-hell friends, Charlotte suspected, for she had never met him. At first Rowan had displayed his usual unwarranted jealousy of anyone who noticed her, giving his friend surly looks. Only when Charlotte had shown a distaste for the man had Rowan relaxed. And then at dinner she had said something to displease him and Rowan had jumped up and announced that he was taking her home—like a bad child in disgrace.

They did not speak all the way to the Portas del Sol.

Still smoldering when they reached her bedchamber, Charlotte told Rowan curtly that she had a headache. At which point he whirled her about to face him.

"I still do not have my apology, Charlotte," he said sternly.

"Nor will you get one!" she flashed. "For none is due!"

For a moment she thought he was going to strike her, but he did not. He stood there hunched over, glowering at her. Then, with a suddenness that astonished her, he seized her and fell with her to the bed, and while she struggled, he ripped every shred of clothing from her body.

Panting and naked, she lay beneath him, surrounded by the ruins of her pale gold gown and the torn lace and cambric of her undergarments.

"Rowan—" she protested, but his mouth crushed down on hers in a suffocating kiss that made speech impossible. She felt his long body move and shift above her own, felt his strong masculinity penetrate her like a spear—and wanted to weep.

This is not the way it should be between a man and a

woman, she thought, confused, *this violent lovemaking without tenderness.* As if in contempt, his body seemed to rasp against her own, making her cringe inwardly even as against her will the inexorable thrusting of his strong masculinity roused her to passions deep within. Torn by conflicting emotions, she felt her pliant femininity respond with a shudder to his tumultuous assault. This was lust, she told herself dully, and knew shame at her body's betrayal even as her senses were lifted and swirled and plunged down into a mindless sea of shivering guilty pleasure. Guilty because she felt shattered by his harsh taking.

Never call it love, she thought bitterly, trying to choke back the moans that rose unbidden in her throat. *For there is no love between us. Only this animal passion that seems to flare up and devour us in its hot flame.*

And then the climax of her own passions overcame her, sending her hurtling over the brink, over the edge of the world, until she fell back exhausted, drained.

Her cheeks were wet with tears when at last Rowan withdrew from her, rising on his arms and staring down into her sad face, cheeks glistening with tears in the candlelight.

"Charlotte, Charlotte, why do you bait me so?" he demanded huskily. "Can you not see that it brings out the devil in me?"

"I do not bait you," she choked. "You take me as if you hate me!"

"No, never that." His dark head came down and he nuzzled with his lips the cleft between her breasts, let his mouth trail over their roundness, tested with his teeth the rosy nipples, felt them tremble. "I could never hate you, Charlotte."

Oh, but you do, she thought, although in her exhaustion she was now too wise to say it. *You hate me for something that happened long ago and that neither of us can ever change. You love me and yet you hate me too, and that hatred washes over you in waves when I least expect it. . . .*

And yet last night he had been a tender lover, wooing her with his body as if it were a song of love.

Hurt and confused, she turned her head away from him. "I am very tired, Rowan." She moved restively as his lips now found her stomach, moved across it. *I am tired of your incomprehensible moods, your sudden angers. If it is going to be like this between us, I wish you had left me in England.* She did not say any of this, of course—it would only bring on another explosion and recriminations and then perhaps her bruised body must endure another bout of frenzied lovemaking. "Very tired," she murmured. "I want only to be allowed to go to sleep."

He straightened up at her tone, all too aware that he had been rebuffed.

"You are a coldhearted wench," he said bitterly, flinging away from her.

She heard him cross the room, banging the door to her bedchamber shut behind him. She waited tensely but he did not return. She relaxed as she heard from below a crash as the front door slammed behind him.

Her husband, having had what he wanted from her, had gone out to enjoy the night life of Lisbon without her, Charlotte thought bitterly. She tossed and turned and at last fell into a heavy exhausted sleep—from which Rowan had shaken her awake and told her to dress, that they would be off to Evora within the hour.

Now beside her she felt Wend's slight shiver. "I wish we hadn't come with him to this foreign place," Wend muttered. "I wish we had stayed back home at Aldershot Grange."

"Oh, but how could we stay, Wend? What excuse could I possibly have given, when Rowan came north specifically to take me to Portugal?"

"He didn't come north to do that," Wend objected doggedly. "He met Livesay on the road when he was riding in and told him that he planned to stay at Aldershot Grange a month and then go back to London."

Charlotte's breath caught. "Did Livesay tell you this, Wend?" Livesay was the butler at Aldershot Grange.

"Yes. I thought he told you too."

"No, he didn't." Charlotte's mind was racing. What had happened to make Rowan suddenly change his mind?

Abruptly she remembered something that had not seemed odd at all at the time. She had been looking out the window and had seen Rowan riding toward the house in the distance. And then, just as she was about to turn away, intending to change from the housedress she was wearing into something more fashionable in which to greet the husband she had not seen for all of six months, she had seen another man riding hard over the brow of the hill on a lathered horse—she could see the foam even at that distance. She had recognized the rider as old Conway from Carlisle, a man who occasionally transacted business for Rowan. The two of them had talked for some time and then Rowan had spurred his mount toward the house and almost collided with his wife in the doorway, ordering her brusquely to pack for Portugal. And looking at her with inexpressible anger.

What had happened between the time he had spoken to Livesay and the time he had burst into the hallway of Aldershot Grange without even a greeting, demanding that she pack at once? Could old Conway on his lathered horse have been racing to tell Rowan something? And if so, what?

What had happened to make him suddenly decide to take her abroad? All at once it seemed to Charlotte of major importance that she find out. There had been something so threatening in Rowan's manner toward her at dinner tonight. And at times this week—alternating with periods of, for him, unusual tenderness—he had glowered at her for no reason at all and she had had the eerie feeling that he was about to burst out with some unwarranted accusation. . . . *What could it be?*

What did she really mean to Rowan? she asked herself, troubled. Sometimes, when he was on good behavior, she had even been persuaded that he loved her. Or had he married her only for her lissome body that had caught his fancy, her face that caused men to catch their breath and turn and watch her wherever she went? Rowan collected beautiful things . . . and sometimes, in those uncontrollable rages of his, he smashed them beyond repair.

Her husband was a formidable and ofttimes frightening
man.

She turned now to Wend and sighed. "I'll never be able
to go back to sleep now, and I don't feel hungry." This to
ward off Wend, who, having been brought up on near-
starvation, thought food was the answer to everything. "I
think I'll walk down to the fish market. It should be
crowded at this hour."

"What, walk alone?" Wend was scandalized. "You'll be
set upon by cutpurses!"

"No, I won't. Dawn is breaking now, the city is waking
up. And perhaps I'll find a chair and have myself carried
down to the waterfront."

Wend looked alarmed. "Wait till I dress! I'll come with
you."

"No need. Go back to bed, Wend. You need sleep too."

She left Wend frowning over the guttering candle she
had brought downstairs with her and went out again,
clutching a light embroidered shawl around her slim
shoulders.

Outside she found Vasco, the servant with the torch,
still leaning sleepily against the wall beside the front door.
Although he spoke fair English, he chose not to understand, and she found she could not wave him away. Stubbornly he insisted on coming with her, lighting her way
with the torch, and it occurred to her that perhaps Wend
was right, there might be cutpurses abroad in the Lisbon
night.

There was no chair to be found.

Coming down from the heights of the Portas del Sol
with the high ramparts of the Castelo de São Jorge looming above her, there was a softness in the morning air that
reminded Charlotte vividly of her childhood in the Scillies,
those fortunate sunny isles off the southern coast of England some twenty-five miles from Land's End. She was
suddenly achingly homesick for her life there and for her
mother, frail charming Cymbeline, who had seemed to
move in grace and laughter through the open-windowed
low granite house she had bought just outside Hugh Town

on St. Mary's Isle a year after her husband's accidental death.

Charlotte passed the twelfth-century Romanesque cathedral and realized that she was now traversing the steep twisting streets of the Alfama, where she had strolled with Rowan and Lord Claypool yesterday. And here again were those ever-present sounds of her childhood, the strident voices of the seabirds piercing the morning air, the winged whir of kittiwakes and gannets and cormorants and puffins and gulls swooping above her. Even the steep terrain brought back the memory of clambering over the rocks of the Scillies.

But that life was gone now, gone forever. It had been replaced long since by life with unpredictable Rowan, who rose from his bed by night to pace restlessly. She could hear him walking back and forth in the next room.

Why? she asked herself bluntly. It was a question she would never dare to ask Rowan. They were married but they had never really been close. It was like a truce between them, this marriage. It always had been. With Rowan watching her with keen burning eyes across the breakfast table as if to penetrate into her mind and discover if she had been unfaithful to him in her dreams.

As indeed she had. The thought no longer brought a blush to Charlotte's cheeks, for theirs was a marriage not made in heaven, but, she sometimes thought, designed in hell.

Still, they had endured together thus far—couples of their class seldom divorced—even though Rowan could not help knowing that she had never loved him, and he had found mistresses, so many of them, for gossip about his wild and wastrel ways in London had a way of reaching even into far-off Cumberland. Charlotte had turned a deaf ear. She was never completely comfortable in Rowan's presence, so it was good to have him away from her, although she was always careful to mask her feelings and to play the devoted wife whenever he returned.

The salt air that blew from the Atlantic up the mouth of the Tagus River rippled Charlotte's blonde hair—that golden hair in which Rowan had seemed to take such delight early in their marriage, never allowing her to cut so much as a wisp of it. Now she brushed it back away from her face with an expensive embroidered peach kid glove, for Rowan, although he neglected her, lavished money unstintingly on her wardrobe.

Concentrating on keeping her footing on this dim narrow balconied street, so steep it seemed to be made up mainly of steps that wound down through the Alfama toward the waterfront, Charlotte puzzled, trying to sort it all out.

Why had Rowan's lovemaking, which had been careless and desultory in this last year before their departure from England, almost condescending at times, suddenly become so fierce? That first night in Lisbon he had taken her in his arms as if he would destroy her, bombarding her with a passion that left her weak and bruised and shaken.

On the ship he had not been like that. Their embarkation had wrought a marvelous change in him. He had seemed lighthearted, as if some great weight had been lifted from his shoulders. And his lovemaking had again been tender and considerate.

When they were at last settled into their house in the Portas del Sol, his lovemaking had become totally unpredictable—a tender lover one night, a bruising brute the next. It was not love, and certainly not affection that drove Rowan, but something else, something that made him cry out in his sleep, angry indistinguishable words that degenerated into restless muttering. Something sinister. And now she felt that something like a prickling in her spine as she held up her skirts to avoid a heavy flowerpot.

It was that prickling of dread that had driven her out in the dawn to think.

Now, in the tortuous twisting of the narrow alleyway, a cat, one of the typical striped tabbies that abounded in Lisbon, darted beneath Charlotte's feet and dashed away with a yowl as she gave a lurch to avoid stepping on it. Now it crouched on the stone steps nearby, looking up at her, its knowing green eyes in its long pointed face flickering in the torchlight. From a distance came the screeching sound of caterwauling cats making love and perhaps war, and the striped tabby sat up alertly.

"Puss," murmured Charlotte ruefully, "I hope *your* lover doesn't treat you like that."

As if finding the sound unbearable, the cat plunged down the steps and then began to walk more decorously, swishing its tail. Charlotte watched it.

Who knew what the cat had been through the night before? Maybe, like her, the cat needed to get away and try to puzzle out life. Certainly *she* had needed to get away this morning, to clear her head, for her body was still aching from Rowan's punishing style of lovemaking of the night before.

She passed a stone fountain tiled in blue-and-white *azulejos* depicting garden scenes. Beside it two heavyset women—stolid early risers in the pale Portuguese dawn—were filling water jugs. Half-dressed ragged children tugged at their skirts, and cats sidled around them, rubbing against their substantial legs. Charlotte was tempted to sit on the edge of the fountain and view this little panorama of life in an exotic city.

But she decided against it. His torch extinguished now in daylight, Vasco still lounged along behind her, though walking now at a respectful distance. Suppose he took it upon himself to clear these people away for the wealthy *senhora*? She could not chance it, she decided ruefully, and moved on toward the busy waterfront.

Ah, this was just what she needed—a brisk uncaring crowd and healthy pandemonium. Around her in the fish market, weathered-looking fishermen were selling their catch to the olive-skinned *varinas*, the fishwives who would pile them in big flat baskets and hawk them lustily throughout the awakening city. How their wide black skirts swished over the cobbles, what brilliant smiles they flashed at their customers as the gold loops bobbed in their ears and the dripping fish they carried in those flat baskets on their heads trickled down to splash on a golden necklace or a cross worn between ample breasts. Here among the *varinas* and the men in their cross-stitched red shirts, unnoticed in the hubbub, she would try to face her problems and understand at last why her husband made love to her as if he were scourging her.

From the waterfront fish market as she wandered through it, the water glistened and white-winged gulls were turned to pink or lavender in the early-morning sky. Myriad craft were moored in the harbor—rakish red and brown fishing smacks, beautiful barges with lateen sails, called *fragatas*; every kind of sailing ship seemed to be represented. One big potbellied merchantman caught her eye, for it flew the English flag. The ship's passengers were just then disembarking, and a wave of homesickness drew Charlotte toward them.

Suddenly in that crowd she was startled to see a familiar face—a man's face, a strong face, bronzed and weathered, with hair so blond it gleamed Viking-white in the pale breaking sunlight. The face was gone almost before she glimpsed it, lost in a sea of disembarking passengers, but the momentary sight of it had caused her heart to lurch violently in her chest. For that was a face she had thought never to see again this side of paradise. And just that one brief glimpse of it had sent her blood racing to old wild rhythms and sent a hope akin to panic skittering throughout her woman's body.

For the man she had just glimpsed—and surely she must be mistaken, for he was long dead—had meant more to Charlotte Vayle than anyone else in this world. Her love for him was deep and tormenting and had haunted her to this day. Indeed, just the sight of a man who only *looked* like him brought back to tantalizing life the memory of green eyes that had smiled into hers, of long-fingered hands that had caressed her, of lips that had melted tenderly against her own.

It was—no, it couldn't possibly be Tom Westing!

But even in her disbelief, Charlotte found herself running mindlessly forward, for she must know, *she must know*.

Blindly she bumped into a cart and barked her shins. She scarcely noticed the pain. A black-skirted *varina* car-

rying a load of fish in a basket on her head swore at her as
she stumbled away from the cart, fighting her way toward
the disembarking passengers.

For the sight of the blond stranger—and stranger he
must certainly be—had brought back to Charlotte a vivid
searing past that she had tried so desperately to forget.
She was swept into a maelstrom of memory of a love that
had had its tender beginnings among the crags and lakes of
Cumberland just below the Scottish border and had flared
into disaster in the golden summer of 1732.

2

Cumberland, England, Summer 1730

Charlotte Vayle would never in her life forget the moment she had first laid eyes on Tom Westing. It had actually been, she later supposed in retrospect, the day she had first realized what it could really be like between a man and a woman, the day she had first given serious thought to having a man's warm arms enfold her naked body and let his fervor transport her to another world and joys undreamt of. . . . But that was later. At the time, her girlish embarrassment had known no bounds.

Charlotte was fifteen—a thin and gangling fifteen with wide expressive eyes that seemed too large for her delicate heart-shaped face. She and Wend, the new serving girl (a feckless time-waster, according to Cook), had strayed from the kitchen and gone idly looking for birds' nests. They were walking barefoot (to save their worn shoes) over warm stones and soft grasses, making their way down from Friar's Crag, a low wooded promontory that rose above the eastern shore of the glistening expanse of that ancient glacial lake men called the Derwent Water. And Wend had been telling Charlotte how at home—waving vaguely toward the countryside in the direction of the Greta— they always hung withered birch twigs over the door to keep out witches.

Although she had been brought up among the dolmens

and standing stones of the far-off Scillies, Charlotte had no
real belief in witches, and had laughed.

"Are you troubled with so many then?" she asked.

And Wend, who was two years older, big-boned and
surefooted, had turned with a sniff. "You never know what
lies in store," she warned. "That's what my ma always
says!"

That had certainly been true of her own life thus far,
Charlotte had felt like saying. *If she had known back in
the Scillies what waited for her in the north of England,
she would have wept!* Watching Wend's browned muscular bare legs move out ahead, Charlotte could not help
thinking whimsically that from the condition of their clothes,
none would have guessed that Charlotte was ostensibly
the mistress and Wend the maid. On the whole, red-
haired Wend was the better-dressed, for Charlotte, child-
ishly small for her age when she had first come to
Cumberland three years before, had shot up like a weed
this past year and her present clothing, for all its good
linen cloth and fine stitching, was much let out and had
long since gone threadbare. The contrast was painful, for
Wend's cheap petticoat beneath her tucked-up skirt was of
a flaunting red color and practically new (bought with her
first wages), while Charlotte's ragged skirts, once sky-blue
above her mended white petticoat, had faded from many
washings down to an indeterminate bluish gray.

Here at the roof of England, where long-forgotten volcanoes slumbered, their hard green slates scarred by frost
and ice, was the great central massif of the Lake District,
rising majestically just south of the pleasant Vale of Carlisle. Around the silvery waters of the lake the tops of
cathedrallike mountains disappeared mysteriously into the
mist on this day of drifting clouds that made a shifting
pattern of shadows across the storied hills. It was a magical
day and there was a kind of solemn stillness about it, as if
all the world were waiting for some great message to roll
sonorously down from the peaks.

Both girls felt it, a vibrant waiting hush that had settled
over the silvery lake and all its surroundings. They had
started out laughing and lighthearted, but the hush of this

summer's afternoon had stilled their voices, and now they found themselves almost tiptoeing through the trees.

"Why don't we visit Fox Elve?" suggested Wend, who had a wayward sense of humor that went well with her fiery hair. "Perhaps the ghost of the Viking Lord will rise up and snatch at our ankles!"

Charlotte, immersed in the haunting unreal somnolence of the countryside, nodded and followed Wend down the steep path that led to the tiny isolated hollow known as Fox Elve. Everyone around there knew the legend of the Viking Lord who on some long-ago raid had been left for dead by his men when their dragon ship had departed for distant fjords. A local girl had found him, so the story went, and had nursed him back to health there by the spring at Fox Elve. But this was no ordinary girl. Her hair sprang pure gold from her head and she rode a white horse and carried a long magic sword that she could wield as well as a man. Perhaps she pitied him, this Golden Maiden. Anyway she gave him back his life there by the spring at Fox Elve. And when he was well again she kissed him on the lips and bade him depart back to the deep fjords of the north from whence he came.

But the Viking Lord had lain in her arms and felt her witchery, and he refused to go—unless she accompanied him. "Why can you not go with me?" he had demanded.

The Maiden, who was strong and beautiful, had stuck the point of her long two-edged sword into the ground and leant upon the hilt. She had looked down at him sadly from her blue eyes.

"Because 'twas I who brought you down," she told him simply, "although in the heat of battle perhaps you did not know that it was I. And because you were the trophy of my own blade, none interfered when I chose to give you back your life. But if I left this place with you, we would be pursued, for I and my Magic Sword are Luck Bringers to Battles and I am considered a great prize in my village. Besides, I am promised to our chieftain. He would never let me go. He would bring a war party charging after us and they would bring you down."

"I care nothing for that," scoffed the Viking Lord, who

had recovered his strength and with it his bravado. "We will steal a boat and be off before the wind!"

"No," sighed the Maiden. "But tonight I will bring you wine and lie with you one more time. Tonight—but you depart on the morrow."

This did not suit the Viking Lord at all, and that afternoon he found some herbs in the forest, and when the Golden Maiden came with her wine sack and her sad, determined face, he managed to slip some of the herbs into her wine, whereupon she fell to the ground in a deep sleep.

And while she was sleeping he lifted her upon her white horse and rode away with her toward the sea. And as they rode, dark clouds began to drift across the sky.

They never reached the coast. The village chieftain had set spies upon them and he and a party of his men were waiting to pounce upon them before ever they reached the northernmost reaches of the lake. With his way barred, the Viking Lord wheeled his horse back the way he had come. He rode at breakneck speed, carrying his golden-haired burden in her trailing white gown until at last he made his stand at Fox Elve, where he had first fallen and where he had been given back his life.

There in the gathering storm, with thunder rolling down from the distant hills, he laid his comely burden down. And there, surrounded, the Viking Lord called hoarsely upon his Norse gods for aid. He called upon Odin, the God of Battle, for victory, and upon Thor, the God of Thunder, to bring down his mighty hammer upon his foes.

As his encircling attackers sprang at him, he brandished above his head the Golden Maiden's magical two-edged sword, and Thor gave forth his thunderous answer. A bolt of lightning sprang from the dark sky overhead, but not to the foe—it was the upraised sword the lightning struck. The circle of attacking warriors fell back, watching in awe as the sword turned fiery red and melted and the Viking Lord was himself consumed by the flame and turned into ashes.

There were several endings to the legend that had come down, told over campfires and before crackling winter hearths, and they were all sad. But Charlotte, wanting a happy ending for the lost lovers, had supplied her own. In her version the Golden Maiden had risen on her long white legs and waved away her chieftain. She had claimed the ashes of the Viking Lord as her own, since it was her blade that had originally brought him down. He was hers. Hers forever.

With his rival turned to ashes, the chieftain had readily acquiesced and turned away, unwilling to bear the grief in his golden lady's eyes.

And after that . . . After that, with her magic she had brought the Viking Lord to life again and they had ridden away together on some highway to the stars—so Charlotte dreamed.

The two girls had almost reached Fox Elve now, silent and breathless. Charlotte had been there many times. She knew there was naught at Fox Elve except a little copse surrounding a spring, and the tiny stream that rippled from it, and a stone cairn that some claimed had been piled up as a memorial to the Golden Maiden who had seized her chieftain's blade in her despair and plunged it hilt-deep into her heart. And nearby, a sunken grave that perhaps held the body of the chieftain, who had taken the same dagger, still warm with his beloved's blood, and—to join her in some netherworld—had dispatched himself with it. Or, some said—and superstitious Wend was one of these— the "sunken grave" was no real grave at all, but a grave-like hole burnt into the ground when the bolt of lightning had immolated the Viking Lord—a hole from whence his ghostly hands might reach up and out and snatch at the ankles of the unwary to drag them down to hell.

Charlotte had never liked any of those suggestions and refused to believe them. She preferred to think that the cairn was a memorial raised to commemorate a love that had defied time and death and that the sunken grave had been dug for someone else long after.

The story of the Viking Lord and the Golden Maiden had always haunted Charlotte, and now that she and Wend were padding silently down into the copse where, legend had it, the long-ago drama had taken place, she was once again spinning fanciful dreams about it.

They were under the trees now, shadowed by the branches, their bare feet making no sound on the soft grass, in an unreal other-world. The haunted cairn of piled-up rough stones was ahead of them over a little rise, and just behind that, the sunken grave lay half-hidden, festooned with blue myrtle and ivy.

Wend headed for that ivied grave and the cairn behind it, with Charlotte in her wake, when, as one, both their young bodies jerked to a violent halt—so suddenly that they almost toppled forward.

There before them a woman's long shapely naked leg was rising from the sunken grave.

The Golden Maiden! was Charlotte's first wild thought. *She's come back!*

Life was certainly there. That disembodied single leg was arching upward with a splendidly luxurious air. Impudently and indecorously it waved before them. As they watched, fascinated, the bare foot twirled around, toes curling to the accompaniment of a high gurgling giggle and a man's low laugh.

The two girls exchanged startled glances. Charlotte opened her mouth to speak, to whisper, "Come away, Wend"—and closed it again as another voice, slightly slurred and female, filled the air.

"Ohh, Tom . . ." murmured that dreamy voice. Then, more urgently, *"Ohhhh, Tom!"* on a rising inflection. And then an ecstatic moan.

Charlotte gave Wend's arm a tug, but Wend was loath to go. Bright-eyed and overcome by curiosity to see who was in there moaning so joyously, Wend leaned closer, and to do so, took a single step.

A twig snapped beneath her foot.

"Come away!" entreated Charlotte.

With her words, the white leg came abruptly down. As it disappeared from view, a man's head and naked shoulders shot up, his face looking startled and indescribably wrathful. Charlotte would never forget how he looked then, his intense green eyes vivid in his tanned face and that shock of pale hair shining almost white as the sun caught it in dappled light through the branches. Beside him now popped up a girl's tousled butter-yellow curls, and then, as she struggled higher, her upper torso was revealed, displaying an unlaced bodice and a pair of round full naked breasts peeking out unleashed. At the sight of Wend and Charlotte, standing there with ludicrous expressions, she broke into a cascade of wild giggles.

"Shut up, Maisey," muttered the man, frowning ferociously at the two young interlopers. Charlotte saw from his shoulder motion that he was clutching at something— very possibly his trousers. He waved a commanding arm. "Be off with you now!"

"Yes, go along with you, Wend," chimed in Maisey irrepressibly. "And take that brat with you. And don't you be telling my James you saw me here!"

Overcome with embarrassment, her face feeling hot enough to fry eggs on, Charlotte gave Wend a solid push. "Oh, do go on, Wend," she cried desperately. "Can't you see they want to be alone?"

Thus urged forward, Wend took a reluctant step away and Charlotte had a last embarrassed glimpse of Maisey's convulsed countenance and the young man's lowering departing glance as the two girls stumbled away.

Not till they had gone a hundred yards from Fox Elve did Wend speak.

"Do you know who that was?" she demanded in a breathless voice.

"No," said Charlotte prayerfully, hoping in her heart that whoever he was, she would never lay eyes on him again—it would be too embarrassing. After all, she and Wend had caught him actually . . . doing it!

"That was Tom Westing," Wend informed her importantly (Wend prided herself on knowing everything about everybody). "Down from somewheres near Carlisle, they say. Good-looking, isn't he?" She gave Charlotte a roguish look. "I wouldn't have minded being in Maisey's shoes myself."

"She wasn't wearing any," pointed out Charlotte in a stifled voice. She was still red with embarrassment, but she agreed in her heart that there was no doubt that Tom Westing—for all the lowering looks he had shot at them—was certainly good-looking.

"Or probably much else," was Wend's comment. She cast a glance back the way they had come. "Fancy them there in that hollow grave together. Makes a nice narrow bed, doesn't it? I'll have to remember that." She chuckled.

"*Wend!*" reproved Charlotte, shocked.

Wend flounced along for another couple of steps. "Maisey's James will be having words with Tom Westing if he hears about this!" Her crinkly eyes sparkled with anticipation.

"Oh, Wend, you aren't going to *tell?*" protested Charlotte. Surely it was bad enough to have stumbled upon the lovers accidentally without babbling about what they had seen to all and sundry.

Wend shrugged airily. "Well, I might not—and then again, I might," she admitted, tossing her head. "I'll think about it."

They were in sight of home now. They had been walking downhill toward the lake. Now before them, dark against the silvery mirror of the Derwent Water, rose the steep roof slates of Aldershot Grange, which had been Charlotte's home for the last three of her fifteen summers.

The house was sturdily built of stone, and large—though not as large as medieval Castle Stroud, which lay out of sight through the trees to the north along the lakeshore. Nor was it Blade's End in the other direction. Still, Aldershot Grange was comfortable. Charlotte had a big bedchamber on the second floor and the house was manned by a skeleton staff of servants—but Charlotte would never consider it home.

Home lay far, far to the south beyond Land's End in the Scillies—and it was forever lost to her.

Aldershot Grange was Uncle Russ's home. Charlotte had never met her uncle until he arrived one day, all the way from London, to bring a suitor to visit her mother.

"Cymbeline," Uncle Russ had argued when the suitor was out of earshot (although Charlotte, lurking nearby, was not), "John Foster is the right man for you. He is still young and you are not getting any younger."

"And . . . ?" asked her mother.

"And he has a house in London and a handsome patrimony in Hampshire," he added in a sulky voice.

"So you will be able to borrow money from him if I wed him," her pretty mother had guessed shrewdly.

Uncle Russ had blustered a bit at that, and her mother had laughed, knowing she had hit the nail on the head. But Cymbeline had liked the attractive ginger-haired John Foster for himself and had at last agreed to marry him. The year was 1727.

Charlotte, then twelve, had realized excitedly that this remarriage of her mother's would bring great changes into her life. For one thing, they would leave the isolated summertime beauty of the Scillies for the bustle and excitement of London. London! She thrilled to the thought. For another, she would have young people about, for John Foster, a widower, claimed to have both a son and a daughter near Charlotte's age.

But lovely fragile Cymbeline had been growing ever more frail that summer of 1727. Although she never complained, Charlotte had seen her clutch her heart and pause to lean against the warm stones of the garden wall. The excitement of the wedding preparations had been too much for her and she had gasped out her last breath almost on the eve of her wedding. How vividly Charlotte remembered that last day. . . .

She had been in her mother's big airy bedchamber helping her select a wedding gown, and the feather bed with its lace coverlet was strewn with clothes. The casements were open onto a sunny day of blue skies and soft white clouds that floated across them like white swans upon a blue lake.

"I had so wanted to wear something light and festive for the ceremony—like this!" Wistfully her mother had held up a fluttery pale yellow gown, hooped and flounced and decorated with delicate seed pearls sewn into ivory satin rosettes. "With ivory kid gloves embroidered in pale yellow silk. And a wreath of yellow roses for my hair."

"Then why don't you?" wondered Charlotte.

Her mother sighed. "John's sister has written to me—and oh, she is sure to arrive tomorrow and disapprove of everything—that I must remember that I am a widow and not some young virgin and she thinks black would be most appropriate!" Cymbeline sounded indignant. "I told John that I simply refuse to be married in mourning, no matter what his sister thinks, and he suggested dark brown or indigo or possibly a deep purple." She sighed again.

"Wear this one and face her down," suggested Charlotte the irrepressible rebel, cheerfully indicating a simple white gown of thin rippling silk. "You look wonderful in it."

"Oh, then she'll accuse me of creating a scandal by making it appear that I am 'being married in my shift'!" Cymbeline's ready laughter pealed.

Twelve-year-old Charlotte was well aware of the prevalent belief that if a bride wore only a single long white garment to be wed her husband could never be held responsible for her debts. "Perhaps you should run away and be married?" she suggested raptly. "Then you could wear what you like."

"Oh, that would be fun and I know it is the fashion, but really, where would I run?" her mother countered lightly. "Gretna Green is far away and so is Fleet Street! No, I must try to get off to a good start with my in-laws—I'll wear this." She picked up a rustling indigo silk with jet tassels and held it up to herself and stood thoughtfully before the mirror.

Then abruptly her face had lost its color and her lips turned blue. "I don't . . . feel so well," she gasped.

Before nightfall she was dead and the rustling indigo silk had become her funeral gown.

Uncle Russ had seemed to feel no grief at his young sister's loss.

Only Charlotte felt this blinding grief for her laughing young mother. Bereft of his bride-to-be, John Foster had promptly disappeared from Charlotte's life. And Uncle Russ, her mother's bachelor brother, simply arrived from the north and took over. He had himself appointed Charlotte's guardian, stripped the house in St. Mary's and sold everything, and swept twelve-year-old Charlotte and her few personal possessions north to his own home of Aldershot Grange near the Scottish border.

Charlotte's first winter there was bleak. With clothing far too thin for the biting cold, she had shivered in the big drafty house, wrapped herself in shawls, and hovered by the hearth. Hopelessly she had watched freezing rain and sleet chatter down on the roof, and snow and ice storms obscure the gray landscape. Like her mother, she was a child of the sunshine, and this land of cold gray mists and frosty air depressed her.

Sometimes that winter she had felt she would die at Aldershot Grange, alone and unloved, for her uncle had simply brought her home and left her there and gone down to London, leaving her with an unsuitable wardrobe in the company of servants. Remembering the warmth and gaiety of the palm-fringed house in the Scilly Isles, Charlotte had night after night cried herself to sleep.

She was to learn in the next three years that her uncle was rarely in residence at Aldershot Grange, that he spent almost all his time carousing in London. And on the few occasions when he was home, he was cold and harsh and in the main ignored her. He seemed to think she needed nothing save food and shelter, and gave her so small an allowance that she could barely buy pins with it. It was fortunate that she had learned to read and write and do sums in the Scillies, for schooling was now out of the question. Gradually Charlotte's clothes wore out, and she would have been left in tatters had not she and Wend one rainy day decided to explore the large attics of Aldershot Grange. Tucked away in a dusty corner, festooned with cobwebs, they found an old forgotten trunk, and when Wend pried open its curved lid, they both gasped. There, carefully packed away in lavender, were some dresses Charlotte's mother had worn as a girl—and left here long ago when she married and moved away.

"Didn't find them none too soon!" Wend chuckled, holding up a pink taffeta apron with an admiring "Look at *this!*"

Charlotte, rummaging delightedly in this treasure trove,

flung it over Wend's shoulder, "You can have the apron,
Wend." And stopped as she found a little broken fan
bearing a painted scene of clouds and cupids. Her mother's fan, beyond a doubt, for her mother had always loved
cupids. Charlotte's eyes misted with tears as she held the
little fan against her cheek. She carried it downstairs atop
a pile of lavender-scented clothing, and got it out and
looked at it whenever she felt downhearted, for somehow
that little broken fan seemed to bring her mother—and
that lost life of the Scillies—closer to her.

The items from the trunk kept Charlotte from going
about in tatters, but they were hopelessly unfashionable
with their great puffed sleeves, and Charlotte, who was
taller than her tiny mother, found herself promptly out-
growing them—and eventually even they grew threadbare. When she asked her uncle if she might not be
allowed some portion of her inheritance to purchase new
clothes, he barked that his sister Cymbeline had had many
debts of which Charlotte knew nothing and the estate had
barely been able to pay them.

Charlotte doubted that last, but she was in no position
to find out—she would simply have to wait until she came
of age.

Or married.

The latter seemed hopelessly far away.

And then Wend—laughing, joking, superstitious Wend—
had come into her life, hired to replace old Glynis in the
kitchen. Wend was noisy and good-natured and she came
like a bright spirit into this new world of the pale unhappy
child from the Scillies. Lonely and lost and sure that she
would never become accustomed to life amid these forbidding northern crags, Charlotte was forever persuading
Wend—who didn't need much prodding—to slip away
with her and go exploring some new or seldom-trodden
path.

As for instance today, when they had come upon the
unrepentant lovers lying in the sunken grave. . . .

The two girls had been out for a long time and they
made their way back into the house stealthily and by
different routes—Wend because she hoped Cook might not

have noticed her absence, Charlotte because she had spotted a strange horse tethered near the house and wondered who their caller might be.

She was not long in finding out. A sharp-featured swarthy gentleman was lounging on a long wooden bench in the hall as if stationed there to prevent anyone coming in from the outside without his seeing them.

"Where is Mistress Charlotte, wench?" he demanded of Charlotte in a harsh impatient voice as she came in. "I've been waiting for her these past two hours."

Humiliated that he should consider her a servant, Charlotte came to a halt before him and rose to her full—though not very great—height. "*I* am Charlotte Vayle," she announced menacingly, the effect somewhat marred by her sudden realization that there was a new long rent in her skirt and hastily trying to cover it.

Startled or no, the sharp-featured gentleman came swiftly to his feet. "Your pardon, Mistress Charlotte," he said smoothly. "It is so dark in this hall . . ."

"That you took me for a serving wench," supplied Charlotte bitterly.

"Oh, never that!" He swept her a gallant bow. "Arthur Bodine, at your service." He straightened up and Charlotte's mouth tightened mutinously as a pair of cynical brown eyes raked up and down her thin still-childish figure.

He is criticizing my clothes! she thought hotly, her fingers clutching the worn faded material of her torn skirt.

But it seemed that was not precisely what Arthur Bodine had in mind.

Over supper, which was served in haste in the dusty long dining room—Mr. Bodine having refused to take so much as a bite until the lady of the house was home—he told her that he was "looking in on her" at the behest of her uncle in London.

"Uncle Russ is too busy to come north this year?" Charlotte guessed, giving her caller a steady look.

"That's right," Bodine agreed affably. He studied her small face, looking peaked and pale beneath the starched ruffled cotton cap that completely hid her luxuriant blonde

hair, with a sigh. "Not for a couple of years, I imagine."
He sighed again, peering at her.

"Why? Why did he say that?" Charlotte demanded fiercely
of Wend when Arthur Bodine had departed. "How could
he know what Uncle Russ would do?" For there had been
something in Bodine's manner that alarmed and upset her,
something she could not quite put her finger on.

Wend, who had served the hasty supper, cast a thoughtful glance at the door through which Arthur Bodine had
departed.

"He was looking at you as if you were a horse he wanted
to buy," she mused shrewdly.

Charlotte shivered.

"Perhaps your uncle sent Bodine to see if you were ripe
enough for marriage?" suggested Wend.

Charlotte gave Wend a shocked look. "But I'm only
fifteen!"

"My two sisters were both married before they were
thirteen," Wend informed her.

"Yes, but . . ." But they were of the servant class and
she, Charlotte, was of the gentry. Charlotte couldn't quite
bring herself to say that but Wend guessed and her young
face hardened.

"The gentry *sells* their daughters," she said truculently.
"They just don't call it that."

Charlotte swallowed. Perhaps Wend was right. Perhaps
Bodine had been looking her over with that in mind. She
gave an involuntary shiver.

"Don't worry," said Wend more kindly. "Maybe you'll
find someone for yourself before your uncle gets around to
it. Maybe you found him today! Tom Westing was looking
at *you* more than at Maisey!"

"Wend!" sputtered Charlotte. "That's not true!"

"Isn't it?" Wend went away laughing.

But it gave Charlotte something to think about, and that
night in her big square bedchamber beneath a threadbare
coverlet—for her mother's bed linens had all been sold on
St. Mary's, and Uncle Russ never thought to buy anything
new for the house, so even the window hangings were in
tatters—Charlotte dreamed that *she* was the Golden Maiden

and Tom Westing her Viking Lord. She dreamed that she was taller, more filled out, that she was wearing a white dress, a sinuous gown of finest silk that moved as she moved, and that they had sunk down together in the dappled shadows of the copse. His handsome face was very near, his breath hot upon her cheek. She felt his strong hands caressing her white skin, heard his low laugh.

And waked with her heart racing, to realize it was the next morning and that what had waked her was Ivy, the upstairs maid, laughing with Wend outside her door.

Wend, who was always seeking some way to get out of work, came into the room as Charlotte was dressing.

"Wend, you should knock," Charlotte reproved her. "I might have had my clothes off, and someone going by in the hall—"

"Nobody upstairs but us womenfolk," Wend corrected her breezily. She flopped down on the unmade bed and watched Charlotte dress in silence for a moment. Then, "Didn't they look funny?" she said.

"Who?" asked Charlotte, but she knew.

"That pair we interrupted making love yesterday," said Wend patiently. "Didn't they look funny, though, interrupted like that? Maisey coming out of her dress and that butter-yellow hair all tangled! And Tom Westing mad as a hornet! He'd probably have jumped up and chased us away if he'd had his pants on, which I'll wager he hadn't!" Her hazel eyes sparkled.

Charlotte looked up from pulling on her petticoat over her chemise.

"Wend, you *can't* talk about them," she said with decision. "It would be too embarrassing for us both to say what they were doing when we found them. Besides," she challenged, "why should we make trouble for them?"

Wend stood up and considered the shorter Charlotte from her superior height.

"That's so," she agreed. "Why should we make trouble?" Then she grinned. "Perhaps you liked what you saw?" she suggested slyly. "And you don't want to see Tom Westing's handsome face get bruised?"

Hot color raced to Charlotte's cheeks. "That's ridiculous, Wend," she snapped. "I hope to heaven I never see Tom Westing again—indeed, I think I should die of embarrassment if I did!"

"Oh, you'll see him again." Wend laughed. "But perhaps not with his pants off!"

And as it happened, she did.

The very next day.

3

The day was hot and beautiful, with fluffy white clouds
floating in an endless blue. Charlotte had come alone to
what she called her "secret place." Although it was not
really far from the house, up near Fox Elve, it could be
entered only through a cleft in the rocks and its entrance
was fully concealed by the branches of an ancient gnarled
oak tree. Charlotte had found it quite by accident during
her first miserable year at Aldershot Grange and had formed
the habit of going there whenever she wanted to be
alone—or when life at the big gray house became too
insupportable. She had never even brought Wend here.

Today she had no companion. Cook had called Wend a
lazy wench and threatened to take a broom to her rump if
she disappeared again when there was work to be done.
Without Wend for company, the "secret place" had seemed
the perfect spot to while away a lazy summer's afternoon.
Charlotte had brought along a leather-bound volume (it
was in reality a racy novel called *The Cuckold's Revenge*),
and to mark her place she had carelessly slipped in a
well-thumbed tract by Daniel Defoe that had been written
six years ago in 1724. The tract was provocatively entitled
"Conjugal Lewdness: A Treatise Concerning the Use and
Abuse of the Marriage Bed, and Married Whoredom," and
it dealt at length with a subject Charlotte found enormously fascinating: trepanning, which was the crime of

34

kidnapping heiresses and marrying them against their will (possibly with the encouragement of guns held at their breasts) in order to gain control of their fortunes. Charlotte had read the tract with big eyes and imagined herself snatched from her bed by a trepanner, bundled into a coach, and whisked away to be married in Scotland at gunpoint. She had imagined herself on such a wedding night—not cowering timorously in her bed, but leaping up dramatically and holding the trepanner at bay with his own pistol, which she had thought to snatch up before she made a dash for the door and freedom.

But of course, Charlotte realized regretfully that she was unlikely to be sought out by a trepanner, since she was not an heiress and had no hope of becoming one. The best she could look forward to was that her uncle would trot out some prosaic suitor and tell her that she must be content with him. Her violet eyes gleamed rebelliously. She would chose her own suitor, that she would! She would not let herself be forced to marry against her will, as were so may aristocratic young girls. She would . . .

What she would do was lost as she caught her skirt in a berry vine and with a little exclamation stopped to wrest it free. It was but a little way farther to a rocky opening behind the old oak, from whence came a faint splashing of water—indeed it was curiosity about that faint musical sound that had first led Charlotte to discover this little sheltered spot, surrounded by rock walls on all sides, where a spring-fed waterfall tinkled down to a little circular trout pool below—a pool that shimmered away through a crevice in the rocks, to appear a few yards farther through the rock as one of the many small streams that laced this broken landscape.

Used to the place, she had scarcely looked around her, seating herself comfortably on a flat rock beside the trout pool. She immediately opened the book and began to read. Oblivious of everything but what was happening on its pages, she was dangling her bare toes in the trout pool and had just reached an exciting passage where the fictional hero discovered his wife's infidelity, when some little extra sound arrested her. She looked up calmly—and her gaze froze.

A tall masculine figure had just stepped out from behind the concealing screen of the waterfall. A figure crowned by a shock of hemp-fair wet hair he was just in the act of tossing back—a gesture that sent out a shower of droplets over his broad muscular shoulders. His handsome face with its expression of total astonishment was familiar, as indeed was his deep bare chest.

It was Tom Westing.

And he was dripping wet and stark naked.

Charlotte's heartfelt gasp was cut into by his voice—not the commanding roar she had heard when she and Wend had broken in on his lovemaking at Fox Elve, but a ripple of pure amusement that seemed to come from the depths of him.

"Well, well," he said conversationally, seeming not in the least embarrassed by his daunting display of masculinity unveiled as he reached down behind a rock to bring up his smallclothes. "It's the little girl from Fox Elve. You *do* seem to have a way of finding me without my trousers!"

Charlotte turned brick red and would have given anything she owned to just disappear. She muttered something incoherent as she scrambled to her feet and turned and darted for the entrance.

She was most of the way to Aldershot Grange before she realized that she had dropped her precious book back by the trout pool.

Nothing would have induced her to return for it. After all, suppose she found him calmly squatting there *au naturel* reading those passages she found most alluring? Especially the part where the hero bent tempestuous Lady Augusta to his will?

Oh, she would *die* if she ever met Tom Westing again!

Afraid she really *would* run across him, for he was obviously hanging around the neighborhood—probably to meet Maisey—Charlotte skulked in the house all that day and spent the next morning wandering around the little walled garden, long overgrown with weeds. Occasionally she would cast an anxious glance in the direction of Fox

Elve, wondering if it would be safe now to go up and recover her book.

About noon Cook told her that the old woman who occupied a tiny cot south of Castlerigg Stone Circle was reported to be down with rheumatism again and remarked that it was a pity she could not spare Wend to take her some broth and rolls, since this was the day of the Great Wash, when all of the laundry for the month was done. Somewhat relieved to have something to do at last, Charlotte took the hint and soon set off with a pail of soup and a dozen rolls tied up in a linen square.

The way to the old woman's house she knew well. It led up and along the side of a rocky crag that rose high above a stream that in spring became a raging torrent. Here the path was very narrow, and Charlotte had always edged along it very carefully, for the rushing stream gushed white and foaming at the base of an almost sheer cliff far below. This day she was cautiously negotiating her way along it when she looked up and saw a few steps above and ahead of her the insolent figure of Tom Westing.

A wave of embarrassment at seeing him again, this man she always seemed to stumble over when he was naked—and the thought of having to pass him at such close quarters, where she would literally have to squeeze by, brushing his body as she went—overcame Charlotte's common sense. She whirled in panic to go back the way she had come, caught her foot on a rock outcrop, and with a wild scream plummeted over the edge, catching onto the only thing within reach—a sapling that had found a precarious hold in a cleft in the rocks. A sapling that now bent with her weight, barely holding her.

"Steady!" called Tom's strong voice. She could hear the slap of his shoe leather as he raced toward her down the path. A moment later she felt his hands seize her in a firm grip. He pulled her shuddering body back over the edge just as the sapling's roots began to tear free, and whirled her about to face him.

Overcome by terror—for she had been looking into death's grinning face in that white water far below, where the linen square and the bucket of broth had long since plummeted—Charlotte felt her breath leave her and she clung to Tom's sturdy form like someone drowning.

"There, there," he said soothingly as he held her against his chest, letting her shiver there. "You're not dead, but whatever made you turn about like that? Don't you know this path is too narrow to turn where you did without the greatest care?"

Charlotte couldn't bring herself to tell Tom why she had spun about, any more than she could control her shivering. She was suddenly aware that she was being comforted in the arms of a strong man and that his masculinity called out to her. It registered on her with a kind of dazed shock that she *liked* being held, that she would be content just to stay here in the circle of those long protective arms forever.

Alarmed that such a thought could cross her mind, she tried to pull away from him.

"Ho, there!" he cried. "You're about to do it again—and this time you may tip us both over!"

Charlotte subsided in shivering embarrassment, and when she could face him again, she looked up beseechingly. "I'm sorry," she said faintly. "You saved my life," she added on a note of wonder.

"Aye, I believe I did," he agreed in a casual tone. "And there's little doubt you will take a lot of saving if you go about in this fashion!" His tone was jocular but he was surprised at the impact her wide pleading violet eyes were having on him, and the feeling that had abruptly swelled through him as he clasped her skinny female body to his breast. She was a child, he reminded himself sternly, and put her away from him—most carefully. "Come," he said, taking her hand. "I will escort you where you are going— just to make sure you get there."

"There is no longer any point to my going," she admitted a bit tremulously. "I was carrying a bucket of soup and some bread to old Mistress Meggs, who lives in the valley just beyond, and now"—she looked over the edge of the cliff with a shudder, down into the white cascading water far below—"the soup and the rolls are both flying away downstream."

"Then I will take you back the way you have come," he said firmly.

"Oh, there is no need. Really." She was all too conscious of a fluttering in her chest and of the warm steady pressure of his big hand enfolding her small one.

"Nonetheless . . ." His tone was crisp.

He led her along the narrow path without speaking, pausing wherever there was a bad step to help her across, and Charlotte was embarrassed, because she had passed this way many times before—always without mishap.

"I have been reading your book."

Charlotte stumbled at this sudden announcement, and he steadied her with a curious look.

"You . . . you have?" she asked faintly.

"Yes. Books are hard for me to come by."

He was poor, then. She had guessed it by the worn look of his russet coat, although it was of a decent cut and fabric. His boots, too, had seen better days. But he could *read*.

"How do you like it?" she ventured.

"It is well enough," he told her restlessly. "I had rather there was more time spent on the hero's sailing ventures and less on toasting Lady Augusta's eyebrows."

"She had very unusual eyebrows," defended Charlotte. "They were—"

"I know. High and exalted." He sounded amused. He turned suddenly and peered down into her face with a grin. "Faith, who would have thought it? We have here a pair of exalted eyebrows!"

Despite her vexation, Charlotte laughed—and Tom laughed with her. He had a laughing face, she decided, sunny.

"Actually," he admitted on a sober note, "it was the tract that interested me most."

"Oh, Mr. Defoe's tract on trepanning?"

He nodded. "I was curious about it."

"So now you are planning to kidnap a young heiress and marry her at gunpoint?" Charlotte guessed merrily.

He gave her an odd look. "I might," he said carelessly.

She caught her breath and color flamed in her young

cheeks. *But I am heiress to nothing!* she reminded herself
quickly. And then the fleeting thought came: *Of course,
Tom doesn't know that.* . . .

The slanted look she gave him through her lashes was
suddenly arch. "They hang men for trepanning, Tom."

"Ah, but it might be worth it," he sighed, and looked
out suddenly into the distance. He had seen a man hanged
for trepanning once. A big blustering fellow who had
swaggered all the way to the gallows. And from a coach he
had seen a girl's white face peering out to watch, and
people had nudged each other and said she was "the one."
Tom thought he had seen a glisten of tears on her cheeks
before her head had been suddenly jerked back to disappear from view as the prisoner was strung up and left to
jerk and dance in the air while the crowd stared and
muttered. Tom had wondered then if it had been a real
kidnapping, or had this pair actually been lovers? Anyway,
the law was clear. Trepanning was indeed a hanging offense.

He turned back to gaze upon this lovely delicate young
girl at his side—and found she was not looking at him but
instead was intently studying the rocks. Her color was
high. Although his tone had been bantering when he said
"it might be worth it," there had been something in the
way he said it that had made her heart beat faster.

Charlotte was growing up.

By the time they had come within sight of Aldershot
Grange they were the best of friends. And on Charlotte's
part at least, a little more than that—she had decided she
adored him. His roguish smile lingered with her long after
he had gone.

When Charlotte came into the kitchen to tell Cook she
had lost her soup bucket and rolls into the gorge, she
found Wend standing in the open doorway watching her.

"Well," said Wend, leaning on her broom and considering Charlotte with new respect, "I see you went out and
got him!"

"I did nothing of the kind!" protested Charlotte. "I
nearly fell over into the gorge and he saved me."

"Clever of you," said Wend admiringly.

Charlotte flushed. "I wasn't trying to be clever," she

told Wend stiffly. "I was trying to turn around because I thought I couldn't get by him where the path was so narrow, and I—"

"Just fell naturally into his arms." Wend chuckled. "I must remember to do that someday."

"Don't be silly, I'll probably never see him again."

Wend snorted her derision.

The next day Charlotte was adjusting the worn window hangings in her bedroom when she saw Tom striding down the slope to Aldershot Grange. As he walked, he was leafing idly through a book, which she guessed was the novel she had dropped in such haste. He cut a handsome figure, she thought with a pang, watching him swing along in the distance in his worn russet coat with his battered hat set at a cocky angle upon his shining fair head. When he came closer he looked up, and Charlotte instinctively stepped back, breathless lest he should see her watching him approach. When she dared to look again, he had disappeared—probably into the kitchen, she guessed from the angle at which he had approached the house.

She ran downstairs, suddenly alarmed lest flirtatious Wend should already have him seated at the kitchen table drinking a tankard of cider. But it was Charlotte he had come to see.

"Mistress Charlotte, I'm returning your book," he said with a courtly bow, and Charlotte thought: *He is a gentleman for all his worn clothes. That bow had a practiced ease.*

"I hope you enjoyed it," she said stiffly, well aware that Cook and Wend were both watching them, bright-eyed. And then, to escape their surveillance, "Would you like to see our garden?" she wondered.

"Very much."

Together they strolled out into the low-walled weedy patch, but neither of them was aware of their surroundings. In the soft air a bee buzzed around his head, but he seemed not to notice. She was giving him a luminous look. Charlotte's heart would have beat faster if she could have known what Tom was thinking on his way over here; he had been wondering about the strange tug on his heart-strings this thin little waif had inspired, and had been chiding himself roundly for taking such an interest in one so young.

Now in the weed-choked garden he was hanging on her words.

"We had beautiful flowers back in the Scillies," she told him wistfully. "I can't quite get used to this north country, the hard winters, all the snow—I guess I'll always love summer too much."

"I was brought up in the Bahamas," he said surprisingly. "So I know what you mean."

"Oh? I thought Wend said you were from Carlisle."

"Only since I was seventeen. My father . . . died and my mother remarried, a shipbuilder. He and I don't get along."

She cast a sudden stricken look at his worn clothing, hardly that of a shipbuilder's stepson. So that was why he had wandered down this way—trouble at home.

"Is that why you're here instead of in Carlisle?" she asked steadily.

He gave her a quick wary look. Actually he had come here in pursuit of a girl—Maisey, whom he had met in Carlisle one market day. But the glow of that little affair was already ebbing, and anyway, he was not of a mind to tell her about that, this too-thin, big-eyed child who had such a strange appeal for him.

"What do you do?" she asked.

He looked out across the garden wall before he answered, and his gaze seemed to skim past the lake's shining surface to the blue sea somewhere beyond their vision.

"By trade I am a navigator," he said. No need to tell her of the slippery decks of the fast furtive ships where he had learned that trade.

"Did you go to sea early?" she asked eagerly.

"When I was ten," he admitted. "I was a cabin boy."

"That must have been a very difficult post to get for one so young," she said admiringly. "I mean, so many lads in seafaring towns must seek it."

"Not really difficult," he said, still looking out to far vistas. "My father was the ship's captain." No need to tell her that he was "Devil Ben" Westing's son or that his father's ship, the *Shark*, was the terror of the seas.

"What trade was he in?" asked the girl from the Scillies, who knew something of the sea.

"Trade?" He turned to look at her then. "Why, mostly the Far East, Africa, India." That much at least was true. The *Shark* had ranged with other freebooters mostly from Madagascar.

"The spice trade!" Her violet eyes sparkled. "How exciting!"

His calm gaze managed to give her no hint of how exciting it had been. He still bore the scars of some of that excitement. "Yes, it was exciting," he admitted, and there was irony in his tone.

She missed that irony. "I have always wanted to see the Spice Islands," she told him.

Not the way I saw them, he thought grimly. *With dead men hanging from the yardarm, half the sails rent and mutiny below!* "They are very beautiful."

"It must have been wonderful, growing up beside your father." She sighed with envy. "Mine died when I was very small."

It had not been wonderful. It had been pure hell. Tom could admire his father's strength and courage, but there had been precious little else to admire. His father's world was not the world of the buccaneers, with gallantry toward women and loyalty to country—privateers, really, whose only enemy was Spain. Tom had learned his trade in an evil world, a world of piracy, where any likely ship was prey if you were strong enough to take it. He had hated that world, and when he was seventeen he had left it, jumped ship and never gone back. Where his father was now, he did not know—and did not care. That Devil Ben would end his life at the end of a hangman's rope, he had little doubt. And Tom had no intention of joining him there.

As he looked down into those trusting violet eyes, the truth trembled on his lips. He yearned to tell Charlotte all about it—of the blackguard his father had been even though he had come of good family once, of how his father had never really married his mother. How, when he was away on one of the long voyages from which he might never return, she had met a shipbuilder and married him and gone to live in Carlisle.

Tom had found out where she was and gone to Carlisle. There he had met a cold reception. He had shipped out, but was now back again—and the reception was just as cold. His mother had three children by the shipbuilder now and she wanted to forget the past—and Tom was part of that past.

"It is true I am by trade a navigator, but in truth I prefer the land," he said. And meant it. Although he had grown up on the rough seas, it was really the land that beckoned him, land and forests and mines. He hoped someday to become a planter, somewhere far from Carlisle. Suddenly he wanted to tell this slip of a girl about that, to share all his dreams with her.

He cursed himself for a fool. She was a child, a wee wisp of a maid, a bud, not yet a flower.

But still he could not bring himself to leave.

They sat on the garden wall with the tall weeds blowing about them and the shining expanse of the lake behind them, and he told her stories—very much expunged—of the sea and the strange tropical lands to the south. Of jungle orchids and of the mahogany that men called rose-wood because when it was fresh-cut it smelled like roses, of flying fish and coral beaches and spice-scented nights beneath the Southern Cross.

He talked to her soberly, as if she were a grown woman.

Charlotte was enthralled.

When Tom left that day, he took her heart with him.

He stopped by once more, two days later, and found her sitting on the garden wall looking dreamily out toward the lake. She turned and looked up rapturously at his approach, for all that he was both dusty and tired.

"I'll be sailing day after tomorrow," he said brusquely. "On the *Mary Constant*. I've signed on for a long voyage." And she was not to know that after that long talk with her in the overgrown garden, he had sat all night on the heights above Aldershot Grange, looking down at the dark pattern of its chimneys against the moon-silvered lake, and fought a great battle with himself. If he stayed, he would do what he had never in his life done—sully a child. For he saw the shining trust in those violet eyes and knew in his heart that she would be easy prey. He was shamed by the thoughts he had had of her—thoughts of bringing her to his bed—and with a wrench he had put them away from him.

And then he remembered her lovely smile, like the sun breaking through the mists above the crags of Helvellyn, and his resolve was shaken.

No, he told himself, he would not do it. He would leave Charlotte as he had found her. Untouched. She deserved to grow up sweet and pure and dreaming.

And the only way she was going to do that was for Tom Westing to put a distance between himself and her. To go away. To sea, preferably, where he could not easily get back in case he weakened. To sea, and on a long voyage. For this elfin half-grown girl with her violet eyes and her wonderful smile had taken such a hold on him as would not easily be broken.

The morning after his vigil on the heights above Aldershot Grange he had made his way back to Carlisle and had signed on the first vessel that needed a navigator.

And now she was looking at him as if her world had collapsed.

"I'll . . . miss you . . ." She faltered.

"And I'll miss you, Charlotte." She would never guess how much! And of a sudden he swept her into his arms and planted a long kiss on those tremulous lips that responded so softly, so vibrantly to his touch.

Resolutely he put her away from him. He was looking down into her eyes, and for a moment he lost himself in their violet depths. Sternly he reminded himself once again of her youth and inexperience. "I brought you something from Carlisle," he said, and gravely took from the pocket of his shabby coat a small gold locket on a delicate chain and clasped it around her neck.

"To remember me by," he said.

As if she could forget!

"Oh, must you go yet?" she cried, distressed, when she saw he was really preparing to leave.

He gave her a wistful smile. "If I stay," he said ruefully, "I'll do something we'll both regret."

She followed him through the garden for a few steps. "You'll come back?" she asked anxiously.

He turned toward her, and all the depth of his yearning reached out to her like a warm soft wind. "Oh, yes, little Charlotte," he said in a rich deep voice that seemed to whir through her senses. "I'll come back."

And then he was gone, swinging away jauntily, heading north along the lakeshore toward Carlisle.

Wend saw it all from the window.

"He's in love with you," she whispered when Charlotte came in. "Any fool can see that! Here, let me see, what did he give you?"

Charlotte held out the locket and gave Wend a misty look.

"He's going far away, on a long voyage aboard the *Mary Constant*. Oh, Wend, do you think I'll ever see him again?" she wondered with a little catch in her voice.

Wend was holding up the locket delightedly. "Oh, you'll see him again," she told Charlotte with a confident chuckle. "But who knows how soon?"

4

Winter 1730

In the great cavernous kitchen of Aldershot Grange, Cook had just burned the venison and the smoke from the big iron skillet was drifting upward past the hanging brass kettles to the blackened beams above. Perched on a three-legged stool beside the enormous stone hearth, where a bright fire was crackling, Charlotte had been listening with the same fascination as Cook and the others to the tale Wend was telling.

Ignoring the smoking mass that was to be their dinner, Wend was still speaking, leaning on her knuckles on the rude plank table, her eyes large and round.

"And when I come walking down by the lake on my way back from visiting my mother, *there it was again!* A woman's white arm reaching up through the ice out of the Derwent Water and beckoning to me—*beckoning!* And I asked myself, *where could it want me to go?*"

Wend's sepulchral voice was accompanied by a sudden shriek of wind that had come down off the crags and was trying to tear off the roof slates, and Charlotte shivered pleasurably. Although she did not really believe in Wend's outrageous stories, it was always fun to hear Wend tell of demons and goblins that stalked the night.

"Where did it want you to go? Why, to the other side of the lake to that lad you're always threatening to run away with!" said Livesay, the butler, who was sitting at his ease

47

at the head of the kitchen board, smoking his long clay pipe. He winked companionably at Wend.

Wend threw him a hurt look. "I've told you twice now that I've broken off with him. Why won't you believe me?"

"But what happened then, Wend?" urged Ivy, the upstairs maid.

"Why, a kind of white light shone over the lake and it fair blinded me!"

"Sun on the ice," suggested Livesay with a grin. "Blinds you every time."

Sleet crashed in a solid sheet against the windowpanes and Livesay's last words were lost in another vengeful howl of the gale.

"But then, Wend?" Ivy demanded. "What happened then?"

"When I could see again, the arm was gone," Wend said sulkily with a dark look at Livesay, who had spoiled her story. "And I come on into the house. That makes twice I've seen it," she added defiantly.

"Wend, you'll be the death of me," sighed Cook, clawing with a long fork at the burnt venison. "You with your tales!"

" 'Tweren't a tale," said Wend with spirit. "*I saw it!*"

Charlotte's slender arms were wrapped around her knees as she listened raptly. Wend's superstitious tales were always a delight. Last week Wend claimed she had seen a headless beast galloping off toward Cat Bells, and the week before that she had seen fierce blue devil's lights burning off Friar's Crag. It was worth eating a burnt dinner just to hear her.

Charlotte's worn old-fashioned clothes had vanished, for on long evenings in the kitchen while Cook dozed by a fire that sputtered on the stone hearth, Charlotte, bending intently over her needle, had taught herself to sew. Not well enough to make her living at it as Wend's mother once had, but well enough to stitch up the simple homespun gown she was now wearing. The cloth she had dyed herself with oak-galls—Cook had shown her how. And although the sunlight had faded it to a rather indeterminate buff, she hoped next year to get enough saffron

crocus blooms to dye a dress saffron yellow to complement
her red-gold hair.

But there was another difference between the girl who
sat at table that December night and the girl who had run
heedless along the watery tarns and becks in early summer. Now Charlotte's violet eyes dreamed and a smile
curved the corners of her soft mouth. For she carried in
her heart the memory of a lover's kiss—at least to her
mind it had been a lover's kiss, and that memory warmed
her on bitter nights when the fire burned out on the
hearth and icicles hung from the eaves and you could see
your breath not just outside the house but inside as well.

"Christmas will soon be here," Ivy said abruptly. "Isn't
it time we drew lots to see who stays with Mistress
Charlotte?"

A miserable look spread over Charlotte's young face, for
she knew that Cook and all the other servants lived
to the southwest in the vicinity of Cat Bells or Buttermere.
In order not to leave her alone in this big house, somebody would have to miss the Yuletide season with family
and friends.

She was overjoyed when Wend spoke up.

"Why don't you come home with me for the holidays?"
she asked Charlotte. "We'd be more than glad to have
you."

Wend's home was on the south shore of the Greta and
they were to arrive on Christmas Eve.

It began to snow shortly before they started out, but
that did not deter them. They were wearing stocking caps
and warm mittens and Cook had prepared for them a
bountiful lunch of cold meat and thick slabs of bread and
scones, which they would eat along the way. She stood in
the kitchen door and waved good-bye as Livesay, who in
this household did far more than "buttle," took them on
the first lap of their journey in the cart.

He let them out hastily when the way worsened, muttering that he'd best get back before the snow got deep or
he'd never make it to Cat Bells this night.

Undaunted and in high spirits, the two girls slogged on
with determination through the snow and made a breath-

less stop for lunch at Castlerigg Stone Circle, which Wend declared was haunted, even though she promptly brushed the snow from one of the stones and sat down upon it to eat her lunch.

Charlotte did the same, and looked around her with interest at the outer circle of thirty-eight snow-capped stones surrounding the inner circle of ten. Around her the mountains brooded. She had been here in summer, of course, when there were soft grasses growing round the lichened stones, but now in winter they looked different. Bleak, unforgiving . . . like gravestones.

She wondered stabbingly if Tom would ever come back. So many men didn't; they were lost at sea. The tall ships weren't called "widowmakers" for nothing. Suddenly the currant-filled scones lost their flavor and Charlotte's thoughts turned grayer than the wintry sky.

"We'd best be off," decided Wend, jumping up with her mouth full. "Snow's getting deep."

It was indeed. They trudged on toward Wend's home cottage, arriving exhausted and grateful to see the smoke from its single stone chimney appear as a smudge through the drifting white flakes. It was a one-room affair with a curtained alcove where Wend's parents slept, and when Charlotte and Wend swept in, bringing with them a shower of snow, that room seemed too small to contain the people in it.

There were shouts of welcome from the children, who clustered around their skirts brushing off the snow. And Wend's mother, who was bent over the hearth stirring up the fire with a poker, turned about to beam at them. Wend's father, crippled from a fall while leading a party up the heights of Helvellyn, tried to rise from his chair—and fell back with a grimace of pain. But his eyes, hazel like Wend's, sparkled through the smoke from his long clay pipe as Wend threw her arms around both her parents, greeting them as if she'd been living as far away as China instead of just down the way at Aldershot Grange.

"And you'll be Mistress Charlotte," said Wend's mother comfortably. "I told Wend to bring you along for Christmas."

Charlotte instantly liked the woman, who seemed like

an older edition of Wend. She told her hostess shyly how much she'd been looking forward to this visit. Wend's mother seemed pleased—it was the first time she'd ever had a visit from "the gentry," and she took Charlotte's mittens and stocking cap and scarf with care and hung them up to dry by the hearth. Charlotte felt deep sympathy for Wend's mother, saddled with all those small mouths to feed, trying to survive on a tiny plot of land in this lonely place with a man who could not help her.

On Christmas Eve, when they sang Christmas carols, Charlotte remembered achingly her Christmases in the Scillies, with her mother gaily playing the spinet and everybody singing, and her eyes filled with tears. If only her mother were here . . .

But her mother was gone, the old happy life in the Scillies was gone, and it was never—any of it—ever going to return. Just as Wend's two brothers who had gone away to sea were never going to return. The singing died away, the supper dishes were cleared, and everybody bedded down, wrapped in heavy wool blankets with snow hissing down the chimney into the dying fire.

They woke to Christmas morning with hugs and kisses and the giving of little homemade gifts—and snow piled up so deep outside that it drifted in over their feet when they opened the door.

They were snowbound the whole week.

Then, just before Twelfth Night there was a brief thaw, which turned all the white surfaces to treacherous glistening ice. And the day after a Twelfth Night celebrated mainly with hot broth and singing, Charlotte and Wend tugged on their stocking caps and mittens and prepared to trudge back to Aldershot Grange.

Just as Wend's mother, who had come outside with a shawl wrapped around her thin shoulders to give Wend a last good-bye hug, cautioned them to be careful, she herself slipped on the ice and fell sprawling, unable to rise.

They got her inside, put her to bed, and decided to postpone their leave-taking until the next day. But the next day Wend's mother was no better; she still could only creep about, stooped over and groaning.

At the door, with her breath making a cloud in the cold air, Wend told Charlotte good-bye. "I've got to stay with Ma," she said. "Else who'll take care of things here?" She hugged her friend and watched Charlotte start out toward Aldershot Grange.

Livesay shook his head when he heard Charlotte's excited scheme of taking Wend's place.

"It won't do," he insisted doggedly. "The master—"

"Uncle Russ needn't know about it!"

"But, Mistress Charlotte, it's not right that you should fetch and carry like a—"

"Wend needs our help, Livesay! She'll be back in the spring—maybe sooner. And Uncle Russ won't even know she's been gone, because you're going to keep on paying her wages and take them over and give them to her." When still he hesitated, she gave him a defiant look. "You don't think I'm strong enough to do Wend's work, but I am—you'll see!"

Livesay shook his head in perplexity and conferred with Cook—as he often did when things got too much for him.

"Mistress Charlotte has a good heart," sighed Cook. "She saw how things were with Wend at home."

"A good heart but not much sense," retorted Livesay. "If the master finds out I went along with this scheme—"

"No need for him to find out," said Cook briskly. "Not if we all swear not to tell."

Livesay groaned, but in the end he agreed that Wend should have her wages, although he remained adamant about not letting Charlotte take Wend's place. Young though she was, he reminded Cook dourly, Mistress Charlotte was still the lady of the house.

That winter and spring marked a time of growing up for Charlotte. Before, she had been a pretty child in a fey half-elfin way. Now she was on her way to becoming a blazing beauty. Even the servants who had known her so long they hardly looked at her anymore remarked it.

And when Wend came back in early summer on a day of blue skies and fleecy clouds and birdsong, she stared at Charlotte and took a step backward in surprise.

"Well, look at *you!*" she marveled.

The two girls eyed each other with new delight, but Charlotte had grown up in other ways too. She no longer teased Wend into slipping away for hours from her job, realizing that Wend's livelihood depended on it. Alone now, even though Wend had returned, Charlotte wandered the glens or climbed the steep rocky paths—and sometimes, as she always had ever since she had found it, she took a book and went to her "secret place" by the waterfall to read and laze the summer days away.

Only now she often found herself laying aside her book to dream.

She dreamed of a tall young man with a laughing face and eyes as green as the sea beyond the Scillies. A man with a magnificent physique and the look of a wanderer to him. A man she knew in her heart she could count on through all the years.

I'll miss you, she had told him, forlorn.

And I'll miss you, Charlotte. The fervor with which he had said that, the vibrant note in his voice, the sudden intensity of his gaze—ah, she would never forget them!

She fingered the gold locket he had given her—and she dreamed of wonderful tomorrows.

Fall came with its crisp days and winter with its mists and snows and howling winds. When blizzards whipped across the Derwent Water and gusts of icy wind nearly toppled the chimneys of Aldershot Grange, when the servants all huddled together by the hearth in the kitchen, Charlotte took long walks in the snow, coming in red-cheeked to stamp the snow off her boots.

Charlotte spent the Twelve Days of Christmas with Wend again that year, but this time they left with more than a light lunch to be eaten at the circle of standing stones. They arrived laden with a whole stuffed goose and wheaten bread and damson preserves and all the apples they could carry from the deep bins in the Grange's cellars—and Charlotte was pleased to find Wend's mother entirely recovered.

Winter whistled by, a harsh winter that froze the lakes and blanketed the valleys in white. Then spring burst forth and Charlotte could again stroll to her favorite haunts, now released from winter's grip, and dream of Tom.

It was on returning from such a walk that she saw Arthur Bodine again. He had come by Aldershot Grange, calling at the house to "look in on her," and from the window he had watched Charlotte strolling back from Friar's Crag, swinging along in her faded homespun dress with her blonde head held proudly, her gait as graceful as the soft-footed deer's.

Bodine, seeing her, marveled. Could this be the thin half-child, half-woman of whom he had reported with a shrug to her uncle, "She is not yet ready—she would make no impression on any man"?

Now, watching her descend the slope, Bodine found that he himself was impressed.

"The wench walks as though her head should wear a crown," he muttered to himself, "though she is dressed more like a serving wench." He frowned thoughtfully, his mind racing.

Hat in hand, he strode toward the door and swung it open to admit this fresh-faced young beauty.

Charlotte stopped at the sight of him. She greeted the swarthy Bodine warily. He had remembered her as frail, but there was a strength in her slenderness, a confidence that surprised him.

Regal, he thought again.

"Mr. Bodine." Charlotte curtsied gravely and with enchanting grace. Then her head lifted and those beautiful violet eyes narrowed. "To what do I owe the honor of your visit, sir?"

Well-spoke, he thought in reluctant admiration. *I am being challenged.*

"I have but stopped by to inquire of your health so that I may report it to your uncle when next I see him," he told her smoothly.

"You may tell my uncle that I am very well but in need of new clothes," said Charlotte crisply.

Bodine's practiced eyes passed over the faded homespun gown, inexpertly made, that Charlotte was now wear-

ing. "Are you saying that you have no better garments
than this?" he demanded in surprise.

"That is exactly what I am saying. And I am sure that is
the reason I have never received an invitation to attend a
ball—I am not presentable!"

"Are there so many balls in these parts?" Bodine asked,
dark brows elevated in amusement.

Charlotte flushed, eyes snapping. She was not to be
mocked on this subject! "I will admit there are none to
speak of." None at all, she might have said, for on either
side of Aldershot Grange were absentee owners who seldom appeared and never really opened their large houses
for entertaining. *"But I should have the proper attire if
one chanced to be given!"*

She looked so pretty saying that, with her young face
flushed and earnest, that Bodine was tempted to laugh.
"Indeed you should, Mistress Charlotte; I am sure you
would grace any ball. I promise to tax your uncle with it,"
he added easily. "It may be that my opinion will carry
some weight."

"I do hope so." But she looked on him more kindly
now. "Will you not stay to sup?" she asked courteously.

"No, I must be getting on while the light lasts." He
swept her another urbane bow. But he cast a last lingering
look backward as he left. *I shall have something to tell
Russ this time,* he was thinking. *The wench is ready!*

The dress arrived at Aldershot Grange shortly after,
brought by a lad who said he could not wait.

Charlotte received the large box in surprise. The most
she had expected from Bodine was to mention her need
for clothing to Uncle Russ—but since the box had arrived
so quickly, Bodine had obviously taken the matter in hand
himself. She chided herself for misjudging her uncle's
swarthy friend—never guessing Bodine intended to charge
Russ double what he'd paid.

The dress the box contained was to Charlotte a miracle.
It was of lissome white voile and very modish, with a skirt
that swirled around her graceful young legs as lightly as a
butterfly's wings. A wide band of heavy white lace at the
base of the three-quarter-length sleeves was finished with

a froth of white voile ruffles from which her slender fore-arms emerged. Below the tight bodice, remarkably low-cut (indeed Bodine had ordered it cut lower, while the seamstress had tightened her lips and muttered darkly that something would "pop out"), the long full skirt of the white voile overdress swung out fashionably, split down the center and both sides decorated with heavy white point lace trailing four inches wide down the length of the skirt, over a bell-shaped white linen petticoat embroidered in white silk and encrusted with lace. Charlotte gasped to see the wide top panniers of the whalebone structure that gave the wide skirt such elegance. Not since she had lived in the Scillies had she seen anything like that. And besides that there was a tiny white lace cap edged with white ribands that fell through her long blonde hair down below her shoulders. And a pair of soft white slippers that actually fit (a lucky guess of Bodine's) and white gloves and a white-painted fan.

The effect, for all the tempting low cut, at which Livesay blinked and Ivy moaned rapturously and Cook muttered, was strikingly virginal and entirely enticing.

Charlotte was so excited she almost wept. She tried the entire costume on and ran downstairs to twirl around the cavernous kitchen to the delight of Wend and the other servants. She broke into a dance her mother had taught her when she was a small child. The steps might be out-of-date now, but her young body was so graceful, her feet in their soft new shoes tripped so lightly across the stone floor, that the servants—even disapproving Cook, who objected to so much of Charlotte's bosom showing—cheered her on, clapping their hands until finally, flushed and laughing, she collapsed onto one of the long benches at the rude trestle table.

"I think I've never been so happy!" she gasped.

Wend, who had been off visiting her mother along the Greta, had come bouncing in while Charlotte was dancing, and stood watching while Charlotte collapsed laughing at the kitchen table.

"Oh, Wend, isn't it a beautiful dress?" she cried, smoothing out the skirt that rippled like cream. "My uncle's friend sent it to me. Oh, Wend, I think I've never been so happy!"

"Oh, I think you could be quite a lot happier," was Wend's lazy comment.

Charlotte shot a look at her. "What do you mean?"

"I mean," Wend said with enormous nonchalance, "that on the way here I ran across Will the Peddler. He was just down from Carlisle, where he'd been buying his goods along the waterfront. He told me a ship had just been sighted coming in, and someone with a glass said it was the *Mary Constant*. She was still far out but she'd be docking on the next tide."

The *Mary Constant*—Tom's ship! The look on Charlotte's young face dazzled even Wend.

Tom Westing was back!

5

Early Summer 1732

That day in early June dawned bright, and Charlotte, who had been far too excited to sleep the night before, was up with the dawn and demanding of a sleepy-eyed Wend how long she thought it would take a man to reach Aldershot Grange from Carlisle.

"That depends on whether he's afoot or riding." Wend yawned.

"Well, I doubt he'll be riding," said Charlotte reluctantly. "After all, he's a navigator and he doesn't own a horse."

"So don't look for him before tomorrow at the earliest."

But of course he could hire a horse, or manage a ride in a cart . . . Charlotte spent all the afternoon half-dressed, watching from her casement, ready to slip into her wondrous new gown the moment she saw Tom's familiar form in the distance.

The sun set without him.

The next day she was certain he'd be here, so she dressed herself in the white gown and went out and sat on the garden wall, arranging her skirts to make a pretty picture for him from a distance. After a while the sun grew too hot for wall perching—after all, she wanted to look cool and fresh when he arrived—so she waited beneath the shady branches of a nearby tree.

Hunger finally drove her inside.

"There's lots of reasons why he wouldn't be here yet," Wend tried to comfort her. "Maybe there was some trouble docking the ship. Or something about the cargo."

"But would that keep the navigator aboard?" wondered Charlotte.

"Who knows?" Wend, who knew nothing of the sea, shrugged. "It might."

Charlotte brightened a little at that, but Cook noted that she scarcely touched her dinner.

The following day, when Tom still didn't come, Charlotte didn't touch her dinner at all. She shook out the lovely new dress and packed it carefully away. To await some great ball, she told herself—and then her eyes filled with tears.

Outside, as if to suit her mood, the weather changed. Overcast days replaced sunny ones. Gray clouds swirled overhead and there was a mist of rain in the air. Charlotte, now back in her buff homespun, wandered out uncaring into the dismal weather. She found her way aimlessly northward along the eastern shore of the Derwent Water, feeling the dampness in her hair, feeling her clothes grow limp.

Tom had not come after all. No doubt she had been a fool to expect him, Charlotte scolded herself. More than a year and a half had gone by since Tom had left England— perhaps he had found another girl somewhere. The thought cut deep.

A low promontory rose just ahead, but Charlotte had not the heart to climb it. She sat down on a rock and pulled up a blade of grass from nearby, tested it with her teeth. It tasted springlike and sour—but no sourer than her thoughts. For until now she had had a lover, if only in her dreams. Now she had no one.

She sat there, head drooping, for a long time. Finally she decided that there was no sense coming in drenched, and she threw away the grass stem she had been twisting in her fingers. She got up and tossed back her wet blond hair.

As she did so she saw a figure silhouetted against the gray sky, a figure in a tricorne hat.

Tom!

Charlotte's heart gave such a great leap inside her chest that she felt it must surely burst her bodice. Before her the figure on the promontory saw her as well and waved. Now he was hurrying down the incline, moving awkwardly, she saw, because he was walking with the aid of a stout stick. *That* was why he hadn't arrived before, he'd been hurt! Charlotte picked up her skirts and ran like a deer toward him.

And came to a halt halfway up the slope, suddenly overcome by shyness.

Not so Tom. At sight of her he gave a whoop and began to run down the slope, tossing aside his stick as he ran. And brought up before her, beaming.

"So you're still here," he said. "I was afraid you might not be."

Charlotte found her voice. "Oh, yes, Tom—I'm still here."

And then—neither of them ever knew later just how it happened or who made the first move—they were in each other's arms, Tom was holding her so close the buttons of his coat bit into her flesh, and Charlotte was saying, "I knew your ship had come into port, and oh, Tom, I was so afraid you weren't coming!"

Tom's grip tightened and his lips were on her wet hair so that his voice was muffled as he said huskily, "Little chance of that!"

It had begun to rain in earnest now, but neither of them noticed.

"When I first saw you, I thought you were hurt!" she exclaimed.

"No, 'tis my shoe," was his cheerful rejoinder. "There's a hole worn in it I could put my fist through. I had stuck a piece of leather in it but I lost it."

"Your . . . shoe?" she asked, fascinated. "But why haven't you had it fixed?"

"I didn't want to take the time." He laughed. "For I had a wench waiting at Aldershot Grange."

"But you've been home a week or more!"

"I've been in Scotland."

She stared at him openmouthed, and tasted the falling rain. *"Scotland?"*

"Aye," he said grimly. "And a fool's chase it was." He explained that they had cast anchor in Carlisle harbor at night and he had gone ashore with the others, meaning to get a good night's sleep and hire a horse to ride to the Grange. He'd had but two rounds of ale with his shipmates before he left the carouse and headed back for his inn. " 'Twas in a dark alley that they set upon me. Five men who'd been lying in wait. I might have managed the four who came at me from the front and sides, but the one from the back near cracked my skull, and my friends found me later unconscious and robbed of my entire ship's wages."

"Oh, Tom," breathed Charlotte. "How awful!"

"Awful it was," he agreed dryly. "And I have naught but my own folly to blame."

"Oh, but you couldn't know—"

"I could," he said, his tone definite. "I'm used to rough towns"—*and rougher men,* he might have added, but didn't—"and I was not taking proper care when I went into that alley. My mind was on a wench." He gave her a whimsical smile that made her heart lurch happily.

"Did they ever find the men?"

He shook his head. "One of my friends found me—and brought me to with a bucket of water and some brandy. I had the damnedest headache. And then we searched the town for the thieves who robbed me. 'Twas late morning before we learned that a party of five who met their description had been seen around dawn setting out for the north. We tracked them over the border and there lost their trail." His voice turned rueful. "Save for the few coins my friends lent me—all spent for hired horses and lodgings along the way—I'm as poor as the day you found me."

"It doesn't matter," Charlotte told him warmly. "I don't care for money at all."

Tom snorted. "Shows how young you are! 'Tis money keeps a roof over your head and the rain out—never say you don't care for money, Charlotte!"

"Well, you know what I mean." She was suddenly aware that water was running down her forehead and into her eyes. "It's raining," she said wonderingly.

Tom laughed and hugged her. "We didn't seem to notice!"

But he let her retrieve his stick and urge him down toward Aldershot Grange, where, she told him blithely, "We'll hang up our clothes and dry off."

His brows shot up at her choice of words, but the idea was so appealing that he went with her willingly enough. She brought him into the kitchen with a flourish.

"I am entertaining a gentleman tonight," she told them all grandly. "We will have supper for two served in the dining room, if you please."

Cook winked at Wend, and Ivy gasped, but Livesay was equal to the occasion. He rose and acknowledged his mistress's order with a deferential nod. "Yes, Mistress Charlotte," he said gravely.

"Oh, and . . . we're both soaking wet."

"We can all see that," muttered Wend, eyeing the puddle in which they were standing.

"I'm going up to change, and I'll need a hot bath. Wend, will you bring it up? And Tom will be wanting a hot bath too. In the green bedchamber, I think. And a dressing gown—one of my uncle's—while his clothes dry by the hearth. Would you see to it, Livesay?"

Again that courtly nod. All the servants loved their employer's young niece, and if she wanted to play hostess, they would do their best to assist her.

Tom limped gingerly over to the hearth and sat down upon a three-legged stool.

"Tom wore a hole in his shoe while he was out chasing the covey of thieves who stole his money and fled to Scotland," she announced regretfully. "I'm afraid we can't do anything about that. My uncle didn't leave any shoes here when he left for London."

Livesay cleared his throat. "I was apprenticed to a cobbler in my youth," he explained. " 'Twas a trade I disliked, which is why I don't talk about it. But there's leather in the stable and I can still mend a shoe. If you'll give me the

shoe tonight, young sir, I'll guarantee you 'twill be fixed
by morning."

Tom's eyes lit up and Charlotte breathed, "Oh, Livesay,
that would be wonderful. I do want to show Tom the
countryside, but how can I if he's limping?"

Everyone in the kitchen beamed.

Charlotte left them and went upstairs to bathe in the
hot water Wend brought—along with word that both Cook
and Ivy were atwitter over Tom's arrival. She dashed away
carrying Charlotte's white voile dress to be pressed by
Ivy, who had a knack for those things. Charlotte soaked
lazily in the metal hip tub and then dried herself on linen
towels. She thought she might not have given Tom time to
get his clothes dry and to climb back into them, but when
Wend arrived bearing the meticulously pressed white voile
dress, she rolled her eyes and warned Charlotte that "Tom
Westing is pacing the hall waiting for you to come down
those front stairs, and you'd best hurry, for I think Ivy has
fallen in love with him!"

Charlotte laughed and Wend helped her into the dress,
and between them they got her long hair—which had
gotten wet in her bath—combed out and tied back with a
riband.

"And if you don't come down quick," Wend warned,
giving Charlotte's hair a last pat, "Cook is going to have a
fit, because she's been waiting supper for you."

Thus alerted, Charlotte ran soundlessly down the hall
on her soft white slippers ad paused at the head of the
stairs to drink in the sight of the broad-shouldered man
who paced restlessly about below. In the wild excitement
of seeing him again she had not realized until now that he
was wearing new clothes. The russet trousers that encased
his strong muscular legs now matched a russet coat that
sported brass buttons instead of wooden. And the coat had
wider cuffs and was of a better cut than the one he had
worn when he embarked (she would have blushed with
pleasure had she known he had bought them both to
impress her at his last port of call).

But new clothes or no, Tom had not really changed, she
thought fondly, looking down at that shock of fair hair, and

jaunty gait. Still . . . there *was* something different about him. She pondered over what that difference was, and it came to her that it was in indefinable *presence*. The wild lad had become a man, no longer a tall stripling gone a-roving, but a strong man to reckon with. And to love.

And the green eyes that looked up and caught her standing there were a man's eyes, hot with passion, yet steady too. Her heart abrim, clad in her lovely new white dress, Charlotte floated down the broad front stairway to meet her lover.

Standing in his stocking feet in the hall below—for he had surrendered his shoes to Livesay—Tom Westing thought he had never seen anything more beautiful. Charlotte had toweled her wet hair almost dry before combing it, and it now cascaded from its riband down her back in a blonde shower of silk. The shapeless clothes in which he remembered her had given little hint of the beauty of her slender form, any more than had the wet bedraggled homespun in which she had greeted him today, but now her young loveliness was deftly revealed by the white voile gown. He had left behind him a child, but he had come back to a woman. He stood the straighter and drew a deep breath. It seemed to him that everything a man could possibly desire in this world was coming toward him down the stairs.

"Charlotte," he said wonderingly, "you've become a beauty."

There would be no compliment in her life Charlotte would ever treasure like that one.

They went in to the dining room, which, under Livesay's supervision, was set out as majestically as if the master was entertaining Lord Pimmerston from nearby Castle Stroud. The board was heavy with silver—most of it tarnished, for there'd been no time to clean and polish it. There was a loaf of sugar and a pair of great salts, and a large white linen cloth—clean but mended, for the master cared little for such things.

It didn't matter really. Neither Tom nor Charlotte saw anything but each other that night.

Tom was looking at her wistfully down the long board.

He had meant to bring his ship's wages and throw them—
along with his heart—at her feet. He had meant to propose marriage and ask her to run away with him, for he
was not fool enough to suppose that her uncle would favor
a marriage between a man like him and the niece of the
master of Aldershot Grange. On shipboard, all those nights
away from her, it had seemed possible, reasonable even.
He would return, she would be waiting . . .

And he had returned, and she had been waiting, and
now none of it was possible because he'd been fool enough
to let himself be robbed in some dark alley in Carlisle.
Now he had nothing to offer her, nothing.

Looking into each other's eyes, they ate Cook's best
hasty supper—and never knew afterward what they ate.

They sat long at table, laughing and talking, and when
they had done at last, Charlotte rose and spoke to Livesay,
who hovered nearby.

"Master Tom and I are going to take a stroll in the
garden if it's stopped raining," she told him. "Please have
Ivy prepare the green bedchamber for him when we return."

Livesay frowned, and when Charlotte ran upstairs to get
a light shawl against the damp, he went up to Tom, who
stood waiting by the garden door. Livesay might not have
been wearing livery these days, but he knew what life in a
gentleman's household should be like—indeed *had been*
like when Charlotte's grandfather was alive.

"I'm sorry to speak out like this, young sir," he began.
"But seeing as there's no proper chaperon for Mistress
Charlotte about the place—"

"I take your meaning, Livesay," Tom interrupted. "Very
commendable of you to mention it. I won't be sleeping in
the house tonight, or any other night, but I will avail
myself of a space in the stables if that's convenient?"

"Oh, most convenient." Livesay looked vastly relieved.
"And there'll be clean sheets on the straw and a pillow
waiting for you in the loft. Timmy, the stableboy, will
show you just where they are. And come morning there'll
be a basin and towels for washing too."

Tom chuckled. "You'll spoil me, Livesay, that you will.

And you can rest easy about Mistress Charlotte. I promise not to overstep the bounds, chaperon or no chaperon."

Then Charlotte appeared and Livesay melted away obsequiously into the background while she took Tom into the garden.

They walked past dripping rosebushes unburied at last from the weeds, for Charlotte had been getting the garden ready for this walk for over a year and a half now. Their feet trod the wet stones of the narrow garden path and Charlotte had to swish her lifted skirts toward Tom's knee breeches to keep them from getting wet from the dripping shrubbery.

The moon cast a silvery radiance over the Derwent Water, and nearby there was the whir of owls; the scent of roses, made clinging by the dampness, filled the air with a heady perfume. Somehow at that moment Charlotte felt more aware of the world around her than she had ever been. Somewhere nearby a bird trilled a single sleepy note and the small questing sound went right through her. The tall man beside her was looking down at her with love in his eyes, and his very nearness made her dizzy.

"God, I've missed you," he murmured, and she went wordlessly into his outstretched arms, felt her knees grow weak as she leaned against that deep chest and listened to the strong regular beat of his heart.

She wanted to tell him how much she had missed him too, but her heart was too full at that moment to speak. The magic of the world was all around her—and then he bent his lips to hers, slowly, tenderly, with grace, and the world disappeared and there was only Tom. Tom, her lover.

She felt his mouth change position over her own, she felt his tongue now delicately probing her lips, finding its way gently, demandingly between them, she felt her young body bent backward until she seemed to be lying on his strong outstretched hand, and she twined her arms around his neck and gave herself up to whatever lay in store.

Nothing lay in store.

Tom put her away from him suddenly and his voice was roughened with feeling.

"You're too much for me tonight, Charlotte. I'll say good night."

Charlotte opened her eyes and looked up into his rueful face. For a moment she felt confused, indignant; then it came to her that he was not rejecting her—in his way, he was *protecting* her. And with the knowledge came a wonderful new feeling, of being precious to someone, and all the joys of being a woman flooded through her.

Still lying back on his spread hand and outstretched arm, she smiled her enchanting smile and slid her arms from around his neck to cup his face in her hands.

"Why, Tom?" she asked with innocent witchery. "Tell me why."

He groaned. "You *know* why, Charlotte," he said firmly, and straightened her up and abruptly removed his arm. "Good night."

He was moving away from her before she said, "You're going the wrong way. The house is over here."

Tom turned. "Aye, it is."

For a dreadful moment she thought he was leaving Aldershot Grange, and the moonlight lost its luster.

"Didn't you like the green bedchamber?" she asked, crestfallen. "It's the one I had made up for you."

His deep sigh reached her across the scent of roses. "I liked it, Charlotte. But I'll not be sleeping in it. I've already told Livesay to bed me down in the stables."

"You'll *not* sleep in the stables!" she flared.

"I will," he said. "And that's final. I've a care for your reputation if you do not. You've no female chaperon here and your uncle's not in residence. Do you want word to get around that you're entertaining a gentleman caller— and one who'd be placed below the salt at that—*overnight*? In the green bedchamber?"

His humorous assessment of the situation brought an answering flicker to her violet eyes, but she was prepared to insist.

"Nevertheless," she said, "you *are* my guest, and—"

"And therefore bound by honor to remain on good behavior," he said lightly. "Should your uncle arrive in the night, I'd not like him to find you entertaining a male guest in the house. Just suppose he arrived toward morning, Charlotte—what do you think he'd do?"

"If he didn't like your explanation, he'd most likely horsewhip you," admitted Charlotte with a sigh.

"Right," he agreed cheerfully. "And he'd be within his rights. No, I'll be better off in the stable loft and you'll be better off if you let me have my way in the matter."

Charlotte pouted, but she bade him good night. From the garden door she watched him head out for the stables.

After all, she told herself sternly, *for all they were in love, they hardly knew each other.* . . .

But all her admonitions to herself faded when she went back to the kitchen to find Cook and Livesay gone—and Tom's sheets neatly stacked on the kitchen table on top of a pillow.

"Well, look at that!" marveled Wend, coming in just then. "Ivy must have forgotten to take those sheets out to the stables when she spilled the drippings and Cook chased her out of the kitchen!" Her smile on Charlotte was bland. "Would you like me to take them out to Tom?"

"Oh, no, you've been fetching and carrying ever since he got here," said Charlotte hastily. "I don't mind doing it, Wend."

Indeed she glowed as she swooped down on the table and swept the bedding up in her arms. For this meant she would see him once again before she went to bed. She spun about so swiftly that her skirts swirled out, and marched through the moonlight out to the stone stable.

"You see?" whispered Wend, watching Charlotte's progress through a crack in the kitchen door. "I did right to tell the stableboy to get lost for a while—just like you did right to 'forget' those sheets, Ivy! Did you see how happy she looked when she ran out the door?"

Ivy, who at Wend's insistence had been hiding in the buttery, now came out.

"What will Livesay say?" she muttered, rolling her eyes.

"He won't know," Wend said coolly. "He's off locking the front door, and Cook's gone out to keep him occupied by complaining about the meat he's been buying."

Wend had a talent for intrigue.

Charlotte, when she opened the stable door into what seemed total darkness, wished she had brought a lantern along.

"Tom," she half-whispered, for she was aware that the stableboy slept here—somewhere, she thought, at the far end of the big hayloft above.

"Yes?" he answered her instantly, almost as if he had been expecting her.

"I've brought your sheets and a pillow. Ivy forgot to bring them."

Tom came down the ladder. Now that her eyes had grown accustomed to the darkness, she could see him vaguely, and when he crossed a shaft of moonlight she walked forward and deposited the bedclothes in his arms.

"Thank you," he said gravely, and with them under his arm he went whistling up the ladder.

Charlotte followed him up.

"Someone must make your bed," she declared anxiously. "And since Ivy forgot . . ."

She made his bed in a shaft of moonlight that came in through chinks in the roof, chinks that the stableboy had complained must be repaired. Tom watched her silently.

She looked so dainty and industrious there, carefully spreading out sheets on the hay, arranging his pillow, plumping it. Every bone in his body ached to claim her.

"Here, lie down and see if this won't do." She threw out an arm, indicating that he should try out the bed.

Reluctantly Tom took off his shoes and lay down.

"There," she said. "That will do nicely." And suddenly she was kneeling beside him. "Oh, Tom, won't you reconsider the green room? I don't want you to sleep in the stables while I . . ."

Her voice trailed off, her face was very near, he could smell the slight perfume of her hair, like wildflowers, and her breath was sweet and light upon his face. His arms seemed to move of themselves, to sweep her toward him to lie across his broad chest. His cheek grazed her own as he pressed hot kisses upon her lips. His hands stroked her back, her arms, and were suddenly easing down her tight bodice.

Charlotte felt a summer madness stealing over her. Tonight she did not care what he did—indeed whatever he did would be right, *must* be right. They loved each other, they would always feel exactly as they did at this moment, and around them the dark stable, moonlit through the chinks in the roof, with only the sound of a sleepy barn owl moving on its roost, and the restless hooves of the horses disturbing the straw below, seemed of a sudden the most romantic spot in the world.

Her right shoulder was out of her gown now and the two top hooks of her bodice had burst open from the strain of his probing fingers. Tom's warm hand was cupping her breast through the thin cambric of her chemise, and she moaned as he pulled the riband that held her chemise and the fabric slid away, leaving her breast bare to his lips, which found and toyed with the shell-pink nipple. It hardened tensely at his touch and she felt her breath coming fast and now faster. She was lying across his hips and she could feel the hardness of his manhood against her thigh. She moved restlessly, swept away by new feelings that crowded about, exhilarating, sweet.

And suddenly she found herself lying on her back on the linen sheet, hearing the soft crunch of hay as Tom's knees on either side of her bored downward with his weight. She was looking up at him with arms spread wide, lips parted, eyes alight, when he jerked himself away from her with a groan and stood breathing hard, looking down at her.

"Get up," he said, and his voice was uneven, husky with desire. "Get up and leave. *Now!*"

Charlotte gave him a hurt look and sat up. She tugged her bodice back up over her shoulder—which was agony for Tom, watching the ripple of her young flesh. And she hesitated deliberately, letting her fingers flutter over the hooks that had pulled free, so that the upper part of her firm young breasts was still exposed to his avid gaze.

"Down the ladder," he said tersely, and took her by the hand and swung her to her feet.

She was being dismissed! With her head high, she moved toward the ladder, welcoming his strong grip on her hand as she felt with her foot for the top rung. She did not say another word to him. After all, she had her pride!

When she got back to the kitchen, still seething with indignation at Tom's sudden rejection of all that she had offered, she had forgotten about those top hooks. She was glad to find that no one but Wend was there.

"Well," said Wend, eyeing the hooks and the hay in Charlotte's disheveled hair, "I see that you fought—and won, more's the pity."

Charlotte flushed and her hand clutched the errant hooks to cover them. "I may never speak to him again," she warned darkly.

Wend's chuckle followed her as she flounced out.

6

The next morning Charlotte sensed a change in Tom, a sudden reserve, as if during the night a wall had been built up between them. They breakfasted on delicious Cumbrian sausages in the long dining room, and Wend kept finding reasons to bustle into the room, even though Livesay was serving them. And every now and then through a crack in the door Charlotte saw Ivy's curious face peering in.

It made her feel awkward, all this surveillance, and after breakfast she determined to get Tom away from them.

"I'll show you Castle Stroud today—if your blisters are up to it?" she suggested.

"I'm up to anything," Tom assured her cheerfully.

But she noticed as they walked along the lakeshore that he was trying not to get too close, trying not to touch her—and wondered why. Could it be that she had offended him last night?

That she could even think such a thing only revealed her youth and inexperience with men. In truth Tom was beginning to be afraid of himself, of what he might do when Charlotte came too close. The light wildflower fragrance of her hair made him want to bury his face in its golden shower, and the lightest touch of her hands made his flesh quiver and yearn for her. It was true he had been a long time at sea, but he had never had this overpowering desire for any woman, and the sneaking feeling that he might lose control unnerved him.

"Are there people living at Castle Stroud?" he asked, having passed by that great stone pile on his journeys back and forth from Carlisle. "I had thought it to be deserted."

"Livesay says it hasn't really been lived in since 1700," Charlotte told him. "He says the last Lord Pimmerston meant to move back in, but then he died and the present Lord Pimmerston divides his time between London and a large estate near Sheffield. He never comes here, but there's a caretaker in residence. He's very nice, he told me that Wend and I could wander through the place whenever we chose, so long as we didn't break anything, for then he'd be held responsible."

Tom smiled down at her earnestness. "And do you come here often?"

"Never in winter," she said. "He closes it up tight. But in summer, yes. Oh, Tom, it's the most beautiful house in the world!"

"Just where you'd choose to live if you could?" he murmured, and something in his green eyes clouded, for he knew *he* could never give her a house like that.

"Oh, yes," she breathed. "The house, yes! But," she added provokingly, "I'd want it all moved to some nice warm place like the Scillies!"

Tom threw back his head and laughed. "Charlotte, Charlotte, quite contrary! So not even that great pile of Castle Stroud is good enough for you—unless it's moved stone by stone?"

She laughed too, her face reflecting the joy of walking beside him as she had longed to do for so long. "Oh, of course it would be!" She gave his hand a little squeeze. "Let's stroll through the rooms and pretend it's ours, Tom!"

Without meaning to, she had driven a barb into his heart. His lady was ambitious, he could see that now— something he had overlooked before. For all her scorn of money, she wanted what it bought—she wanted *more*.

When the medieval towers and battlements and crenellated gray stone walls of Castle Stroud reared up before him, Tom's expression was glum.

The caretaker of the castle, a stooped old man, greeted Charlotte warmly, eyed Tom with twinkling curiosity, and confided his big news—that a stranger had stopped by to tell him Lord Pimmerston might be coming north for a visit soon, and although some servants would accompany his lordship's party, of course, he'd better be ready to round up extra help locally on short notice.

"Isn't that wonderful, Tom?" Charlotte led Tom, almost dancing, through the first of the two courtyards that were divided by the kitchen, banqueting hall, and dining room.

"Wonderful," he echoed without enthusiasm.

"And that means the castle will be full of people, for he'll bring guests from London or at least Sheffield, and we'll have *neighbors*, Tom, at least for a while! We haven't had any neighbors on either side of us since I've been here, because Blade's End to the south of us is tied up in some kind of estate that Uncle Russ once said probably never *would* be settled. Just think, neighbors!"

"Neighbors," repeated Tom stonily. All his life he had been beset by neighbors who lived too close and threw their slops into the street, where one must step warily, neighbors who kept the night lively with marital discord and squalling children and sometimes drunken brawls. He sighed and followed her as she entered the big elaborate dining room.

"I love this room," she breathed. "So much nicer than anything we have at the Grange. Oh, Tom, I wish I could have entertained you here!"

Tom's rueful gaze passed over the dining room's handsome paneling, the alcove's carved medallions, and got lost in the maze of heraldic ceiling paintings.

She gestured. "And above this is the great chamber—it's exactly the same shape. Oh, come along, I'll show it to you!"

Silent now, Tom let her lead him along.

She brought him into the great chamber with a flourish. "Just look, Tom!"

Tom looked. He saw a splendid room with an Elizabethan frieze and handsome roof timbers. Like Charlotte, he suddenly imagined this large room filled with lords and ladies, elegantly dressed in satin and silk, the men fastidiously taking snuff from gold snuffboxes, the women waving delicate ivory fans—and all of them turning away from plain Tom Westing, who had neither newfound wealth nor background to justify his existence.

Charlotte, enchanted with her surroundings, did not see the expression on his face.

"Lord Pimmerston is sure to give a great ball, and the whole countryside will be invited! Oh, wouldn't it be wonderful to dance here, Tom, in this very room?" She left his side and pirouetted gaily across the floor, her thin white voile dress billowing out around her flying feet.

Tom felt a lump form in his throat. He thought she should dance here too—and wave her fan among the elegant company he envisioned occupying this room. *And that was something he could not offer her. . . .*

Eager to show him all the wonders of Castle Stroud, she pulled him along the airy long gallery; she stopped before the great bay windows, some of whose panes bulged outward to enchant the eye with distorted vistas, and pointed out the terraced gardens below, which the last Lord Pimmerston had laid out before he had fallen into the lake and drowned. And Tom looked moodily out at those vast gardens and estimated in his head how many gardeners it would take to keep them up.

Suddenly Charlotte hugged him in her exuberance and he knew an exquisite torture, for with every word she said his world was tumbling down about his ears.

"Charlotte, the caretaker can see us," he said huskily.

"Where? I don't see him." Charlotte peered out through one of the straighter panes.

"He was there," Tom sighed, and turned away down the long corridor. Livesay had done a fine job mending his shoe, but Tom had lost the springiness of step with which he had accompanied Charlotte when they started out.

Charlotte noticed that. "Oh, Tom, I've kept you walking all day!" she cried penitently. "I forgot all about your blisters."

"No matter," he said. "We can sit outside among those flowers and weeds you love so much, and I'll rest my foot."

Charlotte was delighted to accompany him to any part of the castle, inside or out—she loved it all. And as for Tom, to sit beside her on the low stone wall of the terraced garden looking down across the shimmering expanse of the Derwent Water with the blue hills rising in the distance was a stolen delight he could not resist.

He sighed when they rose to leave, and Charlotte took that to mean that he had fallen in with her own mood.

"Oh, Tom, I always do so hate to leave this place," she told him wistfully. "And I can see you hate to leave it too." She looked around her, drinking it all in.

Tom thought she shouldn't be leaving it—she belonged in a place like this, a castle setting. Why hadn't he seen it? Their footsteps turned toward Aldershot Grange and he glanced back at the crenellated gray stone walls and towers and enormous multipaned stone-mullioned windows— Tom had never in his life even lived *near* a house with mullioned windows. As all that grandeur faded away behind them, bitterness pierced his soul. Beside him walked a young aristocrat. He had thought of her only as a girl before, but now, having just seen her in her natural habitat, he knew her for what she was—too good for the likes of him. He could see that now.

He stared down at Charlotte, talking vivaciously. He drank in the sheen of her golden hair and listened to the lilt in her voice, and he asked himself how he could ever have dared to dream that she would be content to share the simple life he could give her.

And when Lord Pimmerston came north with his London and Sheffield houseguests, there would be more than one gentleman among that party who would discover Charlotte's fresh young beauty, and she would be offered the kind of life she wanted in a house like this, beside some other young aristocrat who would take her to wife. A different world. . . . His gaze was bleak.

"I can see you would hate to leave it," was all he said.

And then she was showing him a bank of golden gorse

along the way, and admiring the distant view across the
lake, laughing as a startled rabbit leapt up and ran by
almost beneath their feet, nearly skipping along the path
in her excitement to be spending not just an hour or two
but a whole day with him. And she never realized that her
exuberance, her girlish chatter, which had in reality been
brought on by his very presence, had brought him to
despair.

At supper that night Tom was very quiet, listening to
the musical sound of Charlotte's voice rather than her
words, admiring the way the candlelight seemed to light
up her hair, losing himself in the depths of those lustrous
violet eyes that smiled so winningly at him across the long
board.

Happy and excited, Charlotte did not really notice his
wistfulness—she was already making plans for what they
would do tomorrow. Visit Blade's End, she thought, so
Tom could see what lay on the other side of Aldershot
Grange along the lakeshore.

But when Tom told her firmly in the kitchen that he
would return to the stable alone that night "because it's
beginning to rain," Charlotte found reason to protest.

"I'm not a sugar loaf—I won't melt!" She laughed, preparing to accompany him anyway.

"No, I won't have you getting wet," he said, so firmly
that Cook and Livesay exchanged glances.

Rebuffed, Charlotte fell back. "Good night then," she
said, puzzled.

"Good night, Charlotte." Tom gave her a last lingering
look and was gone into the drizzle.

"Do you think we've seen the last of him?" Cook asked
Livesay when Charlotte had gone up to her bedchamber.
"He had a farewell look on his face, if you ask me."

Livesay shook his head. "No, the lad's a glutton for
punishment. He knows he can't have the likes of Mistress
Charlotte, but like a moth he hovers around the flame."

"And gets singed," said Cook sourly.

"But I don't think he'll be off with a blistered foot into a
rainy night," said Livesay.

Charlotte too had seen that "farewell look" on Tom's

face, and although she hadn't really understood it, it had made her uneasy, and made her sleep restlessly. She dreamed that she and Tom were walking toward Castle Stroud and an eerie darkness fell, followed by a moaning black wind that shuddered through the trees, tore off the leaves and branches, and caught them and swept them apart. She dreamed that she was flying through the treetops calling his name and hearing his voice calling out to her, ever harder to hear as it receded into the distance. She woke with a beating heart to the sound of a shutter banging, and sat crouched in her bed shivering, still caught up in the terror of her dream.

It was as if Tom's spirit was calling out to her, telling her something was amiss.

She did not go back to sleep that night, but waited only for dawn to break before dressing and running downstairs. In the big kitchen Cook gave her a concerned look and Wend looked mutinous. Tom, it seemed, had already breakfasted and was about to leave for Carlisle.

"But you can't!" she wailed. "You've barely gotten here."

Tom looked tired. And no wonder—he had been wrestling with himself all night. At least his better judgment had been wrestling with the rest of him, which considered him a prize fool.

He hesitated. Then, "Walk with me as far as Friar's Crag, Charlotte?"

"Of course, but—" From the restless look he wore, she dared not argue further. He might very well leave without her!

Although she tried to make conversation, Tom's answers were short and glum all the way to the low wooded promontory of Friar's Crag. His face was very set, for he had let Charlotte believe him to be what he was not. He had let her jump to the conclusion that his past would bear inspection, that he had been in the spice trade. Now he would tell her the truth and watch her draw away from him. Better now than later.

"Charlotte, sit down," he commanded tersely. "I have something to tell you."

Charlotte sat.

He did not sit down himself, but stood with his face turned toward the mouth of Borrowdale Valley, where an arched stone bridge crossed the Derwent at a narrow point called the Jaws of Borrowdale. He felt as if those jaws were swallowing him.

"I've never told you the truth about myself," he said quietly. "You're going to hear it now."

Silent, Charlotte listened, ached to hear of the little boy born out of wedlock on a sandspit in the Bahamas. Brought up helter-skelter, surviving as best he could, and then carried away as a cabin boy by his pirate father on the *Shark* to Madagascar. Tom spared himself nothing in the telling, his voice dispassionate—indeed he might have been speaking of someone else, someone for whom he cared little. But all the force of his character came through to Charlotte as he talked, and she saw before her a man who had hated the world of piracy, who had used what gold he had gained to help captives escape their sordid fate and reach their homes, and who had at the first opportunity jumped ship and made his way back to England to seek an honest berth on an honest ship.

When he had finished, there were tears in her eyes but she felt a pride in him so strong she glowed with it.

"So you see, I'm not the man for you," he said quietly. "I deceived you, I let you think I was in the spice trade, perhaps I even let you think I had expectations. I have none. You deserve better than a man like me, and I'll be out of your life now."

Having told her the worst, he could not bear to meet her eyes. He turned to walk away.

"Tom," said Charlotte in a soft voice. "Come back. I don't care about what you've been—I care about what you are now. *And no man could suit me better.*"

Her voice was so rich as she said that, that Tom swung round sharply to look at her. His throat constricted as he saw all the love and trust in her young face—a trust that surely he did not deserve.

"I have put aside the cutlass," he said gravely. "As you can see, I wear no weapon. And when I came back to England this time, I intended to ask you to wife."

Charlotte swallowed uneasily, watching him, aware that he was speaking now in the past tense.

"I meant to toss my heart and all that I had earned from the voyage at your feet." He sighed.

"And now?" she asked fearfully.

"Now I am off to Carlisle, where a ship called the *Annie Clarette* leaves for America day after tomorrow. I was offered a berth on her and now I'll take it. I'll be gone six months—maybe more."

"But . . . must you sail?" she protested. "Couldn't you find some other job, Tom? Something here? On land?"

"Not in Carlisle," he said harshly. "My stepfather has poisoned the minds of all the likely employers against me." *And besides, Carlisle is too close; if I remained in Carlisle, I could not stay away from you. . . .*

"Liverpool then? Or Leeds?"

His jaw hardened. "There'll be trouble with the banns, Charlotte—you know there will be, for we've not got your uncle's permission, nor are likely to get it. Even if we tried, someone would surely write and tell him and he'd come looking for you. You're too young, he'd have us annulled. And then he'd find someone else for you—quick. And I'd have no money to take you away. Like as not, I'd be in gaol for abduction!"

"But I've waited all this time," she said plaintively. "And now you're leaving me again! It isn't fair."

"Life isn't fair." His lips twisted into a crooked smile.

They had not moved; only their low-voiced conversation had disturbed the stillness. Songbirds, gone quiet at their approach, had commenced singing again, soft throaty notes and gentle trills. Between the trees the waters of the lake glimmered calm in the summer sun, and nearby a bee buzzed lazily, plundering the nectar of the wildflowers.

Charlotte had slid down on the grass with her arms behind her head. Lying there on her back in the thin white dress, she looked endlessly inviting.

"If you're going to leave me," she said wistfully. "At least you might kiss me good-bye."

Tom drew a deep ragged breath. "Don't try to break my resolve, Charlotte," he warned, going down on one knee beside her. "It's weak enough already." But his long body bent over hers and he pressed a soft yearning kiss on her upraised lips.

Charlotte reached up and twined her arms about his neck and pulled him down to her.

"Oh, Tom," she whispered. *"Do stay* . . . and if you can't stay another night, at least stay close to me for a little while."

In Tom's opinion he was too close already. His lean body had already caught fire at her touch and he could feel again that aching yearning in his loins to clutch her to him and make her his for all time. Charlotte was nuzzling ever closer to him, content to be held, reveling in his nearness, trying to push the future away. The very nearness of her—for all her innocence—was overpowering his senses.

He pulled away and stood up, his voice slurred with feeling. "I do not hold you light, Charlotte."

"Ah, but we're betrothed, Tom," she protested in a hurt voice. "We're going to spend our whole lives together. How can it matter if—"

He spoke roughly. "All voyages are uncertain—life is an uncertain matter at sea. I could fall from the rigging, I could break my neck, I could drown. Do you think I want to leave you a little gift—a child perhaps? A babe that you could bring up alone after your uncle scorns you for taking up with me and casts you out? Do you think I want that picture before me on stormy nights at sea, Charlotte? No, I want to think of you safe and warm and cared for, even if the vessel I'm on is already sinking or burning down to her waterline!"

He wrenched away from her and stood up, fleeing himself as much as those gentle hands that were caressing his hair.

"That's ridiculous!" she shouted, sitting up.

Alarmed, the birds around them took off with a whir of wings.

"It's not ridiculous," he snapped. "That's the way it's going to be. And you wouldn't think it so ridiculous if something happened to me on this voyage!"

"Then go and don't come back!" she flared.

"You don't mean that, Charlotte?"

"No," she said bitterly. "I don't mean that. Have a fine voyage, Tom, with fair winds to guide you home." But she turned her face away from him.

"I hoped you'd say that." He leaned down and ruffled her bright hair.

"If you really loved me . . ." she mumbled resentfully.

"I'll not leave you with child," he said harshly. "I've seen too much to wish that on you." *At least if the ship goes down I'll not find that waiting for me in hell!*

Then he was gone, swinging away from her through the trees.

She jumped up, for a moment intending to follow him, to make him take her with him.

Then the futility of it closed down around her. That stiff back of his told her he would never relent.

And Charlotte could not know that Tom was at that very instant fighting himself with all his might, and that if she *had* followed him just then, had run after him and thrown her arms around his neck, he would have flung all his good intentions to the wind and made her his on the spot.

It might have changed their lives.

7

So much *might* have happened that morning when Tom swung off on the road to Carlisle . . . but Charlotte was young and confused and she was not sure what was in any man's mind, least of all Tom's. She stayed where she was, turning over and beating her fists on the grass, and sobbed. When at last she sat up and dashed the tears from her eyes he was out of sight.

After a long while she got up, inspected her dress for grass stains—fortunately there were none—and trudged home. Her step quickened when she saw the horses hitched around the front door of Aldershot Grange and her gaze quickly roved over them. There were several carts in evidence—and there was Uncle Russ's big bay horse, she would have recognized him anywhere by his rolling eyes and his lips drawn back over his teeth. Which meant that Uncle Russ, after being absent for more than two years from the Grange, had returned. And there was a small dun horse—not distinctive, it could belong to anyone. Most of the other horses were nondescript too—she guessed they belonged to the grooms, who were doubtless in the kitchen at this very moment quenching their thirst with apple cider.

But to whom did the handsome roan stallion belong? And who had ridden in on the beautiful light chestnut with a coat as sleek and shining as polished sandalwood, just now pawing the ground lightly with his forefeet? Had any of the grooms been present, she would certainly have asked.

And then she caught sight of another cart just now being driven up and saw that its driver wore the maroon-and-gold livery she had heard described as belonging to the owner of Castle Stroud. Her heart quickened. So Lord Pimmerston had come north from Sheffield at last to visit the ancient seat of his family! He might indeed give a great ball and invite the whole countryside.

She put aside the thought of great balls and strangers on dashing mounts. It was important that she get Uncle Russ aside and speak to him about Tom. If she told Uncle Russ how desperately she loved Tom—perhaps he would help. Oh, he *must* help! Maybe he would think of some friend who might employ Tom, and perhaps it would not be too late to overtake him and keep him from signing on the *Annie Clarette* and being gone forever and ever!

She hurried inside through a front door that now stood wide in the afternoon sunlight, realizing suddenly that she was windblown and perhaps even a little sunburned. Fortunately there was no one in the great hall, and instinctively she walked softly, half-expecting her uncle and his friends—perhaps he had brought a lady with him!—to come surging out of a doorway and find her with her hair all mussed. She should certainly go upstairs and comb it before she came down to be presented to the company—on this of all days, her appearance must not shame her uncle.

With that in mind she was tiptoeing past the drawing-room door, which stood slightly ajar, when she heard her name mentioned—and in a way that froze her in her tracks.

"Come now, Russ, if I'm to marry this niece of yours, where is she?" rumbled an unfamiliar voice from the other side of the door.

Charlotte stopped as abruptly as if her feet had suddenly become stuck to the floor, and heard her uncle's familiar voice say, "She'll be along, Pimmerston, she'll be along. Out strolling, according to Livesay."

Pimmerston! That rumbling voice then would be Lord

Pimmerston from Castle Stroud. She had heard he was a roué and vain. Somehow her uncle had managed to arrange a match between her and Lord Pimmerston, whom he doubtless considered to be a great catch. Well, he could disabuse himself of that idea right now, for marry him she would not!

She could hardly wait to tell her uncle so, and her hand was already reaching out to push the door open when Lord Pimmerston's next words gave her pause.

"Are you certain the girl's a virgin?" Again that rumble, sounding petulant.

Charlotte felt a quick rush of scarlet to her cheeks and withdrew her hand as if the door were hot to the touch. How *dared* he?

"Absolutely certain," came Uncle Russ's reply, very solemn. "Charlotte is a virgin, I promise you."

"She could hardly be anything else, trapped in this backwater!" Arthur Bodine's voice, she realized with a start.

Charlotte yearned to kick the door open, and she was contemplating doing exactly that, no matter what the consequences, when with the next overheard words horror washed over her.

" 'Tis absolutely essential she be a virgin." Again that scolding rumble. "For the only reason I'd wed her at all is to rid myself of this 'gallant's disease' I've contracted—and Bodine here insists that marriage to a young virgin will cleanse the gallant's disease from my body."

"And you could find no virgins in London or Sheffield?" wondered a fourth voice, attractive and well-modulated, a voice that Charlotte did not recognize.

"None to speak of!" was Bodine's quick comment, and there was general laughter.

Outside the drawing-room door Charlotte's young face had turned white as parchment. Her uncle had actually come north to bring her . . . this! She felt physically ill. Indeed she would have run away at that moment had not the fourth voice, which held an odd attraction, inquired curiously, "But what of the girl, Lord Pimmerston? After all, this is Russ's niece we're talking about, not some street wench. She'll be eager to wed a man of your stature, no doubt. But will she not contract the gallant's disease from you?"

Charlotte cringed at his lordship's callous response.

"Were not women put on this earth to do men's bidding and assuage men's ills?" he rumbled. "Of what other use are they? The girl will serve my purpose well enough—after all, Russ here vouches for her, and she has a decent background. God's teeth, what's keeping the wench?"

"She will run away once she learns what you have planned for her," predicted the fourth voice indifferently.

Charlotte was indeed about to take flight when she heard Bodine's voice—"Ah, we've taken care of that, haven't we, Russ?"—followed by an unpleasant chuckle.

Charlotte would have dashed back the way she had come and gone out the open front door, but as she whirled, she saw Livesay and the stableboy just now staggering in under the weight of her uncle's chest and a large box. Coming in at that moment, they effectively blocked her way.

"Ah, there you are, Mistress Charlotte!" Livesay's carrying voice held a rising inflection. She saw that he had discarded the countryman's smock he usually wore and was wearing the old-fashioned stained brown velvet coat—one of Uncle Russ's castoffs—that he considered his badge of office. "Your uncle was asking where you were." He was looking at her somewhat accusingly. "And I told him you were out strolling somewhere."

Charlotte knew that Livesay was only trying by this method to warn her that he had not mentioned Tom, but her gratitude for that was outweighed by the fact that his voice had been loud and piercing enough to attract the attention of those in the drawing room, and she heard her uncle say, "Ah, here she is now, Pimmerston. You can view her at last."

Charlotte did not want the occupants of that room to know that she had overheard their conversation, so she flew down the great hall to Livesay with a breathless, "Is that box for me, Livesay?"

"No, Mistress Charlotte." Livesay blinked and trudged on past her.

Charlotte whirled and so appeared to be just coming through the front door as her uncle stuck his bewigged head and ruddy face out into the hall.

"Charlotte?" He looked startled at the change in her. His gaze raked her up and down and a pleased expression spread over his florid features. His chest, in his brown satin coat, expanded. "Come greet our guests." He beckoned with a deep-cuffed arm.

With her head held high, albeit a trifle pale, Charlotte brushed coldly past her uncle with only the barest of greetings to face the three men he had brought north with him.

She would never quite forget the scene that greeted her there in the familiar drawing room of Aldershot Grange:

Golden afternoon sunlight spilled into a room that must have been beautiful during her mother's girlhood but that had long since gone shabby with peeling yellow paint and moldering moss-green wall hangings. Three men were seated upon the faded olive-green velvet of the heavy Jacobean chairs arranged around the cold hearth, drinking ruby port wine. All three came to their feet at the entrance of a beautiful young girl.

Over on her right she recognized the fustian-clad form of Arthur Bodine, not so well-dressed as the others and slightly bowlegged. He raked her with his hard brown eyes, pleased with the gown he had sent her, and his smiling gaze briefly met Charlotte's in a devouring sort of way. Charlotte could not restrain the look of loathing that crossed her face like a shadow, and Bodine's smile faded.

The other two, she saw, were both dressed in the height of fashion.

The thin and languid gentleman on her left could be none other than Lord Pimmerston. His pomaded bag wig was elegantly curled, enormously modish, and of an unlikely golden hue, and the large dark green satin bow at its back was matched by a similar bow at the front, just below his pointed chin. His sallow face was unhealthy-looking and he wore a black patch that seemed to emphasize the

slight sneer his mouth habitually wore. The splendor of his
apparel far overshadowed his countenance, for he was
wearing a bottle-green satin coat with glinting gold buttons enameled in green marching down it from the neck to
the hem of its stiffly flared skirt. The rest of the coat was
entirely overpowered by wide pale green velvet cuffs of
enormous dimensions that covered his elbows and indeed
most of his arms as well, but allowed a rich spill of lace to
fall over his wrists to highlight his bejeweled hands. A
long ivory brocade waistcoat bore a similar march of slightly
smaller buttons that matched those on the coat, and his
trousers were of the same bottle-green satin as his coat.
Like the others, he wore riding boots.

His lordship had just been in the act of taking snuff, and
as Charlotte entered, his nose was twitching. But twitching
or not, to the fashion-conscious his was a daunting figure
and he had risen to his feet and taken a mincing step
forward, expecting to be instantly noticed and admired.

Charlotte ignored him and addressed her sweeping curtsy
entirely to the tall, more soberly dressed gentleman in the
center. On her left, Lord Pimmerston looked affronted.
He snapped his green-enameled gold snuffbox shut and
assumed a pose that had cut a wide swath in London
drawing rooms. When Charlotte still ignored him, his
sneer deepened, while his small eyes peered out at her
with grudging admiration of her beauty and discontent
that she could be so lacking in grace as to overlook him.

The tall gentleman in the center, who occupied Charlotte's complete attention, was doubtless the fourth voice
she had heard in that sunny room, and certainly the only
voice that had expressed any interest at all in her welfare.

Charlotte stared at him breathlessly.

He was a man worthy of being stared at—and used to it,
she guessed, from the amused expression that now crossed
his sardonic features.

He was of a swarthy complexion, lean and tall with very
black hair and a face that Charlotte supposed would be
considered handsome; she was not disposed to consider it
so, for she judged him to be in a minor way one of the
conspirators against her, and she gave him her attention

only to annoy Lord Pimmerston, whose pointy countenance was now covered with an angry flush.

But the effect of this tall fellow before her was indeed
impressive. He wore his white cambric Steinkirk cravat
with an air, pulled loosely through a buttonhole of the
dark riding coat that matched his trousers. Under his
coat, which was open, could be glimpsed a light gray
brocade waistcoat with silver buttons.

"And who might you be, sir?" she wondered. "Since my
uncle does not choose to introduce us."

His dark eyes had widened at the sight of her floating
into the room like a graceful white moth. Conscious that
he had the young lady's full attention, he made her an
elegant leg, sweeping the floor with his dark tricorne
alight with silver braid.

At her words a twitch of amusement altered the expression on what Charlotte considered to be a stern mouth,
and he shot a quick glance at Lord Pimmerston, seething
beside him, but his reply was grave enough.

"Rowan Keynes, at your service."

"Lord Pimmerston." Slightly disconcerted that Charlotte had so far managed to ignore that elegant bird of
plumage in gold-encrusted green satin, who preened,
discomfited, to her left, her uncle quickly seized Charlotte
by the elbow and turned her about to face his lordship.
"My niece, Charlotte."

Charlotte's cool violet gaze swept over his lordship completely without interest and she gave him only the barest
shadow of a curtsy before turning back to the tall gentleman in the center. At this snub, his lordship's face drained
of color save for two spots that remained on his sallow
cheeks as a badge of the indignity he felt he was suffering
from this wench.

The wench appeared already to have forgotten him.

"Have you traveled far, sir?" Charlotte again addressed
Rowan Keynes.

"From Lord Pimmerston's estate north of Sheffield,"
was the lazy reply.

"And Arthur Bodine," said her uncle doggedly, again

turning Charlotte about so that she might not ignore his other guest. "I believe you've met my niece, Charlotte."

At her stare that denied recognition, Bodine's brown eyes narrowed.

"I believe I selected that gown you're wearing," he said in a slightly threatening voice.

"Did you indeed?" Charlotte managed to sound so completely indifferent that a flash of amusement again flashed over Rowan Keynes' dark features. "I had rather selected my own."

"Come now, Charlotte," sputtered her uncle. "Bodine chose well, admit it!" It was not lost on him that all three gentlemen—although the tall dark-haired one was not so obvious about it—had let their gazes rest lingeringly on Charlotte's white bosom and the tops of her pearly breasts, exposed to view in the low-cut white gown.

Charlotte too had noticed, and under the pretext of toying with her hair, she lifted her arm to hide that pale expanse from three pairs of questing eyes.

"We have been awaiting your return," her uncle told her jovially. "Lord Pimmerston is opening up Castle Stroud for a brief stay, and since word of his arrival has already spread along our way here, he is expecting callers throughout the evening. We are invited to be his guests for dinner, and there will be dancing afterward."

"How nice," said Charlotte, speaking up clearly. "It is unfortunate that I will not be able to attend."

"Eh, how is that?" Lord Pimmerston leaned forward, perplexed.

"Yes, what do you mean, girl?" demanded her uncle.

"I mean that this is my only decent dress." Charlotte indicated her new white voile gown. "And I am afraid I may have gotten the back of it badly stained—from lying on the grass." She drawled those last words and gave the company about her a challenging look. She hoped they would put the worst construction on it. Let them think she'd been lying on a grassy bank with some chance-met swain!

Rowan Keynes was the only person in the room who

looked amused, but her uncle roughly brushed her remark aside.

"Nonsense, of course you'll go! Turn around." And when she did half-turn reluctantly, "Why, there's naught amiss with the dress! Stop this missishness, you are accompanying me to Castle Stroud!"

"Well, at least I must comb my hair first," Charlotte insisted stubbornly. "I certainly cannot go out looking like this!" She gave her golden hair a shake, and three appreciative pairs of eyes followed its golden shimmer.

"'You may comb your hair but you will be back downstairs and ready to accompany us in fifteen minutes," her uncle told her in a voice of menace.

"Very well." Charlotte left the room, leaving the door slightly ajar behind her, and leaned for a moment against the doorjamb in the empty hall. She felt weak from the encounter.

Behind her she heard her uncle's complacent, "Well, now, Lord Pimmerston, is Charlotte not everything Bodine told you—and more?"

And his lordship's petulant rejoinder. "Aye, she's a beautiful thing—though she's obviously in need of taming."

"Ah, you'll enjoy that, won't you?" Bodine's voice, accompanied by an evil chuckle.

But his lordship was not to be so easily mollified. The wench had publicly slighted him, and she should pay dearly for it!

"What's this about grass stains on her back?" he added in a disgruntled voice. "She seemed to be making a point of it. I warn you, Russ, if when I've married her she turns out not to be a virgin . . ."

"Why, then I'll make you a widower myself—with my own hand," promised her uncle in so cold a voice that Charlotte shivered.

Oh, they were vile, vile! Sitting there discussing the ruin of her young life as if she were of no account!

The front door was closed now and she had little doubt that if she tried to run away she would be ridden down and dragged to Lord Pimmerston's dinner party by force. Oh, if only she could ride! *Then* she might fling herself on the most likely mount available and thunder away. But by now the grooms, who had probably been enjoying a tankard or two in the kitchen, would be gathering out front to await their masters. There was no chance of immediate escape; she would have to make plans for later. She must get word to Tom.

With that in mind she turned away from the stairway, intending to head for the kitchen, when a large woman in indigo linen, who seemed to appear from nowhere, interrupted her progress. The woman must have stood all of six feet in her striped stockings, and she was built like a wrestler. Her ample bosom and hennaed hair swayed toward Charlotte.

"Mistress Charlotte?" said the woman with a smirk. "I'm Semple, your new lady's maid brought by your uncle to serve you."

"Well, then serve me upstairs," said Charlotte briskly with a nod toward the stairway. "I'll be right up."

"No, Mistress Charlotte." The formidable newcomer stood her ground. "I've been told that you're in my charge and I'm not to let you out of my sight."

So this was what Bodine had meant when he told Rowan Keynes that they had "taken care of" any attempt she might make to escape: Semple was to take her in tow.

Charlotte gave the huge woman a hopeless look.

"Very well, Semple. I will require a basin of water to wash my face and hands."

Semple did not move. Her expression was suspicious.

"There is no need for you to bring it yourself, Semple." Charlotte sighed. "Wend can bring it. Wend!" she called loudly over Semple's shoulder, hoping the girl was within earshot. "Wend, bring a basin of water to my bedchamber —at once!"

She hoped too, as she preceded Semple up the stairs like an animal being herded, that Wend would not take offense at her peremptory tone, which had been intended only to impress Semple, and sulk in the kitchen and send Ivy instead—for the carrying of the water would indeed have been Ivy's job and not Wend's. To her enormous relief, Wend appeared shortly with a pitcher of water that she slopped angrily into the porcelain washbowl in Charlotte's bedchamber.

"Will that be all, my lady?" Wend asked with elaborate deference. Charlotte half-expected her to back from the room bowing idiotically.

"Semple," said Charlotte sharply, "bring me a cake of soap—you'll find the one I want in the chest right over there." And when Semple's back was turned she reached out and caught hold of Wend's skirt as the girl was about to leave and pulled her back. Wend turned with an angry look and Charlotte put a finger to her lips.

Wend caught on at once. She leaned closer.

"Find Tom, he's on the way to Carlisle." Charlotte's whisper was a mere breath in Wend's ear. "They're marrying me off to Lord Pimmerston to 'cleanse' him of the gallant's disease, and Semple's here to guard me lest I try to escape."

Wend gave her a shocked look, and as Semple rummaged about for the nonexistent soap, Charlotte complained petulantly about the water being too cold.

"I'll get some more water," promised Wend, about to scurry from the room.

"No, there isn't time." Charlotte's voice followed her. "I must hurry, so I'll use it as it is. We are leaving for Castle Stroud in ten minutes. Well, don't stand there, Wend. Be off with you. I'm sure Cook must have need of your services in the kitchen."

Wend was off with alacrity—but not to the kitchen. She hurried out the garden door and was off on the run along the lake path, looking for Tom. Later, when Lord Pimmerston's party, which now included Charlotte, passed her, she hid in the bushes.

Rowan Keynes, upon learning that Charlotte was afraid of horses and had never learned to ride, suggested that it was a pity that she must bounce all the way to Castle Stroud on a cart. He offered to take her up before him on his beautiful chestnut horse, and before Charlotte could refuse, her uncle accepted for her—doubtless, Charlotte thought bitterly, to prevent her from leaping from the cart at some likely spot and trying to escape.

With her uncle giving her protesting body a boost, she found herself taken up before Rowan Keynes, her back brushing the dark cloth of his smart riding coat with its stiffened skirts slit at back and sides, the better to fit to the saddle. As the party moved off toward Castle Stroud, Charlotte found herself leaning back against his hard masculine figure to avoid the occasional brushing against her breasts of his arm that held the reins, although sometimes when the way was rough the horse's step threw her forward against his arm or hand. She also found herself brought into intimate contact with his muscular thighs. She felt embarrassed and tried to move about to get into a less intimate position, but that only made matters worse. She felt his arm steady her, tighten suddenly, and behind her his breathing seemed to change, grow heavier.

"Have you always lived here in the north country?" he asked as his horse, which had been dancing sideways to Charlotte's discomfiture, for it tipped her this way and that in his arms, changed pace and moved along sedately behind her uncle and Lord Pimmerston and Bodine, who rode in a little cluster ahead.

"No, I am from St. Mary's." Charlotte was a little breathless.

"In the Scillies? A flower of the south, then."

"And I wish I were back there," added Charlotte bitterly.

"You do not like the cold winters?" he hazarded. "I must admit I am not fond of them either. I spend most of my time in London, where I have a house, but I am fond of the Continent—particularly Portugal in winter."

Charlotte did not care where he spent his winters—or his summers either, for that matter. Between bouts of trying not to sit so close to this disturbing stranger, she was desperately hoping that Wend would find Tom. He would find a way to rescue her, of that she had no doubt. She was scarcely aware of her surroundings as the impressive gray battlements of Castle Stroud loomed up before them.

"From Pimmerston's description, I hadn't expected the place to be so beautiful," murmured Rowan appreciatively.

"It's too far from town for him to appreciate it!" was her tart response.

"No doubt." He had detected that protective note in her voice when she spoke of it. "Do you know the castle well?"

"Very well—and I think Lord Pimmerston is right, he doesn't belong here!"

"Oh, I doubt Pimmerston ever plans to live here," was Rowan's murmured comment.

Just wed here! was Charlotte's unspoken rejoinder.

8

Castle Stroud

Although the servants had done wonders in the short time they had been there, Castle Stroud could not really be said to have been "opened." True, the dining room had been rendered habitable, with fresh white linen cloths and polished silver. And a cook and her helpers had hastily prepared quite a creditable dinner. But the dinner was late, and dusk was upon them when at last they sat down at the long board.

To Charlotte it seemed interminable. All she could think of was Tom, and whether Wend, sprinting up the lakeshore toward Carlisle, had been able to reach him. She gave disjointed answers when spoken to, and sometimes no answer at all.

After being roundly snubbed by her at Aldershot Grange, Lord Pimmerston had chosen not to seat Charlotte beside him, but instead sat with Russ on his right and Bodine on his left. Down the table Charlotte sat across from Rowan Keynes, who watched her with sympathetic eyes.

As the endless dinner progressed from course to course, a sprinkling of guests—alerted along the route of his lordship's impending visit—began to arrive, and Charlotte was duly introduced to them. She realized that for the county this was a great event, the arrival of Lord Pimmerston at his northern estate, and homage was considered due. Her mind in turmoil, Charlotte managed to acknowledge their greetings, but she did not really hear what they had to say.

Due to the lateness of the hour, the few ladies did not withdraw to the withdrawing room, but his lordship announced that there would presently be dancing in the great chamber above, for he had brought with him musicians from Sheffield.

There was a delighted flurry among the ladies at that announcement, for there was not one among them who had ever danced a measure at Castle Stroud. Then Charlotte's uncle spoke quickly to Lord Pimmerston, who ordered everybody's wineglass to be refilled—Charlotte thought her uncle was about to propose a toast to their host, when to her horror he made the ringing announcement that his ward was to be joined in marriage to their host and the banns would be cried on Sunday next—which brought forth a clamor of voices over which her uncle's voice rose in a bellow:

"Let us drink to the health of the happy couple!"

The happy couple! Charlotte choked and dropped her glass with a small crash. Some of the wine spilled on her dress, and she dabbed at it with a linen napkin.

As they left the table, a flurry of well-wishers surrounded her. Charlotte felt suddenly that she might faint. On the pretext that she must wash out the wine stain, she burst out of the group and headed blindly toward the door. Her uncle saw that and sprinted across the room to head her off into the cushioned alcove where heavy velvet hangings would muffle their voices. He caught hold of her and half-dragged her there.

Charlotte had lost all sense of diplomacy. "How dared you make such an announcement?" she panted. "And without asking me my feelings in the matter?"

He looked thunderstruck. "I'd no need to ask your permission! You'll do as I think best." His grip on her arm tightened cruelly.

"You are hurting my arm!" She struggled with him, feeling her feet slide across the floor under his urging. "And there is no point in your dragging me about. I will never marry that diseased popinjay!" White with fury, she was speaking through her teeth.

Her uncle gave her arm a cruel twist and almost threw her into the alcove.

"You'll marry him or I'll be ruined," he snarled. "And unless you want to be tied to a stone and sunk in the Derwent Water, you'll marry him with a smile on your face!"

Charlotte's arm ached from this manhandling, and pain laced her voice with desperation. "You mean you've spent all of my mother's money as well as your own?" she shot at him bitterly. "I don't doubt there are magistrates about who'd be interested in that!"

Her uncle turned on her such a look of menace that she felt chilled, as if touched by a cold metal blade. "Keep a civil tongue in your head," he warned, "or I'll stripe that dainty back of yours where it won't show!"

"Lord Pimmerston will object to your ruining my beauty!" she said sarcastically.

He glowered at her. "I've no doubt he'll stripe it himself," he said softly. "On your wedding night, like as not!"

He turned to Semple, who had witnessed this display and now loomed over them both like a giant shadow of a woman against the candlelight.

"Semple, keep an eye on this wench," he instructed sharply. "Do as Bodine told you—use whatever force you must, but do not let her out of your sight except when she is with one of us." A remark which both Charlotte and Semple understood to include Rowan Keynes.

He turned on his heel and left them, Charlotte leaning against the wall to catch an angry breath, Semple hovering watchfully nearby.

Across the room Rowan Keynes too had noticed this display. With a frown he quickly detached himself from the pack and made for Charlotte and the alcove. On the way to the alcove he encountered Lord Pimmerston, who at sight of Charlotte's violent reaction to the betrothal announcement had spilled wine on his cravat and had returned to his guests wearing a miraculous creation decorated with tasseled beads.

"Oh, very nice, Pimmerston," Rowan complimented his lordship's taste in a bored voice.

Lord Pimmerston ignored Charlotte, glowering in the alcove, and touched his elegant neckwear caressingly. "I had left the one I wanted in Sheffield," he rumbled in a regretful tone. "I've a mind to cane Crouch for his oversight in leaving it."

A picture of slender elegant Pimmerston caning Crouch, his lordship's burly valet, fleetingly crossed Rowan's mind. If Crouch took a notion to, he might turn on his employer and break his effete lordship in half.

"Your betrothed looks lonely across the room, Pimmerston," he commented. "Now that the music's started, d'you object if I claim the first dance with her?"

"For all of me, you may claim the first dance and all the others. I've no intention of leading her out."

Rowan Keynes quirked an expressive eyebrow at Lord Pimmerston. "Don't tell me you have fallen out of love already?"

"Love?" Lord Pimmerston snorted and snapped open his green-enameled gold snuffbox and took a delicate pinch of snuff. "There's no question of love here, as well you know."

Rowan's gaze passed over Charlotte, with perhaps a trace of pity, as she leaned against the wall of the alcove.

"Favor, then? Don't tell me such a beauty could fall out of favor?" he rallied.

Lord Pimmerston had been simmering under Charlotte's slights ever since he had met her this afternoon. At the moment he was in no mood even to concede that she was beautiful.

"Beauty? I hadn't noticed. Headstrong, yes." Across his ancestral hall he gave the recalcitrant Charlotte a lowering look. "Yes, dance attendance on her, by all means, Keynes. Keep her out of trouble." There was a vicious note in his lordship's rumbling voice. "I'll tame her at my leisure. *After* the ceremony."

"I don't doubt you will," agreed Rowan Keynes easily. His smiling gaze rested on Lord Pimmerston almost with fondness.

In the alcove, the pain in Charlotte's arm had lessened now, and she stirred. Hovering almost over her, Semple seemed to tense.

"Well, come along, Semple." Charlotte cast an angry look up at Semple's iron jawline. "Make yourself useful. See if you can find me a fan—I forgot to bring mine."

Semple stood fixed in place, towering over the shorter Charlotte. "I can't leave you," she stated flatly. "Except in the company of one of the four men who brought me here."

"Well, leave me with this one then!" Charlotte indicated Rowan Keynes, who was walking purposefully toward them. "And go find me a fan."

In the minstrel's gallery above—for this had once been a medieval fortress—a trio of musicians began to play stringed instruments. As their music floated down, Rowan Keynes asked Charlotte if he might lead her out for the first measure.

"I do not know the new steps," Charlotte warned him. Now that Semple was temporarily out of the way, she was looking about for an escape route.

"Then I will have the pleasure of teaching you," was Rowan's firm rejoinder as he led her out upon the floor.

Charlotte cared not a whit that everyone was watching her and indeed whispering about this hurried betrothal. Nor did she care whether she trod upon her partner's foot or indeed collided with him. Her whole being was concentrated on escape—oh, surely Wend had been able to overtake Tom! If not . . .

"You don't want to marry Pimmerston, do you?" asked Rowan quietly. "He's very rich, you know." He watched her face to see how this latter piece of news would affect her, for it was possible that she did not understand what a great lady she would become by virtue of this marriage.

For answer Charlotte deliberately trod on his foot and flashed a resentful look up at his dark smiling face. "I don't *intend* to marry him!"

"Indeed?" He deftly avoided being trodden upon again, although it took some fast footwork. "And how will you avoid it, when your uncle seems so determined?"

Charlotte's violet eyes narrowed. They were approaching the door.

"In the wedding ceremony, when I am asked if I take this man, I will shout, 'No, I do not take him, and I will not ever take him!'—and run at once from the room."

"That will be an invigorating spectacle," he said politely. "I shall make sure to attend your nuptials!"

"Oh, do not mock me!" She tried to wrest free of his grasp. It was but a short sprint to the door.

But he kept his hold on her. "I would advise you not to tell your uncle in advance of the ceremony of your intention to refuse your bridegroom in the church," was his cool admonition. There was a glint in his dark eyes—though whether of humor or sympathy, she could not tell.

"Why not?" she demanded truculently.

"Because there are potions that make one more pliable, even biddable."

She stared up at him. "You think he would be able to . . . ?"

"Oh, I've no doubt of it," was his calm rejoinder.

"He's a monster!" she burst out. "Sitting down there in Sheffield making all these terrible plans for me!"

"Hush, not so loud," Rowan cautioned. "Nobody can quite hear your words from where we are, but the expression on your face is creating interest."

Charlotte promptly turned her head away from the other couples dancing sedately about the floor.

"You know that I am a prisoner," she accused. "Bodine and my uncle have brought that awful woman here to guard me until the ceremony is over—although why Bodine should be interested, I'm sure I don't know."

"Bodine is doubtless getting a percentage of what your uncle will receive from Pimmerston for arranging the match," suggested Rowan. And when Charlotte shot a surprised look at him, "Young virgins possessed of such beauty as yours command a high price."

"It's terribly warm in here," she complained.

"You're right," he agreed equably. "Shall we step outside into the garden and cause a scandal? It may be that you will not have to marry Pimmerston after all!"

Incensed that he should adopt a bantering tone over

something so desperately important as her future, Charlotte nevertheless let Rowan lead her outside into the cool night air of the terraced gardens that led down toward the lake. The gardens were overgrown—Lord Pimmerston's servants had been able to do nothing about *that* in the short time they had been here!—and the grassy paths were soft and sparkled with dew beneath her feet, so that she lifted up her skirts to keep them from getting wet. Around them was the heady scent from the tangled vines of the moss roses that spilled over a nearby wall. A mist had risen from the lake and obscured the shoreline. All the world seemed very still.

Then suddenly she saw Tom as a swirl of mist broke away to reveal him standing motionless by a tree at the lakeshore. He must have been studying the castle and determining how best to effect an entry without attracting attention.

She cast a quick glance up at the dark face etched above her in the moonlight, but if Rowan had glimpsed that shadowy figure, he gave no sign.

"Would you mind very much going inside and bringing me a shawl?" she asked with a sudden shiver. "It's so damp out here that it's giving me a chill."

Rowan seemed not to think it odd that from declaring herself too hot she was now declaring herself too cold.

"Are you sure you would not like to return inside with me?" he asked.

"No, the roses smell so nice, and . . . and I don't think I could face all those people right now, babbling about how wonderful it is that I'm about to marry Lord Pimmerston!"

He chuckled. "I can sympathize with that," he said. And indeed he could, for he had just recently been jilted by a young lady of fashion and splendid good looks and had ridden fuming out of London hoping to cool his hot temper in the north country. When in Sheffield he had been invited to accompany Lord Pimmerston, a recent acquaintance, to his nuptials with a wench on whom he had never laid eyes, the situation had intrigued him and he had ridden along to see what would happen. Besides, it was on his way to the coast, for he was involved in affairs about which his host knew nothing—though he would have been stunned indeed to learn of them.

But Rowan had eyes even sharper than Charlotte's; he had not missed that silent figure lurking by the tree. He moved obediently to the garden door, which was conveniently out of sight behind some tall overgrown shrubs, then opened it and closed it loudly—but remained outside to watch through the shrubbery.

The minute Charlotte heard the garden door close, she picked up her skirts and fled across the dewy grass paths to Tom. In the swirling mist Rowan saw her almost throw herself into a pair of arms that closed about her reassuringly.

From the shadows Rowan watched this reunion. A lover, no doubt—he remembered her bland remark earlier about grass stains on the back of her gown and felt a surprising stab of jealousy. He wished he could hear what they were saying.

"Oh, Tom, thank God Wend found you," Charlotte breathed. "We must get away from here!"

"So Wend told me. I've no horse, so—"

"There are plenty of horses here! Take your choice!"

And that would make him a horse thief and subject to hanging. He hesitated, but only for a moment. "The stables will be full of grooms," he said. "We'll have to take the best mount we can find of those horses that guests who do not mean to stay the night have left tethered outside."

He led her to them, realizing grimly that he had already staked out the place where they were tethered for just this purpose. "Put your foot in my hands," he instructed Charlotte. "I'll give you a boost up."

"But I do not ride," Charlotte protested in panic.

"Then we will ride double," he decided, and swung her up behind him. "Hang on," he told her, "and duck when I do, for I'll be taking us into the woods and you mustn't be swept off by a low branch."

Rowan, who had followed silently through the shadows, had watched it all. There was a strange brooding expression on his face, but he stayed rooted where he was until the "borrowed" horse carrying double had pounded away over the wet grass and disappeared into the darkness.

A number of seemingly unrelated things were passing through his mind. This girl, even with her hair unfashionably done and only passable clothes, was even more striking than Katherine Olney had been—and *she* was the toast of London. Clawing memories rubbed his lacerated feelings raw as he saw the dark beauty rise up before him— lovely Katherine with her dark cloud of hair and her mocking eyes and her soft winning manner. Katherine, who had betrayed him, not even bothering to return his betrothal ring before she ran off with young Talybont to Wales. Rowan's handsome face darkened at the affront, and the cruel lines of his mouth deepened. He'd been of a mind to follow and make her a widow—but other matters too important to ignore had intervened, sending him north.

His thoughts returned to Charlotte. It was not just her beauty. What was there about her? Some quality . . . He could not quite put his finger on it, but it was there. *A spirit like a Toledo blade*—yes, that was it, a fine resistance to destruction. He smiled at the aptness of the thought.

For a moment he let his mind imagine Charlotte stunningly gowned, making her bow to London society, being presented at court. . . . And then his mind veered back to his own circumstances. He was due in Portugal soon. This surprise visit to Sheffield and the subsequent journey to Cumberland should surely have convinced the dark, furtive fellow who had been dogging his heels ever since he left London—and who was beyond doubt an agent of the Spanish king sent to defeat his mission—that he was merely off on holiday. He could not afford to stay here long, and yet . . . this girl of the blue lake country was beautiful indeed. His mind kept returning to her.

Where would a runaway couple go from Castle Stroud? Carlisle perhaps, or into the wilds of Northumberland, but more likely Scotland . . . over the border, where marriage ceremonies could be performed by anyone in the presence of witnesses. The swift instinctive way Charlotte had gone into that fellow's arms had not escaped him.

He stood, pensive now, in the cool damp air and imagined himself strolling through St. James's Park with Charlotte dangling on his arm, and meeting dark lovely Katherine

Olney—Talybont now. He imagined Katherine's face, startled, affronted, if she were to meet him so, for he had had a message from Katherine before he left, delivered even while she was on her way to wed young Talybont, and that message had enraged him most of all. Because of her father's penury and her meager dowry, Katherine had written with sweetness dripping from her goose-quill pen, she had been obliged to wed Eustace Talybont, who was enormously wealthy, but they would be coming back to London soon—oh, he could count upon it, she would see to that—and dear Rowan *must* be there when she returned. This sudden marriage of convenience need make no difference between them, they could still enjoy good times together just as they had before. *Damn Katherine!* he thought violently, his fingers clenching until the knuckles were white. *She imagined she could have them both! Oh, how he would like to strike back at her!*

He was staring into the darkness at the exact spot where Charlotte and Tom had disappeared when he thought that. His eyes narrowed and he pulled out his gold pocket watch and noted the time in the moonlight. He would give them twenty minutes' head start. . . .

When the twenty minutes were up he strolled back into the house to find the place in an uproar, with everybody looking for Charlotte.

"Where is she?" demanded Lord Pimmerston, gone almost purple with rage. "You were seen to leave with her!" *And if you have damaged the goods . . .* ! was the unspoken threat behind the words.

"I have been looking for her too," was Rowan's bored response. "She asked me to fetch her a shawl. I started to do so before I realized that I should not leave her alone. I turned about and found that she had disappeared. I have been searching the gardens for her, thinking that she might have fainted and fallen into the shrubbery—or possibly had a seizure." He turned blandly to Russ, who looked choleric. "Is your niece given to seizures, by any chance?"

Russ was breathing hard. "Charlotte is not given to seizures of any kind. We . . . had a disagreement tonight."

"Yes, I noticed that she seemed upset." Rowan was enjoying himself. "She was standing by the lake when I left her. You don't think she could have thrown herself into the lake, do you?"

Russ paled. "Of course not! Neither thrown herself in nor tumbled in—she is far too sensible a girl. Nor was our disagreement that important. It was merely a discussion of her dowry—"

"She wanted one?" cut in Rowan sympathetically.

Russ almost choked. "We disagreed upon the matter!" he roared. "And I'll not discuss it with you, Keynes!" He turned anxiously to their host. "It is possible she may have gone back to Aldershot Grange to sulk."

"Yes, I would not put it past her," snapped Lord Pimmerston, almost beside himself with rage at being thus humiliated in public by the sudden disappearance of his betrothed. "I'll send someone to the Grange at once to check on that."

"My horse is missing!" One of the guests bustled up at that moment to report his loss to his host. "Norah and I rode over and left our horses tethered outside, since we didn't plan to stay long, and when I went out just now, my horse was gone! I was asking about among the servants, and one of them thought she had seen a man and a woman riding away on a horse that fit the description of mine."

"There's your answer, then." Rowan turned cheerfully to his host. "Pimmerston, I do believe your bird has flown."

9

The Scottish Border, Forty-eight Hours Later

Night had closed down again over the border country. From behind low-hanging clouds the moon scudded in and out, gilding a magical countryside of high peaks and rushing streams and cataracts and gorse and bracken. When they had started out from Castle Stroud, Tom had been tinglingly aware of Charlotte's arms about his waist as they rode, and he had had to fight off the sudden urge to find some likely place, dismount, and take her on the spot.

Now, some forty-eight hours later, he still felt his blood surge whenever the rhythm of the horse's gait over this uneven terrain brought her firm young breasts into contact with his back. She was tired now and she lay with her weight sagging against him so that those soft mounds were crushed trustingly against his hard body. And tired as he was after two days of dodging the relentless pursuit that had dogged them almost from the beginning, his back still tensed as his muscles responded to her nearness.

In the woodlands in that first dash from Castle Stroud, they had considered where to go. Tom had been all for heading directly north along the lakeshore, passing south of Keswick and making directly for the coast, where they could find some skiff and work their way south. But Charlotte had pointed out that they could be married in Scotland without a license—indeed Wend had told her that Maisey, on whom they had stumbled that day with Tom at

Fox Elve, had deserted her James and run away to Scotland with a sailor. She'd been wed at a smithy in Gretna Green, with a blacksmith performing the ceremony, strangers for witnesses, and an anvil serving for the altar. Such marriages were perfectly legal, she argued, and once she and Tom were legally wed, her uncle would have no choice but to accept it.

Tom voiced the opinion that her uncle, arriving in force, would promptly try to make her a widow.

"Not if we already have . . ." Charlotte was about to say "slept together," but she blushed and let her voice trail off. "I mean, Lord Pimmerston wouldn't want me then," she said softly.

Tom had smiled but remained unconvinced. "Revenge is always sweet," he countered. Revenge was a pleasure he had seen men die for.

"I don't think Uncle Russ would care about revenge—he'd just consider us a lost cause." She sighed. "I think he's gambled his fortune away, and my mother's too, and the only reason he is trying to force Lord Pimmerston upon me is that he's desperate for money. He told me he'd be ruined if I didn't go through with this marriage." He had told her quite a bit more, but she chose not to say so. "And if *our* marriage was already . . ."

"Consummated," supplied Tom dryly.

"Consummated"—she stumbled shyly over the word—"when he found us, why, then he'd just go home in defeat and prepare to sell Aldershot Grange to settle his debts instead of selling me for them!"

"So Scotland it is." Tom was as ready as the next man to take his chances.

They had sheered away from Keswick, which lay at the head of the Derwent Water, and passed north of Penrith, intending to go around Carlisle to the east and cross the border into the Scottish Lowlands somewhere north of Kingstown, but after riding through rough country all day, Charlotte was so tired and they were both so hungry that when they came down from a steep rise and saw below them a tiny inn with a shingle flapping in the breeze outside, Tom decided to chance it. The horse was near done—after all, the animal had not been fresh when they started.

"Say nothing," he warned Charlotte. "Follow my lead here."

He rode boldly down into the narrow valley, dismounted, and handed Charlotte into the Stag and Horn as the flaking paint of the sign above the door announced.

In the low-ceilinged public room they were the only guests and they seated themselves at the single long board where all travelers dined. Their host, a short pink-cheeked fellow with gray-streaked ginger hair, bustled about in his leathern apron and apologized that there was no proper time to "prepare a bird," but cold venison pie was all his Annie had left when she took the whole family in to market, leaving him behind to mind the inn.

"Have you no guests then?" Tom inquired with just the right degree of polite interest.

The landlord shook his head. "Though there'll be a few lads dropping by later this evening for a drop of ale. Weather's too good to drive them inside yet!"

So the inn was deserted save for this smiling fellow before them. . . . Tom's eyes had gleamed at this piece of good luck. He abandoned his questions and waxed voluble on their own case, explaining that Charlotte was his sister and that they had both come down from Carlisle on their way to visit their mother's cousin, who lived somewhere near Cross Fell, but they had become lost.

"Cross Fell? Ah, then you're going in the wrong direction," the landlord told him.

"After we've eaten, perhaps you would be good enough to point the way?"

"Indeed, young sir, that I will."

"Meantime, I'll feed and water my horse, since you're short of help here today, and you can put it on my bill."

The landlord nodded and bustled away to bring them their dinner, and Charlotte gave Tom a worried look and whispered, "We've no money! How will we pay for it?"

"We won't," muttered Tom. He was glancing about,

hoping to locate a weapon—a musket perhaps—but none was in sight. "And we need a fresh horse too. Just close your eyes and pretend to be napping, in case someone comes in. I'll be right back."

In the stable, as he fed and watered his stolen mount he surveyed the situation. The landlord had a pair of very decent horses; of the two, the dappled gray mare looked like she had more staying power.

Wooden plates were laid, tankards of cider filled, the meat pie was brought, and good brown bread. Tom asked if there were apples to take along on their journey to Cross Fell, and the landlord obliged by bringing him a knotted linen square filled with hard delicious pippins.

Cold food had never tasted so good. They ate their venison pie and brown bread and accepted second helpings. They drank the strong apple cider, and Charlotte, who had been edgy about someone coming in, relaxed and smiled dreamily at Tom across the table and imagined what life would be like once a blacksmith had banged his anvil and pronounced them wed. *It would be wonderful*, she decided happily.

The landlord explained sheepishly that his wife had left only enough of a great tart for one serving (she had meant it for him, but he forbore saying that), and Tom quickly told him to give the berry tart to the lady. And while she ate it, would the landlord step outside and point out the way to Cross Fell?

The landlord would. He led Tom out upon the grassy plot before the inn—which in itself showed that this way was not much traveled—and gestured toward a nearby hill, explaining that if he would go around there to the right—

He never finished, for Tom's fist clipped him neatly on the jaw and stretched him out upon the grass, senseless.

Tom stood over him for a moment. He had hated doing that to this kindly man, but he had to get Charlotte out of here.

"I'll pay you when I can," he muttered to that prone unhearing figure in the leathern apron. "And for the horse too." He turned and beckoned to Charlotte, who was watching horrified from the window.

"He still isn't moving," Charlotte reported fearfully as Tom saddled the dappled gray mare. "Oh, you don't think he's dead, do you?"

"Of course not." Tom sighed. "But I'm hoping he'll stay peacefully where he is until we're out of sight." He was wishing he had the time to search the inn for a weapon, but "some of the lads from hereabout" could come streaming in at any minute and he dared not linger.

Just as they cleared the next rise, they heard an angry bellow from the direction of the inn.

"There's your answer," he told Charlotte ironically. "He's awake."

And then came the boom of a a musket.

"Very much awake." Tom took a twisting course in case the enraged landlord decided to leap astride the other horse in his stable and follow them.

"He'll alert the countryside with all that noise," worried Charlotte as they heard the musket fire again in the distance.

"We must take that chance. At least we've eaten, we've a fresh horse beneath us, and pippins to keep us going— all of which gives us a better chance to reach the border."

But Charlotte was looking back, still upset.

"We'll come back and pay him when we can. We will come back, won't we, Tom?"

"When we can," he answered absently, his mind more occupied with the pleasant discovery that the dappled gray mare beneath him was thundering down the slope as if she liked to run.

"What do you think we should do once we're wed at Gretna Green, Tom? Stay in Scotland or come back to England?"

Tom had been giving that a lot of thought. He answered promptly, "We'll head for Dumfries and sell the horse in the market there and make our way down the coast to Liverpool. And there, if you're willing, we'll indenture ourselves for the voyage to America. Would you like that?"

"Oh, yes," she breathed as they rode away into the

gathering dusk. The bagpipes of Scotland already sang a wild refrain in her heart. Ahead lay the Scottish Lowlands—and freedom!

They carefully skirted Carlisle—and it was there that the first group of pursuers crossed their path. Tom reined in at a shout ahead and a cry of "There they are, lads! Let's take them!"

The mare was skittish but she was fast. Tom would always be grateful for the way she responded to being turned about. She wheeled instantly and plunged along a path through some low woods, running like a deer. There Tom turned sharply east and down through a ravine and then south into rougher country until their pursuers had lost them.

The bands of men pursuing them, Tom realized bitterly, would have had fresh horses at their disposal all along the way, but he and Charlotte would have been ahead of them had the two of them only swooped down on the inn and departed with the mare. Their dinner had cost them their safe, easy passage to the Lowlands of Scotland.

After that it was hide-and-seek among the hills. They catnapped briefly by a stream and let the mare graze. It was a soft pleasant evening and Tom longed to hold Charlotte in his arms, but he was afraid to touch her because if he did he knew he'd go all the way with her, and that, he felt, would be unfair. She deserved a better "first night" than that, hurried and on the run—and she would have one.

They munched their apples and, strengthened, rode on.

But when at dawn they once more made their bid to win through just north of Carlisle, they were again pushed back and they were on the run all day. And now it was night again. They had eaten all their apples and were again famished, and they had almost reached the border when they were again driven back, this time in darkness. It worried Tom that their pursuers had seemed to be gaining in numbers as the day wore on—and seemed to be coming from everywhere.

He had hoped to make Scotland before the mare's endurance gave out, but now he saw that it was not to be. They had been trying to go around a tall mountain when Tom had seen the lanterns ahead—and sheered off. At this point there seemed to be no way to go but over that mountain or back the way they had come, so he started the mare up the mountainside. Climbing steadily, the poor beast made ever-slower progress, wavering on the grassy slope. The horse must have rest—and Charlotte too. She had been clinging gamely with her arms wrapped round his waist, her fingers locked over one of the brass buttons of his coat.

She had not complained, not his Charlotte, but now her head had lolled against his back and her bright hair, loosened by their long ride, was blowing across his face in the freshening breeze.

That breeze brought with it the promise of rain, and Tom was not sure whether rain would be a good thing or not. It would mean they would leave hoofprints here dug into the short grass or in any muddy patches they chanced to cross—hoofprints fresh and easy to follow. And when it began to rain, the rocky ways would become slick and dangerous. But rain would also obscure sound and vision and might allow them to slip between the parties that thrice had forced them back, and let them win through at last to Scotland.

The mare stumbled again and instinctively Tom reached out behind him to steady Charlotte, who might have gone to sleep in the saddle. She had, and she came awake with a start, and slid permissively into his arms when he dismounted and reached up to lift her down.

"Where . . . where are we?" she whispered, afraid the sound of her voice might carry through the darkness.

"If I'm right, this is Kenlock Crag," said Tom. "And Scotland is just over there." He made a sweeping motion with his arm.

The moon came out and Charlotte's gaze swung round, studying the peaks that rose in silvered silence about her. With the great bulk of the mountain obscuring most of their view at this point, there was not even the faint light of a farmer's candlelit window or crofter's hut; they might have been alone in the world.

"I don't hear anyone," she said after a moment.

"No, there were some lanterns, but I think we've lost them down in that last valley." He hoped he was right.

"Tom, if this is Kenlock Crag, then somewhere up near the summit there's a place where we could rest—and hide. Wend's father told me about it last Christmas. He used to be a guide for hunting parties climbing these steep crags—that was the way he got hurt, taking a party up Helvellyn."

"Did he tell you how to find it?" Tom sounded doubtful.

"Only that there was this narrow defile that led up to the top, and that branching off from it was another narrow cleft, and if you followed *that* branch, you would reach it."

Tom peered upward.

"There looks to be such a place up ahead," he said doubtfully.

"Then that must be it," said Charlotte. "He said it was really the only way to the summit."

Which would mean it would be a good place to defend . . . if defense became necessary.

"Shall we go up and see?"

Charlotte nodded. She was fully awake now and ready for anything—and she was sure she could trust anything Wend's twinkling-eyed climber father told her. She trudged along beside Tom as he led the mare on their upward journey.

The defile was farther than it had appeared to be from below, and when they reached it they sank down on the ground to rest before attempting an even more difficult climb toward the summit.

Beside them the dappled mare stood swaying slightly, her head drooping.

Tom studied the defile, which narrowed as it trended upward. He could not see the fork Wend's father had described, but there could well be one up there. It was a chance he felt they had to take, for they could not risk letting daylight find them exposed on the mountainside.

He looked at the horse. Her hooves would ring on the rocks and the sound would carry. He remembered the lanterns. They might be out of earshot of the men who carried those lanterns—or they might not. Anyway, this was where they and the horse would part company.

He stood up.

"She's been a gallant mount, this mare, and she's saved us more than once." Tom stroked the despondent animal's mane. "But she needs to find water and grazing and she won't find it up this rocky way, nor have time for it when we make our bid for the border." In fact a tired, wavering animal would be a liability, for there would be some nearly level terrain to cross between here and the border, and while he and Charlotte could drop to the ground and lie still in reeds or rushes, a horse would stand tall—and it was doubtful that he could persuade a strange horse to lie down on order. "We'll have to manage on foot from here on, Charlotte."

He took the mare's bridle and turned her gently around, gave her a light dismissing slap on the rump. Obediently—thankfully, he thought—the mare sidled off, sliding a little on the slippery short grass, but heading ever downhill.

They were both silent as they watched the mare depart, because without her they had lost so much of their power to maneuver. They were committed to the mountain.

They looked at each other for a long moment and then they started up, climbing ever upward until at last Tom thought that Charlotte could stand no more and ordered her to rest.

"Stay here," he said. "I'll go exploring. If I can find this place Wend's father mentioned, it will be a bit of luck for us."

Charlotte was glad to rest and wait. When Tom came back he looked well-pleased.

"It's a bit tricky to get to," he said, "but it's up there, just like he said."

He led her upward to a place where there was a fork in the defile. He took the fork to the right and she clambered up after him to a place breathtakingly near the summit. It was indeed a sheltered spot she saw as she looked over a low wall formed by a fallen boulder into a scooped-out place that must have been created when the rain washed out a softer section of rock. On three sides the rock walls rose sheer save for a natural overhang that loomed over one side of an almost level stone "floor," scoured almost smooth by rain. Off the main defile that led on up to the crest of this rugged peak, this tiny natural terrace was as private—except for the cleft entrance through which she now looked—as if they were in a small courtyard surrounded on three sides by house walls, a terrace over whose low uneven entrance barrier Tom had already vaulted and where he was now standing.

"Watch out you don't walk too far that way." He waved his hand at the fourth side, where the flat terrace wall seemed to disappear. "There's a sheer drop that goes down forever, with a cascade rushing by at the bottom."

"I can hear it," she said. And indeed she could. The sound was making her thirsty, but there was no water up here. Unless it rained.

Without waiting for him to help her over, Charlotte leapt over the low boulder to join him. Her skirt caught on a jagged outcrop of rock as she sprang, an outcrop split away by last winter's frost perhaps. It caught her by surprise and twisted her to the side so that she landed in a tumble of wide skirts on a pile of loose rocks instead of the terrace floor, worn smooth by rain.

Instantly Tom was bending solicitously over her.

"Are you hurt?" he asked sharply, for an injury now could be a desperate thing.

"No." In the fitful moonlight she gave him a wan look and tried to struggle up, only to fall back with a sharp low cry. "My ankle," she amended bitterly. "I seem to have wrenched it as I fell."

Above her Tom bit his lip and frowned. He bent down and scooped her up. Reproach her he would not, for she had been as gallant as the mare, and full of spirit all of this wild ride into the unknown. He carried her to a sheltered spot cupped out of the protruding rocks above them and carefully laid her down.

"If it rains, you'll have some shelter here," he explained.

"Oh, Tom." Charlotte's voice was uneven and filled with anxiety. "I've ruined our chances, haven't I—getting hurt?"

"Of course not," he said soothingly. But he had a sinking feeling all the same. How badly her ankle had been injured, they would know by morning. Meantime . . .

"I'll climb up to the top and have a look," he told her restlessly.

He made his way over the low boulder that resembled a terrace wall, and back down along the way they had come over this broken pathway to the fork in the defile, and then climbed up the main defile until he reached the summit. There atop the highest rocks he looked out across a vista that seemed to include the whole of the British Isles.

The night wind blew his hair, and the moon was hiding behind a cloud so that the entire wild landscape had a devil's darkness about it, mysterious, remote. From this high vantage point, seemingly on the roof of the world, he could see the lanterns of his pursuers moving about like fireflies in the darkness far below. So many of them. In an irregular line from east to west those lanterns swung, barring the way to Scotland.

It was worse than he had thought. He exhaled a deep slow breath. Penetrating that barrier would be difficult enough for a strong man. For an exhausted girl with a strained ankle it would be impossible. But perhaps they could hide here for a time until the searchers decided they had somehow slipped through the net; perhaps then the searchers would go on a wild-goose chase into Scotland; perhaps—

It was then that he heard the dogs. A faint distant baying echoed in more than one place. First he heard it faint and far off to the east. He cocked an ear and waited tensely. The sound was echoed by a distant baying far to the west.

It was then that he knew that they were lost. There would be no time for Charlotte's ankle to recuperate, no flight into Scotland. No future.

His pursuers below were determined men. With the help of their dogs they would comb these hills, scour them like the rain. The dogs would find the mare he had set free, too tired to be far away, and then the dogs would find *them.*

The thought of his own death did not move him so much—he had faced death with courage on many a slippery deck. But what of Charlotte? He had a sudden horrifying vision of Charlotte being attacked and savaged by dogs and *then* carried away to her bridal bed and a man who only wished to use her young innocence to cleanse himself of the results of his own debauchery.

As if to blot out the picture, he closed his eyes.

And opened them with a savage gleam.

He would fight! When he heard swords clanking or horsemen coming up that narrow defile—and surely he must, for horses' hooves would ring on the rocky surface and alert him—he would hurl down stones upon them, he would loosen boulders, he would send man and beast careening down the mountainside to their doom!

Sadly, common sense returned.

Stones . . . against muskets, against long swift swords. He had foresworn the ball and the blade as emblems of a trade he despised, put them out of his life in an effort to be worthy of Charlotte. Regret for his rashness poured over him. God, to have a cutlass in his hand and a pistol in his belt at this moment! He could not even defend himself properly against armed men!

He would fight—aye, he would do that, he would throw down his boulders, he would dart about trying to dodge the musket balls that would be aimed at him—he would fight, but in the end by sheer numbers they would overcome him. And if they did not kill him on the spot, which was likely, they would carry him off to a magistrate to be hanged nice and proper for horse thievery, or more likely for trepanning, for her uncle would doubtless swear he had kidnapped Charlotte with a forced marriage in mind—and the penalty for trepanning was death. Looking down over those winking lights far below, he had the eerie feeling that he was already dead, that the same evil fate that had placed him willy-nilly aboard the *Shark* had contrived to bring him here to Kenlock Crag so that the gods might laugh to see him struggle against overwhelming odds.

It was only after Tom had accepted the fact that tomorrow's dawn might be the last that he would ever see that he began to think, and after a while his eyes lit up and he glared down into the darkness.

They would have him—naught could be done about that. *But they would not have Charlotte!*

10

Kenlock Crag

Tom came down the short distance from the peak with his mind made up.

"What did you see?" she asked, even as he vaulted over the low wall.

"Lanterns."

Her breath caught. "*Lots* of lanterns?"

He nodded.

She was looking up at him, fear in her eyes. "Enough to bar our way to Scotland?"

"I'm afraid so." He sighed.

They were both silent for a space. He stood looking down at her, thinking how lovely she was, how untouched, and how vulnerable.

"Then if we can't try for Scotland, what do you think we should do?" she asked in a low voice. "Try again to go around the base of this mountain and strike out for Carlisle?"

He nodded again. "It's possible." *And it was, if miracles still happened.*

"We could take a ship from Carlisle," she said wistfully.

"We've no money for passage," he felt constrained to point out. "And now no horse to trade for passage."

"Yes, but your mother lives in Carlisle, Tom. Surely at a time like this she would help us?"

She would not, but why should he spoil the illusion? Let

120

Charlotte dream a little longer. The dream would be over soon enough.

"Yes, we'll go to Carlisle." He tried to sound convincing. "To my mother."

"Shouldn't we be starting?" she asked in a small voice.

"Not yet, there's plenty of time before morning."

Fear crept into her voice at his offhand tone. "And if my foot is better, we could be in Carlisle tomorrow night," she said unevenly. And then, "Oh, Tom, hold me!"

He sank down beside her. It was exactly what he had had in mind. There was only one way to save her once he was done for, and that was to render her no longer a virgin. That would turn away the evil lord who would use her for his disgusting purposes, and there were others, men of wealth and power, men who could take care of her as he could not, who would covet her for her beauty and for all that she was. That tall fellow who had come out with her into the garden at Castle Stroud, for instance—and there would be others. He was not the only man who would fall in love with a girl like Charlotte. At Castle Stroud he had seen the great candlelit chandeliers and heard the strains of music floating out, and he had known what it meant. The gentry of Cumberland had discovered Charlotte now, and hers was a face they were not likely to forget. She could escape her uncle and men such as Lord Pimmerston and find for herself a bright future . . . with his help.

There was time—time enough for his purposes, at least. For there were other mountains about, and the searchers might well waste their time climbing those first. Even if they chose this crag, they might search a long time before finding the narrow defile he had taken—and in any event they probably would not attempt the ascent before morning.

Charlotte had moved over a little to give him room on the smooth rock surface. Hot desire for her welled through him every time he touched her—even brushing her skirt could bring a dark flush to his cheeks—and now . . .

He reached out ever so gently to take her in his arms, and she went into them, burrowing deep, as if to seek cover. Tenderly he stroked her golden hair. Making her

his—even though it was only for a night—would make
death worthwhile, he thought, and felt her quiver as he
leaned down and dragged his lips over her own, traced a
warm line with them along her smooth cheek, over her
chin, and down her pulsing white throat to bury his hot
face in the enchanting area between her young breasts.

Charlotte quivered beneath this sweet assault. Shyly
she rubbed her cheek against Tom's dark hair and moved
her body a little, the better to fit against his own. He was
undoing the hooks of her bodice now, and she made no
move to stop him. There was a purposefulness in him
tonight, and of a sudden the reason for that purposefulness
knifed through her.

"Tom," she whispered. *"You think we're going to die,
don't you?"*

His head came up and he looked into her troubled eyes,
lit by the fitful moon that had slid from behind the clouds
to bathe the border country in its pale radiance. He would
lie to her no longer.

"I don't mean to let them take me alive," he said quietly.

A shudder went through her slight form.

"Then I'll go with you, Tom," she said, lifting her chin
defiantly. "We can stay here through the night, and when
we see them coming in the morning, we can throw ourselves over the edge into the chasm." She nodded toward
the distant sound of white water cascading far below at the
base of the cliff.

*Over the edge to oblivion. . . . His lovely girl, she meant
to die with him.* Tom's eyes misted over.

"I've no intention of throwing myself over this or any
other edge," he said sternly. "I intend to fight for my life."

She was clinging to his coat, holding on to him with real
desperation.

"I promise I won't survive you, Tom," she choked. Her
grip on him was tightening in panic as she spoke.

This sudden urge to join him in hell was no part of his
intention. He took Charlotte firmly by the shoulders, gave
her a little shake.

"But you *must* survive me, Charlotte," he said earnestly. "Otherwise it will all have been in vain and I'll die knowing I've failed you."

Her jaw was set stubbornly. He tried another tack.

"You have a long life to live and you'll soon forget the fellow who stole a horse and tried to carry you off to Scotland. You'll find a better man—and you'll be happy." *God, he hoped she'd be happy!*

Her fierce shake of the head told him where she stood on that.

"At least promise me you won't do anything rash—not right away," he said huskily. "Promise me you'll give life a chance."

"I won't do anything rash right away," she promised. "But"—her eyes glinted—"later I will! I'll join you wherever you are!"

He had to hope that before that happened the right man would come along . . . to replace him in her heart. He tried again.

"Somewhere there's a house like Castle Stroud waiting for you—with the right man inside. There'll be children, dancing, fine clothes, trips to London—you want all that, don't you?"

"Oh, yes," she said sadly. "I want all that. But I want it with *you*, Tom. All the time we were in Castle Stroud together I was imagining what it would be like to live there with *you* beside me." She gave him a sad, almost derisive look. "I could *have* Castle Stroud, Tom—indeed, it's being forced upon me."

But at what cost. . . .

"The right man will find you, Charlotte, if you'll just let him."

Her face seemed to fall apart.

"I don't want them, Tom. I only want *you*." There were tears in her voice and she clung to him like a hurt child.

Her words thrilled him, sang in his brain. For a dizzy moment he felt he could survive anything.

"Don't cry," he murmured, caressing her throat, her shoulders, letting his hand slide along the smooth skin of her bosom. "I've wanted to do this since first I laid eyes on you. Just consider that you're giving me a great gift, one

that I'd die for willingly. And anyway," he added recklessly, for he did not want her "first night" to be spent in
sighs and tears, "let's look on the bright side. We may live
through this—others before us have survived worse."

Of course they had—and she and Tom would too!

"Oh, Tom, we *will* make it—we'll hide, we'll escape
them!" Confidence began to well through Charlotte as
Tom's questing fingers again sought her breasts, released
them from the cloth that bound them, fondled them so
that little warm shivers went through her.

"We'll live together forever, Tom, we'll have children, a
home of our own . . ." He had eased her out of her bodice
now and his hands were warm and tingling on her back,
sliding up and down the smooth skin as his lips against her
breasts worried first one pink crest and then the other.
"Oh, Tom"—her voice broke—*"tell me you think we can!"*

"I think we can," he lied in a slurred voice, and her
body sagged against him in mute surrender as, reassured
by his words, some of the tension left her.

But whatever happens, we'll have this night! was her
thought and his as her skirts were swept up and she felt
his long fingers gliding up her smooth thighs, gently probing her secret places, bringing a soft low moan of desire to
her lips.

Tom took his time. Whatever happened on the morrow,
Charlotte should not be deflowered hastily or roughly or
with lack of care and tenderness. He wanted these moments to be magic moments—for her as well as for him.
And although he did not consciously think about it in the
wave of desire that had taken him in its grip and that soon
would be too much for him to hold back, he wanted to be
remembered. He wanted Charlotte to give a smiling thought
to Tom Westing now and then after he was long gone.

And so, even though he must break the seal of her
girlhood, he would try in the doing of it to bring her joys
undreamt-of. And to that end he stroked her sweet young
body, he teased her breasts, nibbling her nipples to hardness, he dragged his warm lips across the skin of her soft
responsive stomach, he tickled with light caressing fingers

that silky mound of hair above her thighs and explored its
silken recesses.

"*Charlotte, Charlotte,*" he sighed. "*A man could fill his
life with you.*"

"Oh, Tom, we should have forever," she choked. "Not
just a night."

"Hush," he murmured.

Yes, hush! she thought rebelliously. *Hush, lest Fate
should overhear—for it is Fate decides the odds!* But she
did not say it. Instead she clung to him with all the love
that was in her.

Wild new feelings were assailing her senses, surging
feelings deeper than the sea, stronger than the storm
winds racing off the high crags, feelings both wondrous
and new. She was dizzily conscious of his teasing, stroking, tempting her, readying her for his first thrust.

And when it came she quivered with the sudden shock
of it, gasped, and lay for a moment so still he was afraid he
had hurt her too much. And then, as if to tell him he had
not and to give him silent permission to continue, she
stirred in his arms and tried to press her warm femininity
even closer in perfect trust.

He was touched by the innocent ardor of that slight
expressive gesture and went about his work with care and
skill—and strength.

Long pulsing moments later she was no longer a maid
and her world was tumbling about with crazy upside-down
rhythms and dazzling new delights that led her up and up
as her back arched upward to meet him and swept her
down again in joy as he drew back for each fresh thrust.

"Tom," she murmured brokenly. "Oh, Tom, I love you
so." But her voice was hushed by his kisses even as her
body and spirit, joined with his, seemed to soar from
Kenlock Crag out to the farther stars.

And Charlotte came back to the world content, feeling
somehow magically reborn, no longer Charlotte-the-Alone,
but Charlotte-Loved-by-Tom. It was a wonderful feeling.
She felt her whole body tingle as he left her to roll over
and lie beside her at last.

This, then, was fulfillment. And in the blinding splendor of young love, she suddenly could not imagine anything really bad happening to them. The whole world was theirs already—surely they would be allowed to keep it?

"Oh, Tom," she murmured. "We *will* win through. I feel in my heart that we will."

Tom dragged himself up on one elbow and grinned down at her. Her optimism was catching.

"Perhaps. They say the devil protects his own. And I'm surely one of the devil's own!"

"No, you're not!" Her arms were around his neck again. "You're a fine good man who's had bad luck, that's all! And your luck will change, Tom—I feel it. See?" She lifted her foot into the air. "My ankle feels better already. I'm sure I'll be able to walk tomorrow. And then—oh, Tom, we'll elude them, I'm sure we will!"

She nestled against him in the golden ephemeral optimism of the afterglow, confident their world would be righted. And Tom, who had seen the lanterns, took her again—took her with all the fire and fervor and torment of one who knows he lives beneath the shadow of the sword.

It was a night like no other.

11

At dawn Tom rose and checked on Charlotte's ankle. It was red and swollen, and if she moved, it throbbed—there was no question of her walking. Cold water to bathe it would help, and they were both thirsty. He would have to chance being seen searching for water, for it might become impossible later if these hills were swarming with climbers out for his blood.

He was lucky. Only a short distance down the mountainside he found a little bubbling spring that trickled downward over the rocks. He drank thirstily and carried water back to Charlotte in his hat. When she had drunk all she could, he bathed her ankle with the rest of the water and she sank back, insisting the pain had eased.

"We will rest here until the pursuit moves off in some other direction," he told her in a confident voice, keeping up the charade they were playing out between them. "By then your ankle will be better."

"Yes," she said, reaching down and touching her swollen ankle gingerly. "People can live a long time without food," she added. "So long as they have water—and we have water."

Her cheerful courage stabbed him through, and he turned away so that she could not read his face and know what he was thinking.

"Tom," she said, lying back and folding her arms behind

her head. "Tell me about the time when you were a little boy—I want to know all about you."

And Tom, to entertain her and keep her mind off hunger and danger, found himself recounting to this silent solemn-eyed girl things that he had never told a living soul, told her about his failures and his triumphs, what he had thought of when death had loomed near, all his cherished hopes and dreams.

When he had finished, Charlotte's eyes were filled with unshed tears and she sat up and took him in her arms, held him to her like a child. "I never knew it was possible to love anyone so much," she told him in a choked voice.

Tom did not know what he could possibly have said to merit that heartfelt response. He knew simply that he wanted to be worthy of this girl and to get her safely through—wanted it more than anything else in this world.

And on the wings of such feelings their young bodies blended in a silent love song that knew neither time nor place but only a vast tenderness and a caring that healed old wounds and made life seem a wondrous vibrant thing.

When it was over, Tom gently disentangled himself from Charlotte's twining arms and legs.

"I hope I didn't hurt your ankle," he said gruffly.

He had, but Charlotte would have died rather than admit it. "If you had," she told him with a light laugh, "I don't think I'd have noticed!" She stretched luxuriously. "Oh, Tom, tell me they won't find us. Tell me they'll go away and leave us in peace, and we'll make our way to Scotland and be forgotten. . . ."

"They'll go away," he told her moodily.

But not till they've got what they came for, his own thoughts mocked him.

And yet, lying here with her in this sheltered place with the warm sun streaming down and only an occasional bird winging overhead, it was easy to imagine that they would win through. Despite his better judgment, he found himself half-believing it. He propped Charlotte's foot up again on a rock made comfortable by having his hat atop it and watched her go to sleep, curled up in this haven to which he had brought her.

And against his better judgment, he dreamed too. . . .

Leaning against the rock beside her with his long legs stretched comfortably, he sat the whole of the afternoon until the red glow of sunset stained the sky and flushed the faces of the drab-colored peaks around them. The air was hushed with stillness as the world sank into twilight, that magical haunting twilight that falls upon the mountains.

It had been a long time now and there had been no sign of life in any direction. A surge of hope went through him. By heaven's light! If only those armed men prowling below would disperse, he would carry Charlotte out of here! Carry her away somewhere to a feather bed where she could recuperate at her leisure. He wasn't sure just how he was going to accomplish that, but he vowed within himself to bring it about. And then he closed his mind on it.

It was too soon to dream.

As the dusk deepened, he crept down and brought Charlotte more water—and wished he could bring her food as well.

But her wan face was smiling courageously when she finished drinking the water.

"We've lived another day, Tom," she said softly.

At those simple words, he felt as if his heart would break. Beyond speech, he took her in his arms and held her close, close.

At least, he told himself fiercely, they would have another night together.

And a night of splendor it was, a night made for memories as they dallied together, tasting all the joys of love. Physically they seemed made for each other, a perfect match, and there was between them an unspoken tenderness that went beyond desire. Lost in magic as she lay in his arms, Charlotte knew a deep and rich fulfillment, and Tom knew a bittersweet longing and an aching regret, for he realized all too well that these golden moments when he clasped her to him might be all he would ever have of her. They would have to last him all of his life. . . .

He meant to keep watch when finally they lay together,

spent but still aglow; he meant to, but fatigue overcame him and gradually his eyes closed and he slept.

The whole countryside had been aroused by Charlotte's "abduction by a trepanner," for Bodine had seen to it that word was put about that Lord Pimmerston's betrothed was a young lady of vast fortune who had been snatched from the gardens of Castle Stroud by a horse thief who held a gun to her head. This fellow, it was reported, intended to spirit the unfortunate heiress across the border, marry her in haste, and return to claim her fortune and bribe his way out of his thievery.

Such a story was bound to arouse the fury of the county, and from all about, grim men armed with muskets had set out at once to patrol the border country, lest the fiend slip through with his victim.

The horse Tom had stolen from its hitching post at Castle Stroud had by now returned home, but when a fellow who frequented the Stag and Horn chanced upon the landlord's horse grazing peacefully beside a little spring, he rode in haste through the darkness to bring the news to Charlotte's uncle, who, along with Rowan Keynes, had ridden in with a small search party, while Lord Pimmerston and Bodine had raced off for the coast in case the "rogue," as Tom was now called, should try to escape by sea.

As the man who had found the horse approached with his news, a heated conversation was taking place between Charlotte's uncle, astride his bay horse, and Rowan Keynes, sitting easily astride his chestnut stallion.

"The girl sees herself as meant for better things than a man of Pimmerston's age—and eaten away with the 'gallant's disease' as well, and eager to infect her!" Rowan was insisting. "Had either of us been in her slippers, we'd have run away too."

"We're neither of us wenches," was the grumpy response. " 'Tis not for a wench to decide." But he gave Rowan a curious look, for it was the streak of cruelty in Rowan's nature along with his wildness that appealed to men like himself and Lord Pimmerston and Bodine and others of their ilk. The Rowan Keynes he had known rode his horses without mercy, had once horsewhipped his valet insensible for forgetting to relay a message from a lady, and was reputed to have beaten a prostitute in London so badly that she could not work for a month. When asked about the prostitute, Rowan had said frankly that she'd approached him knowing full well that she had a fresh case of the "gallant's disease"—which he'd have got from her had he fancied her, which he didn't—but when he found out about that, he had sought her out and punished her. Tongues had wagged for a while, but prostitutes counted for little, and most who heard about it felt she had gotten what was coming to her. "What's this, Rowan?" Russ demanded with sudden interest. "Why've you taken this tack? Have you gone soft for the wench?"

Rowan frowned at him. *Had* he gone soft for the wench? Visions of Charlotte dancing in her white dress floated through his mind, clouding it.

"Certainly not!" He closed his mouth with a snap. But one thing he *had* decided—*Pimmerston should not have her!*

What else he might have said at that moment was interrupted by the arrival of the landlord's friend from the Stag and Horn, who told them he had found the stolen horse. "So they must be somewheres around here," the man concluded. "For afoot they can't have gone far."

"We'll fan out and search the valley!" exclaimed Russ instantly. "Pass the word!"

But as their messenger galloped away, Rowan's thoughtful gaze turned upward toward the heights.

"If I were fleeing and my horse had given way under me," he mused, "I'd seek high ground and a good defensive position—not go running about like a scared rabbit through the meadows below."

Russ frowned. "What're you saying, Rowan?"

"I'm saying they're up there." Rowan nodded his dark head toward the peak above.

"On Kenlock Crag? Can't be! We'd have seen them climbing up, wouldn't we?"

"Not if they did it last night in the dark."

"But the horse couldn't make it, it's too steep."

"Maybe not. Someone from around here can tell us if there's a good way up." He rode off.

"Wait for me!" cried Russ. "If there's a chance we can pounce on the pair of them ourselves . . ."

Up ahead, riding through the gathering darkness, Rowan did not answer. That was exactly what he had in mind.

They found a pair of local men—climbers both—who knew the rocky defile that led to the top of the mountain. Aye, they could lead them up there—night or day.

"Dogs!" rumbled Charlotte's uncle on a note of triumph. "We'll send up the dogs first. They'll flush Westing out like a fox!"

"Westing's well enough, but there's your niece up there," pointed out Rowan. "You've seen dogs tear foxes to pieces. Suppose they attack her? Do you plan to turn the wench over to Pimmerston bitten and bleeding?"

Russ subsided, grumbling.

Pleased to have won his point, Rowan narrowed his dark eyes.

"We'll go on foot—with the help of these good fellows here." He nodded toward the climbers.

"Very well," agreed Russ with a sigh. "We'll start at dawn."

"We'll start now," corrected Rowan pleasantly. "We'll make the climb at night, when they won't expect us. After all, we don't want them to do anything foolish—as you told me was done by a pair of runaway lovers last year on yon mountain."

His remark silenced Charlotte's uncle, reminding him that last year a maddened father had pursued his runaway daughter and her lover to this very crag. Cornered and desperate, they had locked hands and leapt to their death in the cataract below. Dead, Charlotte would be of no use to him.

"How many men should we take?" he asked in an altered tone. "There's a dozen nearby who'd be glad to volunteer."

"The four of us should be more than sufficient," was Rowan's cool response. He would have liked to say "the three of us" and leave Russ at the base of the crag, but he knew that Russ would never allow that, and there was no point in arousing his ire. But when Russ reached for a lantern, Rowan said tersely, "Leave that. The moonlight will soon be more than enough to light our way."

Carefully, moving like shadows, with the experienced climbers going ahead and leading the way, the two men started out.

They took a long painful time climbing up the defile. At the fork their guides left them and went ahead to the top, moving like ghosts silhouetted against the dark sky.

And then from above, lying along the protruding rock outcrop that overhung the niche that partially covered the sleeping bodies of Charlotte and Tom, a vantage point that could be seen in the distance by the two men waiting at the fork, the experienced climbers beckoned Rowan and Russ toward the low terrace wall where Tom had erected his small cairn of stones to serve as a warning.

Silent and breathless now, Rowan and Russ arrived at the spot simultaneously and their two heads came up over the terrace wall, surveying the lovers' hideaway.

The scene they had come upon in the moonlight was a peaceful one. Charlotte lay upon Tom's spread-out coat. Her head was pillowed on his shoulder. Tom's shirt was pulled out from his trouser top and one fine hand lay with the fingers still touching Charlotte's unhooked bodice, as if it had slid there from caressing the mounds of her firm young breasts that rose bare and pale, their tips caressed by moonlight. As she moved restlessly in her sleep on the hard rock surface, Charlotte's light skirts had ridden up, and Rowan Keynes was confronted with the prettiest pair of legs—for all the slight swelling and redness of one ankle—that it had ever been his privilege to view. Her bright hair was spread out in a shining moon-glittered mass.

It was a very private scene, a scene upon which no man should have stumbled, and for a moment, caught up by the girl's beauty and by a sudden wish that *he* were that long tall fellow lying there asleep, Rowan held his breath.

Beside him Charlotte's uncle had no such finer feelings. He let out a bellow that would have waked the dead, slipped, and clutched at Rowan's coat to save himself.

The spell was broken.

Tom, aroused by the noise, gained his feet in a bound and leapt forward. That put him in range of the climbers from above, who dropped down on him just as Rowan, picking up the top stone of Tom's cairn, flung it with force to smash into the side of Tom's head so that he staggered sideways and fell like a stone at the cliff edge.

At that point Rowan was occupied with keeping Russ's weight from pulling him over backward, for Russ had toppled, lost his footing, and would have skittered down the steep defile behind him save for that death grip he had taken on Rowan's coat.

At the noise, Charlotte too had come awake and seen with paralyzing fear Tom spring up and be struck down by a stone from nowhere even as two bodies hurtled down upon him from above.

With a cry of fear at seeing Tom lying so still on the cliff edge, where he might with any motion topple over, Charlotte came to her feet and, unmindful of her injured ankle, plunged toward him.

One of the climbers from above, seeing her try to lunge past him, and afraid that her impetuous spring forward might carry her over the edge, managed to snatch at her skirts. Her hurt ankle gave way and she went down in a heap. This was accompanied by a loud rip as her skirts parted company from her bodice at the back.

The other climber who had guided the party up seized Charlotte by the arm and yanked her to her feet, where she would have gone down again save for the first climber, who promptly seized her other arm. Together they bore her back to the rock wall, where she stood on her good foot, kicking out at them with her injured one and screaming at Tom to get up and save himself, to get away from the edge or he'd go over!

She made a pretty picture spread-eagled there against the rock wall—and perhaps that was why the climbers continued to hold her thus, devouring her with their eyes— for her firm round breasts rode free above her unhooked bodice, bouncing as her torso moved with each angry kick. Her skirts in the back had torn free and hung down almost like a train, while her chemise—in which her heel had caught in the melee as she was unceremoniously yanked to her feet—streamed down below like a train as well.

In her torn white gown with her hair wild and disheveled and her face flushed, she looked curiously like an embattled bride—and endlessly tempting.

It was in that moment that Rowan decided to marry her.

Rowan, who had missed the early part of this scene as he was pulled abruptly backward by the weight of Russ's body as Russ clawed to regain his footing on the steep defile, had by now managed to regain the terrace, dragging Russ with him. He shook off the other man and vaulted the terrace wall, knocking down Tom's cairn of stones as he did so.

Russ came over next, stumbled on a rolling stone, and was righted by Rowan, who reached out and caught him. Russ was so angry he was almost frothing at the mouth.

"Pimmerston will not want her now—she's no longer a virgin," Rowan told Russ softly. His dark eyes gleamed.

"We don't know that!" blustered Russ. "Could be he didn't get that far. By God, we'll have her skirts up and find out!" He plunged toward Charlotte, who was standing precariously on one foot, being held flat against the rocky wall by the two climbers, one on each side, holding her arms pressed against the steep wall of the crag.

Rowan's long arm barred his way.

"*Ask her*," he suggested pleasantly.

"Did that rogue pierce your maidenhead?" roared her uncle.

"Yes, he did," Charlotte screamed back. "And I'm glad of it! 'Tis better than what *you* had in mind for me!"

"I'll have proof of that!" Russ struggled against Rowan's detaining arm.

Charlotte's face was white when Rowan, hard put to hold Russ back, suddenly said, "There's your proof," and Russ followed the gesture of his head and saw what Rowan meant. In the bright moonlight, the torn-away section at the back of Charlotte's thin chemise, which had left her body and now lay spread out at her feet, was highlighted, and its delicate white surface betrayed a pale stain of watery blood.

His chest heaving with rage at being thus bilked, Russ flung himself back from Rowan's restraining grip, and Rowan, now that Russ was no longer headed in Charlotte's direction, let him go. All eyes were on Charlotte, quivering there, when suddenly Russ turned to vent his spleen upon Tom.

"Bastard!" he almost sobbed, and with the word—and to the accompaniment of a shriek from Charlotte—he aimed such a devastating kick at Tom's body that the very force of it sent Russ himself over on his backside.

The effect on Tom was worse. Caught by such a solid blow, his inert body rolled over, poised for a moment half-on, half-off the cliff edge, and then, almost in slow motion, went over the edge, dislodging a shower of stones as he went, to disappear into the blackness below.

For long moments, with the remnants of Charlotte's scream still lingering in the air, the whole group remained paralyzed. No one spoke, astonished perhaps by this sudden attack upon an unconscious man who could not defend himself. Even Charlotte's uncle, frozen in the act of trying to struggle up, remained mute, as if appalled by what he had done.

But Charlotte, listening to the rattle of dislodged stones that seemed to go on endlessly as they—and no doubt Tom with them—plunged downward, to be lost in the white waters of the cascade far below, never heard the last stone drop.

Overcome by horror, she had fainted, and her half-clothed young body hung slumped against the rock wall, kept upright only by the grasp of the two men who held her.

12

In that moment, when Charlotte sagged senseless against the rock wall and her guardian still sat mute, only Rowan Keynes seemed to know what to do. He stepped across Russ's fallen form and strode to the edge from whence Tom's body had pitched, and stood silently looking down.

"What d'you see?" came Russ's hoarse voice from behind him.

"Nothing." Rowan turned about in time to see Russ bite his lip. Russ's face, he noted, had gone very pale. Seeing Russ sitting there looking so pinched and frightened brought a shadow of scorn to Rowan's hard mouth. Instantly he took command. "Can you manage the girl between you?" He was speaking to the two guides, one on either side of Charlotte's collapsed figure. "She'll be safer if the pair of you take her down the mountain, since you both know the way. Russ and I will follow you. Oh, and remember not to let go of her lest she do herself a hurt—for 'tis plain she's grown fond of this kidnapper who accidentally fell over the cliff to his death just now."

His voice was bland and the pair of them looked at each other uneasily. That was not the way they had seen it, but both of them were dead set against trepanning and both imagined Charlotte to be a silly young heiress stolen away from her rightful betrothed and seduced by a wily fortune hunter. Their worried eyes met and held for a moment, then swung about as they nodded in silent agreement.

Rowan understood those nods: the two would look the other way. "Accident" it would be.

Russ did not speak until the pair of them, carrying Charlotte's limp body, were out of earshot. Then he heaved a deep sigh.

"I've you to thank for that, Rowan."

"Yes, you have," agreed Rowan pleasantly. "And I'll tell you just how you can thank me. I intend to have the girl."

The older man's shoulders slumped. "I'm ruined if I don't let Pimmerston have her, you know that."

"So you plan to palm her off on him as a virgin after all?"

The shrug of Russ's dejected shoulders was ample answer.

"How much is Pimmerston paying you?" Rowan shot at him.

"Paying me?" Russ was prepared to bluster, but the sudden menace in the other man's face shut him off and he muttered a figure that caused Rowan's brows to shoot up.

"So much?" he murmured. "Well, well . . . I'll pay the same price for her, only you'll have to wait for it. There's somewhere I must go first."

"Wait?" muttered Russ suspiciously. "For how long?"

"Not long."

"Better not be long or my creditors will be on me like a pack of dogs."

"Your creditors . . . yes, we wouldn't want them to strip you of your lands, would we?"

Russ made no answer, but his eyes smoldered. "She won't have you, you know," he said bitterly. "She wouldn't have Pimmerston and she won't have you, stubborn wench that she is!"

"Oh, she'll have me," was the calm rejoinder. "And she won't even know she's been bought. But I don't propose to hand over a small fortune for nothing. I'll buy Aldershot Grange from you, together with all its goods. Once Charlotte is mine, I'll give you my note of hand for it and you can have the deed drawn up." As if in answer to Russ's balky expression, he added softly, "And when I redeem

the note and take the deed, I'll give you back a lease on
Aldershot Grange for your lifetime, at a rental of"—laughter
welled up in his voice—"a single blood-red rose, payable
once a year during Whitsuntide."

Russ drew a deep breath and his sagging shoulders
straightened. "I'm willing enough," he said cautiously,
"but my creditors must even now be streaming north—"

"Oh, bother your creditors," said the younger man impatiently. "Disappear, man, disappear! Until I return."

"And where are you going?"

The dark eyes took on an opaque look. "Edinburgh,"
was the glib answer. "There's a man there who owes me
money, and I'm off to collect it."

"Good. I'll go along."

"That you will not. Now, listen to me. Here's my plan."

Before they were a quarter of the way down the mountain, following the distant figures of their guides in the
moonlight, Russ knew what part he must play. He chuckled.

"By the Lord Harry, I believe it will work!" he exclaimed in admiration.

"Of course it will work," was the cold response. "My
plans always work."

Below them they could hear Charlotte, fighting and
struggling now with the guides and passionately demanding to be taken back to the cliff, where she could see
Tom's body below, for could he not still be alive? They
could hear the guides gruffly assuring her that no man
could survive such a fall and live, and besides, one of the
"gentlemen" had looked over the edge and said he was
gone.

"I'm not so sure your plan will work," warned Russ,
suddenly glum.

"It will," said Rowan confidently, reaching out to steady
Russ as a bit of rock gave way beneath the other man's
foot.

When they reached the base of the mountain where the
horses had been left tethered, they found Charlotte seated
on the ground with one of the guides gripping her arm.
She fixed a venomous gaze on her uncle.

"Murderer!" she said through her teeth. "I'll see you hanged for this night's work!"

The guides stirred uneasily. Of a sudden the night seemed darker.

" 'Twas your lover who would have been hanged for trepanning," her uncle told her heavily. "So his death *by accident* was merciful."

With a convulsive motion Charlotte jerked free of the guides' grasp. Heedless of her injured ankle, she tried to spring at her uncle, but Rowan caught her.

"Easy," he murmured, hearing her gasp of pain as her weight went on that ankle. He turned to the two men who had brought her down the mountain. "We can take it from here," he told them. "We both thank you for restoring this lady to her guardian."

"Restored?" cried Charlotte. "I am not 'restored'!" She twisted about, trying to appeal to the guides. "I am brought to this man against my will—I will not have him as a guardian any longer. He is a murderer, he has murdered Tom, he—"

"There, there." Rowan crushed her face against his chest in a way that effectively smothered her words, turning them into an unintelligible jumble. He held her thus while the guides made a hasty exit, muttering to themselves. "Pass the word, will you," he called, "that the lady is found and the searchers can disband."

"How dare you?" Charlotte cried when Rowan loosed his grip enough that she could speak. She struck at his face but he dodged. "Unhand me at once!"

"Yes, unhand her, Rowan," came her uncle's sneering voice. "Give her to me, for I must deliver her to Pimmerston."

Charlotte's accusing face swung toward him. "Pimmerston?" she scoffed in a bitter voice. "I myself heard Pimmerston tell you he only wanted me because I was a virgin—and I am a virgin no longer!"

"He has changed his mind," her uncle assured her calmly. "It seems your running away has inflamed him. He waits for you with bated breath." There was irony in his tone.

"I do not believe you!" she flung at him.

"You'll believe it soon enough," he said sourly. "Here, give her to me, Rowan. I'll knock some sense into the wench before I turn her over to Pimmerston."

"No," said Rowan.

Both Charlotte and her uncle gave him their full attention. "What d'you mean?" blustered her uncle. "I'm the wench's guardian! Turn her over to me at once, man!"

Again that calm "No." Charlotte was looking up at Rowan in surprise. "I'm not going to let you knock her about, guardian or no. Nor give her to Pimmerston either." He could feel Charlotte's body stiffen.

"If you think to have the wench for yourself . . ." Russ sprang at Rowan and was sent sprawling by Rowan's long arm.

"This way, my lady!" Rowan reached for the reins, swept Charlotte up onto his chestnut stallion, and leapt to the saddle after her. "The lads who've been searching for you are heading for home now, and if Russ wants you back he'll have to come for you himself!" He wheeled his horse about, even as Russ scrambled up with a hoarse shout, and thundered off in the direction of Scotland.

"But I can't go with you," Charlotte cried in panic. "Tom may not be dead. I must go back!"

"My lady." Rowan kept his arm firmly about her waist and his sober voice interrupted her. "Tom Westing is dead. I myself looked over and saw his body lying upon the rocks below, almost athwart the stream. The moonlight showed him clearly. 'Twas plain his neck was broken. And as I watched, the torrent took him. If he wasn't dead already, the churning waters of that wild cascade would have broken him against the rocks."

Hope that by some miracle Tom might still be alive had sustained Charlotte during the long journey down the mountain, and now with these words coming from a man who had just proved himself a friend, that hope was gone. A great sob shook her young body and she collapsed weeping against the chest of the strong man who held her.

For a time Rowan let her weep while the horse covered ground at a more sedate pace. When her sobs had died down a little, he said in a reassuring voice, "Have no fear,

Charlotte, Pimmerston shall not have you. Nor will I return you to your uncle, I promise you that."

She moved restively, seeing the world through a blur of tears. "But where . . . where are you taking me?" she choked. For it had come to her suddenly that they were riding through the night to some unknown destination.

"Across the border to Scotland," he said easily.

"To . . . Scotland?" She dashed her tears away and turned to peer up into his face. "Why Scotland?"

"Because we'll be married there. At Gretna Green."

"But that's madness!" Charlotte gasped. "I cannot marry you. I cannot marry anyone! Oh, do put me down and I will find my own way. I will escape my uncle all by myself."

Rowan's response to this rebuff was steely. "I will *not* put you down to wander these hills and vales alone. I will not abandon you to wolves or carrion birds. Nor will I leave you here for Russ to find and drag you protesting back to Pimmerston. To Scotland you will go, and there we will be married."

"No, we will not!" She began to struggle fiercely.

Rowan reined up and brought his mount to a halt.

"Do you wish to be forced into Pimmerston's arms?" he demanded.

"No, I will die first!" cried Charlotte wildly.

"It is harder to take one's own life than you might think," he said in a mild tone.

"It will not be hard for me!" she flashed.

He was staring down at her now with a strange intensity. She could not know the effect her wild loveliness in the moonlight had on him at that moment. Suddenly his wry laugh rang out, echoing across the glen. "I might have known," he told her ruefully. "After this night's work, I will die for nothing!"

Charlotte was bewildered. It was herself who would die, not Rowan. "What are you talking about? Why should *you* die?"

"D'you think your uncle is not already gathering men to follow us? D'you think he'll not charge me with kidnapping you?"

"But I'll tell them what happened," she protested. "I'll charge my uncle with Tom's murder and explain that you were but saving me."

"Who'll listen to you?" he cut in brutally. "Up on the mountain I thought it best for all concerned to call Westing's death an accident and avoid a trial that would shame you, and by now the guides have spread the word far and wide that he died by misadventure, that he toppled over the cliff by himself. D'you think they'll backtrack on that?"

"But *you* know the truth!" she cried. "*You'll* tell them what really happened."

"Who'll listen to me now? I'm the man who got rid of the guides and then kidnapped you from under your uncle's nose. They'll hang me for trying to save you."

Charlotte was staring at him in horror. It was true; her uncle was vicious enough to bring charges against Rowan, and who could tell what a court would do?

"My only chance now," he told her evenly, "is to marry you in Scotland. Once the deed is done, even your uncle must relent. And this way Pimmerston will never have you."

Her head seemed to be whirling into blackness. The events of the night had been too much. Tom was gone, and she would shortly follow him—but Rowan had tried to save her, his intentions at least had been good—she could not bring him to his death! He was watching her intently, stalwart in the moonlight, his dark face close to hers. He was waiting for her answer. Charlotte struggled up from the blackness.

"You knew you took your life in your hands when you carried me away from my uncle," she said slowly. "Why did you do it?"

He sighed. "I should think it was obvious," he said caressingly. "I care about what happens to you, Charlotte." His voice deepened and held a wistful note. "Indeed, ever since this chase began, I have wished that I were Westing."

It was simply put, and the sincerity of it reached her. For a long time she stared at him, her tearstained face pale. Then, "I cannot let them do you harm because of me," she said in an altered voice.

"So you will marry me?" His tone was rich.

She did not answer. Heartbeats throbbed by—so many of them that he began to feel a deep unease. Could Russ have been right? Was the wench so stubborn that she would marry no one, but believe herself tied to a dead man forever?

"I know it is asking a great deal," he said tentatively. "But—"

As if ashamed of her hesitation to aid the man who had aided her at such peril, she cut in, her voice hurried, "I will . . . go through the ceremony with you." And then, lest he misinterpret her meaning, she added in a low voice, "But I cannot truly be your wife, that is asking too much."

Myriad emotions passed over Rowan's face for a moment, were quickly controlled. His jawline was set.

"I will accept whatever crumbs fall from your table," was his sardonic answer. "And now, my lady, if you will lean against me and try to sleep, we'll soon be in Scotland."

But Charlotte could not sleep. The memory of Tom, of all that she had lost, pressed in about her. She sat bolt upright, with the rising wind blowing her hair back against Rowan's shoulder. Every time a strand of it blew against his face, it seemed to burn him like a brand, but he kept hold of himself and even managed not to tighten the slack though watchful grip he kept on his precious burden.

All the rest of the way to Gretna Green they never spoke. The wind was drying the tears on Charlotte's pale cheeks even as she wept. Silent tears for all that might have been.

The wind kept rising; it moaned across the valley, rising in tempo until all the banshees of hell seemed to be wailing in the glen. Charlotte would never forget that wailing of the wind, nor the teardrops of rain that fell upon them in the gray of early morning as they rode into Gretna Green. She felt that even the heavens wept for Tom.

In Gretna Green the smithy had been fired and flames rose against the cherry-red glow of a horseshoe the heavy-muscled smith was pounding into shape. He looked up at their approach, guessing these tired riders to be exactly what they appeared to be—runaway lovers.

Limp with fatigue, Charlotte felt herself lifted down from the horse and leaned against Rowan as the smith's beaming wife came out of the house wiping floury hands on a cotton apron. She was a big buxom woman and came to a halt before Charlotte, looking anxious at the sight of the girl's set face and tragic eyes and torn clothing.

"Is the lass all right?" she asked, casting a worried look at Charlotte's husband-to-be.

As usual, Rowan rose to the occasion.

"My lass's guardian swore she would be wed to no man who is half-Scottish," he told the smith and his wife in a surprising Scots brogue. "He caught us when we were leaving"—here indicating Charlotte's torn dress, which she was holding together with both hands—"and did attack her. For which I laid him low," he added darkly. "So I've brought my lass home to my mother's land—my mother was a MacAldie from Edinburgh—and that's where we're going, to her people. But my lass's guardian will be pounding over the border in hot pursuit, so we hope you can get us wed, and speedily."

"Oh, of course we will!" cried the smith's wife, bristling with anger that a good Scot should be turned down by an English guardian. She almost applauded when Rowan added with a swagger, "Faith, if you've a pen and parchment, I'll pen her guardian a note saying as much. If you'll be good enough to hand it to him, for he's sure to come by this way seeking her."

"Aye, that's the way to do it," she said with approval, and led them inside to a sturdy table, where Rowan dipped the sharpened goose quill she gave him into a dark concoction he hoped was ink and swiftly wrote his note of hand for Aldershot Grange—payable at the time he was delivered the deed on same. He sealed it with candle wax, pressed into it the imprint of his signet ring, and handed it to the smith's wife, who laid it carefully away. "But what about the poor young lass's clothes?" she asked anxiously.

Rowan's gaze swept over Charlotte, who was leaning

exhausted against the wall, holding her bodice together with one hand and her skirt together with the other.

"I've no time to shop for any, but if you've a spare dress and a cloak, I'll pay well."

"I've naught will fit her," sighed the smith's wife.

Feeling light-headed, Charlotte listened without interest to this exchange. The goose quill scratching over the parchment had not interested her, nor did this. What did it matter what insults Rowan penned to Uncle Russ? Her life was over—what did it matter what she wore?

But she submitted to the ministrations of the smith's kindly wife, who took a couple of quick stitches in the bodice and pinned up Charlotte's skirt and chemise to her bodice as best she could, partly covering her handiwork with a clean homespun apron dyed with hazel.

Charlotte looked strangely attired in her torn finery and homespun as she walked out into the darkening weather to take her vows. With eyes cast down, staring dully at the damp trodden grass around the smithy, she took her place beside Rowan, standing before the anvil-as-altar, and listened to the words being sonorously read. To her credit, she went through the ceremony dry-eyed—except once, when she was momentarily overwhelmed by the realization that she was in Scotland at last, Scotland, where Tom had promised to take her, where she was being married just as they'd planned, except that the wrong man stood beside her taking his vows. Tom was dead, his battered body borne upon the crashing white waters of the cascade far away. Her violet eyes filled with tears that spilled over, but she managed to keep her voice almost steady as she murmured low that she would take this man to be her wedded husband.

"My lass was fond of her guardian," Rowan muttered to the smith's wife by way of explaining Charlotte's tears.

And at that moment the heavens opened and the rain that had been threatening all day began to beat down in earnest. Rowan seized Charlotte's hand, waved to the smith and his wife and helper who had been their witnesses, and hurried Charlotte to the horse.

In a steady downpour they made their way to Dumfries,

and on that ride she said, "I did not know your mother was a Scot."

"Nor was she," was his cheerful reply. "But announcing that she was a Scot served me well."

It was the first suggestion she had that Rowan really was a consummate liar.

"Then we are not going to Edinburgh?" she asked tentatively, pushing her soaked hair back from her face.

He laughed. "No, we're for Portugal," he said carelessly.

Startled, with rivulets of rain pouring down her smooth cheeks, Charlotte swung round to face him. "*Portugal?*" she exclaimed incredulously.

There was exultation in the look he gave her, for had not everything worked out exactly as he had planned? "Portugal," he affirmed. "Where none of them will ever find us."

Charlotte turned her wet head away without comment. After that first surprised outburst, she seemed to have lost interest in the subject, he noted with regret. He would have been filled with alarm had he known the depths of her despondency, guessed what she was thinking:

Lost at sea . . . a dark night . . . over the ship's rail to oblivion. Oh, Tom, Tom, wherever you are, wait for me. . . .

13

The High Seas

Doing away with herself had proved less easy than Charlotte had assumed it would be.

In Dumfries Rowan had arranged passage on a ship that plied up and down the coast.

He had arranged for something else too:

In Dumfries Rowan had managed somewhere to find a dress for Charlotte. He left her waiting for him in "Sweetheart Abbey," and when he came back, walking purposefully, with his arrangements for passage already made, he had the dress bundled up under one arm.

" 'Tis the best I could find on short notice," he told her. "Here, we'll find an alcove for you to put this on. You cannot go about in torn clothes concealed by an apron!" He frowned at her present garments.

Charlotte was too tired and despondent to care what people thought. But she was submissive enough to let Rowan find her an alcove and stand guard while she removed her bedraggled gown and donned the simple green and yellow calico trimmed modestly in bands of moss-green grosgrain riband that he had found for her. It did not fit very well. The girl for whom it had been made was much shorter and far plumper, so the dress rode up unfashionably high on Charlotte's trim ankles and hung depressingly loose in the bodice.

Rowan winced at sight of her when she came out of the alcove and turned about listlessly for his inspection.

"Well, there's no time to do anything about alterations now, for we must hurry aboard," he muttered, sounding harassed. "We were lucky as the devil to find a ship that was just leaving." He frowned down at her. "We'll see what can be done about the fit aboard ship. At least we'll rid you of this!" He snatched the torn white gown from Charlotte's fingers and tossed it atop the apron into a corner.

Charlotte, uncaring about her appearance, turned to take one last wistful look at the little heap of white voile lying there forlorn. She swallowed. That dress had been to her a wedding gown.

She closed her eyes and let Rowan take her arm and lead her away to the ship.

Out of the Nith River they sailed, into the Solway Firth—and terrible weather. The light coastal vessel they were on had bobbed like a cork on the churning seas and made almost everyone on board seasick. The few accommodations the ship afforded had all been taken up by a single family removing from Dumfries to Liverpool with all their goods, and Charlotte had found herself sandwiched into a tiny cabin with three of the daughters—every one of them at least as sick from the ocean's buffeting as herself. When they reached Liverpool she was pale and tottered ashore only to discover with a groan that Rowan, who was never seasick and who had spent most of the voyage on deck enjoying the gale, had once again had "rare luck"—a ship bound for Lisbon was leaving on the evening tide.

And so an exhausted Charlotte found herself almost no sooner landed than bundled on board another vessel, this one a fat wallowing merchantman called the *Ellen K.*—and this time with a cabin of her own. Rowan had managed *that* by explaining to the captain how seasick his young wife became and by conveniently having the money on hand to pay for the extra accommodation.

Charlotte was looking wan as they went aboard.

"How did you happen to have passage money with you for such a long journey?" she wondered as they went aboard.

Rowan gave his bride a sardonic look.

"I am usually prepared," he told her in an amused voice.

She was to learn that Rowan always carried gold with him, sometimes quite a lot of it, and that he *did* seem always prepared for anything. At the time, dull and exhausted and brokenhearted over Tom, she did not really think it so strange.

They stood on deck as the ship drove out of the Mersey into the Irish Sea, sped onward by a brisk wind that billowed her sails. Charlotte would have liked to go immediately to her cabin but she did not protest Rowan's desire to be out in the fresh open air after the long gale they had endured on the way here. She no longer felt ill, merely weak and tired.

"Dinner will give you strength." Rowan assessed her condition with a smile. "It will be served as soon as we stand well out to sea, and we are to be the guests of the captain in his cabin."

"Oh, no, I don't think I—"

"It would be very rude of us not to accept his hospitality," Rowan said firmly. "After all, he went to considerable trouble moving people about in our behalf so that you might have a cabin to yourself."

Charlotte nodded wanly. She would dine with the captain.

Captain Scaleby proved to be a bluff, good-natured Cornishman, full of entertaining stories about the sea. He was delighted to learn that Charlotte was from the Scilly Isles and told her warmly that he was glad to have a pretty woman on board for the voyage.

Sitting in the captain's roomy though unpretentious cabin, listening to Rowan conversing easily with Captain Scaleby for all the world as if he might have been an old "sea dog" himself, Charlotte felt her strength coming back to her. She found herself savoring the excellent dinner, complete with fresh fruit and vegetables, which their host assured them had been "newly brought on board this very day."

It was still early when they rose to leave, and Captain
Scaleby, having drunk one last toast to the "beautiful
bride," came up with a sudden bit of information that
brought Rowan to attention.

"There's a gentleman named Flint on board," he volunteered, "who's just back from Portugal. He could tell you
how matters stand there."

"Thank you. I'll have a talk with him tomorrow."

"Best do it tonight. We're letting him off at Anglesey
tomorrow. He won't be accompanying us on the voyage.
But you'll be able to find him dining with the rest."

Rowan nodded. "I'll do that."

They thanked Captain Scaleby for a fine dinner and
Rowan had already escorted Charlotte onto the deck when
the captain called him back. Although their conversation
was low-voiced, it was a quiet evening, the passengers had
not yet left their supper to come out onto the deck in the
dusk, and Charlotte could hear the captain's nasal voice
clearly.

"I'm sorry to tell you this, but Morrison's gout is acting
up on him and he's refused to give up his cabin and move
in with Wetherbee as he promised. So I'm afraid your
bride can't have a cabin to herself after all. But the weather
is clear and I don't think she'll be seasick—she seemed
well enough at dinner."

Charlotte could not hear Rowan's low-voiced response
but she took a couple of steps away from the cabin door
lest he be aware that she had overheard when he joined
her. Her heart was beating fast. They were to share a
cabin after all. . . .

She waited for Rowan to tell her that, but he did not.
He merely escorted her to her cabin door and told her
that he wished to have a word with this fellow Flint, who'd
have the latest word on how things were in Portugal.

How things were in Portugal meant nothing at all to
Charlotte. What *did* mean something to her was the sight
of the single large bunk that seemed to occupy most of the
space in the small cabin about her. She approached it
gingerly. And suddenly it seemed to signify everything

that was wrong with this ill-considered marriage she had gotten herself into. Marrying Rowan had seemed the only thing to do at the time. Now suddenly it was all wrong.

Set-faced and silent, she stared at that bed—a bed such as she and Tom might have occupied in bliss together had things gone differently. She began to pace the floor, thinking of all that might have been, all that her uncle's sudden vicious kick atop Kenlock Crag had robbed her of. She remembered the feel of Tom's arms, so strong and warm and loving. She remembered the tenderness with which he had held her, the depths of those clear green eyes that had probed so deeply into her own. She thought with a pang of how unerringly Tom had turned back to save her when he knew how slim their chances were, when it would have been so easy for him to just keep going and let himself forget a girl who could only bring him disaster. Indeed he could have left her at any time on that wild ride to freedom and made his escape. Loving her had cost Tom his life.

A great sob escaped her and she pressed shaky hands to her mouth. *She* had been Tom's undoing—she alone. And now tonight she was to share a bed with a man who— trumped-up marriage or no—was really a stranger. She flinched at the thought.

Outside her door she now heard footsteps. The passengers were returning from supper. But Rowan was not among them—doubtless he was still with Flint, seeking information about matters in Portugal, although God alone knew why he cared.

Since this small stuffy cabin had no window, it was illuminated by a swinging overhead lamp even in the daytime, but she knew it must have grown dark—and still Rowan had not returned.

Charlotte's hands twisted together and her lovely face now wore a hunted look. She belonged to Tom—and only to Tom. And somewhere, somewhere Tom was waiting for her. She had to believe that. And outside was the sea, endless and deep, waiting to receive her.

She opened the door.

Outside, the darkness was pierced by a slender moon that shed its pallid light across the broad expanse of wooden deck before her. There was no one about.

Like a wraith, she drifted to the ship's rail, drawn as if by a magnet. She rested her hands upon its smooth solid wood and stared down at the moon's pale glimmer upon the dark waters. About her the night was very still. And who was to say Tom's winging spirit was not waiting for her somewhere out there? Perhaps he was even now calling out to her and her earthbound ears did not hear him. Perhaps she would find him again if she seized her courage in both hands and dived deep into the dark waters that lapped the side of the ship.

Caught up in these destructive thoughts, she leaned over the rail a little farther, fascinated by the sight below. Only a little farther and it would all be over, the die would be cast, her earthly travail would be over and she could soar on wings of her own, seeking Tom. . . . *Only a little farther* . . . She threw a foot up and over the rail and prepared to take the plunge.

And was abruptly jerked back from the rail, jerked back so roughly that she lost her balance and plummeted backward against a solid body. She heard Rowan's voice, low and furious: "Are you mad that you would throw yourself off the ship?"

"Let me go!" she cried.

She thought she heard his teeth grate, but her own voice was smothered, choked off as he whirled her about and clenched her against his coat. Dizzy with what she had almost done, confused by his sudden appearance, for, lost in concentration on those dark lapping waters, she had not heard him come up behind her, she let herself be dragged back to her cabin, watched him close the door behind them. In the lamplight she could see that Rowan's face was white and she could feel through the fierce grip he still kept on her that he was trembling.

"What is this urge you have to destruction?" he demanded.

"I heard what the captain told you," she gasped. "That we would be *sharing* this cabin."

"And you thought . . . ?"

Charlotte shivered. "Yes, there is but the one bed . . ."

She thought she saw his shoulders flinch but she read only fury in the dark eyes fixed so intensely upon her.

"And so you thought to take your life lest I thrust myself upon you?" His voice lanced at her with cutting sarcasm. "Tell me, have I offered you some hurt? Have I so much as laid a finger on you since I wrested you from your uncle's machinations? God in heaven, I am cursed by my own folly! *Why are you so intent on taking my life?*"

She fell back, startled. *"Taking your* life?" she demanded incredulously.

"Yes, did you think you would die alone and I would go merrily on? In Cumberland you nearly let me go to the gallows for kidnapping, and now—*now* you would have the world think I have murdered you!"

"But there could be no thought of that!"

"Could there not?" His grip was cruelly tight; his dark eyes blazed into her bewildered violet ones. "The deck watch heard you cry 'Let me go!' I saw him turn in our direction. And now I've no doubt from the rebellious look of you that you plan to try for death again the moment my back is turned. The world will think I have given you some injury, they will remember that in Scotland you were a dejected bride weeping at your own wedding, the deck watch will remember that you cried out to me at the rail to let you go—they will have heard that you are an heiress, because Bodine spread the word that you were, and they will believe that I wed you for the wealth you do not possess and that I killed you when I found you had none!"

Charlotte felt the trap closing about her.

"I told you that I cannot be a wife to you!" she cried despairingly.

"No, nor to any man!" he said gratingly. "But before you see me in hell, I will have some recompense for my folly in having troubled to save you."

With the words he abruptly tossed her to the bunk and followed her there, tearing at his clothes as he did so. Her attempt at a scream was instantly silenced by a hard mouth that covered her lips and almost cut off her breathing. Fighting him for all she was worth, Charlotte felt her wrists confined in a cruel grip and her skirts yanked unceremoniously upward. She heard the calico rip and felt her undergarments tear away from her. She struggled anew as her legs were thrust apart, and in rising panic she tried to slip sideways beneath him. Rowan countered this by landing on her so that together they slid to the side of the bunk and were brought up hard against the cabin wall. Trapped and fighting, Charlotte tried to bring up her knee, but it was crushed triumphantly downward and she heard Rowan's short angry laugh as he bore it down into the mattress.

A moment later her entire young body shuddered as she felt Rowan's hard masculinity plunge into her and she seemed to be swept this way and that, the better to please him.

And then as quickly as it had come, Rowan's fury seemed to subside, and even though his grip was still as firm, his demeanor toward her changed. His lips no longer bruised her mouth but moved softly across her own, allowing her straining lungs a gasping breath. His long body, which had crushed her into the mattress of the bunk, was now raised on one elbow, and she felt with a shock the pleasurable sensation of his dark-furred chest moving lightly across the soft mounds of her breasts, teasing her tender nipples, bringing them to hardness. His narrow hips—of a surprising sleekness—rubbed like heavy satin against her own tingling skin as he moved luxuriously, lazily, within her.

And to her shame, Charlotte felt her resilient young body respond to him. Although she tried her best to remain rigid, her very stance a protest, she could feel herself going pliant in his arms and shivering against him. If he felt this change in her, he took no notice, proceeding as if she was his by right—as indeed in law she was—letting his free hand slide down beneath her rounded buttocks and press her upward against him as he moved inside her with long, slow, tantalizing strokes that brought a gasp to her lips and a low moan deep in her throat.

Charlotte's was a passionate nature. She was made for love—as all men knew who looked at her. And tonight her fragile body overcame her indomitable spirit and she melted into an all-enveloping warmth that glowed through all her senses, setting them ablaze.

Rowan's touch was magical, stirring—he was experienced with women. And the wildness of his nature reached through to her as if his spirit, caged within him, now fought free and took her, his mate, with him through pathways unexplored by other mortals, soaring over mountains far and free, riding the winds, alone together and needing no one else, wanting no one else, only each other, perfectly matched and reveling in that perfection.

In Rowan's arms Charlotte forgot everything, she became another person altogether, a woman who moved as he moved, breathed as he breathed, wanted what he wanted, wanted *more*. Somewhere she had shed her controlled self-flaying outer self and become only the woman inside her, a reckless spirit meeting this wild lover more than halfway, giving him back joy for joy, straining in his arms and savoring every moment.

Swiftly their passion crested, but still he held that last great bursting moment at bay, carrying her ever upward with him until it seemed to her that she could stand no more—only to crest the next wave even higher. She was a mad thing in his arms now, panting, moaning, desperately seeking. Her hands no longer needed to be held lest she do him an injury. Like her body, they seemed to belong to him now, they clutched at life, they clutched at him, trying to draw his long body ever closer. She had forgotten in whose arms she lay. She was devoured by heady passions that obscured her view of life and left the world out of focus somewhere beyond these cabin walls.

She was his. Utterly.

At least for the moment.

With a last frenzied effort their bodies seemed to crash together in a wild crescendo of passion that brought a cry to her lips and a groan from Rowan. Her world exploded and she was lost in a wild splendor that seemed to go on and on, filled with tremulous ecstasy that dimmed the vision and clouded the brain.

At last she lay beneath him spent and glowing.

And as the glow receded a little and the world came back to her, she realized what she had done.

She had been untrue to Tom. She had let another man have his way with her. Worse, she had enjoyed it, been thrilled by it! A shame such as she had never known washed over Charlotte and her closed eyes filled with hot tears that ran in silence down her smooth young cheeks.

Rowan, his face pressed against her cheek, felt those tears and slowly sat up, gazing down at her.

In all his life he had never experienced anything quite like this young girl's openhearted fervor. She had made him feel triumphant, a superior being, godlike.

And now she lay crying in his arms.

He pulled away from her with a curse, his face gone pale and set.

"I will leave you to sleep alone," he said bitterly. "And if you think to kill yourself, you can forget it, for I will take charge of all the sharp objects in this room!" He was moving around, grasping objects as he spoke. Charlotte's eyes were still tightly closed but she could hear the slight clash of metal objects.

She turned over, pressing her face down into the pillow. Kill herself? What need to do that now? She had dishonored Tom. And in her fatigue and shame, she felt herself to be already dead.

All that long night she lay there grieving until, toward morning, sleep and exhaustion claimed her.

When she awoke she saw Rowan, fully dressed, standing there looking down at her. She could not fathom the expression on his face but she realized of a sudden that her clothing was gone somewhere and that she lay quite naked to his gaze.

With a quick indrawn breath she snatched at the coverlet to draw it over her. And then the memory of last night's wild joining came flooding in and her face turned crimson and she shrank back beneath the coverlet.

Rowan noticed that slight edging away, the sudden darkening of her expressive violet eyes.

"I have come to say what I have never before said to a woman," he said slowly. "I am ashamed of my action last night and I would tell you that I am most heartily sorry."

Charlotte swallowed. She watched him warily. She was afraid of him; she was afraid of herself, for last night had shown her how treacherous her body could be.

"When I saw that you were about to throw yourself into the sea . . ." He brushed a hand across his face as if to shut out the memory. "I . . . Something came over me." He leaned down. "It is my intention to bring you safe to dry land, and I will offer you no affront or repetition of last night's performance. As God is my witness, Charlotte, I will bring you back to the land of the living. And when I have done that, you may walk away from me—I will not move to stop you. *I only want you to live.*"

It was a very handsome declaration, she realized, and one she could not match, for perhaps he expected her at this point to assure him that everything was all right and that they could begin anew as man and wife. *But they could not begin anew, they could never be man and wife— Tom's memory stood squarely between them.*

Charlotte's voice was barely a whisper, a wisp of sound. Rowan bent forward to hear it.

"I cannot be a wife to you, Rowan."

As if she had slapped him in the face, he straightened up. "That much is clear," he said harshly. "Nor do I ask it of you. I only ask that we strike up a truce. Can you unbend that much?"

"Where . . . did you sleep last night?" she asked him.

"On the floor." He nodded at the door.

"I . . . I will sleep on the floor," she volunteered.

This time she was sure she heard his teeth grind together. "You will not!" he exploded. "You will sleep in that bed in which you now lie! And you will stay in it until I can find you a needle and thread, for it would seem that I have torn your present garments from your back." He sighed. "I will be back presently, Charlotte, at least with some pins."

He left, closing the cabin door rather hard behind him.

Alone now, Charlotte covered her face with shaking hands and felt scalding tears trickle between her fingers. She had loved Tom so much and she had betrayed him. Worse, under the spell of Rowan's powerful physical attraction she had *enjoyed* her betrayal! God might forgive her, the world might forgive her, but she knew she would never forgive herself.

14

Kenlock Crag, Cumberland, England

When Charlotte's guardian had booted Tom Westing's inert body over the cliff edge on Kenlock Crag, he had not gone personally to view from that edge where Tom Westing's body had gone.

Rowan Keynes had done that for him—and what Rowan had seen there, he had chosen not to report.

In the moonlight he had seen Tom Westing's body, not as he had reported it later to Charlotte, lying with a broken neck at the bottom "athwart the stream," but caught upon a narrow ledge some twenty feet below. He had actually opened his mouth to tell Russ to rest easy, Westing was not dead after all. Then abruptly he had closed his mouth again. The girl would not be tractable if she thought Westing were alive. And if they somehow managed to drag him up topside—though he doubted they could do that without ropes—she would fight for him like a tigress.

Better for all of them that she think Westing dead. So he had gone away with the others, callously leaving Tom Westing to die. And indeed for many hours Tom had lain like death where he had fallen.

At last his long body stirred. The rays of the hot afternoon sun seemed about to blister his back as he lay there prone on the warm stone floor of the ledge.

Confused as to his surroundings, he essayed to sit up—

and sank back with a groan as a pain like a scimitar seemed to split his skull apart. Indeed the very act of his sitting up had almost toppled him off the narrow ledge, and his vision, wavery and blurred by the pain in his head, gradually cleared and showed him the raging cataract far below. Clutching his head as if it might come off, he pulled back abruptly from that vision of impending death below— and felt his shoulder strike the hard rock wall that rose sheer above him.

After a while, as he slumped there, the pain eased and all that had transpired to bring him to this pass struck him with blinding force.

He remembered something, a weight—no, *someone* dropping on him from above, he had a flashing memory of two men—Charlotte's guardian and the tall man who had come to the garden with her the night she had fled with him from Castle Stroud—and he had seen her guardian's arm drawn back to loose the stone that had felled him, but he remembered nothing after that. *Charlotte, what had they done with her?* The thought brought him staggering to his feet to lean weak and sick against the smooth stone wall from which the narrow ledge on which he stood jutted.

After a moment his wits began to work. He listened intently. No sound came from above; no murmur of voices broke the absolute stillness. His head turned slowly, scanning the countryside. There had been mounted men, flickering lights down below. Now it was light, but not a person, not a horse or a deer or a sheep moved throughout the long vista spread out before him.

They had taken her away. . . .

Dizziness overcame him and brought him back down on his knees to the floor of the ledge. There was a thrumming in his skull like a background chorus to the pain that went through his head when he moved.

He must find Charlotte, save her.

He tried to stand again, and a great blackness came over him. His body crumpled to the floor of the ledge and lay there immobile while the shadows lengthened and the moon waxed and waned.

With the dawn he waked again, and this time he had more strength and he was very thirsty. On his feet now and moving with a sore shoulder where Russ had kicked him, he assessed the situation. Above him, twenty feet of sheer rock face mocked any efforts to ascend. On either side lay oblivion, for the ledge was a mere shelf created when last winter's ice had collected in a long crevice and broken off in the spring. There was a tiny cleft now where it joined the rock face that told him that part or all of even this narrow shelf might not be here come next spring.

There was no way to climb up, that much was clear, no way out on either side. He considered trying to climb down, but the rock face below dropped away sheer and as smooth as glass—and in the depths below rushed the torrent, sending up plumes of white spray as it cascaded through the narrow gash between the rock walls.

His present situation was hopeless and there was no point in trying to hide. Better far to rot in some jail, where he would have at least a chance of escape, than to remain here immobilized.

He cupped his hands and called out a long halloo across the valley.

Only an echo answered, reverberating and diminishing until the sound died away and all was still again.

He took off his shirt and tried tying it to his belt to make a kind of flag to flutter in the breeze—but it was no good. The wind forced it back against the rocks.

His pockets yielded something better: a small piece of brilliantly polished metal which he had sometimes used as a mirror to shave or as a knife to hack off his hair when it grew too long to suit him. He had been shipwrecked once in the southern ocean with that piece of metal in his pocket and it had proved lucky for him—he had used it to signal a passing ship. Perhaps it would do the same for him here.

He took it in his hand and held it in the sunlight, turning it about to focus on the nearby hills and vales. Someone, *someone* must be down there in those wastes. Someone who would look up and be blinded for a moment and then become curious and investigate.

He sat there for half a day beaming that small beacon out into the empty spaces below, and now and again hallooing.

Nothing happened.

By the next day his voice was cracked with bellowing and his arms tired from holding and turning his shiny bit of metal for hours on end. Thirst tore at him and his throat was becoming too dry to make a respectable shout. He looked out into the blue distance and it came to him morosely that he was going to die here on this lonely crag, isolated from all the world, and he wondered if those who had brought him down had intended it thus. Probably so, he reasoned, for his death up here would save them the notoriety of a trial.

He began to think of death more quietly, remembering all the times he had eluded it—in the Bahamas, in Madagascar, aboard the *Shark*, where they had said Devil Ben's son led a charmed life, and lately here in England. He tried to keep his mind from tormented visions of Charlotte struggling in the arms of Lord Pimmerston, visions that made his hands clench and his blood roar in his veins. He hoped that deflowering her had saved her from that, but it would not have saved her from her guardian's wrath. Just thinking what form that wrath might take made his hands grow clammy with sweat.

Perhaps she had gotten away. Oh, Lord, he hoped she had, his brave and dainty lass. She deserved better than Pimmerston, better than himself for that matter. He grew a little light-headed just thinking about it.

On the night of the third day it rained and Tom took full advantage of it, thankfully soaking up water in his shirt, drinking greedily from a little rivulet that ran down over the edge of the cliff above.

Hunger assailed him. He chewed on the leather of his belt, but it did him little good. He was weakening and he knew it. Still he continued to force himself to flash the piece of shiny metal all about him at the nearby hills and to manage now and then a cracked halloo.

Above him now large birds circled lazily against the sun,

riding the air currents on broad powerful wings. Vultures, probably, waiting for him to breathe his last. Perhaps not even waiting for that. One swooped down and landed suddenly on the ledge, staring at him with red eyes and taking off with a squawk when he lunged at it, trying desperately to catch it, for even a vulture was food.

That lunge nearly carried him over the side, and he lay there panting and discouraged. He pulled out the bit of shiny metal and tried again, flashing it all about. And then, tired of staring into the sun, he fell asleep.

What woke him, he was never sure. When he opened his eyes the vultures were still there, circling against the blue, but there was something else up there as well. Above him, stuck out over the edge of the cliff, were the faces of three sheep, peering down at him with woolly impassive dignity.

Where there were sheep, there must be a shepherd. Tom drew a deep breath and managed a respectable halloo.

He received a rather breathless halloo in return. And then, amid a scattering of stones—he decided that must have been what had waked him, the shepherd's ascent— the shepherd's face appeared. A friendly face, browned with the weather.

"Fell, did you?" was his cheerful assessment from atop the cliff. And at Tom's nod, "I almost fell off this place myself once—never came near it since. Wouldn't have come near it this time except that I was looking for my sheep. Are you hurt?" And at Tom's shake of the head, "You're in luck. I've got a rope here—need it for the sheep. Sometimes they fall or get themselves wedged and I have to climb down and hoist them out."

As he talked, he was letting down a coil of rope secured to a boulder. Seaman that he was, Tom had no difficulty making himself fast to the line, and marshaled his remaining strength for the climb up. He tumbled over the top exhausted and lay flat.

"Water!" he gasped.

The shepherd obliged with a water skin and watched Tom drink thirstily. "You must have been one of the search party looking for that heiress and her kidnapper, to get yourself stuck up here," he observed.

"I was left behind," Tom acknowledged, taking another long draft from the water skin.

"Funny about that pair," said the shepherd, who hadn't seen this much excitement in these peaceful hills in years. "No sooner was the heiress found and her kidnapper fell off the crag to his death than she took up with someone else, one of Lord Pimmerston's guests, I'm told, and rode away with him."

Here was his chance to learn what had happened to Charlotte!

"I was left behind when they were taking her down," he improvised hoarsely. "I struck my head in the fall, and when I came to they'd all gone. They must not have missed me. You say she rode off with someone else?" he added, incredulous.

The shepherd nodded energetically. "Rode off with him and got married, they do say, in Scotland."

Married! Tom's gorge rose and he began to retch.

"Knew you'd do that, drinking that water as fast as you did," was the shepherd's cheerful comment.

Tom didn't believe Charlotte was married. He didn't believe it for a moment. The fellow had got it all wrong. When he left the shepherd, he made for Scotland—and found a tiny out-of-the-way inn tucked somewhere along the way. Hoping for news of Charlotte, he hurried to the inn door, but found the place deserted save for the landlord. He told the landlord he was just down from a visit to Edinburgh, where his purse had been lifted, and he'd never return again to such a wicked place, it was England forever for him.

With the quick sympathy of a border dweller for his own side of the border, the landlord nodded approval. " 'Twill teach you," he said briskly, "which side of the border to stay on." He poured out some ale and slammed down a pewter tankard before Tom with a flourish. "Robbed or no, there's no denying a draft to a thirsty man at this inn," he said heartily.

Tom thanked him, lifted his tankard with a smile, and wondered what the news was in these parts.

The landlord was not loath to give it.

"Most of the talk is still about the horse thief who ran off with Lord Pimmerston's intended," he said, and drained half of his own tankard at a swallow.

"And did they catch him?" wondered Tom blandly.

"Aye, but not before he'd raped the girl." The landlord wiped his mouth with his sleeve. "Oh, they did for him, all right. Some of the search party came through here on their way back home, and they told me all about it. They said he showed fight, did the horse thief, but he was hit with a stone and fell over the cliff at the edge of Kenlock Crag, and what was left of him was carried off in the torrent below."

Tom considered that, lifting his ale to his lips and taking a long thirsty swallow. *So they thought him dead, did they?* He set the tankard down.

"And did they recover Lord Pimmerston's intended?" he asked in a casual voice.

"Not that I heard." The landlord finished his own tankard at a gulp. "She ran off with someone, headed for Scotland."

Tom headed there too, and reached Gretna Green in daylight. Gretna Green, where he'd meant to marry Charlotte. He looked bitterly about him, inquiring at the first smithy he found. The smith's buxom wife told him eagerly about the marriage.

"Fine gentleman, he were, and tall," she recalled. "But the bride looked sad, I thought, and her clothes were all torn."

Tom's fair head lifted alertly. "He was *forcing* her to marry him?"

"No, she was pale but willing. She spoke her vows clear enough, and they went away together."

Those words went right through Tom, to gnaw at his very soul.

"And that was the end of it?" he asked dully.

"Well, not quite," ruminated the smith's wife. "Her guardian did come looking for her after, and he told us the

English lord—her betrothed—had a stroke after he learned
she ran away the second time, and with one of his guests.
He said the English lord wasn't expected to live. He
followed her to Dumfries—"

"Who followed her?" cut in Tom hoarsely.

"Her guardian. He came back this way and told us she'd
disappeared, and her bridegroom with her, nobody knew
where."

Tom thanked her and turned away, heartsick.

*Fine gentleman, handsome and tall . . . Lord Pimmerston's
guest. . . .* That would no doubt be the tall man he'd seen
bending over Charlotte so solicitously in the garden that
night at Castle Stroud—and again with Charlotte's guardian on Kenlock Crag just before the stone felled him. At
least the fellow had had the sense to wrest Charlotte away
from Lord Pimmerston's clutches.

Charlotte, he told himself dully, had taken the only
sensible way out. She had found herself a protector and
married him. None could blame her for that. But his heart
ached for her, and if he had known her whereabouts at
that moment he would have been off to join her like an
arrow shot from a bow.

Despite God and constables.

But—it was too late. Charlotte had made her choice,
and even though that choice had been forced on her at the
time, by now she was doubtless glad of it. She didn't need
a dead man to rise up and try to claim her. Above all, she
didn't need Tom Westing to come prowling back into her
life.

Bearing a wound deeper than he had ever sustained in
battle, Tom, knowing England was dangerous for him just
now, forged farther north into Scotland. In the seafaring
town of Glasgow he took the first berth offered. On the
Heron, bound for Curaçao and—ostensibly—a bit of trading with the Dutch. Tom doubted that that was indeed her
purpose, for the *Heron* was slim and sleek, built for swift
strikes and fast getaways. Tom told himself he did not
care. He had thought to become a fine upright fellow, one
worthy of such a girl as Charlotte. Now that she was gone,

what did it matter what happened to him? He would let fate, which had so battered him, waft him where it would.

Charlotte would have been dumbfounded to know that Tom had survived and that his ship had even for a while followed her track down the Irish Sea before their ways split and Tom's ship shot westward toward the Azores while her sturdy merchantman beneath a full head of sail moved serenely south toward the Iberian Peninsula—and Lisbon.

15

Lisbon, Portugal, Summer 1732

Lying like a many-faceted jewel at the mouth of the Tagus River, Lisbon—that westernmost capital of mainland Europe—glittered in the morning sun. Although it was early, the old city, its Moorish influence still visible, was already a hubbub of activity. On the Mar de Palha, the "Sea of Straw," the lateen sails of rakish *fragatas* flashed red and brown and orange as they took advantage of the brisk breeze that came up the tidal estuary from the Atlantic, which here seemed only a breath away. Colorful crowds jostled each other along the waterfront. Black-skirted barefoot *varinas* hawking trays of fish carried on their heads darted in and out among passengers from incoming vessels. University students from Coimbra, sweltering in black capes over their black frock coats, shouldered by gaudily painted harlots intent on snaring foreign sailors. Dominican "Black Friars" wound through the crowd in their hooded black habits over white woolen garments, dodging donkey carts piled high with vegetables and fruit, while veiled women from the south—a living reminder that the Moors had left their stamp on the city—rubbed shoulders with elderly flower vendors shuffling along with mountainous baskets ablaze with enormous red and pink and yellow blooms.

Looming over the city from the heights, the storied battlements of the Castelo de São Jorge looked down over the myriad churches of the Alfama, or Old Quarter. Here steep twisting alleys, some so narrow that only two donkeys could squeeze by at a time, were decorated with flapping laundry and graced by iron balconies that hung out over the street, trailing vines and flowers from large earthenware pots. Everywhere were tiny hidden gardens and gracious courtyards filled with fragrant fruit trees and palms and scampering laughing children and dogs and cats.

This was the great port city of Lisbon where the *Ellen K.* had made landfall last night.

Lost in gloom over Tom's loss and still crushed by her "betrayal" of him, Charlotte had given Portugal scarcely a thought during the voyage. All the way up the Tagus estuary she had moped in her cabin, although she could hear excited cries from the passengers on deck. Even on disembarking, she had kept her violet eyes downcast, ignoring the lights of Lisbon—as if she felt she was unworthy to share in the joy others felt at making port safely after a fair voyage.

Charlotte had not cut a very good figure as they landed, for her gown, which had been hastily mended on the voyage, was both unfashionable and ill fitting. That, combined with her determinedly downcast manner, had caused brows to lift as they disembarked, and Rowan had scowled fiercely back, as if to challenge the opinion of his fellow passengers.

Unwilling to parade Charlotte through the common room of one of Lisbon's more elegant hostelries until she had better clothing, and unhampered by luggage—for unlike most of the passengers on the *Ellen K*, he and Charlotte had traveled almost embarrassingly light and had no need to wait for drays or heavy carts to transport their baggage— Rowan had hoisted his saddlebags himself and led Charlotte to a nearby low-roofed whitewashed inn where he took rooms for them both.

But when Charlotte had promptly sunk down on the bed and announced in a bleak voice that she was not hungry and would go straight to bed, Rowan had lost his patience.

"You will eat something if I have to force every bite down that white throat!" he snapped.

"But I don't wish to go downstairs," Charlotte protested. "You can see that I am too tired," she added defensively.

"Very well, you will eat here—but eat you will!"

Charlotte had sighed and viewed without enthusiasm the bowl of *caldeirada*, a kind of Portuguese *bouillabaisse*, redolent of onions and paprika, which was brought up to her. "Aren't you going to join me?" she asked.

"No, I shall seek more lively company," was his cold rejoinder. But he stood ruthlessly by while she consumed the very last spoonful of the *caldeirada*. He even insisted that she finish the glass of wine he poured for her.

That he had slipped a mild sleeping potion into the wine he gave her, Charlotte had no way of knowing, for she was unused to wine and did not notice its slightly altered taste. Rowan watched her drink it, knowing she would assume it was the wine and not the potion that would keep her asleep through the night and well into the next morning. Then he had locked the door and left her. And gone to prowl the town looking for word from the man he was to meet in Lisbon. He found none.

Annoyed by that failure, he had come back after being out all night to find Charlotte sleepily rousing. Abruptly he had decided that, presentable or not, he would take her out now to view the town. Perhaps that would breathe some life into this listless creature!

When Charlotte had stepped outside the whitewashed walls of the inn and been handed into an open carriage, she had been amazed.

She had come in darkness into a city of light.

The streets were clean, the skies a vivid blue, the air off the Atlantic clean-washed and tangy. Buildings of soft-hued stucco were all around her, pastel pinks and watery greens and hazy blues. And scattered proudly among them— some still under construction—were marble palaces built in a splendidly rococo style with windows that flashed in the sun. Indeed, as they continued around the great central plaza, the very buildings seemed to blaze about her, each more magnificent than the last.

And they seemed to her enchanted gaze to rise forever, terrace upon terrace of them, sweeping up over the low hills above her. It was a dizzying vista and Charlotte was sharply aware of how different it all was from anything she had ever known. All the splendor of a great city was opening up about her and she found herself caught up in it, swept away from her dismal thoughts.

Now they were turning into a broad avenue whose traffic consisted predominantly of coaches and carriages with occasional handsomely caparisoned riders, some in glittering wide-brimmed sombreros, who passed by on dancing mounts with jingling spurs and silver-studded saddles. But it was the coaches on which she chose to feast her eyes—so astonishingly many of them! There was a blue one, its door emblazoned with a coat of arms of snarling leopards, there a giddy-looking coach encrusted with delicate garlands of painted ivory and gold and with more glass than she had ever imagined a coach could have, and just passing was one with a sleek maroon leather body and bright yellow-green wheels, and just ahead—oh, just ahead was a truly magnificent coach adorned with gilded mermaids that gleamed gold in the sun.

"Why, it is a city of coaches!" she exclaimed breathlessly.

"And other wonders," agreed Rowan in a slightly sarcastic voice, for the determinedly downcast demeanor of this bride-who-did-not-want-him had brought a look of amusement to the narrowed eyes of a harlot he had scorned as he went into the inn. He was still smarting from her worldly assessment of him.

Charlotte, immersed in the wonders within her view, did not notice his tone.

"And it is a city of palaces," she added, impressed. "And so many of them look *new*. Look at that one—and the one over there. They are just now being constructed!"

"All built by the gold that flows from the mines of Brazil," he told her carelessly.

"It's glorious," she sighed, sinking back in contentment.

Rowan turned an amused look upon his bride, and that

swing of the head brought into view another carriage just then passing. It bore an opulent couple, the gentleman in gold-embroidered lavender-blue silks, the lady in a striking gown of crimson taffeta ornamented in black grosgrain and wearing a spectacular hat that set off to perfection her cloud of raven-black hair. Their heads were both turned away, for the gentleman seemed to be pointing out something in the street beyond, but in the brief moment as they flashed by, the lady's handsome profile came into full view and Rowan drew in his breath sharply.

Katherine. A pang went through him. Katherine, the woman who had cast him aside the moment a better offer came her way. Bitterly he remembered the fancied smirks of his London friends and acquaintances, all of whom, he had no doubt, had laughed when they heard about it. Ah, she had made a mockery of him in London, had Katherine, and now here she was riding gaily by in Lisbon all decked out in a carriage, her dark loveliness attracting attention—just as she meant it to.

And lounging beside her, that graceful fop of a young husband of hers, Eustace Talybont. Well he might lounge about, secure in the knowledge of the inherited acres that would one day be his! Rowan had not been one of those fortunate ones blessed with an ancestral seat and no need to make a living. He recalled that Talybont was supposed to have made a jest about Katherine's rejected suitor. The "money-grubber" Talybont had called him, referring to Rowan's onetime stint as manager of an elderly lord's estate—a position from which he had been hurriedly ousted when the old lord died and his sons had shouldered Rowan out. Rowan's hands clenched at the sting of that remark. Indeed, had Talybont been in London when Rowan heard what the man had called him, he would have sought him out on the spot and sampled with his blade the color of that arrogant blue blood! He toyed with the idea of doing so now, of ordering the driver to draw up alongside the carriage that had just passed them and then rising in his seat and leaning over and slapping his glove across Eustace Talybont's self-satisfied face.

The temptation was great, but better judgment stayed his hand, though it did nothing to cool his hot temper.

He dared not do it—not now, not here. Dueling with Talybont—most certainly if he killed him—would bring Rowan Keynes too forcibly to the attention of the authorities. He might find himself imprisoned or—worse in his view, for he was contemptuous of prisons, having escaped from several—he might be cast out of Portugal, and it was harder getting a ship's captain to turn his vessel about than it was to bribe one's way past prison bars.

Of a sudden his dark eyes gleamed and he cast a quick look down at the excited girl beside him. A plan was forming in his mind and it came to fruition as he noted the fashionable inn the Talybont carriage drew up before. Quickly he told his driver to drive on.

"Charlotte," he said.

Charlotte, who had been craning out of the carriage the better to view, on the highest hilltop above her, the great outer bastions surrounding the lofty pile of the Castelo de São Jorge, turned reluctantly.

Her violet eyes were shining, Rowan noted approvingly.

"Charlotte," he said gravely, "I have a request to make. The woman just alighting at that inn—no, don't look now, she is turning about"—he ducked his head until he again had a back view of the lady's coiffure—"I want her humbled."

Charlotte came out of her fascinated survey of the city with an effort. "What do you mean, 'humbled'?"

Rowan's mouth formed a grim line.

"That woman is Katherine Talybont. She broke our engagement, kept my betrothal ring, and married that fop up yonder"—he nodded toward Eustace Talybont, just then helping his wife to alight—"and made me the laughingstock of London." He paused, "I want her humbled."

"How?" wondered Charlotte.

"I will tell you later," he said, and sat back.

Charlotte considered him sidewise through her long lashes. Rowan was indeed a very handsome man and she was surprised to hear him speak so bitterly about being jilted. He was so erect, so vital, so manly—how could any

woman leave him for another? she wondered. Any woman
who loved him, that is. She cast a quick backward look at
the woman, who had now left her carriage and was sweeping into the inn with her hand resting lightly upon a
lavender-blue-silk arm. Even in that brief glimpse she
could see that Katherine was very beautiful.

"Did you love her very much?" she asked wistfully.

The answer was controlled, self-mocking. "I thought I
did."

"And she loved you?"

"Oh, she was forever declaring it." He gave a short hard
laugh. "But Talybont"—he nodded back toward the inn—
"was the richer."

Charlotte digested that. She considered the face, now in
profile and looking carved from granite, of this man with
whom she had made a hasty marriage of convenience.
After overwhelming her with unwanted attentions that
first night on board the *Ellen K.*, Rowan had kept his word
to her. He had slept across her door on shipboard—the reason for this, she knew, was to keep her from dashing out
in a paroxysm of grief and hurling herself overboard—and
he had offered her no hurt. Indeed, save for rather fiercely
insisting that she eat her dinner and drink her wine last
night, he had been unfailingly courteous. He had, now
that she thought about it, saved her from both Lord
Pimmerston and her uncle—and he had done it at the
possible cost of his life. All of this she had accepted from
him and given nothing in return—that is, if you discounted
that brief wild bout in the cabin of the *Ellen K.*—and she
realized now that she must have frightened him half to
death by almost going over the rail of the vessel. She had
driven him too far, and his control had snapped, but later
he had seemed heartily sorry and ashamed of himself and
had thenceforth acted as a perfect gentleman. And had he
not taken separate rooms for them at the inn last night?

Rowan had been ill-rewarded for nearly throwing his life
away for her, and now he was asking her a favor—just
what favor was not yet clear.

"I will do all I can to help you," she said with such

fervor that his eyes gleamed. "What do you want me to do?"

She had half-expected him to say, "Go to Katherine's inn and pretend to be a serving girl and find my betrothal ring and bring it to me," but he surprised her.

"First," he said in a gentler tone, "I am going to take you shopping."

Rowan was an extravagant man. She found that out at once, at the first shop he took her to—a cobbler's, from which she emerged handsomely shod. Next, to buy fragile underthings, silk stockings, a dainty lace chemise as fine as any her mother had ever owned. And to a milliner's, where he selected several hats to be held for them until he could discover what sort of gowns she would be wearing. The milliner, Charlotte noted, was most respectful and promised that the hats would be held until tomorrow.

But buying the gowns—*that* was a revelation. The ladies on St. Mary's Isle had gotten themselves up bravely for their balls and routs, but they were mainly conservative in dress. Not so Rowan. In a shop with, surprisingly, an English shop mistress, he chose her clothes for her and Charlotte could not believe her eyes. Set out for their inspection was a large array of the latest "fashion dolls" from Paris, for France was now the acknowledged leader of the fashion world, just as Spain had been in the last century, and French styles and French laces were as eagerly snapped up in Lisbon as they were in London. The stiff little dolls were dainty miracles of fabric and lace, and, copying their tiny elegant gowns, local dressmakers would whip up full-size copies for ladies of flair and fortune.

Charlotte's interest quickened as Rowan selected a slim-waisted full-skirted gown of a tawny gold that matched her golden hair delightfully. It was cunningly made, narrow from the side view but with a very wide skirt held out by light metal hip panniers. It was very sporty, its sleek tailoring giving it the look of a riding habit, while also managing to display Charlotte's feminine charms in delectable fashion.

"Where will I wear it?" Charlotte asked, half-expecting Rowan to say they would save it for some distant occasion.

"Why, you'll use it for riding about and for everyday wear," he answered her absently. "It will look well with the bronze tricorne hat I selected for you back there and with those bronze leather slippers you are wearing."

Charlotte took a deep breath. On St. Mary's Isle not even her mother would have considered donning such a gown for everyday wear.

"I doubt I will be able to wear it riding about," she told Rowan ruefully, "for the skirt will take up more than the whole width of a carriage!" She estimated that the skirt must be almost four and a half feet wide across the front, more than double its width from the side view.

"The panniers that hold it out are flexible and will bend," Rowan assured her absently.

"And fashion decrees broad at the front, narrow at the side," put in the shop mistress in a reproving voice, as if Charlotte should know that.

"You will need gloves," Rowan said, "but I believe we will purchase those from a glover."

"Oh, but we have some very fine . . ." began the shop mistress, and let her words dwindle away at Rowan's cold look.

"A glover," he repeated firmly. "For I see you have nothing in bronze kid."

Charlotte watched dizzily while Rowan added to their purchases a silken purse, some delicate handkerchiefs, and told her to remind him that they would also need pomades, perfumes, a comb for her hair, some hairpins so that it "would not fall down in that disagreeable fashion," and perchance a bit of black court plaster to add emphasis to the whiteness of her skin.

Speechless as dolls in ball gowns were paraded before her, Charlotte overlooked that bit about her hair falling in "disagreeable fashion."

"Which gown do you like?" asked Rowan.

"The pink brocade, I think," she said tentatively.

"No, you shall have the lavender satin with the silver lace. Its hue complements your violet eyes and will"—his sudden laugh jarred her—"go well with Talybont's blues. I am told his friends have nicknamed him Blue because he never wears any color save blue or lavender."

"To match his blue blood?" Charlotte quipped.

Rowan gave her an odd look. She had cast off her dreary expression and was entering into this thing. His dark gaze kindled. "Exactly," he said softly. He turned to the shop mistress. "When will these be ready?"

"Well, we are very busy, sir," was the nervous answer. "In a fortnight, shall we say?"

"No, we shall not say a fortnight. The day gown must be ready by tomorrow morning, and as for the lavender satin, my wife needs a gown to wear *tonight.*" He rose and fixed the shop mistress with a stern gaze. "I see we will have to go somewhere else, Charlotte. Someplace that can accommodate our needs."

"But, sir!" The shop mistress was upset at the loss of so much patronage. "I suppose I could have the day dress ready by tomorrow morning," she admitted doubtfully. Her mind was working rapidly. If she brought in her assistant's two younger sisters—yes, they could do it. "But the lavender satin has those intricate rosettes—it will take longer." She was very definite about that.

"Then we must forgo the lavender satin," Rowan told her ruthlessly.

She bit her lip. "Perhaps"—she sounded reluctant—"perhaps I have the answer, sir." She clapped her hands and her assistant appeared. "Celeste, bring me the blue gown we have just finished."

"But that gown is for Madame Monserrat," was her assistant's scandalized protest. "We made it up from a fashion doll that she herself had sent from Paris!"

"I know, I know, but Madame Monserrat has not paid her bill from the last time." The shop mistress's voice hardened. "And the gentleman is paying cash, is he not?" Her questioning gaze sought Rowan, who nodded. "And we have already kept the gown for two weeks because Madame Monserrat has left for Oporto. We will deal with the matter when she returns. Hurry, Celeste, the gentleman must not be kept waiting!"

The gown Celeste brought out was of a delicate blue

that Charlotte's mother had called "Prussian blue" but which Rowan called "Copenhagen blue." It reminded Charlotte of the skies over the Scillies. The fabric was almost tissue-thin. "Real Italian silk," the shop mistress assured them with pride. "And"—she studied Charlotte's slim figure—"with a little alteration it should be a good fit."

"Try it on," commanded Rowan, and Charlotte retired to a small dressing room and had the gown pinned up—for Madame Monserrat had not been blessed with Charlotte's tiny waist, and was a shade taller—by the shop mistress herself and by two seamstresses who had magically appeared from a back room, one with a mouthful of pins. The gown's wide flaring neckline just missed Charlotte's shoulders. It was shield-shaped and executed a slightly dipping V directly over Charlotte's forward-thrusting young breasts. Indeed it was cut so daringly low that it was Charlotte's opinion that it revealed more of her breasts than it hid. Still, daring or not, the effect was devastating. Pearly white, the tops of her breasts rose and fell, the pink nipples barely obscured by the sheer material. At the point of each shoulder was a large lace rosette set into a frame of pale blue satin ribands, giving the effect of a small corsage on each shoulder. A delicate blue ruching marched down the tightly fitted bodice and when it reached the skirt became abandoned, with fluffy blue silk rosettes peeking here and there from great scalloped flounces. Brilliants were set here and there, making the dress sparkle as she moved, and the upper part of the three-quarter sleeves, which became a spill of white lace at the elbows, were frosted—along with the tip of the bodice—with tiny clear beads that gave Charlotte, standing before the French cheval glass, the appearance of rising from a flower-filled blue lake with tiny droplets of water glistening from her shoulders and bust and cascading spectacularly downward. Some of the beads were sewn on in short iciclelike groups so that they dangled, and the effect was that her young breasts seemed to quiver at the slightest breath.

Charlotte had never even imagined a dress like this.

"And with your hair up—so," said the shop mistress, lifting Charlotte's hair impatiently when they came out for

Rowan's viewing. "And with—what do you think, Ada, a small coif?" And when the seamstress with the mouthful of pins shook her head, "No, I suppose not. Perhaps some lace ruffles for her hair?" she suggested to Rowan.

Rowan was studying his dazzling wife with pride. "No," he said with decision. "A plain blue satin riband to twist in her hair, long enough to allow it to cascade down over her shoulder. And blue kid gloves—with brilliants if you have any. And then we must hurry back to the cobbler, Charlotte, for now you will need pale blue satin slippers with very high heels."

"Ah, perfect!" cried the shop mistress, clasping her hands as if in prayer. "The alterations will be completed by tonight—it may be a trifle late," she added anxiously.

Rowan paused and frowned. "No, it must be ready this afternoon for my wife to wear to dinner," he said. For who knew when the Talybonts might leave Lisbon? Who knew, they might be booked for sailing on the morrow!

"Oh, but, sir!" cried the flustered shop mistress. "My ladies"—she indicated the seamstresses, who were looking at each other with resignation—"would have to drop their other work that is promised for this afternoon—"

"Even so," Rowan cut in with a shrug. "Unless you can have this gown ready in *under two hours*, I will have to take my custom elsewhere."

"It will be ready for you, sir," gasped the shop mistress, and turned to her henchwomen. "Drop everything you're doing, Ada, and come with me. You too, Rowena."

Before their shopping expedition was over, Charlotte found herself laden with more slippers, a pale blue feather fan, ribands, pomades and assorted cosmetics—"Which I hope you will know how to use," was Rowan's comment. "For you need very little, if any. Perhaps just a touch of lip rouge, and you can pinch your cheeks to make them red."

Charlotte flushed. "I assure you I can do something myself!"

Rowan chose to ignore her outburst.

"Observe the wig in this shop window," he said, bringing her to a halt on the cobbles. "Do you think you can manage that coiffure, or will you need help?"

"I think I can do it," Charlotte said doubtfully.

"We will get help," decided Rowan, noting her hesitation. "Observe the way it is done so you can copy the style yourself when help is no longer available."

And so, powdered, pomaded, and with her gleaming gold hair arranged in an impossibly difficult but altogether lovely style, Charlotte tripped downstairs in her high-heeled blue satin slippers alongside Rowan, who had bought for himself only a fresh cravat and shirt and a new pair of white silk stockings to display his calves below his fashionable dark knee breeches.

"Good tailoring takes time," he explained. "I have no intention of buying anything that takes less than a week to fashion."

Charlotte regarded him in awe. She had never heard any man speak like that. She decided Rowan was half-warrior, half-dandy.

"And now as to what you will do," he said as they got into the carriage after leaving their inn. "I wish you to humiliate Katherine by drawing her husband's attention— yes, and the whole room's attention if possible—away from her and to yourself."

"You want me to flirt with him?" demanded Charlotte in surprise.

Rowan looked down into those clear questioning violet eyes.

"Yes, I want you to flirt with him," he growled. "You know how to flirt, don't you?"

"I suppose so." Charlotte bit her lip.

"With a face and figure like yours, you should have little difficulty going about it," he added in an almost gloomy voice. Charlotte was not to know that his gloom was occasioned by his vision of seeing her play up to another man. "Just keep turning about this way and that," he counseled. "Talybont's eyes are sure to follow you."

Charlotte regarded him doubtfully. She had never considered herself such a beauty, but seeing herself in this blue gown in the cheval glass had been a revelation.

Perhaps Rowan was right, perhaps she could attract the attention of a man on his wedding journey beside a strikingly beautiful bride—but she was not sure. Anyway, she would soon find out.

"And," he told her, "we are going to change inns. We will be staying at the Frango Real—that means Royal Cockerel," he added absently.

"Where the Talybonts are staying?" she guessed.

"Just so." He nodded—and at that moment she was not quite sure she liked the look in his dark eyes.

16

Rowan and Charlotte arrived by carriage at the fashionable Royal Cockerel, where the Talybonts were staying. The inn was three-storied, whitewashed, with a side door leading out onto a cobbled alley. The shutters were painted a charming blue, and blue *"azulejo"* tiles decorated the wide entrance. They alighted in a busy courtyard and their boxes were immediately snatched up by a dark-skinned servant wearing a red cross-stitched shirt, who carried them into the common room, set the boxes down, and stood stolidly waiting.

People churned about, conversations in many languages mingling. Nearby they could see the harassed landlord explaining to a couple who seemed to have no fewer than fifteen children that the inn was indeed full.

"Wait here." Rowan made way through the crowd for Charlotte and seated her on a long painted wooden bench near the entrance. A rather plainly dressed woman in tabby was already seated there, and she moved quickly down the bench to make room for this elegant newcomer whose wide skirts threatened to take up the entire bench.

Charlotte smiled her thanks at the woman, who seemed to speak no English, and looked up to see that Rowan was on a direct collision course with a tall thin woman dressed in black, who was moving fast through the crowd and carrying two large boxes, one atop the other, which partially obscured her vision. Before Charlotte could call out to him, they collided and the boxes fell to the floor. Both flew open, spilling out a lady's rose-pink hat and a gentleman's distinctive tricorne in vivid blue and gold. The woman—Charlotte could now see that she was wearing a lace-trimmed white cap and a neat white apron, which had been gathered up in her hands as she held the boxes and which probably marked her as a lady's maid—seemed quite startled and waxed voluble as Rowan bent to help her retrieve the hats and stuff them back in their boxes. Although in the hubbub Charlotte could not hear what the woman was saying, she saw the woman smile her thanks at Rowan and then, boxes in hand again, hurry away up the wide stairway.

Charlotte lost interest in the woman and turned to watch Rowan, who was now talking rapidly to the innkeeper, a short wiry man who was shaking his head and making despairing motions with his hands. Into one of those hands Rowan now dropped several coins, and the innkeeper's head stopped shaking negatively.

He beckoned, and Rowan, with the servant trailing after him with their boxes, followed the landlord upstairs. It seemed only moments later that he was back again, moving through the crowd toward her.

"We will not have the best accommodations," he told her. "But we will have a side room on the second floor, which is the best we could expect to get in this crush. I told our landlord that these boxes are but the fruit of today's shopping, that our main luggage will arrive later," he added with a grin.

Charlotte was a little daunted by Rowan's taking only one room. But his face was bland.

"We must hurry," he said before she could speak. "The dining room will be filling up." He piloted her skillfully toward a large frescoed room in which she could see numerous tables. "Now, drop your fan," he murmured when they reached the dining-room door. "I want to make sure everyone remarks you."

By "everyone" Charlotte presumed he meant the Talybonts.

She let her new fan slide negligently from her fingers, hoping it would not be damaged by the fall.

"Ah, wait, Charlotte, you have dropped your fan!" Rowan said in a ringing voice that turned nearby heads to watch him. He retrieved the fan with a flourish and Charlotte dimpled and made him a half-curtsy as a reward. By this time most of the dinner guests were aware that a beautiful young woman had entered the room in the company of a tall, somewhat dour gentleman who wore his sword as if he meant it. A servant appeared to lead them to their table.

"No, I do not think that table will do for Mistress Charlotte," objected Rowan in a strong voice. "I believe it will prove too drafty." The next table was much too ill-lit— why, they would not be able to see their food. Finally a suitable table was found—"That is, if you position it a little more this way, to give Mistress Charlotte a better view of the room."

By now there were covert smiles all about as the diners watched Rowan fussing over the beautiful girl who languorously waved her fan and did her best to gaze up at him adoringly.

Katherine and Eustace Talybont, late diners ever, had not yet arrived when Rowan and Charlotte made their entrance. They arrived as Rowan was pulling out Charlotte's chair at their final table.

Charlotte felt Rowan tense, for the chair seemed to waver under her for a moment and she looked up to see a vision of dark loveliness that was enough to shake her own confidence. Katherine Talybont was a classic beauty, a trifle cold perhaps, but then, her beauty was of a type much admired. Her skin was creamy satin, her big dark eyes endlessly appealing, her rouged lips wore a slightly challenging pout, and her carriage had just the suggestion of a slither that made her seem to undulate in her silken gown. That gown was of a deep crimson, its skirt as wide as Charlotte's and heavily trimmed in rich black lace that seemed to augment the beauty of Katherine's own black satin tresses. She was wearing a necklace of heavy jet, and long jet earrings bobbed in her ears.

"She's wearing rather a lot of jet jewelry, isn't she?" murmured Charlotte, staring at the massive display, which, she thought, rather spoiled the effect of Katherine's low-cut gown.

"She hasn't got the Talybont rubies yet," muttered Rowan. "Nor is she likely to!"

"Why?"

"Talybont's parents didn't much like the marriage—they had someone else in mind for Eustace."

Charlotte studied the long jet earrings—that one day might magically become rubies—dangling from Katherine's ears; the flashing rings that adorned her fingers (perhaps they were paste, who knew?); the cleverly affixed brilliants that lit up that lustrous dark hair.

And Rowan wished her to outshine *this*. Well, she would do her best.

Charlotte, with no jewels but only a long blue satin riband, twirled it languidly so that its silken sheen raced in and out across her golden hair, and waited for this wonder to approach them.

The wonder did not approach. The wonder, absorbed only in herself and expecting her spectacular good looks to make her the center of attention, was just then indicating a table in a position of vantage to show herself off. And the tall man dancing attention beside her, a man who at first glance looked not unlike Rowan with his dark hair and almost military bearing, was completely absorbed in assisting her in her design.

"Katherine!" Rowan's hearty voice rang out across the room—and the wonder stopped in her tracks and turned to look at him in amazement. Beside her, Talybont, clad in sky blue, frowned. A moment later Rowan was striding toward them. "Katherine, it is good to see you and . . . Talybont, isn't it? Yes, I thought so. But you must dine with us, naturally. We are just over here." He was propelling them toward Charlotte even as he spoke, and they were brought up before her at the table. From this nearer view Charlotte could see that Eustace Talybont's resemblance to Rowan was only superficial. He had dark hair and was about the same height and weight—and perhaps,

she thought, that was partly what had attracted Katherine
to him—but there was a certain slackness to his mouth, a
vacant look in his watery blue eyes. He did not measure
up to Rowan, she thought proudly.

"Charlotte, may I present Katherine Talybont and her
husband, Eustace Talybont? This is my bride, Charlotte."

What else was said at that moment, Charlotte was never
sure. She was aware of a dazed expression on Katherine's
classical features and of an admiring. "Well, I do say!"
from Eustace. Katherine's mouth opened and closed again,
and abruptly she sank down in the chair Rowan pulled out
for her. Eustace sank gracefully down in the other chair.

"Well, what luck is this?" said Rowan even more heartily. "What better chance than to run into the pair of you
like this! I take it you have extended your wedding journey since we find you here in Lisbon?"

Katherine did not feel obliged to answer that. Instead
she bored in on the main question. "Have you been married long?"

Rowan laughed. "Not long. Charlotte was Lord Pimmerston's betrothed, but the moment I laid eyes on her I
knew I had to have her. We ran away and tied the knot in
Gretna Green."

"In Scotland?" murmured Katherine unbelievingly. "How
very romantic of you, Rowan." Her voice was laced with
irony. How long ago was it, she asked herself resentfully,
that she had held this man in the palm of her hand and
made him dance to her tune as if he were a puppet on a
string?

Charlotte felt she should do something. She moved
restively, causing the tiny clear beads dangling on her
bodice to stir and ripple. Eustace Talybont immediately
noticed those rippling breasts, and his eyes never left
them. He answered a sharp question from Katherine
abstractedly.

"I *said*, Eustace, what do you propose to order for
dinner?" she repeated in an irritated tone.

"Dinner? Oh, yes . . . er, whatever our host recom-
mends," he said vaguely.

"But let us drink first, a toast," proposed Rowan, lifting his glass. "To friendship."

Lifting her glass caused Charlotte's beads to ripple magnificently. Under other circumstances she would have placed her fan directly between those pale bare mound-tops and Eustace Talybont's devouring gaze, but tonight she was pledged to bewitch him. She wafted her fan coquettishly and laughed a little rippling laugh, then leaned down a trifle to intercept his gaze and beamed a brilliant smile directly into his face.

The full force of that beautiful smile, those sparkling violet eyes, those even white teeth, caught Talybont like a blow. He seemed to reel from it. "By the Lord Harry, however did Keynes find you?" he muttered huskily.

His bride was very annoyed.

"*Really*, Eustace! He 'found' her somewhere in the north of England, one must suppose. Or was it"—she challenged Rowan—"in London?"

Amused that the wily Katherine was half-convinced he had been carrying on with Charlotte even while betrothed to her, Rowan supplied simply, "In Cumberland." And added, "Where the beauty of the scenery is a fitting setting for such a one as my glowing bride."

Charlotte was indeed aglow. Her gorgeous gown, the heady atmosphere, this frescoed room, her determination to help Rowan in this strange mission, the wine—all contributed to that glow. No one in the room, and certainly no one at their table, was unaware of it. She was vivid, vivacious, completely alluring. And Katherine could not help but see that there was a freshness to this girl, a sheen—the shimmer of untouched youth. Charlotte was undoubtedly younger than Katherine, whose age almost matched Rowan's—*and she looked it*. Katherine gave her black lace fan such a violent wave that she nearly snapped its delicate ivory spokes.

"Excuse me," said Rowan abruptly. "I see a man I must speak to. I'll be right back." He smiled benignly down upon Katherine. "I trust you'll keep my bride amused while I'm gone?"

Katherine's little white teeth ground ever so slightly. "We will do our best," she said in a stiff voice.

Left alone with the Talybonts, Charlotte almost succumbed to panic. But the smoldering fury in Katherine's face stiffened her resolve. She turned her full attention to Eustace.

"*You* have certainly never come up to Cumberland," she remarked sweetly. "For I would certainly have remembered you."

Eustace threw out his chest. "I've been told people do remember me," he admitted.

Beneath the table his wife kicked him with the toe of her slipper and he gave her a confused look. Her warning glance told him nothing—Katherine was always giving him warning glances. Charlotte again moved her delectable shoulders, the tiny glittering beads rippled, her breasts seemed to quiver, and he returned to his fascinated study of them, ogling her over his glass. Ah, what a piece of work she was! How had Keynes found her—and so quickly? He reminded himself that Keynes had found Katherine too—and found her first. He began to respect Keynes.

"But how could you *not* come to Cumberland?" Charlotte was reproving Eustace with a seductive little pout.

"Because Eustace prefers balls and gaming hells to chilly lakes and sheep," Katherine answered tartly for him.

Charlotte batted her eyes at Katherine for Eustace's benefit, showing off the full glory of her long lashes. "But we have so much *more* in Cumberland," she declared, her voice a purr. "The air is so crisp and clear and the whole countryside is so *private* that in summer girls sometimes take off all their clothes and dance naked in the sun on the crags."

Eustace Talybont's breath was coming a little faster now. "And do *you* dance naked on the crags?" he asked, fascinated.

Charlotte gave a little deprecating laugh and tweaked her long blue hair riband. It slid obediently down over her bosom and nestled in the cleft between her breasts. Across from her Eustace Talybont licked his lips, imagining her naked, dancing above him on a crag, beckoning him to come up and join her.

"Oh, of course *I* couldn't do such a thing," Charlotte said with a little laugh that gave the lie to her words. "My guardian always warned me that *heiresses* must be very careful because the world is full of kidnappers who will hold a gun to their bosoms and carry them off!"

"You are an heiress then?" Katherine's voice was sharp.

Charlotte turned her violet gaze upon her. "But *of course*," she said gently. "I supposed all the world knew *that!*" She enlarged upon that theme, mentioning rather vaguely how well her uncle had managed her estates in Cumberland and Westmorland, her shipping interests, some ventures in the wool trade. She had about run out of things to dazzle Katherine with when Rowan returned at last to the table.

"Couldn't catch the fellow," he told them in a sunny tone. "Chased him halfway down the street!"

He resumed his seat beside Charlotte and under the table took her hand and she felt a ring slipped upon her finger. She threw him a confused look, which he ignored. He kept her small hand confined in his own big one while he talked.

Presently, "Show them your betrothal ring, Charlotte," he suggested carelessly. He brought up Charlotte's hand, smiling into Katherine's eyes. "I think you will both recognize it. It is nice of you to return it to me, Kate."

At sight of the ring, which was a sapphire set in heavy gold, Katherine gave a small scream of dismay and leapt to her feet, while Eustace Talybont grew red and stuttered, "I say, how did you—"

"Thief!" choked Katherine, reaching across to take back the ring.

Charlotte's hand was swiftly withdrawn.

"Not a thief, Kate, a former suitor," Rowan corrected her.

"I will have that ring back!" cried Katherine, raising her voice. "Eustace, call the innkeeper and tell him that I have been robbed!"

Rowan half-rose. He leaned across the table, seized

Katherine's arm, and pulled her back into her chair. "Not unless you want the whole world to know of your perfidy," he told Katherine in a sunny voice. "Discarding a betrothed and then keeping his betrothal ring, forsooth! What will the world think of you, Kate?" He was keeping a tight grip on her as he spoke, and she tried to wrench free.

"I say there, let go of my wife!" bellowed Eustace Talybont, scrambling to his feet. "I'll call you out! By God, I will!"

Rowan regarded his adversary with contempt.

"You need cooling off," he said, and dashed his wine into Talybont's face, glass and all. And then, while Talybont stared at him in openmouthed fury, with the red wine dripping down his face to stain his expensive sky-blue silks, Rowan, with scorn in his voice, gave him a piece of advice. "I am a better shot than you, Talybont, and a better blade. I suggest that you think that over before you challenge me for taking back what is mine. And as for you, Kate"—he gave Katherine's wrist, which he still held, a cruel twist that made her flinch—"I suggest that you remember that this lad's fortune is not yet his. He has a younger brother, and if I make you a widow, you will not be a rich widow, you will have to hasten about to find some other wretch to cozen!"

"Be damned to you!" bellowed Talybont, now purple in the face. He would have lunged at Rowan but that several gentlemen who had risen from their seats and were crying out that the dining room was no place for a brawl leapt between them. And Katherine Talybont, who had by now been released from Rowan's savage grip and whose white face showed that she had got the full import of his words, flung herself upon her young husband in a panic.

"Oh, Eustace, let him go. Please do not become embroiled. What do we care what he says? Eustace, for love of me—"

The innkeeper and several waiters had by now inserted themselves between the combatants. Shouldered aside, Rowan cut in crisply, "Let us take our leave, Charlotte."

Charlotte rose with alacrity, glad to be gone from this place where everyone was staring at them, and where

most of the men were on their feet, aware that this inter-
change might erupt into swordplay. Even above the hubbub, Katherine Talybont's penetrating voice carried to
her, assuring Eustace in plaintive tones that there should
be no warring on her account, that it was true that she was
the sweetest, gentlest, most forgiving of women and that
even though she had been cruelly used . . . Her words
were sometimes obliterated by her husband's oaths as staff
and diners surged forward to hold him back. Charlotte's
face was stained with color but she kept her head high and
was escorted from the dining room by a smiling Rowan,
who swaggered along beside her, delighted with the havoc
he had caused.

Back upstairs in their room—and for the moment Charlotte had forgotten that it was *their* room—Charlotte sat
down on the bed and studied by the light of a candle the
ring that Rowan had spirited away from Katherine.

Rowan watched her for a moment. Then he sat down
upon the bed beside her and reached around her, holding
her hand up to the light.

"It is too large—your fingers are more slender than
Kate's," he observed critically, and Charlotte half-expected
him to say, "I will have it sized for you tomorrow." But he
did not. Instead he drew it gently from her finger. "You
do not want to wear another woman's betrothal ring,
Charlotte."

"No, I . . . Of course not." But she gazed rather wistfully
at the gold ring with its beautiful blue stone.

"I will get you a better one another time. I have a use
for this one right now."

"A use?" Her high arched brows shot up questioningly.

"Yes," he told her calmly. "Tomorrow morning I intend
to convert it into cash, and I will use the proceeds to pay
for everything I bought you today."

Now she remembered. Rowan had said he would pay
cash but he hadn't actually done it. And Katherine's betrothal ring was going to pay for *her* new finery! Charlotte
dissolved into laughter.

"Oh, Rowan, I have never had such an evening!" she
gasped.

"You seemed to be enjoying leading Talybont on," he observed, eyeing her narrowly.

"Eustace Talybont? *That* poor stick?" Charlotte collapsed into laughter again. "Why, he's naught but a male French fashion doll," she scoffed. "I can't imagine why Katherine married him."

"Money," supplied Rowan crisply. "Eustace is the Talybonts' oldest son and most of what they have will one day be his. My fortune-hunting Kate has gotten her claws into him and she will never let him go."

Charlotte controlled her mirth. She thought she had detected a note of pain in his voice.

"Money isn't enough." From the circle of his arm she gave him a very steady look.

He seemed to relax.

"No, for you I don't think it would be," he observed, and his voice softened. "Once I thought that of Kate, but I was proved wrong—and now I thank God that I escaped her, that it's Talybont who must dance to her tune and not I!" His dark head was inclining down toward her as he spoke, and suddenly his other arm was about her as well, holding her lightly.

"Charlotte, Charlotte," he murmured against her hair. His hot breath rippled strands of it, making little tingles of feeling march down the nape of her neck. "You are all the things I thought Kate was—and learned she was not. Thank God I found you."

It was very lovely to be held in his arms like this, to hear words like these. His voice was soft, tender, sincere. And Charlotte felt a warm glow of sympathy for him tonight, a kinship, for in a way, Rowan had lost a love too. And she was grateful to Rowan as well—for saving her in England, for bringing her here to Lisbon, for making her want to live again. In the glow of those feelings she brushed her soft lips across his cheek and for a wavering moment yearned toward him.

Rowan needed no second invitation. His arms tightened about her fiercely, and when she stirred in his arms and would have remonstrated with him, he pressed his mouth down firmly upon hers and effectively silenced conversation.

It seemed to silence her resistance too, for her world seemed to tip and she felt the wall she had tried to build up between them crumbling, crumbling. . . .

Rowan kissed her, and for long moments they swayed together atop the big bed. Then all her defenses seemed to come down at once. She clung to him and murmured his name.

She was hardly aware of how the blue dress left her body. It departed quietly, gently, sliding away from her in little silky tugs. Rowan was a master at handling delicate fabrics—and a master at touching delicate skin. This time there was no haste in him. He lifted her with one hand while he whisked the fabric away beneath. He removed the clothing from her slim body as he might have slipped the petals from a rose—and where his hands had been, he followed with his lips, teasing, tasting, tempting. And then fiercely demanding, so that when he eased her back gently upon the light coverlet, her own passion had already risen to fever heat.

But even that was not enough for him. He dawdled with her, teaching her some of the wicked byroads of love, assaulting her senses so that she was trembling and almost crying out beneath his ministrations before he entered her, her entire body a searing swaying reed, pliable in his arms, born for this moment. Rowan seemed suddenly a being larger than life, a tall sturdy spire to which her entire being could cling forever. Almost worn out by desire, she felt herself blown this way and that before the hot winds of the passions that consumed him before he brought them finally to a tense and desperate and wholly satisfying fulfillment.

Charlotte had never known such a night.

Morning came all too soon. There in the big square bed Charlotte had slept blissfully, peacefully. She might come to grips with her demons in the morning, but for tonight she slept like the young bride she was, nestling against the long naked body of her bridegroom.

She came awake gradually, aware that Rowan was not there beside her. When she managed to get her eyes open, she saw his tall figure, already dressed and standing before the window with the sunlight pouring in and gilding his outline. She supposed he had been out disposing of the ring.

"Rowan?" she asked questioningly and rose on an elbow.

He did not turn but his voice reached her.

"Charlotte," he said, "I have taken you to wife and whatever has gone before for each of us is past all undoing. I choose to forget that there was another man before me, just as you must forget that before you there were other women. We will start fresh. Is it agreed?"

Charlotte studied that long frame silhouetted against the late-morning light.

"It is agreed, Rowan," she said softly.

She meant every word. She had made her vows to this man, not back in Scotland—those were lying vows, forced on her by the desperation of the moment. They no longer counted. These silent vows were the vows she would live by. She felt no need to say it, but she had made her vows to him last night in the full glory of her ardor. And this morning she knew that she would keep her bargain. Tom was gone, forever lost to her. She would always keep a candle burning for him in her heart, but Rowan was here and he loved her. Of that, she felt that his body had given her no reason to doubt.

Still he did not turn. His voice was almost dispassionate.

"But although I will condone what has happened before, I will tolerate no future slips. Is that understood?"

"Of course." Charlotte sounded wounded.

He whirled about. *"Is that understood?"* he demanded with such violence that she shrank back before the naked intensity of his gaze. "We are on even terms now, a man and a woman. You have chosen to be mine *and you will remain mine*. Is that understood?"

He strode across the room and Charlotte watched him in bewilderment. She felt suddenly hunted. "Of course it is, Rowan," she said placatingly. She felt she should say something more, for he was bending down, staring into her face as if to read something there—some reservation perhaps. "You have been honest with me and I will be as honest with you," she said, lifting her chin and giving him back gaze for gaze.

His long body relaxed and he sank down on the side of the bed.

"Beautiful Charlotte," he murmured, and reached out to caress her soft young breasts, exposed to view as she lay on one elbow. "You are a miracle, you know." His head bent down to nuzzle those pink-crested nipples, to make her shiver and fall back, letting her arm go around his neck. "A perfect woman—sheer perfection, had I but found you first."

Charlotte didn't feel perfect and certainly not "a miracle." But she had no time to ponder his last words—"had I but found you first"—for Rowan was already tempting and teasing her into desire. His trousers were open now. His strong hands cupped her buttocks, lifted her and brought her hard against his ready manhood. His lips caressed her, his body strained against her own.

Charlotte closed her eyes and let her quivering senses take her where they would. She moaned beneath Rowan, trying to force her slender body upward against him, seeking, finding. Like birds in flight their bodies beat to a wild sweet rhythm that left them spent but somehow refreshed.

She told herself that this was love.

17

The moments of making love were precious, but Charlotte found the afterglow cut short, for Rowan rose almost immediately. "Come, rise to face the day—it's late." But he sounded happy, his voice bantering.

"And what does the day hold in store, pray?" Charlotte stifled a luxurious yawn as she threw her feet over the edge of the bed.

"This morning I am going to take you shopping."

Charlotte paused with her feet midway to the floor. "*Again?*" she demanded incredulously.

Rowan was grinning down at her. "Not for clothes—for pottery."

Charlotte began to dress hurriedly in her smart new gold silk. "I didn't know you were interested in pottery, Rowan."

He shrugged. "I have been told of an interesting shop."

Confused, because she could not imagine Rowan having much interest in pottery—silver, yes; gold, yes; jewels or swords of fine workmanship, yes; but pottery, no—Charlotte hardly touched the bewildering array of fruits that had been brought for her breakfast and soon found herself accompanying Rowan to a shop whose low entrance belied its large interior.

They moved about among the tall wooden racks displaying wares from different regions. The finished product differed in color according to the clay from which it was made, a clerk explained to them earnestly in Portuguese, which Rowan translated into English for Charlotte's benefit. Those pearly-gray jugs, for instance, were made in the countryside hereabout, but those red earthenware pots were from Alentejo—note the Roman form of them—while those black clay pitchers were from Nisa and those vivid green and off-white ones were from . . . Charlotte never learned where they were from for Rowan's voice suddenly lowered and his tone became urgent. "Turn about with your best smile."

Charlotte did as she was bid, parting her lips so that her white teeth flashed, but she did so with a sinking feeling. There, just arriving at the other side of the rack, were the Talybonts, Katherine gloriously got up in cascading plum silks to complement her husband's silver encrusted pale-blue suit.

Eustace Talybont stopped dead at the sight of them, bringing Katherine, whose arm was tucked in his, to a halt beside him. He got the full impact of Charlotte's smile as she turned about, and so dazzling was the effect that in spite of himself he sucked in his breath. Beside him Katherine's face turned a dull angry red.

Rowan favored his former love with a mocking bow, which was not returned. "It would seem we have the same taste, Katherine," he gibed. "Up early with the pots!"

Katherine's lips quivered but she chose not to answer.

"Come, Eustace, we are leaving!" Katherine turned about so quickly that her elbow caught one of the big earthenware jars and in its fall it knocked off two slender pottery water pitchers that joined it in crashing to the floor. "Oh!" she cried in a fury, and kicked at the fallen sharp-edged debris that now surrounded her thin-soled slippers.

"You really should be more careful, Kate," drawled Rowan. "And hold in check that temper of yours. Eustace will have to pay for those pots, you know."

Katherine whirled, and for a moment Charlotte thought she was going to snatch a piece of pottery and throw it at him. But when Eustace, who had watched sullenly, took a determined step in their direction, she clutched his arm and began to talk to him very fast in a low voice. Charlotte had the feeling Katherine was desperately trying to hold her husband back.

On that note Charlotte and Rowan departed, just as the shopkeeper came bustling up to the infuriated Talybonts to collect for the broken pots.

"You did not wish to buy anything?" Charlotte cocked her head at Rowan when they reached the street outside. "Indeed, you never intended to, did you?"

"My interest in pottery was never very strong," he admitted, "and now it is entirely exhausted. But"—he turned to give her a wicked look, for the incident had delighted him—"I have been told that Talybont's mother collects pottery and he must needs visit the shops to further her collection."

"I would be curious to learn how you know that." Charlotte stepped aside to allow two women carrying water jugs from the nearby fountain to go by. "I was under the impression that you did not know Eustace Talybont."

"Nor did I," he admitted. "But it is common knowledge."

Charlotte had to be content with that, although it sounded unlikely.

They were now some distance away, circling the fountain so that Charlotte could study the scenes of mythical characters depicted on the worn *azulejos*. Charlotte looked up and saw the Talybonts burst from the shop, obviously arguing. Katherine came to a halt and stamped her foot, and when her husband—much too far away for them to hear what he was saying—appeared to remonstrate with her, she struck him in the face with her fan, at which point a carriage drove up and received them and they rode away in high dudgeon.

Rowan leaned against the fountain and laughed. Charlotte was not so certain it was funny. She would have preferred to forget the Talybonts and get on with their lives.

"Would you like a bite of lunch?" Rowan asked, adding expansively, "I will take you to an inn where the cook specializes in shellfish—and surely Portugal has the best shellfish in all the world!"

Charlotte said she would like that very much. Indeed, after this morning's encounter, she felt it would be good to go anywhere the Talybonts were not.

Rowan took her to a small rose-painted inn festooned with iron-lace balconies. Its huge dining room faced the sea and was decorated with old glazed tiles in mermaid designs. As usual, Rowan did not ask her what she wanted—he always ordered for her, assuming that whatever he chose would be the right thing. They sipped *vinho verde*, that delicate fruity "green wine" for which Charlotte was acquiring a taste. The food was brought by a supple barefoot waitress wearing a full skirt held out by multiple petticoats with a hint of lace showing about her strong muscular legs. Her posture was superb and Rowan told Charlotte that the girl's pale Celtic eyes and amber skin probably meant that she was from Nazaré, to the north.

Charlotte found herself eating *santolas*, which she readily recognized as stuffed crabs, although she could not identify the tiny shellfish Rowan called *ameijoas*. She took her first bite of the delicious steamed Portuguese crayfish known as *lagosta suada* and looked up to tell Rowan it was delicious—and there were the Talybonts, both of them looking rather fierce, as if they had just had a quarrel, coming through the door.

"It would seem we have company," remarked Rowan.

"You *knew* they were coming here," Charlotte accused.

"An informed guess." He chuckled. "Katherine is very fond of shellfish."

At that moment Katherine discovered them. She hesitated, glaring at Rowan. Then abruptly she turned on her heel, colliding with her husband, who staggered back a step and then turned to stare angrily in their direction. He leaned down as if admonishing his wife, who charged on past him, and he followed her helplessly out of the restaurant.

"Too bad," mused Rowan. "I had hoped they would stay long enough that Talybont could admire your beauty and compare your sweet smile and charming ways with Katherine's arrogance and bad manners."

"Rowan," said Charlotte bluntly, putting down her fork, "what it is you want of me?"

He turned and his dark eyes were no longer playful. There were devilish lights in them.

"I want you to make Eustace Talybont fall in love with you," he said in a cold voice. "I want him to *want* you, and I want Katherine to *see* that he wants you and to be humiliated by it."

Charlotte recoiled. "But surely enough has already happened to—"

"I want her to suffer," he cut in silkily. "As she made me suffer."

Privately Charlotte doubted the possibility of a man who always seemed to be on his way elsewhere ever falling in love with her, but she did not voice it. Somehow the crayfish had lost a little of its flavor. . . .

That afternoon they wandered the stores, looking at beautiful wool embroideries, the designs of which, Rowan told her, were based on rugs from the Orient, which reminded her once again that Lisbon was a trading city and that great Portuguese carracks had opened up the spice trade with the Far East. Happily, the Talybonts did not make an appearance, although Charlotte strongly suspected that this was to have been their destination, aborted because they had retired to their inn quarreling.

Charlotte and Rowan arrived back at the Royal Cockerel fairly late, and Rowan told her she would have to hurry and dress if they were to secure a table.

As they went upstairs, Charlotte saw a tall thin woman hovering at the head of the stairs. Why, it was the same woman who had crashed into Rowan with her boxes yesterday. Now she was running down the stairs past them at just the moment that several youngsters were running up. They charged against her skirts and she would have fallen but that Rowan reached out and caught her. She smiled up into his eyes, the smile momentarily lighting her harsh pointed features, and began to thank him in a veritable outburst of low-voiced French.

Charlotte didn't speak French, but it did seem to her that the woman was protesting overmuch. Her black eyes too had a soft gleam when she looked at Rowan—but then, women often looked at Rowan like that, even those who had never met him. Charlotte was becoming impatient.

"Come, you said we must hurry," she interrupted.

Rowan shrugged and paused yet a moment longer, listening to another long flurry of words. Then he hurried alongside Charlotte up the stairs.

They were late to dinner, but the Talybonts were later. Charlotte watched them make their appearance, a pale Katherine in vivid emerald-green silk sarcenet being almost dragged into the room by her irate young husband, very red in the face and looking petulant. They looked neither to right nor left but took the first table offered and kept their eyes on their plates as they ate.

"Her hand is shaking with fury," murmured Rowan. "I am surprised it will carry food to her mouth without spilling it." He was lounging gracefully in his chair, drinking ruby-red port wine, as he said that, for he and Charlotte had already finished their dinner and were dawdling over their wine. "Too bad Talybont has his back to you," he added regretfully.

Charlotte was glad. She had been a little ashamed of her performance yesterday and she was again wearing the blue dress that made her young breasts appear miraculously to be in motion even though she was sitting still. The slightest breath made those dangling beads sway and glitter.

"Ah, well," Rowan sighed. "We will have to provide our own entertainment, I suppose."

He beckoned to the pair of guitarists who were discreetly serenading the patrons with their music for what coins they could garner, and the musicians came quickly to their table. Rowan promptly gestured them to the other side.

He is placing them so that they will make a backdrop for us in case the Talybonts should look this way, Charlotte thought resignedly. She took a quick sip of her malmsey wine, which was heavy and sweet.

"What strange guitars," she murmured, noting the shape of the instruments.

Rowan gave them a casual glance. "Yes, they are Portuguese guitars. You have probably seen only the Spanish guitars, which have six strings. These have eight or"—he looked more closely—"twelve by my count, and the shape is somewhat different."

Charlotte was surprised by the breadth of his knowledge—she always would be. Rowan seemed to have the knowledge of the world at his fingertips.

She was about to ask him rather wistfully about his childhood and where he had gained all his lore, but he was speaking in Portuguese to the two guitarists, who looked pleased and struck up a lovely tune that stirred the senses.

"It is a love song," Rowan told her, reaching across the table to take her hand caressingly. "It is about a man who searches the world over until he finds the perfect woman. The song is very old and is usually sung by a woman, but I will do my best."

To Charlotte's surprise, he began to sing in a low voice that nevertheless penetrated to the farthest reaches of the room. He had a beautifully melodic voice, timbred, rich. Gradually conversation in the dining room ceased while the patrons turned about in their chairs to watch the singer. In the candlelight the scene made a charming tableau, Charlotte in her glittering blue gown with her golden hair bathed in lamplight, her breasts rising and falling with her breathing, causing her beaded bodice to sparkle, her lips softly parted, Rowan with his dark head bent eloquently toward her. They looked young and handsome and lost in love.

Across the room where the Talybonts were sitting there was a sudden clatter, as if a glass might have been turned over and some cutlery dropped.

When Rowan finished the song there were smiling nods of approval and light applause from the dinner guests. Somewhat flushed from all this attention, Charlotte looked about her.

The Talybonts' table was empty, their dinners left half-eaten on their plates.

Rowan seemed vastly pleased.

But pleased or not, he was out again that night prowling the taverns alone, searching for the man he was to meet in

Lisbon. Charlotte knew nothing of this meeting—she only knew that her husband went out every night, often waking her when he came home and making love to her. Rowan could get along with very little sleep, she had learned.

All that week he kept up his relentless pursuit of the Talybonts. And although by now the Talybonts promptly turned their backs or made their escape whenever Charlotte and Rowan appeared, it was clear that Katherine was hard put to keep Eustace in check.

One afternoon they met face-to-face at the bullfights, where for a dreadful moment Charlotte thought that Eustace, his face contorted with rage, was going to charge at Rowan head-on. Katherine obviously thought so too, for her face went white and she pitched forward in a faint, sagging against her husband so that he must perforce catch her and so lost sight of Rowan and Charlotte in the crowd.

Something would have to be done about this situation, and soon, Charlotte decided, for Katherine could not always pretend to faint and Eustace now seemed in a perpetually ugly mood, ready to challenge Rowan even if he died of it. She intended to speak to Rowan about it when they returned to their room at the Royal Cockerel. Rowan must have seen something in her face, because before she could speak he said, "I had best go down and pay our landlord something on account—wouldn't want him to start worrying about us."

Deciding she could speak to him later about it, Charlotte watched him go. Then suddenly she remembered that the seam of Rowan's cuff had been ripped in the crowd at the bullfight. She opened the door to call to him to ask for a needle and thread to be sent up, for she meant to stitch up the seam herself when he returned, when she saw him standing near the head of the stairs deep in conversation with the thin woman in black.

Charlotte stopped, puzzled. There was something very friendly in the way they stood there together, as if they knew each other well.

She forgot the torn cuff.

When Rowan came back, Charlotte asked carefully, "Who

was that woman and what were you saying to her just now?"

Rowan's dark brows lifted, but he answered her frankly. "Her name is Annette Flambord. She is French. And I stopped to ask her if she had found a husband yet."

Charlotte was not to be distracted. "She is Katherine Talybont's personal maid, isn't she? And that is how we know so much about the Talybonts' movements. You were asking her about where they will be tomorrow and the next day and the next."

"Oh, I had no need to ask her that," he said carelessly. "Annette volunteers such information very readily."

Charlotte caught her breath. Sometimes her husband's coolness astonished her.

"Are you not afraid you will cause her to lose her job?" she shot at him.

He laughed. "There is probably no better hairdresser in all of Europe. Do you think Katherine would let her go for a mere indiscretion? Indeed, I am amazed that Katherine has been able to keep her so long!"

Charlotte studied Rowan. Handsome, dashing, an arresting face, and a manner that swept all before him. A dangerous, dominating man. "Maybe *you* had something to do with it," she suggested.

"And what do you mean by that?" he asked, amused.

"Perhaps this hairdresser is in love with you," she offered doubtfully.

Rowan came a step closer and there was real mirth on his face now. "Annette," he stated, "is in love with gold. She has never been able to get enough of it to please her. It is a standing joke between us that whenever she does get enough gold for her *dot*—that's a dowry, Charlotte— she will go back to France and marry the man who seduced her and abandoned her in Marseilles and make his life miserable forever. I think she should do it."

Charlotte was a little daunted by this worldly view shared by Rowan and the Frenchwoman. "Is Marseilles where she learned her trade?" she inquired.

"Yes, she was a wigmaker's assistant there and became expert at curling and dressing wigs. I have told her that her skill would bring her fame if she would find herself some great patroness."

"But she already has Katherine Talybont," protested Charlotte.

Rowan chose to ignore the irony in his wife's tone. "Someone far beyond Katherine," he said airily. "At least a marchioness—possibly a duchess. But you have doubtless noticed Annette's skill by the elegance of Katherine's coiffures." He gave Charlotte's golden hair a fleeting glance. "Perhaps I can persuade Annette to dress *your* hair someday when Katherine is out."

Smarting under the implied suggestion that her own coiffure was not as elegant as Katherine's, Charlotte stiffened slightly. "Perhaps *you* should find Mademoiselle Annette this great patroness she needs," she said in a hard voice. "Or do you find your other uses for Mademoiselle Annette too absorbing?"

Rowan was looking angry now. "Be careful, Charlotte, or you will say something you regret. Annette has nothing to do with you."

"Oh, I know she has not." Charlotte sighed. "It is just this . . . this endless pursuit of the Talybonts that has set me on edge. And Annette is part of that. I wish she would go away—I wish they would all three of them go away!"

"Come to dinner," he suggested sympathetically. "And rest easy. I have just been told that the Talybonts are not coming down. Katherine is sulking and Eustace is stomping about the floor railing at her."

Charlotte enjoyed that dinner more than any she had ever eaten at the Royal Cockerel.

But after dinner, as was his wont, Rowan again went out on the town. Charlotte wondered audibly why he did not take her with him. Lisbon by night, he told her, was a city of men. There were few women abroad. If Rowan's behavior was typical, she could well believe it.

Hardly had he left before there was a soft knock on the door and a French-accented voice murmured in English, "Madame, are you there?"

Charlotte opened the door to admit Annette, who slipped by her like a shadow and closed the door behind her.

"I do not know what to do," Annette said quickly in very good English, and Charlotte had a chance to study her face by candlelight. The golden light on those sharp sallow features made Annette's mouth seem sly, her black eyes too watchful. And "thin" was not quite the word for her—"lithe" seemed more appropriate; her step was light, she moved with the easy grace of a Toledo blade. "From the window I saw Rowan leaving," Annette explained. "But he disappeared into an alley, and in the darkness I knew I would have difficulty catching up with him."

"That is undoubtedly true," agreed Charlotte. "But why would you *need* to catch up with him?"

Annette's voice was hurried. "The Talybonts have been quarreling all day. They wrangled over dinner and he ended up by oversetting the table and all the food was thrown on the floor."

"Spare me," said Charlotte with irony. "My husband is far more interested in the Talybonts' activities than I. But I note that you call my husband by his given name. Are you then such old friends?"

The other woman considered her thoughtfully. "Yes— old friends," she said. "He saved my life once in Marseilles."

As he did mine in Scotland and again on shipboard, Charlotte thought suddenly. *We have something in common, Annette and I.*

There was a little flicker, perhaps of amusement, in the shrewd black eyes facing her. Annette's voice had an impish quality.

"And I saved *his* life in Paris."

Charlotte was taken aback. Somehow it did not occur to her to disbelieve that statement. It had been thrown out almost tauntingly, as if to say, *You may think me a servant, but we are equals, Rowan and I. We have always been equals.*

The Frenchwoman was still studying her, as if expecting her to say something. Charlotte obliged.

"Tell me how you came to know my husband."

Annette shrugged. "He must tell you himself, madame. But I have been long his friend. The Talybont woman is anxious to speak with you. She has sent me to fetch you. I do not think Rowan would like that."

Charlotte frowned. She didn't think she would like that either. She had no desire for a confrontation with Katherine Talybont; certainly there was nothing to be gained by it.

Noting Charlotte's hesitation, Annette said, "Perhaps I could say that you are out, that you did not answer my knock?"

"No, I will not hide from her," decided Charlotte. "But I will not go to her either. Tell your mistress, Annette, that if she wishes to speak to me she must come here. I will not retire for the next hour."

Was that a flicker of admiration in Annette's black eyes? Charlotte could not be sure.

"Very well, madame. I will tell her." Annette was gone like a shadow.

Moments later there was a crisp knock on the door. Katherine Talybont, no doubt. Charlotte rose with a sigh to meet her enemy.

Katherine swept in with the air of an injured duchess. She was wearing a loose-backed gown of thin rose damask that swept away from the back of the shoulders into a slight train. She kicked that train aside as she came through the door, and stood in the middle of the room regarding Charlotte with her rose-damask bodice rising and falling in annoyance.

"I think you know why I have come," she stated regally.

"I haven't the least idea," was Charlotte's airy response. She noted that even if Katherine's coiffure had been arranged by "the best hairdresser in Europe," the curls were damp across her forehead and pulling loose in several places. She wondered if Katherine and Eustace had actually come to blows at some point in the evening. "Won't you sit down?" she asked, and waved Katherine to a chair.

"Thank you, but I prefer to stand."

"Very well, but *I* intend to sit if you do not." Charlotte sank down gracefully into a chair and raised her high arched brows questioningly at her visitor.

Katherine was a little nonplussed by Charlotte's aplomb and by being thus received, as if she were a commoner in the presence of a queen, but she came straight to the point.

"Rowan cannot forgive me for breaking our betrothal at the last minute and—"

"Yes, why *did* you do that?" Charlotte cut in smoothly.

Katherine looked vexed, but she answered. "Eustace pursued me and I was swept off my feet," she ground out. "And *you* should be glad I was," she added crushingly, "else you would never have had a chance at Rowan."

Charlotte permitted a look of polite amusement to cross her face and be replaced by her same cool questioning stare.

Katherine leaned forward, intent on her adversary. "I came to ask you to take Rowan away—take him *anywhere*, back to England, but somewhere else."

"And why should I do that?" wondered Charlotte.

"Isn't it obvious?" exploded Katherine. "Don't you realize that husband of yours is trying to goad Eustace into challenging him to a duel *so he can kill him?*"

Charlotte came to her feet. "Rowan wouldn't do that!"

"Would he not?" Katherine's face went haggard, and for a moment Charlotte was almost sorry for her. "You know nothing about Rowan," she said bitterly. "You do not know his *depths!*"

"I think I may know a bit more about Rowan than you do," countered Charlotte. "After all, I am his wife. And I say to you that Rowan would do no such thing."

"Oh, he would, he would!" Katherine's hands were clenched.

"Then if you believe he would," Charlotte countered fierily, "why don't you persuade your own husband to leave Portugal?"

Katherine's hands found a chairback. She leaned upon it with a groan. "Do you think I have not tried? I beg him every day to leave this accursed city! Eustace considers Rowan's presence here in Lisbon to be a constant affront— and especially the way you both hound us. He very nearly assaulted Rowan today—and of course that would have brought on a duel, which is exactly what Rowan wants, he just wants to make sure that Eustace challenges *him*, he wants the world to believe Eustace to be the aggressor. Oh, I know how Rowan's mind works!"

"I doubt that you do," said Charlotte distantly.

Katherine was not disposed to argue the point. She raced on. "Eustace will not go because he considers that if he left at this point it would be an act of cowardice, so it is Rowan and you who must leave!"

"I do not think Rowan will care to leave Lisbon just to convenience you," said Charlotte coldly.

Katherine straightened up and gave her an exasperated look. "If you do not," she warned, "I will have to find some other way of dealing with the matter." Before Charlotte could say, "Just what do you mean by that?", Katherine had spun on her heel and gained the door. She turned to fling back over her shoulder, "And one more thing. I would appreciate it if you would stop these ridiculous attempts to seduce my husband. Making eyes and simpering —you are making fools of us all!"

She was gone through the door with that parting shot, and Charlotte sprang forward and slammed the door after her, then stood against it breathing hard.

Katherine was waspish, she was selfish, she had a cold heart—but in this case she was right: Charlotte and Rowan *should* leave Lisbon—or at least leave this inn— before the trouble between the two men worsened so that neither could in honor extricate himself.

And Charlotte *did* feel that she had been making a fool of herself by covertly smiling at Eustace when they met and coquettishly waving her fan. She had done it only to please Rowan, but it was wearing rather thin. Surely this affair with the Talybonts had gone far enough.

Charlotte feigned sleep when Rowan returned home, for she had no desire to be clasped in his arms and told on brandy-laden breath that whatever was between him and the Talybonts did not concern her. She wanted to confront him with Katherine's visit in the sunlight, and in sunlight the next morning she brought up the subject.

It was another beautiful day in Lisbon, with gulls and

cormorants wheeling in a cloudless sky and a fresh tangy salt breeze blowing in from the Atlantic. After breakfast Rowan had engaged an open carriage and they were driving in leisurely fashion along the waterfront. It was Rowan's habit to drive slowly up and down the waterfront when the tide was in, noting the passengers arriving from the ships that dotted the harbor.

"Who knows?" he would say lightly. "Someone we know might be arriving—your uncle perhaps." And he would chuckle.

Charlotte did not join him in mirth over that private joke. She hoped sincerely that she would never see her uncle again.

Today she had other things on her mind. She spoke boldly.

"I think you are driving Eustace Talybont too far in your efforts to get back at Katherine."

A shadow of grim amusement passed over her husband's mouth. "Do you now?"

"Yes. Katherine visited me last night to implore me to make you see reason and leave Lisbon."

Their carriage was now weaving through groups of fishermen in bright-colored shirts and darting *varinas* with gold earrings swinging from their ears, their raucous voices calling out that they had fresh fish for sale. Rowan waited until they had broken through before answering, and by then his grim smile had deepened.

"Did she indeed?"

"Yes. Don't mock me, Rowan. This has all gone far enough." Charlotte was becoming irritated with her sardonic husband, who seemed to be watching her in dark amusement through narrowed eyes. "Throwing myself publicly at Eustace Talybont in the way you desire makes me feel like a . . . like a . . ." She sought for a word and found none.

"Whore?" he suggested mildly.

Charlotte flushed. "Don't joke about it. Katherine accused me of trying to seduce him in public, and I am ashamed to say that there was some truth in that. She insists I am making fools of us all."

"Really? Your desire not to thrust yourself upon Talybont becomes you. What else did Katherine say?"

"Just that we should leave Lisbon, since her husband will not because he feels it would be backing down somehow and he doesn't wish to appear to be a coward. She feels it will all end in a duel if we stay."

"And she fears for her husband, I take it?" was Rowan's sardonic comment.

"Yes, she is afraid you will goad him into challenging you and that you will then kill him. I told her you wouldn't do such a thing."

"You told her that?" Rowan looked mildly astonished.

"Of course! You have nothing against him other than that he married Katherine."

"And made sport of me in London," he added in a hard voice. "Behind my back, of course."

There was a chill in Rowan's manner that made Charlotte suddenly afraid for Eustace Talybont. She realized that Katherine's assertion might have some basis after all.

"You *won't* kill him, will you?" she asked anxiously, and was aware that he was no longer looking at her, but that his vision was focused with sudden intensity upon a wiry fellow whose travel-stained brown clothes stood out against the clean white or vivid red cross-stitched shirts of the men around him. He was not one of them, that was clear, and his quick darting eyes were scanning the crowd about him from beneath a shock of unruly black hair topped by a dirty brown tricorne.

Rowan's gaze was fixed for a moment. *The man was here, had followed him, this fellow who had dogged his trail across half of England. Rowan had not lost him in Scotland after all. . . .*

"Do you know that man?" asked Charlotte, impelled by the intensity of Rowan's gaze.

"No." But those roving eyes would soon find *him*, and the travel-stained fellow would fall in behind their carriage, pacing them. For this was no ordinary pursuer; this man would be a skilled assassin. And even if he did not strike now, his very presence would endanger Rowan's mission.

They were just then passing a flower vendor carrying a great basket of red and yellow flowers. Suddenly Rowan leaned out of the carriage and scooped up an enormous bunch, dropped coins generously into a damp brown palm, and brought the flowers up just in time to shield his face and Charlotte's from the roving eyes of the travel-stained man.

Startled by having what seemed like a wall of flowers suddenly thrust upon her, Charlotte felt she was being somehow bribed by their loveliness to abandon this discussion. But she could not help exclaiming, "Oh, Rowan, they're lovely!" and burying her face in their petals, drinking in the heady fragrance of the blossoms. Beside her Rowan's dark face too was half-buried in the blooms, screened from sight of the dark wiry man whose head swung about so alertly.

The carriage moved on. A heavy dray hauling wine barrels now obscured the view behind them. Rowan brushed aside the flowers and sat back.

"You have complained that our room, having but one window, is stuffy," he observed. "Now you will have something to scent the air."

Charlotte looked up. "And you promise you won't . . . ?"

The dray had now been replaced by a coach whose driver was shouting impatiently. They were drawing away from the waterfront. Rowan took a quick glance behind him. The wiry dark man in brown was nowhere in sight.

"No, I will not kill Talybont, Charlotte, since the thought gives you such pain," he said in an absent voice. "And you will no doubt be glad to learn that the Talybonts are nowhere near us at this moment. They are out on the Tagus seeing the Tower of Belem and other sights and are not expected to return until tonight."

"Did Annette tell you that?"

He turned to give her an ironic look. "Does it matter how I know? I am not planning to take you out upon the river today, if that is your concern."

Charlotte felt relief well through her. For a moment she had thought . . . But of course that was ridiculous. Rowan was not planning to kill Eustace Talybont, he had never intended to kill him. It was just her vivid imagination that had made her think . . . She turned to Rowan again, her words spilling out breathlessly.

"And you *will* change inns, will you not? So that we will not be constantly brushing up against the Talybonts?"

She made a lovely picture sitting there, her violet eyes filled with mute appeal, her soft lips parted, her golden hair turned to flame in the hot sunlight beating down over Lisbon. Rowan smiled down at her. "That I will do this very afternoon," he declared.

Charlotte's worried face broke into a smile.

At that moment she felt herself to be both loved and cherished.

18

They promptly returned to the Royal Cockerel, with Rowan leaning forward urging the driver to go faster. But he did not immediately pay the landlord and whisk Charlotte away to another inn. Instead he hurried her upstairs and told her that with the city so crowded he must needs prowl about and find what accommodations he could. She was to wait for him up here, not down in the common room—he was very specific about that.

Charlotte, her arms full of red and yellow flowers, nodded happily.

Time passed. In the afternoon heat Charlotte unloosed her bodice and drowsed upon the bed.

She woke with a start. Dusk was gathering outside, a long bluish light. How long had she slept? She leapt up and realized she must have been waked by an insistent knocking on the door.

"Madame?" It was Annette's voice, coming to her through the door panels.

Charlotte threw the door wide and Annette came in quickly without being invited and closed the door behind her.

"Rowan has asked me to escort you to your new inn." She spoke with soft urgency. "Please do not ask questions— just come with me." And when Charlotte hesitated, "It is his *wish*."

Somehow that quiet sentence had the force of a command. Charlotte gazed at this lithe sharp-faced Frenchwoman with the bitter dark eyes and wondered what she was to Rowan—really. A mistress out of his past perhaps? No, she was not pretty enough. Rowan liked beautiful women.

Charlotte sighed and capitulated. "Very well, Annette. I will get my boxes."

"No, I will get them, madame." Annette stepped forward. "Rowan has not yet settled the bill," she explained. "There might be questions if you appear to be leaving the inn with all your possessions. But *I* am always to be seen about carrying boxes for the Talybont woman, who spends half her time shopping. No one will notice me."

Charlotte could see the sense of that. What she could not understand was this unwonted hurry, this haste to get out before the bill was even paid, and most of all she could not understand Rowan's not coming for her himself.

Annette already had Charlotte's boxes in hand, along with Charlotte's bronze gloves, which she had snatched up from the bed, and was gesturing her toward the door.

"We will go down separately, madame. Please use the side stairs and go out the side door into the alley below— you can see it from your window. A carriage is waiting for you there. Get in it and I will join you."

Charlotte frowned. It was one thing to be assisted in her removal by a woman who was an old friend of Rowan's— and quite another to steal out of the hotel like a thief. Still, it must be Rowan's desire, for this Frenchwoman seemed to be more in his confidence than was his wife!

"Won't Katherine Talybont miss you?" she demanded. "Suppose she looks out the window and sees us together in a carriage? Won't you lose your job?"

Annette shook her head irritably. "The Talybonts are dining out and will not return until late. Please *hurry*, madame!"

Thus admonished, Charlotte took the side stairs, carrying her flowers. Outside in the alley a carriage was indeed waiting, and after a moment's hesitation she climbed into it. She could see Annette hurrying around the corner of the building with her boxes, and a moment later Annette had joined her.

As they turned the corner into the broad avenue on which the Royal Cockerel fronted, Charlotte glanced back—and sat transfixed.

There, just entering the inn, she saw Eustace Talybont —no, it was Rowan! And he seemed to be wearing one of Eustace Talybont's suits! He was clad in the very same sky blue that Talybont usually affected, and he was even wearing the distinctive blue-and-gold tricorne that seemed to be Talybont's hallmark—a hat he obviously had duplicated, for it was assuredly the same hat, or one just like it, that had spilled out of its box from Annette's arms that first day when Rowan had crashed into her in the common room.

"That's Rowan!" she cried in bewilderment. She tried to rise to call to him before his tall form disappeared into the inn, but Annette, with surprising strength, bore her back down.

"*Estou com pressa!*" Annette cried, to hurry the driver. And then, more urgently to Charlotte, "Please do not ask me any questions, madame." Her voice lowered. "One cannot be sure about the driver."

Charlotte was seething with questions. "Where are you taking me, Annette?" she demanded.

That much at least Annette was willing to volunteer. "The Pico de Ferro, madame. That means the Iron Crest. It is a very good inn." She smiled reassuringly at Charlotte.

Charlotte was not to be beguiled. In stiff silence she allowed Annette to carry her boxes up to her room at the Iron Crest, which, although smaller than the Royal Cockerel and lacking the extravagant blue *azulejo* tiles at the entrance, was in her estimation a handsome inn—and here they enjoyed a large front room, for which Rowan must have paid dearly. Perhaps, she thought suddenly, he wanted a good view of who was coming and going—and was willing to pay for the privilege. The thought unnerved her.

She turned abruptly to ask Annette—and found her gone.

It was some time before Rowan arrived, and she saw in surprise that he was again wearing his own clothes.

"But . . . I saw you in a blue hat and blue suit going

into the Royal Cockerel!" she exclaimed as he entered. "How on earth . . . ?"

Suddenly his eyes had a cold look. "You were mistaken, Charlotte. I have been nowhere near the Royal Cockerel."

"But of course you have! I saw you there."

"In the dusk one's eyes play tricks," he told her firmly. His eyes strayed to the flowers, now reposing in an earthenware vessel that a serving wench had brought. "Nor have I yet settled our bill at the Royal Cockerel. You considered the last room stuffy; it may be that you will prefer it to this one, which, with the windows open, may smell of fish since it is nearer the waterfront and the *varinas* are constantly parading by. It may be that you will prefer to go back to the Royal Cockerel."

"Oh, no, of course I won't! And I do not understand . . ." She was beginning to doubt that she had seen Rowan. It had been only a glimpse; could it have been someone else who looked strikingly like him? "I do not understand why you asked Annette to bring me here or why—"

Her voice halted as he held up his hand. "Charlotte," he said, "spare me all this. I have received a message from the man I was to meet here. It seems his plans have changed, and I may have to leave—perhaps tomorrow— for Evora."

"Then why change inns?" Charlotte was bewildered. "If we are leaving Lisbon so soon, why—"

"I had already made the arrangements here when I heard," he cut in. "And having gotten accommodations here, I met some English people I thought you might like. They're staying here—right down the hall in fact—and we are to meet them downstairs for dinner in"—he consulted his gold watch—"five minutes."

"What?" cried Charlotte, delighted at the idea of meeting people who—hopefully—would never have heard of the Talybonts. Perhaps, she told herself as she hastened to smooth her hair and get all her hooks properly fastened, that episode was at last over and the Talybonts and Annette would drift out of their lives.

"Are you ready?" he asked impatiently.

"Yes . . . no, I can find only one of my gloves. I saw

Annette pick them up and I thought she had put them down on the bed here, but there's only one."

"Never mind. Charlotte, we must not keep our new friends waiting. If you have lost one of your gloves, we will search for it tomorrow—first in this room, and then, if necessary, at the Royal Cockerel."

Thus scolded, Charlotte scurried from the room after giving one last despairing glance back at the one glove reposing on the bed.

The English people were named Milroyd. They were from Lincolnshire, and this was their first trip to Europe. There were actually nine in their party, but Charlotte met only three because the nursemaid and five children were taking dinner upstairs in their room. But Preston Milroyd, his plump wife, Alice, and his sister Mary were very pleasant and cordial, if a trifle dull. Preston Milroyd, despite his drooping mustache and sleepy expression, seemed to regard himself as a great rake, and after dinner he snapped up Rowan's proposal that they "take in the town" while the ladies "sip wine and rest here at the inn."

"Perhaps the ladies would enjoy 'taking in the town' as well!" said Charlotte tartly, and was disappointed when both the Milroyd ladies tittered, taking her remark as a great joke.

Preston Milroyd fingered his mustache and regarded Charlotte tolerantly. "Quite a little high flier, your wife," he told Rowan in a jovial voice. "Well, don't wait up, ladies!"

"No, don't wait up." Rowan threw Charlotte a quelling glance, which was greeted by a toss of the head.

Why was he forever off somewhere? she asked herself. Where did he go every night? She started, realizing that one of the Milroyd ladies had spoken to her, and tried to gather her wits to cope with, "Do you prefer cross stitch? Or would you rather crochet? For myself, I find embroidery more satisfying, don't you, Alice? Alice favors blackwork."

They were off to a boring evening, but they were the first English people she had met here, barring the Talybonts, and Charlotte made a sincere effort to win their favor.

They bade her good night warmly at her room, made little clucking sounds over "getting the bride safely tucked in," and made their way to their own quarters, which, she understood, took up all the rooms on one side of their floor of the inn.

Charlotte searched every cranny of the room, but her search did not turn up the missing glove.

At last she went to bed, but not to sleep. Occasionally she got up and went to the window, watching parties of noisy roisterers on the street below staggering back to their inns. Rowan was right, she thought bitterly—Lisbon by night was a man's town. The only women she had seen on the streets tonight were obvious bawds.

Rowan came in with the dawn and found her still awake.

"What on earth did you and Preston Milroyd *do* all this time?" she demanded, and Rowan laughed.

"Drank, told stories, made the rounds of the taverns. Preston Milroyd is a man of parts. Couldn't stop telling me swashbuckling stories about his adventures as a young blade in Lincolnshire." He chuckled.

"I couldn't find my glove," Charlotte said sulkily.

"Ah? Then we must dash over to the Royal Cockerel and look for it at once. Milroyd is still down in the common room—he couldn't make the stairs. We'll escort you, my lady!"

"At this hour?" Charlotte wondered if he was half-drunk.

"Certainly at this hour. I'll pay my bill before the chambermaid discovers the room is empty and the landlord decides I've taken French leave, you'll find your glove, and we'll be back in time to breakfast with the Milroyd ladies, both of whom, Preston tells me, are early risers, up at cockcrow!"

Charlotte could hardly believe they would go out at dawn to look for a glove. She dressed in haste and was whisked away to the Royal Cockerel by a half-awake staggering Milroyd and Rowan, who in the outside air seemed, save for a certain overbrightness of the eyes, to be as fresh as the morning.

At the Royal Cockerel they burst in on a most astonishing scene.

Katherine Talybont, clad in a red satin dressing gown, her long dark tresses spilling over her shoulders, stood in the middle of the room. Her back was toward them as they entered the common room, and from her lips emitted a high keening wail. About her a number of men shuffled their feet and looked embarrassed—among them the landlord, several lackeys, some men who appeared to be guests of the inn, and two who looked to be members of the local constabulary.

"What has happened?" Charlotte gasped.

The landlord, who upon seeing them enter had promptly crossed toward them, answered her query.

"The English gentleman, Eustace Talybont, is dead," he replied gravely. "Killed by a footpad at my front door, I'm sorry to say, although whether he was coming in or going out isn't too clear, and the lady seems too hysterical to help us. His body lies upstairs but his wife refuses to go up there. A doctor's on his way and we're hoping he can persuade her."

"This footpad, did they catch him?" demanded Rowan.

"Oh, no need. Talybont apparently killed him himself. They were found lying together outside. We've taken Talybont's body upstairs and deposited the footpad's body at the side door. It will be terrible for the guests to look out the window and see him there. We're waiting for the authorities to come and take him away."

"Terrible." Milroyd hiccuped. "Terrible."

"I've come to pay my bill, for we're joining friends in another inn," Rowan told the innkeeper.

"I fear there'll be many others who will find another inn this day." The innkeeper sighed. "After what's happened here."

"When did it happen?"

"Toward dawn, we hazard. The Talybonts had some kind of argument at the place where they dined, and the wife"—he nodded toward Katherine's red satin back—"left Talybont and came back to the inn in a coach with some other members of their party who left early. Talybont came back much later—and never made it through the door, apparently. We think this footpad must have been lying in wait to spring on someone in the darkness."

"Darkness?" asked Rowan sharply. "But there is a lamp outside the inn."

The landlord sighed. "It had gone out—or else the footpad managed to extinguish it—because it was very dark outside and Talybont's body was found when one of the servants, noting that the lamp outside was not lit, went out and tripped over the bodies. We surmise that the footpad, seeing Talybont approaching the door, seized him from the rear and drove a dagger into his heart. But Talybont, being quick, brought up his own dagger as he was dying, drove it into his attacker's side, and ripped upward. It all happened silently. No one in the common room heard a thing. We were hard put to mop up the blood. It—"

Charlotte shuddered. "I have lost my glove," she interrupted, thinking to be gone from this place as quickly as possible. "While you settle the bill, Rowan, I will go up and search for it." She had already started away when Rowan called to her.

"No, wait, Charlotte," he said sharply. "I will accompany you as soon as I have paid."

His peremptory call to Charlotte apparently carried to Katherine, as their low-voiced conversation with the innkeeper had not. Her keening wail cut off so abruptly that the room of a sudden went eerily silent. She seemed to grow taller, and she brushed aside an object that was being held out to her.

"That is not my husband's dagger. My husband did not own a dagger!" She pushed at the shoulder of a man who blocked her way. He stepped hastily aside and Katherine charged across the room and brought up before Rowan. She did not seem to see anybody else.

"This is your doing!" she panted. "You could not bear to see me happy!" She drew back her arm and struck him a stinging blow in the face.

Rowan never even flinched. "Kate, you are hysterical," he snapped. "Making a scene will not bring Eustace back."

For a moment Katherine looked as if she might faint. She wavered on her feet. Then she turned and waved the group toward her.

"This is your man!" she cried. "This is the man who killed my husband—not that lackey outside! Footpad indeed! Was my husband robbed? No! I tell you they were both murdered—by Rowan Keynes!" She pointed dramatically at Rowan.

Uneasily the men converged on Rowan.

Charlotte found her voice. Rowan was not defending himself—*she* would defend him!

"This woman is mad!" she cried. "My husband and I spent the entire evening with this gentleman and his family at the Iron Crest." She seized Milroyd's arm as if presenting him to the company. "And after we ladies had retired, the two of them were out until dawn—until just before we came over here, in fact."

"That's true." Milroyd was nodding his head. "Lots of witnesses everywhere."

Katherine stared at him. She seemed suddenly to collapse.

"Murderer," she whispered, glaring at Rowan. "You will burn in hell for this night's work!"

"No doubt the devil will find us both, Kate. But if anyone charges that I murdered Talybont . . ."—his voice rang out and his dark head swung about, challenging everyone in the room—"you'll find dozens of people who'll remember us in the taverns right up to dawn, when we came over here."

"And I'll tell you where to find those dozens"— Milroyd hiccuped—"for I bought every last one of them a drink!" He wagged a finger in officialdom's face and began to enumerate the taverns they had visited and the names of some of the men they had talked to.

Rowan, content that he was not to be charged with anything despite Katherine's outburst, was counting out money into the landlord's hand. When he had finished he told Milroyd, "We'll meet you out front. I must take Charlotte up to look for her lost glove."

A chambermaid accosted them outside their bedroom door. "Is it true, sir, that the people down the hall were murdered last night and that the lady's maid has fled?" she asked, big-eyed.

"No, only the gentleman was murdered," Rowan replied irritably. "And how do they know the maid has fled? It is early, perhaps she has found a softer bed elsewhere in the inn and is loath to leave it!"

The chambermaid giggled and Charlotte gave her a look of distaste. She herself was still very shaken by what had occurred downstairs.

"Open the door, please, Rowan," she said crisply. "I have not the key."

The bronze glove was lying on the bed where Annette had apparently left it. Charlotte stared at it, confused. She had a distinct memory of that coverlet being smooth and empty when she had left yesterday.

She picked the glove up. One of the fingers seemed to be stiff, stuffed with something.

Before she could investigate, Rowan took the glove gently from her fingers. "I will take charge of this until we get back to the Iron Crest," he told her calmly. "We cannot have it getting lost again. God knows what new excitement may lie in store!"

"I can't understand why Katherine would accuse you," Charlotte said unsteadily. "I mean, you might kill him in a duel, but not . . . not like this. It was dreadful of her."

"Yes, she has her dreadful moments, has Katherine," he agreed cheerfully. "Come, we will go out the side door and avoid another scene with her."

Charlotte followed him reluctantly, for in that direction lay a corpse. There was a grim-looking servant standing guard beside it. She tried to move on by very fast, but she was caught up short by Rowan stopping to gaze down at the body. Very still it lay in its travel-stained brown clothing, with a worn brown tricorne lying over the face, obscuring it from the view of passersby.

Very deliberately Rowan reached down and removed the tricorne, looked into that dead face.

When it came into view, Charlotte thought for a moment she was going to faint.

The man who lay there was the same man that Rowan had stared at so intently at the waterfront just before he had bought her that enormous bouquet of flowers that now adorned their room.

At that moment Milroyd came round the corner of the Inn and joined them. He was sobering up in the clear morning air. He stared down curiously at the body of the footpad. "Villainous-looking fellow, isn't he?" he remarked cheerfully.

Rowan nodded and dropped the hat back down to cover that dead face. "Villainous," he agreed.

"Awful of that woman to accuse you of her husband's murder," Milroyd said as they rode back toward the Iron Crest. "Poor hysterical creature, she couldn't have known what she was saying."

"Katherine was overwrought," said Rowan. "We were betrothed once and she has a vengeful nature. I am afraid her tirade has quite upset Charlotte." He looked down at his pale young wife, sitting silently beside him.

When they were at last alone, back in their big front bedchamber at the Iron Crest, Charlotte gave her husband a level look.

"Rowan," she said, "what have you done? *What have I helped you do?*"

He was looking down at her with a mixed expression on his face. "Charlotte," he said, and there was an earnestness in his voice, "I have done nothing. I swear to you that I did not know that footpad who waylaid Eustace Talybont."

His voice held such a ring of truth that Charlotte was hard put not to believe him.

"Do you swear to me before God that you had never seen that man before?" she demanded.

"Seen him before? Certainly I had seen him before. Yesterday morning at the docks I saw him—so did you, I think. He stood there in that motley crowd looking like a stranger in a foreign land, and for a moment I thought I had seen him before. But I had not." He sounded almost regretful. "I took a good look at him just now and he was a complete stranger to me."

"And Annette is missing," she added bitterly.

"We don't know that." He sounded impatient. "But under the circumstances I think I will stay away from the Royal Cockerel. I do not wish to seem to be conspiring with Katherine Talybont's maid."

Charlotte closed her eyes. She had to believe him. She had to or she would surely go mad.

But that remembered sight of Rowan—or of a man who looked precisely like Rowan—in a blue suit and hat that were the very mirror of Eustace Talybont's, entering the Royal Cockerel yesterday, would not leave her.

She fingered the bronze glove that Rowan had given back to her. All of its fingers were quite supple now—empty of whatever the glove had contained.

In spite of herself, she had begun to feel afraid.

"Charlotte." Rowan interrupted her thoughts. "I am glad that we have struck up an acquaintance with the Milroyds, for I will feel safe leaving you in their care."

"*Leaving* me?" She felt dizzy.

"Yes. I told you I must go to Evora. The trip would be arduous for you, and since you do not ride, arduous for me also. I will be back in a week, possibly two. I have paid for your accommodations in advance and I will leave you in pocket money. Milroyd has promised to take care of you."

"When are you going?"

"This afternoon—but do not worry, I will take you to lunch first, and after that Milroyd seeks my advice on some tiles he wishes to ship home to his estate in Lincolnshire."

Lunch hardly seemed to be the problem—the world was moving too fast for her.

"What will I tell the Milroyds?" she demanded. "About the reason for your leaving so suddenly?"

"Oh, say that it concerns an inheritance and that I was startled to learn of it and have told you nothing because I cannot yet believe it myself, and if it turns out to be true, I want to surprise you with it."

He was so glib, she thought wonderingly. Lies rolled so readily off his tongue.

But squiring his wife to lunch and helping Milroyd select tiles were not all Rowan chose to do that day. Indeed he and Charlotte spent the day very publicly, going about everywhere. Charlotte had an uneasy feeling that was the reason Rowan was escorting her to so many places—to be seen. Perhaps to appear to be above reproach, a man with nothing on his conscience. And the day wore on into dusk.

The lamps were already lit and candles flickering in holders when Rowan, staring moodily out their bedchamber window into the courtyard below, announced that late though it was, he must get started.

"What?" Charlotte was startled. "Surely you are not going to start out at night?" In her world travelers left at dawn. Or sometime during the day. Never by moonlight.

"The sooner gone, the sooner back," he quipped. And almost with the words he was gone; she could hear his footsteps echoing down the hallway and disappearing down the stairs.

She stood at the window of the Iron Crest and watched him go out into the courtyard. A dim circle of light from the windows showed him climbing aboard a horse that seemed already to have been brought. As she watched, he started off down the street, and just before he disappeared from her vision another rider came out of the darker shadows and joined him.

Charlotte craned from the window, trying to see. The two horses, moving along briskly, passed a lamp shining before a tavern, and for a moment the riders came into view.

There was something familiar about that other figure. Charlotte caught her breath. Although the rider was dressed as a man, it was a woman. A lithe woman with an almost gamin quality in the way she rode her horse.

Annette.

Charlotte closed her eyes. Whatever was between Rowan and the Frenchwoman did indeed go back a long way— and reached into the present and perhaps the future. *And had they—together, Annette and Rowan—killed a man last night?*

When she opened her eyes again, the world seemed to have darkened.

19

In the days that followed Rowan's departure, Charlotte did much soul searching—and arrived at nothing. Rowan was a mysterious man—and perhaps a deadly one. But he had saved her life twice, he had for her an overpowering physical attraction, and in her heart she was sure he loved her. But if he had done the things she suspected him of, could she stay with him?

The Milroyds helped. They were always there urging her to go with them on some new sightseeing junket. Glad to get away from her own nagging thoughts, Charlotte accompanied them willingly. The Milroyds never tired. Through what seemed to Charlotte at least a hundred resplendent churches in the elegant Manueline architecture, their eager feet hurried.

Nor did weather deter them. Undaunted by mists, they set out on the moss-covered road to Sintra. Twice they lost their way in the deepening fog and once the ladies alighted from the large hired carriage which Preston Milroyd had masterfully insisted on driving without a guide, only to shriek as lizards darted suddenly beneath their feet. They found their bearings again at a favored royal residence along the way, seeing the rococo palace of Queluz loom suddenly out of the white silence. And at last, as they drank in the scent of magnolias—a scent somewhat overpowered by the dank smell of moss and wet bark—a sudden change in the winds tore the mists apart and showed them the sweating stone tiles and winding streets of Sintra, and rising on the heights above them the crumbling ruins of the seventh-century stone castle the Moors had thought impregnable—until it fell in 1147.

With the others, Charlotte had climbed the sentry path with its sweeping view all the way to the sea pounding the coast. At the top, out of breath, they had struggled through brambles and trailing vines and disturbed the birds nesting in its empty battlements. Even the exuberant Milroyds had been silenced by the vast loneliness of this high place and shivered at the sound of the wind moaning through its empty cisterns.

To Charlotte, looking down across the plain, her feet upon a stone where some long-ago Moorish girl might have stood on tiptoe to kiss her lover, this crumbling ruin was more than a mere reminder that conquerors came and went. It was a reminder that the past did not come again.

Her brooding gaze found the blue glitter of the sea, far away. Somewhere that sea lapped other shores, somewhere it lapped the English coast, where she had left a lover who would not come again.

Her eyes grew moist and her heart ached for Tom.

"Charlotte, you're wool-gathering!" cried Alice Milroyd nearby. "Preston says if we hurry we might have time to see that abandoned monastery they told us about—the one with cells lined with cork to keep the dampness out."

The Milroyds could always be counted on to bring one back to the mundane present—and at that moment Charlotte was very grateful. She spent too much time these days brooding about Tom, and she knew it. Perhaps it was her defense against her fears about Rowan, she told herself.

She was only half-listening when, on the way down from the Castelo dos Mouros, Alice Milroyd told her gaily that Sintra was where King João had been caught long ago kissing one of the queen's ladies-in-waiting and had airily sworn the kiss was *por bem*, which meant "without consequence"—and the words had crept into the language.

"I wish some of Preston's kisses would be 'without consequence,'" she had leaned forward to whisper laughingly to Charlotte. "It seems to me that every time Preston deigns to join me in our big four-poster back home I have another child! Ah, but soon you will have children of your own and you will know what I am talking about," she added conspiratorially.

Charlotte joined in her mirth, but her own laughter was halfhearted. She had of late been wondering about the "consequences" of her own late-night activity. She had been feeling queasy at breakfast these last few days, and she wondered if that meant something.

But the Milroyds were soon to leave, and they took Charlotte along with them on their "last journey," as they called it, riding along the rocky coast west of the city, leaving the fairy-tale structure of the mighty Tower of Belem behind them, lapped by the waters of the Tagus, and striking out for Estoril and the Boca do Inferno, the Mouth of Hell, stopping overnight along the way.

Charlotte had not been feeling well the morning she waked in the little green-shuttered inn on the road to Estoril, and the jouncing ride in the carriage, rough except when they moved along the white beach sand, had made her feel no better. And when, amid the ohs and ahs of the impressionable Milroyds, she had looked dizzily down into that awesome chasm they called the Mouth of Hell, down into a churning whirlpool where the sea's inrushing water turned into a whirling creamy torrent as it was sucked down, she felt a sudden blackness steal over her and crumpled to the ground.

The Milroyds gathered round her, instantly solicitous. They insisted that shade must be found, and smelling salts, and her hooks must be loosened and water found to dampen a kerchief to hold against her brow. And Alice Milroyd whispered roguishly as the world came back to her, even though she was still gripped by that black nausea, that, "Ah, this is your first one—you'll get used to it as I have! Pray that it is not twins—my oldest sister had two sets, one after the other, and that on top of already having eleven! Her house is a constant din!"

Charlotte sat up, surprised that the nausea that had come upon her so suddenly was as quickly gone.

"Oh, I do not think it was that," she said with a sigh.
For in her heart she thought that it was the sight of those
cascading waters far below down the rocks that had brought
back memories of Kenlock Crag and the white cascade of
death that had battered Tom's body to pieces somewhere
beyond her vision. She closed her eyes at the hurtful
memory.

"That's right," said Alice Milroyd comfortingly. "Just sit
back against those rocks and rest for a while. "You'll feel
better soon."

But summer was ending and the Milroyds must get
themselves home to Lincolnshire, and, Alice Milroyd confided, she feared she was already pregnant again and she
would not wish anything to happen so that she would be
confined to her bed and end up having her latest in a
foreign country. They bade Charlotte a warm good-bye at
the ship and sailed out of her life forever.

And Charlotte, alone now, for she had met nobody
through the Milroyds, took long walks and ate silent sup-
pers at the inn and faced the truth:

She was pregnant. All the signs were there. And the
burning question was: Was the child Rowan's? Or Tom's?
And if the child should *look* like Tom, would Rowan
accept it?

The days sped by, and now there was more of a nip in
the breezes that swept in off the Atlantic. Autumn was
coming to Lisbon, and Rowan was still not back.

She began to wonder and worry that perhaps he was not
coming. Or perhaps something had happened to him. And
then what? She began to regret that she had not asked the
Milroyds to let her accompany them back to England,
perhaps as a governess—although she doubted they would
have done it; surely they would have pooh-poohed the
idea that Rowan might not return to her.

But it was not Rowan who came back to the Iron Crest—it
was Annette.

Annette was waiting in Charlotte's room one day when
Charlotte returned from one of her solitary walks through
the narrow twisting iron-balconied streets of the Alfama.
Charlotte opened the door and stopped dead at the sight

of Annette sitting upon the bed. Indeed, she must have been reclining there a moment before, because the pillow, which had been plumped up when Charlotte left, was now rumpled with the imprint of a head.

"What—?" began Charlotte, when Annette interrupted with an imperious gesture toward the door.

"First close the door, madame."

Charlotte closed the door and advanced upon Annette. "Where is my husband?" she demanded in a tight voice.

"Unfortunately, he could not come for you, madame. He sent me instead."

She had been right about them all along—they were *in league* together in some foul scheme. Charlotte felt dizzy. "Why? Tell me why?" she managed.

Annette sighed. "You have every right to ask why, madame. And I am sure you suspect me of terrible things— Rowan told me you did."

"I suspect you of having something to do with Eustace Talybont's murder!"

"Ah, there you have it. But that is why I fled—because of what happened *before*."

Annette's tone was convincing. Charlotte sank into a chair. "Suppose you tell me about it."

"After the Talybont woman left your room that night, she came back in a fury and stormed about—I could hear her through the wall. And then she came into my room and told me she knew I had once lived in the forest in France and she began to ask me about poison mushrooms—if I could tell the good from the bad. I think she intended to do away with you both."

Charlotte's quick intake of breath sounded loud in the sudden silence. "But surely you are mistaken," she cried. "Why would she go to such lengths?"

"She was not getting any younger. If Eustace Talybont fell out with her, abandoned her, she would be left without funds, for she had no money of her own and his parents had given him nothing. He was using up a small inheritance left him by an uncle. And she feared a duel that would leave him dead and her penniless."

Yes, Katherine had mentioned that. Her fear of a duel had been very real.

"She went further, madame. After she left the next day, I found a note asking me if I could procure the items we had discussed last night—she meant *could I procure poison mushrooms.*" Annette had Charlotte's full attention now. "At that point I realized that she would stop at nothing and that she would manage to involve me somehow, perhaps as a scapegoat, and I knew that I must leave, go back to France. I found the note after I left Rowan, and I wanted to warn him—"

"Why didn't you tell me?" interrupted Charlotte. "I was right there in the carriage with you, and you didn't say a word!"

"I was afraid you would become hysterical and make such a fuss that I would not be able to slip away," admitted Annette. "So I left a note for Rowan in your glove."

The glove she had found at the inn with one finger stiff with stuffing! Charlotte had been sure at the time that it contained a message.

"I already had a horse waiting when I left you. I rode north at once, but my horse was a poor one. Rowan overtook me at Coimbra—I was surprised to see him."

"But he was bound for Evora, and Evora lies to the east," said Charlotte sharply.

"I know, madame." Annette sighed. "But the man he was to meet in Evora was dead when he got there, and he rode north in great haste. It was fortunate that our paths crossed, because we slipped into Spain together and I was able to help him there."

"And where is Rowan now?"

"Somewhere upon the sea, madame. He had to hurry back to England and he took ship from Oporto. He sent me down to Lisbon with money for your passage. He said I was to put you on the first ship bound for London and you are to inquire for him at the Gray Goose Inn in Southwark. He will be waiting for you. In London."

So if Annette were to be believed, she and Rowan were both innocent of Eustace Talybont's death. Charlotte had been mistaken about the dark rider, mistaken about the

man in the blue suit and distinctive blue tricorne being
Rowan. It had all been explained away. . . .

"Annette,' she said quietly, "why do you do all this for
Rowan?"

Annette did not answer for a long time. A sad little
smile curved her hard mouth. Then, "I should think you
would have guessed, madame. I love Rowan. I have loved
him from the moment I met him, the day he saved my life
in Marseilles."

Charlotte breathed a long sigh. She supposed she had
known it all along, but there it was—out in the open.

"It need not concern you, madame. It was all over
between Rowan and me a long time ago." A shadow of
such hunger passed over her eyes at that moment that
Charlotte thought with sudden compassion, *But for you it
will never be over, will it, Annette?*

"You would do anything for him, wouldn't you, Annette?" she asked softly.

"I *have done* anything for him, madame," was Annette's
sad admission. "And yes, I would again."

"You are a loyal friend, Annette." Charlotte leaned forward. "Rowan does not know it yet, of course, but we are
to have a child."

There was a look of sudden raw envy on Annette's face.
It was swiftly gone. "I am glad for you both, madame. But
as for me, I must not remain in Lisbon. I have booked
your passage, madame, on the *Cormorant*, and I have
brought you a cloak so that you may leave the inn by night
and go aboard. Rowan would not wish you to be followed."

Again that shadow of danger that seemed to follow Rowan
wherever he went.

"Thank you, Annette," said Charlotte. And that night,
when, muffled in a long dark cloak at the Lisbon docks,
she was about to go aboard the London-bound merchantman *Cormorant*, she turned impulsively to Annette. "Will
we see you in London? You are always welcome."

Annette shook her head.

"No, madame," she said in a low voice. "I think I am
leaving Rowan's life now. We will go our separate ways. I
am for Paris, where I will probably open up a millinery

establishment, for I am tired of dressing hair. And perhaps now that he is to have a family, Rowan's life will take some other direction. I wish you well, madame."

"And you too, Annette," said Charlotte warmly. "I thank you for all you have done for Rowan—for all you have done for us both."

"Just one thing." Annette's voice had changed slightly, and Charlotte, about to leave, turned back. *"Make him happy."* There was a warning note in the words.

"I will try." Charlotte smiled at her.

Then Annette was gone in the darkness. Charlotte stood looking after her with a brisk wind blowing her golden hair—the same brisk wind that would fill the *Cormorant's* sails and carry her back to England. She doubted she would ever see Annette Flambord again.

20

London, England, Autumn 1732

London was not at all what Charlotte had expected.

The voyage home to England had seemed interminable, enlivened only by the merry conversation of a quartet of Cambridge students who had been summer tourists in Portugal and were now wending their way home, late, browned by the hot Portuguese sun, and bursting to tell her—and anybody else who would listen—about their travels, their first abroad. In her worry over Rowan and her pregnancy—thank God she didn't yet show!—Charlotte had speculated very little about what her own country's capital would be like, and London burst upon her as a complete surprise.

After Lisbon, with its pink palaces and pastel-painted houses and gaily tiled fountains, it was like going from summer directly into winter, and Charlotte felt the change long before the Tower of London or the Houses of Parliament rose up before her.

Here was a cold gray city of commerce, shrouded in fog, swept by the winds of autumn—a center of trade. Here there was no great inpouring of diamonds and gold from rich colonies overseas. Here apprentices thronged and men went about their business in a businesslike way. Nor was the Thames like the Tagus with its colorful lateen-sailed *fragatas*—here sober river barges and stately ships rode at anchor or moved upriver past the dangerous currents at London Bridge.

If Lisbon was a city of coaches, London was a city of hackneys and Charlotte—with the Cambridge students calling hearty good-byes—took one of those hired hacks to the Gray Goose Inn in Southwark, the inn Annette had told her Rowan had designated.

Although she had not expected to be met at the ship, sailing dates being uncertain and the *Cormorant* having arrived unexpectedly early, it was daunting to alight from her hack at the Gray Goose Inn and to find no word left for her.

"Who did you say is expecting you?" demanded the innkeeper, a slight swarthy man whose cold eyes Charlotte did not entirely like.

"Rowan Keynes," said Charlotte anxiously. "Do you know him?"

The swarthy innkeeper grunted. Whether that grunt meant yes or no, Charlotte could not tell. "Wait here," he told her, indicating with a sweep of his arm the common room. "I will see what I can find out."

With her baggage piled about her, Charlotte sat for a good two hours before the innkeeper bustled up with a hard-faced giant of a man dressed in rusty brown, who he told her was Yates, Mr. Keynes' man.

Yates had nothing at all to say for himself. He looked Charlotte up and down, his pale eyes expressionless, and silently carried her baggage outside to a small dark leathern coach. And in that coach she rode to Grosvenor Square and alighted at number forty-three. Its plain facade told her nothing, and Rowan was not at home.

"When will my husband be back?" she asked Yates.

He only shrugged. "Ye're early," he grunted, as if that explained everything, and set her luggage down near the front door, as if it might not stay.

Charlotte took a deep breath. This giant with his lowering expression and large hands and feet was only Rowan's "man"—he must not be allowed to intimidate her.

"Yates," she said in a voice of authority, "you may take

my bags upstairs. I am sure Rowan must have had a bedchamber prepared for me. If not, I will select one."

Yates gave her a sharp look, but without comment he carried her bags up the stairs and opened the door of one of the two front bedrooms, set down her bags, and departed.

Charlotte looked about her. What she had seen of the downstairs had had a rich, luxuriant look and was very tasteful—walls and wainscoting in muted tones, rugs from the Orient, handsome paintings. This room had the look of being freshly done and waiting for its occupant. There were no small possessions, no personal objects. Even the walls were bare of pictures, as if those too would be brought in. The armoire in the adjoining green dressing room was bare of clothing. And the colors startled her: the obviously new bedroom draperies and coverlet were of a brilliant crimson, the Oriental rug beneath her feet a darker crimson—hardly *her* colors.

And then she saw it, what she had overlooked in scanning her new domain: a large K was embroidered into the red satin coverlet and a smaller K had been embroidered into the corners of the rich damask draperies that reached the floor.

These were Katherine's colors, this flamboyant red room and that vivid green dressing room. Katherine had probably selected everything in it.

Charlotte sat down on the bed, feeling suddenly depressed. Rowan had redecorated for his late betrothed but he had not bothered to redecorate for his bride. Perhaps he had not wanted even to enter this bedchamber where he had meant to bring Katherine. It brought back to her sharply those last troubled days in Lisbon before Rowan rode away in the night to Evora.

Well, there was no use moping here. Briskly she got up and prowled about, surveying the house. The furnishings were handsome and elegant—all chosen by Rowan, she had no doubt, for his taste was impeccable. His bedchamber she did not see, for his door was locked, and so were the desk and most of the cupboards downstairs. She did find a rather daunting array of sword canes in a dark corner, and there were matched dueling pistols in a drawer of the library table—but those were understandable enough in a day when gentlemen warred politely with one another and beat off footpads who sprang from dark alleys.

She would have liked to question the servants, but all of them appeared to be out, although there was a savory pot of stew simmering in the kitchen. She wondered if taciturn Yates had prepared it.

She was wondering uncertainly whether she should eat a bowl of the souplike stew when she heard the front door open. She hurried toward the sound and met Rowan, looking travel-stained and tired, just coming into the house.

He stopped in surprise at the sight of her.

"Charlotte! But you were not due until next week!"

"I know, but we had favorable winds." She felt suddenly shy with him; it had been a long time since she had seen him.

"Have you eaten?" And when she shook her head, "Well, I will take you out to dinner and you can tell me all about it."

"Wait, I will get my hat," said Charlotte breathlessly. By the time she was back downstairs, she realized that he was slipping back into her life as if he had never been gone. His greeting had been easy, almost casual, as if they had been separated for hours instead of for long weeks.

"Why did Annette tell me to meet you at the Gray Goose Inn instead of at your home in Grosvenor Square?" wondered Charlotte, when they were enjoying a candlelit dinner at one of the fashionable inns near Drury Lane.

Rowan, who between bites had been keeping up a running conversation on trivial matters, hesitated for a second, and shutters seemed to close down on his dark eyes, but his answer was glib enough. "I had promised the servants their holidays at this time and I had thought you and I might take a trip—I could show you the south of England as winter approaches. Unfortunately," he added with just the proper note of regret in his voice, "I find I am now too busy for that."

Charlotte could not fault his answer, but she had a deep feeling that it was not the truth.

Later, when he took her home and she threw open the

door to the red bedchamber that had so obviously been prepared for Katherine, Rowan drew in a harsh breath.

"I had meant to have all this stuff cleared out," he said frankly. "And *would* have, before you arrived, had your ship not made port early. You shall select for yourself the hangings and furnishings for this room."

Perhaps this was the right moment . . .

Charlotte gave him her most winsome smile. "It would be much nicer to make my own selection," she admitted. And then, ruefully, "I might have managed staying here with all these K's without complaint, but it would be hard to bear my baby beneath a coverlet lavished with another woman's initial!"

She had Rowan's full attention now! "A child?" he murmured, almost unbelievingly.

"Yes, Rowan. *Our* child. In the spring." For whether the baby was Tom's or Rowan's, Charlotte felt she must brazen it out so that her baby would be certain of acceptance, so it would have a father's love and protection.

"Our child. . . ." She could not tell whether he was pleased or not. Suddenly he laughed. "I will be honest with you. I have never given much thought to becoming a father." He looked about him with distaste. "You shall not spend your first night here in a room that bears another woman's stamp. You shall sleep in my room, with me."

They were over that hurdle; Rowan had asked no questions about *when* in the spring. Charlotte felt almost dizzy with relief. She accompanied Rowan into his bedchamber, which was a room that puzzled her. That he kept it locked she already knew, for he had to insert a key into the lock to open it now. The furnishings were handsome, but while those downstairs were exquisite with a French elegance, these were heavier, sturdier, the four-poster canopied and of solid oak, the chests and cupboards looking formidably strong, and . . . Could that be a rope ladder casually attached to a solid metal ring at one of the front windows? What earthly purpose could it serve there unless . . . unless Rowan thought the day might come when armed men would rush up these stairs and break down his bedchamber door, and he wanted a swift way out to the street?

She tore her eyes from the rope ladder and looked about her at the walls, all lined with maps.

"I see you prefer maps to family portraits," she said, smiling.

"Family portraits are for those who have ancestors," was his light rejoinder. "I am remarkably short on ancestors." She noted uneasily that he had crossed to the window and was unobtrusively kicking the rope ladder under the long cinnamon velvet draperies as he spoke.

That night he made love to her with a gentleness she had not known he possessed.

"My perfect woman . . ." he murmured, drinking in the perfume of her blonde hair as he buried his face in it. "And now you will bear me a son. . . ."

Or perhaps a daughter, thought Charlotte, but she did not voice it, for Rowan's new gentleness had given their lovemaking this night a wonderful dreamy quality and she did not want to break the spell.

But she slept only three nights in Rowan's room, for the very next morning Rowan had the red bedchamber and the green dressing room stripped. The red damask on the walls was replaced with delicate blue-and-white French wallpaper, the woodwork was painted a misty blue, and Charlotte was amazed to find that not only was the fragile French furniture she selected from a ship in the harbor whisked immediately in, but even the sky-blue silk draperies and blue silk coverlet were in place before the end of the week, and now her feet trod upon a blue-violet Chinese rug, flower-figured and so deep her feet sank into it. Where the crimson rug and the furniture that had formerly been in the room went, she did not know. She guessed that it had been sold. Anyway, like Katherine, it was gone, hopefully forever.

"I was lucky to get this house," Rowan told her. "They began the development of this six-acre tract here at Grosvenor Square seven years ago and built the east side first, with that large house with the pediment in the middle. On this side we've a jumble of houses, and the mansions about us went begging for a time because the wealthy were all building country houses. I didn't really want one of the big ones, too large for a bachelor, but this one is just right. And," he added proudly, "you'll be interested to learn it was the home of the Duchess of Kendal."

Charlotte gasped. "The Duchess of . . . You mean the Maypole?"

"She was the king's mistress," Rowan said stiffly.

"I know, but . . ." As a child growing up in the warm sea breezes of the Scilly Isles, Charlotte remembered her merry widowed mother, Cymbeline Vayle, laughing herself breathless over tales of German George I's strikingly homely German mistresses—the enormous uncorseted fat one that everyone surreptitiously called Elephant and Castle and the tall scrawny one they had dubbed the Maypole, with whom he had spent pleasant evenings cutting patterns out of paper. She had always thought those tales excruciatingly funny, but plainly her husband took a different view. "So it's a celebrated house," she managed in a somewhat muffled voice.

"In a small way, yes." The look of disapproval on Rowan's face was unmistakable. He took his royalty seriously, she saw—at least German George.

"What did you think of him?" she ventured. "German George."

"I thought he was what England needed at the time," he said heavily, closing the subject.

She realized she had made him angry and launched immediately into engaging tales of her explorations with the Milroyds of the environs of Lisbon, which brought him back into a good humor.

"They were very good to me. I should like to write and ask them to visit us," she finished.

To her surprise, Rowan shook his head. "They were well enough in Portugal," he said with a dismissing shrug. "And they were people I could leave you with. But here in London they would be no asset."

He uses people, she thought. And realized guiltily that in a way *she* was using *him* as well, for the child she carried might not be Rowan's. *And suppose it looked like Tom?*

With that in mind she began a careful campaign.

"I have often regretted my coloring," she told him as they shopped for clothes for her—for she would be needing things soon with waistlines that could be let out.

"*I* regard your coloring as perfect," he said, cocking an eyebrow at her. "In what way would you have it changed?"

"My mother's hair was so much lighter—white as moonbeams, and it glittered in the sun. I used to long for hair like that." She sighed. "And my father had wonderful green eyes, so clear. While *I* ended up with this sort of murky violet."

"Clear violet," he corrected.

"Very well then, clear violet—but I'd much rather have had green." She brightened. "Perhaps the baby will."

In point of fact her mother's hair had been darker than hers and her father's eyes a vivid blue—but then, there were no portraits left of either of them; Uncle Russ had sold them off along with the rest of the furnishings long ago in the Scillies, so Rowan would have no way of knowing.

She felt reassured when Rowan said mildly, "If 'tis a girl, I'd hope she would have your coloring, but we'll take what we get." He grinned. "Just so she doesn't look like Russ!"

"God grant I never see his face again!" exclaimed Charlotte violently.

But she did—the very next night.

It was a bad day for both of them. Morning sickness had struck Charlotte at breakfast and left her feeling shaky. But the weather was perfect, brisk and sunny, and Rowan had insisted on a drive through the park in an open carriage "because a breath of the outdoors would do you good, and besides, I want to show you off in that new lettuce-green gown I just bought you."

When he put it that way, Charlotte could only give him a wan smile and agree. After all, she would soon be so thick around the middle that Rowan might not care to take her out to "show her off."

They had gone scarcely three blocks before they were hailed by two young men who zigzagged excitedly through the traffic to come up beside their carriage. Laughing, Charlotte introduced two of the Cambridge students who had brightened her voyage home.

As she leaned back to wave good-bye to them, Rowan spoke through tight lips. "It would seem you made the most of your voyage from Portugal."

The words struck Charlotte like a slap, and one look at his hard expression told her he imagined the worst.

"It was a lonely voyage," she sighed. "I was grateful to them for making it bearable. They were merry and always joking."

"And so good-looking," he added cuttingly.

"Really?" Charlotte sank deeper into gloom. "I hadn't noticed."

Rowan gave her a sharp look and she faced him squarely. "Rowan," she said, "I have done nothing to . . ." Suddenly her voice faded away, for a woman was just passing in a carriage, a dark-haired woman in crimson velvet. "Oh, dear, isn't that . . . ?"

Rowan followed her gaze and turned a quizzical look upon her. But Charlotte now saw that the woman was a stranger.

"I'm sorry," she said. "I thought it was someone else."

"You thought it was Katherine." He sounded amused.

"Yes."

"Well, you can set your mind at ease. Katherine is nowhere hereabouts. I am told she is somewhere in the wilds of Dorset, arrayed in widow's weeds and trying to persuade her late in-laws to give her an allowance."

Charlotte shivered at his cold amusement. *Did Rowan never forgive anyone? Surely—whatever she had done—Katherine had suffered enough. He didn't need to gloat.*

The two incidents, small though they were, spoiled her day. When they came back, after dining out in one of Rowan's favorite places, she said she didn't feel well and would go right to bed. Rowan said he would be up shortly.

She had changed into a dark blue velvet dressing gown and was poking up the fire, for the night was cool, when she heard the metallic clang of the front door knocker. It was late to receive guests. Curious, she drifted down the hall to the head of the stairs, still holding the poker. The sight below made her grip the poker's brass handle until her knuckles were white.

In the hallway below, confronting Rowan, who had gone to the door, and looking as if he had just been blown in by the wind on this harsh autumn night, stood her guardian. Feet planted broadly apart, he stood there in his brown coat looking surly—he also looked somewhat unkempt, but in the shock of seeing him, Charlotte didn't notice that. It was his words that froze her where she stood.

" 'Tis about time you got back," he was snarling at Rowan. "I've been hiding out from my creditors waiting for you to pay this note of hand you signed!" He waved a paper in Rowan's face. "Honor it, man—or d'you think I'd not use it against you in a court of law?"

"I don't doubt you would," was Rowan's cold rejoinder. "But I've since had Charlotte's affairs looked into, and it would seem she was left a fair sum by her mother—money you squandered!"

Even at the head of the stairs Charlotte could hear her uncle draw in his breath with a hiss.

"You dare—" he began.

"Oh, yes, I dare," cut in Rowan's bored voice. "But I'm a reasonable man. That's a large sum I promised you there." He inclined his head curtly toward the parchment in his adversary's hand. "But since you won't want countercharges of misappropriation of your ward's fortune brought against you, I'm prepared to settle for half—enough to pay off your gambling debts. And the rest of the deal still stands."

"The devil you say! I'll collect on this in full or have the bailiff here tomorrow!"

"And find me gone." Rowan smiled. "And by then your creditors will have found you, for I'll see to that. And there'll be charges and countercharges while you languish in debtors' prison."

"The charge should be murder!" Charlotte's voice rang out from the head of the stairs. Below her in the hall, looking up at her in surprise, was Tom's murderer. A man who had stolen her fortune, killed her lover, and tried to sell her in marriage!

Without conscious volition, without even being aware that she was doing it, she threw the poker like a spear. Down the stairwell it shot, whizzing past the chandelier to strike through the stiffened skirts of her uncle's coat and pin him—unhurt but frightened—to the heavy panels of the front door.

Rowan shot a look upward at his lady. She stood like an avenging angel, he thought, leaning over the stair railing as if she would fly down on dark velvet wings and tear at Russ with her talons. A wistful look passed fleetingly across his hard features—he was wishing her violent action might have been on *his* behalf, and not another man's. Still, he turned in amusement to Russ, ashen-faced at his narrow escape and struggling to remove the poker from his coat.

"Knowing how she feels about you, d'you want her back?" he mocked.

"A hellcat she is, like her mother before her!" yowled Russ, his voice cracking in rage and fear at his narrow escape.

"So we've a deal, then? You don't wish her back? I'll meet you on Fleet Street tomorrow—at Child's." Rowan saw that Russ had torn the poker free from his coat and flung it down, and he threw open the door to let him out. "Be glad her aim was not as good as her intentions, Russ," Rowan said with a chuckle.

"But if I see you in this house again," Charlotte leaned over the second-floor railing to warn Russ, "*my aim will be better!*"

Russ made his escape gibbering, and Rowan closed and locked the door behind him. He looked upward, but Charlotte had disappeared, gone back to her room—perhaps to weep, perhaps to shudder that she had nearly killed a man, perhaps to stalk about in rage that her aim had not been better, that the poker had not found Russ's flesh. Rowan was not sure which it would be with his wild Lake Country wench, but he understood violence, and his heart had known a kindling sympathy when she had thrown the poker like a spear. For some odd reason, he felt closer to her at that moment than he had ever felt before.

And because he respected her action and how she must feel, he left her to her own devices and repaired to his room without disturbing her that night.

In her bedchamber Charlotte was standing before the window in the dark. She was shaking. Just now, when her guardian had looked up, she had seen him, not as he stood quarreling with Rowan, but killing Tom. And instantly she had hurled the poker. She had come near to killing a man tonight. The thought made her feel suddenly weak.

In the days to come, Charlotte learned much—mainly by inference—of what occupied her husband with odd visitors and at odd hours. Robert Walpole, who had resumed the post of First Lord of the Treasury in 1721, and whose power far exceeded that of the king, was determined to hold England on a course of peace and prosperity —and was willing to meet the demands of corrupt parliamentary politicians to do it. "Every man has his price," was Walpole's cynical and outspoken belief, and he employed the services—at whatever price required—of those skillful enough and able enough to effect his new designs, which included intricate intrigues in Europe, where wars were always breaking out.

Rowan—who had not, she had by now learned, any great fortune, despite his extravagant manner of living— was one of these men. He was sent on mysterious missions, sometimes to Europe—and came back enriched; Charlotte learned not to ask why, or what he had done to deserve his new wealth.

The only time she asked him was one evening in the dining room. Rowan had a glass of ruby port in his hand and he looked across it with deliberation at his earnest young wife before answering her, all the while keeping her under the scrutiny of those intense brooding dark eyes.

"You might say that I am a creature of the First Lord," he told her dispassionately. "Walpole considers me mad— but extraordinarily useful. In truth, I suppose I am an Arranger—I arrange for those to meet who cannot meet and perhaps should not meet, I arrange for secret talks and negotiations which ambassadors must keep clear of. I find people who cannot be found. I bring messages and receive information and sometimes pass on large sums of money."

"You are a spy."

He sighed. "No, I am much more. Sometimes I even make things happen." He touched his sword significantly.

Charlotte stared at that sword. "You are an assassin?" she breathed.

"An ugly word." He tossed off his drink and waved his hand carelessly. "Let us say that when I am presented with a problem by the First Lord, I assess what is best to be done to correct the situation."

"You are a statesman," she amended, fascinated.

He gave her a droll look. "Occasionally—and more. When I have decided how best to gain an objective, I carry it out with dispatch. At whatever cost." It was tempting to brag before this beautiful woman whose clear honest gaze was so puzzled. "The rewards are phenomenal," he added dryly, and then his gaze hardened. "You will never mention to anyone this conversation between us."

"No, never," she murmured, looking down into her glass.

"You will forget what I have said. It is a side of my life about which you need know nothing. It need not concern you."

And she had to be content with that. But when she saw flickering candlelight coming through to her bedchamber from the dark hall outside and heard footsteps and then saw the light fading away, she came to realize that it meant that Yates had rushed upstairs to wake Rowan in the bedchamber next door and that Rowan had slipped away downstairs to meet some furtive messenger, or perhaps to accompany him into the dark byways of London. Sometimes he was gone all night, sometimes longer. He never mentioned where he had been or that he had been gone at all. She was expected to accept his comings and goings without interest, as normal. That too was hard to do.

I loved a man who had come from a wicked life and sought an honest one, she thought wryly. *And now I am half in love with a man who came from an honest life and prefers to seek a wicked one.* It was a strange realization for the lighthearted girl from the flowering Scilly Isles to come to. And she thought on it soberly, remembering Tom's willingness to help another creature—once he had winced from an old leg injury and told her he had gained it from trying to save another man who was falling from the rigging, and both had crashed to the deck together—was that not why he had torn his leg falling from the rigging, to help someone else? Was that not why he had been kicked over a cliff, trying to save her? Just as the shining qualities she had seen in Tom had brought him to his death, so Rowan's single-purposed violence—despite all his self-evident brilliance—would one day bring him down.

She supposed there was no way to stop it. Not Tom, not herself, not Rowan—no one could be saved from the onrushing winds of fate.

She wondered suddenly what would be *her* fate—and found no answer.

21

Just before Christmas they received word of Russ's death. He had left a gaming hall drunk and sodden, fallen off his horse in the darkness, and frozen to death in an icy alley. When he was found the next morning his purse was gone, along with his hat and his coat and his boots. The thieves that had left him unprotected against the bitter weather were long gone.

Yates brought them the news as they sat at the breakfast table. Charlotte was wearing a shawl, for despite the fire, drafts crept in from the cold hall and the room was cold. Outside, through the windows they could see sleet beating down on streets still iced and slippery from last week's storm. The kind of weather that men shivered in—and sometimes died in.

"I will not mourn him," Charlotte said through her teeth when she heard. "I shall wear no black, no mourning ring. Nor will I alter one whit our Christmas festivities!"

Rowan was amused. "Not a hypocrite, at least," was his comment. "Although it might be more politic to do so. Russ's friends will be shocked to hear of your hard heart." He chuckled.

"He was an evil man. You know. You told him to his face that he had stolen my fortune."

"A guess only," he told her blandly. "I had not enough money at that moment to pay off the note of hand he brought. Luckily, my wild stab struck home."

Charlotte caught her breath. Rowan could always surprise her. "With my own eyes I saw him do murder!" she flashed. "He kept me in rags, he tried to force me into a frightful marriage. I will not pretend to grieve—indeed I should celebrate!"

In her fury she had risen to her feet, almost knocking over her chair. And now Rowan came around the table and took her by the arms, laughing down at her. "No matter," he said. "We will have the body sent back to Aldershot Grange for interment in the family plot. I will announce that that was Russ's wish. In your condition, you will not be expected to travel so far."

"Nor will I wear mourning nor drape the house in black!"

He shrugged. "I will say that black frightens you because of your impending confinement. I myself will wear a black band on my sleeve to show proper respect."

"Ha!" said Charlotte bitterly. She pulled away from Rowan and paced around the room, breathing hard as she remembered her uncle's perfidy.

"I will also say that he has left Aldershot Grange to you."

"To me?" Charlotte stopped pacing indignantly at her husband's smooth words. "Indeed he would not! I am convinced he hated me—or at the very least despised me as being beneath notice."

"I bought Aldershot Grange from Russ," explained Rowan. "And then gave him back a life tenancy." He laughed wryly. "Which I did not expect to be of such short duration."

"Why . . . why did you do that?" she faltered. "Why did you buy Aldershot Grange?"

His dark gaze was unfathomable. "It was a condition of our marriage."

"Then . . . then you had no need to fear pursuit when we fled to Scotland and were wed at the smithy?"

"No need at all," was his cool reply. "It had all been arranged while you lay swooning."

Charlotte took an involuntary step backward. Rowan had betrayed her! His "note of hand" had not been given to Russ for some gaming debt, as she had thought, but for *her*! Rowan had bought her from her uncle just as surely as Pimmerston was going to!

Fury swept over her. "Then you lied to me!" she accused. "For at the time you said—"

"I lied to gain a wife," he cut in. "A beautiful one that I cherish. Had I not made the deal that night on Kenlock Crag, Russ would have tried to palm you off on Pimmerston anyway. Would you have preferred that, Charlotte?" His voice sharpened.

Charlotte hardly heard him. Her blood sang in her ears. She was overcome by a wild desire to fling something at this man who had tricked her into marriage, and then to storm out of his house forever. She was about to turn on her heel and make for the door when sanity returned. Cold and merciless.

Things were different now. She was pregnant . . . there was her unborn child to think about.

She closed her eyes to shut out the sight of Rowan standing before her. But his voice still beat at her. "Would you have preferred Pimmerston, Charlotte?" he demanded savagely.

Trembling, Charlotte remembered Russ's cold promise to Lord Pimmerston that if she turned out not to be a virgin, he would himself make Pimmerston a widower. A shudder went through her slender frame. Very possibly Rowan, "the Arranger," as he styled himself, had saved her life by "arranging" to buy Aldershot Grange. She could see that Rowan might prefer that fact not to come out—it would make them the talk of London and cast doubt on her "inheritance."

"No," she admitted in a muffled voice, "I would not have preferred Pimmerston."

"Look at me when you speak to me."

Charlotte opened her eyes. Rowan was regarding her stonily. She realized in panic that she must not be cast out, she must get along with this man—whatever she now thought about him.

"I am sorry, Rowan," she mumbled, trying to force sincerity into the words. "I did not think. I . . . I had forgotten about Pimmerston."

"No, you did not think." His voice grew suddenly tender, indulgent. "Perhaps that is what so charms me about you, Charlotte. You throw yourself fiercely into the fray, no matter what the cost. It is a laudable but"—he sighed— "perhaps an unlucky trait, and one which I hope you will not pass on to our son."

Charlotte felt drained. "How do you know it will be a son?" she asked dully.

"I spoke in jest. Indeed I do not care whether you bear me a son or a daughter—I would welcome either one."

And he must keep on thinking that. . . . With an effort, Charlotte managed a wan smile. "I will at least stay close to the house," she promised, "and in that way not shame you for my lack of respect for my uncle's passing."

"It would be wise for you to do so anyway in this bitter weather," he counseled. "Those who venture out invite frostbite."

So their Christmas was celebrated snugly there in the house in Grosvenor Square that had once sheltered a king's mistress. They ate roast goose stuffed with chestnuts, and a blazing plum pudding, and toasted each other with eggnog and smuggled brandy—for England was still groaning under the heavy excise tax. Nobody came to call, and Charlotte was not surprised, for she had already learned that Rowan's "profession," if one could call it that, did not fit in with the kind of warm friendships that had people running in and out of the house at all hours. They did go out during the Twelve Days of Christmas—to music halls, to plays, to dine at inns. They shared in the gaiety of public places, laughed with strangers—but Charlotte could not but feel a pang when she saw parties of revelers laughing and calling out to each other as they trudged by on foot or dashed by in sleighs. And once or twice her violet eyes filled with tears when she heard the sound of Christmas carolers and remembered how in the Scillies her hospitable mother had always invited the carolers in for tea or hot chocolate—a practice that Rowan deplored.

"We will not fill up the house with strangers," he told her firmly, intercepting her as she was about to open the front door.

"But, Rowan, the carolers are outside, and cold. They—"

"No. We do not know who they are." He shot the bolt so hard that it made a noise the carolers must have heard and wondered about.

Charlotte turned away confused and feeling depressed.

"Cheer up," he said. "We will attend a play for Twelfth Night."

Charlotte forbore saying she would rather have opened up their doors to the world and invited the carolers in.

Since Rowan never chose to introduce her to anyone (she had decided that the set he had belonged to in London must be made up entirely of gamesters he did not particularly want his wife to meet), she found herself entirely dependent upon him for companionship, and it was a blow when he told her he would be taking a trip right after Twelfth Night.

"Will you be gone long?" she asked forlornly, for she knew these last three months of her pregnancy would find her far less mobile and it would be depressing without him.

"I don't know," he said. "But you will be all right. Yates will take care of you. If you are asked, say that I have gone north—to Aldershot Grange."

She looked up quickly. "Will you sell the property now?"

"No," he said surprisingly. "I intend to keep it."

But perhaps that too fit into the plans of one who made hurried secret journeys in and out of the country, she decided. Rowan could disappear from London at any time on the pretext of visiting his "north-country estate," and who would make that long trek to check up and find out if that were true? Indeed he could *go* to Aldershot Grange and have Livesay announce to all and sundry that he was ill and keeping to his room—and actually be off to Europe on some mission for the First Lord.

She wondered suddenly if she would ever see the north country again.

Rowan departed into a cold gray dawn right after Twelfth Night, and Charlotte was left to cope. And that wasn't easy.

Indeed she was entirely baffled by Rowan's household—both by its lopsided opulence and by all the things it seemed she was not to change. Of the servants, only Yates, the butler, and Clover, the cook, lived in. Clover was a picturesque woman, plump and ruddy-cheeked and taffy-haired and with a warm sunny smile. She was a mute as the result of some childhood accident and could neither read nor write, but she was quick and clever and understood orders well.

The giant Yates, she knew, she would never like. She found him taciturn, answering questions in monosyllables, and she did not like the way he looked at her—with only half-concealed distaste, as if he did not approve his master's choice of brides. Yates never changed, nor did relations between them ever improve. He was loyal to Rowan only—Charlotte was not included. Yates hired the servants—Rowan had told her she was not to interfere in that. And he kept them in awe. He hovered over the chambermaids and scullery maids, a changing group who came in only by day, until they scurried away. And if he found any of them chatting with the mistress of the house, they were promptly dismissed.

Charlotte found it hard living there on Grosvenor Square, for she had practically no communication whatever with other human beings: Cook couldn't talk, Yates wouldn't talk, and the chambermaids were afraid to talk. On the several occasions she tried to strike up conversations with them, they seemed very subdued, and melted away at Yates' approach.

"Yates frightens people," she had once complained to Rowan. "He's so huge and his manner is so menacing."

Rowan had cocked a sardonic eye at her. "That too has its uses," he had told her cryptically.

But useful or no, Charlotte found life cooped up in a household that went silent at her approach unbearable, and sometimes—despite the weather and her advanced pregnancy—she ventured out on chilly wind-buffeted walks around the square.

On a late-February day, feeling desperate after being

housebound by terrible weather for a fortnight, she decided to go still farther.

"Yates." She caught up with the giant in the lower hall. "Please have the coach brought round. I'm going shopping. You can take me to Cheapside and I'll take a hackney back when I've finished."

Yates looked as if he might say no. He eyed her thickening figure warily. " 'Tis icy," he demurred. "The master wouldn't—"

"The master is not here, Yates. *I* am in charge." And when still he hesitated, "If you do not bring the coach at once, I shall have one of the chambermaids find me a hackney coach."

Yates shrugged and soon their coach was making good time toward Cheapside, considering the icy roads, the traffic, and the insolent sedan-chair men who were supposed to keep to the center of the road but seldom did. Charlotte could hear one of them swearing at Yates in an angry Irish brogue as they rounded the imposing domed pile of St. Paul's Cathedral. She was surprised when he let her off without a murmur.

The weather had turned warmer, and despite the hazard of melting ice underfoot, Charlotte was enjoying her walk and the crowds. She had never really intended to go shopping—indeed she had no desire to carry packages, she felt heavy enough already, but she wanted to be out in the bracing air. She strolled along admiring the big iron-framed signs that protruded out over the street on long brackets. Even more she enjoyed the carved wooden or molded ironwork that identified the kind of shop: three hats to signify a hatter, three sugar loaves to designate a grocer, three great golden balls to identify a goldsmith. As the afternoon wore on, the wind came up, whipping through the crowded streets, loosening the roof tiles, one of which rattled down upon the icy cobbles nearby, causing passersby to jump nimbly away.

Charlotte was about to signal a hackney coach to take her back to Grosvenor Square when above her there was a cracking noise, then a sharp cry of "Look out!" and she was abruptly seized from behind and jerked backward off her feet by a strong arm—just as a huge iron-framed sign commemorating a chocolate shop, and thick as a paving stone, crashed to the street where she had been standing a moment before.

A crowd gathered instantly, some claiming they had been injured by flying debris as the sign broke up on the icy cobbles, and the chocolate shop's owner rushed out to survey the damage. But Charlotte, gasping over her narrow escape, was suddenly aware that even though the wind was sweeping under her skirts and trying its best to tear her velvet hat from her head, she was resting in a pair of most reassuring arms and a pleasant square-cut masculine face lit by warm intelligent brown eyes was looking down into hers with concern.

"Are you hurt?" he demanded. And when Charlotte shook her head, "You should not be out in this weather in your condition."

"I think you are right," Charlotte said shakily, gaining her feet again with his assistance and finding that she was trembling. "You have saved my life, sir, and I do thank you."

"You are very pale," he observed. "I think a cup of hot chocolate might restore you."

He led her into the now empty shop, for curiosity had driven the patrons into the street. But the cold wind soon drove them back again, and Charlotte, seated across from her tall savior, was glad to be in a room full of people, buzzing with conversation. As she felt the warmth of the hot chocolate bringing life to her cold limbs, she smiled at him, and it occurred to her that he looked vaguely familiar.

"I am glad you came along when you did, else I might at this moment lie crushed beneath that large sign out there," she told him ruefully. She was assessing him as he spoke: strong, masterful, about Rowan's age, and dressed as a gentleman in olive velvet lightly accented with gold embroidery and gold buttons.

From across the table he was peering at her keenly. "I believe I know you," he murmured. "You are Rowan Keynes' wife."

"Yes." Charlotte regarded him with interest. "Do you know my husband?"

He nodded. "Indeed I do. What is Keynes thinking of, letting you wander about in this weather unescorted?"

"Oh, he didn't know." Charlotte rose quickly to Rowan's defense.

"If you were mine," he said softly, "I would know where you were at all times—for you are such a lady as might be stolen away from a man."

Charlotte caught her breath. It was the first charming speech she had heard from a gentleman not her husband since her pregnancy had become noticeable. "I thought you looked familiar," she said. "Tell me, have we met?"

She was sure they had not, and he shook his head regretfully. "I have but admired you from a distance, I am afraid. Your husband is known to have a high temper and a jealous nature. Indeed, he holds his ladies as close as if they were in a seraglio," he added humorously.

"I am sure he did not hold Katherine that closely!" she said in a tart voice, for the idea of Katherine in a harem was ludicrous—she would break out!

"No, not Katherine," he mused.

So there had been other "ladies" in Rowan's life who had been held close. She wondered briefly who they were. Actresses from Drury Lane, dancers from the music halls perhaps?

"I have seen you walking about Grosvenor Square," he said. "I have rooms not far from there."

"So that is where I have seen you, walking about the square. You do not sound quite like a Londoner. Does your wife enjoy London?"

He smiled at the question. "I have no wife and you have a keen ear. I thought I had lost my West Country accent after all these years in London. But my time here may be fleeting. I have a sister in Kent who insists that I join her there until her first child is born, and a sister in Cornwall who insists that I return for her wedding, and a sister in Lincoln who insists that I come and make peace between her and her husband. As a man afflicted with too many sisters and afraid to make a choice, I remain skulking in London!"

Charlotte found herself laughing heartily for the first

time in weeks. By the time they had finished their second cup of chocolate, they were fast friends, she had learned that his name was Francis Tremont, and she had invited him to tea the next day.

He squired her home in a hackney coach, bowed deeply at her front door, and departed. He arrived early for tea the next day, his costume refurbished by a fancier cravat and a gold-headed cane—and he brought her a book to read. Charlotte seized on the book with delight—it was *The Fortunate Mistress*, by Daniel Defoe, who had died a year ago in his London lodgings with his last days shrouded in mystery. When two days later a dimpling Charlotte told Francis Tremont how much she had enjoyed the romantic entanglements of its heroine, Roxana, her newfound friend promptly returned with another picaresque novel by Mr. Defoe entitled *The Fortunes and Misfortunes of Moll Flanders*.

On learning that Rowan was away at their "north-country estate," Francis Tremont gallantly declared himself at Charlotte's service "to take her anywhere she wished to go." With the arrival of the baby just over two weeks away, Charlotte was not eager to go anywhere but to childbed to get it over with, but she forbore saying that.

Francis was interested in the house and she showed him about the downstairs, telling him the Duchess of Kendal had once lived here.

"The Maypole? Yes, I know. They tell me her bedchamber was a scandal—baroque and full of fripperies."

"That is Rowan's room now," she said, thinking how greatly changed it must be, stiff and masculine as it now appeared, with its sturdy furnishings.

His grin flashed. "Tell me," he asked conspiratorially, "could I see it?"

"He keeps it locked."

He laughed. "Oh, I might be able to manage that! I've a way with keys."

Charlotte laughed too, for his warm ingenuousness was catching. "I'm afraid I couldn't make the stairs again today," she admitted.

"Oh, well, perhaps another day," he said. "I should like to brag to my friends that I had seen the Maypole's bedchamber!"

He was very pleasant, she thought, full of light banter. He asked her occasional questions about Rowan, but not, she thought, too many. His behavior toward her was impeccable, although his merry eyes told her that *if* she were not far gone in pregnancy, *if* he were not Rowan's friend, he well might be romancing her. She found his company stimulating, for he was both knowledgeable and well-read and full of quips about London personages about whom Charlotte had heard. Francis Tremont, she realized, could easily become a habit.

She did not ask herself what Rowan would think about her entertaining one of his friends at tea so often while he was away. She also ignored the whispers and rolling eyes of the chambermaids and Yates' black looks and mutterings.

Her time was very near now. She lumbered about, despondent, wishing it was over. But when Francis Tremont dropped by for tea, she decided to make it downstairs— one more time.

He was at his best that day at tea. Resplendent in a new coat of mustard velvet that went well with his olive trousers, he insisted on showing her a new parlor game—and accidentally knocked over her teacup. When one of the chambermaids came in to sop up the tea from the rug, he told Charlotte, rather grandly, that he would pour her next cup himself—to make amends. And he did so, while Charlotte leaned over instructing the maidservant in the cleanup, because she was sure Rowan prized that rug.

She drank her new cup slowly, listening with fascination to some details of scandal at court, and suddenly felt dizzy. *It is the baby coming!* she thought in fright, and rose. "I must get to my room," she said abruptly. "I do not feel well."

Francis sprang forward, all solicitation. Charlotte took an unsteady step, her world turned black, and she keeled over in his arms.

He was halfway up the stairs, carrying her at a brisk clip, when Yates, who had been upstairs, dashed down with a roar and yowled for Cook. She came and held the unconscious Charlotte propped against her while Yates, who had seemingly turned into a wild man, all but pushed Francis Tremont out the front door. Then he got her upstairs and two chambermaids put her to bed.

But it turned out to be a false alarm. Charlotte woke groggily but her labor pains did not begin until the next day. They began insidiously, progressed to gritting-the-teeth-just-bearable, and moved on into a black agony that seemed never to end. Finally Charlotte brought into the world a daughter—a delightful, squirming little red-faced bundle who cried lustily and whom Charlotte clutched weakly to her bosom in a kind of joy she had not known existed.

That was a day when Francis Tremont was not received at tea. Indeed Yates shut the door in his face and informed him that the mistress of the house was upstairs producing an heir.

"You should not have any more children," the doctor advised her bluntly. "It is dangerous for you. And you must spend the next three weeks in bed—maybe more."

Charlotte, absorbed in this new and lovable creature in her arms, only nodded. She felt no disappointment at being told she should bear no more children. This one lovely child was surely enough for anyone.

"I shall name you Cassandra and hope that you will know more of the future than I," she whispered against the baby's smooth cheek.

Rowan came back the last of March. Charlotte, still in bed on doctor's orders, with some trepidation, heard him come bounding up the stairs, for by now she knew the truth. The baby's eyes held more than a hint of green and the feathery down on her head was almost as white as goose feathers—Cassandra was Tom's daughter, not Rowan's. Charlotte was glad that on this first meeting a wet nurse was suckling the child in the nursery.

She lay back against the pillows, making a lovely picture there. The rich glow of the firelight cast an orange glow over her soft peach velvet dressing gown and made fiery highlights race across her golden hair so that it seemed to smoulder.

"Yates tells me you have named our daughter Cassandra." Rowan, looking very fit, was pulling off his gauntleted riding gloves as he spoke. He had come leaping into the room, obviously dashing by Yates, and now his dark eyes lit up at the sight of Charlotte, looking so lovely there among the pillows. "For the woman who predicted the fall of Troy and was not believed, I take it?"

"Yes," said Charlotte soberly. "I hope that my daughter will read the future better than I ever did. How are you, Rowan?"

He laughed boyishly. "Never better. Where is she? I would see her."

"She is being fed—I have employed a wet nurse."

"Ah, very wise." He bent down and planted a kiss on the top of her white breast, pushing down the velvet dressing gown with his lips as he did so. "We will be able to go about more easily if you are not tied down by having to nurse the baby."

"Yes, I thought that would please you." She spoke mechanically, because she had dreaded this moment, lain awake at night worrying about it. Now she could hear the wet nurse's heavy footfall outside, and she steeled herself.

The plump wet nurse—a young farmgirl actually—brought the child in, smiling, and held her out for Rowan's inspection.

He looked down upon Cassandra with approval, touched her small face with a tentative finger—and was rewarded by a lusty wail.

"Strong lungs and a feisty temper." He chuckled.

"Yes, she is like you in that," Charlotte said, amazed at how readily sugared lies spilled off her tongue to protect that small helpless bundle held in the arms of the young wet nurse.

"And how are you?" he asked cheerfully. Plainly he had seen nothing wrong in the way the child looked.

"I am ordered to stay abed another week. The doctor warns me not to have another child. He says—"

"Oh, bother doctors." Rowan shrugged. "They are wrong as often as they are right." He watched with approval the graceful way she took the baby from the nurse's arms, the glow of happiness that made her lovely face even more beautiful.

He could not know how she was thanking God at that moment. Her prayers had been answered—Rowan had found nothing amiss.

He stayed with her all that evening, ignoring the prowling sounds Yates made downstairs. His latest venture—he did not say what venture or where—had been successful, very successful. They could afford a bigger house if she wanted one. Charlotte shook her head.

"Just so you are back safe," she said—and meant it.

Rowan smiled deep into her eyes. "Another week in bed?" he murmured.

"Yes, and the doctor warns me—"

"Not to have more children." He grinned. "Well, I'll let you get your sleep then." He left her and she heard him whistling as he unlocked the door to his bedchamber. Yates apparently had given up and gone to bed.

Charlotte closed her eyes in thankfulness that this day had ended well, and slept—right through breakfast.

After breakfast, Rowan thundered up to her room.

"I hear you have been entertaining Francis Tremont." His hard gaze raked her.

Yates had been talking to him!

"I thought he was your friend," she said in defense. "And he saved my life in Cheapside when a great sign crashed to the street directly where I'd been standing—it seemed little enough to offer him tea."

"What were you doing marching about the town alone?" he demanded.

"I couldn't stand it cooped up here alone with servants who won't talk to me," she cried in desperation. "And you have seen to it that we have no friends—at least none who come to the house."

The front door knocker sounded down below. Rowan looked thoughtful. "That will be . . ." He never finished telling her who it would be. "I must go out and I may be back rather late, so dine without me. We will speak of this later," he added grimly.

Charlotte got up and went to the window. Through the

panes she could see Rowan leaving—with Yates and another man. Alarmed by what she thought was his jealousy, she decided to dress and go downstairs. She was feeling stronger today, and since they could not make love just yet, she might be better able to win him over if she met him at the door looking her best. Rowan loved beauty—everything in this house told her that. And she certainly couldn't look beautiful with her hair tousled, lying in bed all day.

Right after the baby was born, Charlotte had used a trick her mother had told her about in the Scillies: she had taken a stack of linen squares and placed them over her stomach and bound them tightly to her body—despite the doctor's frown and mutterings about vanity. Not for her, a sagging stomach! Now, as she dressed she was glad she had done it, for her figure was almost as lissome as it had been when Rowan had carried her north to Scotland.

She chose a pale blue brocade gown delicately edged with silver—ah, that would catch the candlelight this evening! And swept her hair up and let it fall down fetchingly at the sides, with a pale blue satin riband. And went downstairs.

She had dressed swiftly so that if Rowan came back for something, he would find her dressed and looking lovely. Hardly had she reached the foot of the stairs before the door knocker sounded. Yates was not in, and none of the chambermaids appeared. Charlotte opened the front door herself.

Francis Tremont stood there smiling. He had a book in his hand.

"I thought you might like this." He held up the book. "It's all the rage—everyone's reading it."

Charlotte was caught in a dilemma. Every instinct warned her to snatch the book, mumble her thanks, and retreat, shutting the door in his face. But here was a man who had done no wrong, indeed a man who had saved her life—and helped her while away otherwise boring afternoons.

Ever reckless, Charlotte chose the dangerous path. She greeted Francis Tremont warmly. After all, what was the harm? Rowan was away, she could explain diplomatically that the baby was now taking all of her time—Francis would understand. And he would disappear pleasantly, regretfully from her life, and seek some other lustrous— and, one hoped, unmarried—lady. "Do come in, Francis," she said. "Can I offer you a cup of tea?"

He accepted with alacrity and Charlotte showed him into the drawing room and rang for tea. It was brought immediately and Charlotte poured them each a cup.

"As I came in I thought I saw one of the royal coaches just rounding the corner of the square," he said conversationally. "It should have just about reached the house by now."

"Oh, really?" Charlotte came to her feet. She had never seen either the royal coach or the royal family. She hurried to the window, stood peering out, while Tremont lingered by the teacups. "I don't see it," she reported in disappointment.

"It must have gone the other way, then," he said lightly. "But I am sure I saw it. Come back, your tea is getting cold."

Thus bidden, Charlotte returned to the tea table and sat down. Francis lifted his cup. "I will make you a toast in tea," he said humorously. "To royal coaches—even those that disappear!"

Charlotte laughed. Francis was always good company.

A cold voice from the door said, *"Don't drink that!"* And Charlotte turned in amazement to see Rowan standing in the doorway with Yates just behind him. They could not have come in by the front door—she would have heard them. They must then have gone round and crept in the back way! Across from her Francis Tremont had come to his feet.

"Exchange your cup with Tremont's," suggested her husband sardonically. *"Then* drink your toast to royal coaches."

Charlotte stared down into her untouched teacup. Wordlessly she proffered it to Francis. But he made no move to take it. Indeed he was already setting his cup back on the table. "I think I had best take my leave," he said jauntily. "It is good to see you again, Keynes."

"Is it indeed? Well, since you have been enjoying my hospitality these past weeks, the least you can do is drink the tea my wife proffers you!"

"Thank you," was the sunny answer. "But my presence here seems to be causing marital discord. I'll just make my way out, if you please—"

"I don't please." Rowan's tall figure blocked his way. His hand was resting on his sword. He looked formidable.

"Rowan," cried Charlotte. "Let him go!"

But even as she spoke, Francis Tremont's sword snaked out of its scabbard. "You're frightening your wife, Keynes," he said mildly.

"Perhaps she deserves a little fright," was the cold rejoinder.

"*Stop!*" wailed Charlotte.

"Yates," commanded Rowan, "ease around behind me and take my lady out. Then give us room."

Yates did as he was bidden and Charlotte in her nervousness dropped both teacup and saucer. The small crash on the floor went unnoticed by both men, who were now slowly circling each other.

She was already out in the hall when she heard the swords clash. She would have run back but that Yates held on to her, swearing under his breath. Inside the drawing room there was no conversation whatever—just the clash of steel on steel, the crash of chairs and tables being overturned, ornaments broken, the hard breathing of the participants, and an occasional light thump as one or the other leapt over some fallen object.

Those minutes spent in the hall with Yates were some of the longest in Charlotte's life.

It was quickly over.

"Yates," came Rowan's quiet voice. "Send someone to clean up this mess." He came out wiping blood from his blade on a kerchief.

"Oh, you haven't . . . you haven't . . ." Charlotte's voice quavered.

"No, I haven't killed him," said Rowan savagely. "But only because he pulled you from beneath a falling sign.

Patch him up, Yates, and then find a sedan chair and pack him home to his lodgings."

"What . . . what was in the cup?" whispered Charlotte. "Poison?"

Her husband gave her a scathing look as he shot his sword back into its scabbard. "The same sleeping draft he gave you earlier, probably. He'd watched and seen us leave and he was going to render you senseless while he searched the house."

"But why?"

Rowan ran a hand through his dark hair. "D'you not know the manner of man you have been entertaining?" he demanded, exasperated. "Francis Tremont is a well-known agent of the First Lord's enemies. He was using you to get access to this house, to learn about my movements. Good God, have I married a fool?"

Charlotte was too taken aback to answer. A moment later Rowan had slammed out—doubtless to meet the man who had come to the door earlier, and with whom he and Yates had left.

She felt she should go in and help Yates, but she was too unsteady on her feet. It had all crashed in on her, how it had really been. Of course Francis Tremont had looked familiar; he must have gone by the house many times—*stalking her*. And he had been able to save her life that day *because he had been following her*. The falling sign was just a piece of luck that had enabled him to strike up an acquaintance. Now she remembered his casual questions about Rowan—how pointed they now seemed. And he had tried to get upstairs—he had wanted to be shown the Maypole's room! A chill went through her that she had actually considered trying to show it to him! Oh, he had seemed so nice, so plausible, so *friendly*.

Now she saw why Rowan never brought people home with him, why he did not introduce her to people who would promptly come to call. He needed a hole to hide in, a place to catch his breath between his dangerous missions. This house on Grosvenor Square wasn't a home in the ordinary sense—it was a lair.

And that was something she had not fully understood.

Drained, she trudged upstairs and threw herself down upon the bed. After a while she got up and sought out the baby, held the child to her for a long time before giving her back to the young nurse to be fed. She wandered back into her bedchamber and sat there while darkness fell. A chambermaid knocked. Charlotte refused food. She had to think out her life, how it was going to be.

She could see there would be other days like this. She would make mistakes; the world was full of pitfalls for her. And Rowan, versed and hardened in his way of life, would not understand. He would never understand. She saw it all ahead of her, the silent households, the loneliness, the wondering, whenever Rowan went out, if he would ever return. . . . *She was not the woman for this kind of life*. The moon was up but Charlotte's head was sunk in her hands and hot tears spilled down over her young face.

"What, crying over Francis Tremont?" came Rowan's harsh voice.

In the bright moonlight Charlotte spun around. She had not heard the door open—and where had he learned to walk soft as a cat?

"No," she gasped. "I was crying for myself, for us, for this life we have to lead."

"It is this life that brings us that gown you are wearing." He had crossed over to her and now stood ruthlessly above her, studying her pale face that glistened with tears in the moonlight. "It is this life that brings us servants and a fine house and the freedom to travel. *Do you think that blasted fellow you ran away with could have given you a coach and six?*"

"I don't want a coach and six," said Charlotte bitterly. "I just want an ordinary life."

"With perhaps a silver spoon thrown in? Is that why you are sitting here mooning? Doubtless you'd have preferred some younger son like Tremont who may one day come into a barony if the dice fall right."

"No, I—"

His dark face was very near to hers. "You had your chance. *Why didn't you take Pimmerston?*"

"Oh, damn you!" wailed Charlotte. "Why didn't you keep Katherine? You'd have got on with her better!"

She could hear his teeth grate. "You came near to oversetting us this day. There were papers in my room that would have . . ." He seized her by the shoulders. *"Look at me when I'm talking to you!"*

"I don't want to look at you! I'm afraid of what I see!"

With an oath he spun her about. "Perhaps you'd prefer Tremont!" he ground out, and flung her across the bed.

A moment later he lay atop her.

"No!" cried Charlotte. "The doctor said—"

"Be damned to all doctors," he said thickly. "I've been away a long time—I deserve a homecoming." And he buried his face in the soft column of her throat.

She felt the roughness of his beard scratch her skin, for Rowan had a dark jawline and he had not shaved since morning.

"No!" she cried. "I won't." And with all her strength she began to fight him, clawing at his face, struggling, turning her head sharply away, trying to kick at him.

Her resistance seemed to madden Rowan. His hand cracked across her face, momentarily stunning her while he wrestled with his trousers.

Charlotte tried to scuttle away from him across the bed. "It's *too soon*, Rowan!" she wailed.

But he did not seem to hear. He was lost in lust for her, greedy for her body, deaf to her entreaties. He made no effort to arouse her—he thrust direct. Charlotte still struggled feebly, but it was no use, he would have his way with her this night whatever she said or did. His hard masculine body was savoring her sweetness—but vengefully, it seemed to her, without love. When she gasped in pain at the roughness of his handling, he seemed not to care. He was oblivious to the shudders that racked her body, for she was too proud to cry out. Indeed he seemed to take joy in hurting her, and after one last explosion of pain that left her weak, he surged away from her without a word and she heard the door to his room slam.

Charlotte lay sobbing upon the bed, too tired and mauled even to struggle up to see to the baby.

Morning brought a new shock.

Rowan appeared at her door. He looked hollow-eyed, forbidding.

"Get up," he commanded. "You are going north. To Aldershot Grange. You will barely have time for breakfast."

Charlotte sat up. There were dark circles of pain under her eyes, but her manner was defiant. "I will do no such thing!"

"If necessary I will drag you from that bed and send you north in your nightrail!" The words grated. "Now, rise and prepare for your journey."

"The baby is too young to travel. She—"

"Will stay here. The wet nurse can take care of her, and Cook has agreed to help."

Charlotte stared at him speechless. She leapt from the bed and tried to dart around him and run from the room. Rowan blocked her way.

"I have learned that I have to leave London again," he said menacingly. "And I will not leave you here to consort with such as Francis Tremont."

"Oh, but, Rowan—"

"The baby and I will join you in June—or July at the latest. Now *dress!*" He flung her away from him.

And so on a sparkling April day Charlotte found herself careening north in a locked coach from which she could not escape. She had tried to scream as she was bundled unceremoniously into it, and Rowan had clapped a hand over her mouth and promptly bound and gagged her. He had pulled down the leathern flaps over the coach windows and she heard him tell Yates that her bonds and gag were to be removed once they were well out of London and on the open road.

"My lady will be sensible then," he said warningly, turning to look at Charlotte.

Unable to speak, Charlotte had glared at him from the coach's dim interior, and struggled with her bonds.

Yates had laughed.

22

Aldershot Grange, Summer 1734

Aldershot Grange seemed much the same. Charlotte looked around her at the big gray stone house with its steep roof slates mirrored in the silvery Derwent Water and had the eerie feeling that she had never been away. Livesay was still there, and Cook—and Wend came running out when she saw who it was leaning out of the dark coach and waving.

They greeted her with tears of joy.

"We thought you'd never come back," Wend confided, cocking her head and adding, "You look awful."

"I'm sure I do, Wend," Charlotte sighed. She'd scarcely slept on the journey north, jolted and bruised and grieving for her child back in London and for all that would never be. Yates had kept up a grueling pace, and now he came down from the driver's seat, leering at Wend, who took a step backward away from him.

"This is Yates," Charlotte told them harshly. "He's my husband's manservant and he doubles as butler in our London house. But he won't be replacing you, Livesay. I'll see to that," she added with a vengeful look at Yates.

They had never heard her speak thus to an underling, and troubled looks were exchanged.

But Yates was not staying. He left the following morning. Charlotte was heartily glad. She hoped never to see the taciturn giant again.

Other things *had* changed around the Derwent Water: Lord Pimmerston was dead—the gallant's disease had not got him after all, he had succumbed to a stroke. His nephew who had inherited his lands and his title never came to Castle Stroud at all, Wend told her. The caretaker's joints were too old and creaky to allow him to care for the place properly. Once, passing by, Wend had seen bats flying out of a broken upstairs window.

Charlotte thought that was a shame, because Castle Stroud was the loveliest house she had ever seen.

Wend's family were all gone now. Her father and the younger children had been swept away by fever in the spring and her sister had shown up suddenly from nowhere and taken Wend's mother away to live with her in Lincolnshire, where she had married a draper.

Charlotte never quite forgave Rowan for sending her north in the manner he did, and when in June she realized reluctantly that she was pregnant again, she told herself fiercely that if she survived she would always consider this new baby the child of rape.

Rowan came north in July and brought with him Cassandra and a new wet nurse, who seemed to adore the baby. Charlotte gathered the child in her arms but gave Rowan a level look and turned away. She had thought long and hard these past months—and had liked nothing she saw in her future.

It was a stormy beginning to their life in the north of England.

Rowan had missed her. He had at last come to terms with her youth and inexperience and was eager to make amends.

"I was hard on you, Charlotte," he admitted when at last they were alone in the big square bedroom where she had spent so much of her youth.

"Yes. You were."

"But I will make it up to you."

"How?" she asked woodenly. "I am pregnant again, Rowan. A souvenir of our parting."

He was taken aback, and for once a guilty flush spread over his hard features. "I did not think that one night—"

"Oh, did you not? My mother told me that babies were easiest conceived right after birth and that it was a time to be careful. But did you care? No!"

"It is too late to say that I am sorry," he said gravely. "But at least I can make a better home for you and Cassandra."

Cassandra—*Tom's child*. Charlotte realized suddenly on what perilously thin ice she skated. If Rowan were to turn against Cassandra. . . .

"Yes," she said, turning away. "I am very tired, Rowan," she cast over her shoulder. "I had not recovered my strength before you sent me hurtling north. And now this new life within me needs all I can give it. I must rest. I will see you at dinner."

Frowning, he let her go. But in the days that followed, he proved that he meant what he said. He hired workmen, he made repairs, he had Aldershot Grange painted and refurbished until even Livesay looked dazed at the change in the place. He bought Livesay new livery, and a trim indigo costume with a white apron and white cap for Wend, whom he now styled as lady's maid to Charlotte. Wend was ecstatic.

"Me in these new clothes—and you in silks and satins!" she marveled. "It's a wonderful change, isn't it?"

Charlotte smiled at Wend and kept her own counsel. She'd have traded her silks and satins for homespun any day, could she just have turned back the clock.

Summer slipped into autumn and Rowan disappeared again, going she knew not where. Back to London, she told everyone. Back to the house on Grosvenor Square, where Yates lorded it over Cook and the chambermaids. . . . And another Yuletide was celebrated at Aldershot Grange, celebrated quietly, for Charlotte was expected to give birth before Twelfth Night. She did. On the last day of December it began to snow, and with the first flakes Charlotte's labor pains began. At first it was as if the pain walked round her, testing her—and then, as the snow outside deepened, the pain came in whirling gusts like the wind that shrieked down the chimney. A great gale from the cold North Atlantic tore through the Lake Country, snapping off tree limbs, blowing off roof tiles in a torrent of white. And in the big square bed in Aldershot Grange where Charlotte fought for her life, the all-consuming pain blotted everything out until her world became one long unending scream.

"She's going," muttered the sweating doctor. "I can't bring it. And she's weakening."

"Here, let me." With surprising strength, Wend pushed him aside. "Charlotte." She gripped Charlotte's hands in her own, and her anxious voice penetrated through the red sea of pain that roiled in Charlotte's head. "Take strength from me," whispered Wend. "I've got plenty. *Try.*"

And somehow Charlotte did seem to take strength from Wend. The doctor later said it was a miracle. He had been sure her failing strength would never be enough to bring forth the baby. But it was.

So Baby Phoebe, named for Charlotte's grandmother, was born on the first day of January.

"I don't think you'll ever be able to bear another child," the doctor told Charlotte as she lay back weakly with her eyes closed, pale and soaked with perspiration from her endeavors. "Nor should you," he added sternly.

Nobody had to tell Charlotte that Death had brushed her with its dark wings. She was grateful to live to face the new day—and to clasp her new daughter in her arms. A daughter as dark as Cassandra was fair.

Rowan came home on a freezing February day. He never wrote, so it was always a surprise to see him. This time Charlotte could greet him with a child who was truly his.

"She has your coloring," she said. "I think she looks like you."

"God help her then!" He grinned. But he picked up the baby and studied her approvingly, and when he gave her back to Charlotte, his dark eyes glowed.

He had brought her a gift, a beautiful red-embroidered white shawl carefully folded up in his saddlebag.

"Would you like to go back to London with me?" he asked.

Charlotte thought about that gloomy silent house on Grosvenor square. "Not yet," she hedged. "The doctor feels I am still too frail."

So Rowan went back alone.

In the years that followed, Charlotte ventured down to London only twice—and both occasions ended in disaster.

The first time, as they were leaving a music hall, that famous womanizer Lord Kentridge, more than a little drunk, had detached himself from a noisy group and swayed to a stop before Charlotte. Entranced by her beauty, he turned to Rowan and hiccuped. "You're Keynes, aren't you? Heard your wife was smashing—and she is!"

Rowan had promptly seized the opportunity to strike up an acquaintance with Kentridge, and he and Charlotte had accompanied the reeling peer home to his house in George Street, where he told them he was "batching it" while his wife sojourned in Bath.

Rowan evinced an interest in his lordship's library and told Charlotte in an undertone to maneuver Kentridge to the music room and keep him occupied.

Flustered and confused by this strange request, Charlotte nonetheless endeavored to do so. She succeeded far too well.

Rowan came back—from searching Kentridge's desk for some papers that interested Walpole—to find that Kentridge had a burning-cheeked Charlotte backed up against the spinet and was trying to pull her bodice down by main strength. Rowan, who had not found the papers and was in a bad mood, wrenched Kentridge off so roughly that his lordship's handsome mauve silk coat split clean down the back. Indeed Rowan thrust Kentridge away from Charlotte with a force that sent his amorous lordship careening through the music room's open French windows into the thorny arms of a rosebush in the garden outside. His lordship, sobered by his fall and all too keenly aware of Rowan's reputation for swordsmanship, had prudently fought his way free of the thorns, dusted himself off, and returned without a word to put on another coat.

Back at Grosvenor Square, the incident had put Rowan into a black rage.

"I told you to *distract* Kentridge, not *seduce* him!"

"You told me to keep him *occupied*," Charlotte flashed. "And I did! He had chased me all about the room and finally cornered me at the spinet. I was about to slap his face and make my escape when you arrived."

Rowan only growled.

"I will take you north," he said stiffly. "To a background where you will be better suited."

"Perhaps that would be best," sighed Charlotte. "For I do not seem to get on in London."

Charlotte's next London venture was equally disastrous.

Young Lord Stamford, whom they met at a rout held at one of the big German-style houses in fashionable Hanover Square, promptly fell head over heels in love with Charlotte and followed her about, calf-eyed. This irritated Rowan out of all conscience. Since Lord Stamford was more a contemporary of Charlotte than of Rowan—he was but twenty and singularly handsome in a melancholy, poetic sort of way—Rowan could not justify challenging him to a duel, but the young lord's desperate infatuation with Charlotte, which produced titters everywhere, became a source of bickering between them.

"Must that boy always follow us about?" Rowan demanded testily.

"I have done nothing to encourage him," Charlotte insisted.

"He writes odes to your eyelashes, your lips, your love-locks, your earlobes!"

"Oh, don't be anatomical, Rowan! He fancies himself to be a poet."

"He sends copies to his friends. They are read and laughed at in the taverns."

"If they are, it is no fault of mine."

But came the night London would never forget. At a large ball in Burlington House, Lord Burlington's recently erected Italian-style *palazzo* in Piccadilly, just as Charlotte descended the grand staircase, young Lord Stamford, the worse for wine and frantic at Charlotte's most recent rejection, lurched forward from the crowd, fell to his knees,

and reverently kissed the hem of her petticoat while loudly
imploring her to pity him.

Charlotte, gone scarlet with embarrassment, snatched
her skirt away and ordered Lord Stamford to get up on his
feet *at once*. But the incident made juicy reading in the
Gazette and convulsed London.

It was too much for Rowan. Again they retired to the
north. Never again did he take her back to London.

On the whole, Charlotte was glad. Her little girls absorbed her time—Cassandra, bright and sparkling and ad-
venturous with her thick shock of luminous pale hair and
her brilliant green eyes, little Phoebe, dark and tempestuous and cunning like her father—and Charlotte was rather
relieved to be free of arguments with Rowan, who, although he doted on the children, spent less and less time
with his family. As time went by, stories of Rowan's mistresses and chance alliances drifted north, but Charlotte
ignored them, reminding herself that Rowan was a man
with many enemies.

And that was how matters stood in the spring of 1739
when Cassandra was barely six years old and Phoebe not
yet five.

It had been a harsh winter in Cumberland and those
who lived along the Derwent Water had shivered through
it, keeping close by blazing hearths when the wind howled
down through the chimneys. Now spring had burst like a
green blessing upon the land and the damp fragrant earth
seemed sweet and fresh and full of promise.

And into that land of cold nights and crisp clear days
and singing birds came Rowan, riding north from London
to greet a family he had not seen for six months.

Hardly did he pause to greet Charlotte. Brusquely he
ordered her to pack. They were leaving at once for Portugal.

Coming out of the blue as it did, it took Charlotte's
breath away. But after the bitterness of last winter's weather,
she looked forward to a land that seemed to her one of
perpetual sunshine and flowers. She and Wend made haste
to pack, and with the children in tow departed Aldershot
Grange—departed so swiftly that Charlotte was tempted

to ask Rowan if this sudden move meant that he was *fleeing* England, perhaps for his life?

But on shipboard his lowering mood had changed abruptly. There Rowan seemed to relax. He was of a sudden almost the lover he had been those first golden days in Lisbon—teasing, beguiling, and always somehow with a dramatic flair that caught at her senses. A man of whom a woman could never tire, for there was always a freshness in the way he took her.

This was the old Rowan, the man who once had been. Charlotte felt as if she were greeting again someone who had been away a long time, someone she had not expected to meet again. But in the seven stormy years of their marriage, she reminded herself, nothing had lasted. Despite endless truces, they had always been back at each other's throats.

Like a great white bird the tall ship fled across the sea-green wastes of the North Atlantic and Charlotte leaned silent upon the rail, watching the prow cut through the water. The tangy salt wind whipped her wide skirts and her golden hair as she tried to put aside her dark memories and come to grips with the future. Perhaps in Lisbon, that city of light, she and Rowan could recapture—and this time hold—the magic they had so briefly known there . . . before the dark beauty Katherine Talybont had come into their lives and everything had changed. Perhaps . . .

But Charlotte had a strong streak of fatalism in her nature. What would be, would be. And whatever her fate, for her all roads had led to Lisbon.

23

Lisbon, Portugal, Summer 1739

On a glorious day, with seabirds screaming and diving from an endless vault of blue above the white sails, their ship made its stately way up the Tagus River, past the gray rococo structure of the Tower of Belem, rising in embattled beauty to guard the entrance to the town.

Wend's eyes rolled as the skyline of Lisbon, topped by the tall gray ramparts of the Castelo de São Jorge, rose up before them.

"Remember, I told you you'd be surprised!" murmured Charlotte.

Around them the ship's passengers crowded forward, eager to disembark. Rowan stood little dark-haired Phoebe upon the ship's rail and with his arm around her pointed out the magnificent churches whose towers and steeples rose above the palaces and pastel-painted houses.

Cassandra, in a yellow dress, clamored to get up on the rail too, but Rowan took no notice. Charlotte wondered when Phoebe had become his favorite; she hadn't noticed it before. Still, she supposed it was but natural, for Phoebe was truly blood of his blood—and so like him, bright and beguiling and often infuriating. Between them she and Wend boosted Cassandra up, and her yellow hair ribands blew through her frosty blonde hair as they steadied her to get a better view of the fast-approaching port city.

"We'll get lost there," predicted Wend darkly, and Char-

lotte laughed. Indeed, just seeing this City of Light gave
her spirits a lift.

She had assumed that they would disembark with the
other passengers, but Rowan would not allow that. He
said the town might be crowded and he would not drag
the children about in the hot sun from inn to inn as he
made inquiries. He did not ask Charlotte to go with him,
and although she was disappointed, she did not insist.

He came back at dusk and told them he had found a
place for them at an inn but they must stay on board ship
tonight. The English party who were vacating the rooms
would not be leaving until tomorrow.

Wistfully Charlotte watched the lights of Lisbon shining
gold against the velvet blackness, for after dinner Rowan
went into the town again—alone.

As they climbed, bag and baggage, into a coach next
morning, Rowan remarked that the inn was rather far out.

"Rather far out indeed!" said Charlotte when their coach
finally seemed to lose the city altogether and lumbered
out into the countryside. "Good heavens, Rowan, are we
on the road to Evora?"

"The only accommodations I could find in town were
not suitable for the children," he explained. "I think you
will like the place I have found—it is very picturesque."

Picturesque it certainly was. And isolated. The low whitewashed building with shutters painted a dull blue was
almost hidden in a grove of eucalyptus trees. But it was
scrupulously clean, and the food, he promised, was
good—he had already lunched here.

Charlotte did not want to complain before Wend and
the children. "But this is so far *out*, Rowan," she protested
when they were alone. "The children will want to see
everything, and it will take us *forever* to get into town!"

"The sights can wait. All of you need rest after our long
voyage. I will hire a horse and ride back and forth, but you
will stay here."

"Well, the children can stay here, but *I* would certainly
prefer to spend my days shopping or sightseeing."

"Charlotte, spare me." He held up his hand. "I will find
us a house, and speedily. In the meantime, please remem-

ber that Wend is a green girl in a foreign land where she does not speak the language. You must stay with her, of course. Suppose one of the children is hurt or gets sick? Wend would not know how to find a doctor."

"You are right, of course," Charlotte murmured, biting her lip. But she looked out the window longingly as she watched Rowan ride away toward the city.

The children were delighted, playing among the eucalyptus trees, sending Wend scurrying after them as they broke into the open and raced toward one of the squat round-towered windmills that dotted the countryside.

On the third day of this rustic life in an inn where they seemed to be the only guests, Rowan reported that he was still looking for a house.

How she would enjoy helping him do that!

"Wend and the children are well-settled-in now," she told him. "I could go with you, Rowan. Indeed I would like to."

"No." He was very firm on that.

Charlotte gave him a mutinous look. "I do not know why you brought me along at all," she mumbled.

"Walpole's power is tottering," he told her gloomily. "He has made a treaty with Spain to indemnify our English sailors who have been harassed on the high seas, but his opposition—Bolingbroke and the rest—mocks it. If war comes—and it may come sooner than we think—he may well be forced out of office. If he goes, I go with him, of course."

"Go . . . where?" she asked, wondering if he was planning to follow Walpole into some other endeavor.

"To perdition, I suppose, for I will not work for Bolingbroke and his cohorts." A shadow of a smile crossed his face. "Not that they would have me, of course."

"So what will happen to us?"

"Nothing, I hope. I have some money put away, and this present mission should gain me more."

Mission? That put a different light on things.

"But you never take me along on your missions!" She peered at him. "You were afraid to leave me in England," she said in an altered voice.

He frowned. "If the wrong men came to power and I were away at the time . . . They *could* come north seeking me, and finding me not in Cumberland, they might take you away for questioning." He spoke reluctantly.

Taken away for questioning! Charlotte could almost hear chains clanking. "But . . . but I know nothing, Rowan," she protested.

"They do not know that," he said dryly. "And Lord Kentridge, who once tried to force his attention upon you, is one of them. Not to mention young Lord Stamford's grandfather, a man of power."

"But I have never harmed either of them!" she cried, bewildered. "It was not my fault that foolish boy fell in love with me!"

"We know that, but that 'foolish boy's' widowed mother chooses not to believe it. She tells everyone who will listen that you led her son astray. Being a woman, I cannot call her out—and young Stamford has been banished to Oxford, so he can't refute it."

"Are you saying"—Charlotte moistened her lips—"that we cannot return home, Rowan?"

"No," he said equably. "I am saying that I did not wish to leave you in England alone." She looked so upset that he spoke more gently. "I have heard of a house in the Portas del Sol that may be to let. Tomorrow I intend to look into it."

Four days later they moved in.

It was an impressive house, quite new—and the Portas del Sol was a fashionable district looking down upon the terraced labyrinth of the Alfama. Charlotte drew in her breath as they drove up before the flat-fronted stone mansion, and felt a little shiver of delight go through her as the massive oak door was swung open by a wiry dark fellow.

"This is Vasco," Rowan told her. "Our other footman is named João. You will meet him presently; he is bringing our luggage."

Besides which there were a cook, a scullery maid, and two chambermaids. Rowan had indeed been busy, she thought—he had already hired a staff. Wend was upset that they spoke only Portuguese, but Charlotte knew enough Portuguese to give simple orders.

Relations between herself and Rowan had been strained these days, for on arrival in Lisbon he seemed to have turned into a different man. He had been ever the gentle lover aboard ship, but his lovemaking now often had a ferocity that frightened her. There seemed to be a caged tiger inside him, fighting to get out. Charlotte had tried to tell herself his nerves were jangled from worrying about matters back in England, about Walpole's probable loss of power, about his mission—doubtless an important one— and it must be irritating to him to have to ride back and forth such long distances every day. Now, as she roamed through the airy high-ceilinged rooms, eager to see everything and pleased by what she saw, she was filled with hope. This was a beautiful house; the furnishings—for Rowan had taken it furnished—were handsome enough even for Rowan's impeccable taste. From its spaciousness she gathered that he wanted to entertain—and she would do that too, graciously, happily, for the staff was more than adequate. If Rowan wanted, for his own purposes, to fill their house with the elite of Lisbon and perchance travelers from foreign lands, she was ready to do it with a flourish!

Bubbling over with enthusiasm, she turned to tell Rowan, "We should go out to dinner tonight and celebrate finding this wonderful house!"—and found him gone.

He did not return until after the dinner dishes were long cleared away. And he returned filled with some inner anger that lashed out at her through his body after they had gone to bed. His body crushed hers with a fever of desire—but it was a rough taking, bruising but swiftly over, and one from which Charlotte knew no fulfillment.

She lay in the dark, her body pulsing and unsatisfied, and her hopes, which had been so high, wavered within her.

Now that they had a house of their own, Charlotte had confidently expected to find herself driving out next day to see the sights of Lisbon, while Wend supervised the servants in setting things to rights.

Rowan, it seemed, had other plans for her. He insisted that the house needed her personal touch, and Charlotte, feeling it was his right to demand that, spent the next few days supervising her small staff in bringing the pleasant sunny rooms to the peak of perfection. Rowan remained unpredictable, going restlessly in and out—indeed, if the idea had not been so ridiculous, Charlotte would almost have been persuaded that he was checking up on her.

With the house at last in perfect order, they sat down to dinner across a gleaming board and Charlotte spoke eagerly of all the places she wanted to visit—then stopped, puzzled, for across from her Rowan's brows had drawn into a straight line and he had fidgeted, eventually oversetting his wineglass.

"Time enough for all that when we are settled," he muttered.

"*Settled?*" Charlotte stared at him. "Rowan, I should think we were *settled* enough already."

"We will see," he said restlessly, his gaze roaming the heavy-framed oil paintings that the owners had left behind, looking somehow stark against the soft chrome-yellow walls. "Meantime, Charlotte, I have ordered the drapers for tomorrow, and I am not sure what time they will arrive."

"*Drapers?*" Charlotte was amazed. "Rowan, these draperies are well enough. After all, we do not expect to live here for years and years. We are only *visiting* Lisbon!"

"Nevertheless, the drapers are coming, and I expect you to be at home to receive them and to select something more attractive than this faded buff brocade." He shrugged toward the tall dining-room windows with an expression of contempt, and Charlotte was reminded sharply of Rowan's love of beauty, of fine things, of perfection.

She sighed. "Very well, Rowan, I will do as you ask."

But the drapers had not come. Rowan had suggested indifferently that they would come the following day, and then the day after that he said that he had forgotten to tell her that he had told the tardy drapers not to come at all, that he had sent for other drapers. Those did not come either. And after that it was the erection of new shutters for her bedchamber—these present ones were a disgrace, and Charlotte must see to them, for it was well known that workmen never did anything right without supervision. Every day some new excuse to keep her there.

Finally, she had exploded.

"I am tired of sitting in this house looking out at the world," she had told him despairingly. "Indeed I do not care if the drapers never come or if we have new shutters or old. If you will not take me, I am going out alone. Now!"

In a surprisingly pliant mood, Rowan had quickly agreed. And together, in a hired coach—Rowan was ever extravagant —they toured the city, revisiting the parts she liked best, clip-clopping past palaces trimmed with gold leaf and magnificent homes that owed their existence to the spice trade and the great caravelles manned by Portuguese sailors who had made the long treacherous voyage to India. Past buildings washed in pale colors, muted pastel shades of pink and apricot and gold, they rode, past overhanging ironwork balconies filled with flowers, past stone fountains where fishwives scrubbed the fish baskets they carried about on their heads.

At her insistence Rowan took her to view the wide lagoon the natives called the Mar de Palha, or Sea of Straw, that lay northeast of the city. Sparkling blue in the sun, it was alive with the beautiful lateen-sailed barges know as *fragatas*.

And when finally at a street corner Charlotte, enchanted anew by Lisbon's beauty, threw open the door of the coach and leapt down to the cobbles, she was reminded poignantly of the good times in the early days of their marriage, when he had seemed a different man, light-hearted, almost boyish, in love.

"I want to see it all again!" she cried, with a rapturous gesture that encompassed even the hills above the city. "Oh, Rowan, I had forgotten how much I liked it here!"

Rowan's smile deepened at her delight. He dismissed the coach and together they strolled through arcaded streets and squares where fountains tinkled in the warm sunlight.

From one of the many jewelers along the Rua do Ouro, or Street of Gold, he bought her a ring set with an alexandrite "to match your violet eyes." Laughing, he bought her a pair of strange-shaped silver goblets, "lovers' goblets" the silversmith called them, from one of the shops displaying plate along the Rua da Prata, or Street of Silver. And on the Rua dos Douradores, or Gilders' Street, she admired a pair of fine gold-leaf frames, which Rowan promptly ordered sent to the house to replace the heavy ones in the dining room that so displeased him.

And then, in the main square, at the stall of an elderly black-garbed flower vendor, he had just heaped into her arms a fragrant bunch of white and yellow roses to match the pale Chinese gold silk of her gown, with its frosting of heavy white point lace, when they heard a hail from across the square and a voice called, "Ho, there, Rowan!"

Charlotte, whose face had been pressed ecstatically into the fragrant rose petals, looked up to see a florid, heavyset man in bottle-green satins and a ginger wig bearing down on them. He clapped Rowan on the shoulder and wrung his hand. Charlotte smiled at him over her flowers and made a light curtsy when Rowan introduced his old friend Lord Claypool, whom he called Ned.

"What, you've been in Lisbon a fortnight and not let me know?" Claypool demanded in a jocular tone.

"I did not know you were here, Ned," protested Rowan. "I assumed you to be still in Sussex."

"We have been so busy getting settled," Charlotte supplied in defense of her husband. "But now we have quite settled in and are ready to entertain."

Lord Claypool's gaze rested on her with approval. He promptly affixed himself to Charlotte's other side and insisted on accompanying them on their stroll. He'd show her the sights!

When Charlotte said demurely that she had been here before on her wedding journey, Lord Claypool gouged Rowan in the ribs and winked. "Then she'll have seen naught but the bedchamber ceiling of her inn, eh, Rowan? Now you shall see Lisbon, my lady!" He waved energeti-

cally at the Tagus River flowing by on Lisbon's southern
shore. Had Rowan told her that the great Spanish Armada
had sailed out of the mouth of the Tagus River to attack
England 150 years ago, only to be defeated by Drake and
Queen Elizabeth's other "sea dogs"? No? How remiss of
Rowan!

Lord Claypool guided them into the narrow twisting
streets of the Alfama, alive with children and stray dogs,
the overhanging balconies above hung with laundry, and
some of those streets so narrow and steep that they were
more like winding staircases than streets.

And then into more fashionable districts, where Charlotte admired the black-and-white mosaic patterns of the
pavements, and, on the house fronts everywhere, on the
public fountains, the elaborate hand-painted glazed blue-
and-white tiles called *azulejos*, for which Lisbon was famous.

Lord Claypool walked them about everywhere, talking
volubly the while. And nothing would do but they must
dine with him at his inn, which served marvelous food—oh,
they would find nothing like it in the city, did Rowan not
remember? Protesting, Rowan agreed, and Charlotte ate
her first meal out since she had come to Lisbon.

The inn's dining room was commodious and crowded,
filled with satins and laces, perfumes and conversations.
Charlotte was grateful that their host had not insisted on a
private room. It was nice having other people around for a
change, listening to laughter and the clink of glasses, instead of fidgeting under Rowan's brooding stare as she
toyed with her food. She looked with more approval upon
corpulent Lord Claypool, leaning back resplendent in his
bottle-green coat with its wide lettuce-green satin cuffs
braided in gold.

"So you have brought your wife along this time, eh,
Rowan?" But Lord Claypool was not looking at his lean
dark friend, but at the lovely lissome woman in soft Chinese gold sipping her wine across from him. "Faith, if I'd
known you had such a lovely wife, I'd have asked you
where you were keeping her!"

"And how is *your* wife, Ned?" was Rowan's silky response.

"Oh, Maggie's fine, fine." But he answered absently, his gaze still on Charlotte.

"And where are you keeping *her?*" asked Charlotte, glancing around as if expecting to see Lady Claypool come suddenly into the room.

Across from her, Lord Claypool's ginger brows lifted in surprise. "Oh, in Sussex," he replied hastily. "She never leaves Sussex."

So Lord Claypool—a chaser after skirts if ever she had seen one—kept *his* wife tucked away in the country too! Her warmth toward Lord Claypool abruptly cooled.

"Doesn't she ever wish to accompany you?" she shot at him.

"Oh, sometimes she mentions it, sometimes."

"And yet you never take her with you?" Charlotte persisted.

Lord Claypool's shoulders moved restively inside his tight-fitting waistcoat. "She does well enough in Sussex," he muttered.

Charlotte's gaze met his squarely. "How sad for her!" was her comment.

By now Lord Claypool's countenance had acquired a hunted look. He turned to Rowan for help. "What brings you to Portugal, Rowan?"

"A holiday." Rowan shrugged.

His friend's significant gaze passed over Charlotte and back again to Rowan with some commiseration.

He is signaling with that look his sympathy that Rowan had to bring me along! thought Charlotte hotly, and her heart went out to Lady Claypool, stuck in Sussex, and to all other neglected wives.

Sensing her hostility to his friend, Rowan seemed to relax. Charlotte sighed inwardly. With Rowan it was always that way. He had a ferocious jealousy of her, which amounted to mania. She had begun to realize that while Lord Claypool, who was even now admiring a raven-haired lady at the next table as if she were a sweetmeat to be devoured as dessert, might leave his wife at home in Sussex in order to pursue his womanizing without interference, it was different with Rowan.

*He keeps me isolated in the north of England so that I
will not meet anyone,* she realized suddenly. *If I do not
meet any men, I cannot possibly fall in love with one of
them and so be unfaithful to him. If we lived in the Near
East, he would have me walled up in a seraglio, I suppose.*
The thought was depressing. She sighed and fell silent as
she ate the sugared black pudding and the *lulas* Claypool
had recommended, which turned out to be cuttlefish cooked
in lemon butter.

By the time Charlotte, who had a sweet tooth, was
eating her *crème caramel,* the two men, who had both
refused dessert, were working their way through a second
bottle of the ruby-red port wine that came from Oporto, to
the north of Lisbon. And as he drank more, Rowan's mood
darkened.

"We should drink a toast to Portugal's king!" Claypool
exclaimed recklessly. "A fellow as stupid as was England's
own George I!"

Most Englishmen would have agreed with Claypool about
the German George I, who had come reluctantly from
Hanover to rule the English people—and had soon secured
their ridicule by his odd habits, such as keeping turbaned
Turkish servants rather than plain English ones, and by
wondering aloud if he might not close down St. James's
Park to the public and plant it instead with turnips. Most
Englishmen—but not Rowan. Across from Claypool, Rowan's dark face flushed.

"I will drink a toast to his glorious majesty, our former
and much-mourned King George I." Rowan's tone was
menacing.

Oh, dear, thought Charlotte. *This satin-clad fool has
affronted one of Rowan's heroes, and the evening will be
ruined!*

"As you like." Claypool, far gone in his cups, shrugged,
and his voice was slurred. "Only damme, Rowan, I can't
see how you—who took a beauty to wife—can champion
a king who had an eye only for ugly women. And who sat
about evenings cutting out paper dolls with one of his
mistresses."

Rowan's scowl deepened, and Charlotte stepped quickly into the breach.

"Oh, come now, Rowan," she chided reasonably. "Everyone talked about those women at the time, you know that! And cutting out paper patterns is harmless enough," she added, "even if it isn't very kingly."

She had diverted Rowan's wrath from the inebriated Lord Claypool, who had settled back in his chair with a fuzzy expression on his slack-featured face, but now that wrath was turned upon her.

"One would suppose you had delighted in listening to amusing stories ridiculing our late majesty?" said Rowan stiffly.

His tone irritated her. "Some of the stories were not so pretty," she said sharply. "And certainly not amusing!"

"Such as?" Rowan prodded.

"Such as his having his wife's lover hacked to pieces and buried under the castle floorboards!" retorted Charlotte recklessly.

Rowan's intense dark eyes were upon her. "Sophia Dorothea betrayed him," he countered. "What he did was right!"

"Right? How can you say that, Rowan? To divorce his wife, keep her from her children forever, and confine her in the Castle of Ahlden *until she died?*"

"She betrayed him with a Swedish colonel of dragoons. They both deserved their fate!"

Charlotte shivered. She remembered how in the Scillies when she was very small she had heard that the young Prince of Wales had flared up and said bitterly that he was eager for his father to die so that his mother could be released from her long imprisonment. And later Charlotte herself had piped up that she agreed with the prince—and so earned the enmity of one of her mother's suitors, a gentleman from Cornwall whom her mother was considering marrying at the time.

"Your child is a loose talker," the Cornish gentleman had told Cymbeline Vayle indignantly.

"Charlotte but speaks her mind," her mother had answered him in her sweet light voice. "And I will tell you now that I encourage her to do so."

"You should not encourage her, Cymbeline," was her suitor's blunt observation. "She will make trouble with her tongue one day."

"For me perhaps, but not for you," was his lady's brisk reply, and that disagreement had put a wedge between them that was to last for a number of huffy months while Cymbeline fell out of love with him.

He had not been a bad man, that Cornish gentleman, and Charlotte had always later felt rather guilty that her aversion to the German George I should have come between them. As now it was coming between her and Rowan. But her distaste for the late king was such that she could not seem to help herself.

"I do not think *any* woman deserves to be locked up for thirty-two years merely because she happens to look at another man!" she protested.

"*Merely?*" Rowan seemed to ponder that. His eyes narrowed. "Sophia Dorothea broke her marriage vows, and yet you would champion her?"

"Oh, how do you know she broke her marriage vows?" cried Charlotte in exasperation. "Were you there? The poor thing had a cruel, jealous husband and he may even have imagined all those things about her. Suppose there was no truth in them?" She shivered at the idea that poor Sophia might have been imprisoned all those years because of a misapprehension.

"Oh, there was proof enough of her adultery," Rowan drawled.

"But *thirty-two years*, Rowan?" It seemed to Charlotte incredible. Surely the punishment did not fit the crime! "And what of George I, was he so pure?"

Rowan's voice was heavy. "To have released her would have been a sign of weakness on his part."

Too late Charlotte realized how deeply she had become involved in this conversation and that somehow she had been made an adversary of the late king in Rowan's mind. She held her ground.

"I do not consider mercy to be weakness, Rowan."

"Do you not?" he mocked. "I am shocked that you would champion the Adulteress!"

"Oh, how can you call her that?" Charlotte threw prudence to the winds.

"You have insulted the good name of his late majesty—"

"Oh, I have not! I have only repeated what others have said about him."

"And if I do not have your apology here and now for this affront to him, I will take you home!" he finished threateningly.

"Then take me home," sighed Charlotte. "For I will not praise a man I have always considered nothing less than a monster."

Infuriated by her defiance, Rowan rose with such speed that he knocked over his chair, and Claypool, far gone in drink, for he had been pouring and swallowing all the while this exchange had been going on, gave him a dazed look. "What, leaving now?" he asked in a slurred voice. "Egad, man, the evening's just begun!"

"Not for my lady," was Rowan's curt rejoinder. "For her the evening has just ended. Come, Charlotte." And when she did not at once respond to his icy command, he reached out a hand and jerked her to her feet. His cruel fingers numbed her wrist until he got her to the street and into a passing chair. Having seen her into it, he stalked along beside her through the night air, not speaking.

He was taking his erring lady home.

They did not speak all the way to the Portas del Sol.

Charlotte felt humiliated. She was wild to retaliate, even though common sense forbade it. Life with Rowan was incredibly difficult at times, full of sharp corners and murky waters where even the most careless observation could take you beyond your depth. She did not speak to him when she alighted from the chair. Instead she ran upstairs and began undressing for bed in angry silence, turning her back when Rowan appeared in her doorway and stood staring at her.

"You have given me a headache," she flung over her

shoulder when he did not go away. "I would be obliged if you kept to your own room tonight."

"A headache, you say?" As if that was the trigger that would set him off, he crossed the room in a quick stride and whirled her about to face him. "I still do not have my apology, Charlotte," he said sternly.

"Nor will you get one!" she flashed. "For none is due!"

Too well she knew that look on his face. For a moment panic seized her, but she stood her ground, glaring back at him.

And that was her undoing. Rowan fell upon her, tore her clothing to shreds, and took her with a violence that left her reeling. How could a man treat his wife as an adored mistress one moment and a scorned waterfront whore the next? Rowan had not even bothered to remove his boots when he plunged on top of her—and she had the bruises to prove it. And all of this just when she had thought that somehow the magic of Lisbon would heal old wounds and bring them together again. . . . After he had gone back to his own room, Charlotte lay upset and trembling, letting the light breeze from the Tagus dry the tears that glistened on her cheeks.

And then she heard a crash as the front door slammed below. Rowan was going out. . . .

Harsh thoughts crowded in. Unbidden, the memory of a big black stallion rose up before her. Rowan had brought the great beast back with him from a trip to Ireland—another of those wanderings on which she had not accompanied him—and the horse had been his pride and joy. He had bragged about Midnight—for that was the name he had given the horse—everywhere. The horse was very high-spirited, but Rowan was an excellent rider and liked to demonstrate his control.

And then, before a crowd on market day in the little village of Cat Bells, Rowan had mounted the horse, prepared to ride him home to Aldershot Grange. Without warning, the horse had thrown him. And Rowan had landed on his splendid backside in the mud. A titter of amusement had rippled through the crowd as Rowan wrenched himself up from the mire that clung to his new suit—and his face had darkened. Charlotte knew that because Livesay had been there and had told her about it.

Rowan had ripped out a curse and then suddenly had pulled out the dueling pistol he carried and shot the horse between the eyes. The beautiful animal, standing there trembling, had dropped like a stone—dead.

It was only afterward that they found the burr that some prankster or ill-wisher had slipped beneath Midnight's saddle.

Rowan had come home ashen-faced that day, speaking to no one, to lock himself in his room. Passing by his door, Charlotte had thought she heard muffled weeping, but there was a steady grumbling of thunder from the hills and she could not be sure. And when Rowan had come out of that room he had come out set-faced and dressed for travel and had ridden away into a blinding rainstorm without a word. Later she learned that he had gone to London.

He never mentioned Midnight again.

Rowan's possessions did not last long if they failed to please him. And his pets were short-lived if they showed marked preference for another. His favorite hunting dog, Chase, had kept leaving his side, preferring the company of Livesay, who constantly fed him tidbits from the table. One day as the dog dashed by Rowan and came running up to Livesay wagging his tail, Rowan had growled that the dog was a sheep killer and had strung the dog up there and then and cut the animal's throat.

Everyone in the household had wept, for they had all loved Chase, who had endearing ways.

Rowan had dashed away to London then too.

He is often sorry for what he has done when it is too late to do any good was Charlotte's last unhappy thought when finally she drifted off into a troubled sleep.

From which she found herself roughly shaken awake.

"Up, up!" Rowan was saying. "Dress yourself. We leave within the hour."

"But . . . but it's the middle of the night!" protested Charlotte, blinking into the light of the single candle that lit the darkness. "*Why* am I to get up? Where are we going?"

Rowan, who had certainly never confided in her before about his missions, chose this time to enlighten her. Still clinging to the bedcovers, Charlotte listened groggily as Rowan told her they were off to Evora, a town in the Alentejo, where he would keep a tryst with an emissary of England's ambassador to Spain, who was even now riding hard toward them from Madrid via the Pyrenees, bringing a message of utmost importance from His Excellency that Rowan would make sure was conveyed to England.

By now Charlotte was fully awake. Living as she did in the almost inaccessible reaches of England's North Country, she found it difficult to keep track of the political intrigues of the time, but she knew as did everyone else, of the great uproar caused last year when an Englishman named Captain Jenkins had brought one of his ears in a box to the House of Commons—an ear he claimed was cut off by Spaniards who had illegally boarded and searched his ship, then scornfully bidden him to take his severed ear and his grievance to the English king!

As she pulled on her clothes, she realized with a little surge of excitement that Rowan, out late and alone, had learned something—received some message, perhaps from Spain. And was acting on it with characteristic swiftness. How unlike him to have told her about it. And how doubly unlike him to be taking her with him on such a mission. Her fingers paused momentarily in the act of hooking up her apricot silk gown. Could it be that Rowan was sorry for the way he had treated her, and this sudden confiding, this taking her with him, was an olive branch that he was holding out to her?

Enlivened by that thought, Charlotte hurried downstairs. Her lacerated feelings were eager for a reconciliation initiated by *him*. Long ago she had thought she could make a success of this marriage—with time, with effort. Lately—and especially last night—she had begun to despair. Yet now it seemed, incredibly, there might be a chance. . . .

She had reached the front door and was just in the act of

pulling on her peach kidskin gloves when she came to a halt—there was no coach waiting. And Rowan appeared to tell her sardonically that he was not taking her with him after all. He had changed his mind!

Speechless, Charlotte stared at her bewildering husband. Then from behind her came Wend's grumbling protest: "Why did you wake Mistress Charlotte if you wasn't taking her with you?"

The dark eyes in that satanic face swung toward the speaker with such intensity that Wend's ruffled cap retreated into the darkness of the doorway.

"If you raise your voice to me again, Wend," came Rowan's warning voice, "I will dismiss you without notice!"

"Be silent, Wend." Charlotte spoke sharply, for she was all too aware that Rowan, with his mercurial moods and sudden wild tempests, was entirely capable of doing just that—dismissing Cumberland-bred Wend on the spot and driving her away to fend for herself in an alien city. "I am wondering the same thing, Rowan. Just why *did* you change your mind about taking me with you?"

Rowan's daunting gaze played over Charlotte for a few moments before he spoke. Then abruptly he laughed. "Perhaps I decided that I did not desire your company after all, Charlotte." And added negligently, "I leave you to imagine why."

When Charlotte said that she did not know why, he admonished her for quarreling before the servants. And followed that up by telling her that he would be gone at least a week, maybe longer, and that she was not to roam around Lisbon, but to stay indoors until he returned.

Pale with rage, Charlotte watched him go clattering off over the cobbles into the darkness with the mounted servant João following. Charlotte and Wend talked for a while—but that resolved nothing. And Charlotte was too keyed up to go back to bed, as Wend urged.

"I think I'll walk down to the fish market," she said abruptly, noting that dawn was just now breaking. Adding that perhaps she could find a chair for hire and have herself carried down.

Ignoring Wend's protests that there might be cutpurses about, Charlotte clutched her light embroidered shawl around her and went outside. There she found Vasco, still holding his torch, leaning sleepily against the wall by the front door. Good servant that he was, Vasco insisted on following her, lighting her way with the torch as she made her way down from the heights of the Portas del Sol.

Still confused and upset as she picked her way downhill, Charlotte was trying to get her thoughts straight, asking herself what she could have done differently, how she could have made this impossible marriage work.

Rowan had been such a tender lover on shipboard, she had been lulled into a false sense of security. She had been totally unprepared for the change that had come over him on dry land, for on arrival at the inn he had dragged her to bed right after supper every night and leapt upon her almost before she could get into her nightdress, sweeping her protesting form across the inn floor and into the lumpy bed to throw his full weight upon her and maul her—yes, that was the word, she thought resentfully, he *mauled* her. And last night—!

Last night he had left marks upon her body that made her grateful for three-quarter sleeves and long skirts. Last night he had not even taken his boots off but had taken her like some whore in a waterfront brothel, and her shapely calves bore bruises which—thank God!—were covered by the silk of her stockings.

Was there no common meeting ground with Rowan? Must he always leave these wounds upon her heart? *Oh, she would gladly forgo all the material things Rowan gave her*, she thought wildly, *if only he would change, if only . . .*

But she knew in the depths of her that it was not to be. Rowan could not change just as *she* could not change. They would both always be what they were today—with the rift between them widening, widening, until it became a chasm no one could cross.

Down through the twisting streets of the Alfama she hurried, with Vasco in attendance behind her. Past tiny patios and private gardens, beneath overhanging balconies and dangling forgotten laundry, sidestepping sleeping dogs and occasional prowling cats, walking sometimes on cobbles and sometimes on steps, for the streets were steep and so narrow that in some places she doubted two stout men could pass abreast.

Down into the hubbub of the fish market she went, thinking, worrying, wondering what she should do—if indeed there was anything she could do. Her feelings were rubbed raw and smarting and she needed to be made whole again. If there had been even a straw of hope at that moment, she would have snatched at it.

And then in that crowd of strangers disembarking from a vessel in the harbor she saw a face she had never expected to see again this side of paradise. Tom's face. It surfaced for an instant and then was lost in the crowd. But Charlotte was running blindly toward the spot where he had been, mindlessly crashing into people as she went. "*Desculpe-me,* excuse me!" she kept crying as she burst through, thrusting people aside.

And then her frantic gaze found him again. A tall broad-shouldered man clad in a scarlet wide-cuffed coat encrusted with gold braid and brass buttons. His profile was toward her now as he shouldered his way through the crowd, and she could see that his face was deeply tanned, in sharp contrast to his shock of fair hair that gleamed in the early-morning light. There was the stamp of the adventurer about him—Charlotte did not need to see the serviceable sword that swung against his lean thighs to know that it was there.

And now he was breaking free of the crowd with that long, familiar stride. Charlotte, enmeshed in a swirl of people, knew that she would never catch him. In another moment he would be gone from view, vanished from sight just as her dreams of him were gone with the early-morning light. . . .

Of course it couldn't be Tom. Tom was dead. This had to be just some handsome look-alike, but the resemblance was so striking and the effect on her heart so devastating that . . .

"Tom!" she wailed despairingly, one peach-gloved hand held out in mute appeal. *"Tom Westing!"*

The tall figure swung about, his alert gaze raking the crowd. And there he was, looking at her from that dear familiar face, his green eyes glazing with delighted recognition.

"Charlotte!"

The blood left Charlotte's face in a single rush, she felt her knees give way, and even as he sprinted toward her, she crumpled in a billow of apricot silk against a stand of oranges, whose owner, astonished, caught her as she fell.

24

When Charlotte came back to consciousness, there was
Tom's face above her, Tom pressing a flask of a burning
liquid she identified as brandy to her lips.

"I don't believe it," she whispered. "They told me you
were dead!"

He shrugged. "Only left for dead."

Charlotte swallowed. "How is that possible?" she protested. "Rowan told me he saw your body down below on
the rocks, that your neck was broken."

"Do I look as if my neck was broken?"

So Rowan had lied to her even then. . . .

"I still cannot believe it is really you," she marveled.

"Why, have I changed so much?" he countered, smiling.

"Oh, no," she said hastily. "You haven't changed at all."

"Nor have you." The words were a caress.

"Haven't I, Tom?" Charlotte's gaze on him was wistful.
She felt so battered by life. Tom helped her up and she
smoothed out her apricot skirts. "Oh, I *must* have changed,"
she sighed.

"Not to me," he said in a timbred voice. And it was true.
She was lovelier than any woman had a right to be, he
thought. So lovely it hurt his heart. "Come, Charlotte."
He attempted to cover that sudden huskiness in his voice
with brisk cheerfulness. "If you are restored enough, we
can walk about the market and you can tell me how you

have fared since last we met." With what he hoped would seem casual gallantry, he offered her his arm and Charlotte promptly took it.

Together they strolled through the big open market. Charlotte's fair head was tilted backward, looking up into Tom's face, and she could not keep the soft light out of her violet eyes. For his part, he stared down at her, enchanted, enmeshed as he had always been by her nearness, by all she was or had ever been. Thus with gazes locked they moved through the busy stalls unseeing, as if caught up in a dream, and those who observed them imagined them to be newlyweds or lovers.

They had indeed gone back in time. And between them the tension of a sharp physical awareness was building, building. Charlotte had never felt so vibrant, so alive. When a hurrying fishwife dashed by so that Charlotte had to take a quick step toward Tom to avoid being brushed by the tray of fish, and her slim hip came into sudden contact with Tom's lean thigh, she found herself starting violently at the encounter.

"Have you breakfasted, Tom?" she asked hastily, to cover that sudden start and the fact that her nerves were strained to the breaking point, for she was hastening to remind herself that while *she* had remained visible, it was Tom who had disappeared, had let people account him dead, Tom who had neglected to let her know all these years that he was still alive.

"No, I've not breakfasted yet—I was tired of shipboard food."

"Ah, then you must try one of these figs—they are from the Algarve, to the south of us." She gave him a hurt look. "Why did you not let me know you were alive, Tom?"

"Because I was told you had married." He bit into a fig. "And I had nothing to offer you, Charlotte."

Nothing to offer! She looked at him wistfully. "There was yourself," she pointed out.

He laughed. "That's little enough!" He peered down at her keenly. "The man you married, was he the tall fellow I saw you with that night in the garden at Castle Stroud?"

She nodded. "His name is Rowan Keynes—we have two

children." This was not the moment to say, *One of them is yours, Tom!* "Have you married?"

"No." And then, perhaps because he still harbored a little resentment that she had so swiftly forgotten him in another man's arms, "My circumstances never warranted it."

His cool response chilled her a little. She looked away, toward one of the stalls. "Ah, there are some peaches from Alcobaca—you must try one, Tom, they are delicious."

She, in her apricot gown with her peach-bloom cheeks, looked more delicious to Tom than any peach, but he bit into an Alcobaca peach to please her. "Have you been happy, Charlotte?" he asked softly.

She looked away, not meeting his gaze. "Sometimes." She pushed away thoughts of her miserable life with Rowan. "But what of you, Tom? Where have you been all this time?"

"In the Bahamas mostly. I slipped back into my father's trade. It has its ups and downs."

His father's trade of piracy—oh, he must have hated that. Her heart went out to him.

"Take me somewhere and tell me about it," she said steadily.

With alacrity Tom found a nearby inn, and over coffee in a corner of the low-ceilinged common room, Charlotte considered him. Now, on closer inspection, she could see that although his scarlet coat was fashionable, the seam of one cuff was pulling apart, the brave gold braid was a trifle tarnished, and one of the brass buttons was missing. Plainly no woman was looking after him, she thought with a catch in her heart.

She studied him yearningly as she stirred her coffee, drinking him in. Light poured over him through a small-paned window beside her, showing him to be even broader of shoulder than she remembered, deeper of chest. His eyes, though, were just the same, steady, brilliant as emeralds, and as startling against the bronze of his tan as was the sudden flash of his even white teeth when he smiled. The same casual jauntiness she recalled so well still clung to him. But there was a rakish look to him now, a cynical worldliness that made him seem older than his years. There was a new scar on his cheek—Charlotte did not need to be told it had been made by a sword or cutlass. She resisted the urge to trace its short length with gentle fingers.

"How did you come by your scar, Tom?"

He shrugged. "I think I told you I was never cut out for the trade, Charlotte. We were cruising Bahamian waters and having indifferent luck when we chanced on a small merchantman foundering off the eastern coast of Cat Island. We got her people and her cargo aboard before she sank, and by nightfall our crew was drunk on stolen rum. One of the passengers we'd rescued was a beautiful girl." Charlotte felt a twinge of jealousy go through her. "Despite our captain's promise to ransom her unharmed, around midnight our first mate"—his somber voice recalled the size of that great hulking brute—"decided to take her to his bed." His jaw tightened. "By force. I stopped him—with six inches of steel through his heart. But not before he raked me with his knife."

"What happened to the girl?" wondered Charlotte.

"I was guarding her when a storm came up in the night. As I said, our crew was dead drunk, and we broke up on a reef off Eleuthera. Everybody drowned—it was a miracle that the girl and I got through." Not quite a miracle—he could remember nearly drowning himself as he plowed through crashing waves dragging her senseless form with him. He could remember sagging down with her, battered and half-dead, upon the wet sand of a strange beach . . . he could remember the gold he found the next morning, washed ashore in a wooden box that had broken open and deposited gleaming coins across the sand. And that was the gold that had brought him to England, and now had brought him here. . . .

But Charlotte was interested only in the girl, alone with Tom in a tropical paradise.

"This girl you saved, was she . . . grateful, Tom?" she asked ironically.

Tom gave her an amused look. "Not very. Mistress Prudence was a spoiled schoolgirl returning to Spanish

Town, Jamaica, where her father was a planter. She blamed me for everything—the storm, the sea, the breakup of both ships." He began to laugh. "I managed to salvage food from the wreck, and I rigged up a boat of sorts from the debris that washed ashore and sailed us to a port where I could send her back to her father." Some of those golden coins had gone to that. . . . "And I realized then that the trade wasn't for me, never had been. So I didn't go back."

He hadn't cared about the girl after all! Charlotte felt unreasonably heartened.

"Out of the trade you may be." She smiled. "But with that scar, Tom, you still look like a brigand!"

His answer was flippant. "Call me, rather, an opportunist."

No . . . Charlotte had married one of those. And now she was wiser about men. This dangerous-looking fellow across from her wasn't that. She cocked her head at him. "Perhaps a rake," she suggested humorously.

Tom laughed. A laugh that had lost its bitter tinge, gone suddenly young and carefree. Just as his heart had rebounded with joy on seeing her again.

She leaned toward him, serious again. "But I do not understand how you escaped, Tom. I *saw* Russ kick you over the edge of the crag as you lay unconscious on the rim."

He watched her face go white as he told her how he had lain on a ledge some twenty feet below the rim, how he had shouted himself hoarse, how he had weakened, how he had despaired of ever escaping the trap into which he had fallen.

"Oh, Tom!" Charlotte's voice came in a soft sorrowful rush. "You are telling me I left you to your death!"

"Not you," he said quickly, his big hand closing warmly over hers. "For you didn't know." She looked so shaken that he was afraid she might faint.

As the truth of what had happened that night on Kenlock Crag surged over Charlotte, the depths of the trap into which she herself had fallen appalled her. Rowan had lied to her, maneuvered her every step of the way. "Arranger" that he was, he had arranged that she would fall willingly into his arms. In that moment she hated herself for being such a blind fool, a pawn of his masterly game—and a wave of impotent fury at Rowan for his callous deception engulfed her.

But to Tom, even as he worried over the effect all of this was having on Charlotte, this was a moment of triumph. It had wounded him deeply that she would so soon forget, but now he knew why she had so quickly wed. They had deceived her into thinking him dead! His lady had not forgotten him after all. The thought floated by on bright wings. It was easy now to tell her about the days when he had not cared what happened to him, about the long nights at sea without her. Listening, swept up by him, by his nearness, by the love she had always borne him, Charlotte tried to force herself to remember that she had another life now which did not include Tom—and found she could not. *Tom* was her very life.

She moistened her lips, tried to control the emotions that surged through her.

"What brings you to Portugal, Tom?"

He looked deep into her eyes and told her the truth. "I came seeking a lady," he said. "A lady who had left England, it seemed, even as I arrived."

Charlotte stared at him. *That* was why Rowan had taken her to Portugal so suddenly! Oh, he might very well be on a mission—who ever knew with Rowan? But he had brought her along to Lisbon so she would not meet Tom! *That* was the news old Conway had brought him back at Aldershot Grange that had changed his mind!

And that accounted too for Rowan's strange moods, for the callous violence of his lovemaking—he was jealous! *Of Tom!*

Pain must have racked her face at that moment, for Tom leaned forward. "What's the matter, Charlotte?"

"Nothing." She made a slight gesture as if to brush away cobwebs. "I am honored, Tom, that you came seeking me." *But it is too late, too late.*

"And found you, more desirable than ever. Rowan Keynes is a lucky man, Charlotte. You would fill a man's life."

"Not Rowan's," she said bitterly, stirring her coffee.

"Oh?" He looked up alertly. "You are not happy, then?"

She thought of last night's hurtful lovemaking, of this morning's insults. "No, I am not happy," she admitted huskily.

His big hand still covered hers, warm and protective. "I have never stopped loving you, Charlotte, not for a moment. And the day came that I had to see you again, to know how you were, to make sure you were all right. On that day I sailed for England."

"Oh, Tom." Her voice was choked.

"I know you have another life now." He spoke gravely. "And I would not take it from you. But if there is ever aught that I can do . . ."

Oh, there is, there is. You could take me in your arms, you could make my heart whole again!

"I cannot ask you to the house," she said. "Rowan would hear about it and he is wildly jealous of me. Scarcely can I speak to a man that he does not rush me away somewhere. I am sure that the reason he brought me to Portugal is that he heard that you were back in England."

"Then I am endangering you—something I would not do."

He looked about to rise from the table and depart from her life again—*oh, not yet, not yet!*

"Rowan has left the city," she heard herself say. "He will be gone a week or longer."

She saw his eyes kindle and his hand on hers tightened. "Then we might . . . see something of each other?"

Charlotte looked at Tom. The world fled away. . . .

"Hire a coach," she said. Her voice was almost harsh. "We will stop by the house and I will tell Wend . . . Oh, I do not know what I will tell her, but something. We will go south, Tom, across the Tagus toward Setubal. It is a land of sand dunes and orange groves and little villages crowned by ancient castles." *A land for lovers . . .*

His eyes were alight and his hand held hers in a grip that almost hurt. "It is more than I hoped for," he said hoarsely.

And more than I should dare. . . . But there was a madness in her today, a restless longing that would not be brooked. Tom's return was a dream come true, a wonderful impossible dream. A wondrous flower-stitching in the plain weave of her days. She knew herself to be hopelessly entangled in Rowan's web, held fast by her children, who must have a settled home and grow up decently. But that lurking knowledge was submerged in the joy of having found Tom again. She knew it could not last, she knew that Tom would go away once more, out of her life, this time forever. But oh, what fate would be so unkind as to deny them these few precious hours together, hours that must last through a lonely lifetime without him?

Tom hired a coach and they went directly to the house in the Portas del Sol. Charlotte ran in, looking radiant. As she was throwing some night things and a change of clothes into a bag, Wend came in.

"You are leaving him?" Wend asked sharply.

"No," said Charlotte. *Although God knows I would like to!* "I have run across some old friends, the Milroyds. They have invited me to stay with them for a while." And in response to Wend's puzzled look, "I will be gone only a couple of days, Wend."

Wend's puzzled look followed her as she left, running downstairs to get into the coach with Tom.

"Was everything all right?" He was concerned.

"Yes." *I have covered my tracks, Tom. I am about to do what I thought never to do—break my marriage vows.*

It was very silent in the coach. Too moved to speak, Tom took her in his arms.

The world fled away, and Charlotte was seventeen again and deep in love. . . .

At the Tagus River they dismissed their coach as too cumbersome. They crossed the Tagus by ferryboat, hired a cart, and meandered unencumbered into the unspoiled countryside. When they found a fishwife cooking *salmonetes* or red mullet over a little earthenware pot, keeping the charcoal aglow by wafting a straw fan, they stopped to watch, then bought some from her, along with brown bread and a wineskin of *vinho verde*. And lunched upon the fine sand of an empty beach, watching little distant fishing boats bob up and down on the horizon. They spoke of the time Charlotte had surprised Tom by the waterfall—and laughed, and remembered. . . .

After lunch their cart plunged into the pine woods and they turned off the road and found a lonely spot where the pine needles were thick underfoot and low branches swept gracefully down overhead like a curtain.

Tom reached down and piled the pine needles thickly. "Will you sit, my lady?" he asked.

Charlotte smiled and sank down with her apricot skirts billowing about her. "Why couldn't life have been kinder to us, Tom?" she murmured.

"It is being kind to us now," he said huskily, and took off his coat.

"Oh, Tom . . ." She held out her arms in yearning and he went into them, cradling her head in his hand as he bore her gently backward onto the natural bed he had made. The air was fragrant with the scent of pine.

He stroked her hair with a gentleness she had not known for a long time—for Rowan was seldom gentle. He kissed her cheeks, her eyes, her lips, as if he could not believe his luck.

"Charlotte, Charlotte, how I have missed you. . . ." His voice was timbred, soft.

Charlotte closed her eyes. She had missed him too. Ah, how she had missed him! She felt his hand, moving delicately among the hooks at the front of her bodice, release her breasts, and gave a little gasp as his left hand cupped her right breast and he bent down to nuzzle its rosy crest with his lips.

Sweet passions coursed through her at his touch, and she felt her clothes slide away without regret. Tom's long body fitted to hers as if made to her measure, and she moved gracefully to welcome him. Swaying upon their soft bed of pine needles, he slipped inside her gently, tenderly. *This was a lover. . . .*

Charlotte was thrillingly aware of the reverence with which he claimed her, of the love she could feel in his every touch. There was a dreamy, unreal quality to this love they found again here in the fragrant pine woods, and a tingling sense of destiny, as if all their lives had been channeled to this moment.

Then passion swept them up and sent them soaring. They were like wild things with wings beating here on their scented bed of pine. With every thrust she held him closer, closer, as if she would never let him go. With every retreat, her body quivered, wanting him, needing him. With each return, new heights were reached, distant, unattainable. This was a magic world they wandered in, a world Eve had known, and Adam. They were lost here, man and woman, swept up beyond themselves into an ecstasy that seemed to know no end.

Until at last in one mad rush they were swept over the brink into a last wild shattering sweetness and drifted down, fulfilled, to lie together upon the pine needles and breathe the fragrant air.

"Tom." Charlotte lay upon her back, looking up at sparkles of sunlight that glittered down through the dark fluffy branches. "I want you to know that if I had known you lived . . ." Her voice broke.

"I know," he said, moved, and stroked the silken skin of her breasts. "I never believed otherwise."

She turned to him with a little sob and pressed her naked body against him, felt the strong beating of his heart.

"Oh, Tom, what has life done to us? Why did I have to hurt my ankle that day? Why couldn't we have slipped over the border to Scotland? I was married at Gretna Green, you know. Rowan had knocked down my uncle and carried me away, and he told me I must marry him or he would be hanged for trepanning—I thought I was saving his life!"

She felt his muscles ripple and he held her closer.

"I meant to throw myself into the sea," she choked. "I did not want to live without you. And I almost did—but Rowan dragged me back. And then in Lisbon, so far away from all I knew, I found I wanted to live again."

Pressed close against her, Tom understood. She was young, she had wanted to live. In that moment he thanked God for Rowan, who had saved her from the sea. . . .

Saved her so that he, Tom, might hold her in his arms again.

"And then when I learned that I was pregnant . . ." But she could not tell him that Cassandra was his child, it would be too bitter to send him away—as send him away she must—with the knowledge that he was leaving not only herself but also his daughter to another man.

"Hush," he murmured, making it easy for her. "I understand. No man could have asked you to do more than you did."

"Oh, Tom!" She melted against him, feeling hot tears spring to her eyes, that he should have no blame for her. *Her Tom, her wonderful Tom. . . .*

They dallied there through the long summer afternoon, and in the lavender dusk found a tiny inn. There on a crunching straw-filled mattress, with the heady scent of blossoms wafting in through the open window, they made love beneath a white crescent moon to the sound of frogs croaking in the nearby rice paddies. *It had been so long, so long since they had been torn apart, their world shattered. They could not get enough of each other.*

The moon waned and morning came, bright and clear. Tom waked before Charlotte did and leaned over and kissed her awake.

"You were smiling in your sleep," he told her.

Charlotte stretched in his arms, her body moving luxuriously against him. "I was dreaming, Tom. Dreaming that you and I were somehow in possession of Castle Stroud." Her voice caressed him. "And we were the happiest couple in the land, living in the loveliest place." She was aglow with remembering.

Tom's face clouded, for there were no castles in his future. Faith, he could not even give Charlotte the equal of what she had now, that fine house in the Portas del Sol.

Charlotte saw that look and quickly twined her arms about his neck. "Oh, Tom, it was only a dream. Reality is better. Just having you with me is better."

Tom made a soft sound in his throat. His wonderful Charlotte, she would never change. Once she would have thrown her world away on him. He would not let her do

that now. But she was endlessly tempting. He buried his
face in the hollow of her smooth neck, savoring as always
the delicate texture of her skin, marveling that he should
be here with her at all. Surely he did not deserve such
splendors!

Lost in love, Tom and Charlotte stayed snug in their
tiny inn near the rice paddies for two more enchanted
days.

Then they drifted on to the village of Azeitao. There
beside a beautiful stone fountain for which the town was
renowned they ate ewe's milk cheese and drank muscatel
wine. The air was soft and heavy. Reluctant to leave, they
drove on past ancient houses and turned toward Palmela,
watching along the sunlit road as a stork swooped down
upon the croaking frogs. They were content, happy in
each other's company.

At Palmela the inn was full, but they found a room in
one of the low whitewashed houses that lined the cobbled
streets. It was small and not very comfortable and smelled
a little of olive oil and overripe fermented fruit. But they
had brought their magic with them and it lingered through
a starlit night and into the next day, when they climbed up
toward the huge medieval Knights Templars' Castle that
crowned the heights, and paused to catch their breath,
looking out toward Lisbon, where the Sea of Straw caught
and reflected back the light.

Lisbon. . . . The sight of it brought home to Charlotte
that she could not stay here forever, that she must be
getting back to the house in Portas del Sol. But not yet,
surely not yet. . . . A dim foreboding filled her at the
thought of returning. She shivered suddenly, as if the
breeze had turned chill.

"Are you cold?" Tom asked, surprised.

"No—oh, no." What was it Wend had so often said back
in England? *When you feel a cold wind and there's no
wind blowing, it means there's a death soon to be.* Ah, but
that was ridiculous, and not a thought to brook on such a
beautiful day. She turned her back upon the ominous
dazzle of the Sea of Straw and let Tom find them a se-

cluded place to lie in each other's arms there in the cool shadows of the castle's battlements.

The sun was hot, scorching, a breathless day. Damp and straining, concealed by luxuriant palm fronds from prying eyes, their bodies seemed to become one—and today there was a desperation in their lovemaking, for they both knew it was all coming to an end.

Panting, they fell apart at last. Happy, exhausted, fulfilled. Seabirds screamed by overhead. Bees buzzed lazily. They lay in the patterned shade, resting in the golden afterglow of their lovemaking.

Abruptly Tom raised himself upon an elbow. "When did you say your husband would return?"

"He said a week, maybe more. But—"

"I must not ruin your life, Charlotte. I must get you back to Lisbon." He stood up, his face wearing a hunted look. "God knows," he said slowly, "I want nothing more in this world than to take you with me, Charlotte, and live with you to the end of my days. But what can I offer you and your children? I am running out of money—I had barely enough to get me to Portugal. I must take the first berth offered."

She looked at him with large reproachful eyes.

He turned to her with a wild gesture. "What can I do, Charlotte? I cannot take you with me to my haunts in the Bahamas. It is not fit for a woman there. And the pirate's trade is not flourishing—nor will it flourish, for the law will swoop down one day upon the last of these cutthroats and finish them off." He spoke moodily, his tone telling her how much he hated this trade he had grown up in. "So I must take you back, Charlotte, and leave you with this man who saved you from your guardian when I could not."

"Tomorrow," she whispered. "Not till tomorrow."

"Today," he said firmly. He ran a hand through his white-blond hair and his voice went husky. "Because if I lingered another day with you, Charlotte, I don't think I could ever let you go."

She thrilled to his words, to the timbre of his voice as he said them.

She opened her arms. "Don't think about it."

"No." He shook his head. "I am in deep enough now. Your husband may return early, Charlotte. Do you want him to find you gone?"

Charlotte looked at him yearningly. She almost said, *Yes, I want him to find me gone. Take me with you, Tom—wherever you go.* But of course that wasn't possible. Tom could not find employment here in Lisbon—nor could they even stay in Portugal if she left Rowan. Too well she knew his implacable nature—he would seek them out, he would find a way to destroy them. And she didn't want Tom destroyed.

Nor could she go with him when he left, for he would leave as a working ship's officer, but not high enough that he could take along a wife. And besides, there were the children to consider. Little girls who were used to nursemaids and tender care. How could she even imagine blasting away their future? She would not let the scent of orange groves or the smell of fragrant pine woods beguile her. She would see the future as clearly as Tom did, and face it as bravely as he did.

"You are right," she said, rising and brushing off her skirts. "Fate gave us grace for just a little while, Tom. And now we must go back." Her voice was flat, her eyes downcast.

Tom took her in his arms, held her close to him.

"I doubt I can ever match the life Keynes gives you, Charlotte, but if ever I can, *I will be back for you.*"

Her senses wavered. It would be so easy to say, *I will go with you anywhere. Now. We can drift south, perhaps into Spain. Rowan will never find us. We will find a way to live—somehow. Oh, we must seize our chance now, Tom!*

She did not say it. The faces of her children rose up before her. She could see the way it would be if she snatched up the children and went with Tom now. She saw them tired, hungry, hiding, waiting for him to come back from some voyage from which he might never return. They would never have advantages, make good marriages. With Rowan they would have an education, fine clothes, a brilliant future.

Her throat was dry. "You are right," she whispered. "We must go back."

Still reluctant to part, they wandered through the orange groves, drinking in the heady scent, brushing through the dark green waxen leaves, still lost in the magic they were soon to lose. Not till dusk did they go back to Lisbon, lingering along the way so that the moon was out and torchlights flared and cast their wavering light when at last they reached the flat-fronted mansion in the Portas del Sol.

They had released their carriage a short way down the street, for, as Tom pointed out, the clip-clop of horses' hooves rang very loudly on the cobbles at this time of night and there was no use attracting attention. Charlotte agreed. She could imagine that some neighboring serving wench peering out through the shutters would see them there in the pale moonlight and mention it to Vasco, who would certainly tell Rowan.

Walking—and silent now—they approached the house.

Charlotte found that her hands were clenched as they reached the door. All the way back in the coach she had been warring with herself, unwilling to face losing Tom, knowing she must. And now she was—reluctantly—contemplating the long years ahead with Rowan. A man totally unpredictable, violent, and cursed with a consuming jealousy. Facing the future beside such a man filled her with foreboding.

She felt trapped, hopeless.

They had said their good-byes in the carriage, but now she found herself hanging back at the door, caught up by a sudden sense of panic, unwilling to enter.

She got hold of herself. There was no sense waiting. She must go in.

The house was very dark. The outside torch had not been lit; she would have to speak to Vasco about that. Wend must have gone to bed early or surely she would have noticed it. She cast her gaze upward toward the second-floor windows. Her own room was dark, and so, thankfully, was Rowan's. So he had not returned, as Tom feared. Wend and the children occupied rooms in the back of the house, so she would not in any case be able to see their lights from here.

Tom was frowning. "It is too dark." He said it flatly. "I will go in with you."

"No-no, you must not." Her light hand on his arm stayed him. "I do not want Wend to see you, and she might. Nor the other servants, who could describe you later." She felt ashamed to be talking like this, but it was the truth. If she was going to stay here, she could not afford to let stories find their way back to Rowan.

"Then I will wait here until I feel you are safe," he said gruffly.

Charlotte grasped the heavy iron knocker—and felt the door give as she did so. It was not locked! Wend must have left the job to Vasco. She began to feel uneasy. She swung the door wide, saw only the empty staircase sweeping upward into the dimness, lit only by a shaft of moonlight that sifted down, from a high window.

"There is no one here," she said, feeling a sharp sense of relief.

"When you have lit a candle upstairs, come to the window and wave," said Tom tersely. "Then I will know you are all right."

"Yes." She had almost started in when suddenly it was borne in upon her that this might be the last, the very last time that she would ever hear his voice or see his face. Almost had she stepped inside when she whirled about and ran back in panic to fling her arms about him. "Oh, Tom, I cannot let you go," she said brokenly.

He held her tightly for a moment, and when she looked up, she saw that his face in the moonlight was very white and set.

"Go now, Charlotte," he said huskily, and put her away from him.

Walking backward now, seeing him through a veil of tears, she again reached the door and went inside. She did not lock it, she did not have the key, but there was a finality in its closing that made her stop for a moment and lean against it. A chapter of her life was closing with that door. . . .

There was not much furniture in the great hallway, and Charlotte moved forward surefooted to find the stairs, pooled in moonlight from a high window. She forced herself to hurry up them, afraid her resolve would break and she would turn once again and run back to Tom. Now she had reached the top—and she came to an abrupt halt.

A door had swung open, and silhouetted against the candlelight stood Rowan, tall and menacing.

For a moment Charlotte hesitated, her light apricot silk skirts swirling with indecision, poised like a butterfly on the top step. Rowan . . . was back. And advancing upon her.

She summoned her courage. "I have been out all day," she said, trying to sound casual. "When did you get back?"

"I never left," he said in a colorless voice.

She realized her error then and turned in panic to run. Rowan's long arm snaked out and seized the pannier of her skirt. The thin fabric held sufficiently long for him to swing her around to face him before it split with a rip.

"I have ransacked the city looking for you," he grated. "*Where have you been?*"

Desperate, she tried to brazen it out. "With the Milroyds. I left word with Wend, did she not tell you?"

"Liar!" His hand clamped down on her arm. "I was gone but a matter of hours *and then returned here*. There are no Milroyds! You have been with Westing. Admit it! My God, how long had you been planning it?"

Charlotte's eyes were great dark pools.

Rowan had set a trap for her.

And she had walked into it.

"I am not the only liar," she said from between white lips. "You told me Tom was dead. *You left him there to die!*"

He brushed that aside with a shrug of his shoulder. "That does not signify. You are my wife. I told you long ago that I would not look back to what you did before you wed me, but that I would not forgive a further slip." He towered over her.

Charlotte held her breath. *Oh, Tom, Tom, leave quickly!*

she said in silent prayer. *Go now while you still can! There will be other days for you, but this man is going to kill me!*

Suddenly Rowan barked a command, and four men came through a doorway below and stood on either side of the closed front door.

Charlotte felt her breath leave her body as she saw them, for their presence there could surely mean only one thing.

"Let him go," she whispered. "Let him go, Rowan, and I promise you—"

"Be damned to your promises," he cut in bitterly. "You are a lying, faithless wench and I was mad to take you to wife. Call Westing in," he added brutally. "Open your mouth and call his name."

"Tom!" she screamed. But before she could utter her next words, which would have been, *"Run, it's a trap!"*, Rowan's big hand had closed over her mouth, stifling the words.

On the street below, Tom heard her call his name. He came through the door in a rush—and was attacked from both sides. His attackers used no weapons but their fists and boots, but the blows they struck were quick and hard. Overwhelmed by numbers, Tom never had a chance. He went down groaning to the floor and was kicked into unconsciousness.

"Oh, stop them, stop them," Charlotte moaned, writhing in Rowan's iron grasp. "Can't you see they're killing him?" And then, to bring Rowan to his senses, "You'll be accounted a murderer—I myself will accuse you!"

At her words an expression so ugly crossed his face that at any other time she would have blanched before it. "I have no intention of killing your lover, Charlotte," he drawled, and called down sharply to the men below to desist.

"Then what do you intend?" she cried, terrified.

"I intend to have him thrown upon a ship in irons and transported far away," he said coolly, and she realized with prickling skin that he had given this considered thought, that while she had been lying in Tom's arms in the velvet darkness, Rowan must have been pacing the night, making his plans.

She closed her eyes, trying not to see the future—and opened them again at the scrape of boots and saw them dragging Tom's inert body to the door.

Rowan's voice held devilish amusement. "He will wake up on the high seas, penniless, chained, and with his body a torment to him." He seemed to relish the shudder that went through her. "He will wonder what has happened to you." That stabbed at her too, for she was suddenly caught by the certainty that she would never see Tom again.

Love had left her life. It would not be back.

"I will not kill your lover, Charlotte—others will do that." His voice was like a whip flicking an open wound, and Charlotte stared at him in horror.

"What . . . what do you mean?" she faltered.

Rowan was pleased to explain. "The captain's instructions are to take Westing five days out to sea and there drop him overboard sewn in a sack. He is one of those Madagascar blackguards, and I have paid him well—never doubt that he will do it."

Charlotte recoiled from him. "You are lying," she said at last, but she said it without conviction. "Tell me that you are lying, Rowan!"

His short laugh was answer enough. "The ship sails within the hour. You do not believe me? Come, I will escort you to the waterfront, that you may view her departure."

Charlotte was dragged down the stairs screaming. At the front door Rowan thrust his handkerchief into her mouth, wrapped a scarf around her wrists, tied cruelly tight. He himself carried her into a waiting coach that seemed to have appeared from nowhere, dumped her contemptuously upon the cushions, and sat staring at her the whole way to the waterfront.

There he pulled aside the coach's curtain so that she could see in the dawn's pale light a tall ship just now making her stately way down the Tagus toward the sea. It was too far to read her name, but her white sails billowed in the freshening breeze.

Not till then did Rowan free her hands and jerk the gag from her mouth.

"Have you nothing to say for yourself, Charlotte?" he demanded harshly. "Do you not care to weep, to supplicate?"

Desperate, Charlotte leaned forward. She was trembling, and there were tears in her voice. "Find a fast skiff, overtake the vessel, bring Tom back! Give him back his life, Rowan, and I will do anything, *anything*, I promise you!"

The sneer that passed over his dark features was not pretty to see. "It is too late to ask me to save Westing," he told her brutally. "I thought you might wish to plead for mercy *for yourself*."

Too late . . . too late. . . . The words rang like a funeral dirge in her ears.

"Murderer!" she screamed at him. "Murderer!" Panting, she flung herself upon Rowan, scratching his face, beating her fists against his chest. When he seized her wrists, she sank her teeth deep into his hand. With a howl of pain he flung her from him, flung her with such force that her head struck the side of the coach and she slumped unconscious down into the cushioned seat.

25

The Prisoner of the Alfama, Summer 1739

Charlotte was kept aboard a vessel in the harbor for several days, bound and gagged, lying in darkness, listening to the rats creep about. She almost went mad during those days, but was sustained by the thought that if she were indeed on a vessel—and the rasping of the hawsers and the sounds that drifted down to her assured her that she was—then she must be going somewhere and there would surely be an end to the voyage.

And when the voyage ended, she told herself with clenched teeth, trying to hold on to her sanity while a curious rat nibbled at the toe of her shoe, she would burst forth somehow and find her children and sweep them away. She would hie herself to the English consul and tell him how she had been treated—she would win his sympathy and institute divorce proceedings against Rowan. Surely, even though the world would judge her an adulteress, people would realize as well that she had been tricked and duped and treated with inhuman cruelty—the rats were proof of that!

But the captain of the small vessel found time to look in on her with a lantern, saw the rat, and forthwith dispatched his cabin boy to sit by her and scare the rats away. When the boy removed her gag to give her water—nobody offered her any food—she tried through dry lips to question him, to ask where the vessel was bound. But he spoke a language strange to her and she could not get through to him.

At last, when she felt she must surely starve, a coarse blanket that smelled of ship's biscuit and moldy cheese was thrown over her and she was carried away under cover of darkness. She was lifted up—she thought into a coach, for there was a cushion beneath her, the vehicle lurched over the cobbles, and she could hear the clip-clop of the horses' hooves. She knew that they were passing through city streets but she did not know what town it might be—perhaps some fishing village along the coast, where she could make her escape.

At last the conveyance stopped and she was carried into a building, for she heard doors open and close, and up a flight of stairs. Her skin prickled with fright. Could it be that she was being locked up in a tower somewhere? Then she was abruptly plumped down.

It was a terrible shock to have the blanket removed and to find herself sitting in a chair in her own bedroom in the house in the Portas del Sol and to see by the light of a single candle, Rowan standing there with his legs spread apart and an evil expression on his dark face, looking down at her.

"Well, I see you are none the worse for your nights aboard ship," he remarked conversationally, reaching out to remove her gag.

None the worse? Filthy and rumpled and starving, with her hair matted and uncombed? Charlotte stared at him in wonder. Did he intend to act as if nothing had happened?

"I am famished," she said shortly. "And eager to see the children." It came to her suddenly that the house was very quiet. Too quiet. "Where are the children?" she asked in sudden alarm.

Rowan shrugged and she saw that he was dressed for traveling. Indeed she now realized that the doors of the great armoire stood open and that it was empty—her clothes had been removed from it! And there was a heavy chest with a curved top lying near the door, as if waiting for removal.

"Where is Wend?" she demanded.

"Wend and the children are already aboard ship."

"We are going back to England then?" she inquired as calmly as she could.

"*I* am going back to England. You will stay here. A mad wife will be of no use to me there."

Numbed though she was, new prickles of alarm went through her. "I am not mad!" she protested.

"No, you are dead," he said softly. "Your funeral was held the day before yesterday, and now the house is being closed up. It was a problem what to do with you, for the quarters you will henceforth occupy are not yet ready. But have no fear, they are promised by tomorrow. You will be taken there tomorrow night, and afterward my key will be turned back to the owner of this house. For myself, I sail in an hour. Meantime, I will leave you here in the care of these good people." He nodded toward the closed door. "Their name is Bilbao."

Charlotte's wits began to work. "People will say that you have murdered me!" she warned.

His dangerous smile deepened. He seemed to be enjoying himself. "The funeral was swift because the doctor certified that you had gone mad and that some dangerous malady might have caused your illness—it seemed best to inter you quickly. So I have buried an empty coffin and even raised a stone to you. That should quiet any well-wishers you may have who come poking around. Ned came by to offer condolences—and left in a hurry when I told him there was fear of contagion." Rowan's tone was sardonic. "I told him I was taking my broken heart back to England to mend. And he'll bear witness that he found me in deep mourning for my beloved wife—as indeed you see me now!" He spread out his arms and Charlotte realized that he was wearing funereal black; even his cocked hat was as black as his boots.

"You make sport of me," she said bitterly. "Loose me at once."

His brows shot up at this show of spirit.

"I had thought you might ask me why I did not fill that empty coffin with your strumpet's body."

"Very well," she snapped. "I do ask you."

"Because, my dear"—he was always at his worst when he called her "my dear"—"I have no thought to be accused of your murder. You will take care of that for me yourself when you assess your situation and decide to take your own life. I leave the method to you—you are very inventive, so I am sure you will find a way to end it successfully."

"I will never take my own life!" she flared. "Release me at once or I will scream the house down!"

His gaze upon her was almost fond. "I am sure you would delight in doing that," he said. "For 'tis clear your spirit is not yet broken. But it will be, I assure you, although regrettably I will not be here to see it. If you scream, you will be promptly gagged again. I am sure you have had enough experience of that to make you prudent."

Panic welled up in her. "Rowan, this is monstrous! Surely even you—"

He cut through her protests silkily. "In the unfortunate event that you are discovered here in Lisbon after I have gone, my only crime will be that I have set up a sham funeral and left my mad wife in the custody of kind servants to avoid the humiliation of parading her back to England to be held up for ridicule. I have sworn statements from the doctor and two other witnesses that you were raving mad before you 'died.'" He paused in the doorway, those dark gleaming eyes devouring the stunned expression on her white face. She saw in them the same look—was it triumph?—that he had worn when Katherine Talybont had whirled upon him that night in the inn, accusing him of murdering her husband. And, sure enough, he spoke of her. "I thought Katherine was bad, Charlotte, but you are worse. Katherine broke only her promise to wed. *You* broke your marriage vows."

"I came back to you," she pointed out dully.

"Back to me?" He brushed that aside with scorn. "But only until Westing whistled you away again!"

It was true, it was true. If Tom had been able to take her away with him, she would have gone—and gladly. She was silent before the truth of it.

"I searched for you throughout the city. God, I was

gone only a matter of hours. You must have arranged ahead with him, you must have been waiting for the moment when I would leave."

"No, it was a chance meeting." *But she knew he would never believe her.*

He seemed not to have heard. "And then it came to me that I had no need to storm out into the countryside to find you. You would come back for the children. I had only to wait."

She gazed at him hopelessly. "I had told Tom good-bye. I never expected to see him again."

"Oh, spare me further lies, Charlotte!" he said impatiently. He turned to go.

Charlotte made one more desperate try. "Katherine Talybont will put it about that you have done away with me," she warned. "If only to reinforce her claim that you instigated Talybont's murder." Her eyes narrowed. *"Which now I know you did."*

That seemed to reach him. He did not even bother to deny it. He strode back and stood towering over her. "How many lies I have had to weave to make you feel comfortable in this marriage!" he marveled. "You, the adulteress! You, whom I set upon a pedestal and worshipped at your feet!" His teeth ground. "You are another Sophia Dorothea and you deserve the same fate! *And shall have it!*"

Charlotte leaned forward. "You are a devil," she said through clenched teeth. *"Straight from hell."*

For a moment their blazing eyes locked and held like the blades of duelists, locked hilt to basket hilt. Then he flung away from her and his contemptuous laughter floated over his shoulder as he left the room. Not until she heard his boots clatter down the stairway, heard the front door shut behind him, did a sob well up in her throat.

As if on signal, when the front door closed, a heavyset woman came in carrying a bowl of broth. "I am Alta Bilbao," she stated.

"That monster is taking my children away!" Charlotte cried tearfully. "Untie me, I must go and stop him!" In her anxiety, she had spoken in English, and as the woman set down the broth and untied her wrists, she tried to repeat her words in Portuguese.

The woman looked upset. She spoke in Portuguese so fast that Charlotte could catch only a word here and there—but what she made of it was that the *senhora* was not to concern herself, it was only for a little while—until she was better! Desperate to reach the ship before Rowan sailed away with Cassandra and Phoebe, Charlotte tried to untie her own ankles. At this point she was pushed back firmly into her chair and broth was proffered. When Charlotte struck away the broth, Alta sighed and seized Charlotte's wrists and, despite Charlotte's struggles, tied them up again.

When the woman had gone, Charlotte sagged against the heavy chair and deep sobs racked her body. Rowan would sail in an hour . . . with the children . . . her lovely little Cassandra, her tiny Phoebe. In an hour . . . in an hour . . .

The next morning Alta Bilbao again brought the broth, and with it a large slab of bread.

This time Charlotte ate it.

That night, gagged and wrapped in blankets, she was again moved to a new location—to some hilly spot, she judged, from the lurching gait of the donkey or whatever it was her shrouded body had been thrown across. Cramped and half-suffocated, it was almost as if she had been sewn in a sack—and that made her think again of Tom. Had five days gone by? she asked herself wildly. Was Tom, even now, sinking into the green depths, drowning in a sack?

It was indeed the fifth day.

Tom had awakened with a groan and a sickeningly throbbing head in the darkness and stench of a filthy hold. He was aboard ship—too well his nose knew the smell of rotting fish and ship's biscuit and moldy cheese, too well his ears picked up the creaking of the timbers and the crack of the sails. For a moment he was disoriented, seemingly suspended in time and space.

Then a cultivated voice out of the darkness nearby said, "Ah, you're awake. I was here when they brought you in—'tossed you in' might be more accurate. I am Sebastião da Severa."

"Tom Westing." As he spoke his own name, it all came back to Tom—all of it, hearing Charlotte scream and rushing into that flat-fronted mansion and being attacked from all sides, and then the world exploding and dropping him into a bottomless pit. He tried to sit up and found that he was clanking chains—indeed he was firmly chained by the foot to a huge iron ring. He tugged at that ring and began to curse.

"Ah, that is how I felt when they first brought me here," observed the same cultivated Portuguese voice that had spoken before. "Now I am more sanguine, my friend. If one is to die, one may as well accept it in good grace."

"Why are you here?" demanded Tom harshly, his voice rasping because the sudden exertion on top of his head injury had made him feel sick.

He could almost feel the other man's shrug. "I have enemies," was the response. "Enemies who lured me to Lisbon so that they could finish me off and then find a way to claim my lands in Brazil." The voice was wry. "It could be said that I walked into a trap."

"So did I." Tom was thinking about Charlotte. Her desperate scream still rang through his mind. God, what had they done to her? "Have you thought about getting out of here?" he inquired.

"I have thought of nothing else. Indeed, it seems forever that I have been in this dark hole. From time to time I have been brought water and bread. But the sailor who brings it is a mute and cannot answer any of my questions."

The timbers creaked again and there was a sharp slap of sails overhead.

"How long since we cast off?" asked Tom.

"Some hours now. I think our captain must plan to take us out to sea and there dispose of us."

Yes, that seemed likely. Tom's mind was racing. "You say you have lands in Brazil, Senhor da Severa. Have you tried bribery?"

"I would," sighed da Severa, "if I could talk to someone."

As time went on, they got to know each other rather

well, these two unfortunates, as they ate their coarse brown bread, and grew to like each other. Da Severa was a wealthy landowner—he did not say how wealthy, but Tom gathered that his wealth was considerable. He was a childless widower who had chosen not to marry again. In Lisbon his nephew—who had refused all offers to come out to Brazil, since it was clear that that might entail work—had plotted against him with a man called Cortinas. And one night da Severa had been set upon and placed aboard this vessel. If her captain could be persuaded to sail for Brazil instead of wherever he was bound, da Severa could pay him more than whatever sum he had had of Cortinas.

Tom took note of that.

On the fifth day the mute disappeared and a cabin boy brought in a bucket of water and a dipper. And a broken slab of brown bread that the prisoners could share between them. "Wind's coming up," he reported. "Looks like a gale."

"What ship is this?" asked Tom.

"She's had half a dozen names since I've been aboard her," was the lad's cheerful reply. "Scrape and paint, scrape and paint. Just now she's called the *Douro*."

Named for a Portuguese river.

"What was she before?" asked Tom.

"She was *La Lune*." He laughed.

La Lune. The name meant nothing to Tom. "And before that?"

"The *Swallow*. And before that the *Merrie Harlot*."

Ah, there was a name that rang a ship's bell in Tom's mind. "She's been the *Merrie Harlot* more than once, I'll wager," he said softly.

"How would you know that?"

"Because that was her name a long time ago, when she sailed the waters around Madagascar."

"Won't matter to you none," said the lad uncertainly. "Because now that we're five days out, they're going to throw you both overboard. Tonight. The captain sends you his compliments and tells you both to be sayin' your prayers."

"Does he indeed?" Tom's voice was ironic but his heart was beating fast. "Tell your captain—"

"Tell your captain what?" boomed a rough voice, and Tom found himself blinking into yet another circle of light. In the lantern's tawny light a graying man, built like a barrel, came in and stood looking down at him. "I've been commissioned to drop you overboard in deep water, sewn in a sack," the man said abruptly. "And I've a curiosity before I do it to know the why of it. What's your crime, lad?"

Blinking into the lantern's light, Tom looked up warily at his captor.

"No crime," he said. "I loved a woman—and her husband objected."

"Oh, so that's the way of it." The harsh voice above him had gone humorous. "Some husbands have no sense of humor about their wives dallying!"

"She was mine before she was his," growled Tom. "He and a gang of murderers set upon me and pushed me over a cliff. They thought they'd done for me and they told her I was dead. He got her by a trick."

"Clever of him," was the cool observation above him. And then, more thoughtfully, "I took him to be a clever man."

"I came looking for her," Tom told him moodily. "And now he's got you to do for me, and God knows what he'll do to her."

"Like as not," was the callous agreement.

That brusque indifferent voice, that burly neck, that way of standing—a few more scars, maybe, but it was the same man.

"Could it be you're Captain Yarbrough?" Tom wondered.

"Aye, you'll have seen me around."

"That I have," agreed Tom. "But not here. In Madagascar."

"What do you know about Madagascar?" the captain asked sharply. He was peering down at his captive now with more interest.

"I've dined with you there and shared a few bottles of rum when this ship was called the *Merrie Harlot*. Don't you remember me? I'm Tom Westing, Captain Ben Westing's son. I shipped out to Madagascar with him aboard the *Shark*."

"Devil Ben's son? I can't believe it. Ben Westing told me you'd jumped ship somewhere, he hadn't seen you since."

"Aye, I was chasing a skirt," lied Tom.

Above him, Captain Yarbrough swore softly. He pointed a finger at Sebastião da Severa. "You've got a reprieve for the moment, Portagee. I want to talk to this lad!"

An hour later, bathed and shaved, Tom was sitting across from Captain Yarbrough in his great cabin and the captain was pouring him out a glass of Madeira wine.

"When did you last see my father?" Tom asked, sipping the wine.

"Just before his ship went down—with him on it. Broke up on a coral reef near the isle of Nosy Be. None was saved, not one."

Tom felt a ripple of misery go through him. His father and he had never seen eye to eye, but it was a shock to learn that Devil Ben was dead. Lost in the Indian Ocean. . . .

"Sure it's sorry I am to be the one to have to tell you," said Captain Yarbrough morosely. "Have some more wine, boy."

Tom watched the golden wine splash down into his glass. Memories flooded back, not all of them bad. His father had loved Madagascar. For a moment Tom remembered the sights and sounds of the place: impossibly blue water washing white beaches with their fringe of waving coconut palms, the overpowering sweetness of the yellow-green ylang-ylang flowers, clove trees, aromatic lemon grass, vanilla . . . a world apart. A world bloodied by the sword and drunk with rum.

"What did Keynes pay you to haul me out to sea and dump me overboard?"

Across from him, with his feet propped comfortably on the heavy teak table, the old pirate laughed. "Enough," he said. "Enough. And of course," he added indifferently, "I'm honor-bound to do it."

Tom felt a creepy sensation in the back of his neck. This stolid fellow before him might very well do just that.

"Of course, you'd be losing a good navigator," he murmured. "My father tried to teach me all he knew about navigation."

" 'Tis true, it never hurts to have an extra navigator on board," mused Yarbrough. "Still, like I say, I'm honorbound to throw you overboard."

There was a silence between them while Tom eyed the brace of pistols hung on a nail on the wall behind Captain Yarbrough's sturdy back. He wondered if they were loaded, decided any gun in this old pirate's cabin would always be loaded. He was just contemplating the odds on whether he could upend the heavy wooden table, oversetting his host, and snatch one of those pistols from the wall when Captain Yarbrough spoke again.

"O' course, I only promised Keynes I'd do it—I didn't say exactly when. He thought five days, but seems to me there's no hurry. Could be years from today—twenty, thirty, forty." He laughed at Tom's expression, brought his heavy hand down on the table with a slap that sounded like a gun's report. "You're safe from me, boy. Devil Ben's son, fancy that. I'm glad to have you sailing with me, navigator or no."

Tom relaxed. It was the first time he had ever been glad of his sojourn in southern seas slashed by the Tropic of Capricorn. In silent acknowledgment of being given back his life, he raised his glass to the captain.

"Where are we bound?" he inquired.

Captain Yarbrough shrugged. "Madagascar—where a man can still practice his trade. Unless of course something better comes along."

Tom gave him a speculative look. Desperate as he was to get back to Charlotte, he was all too aware that any attempt to leave the *Douro* at any port she touched might change the mind of the old pirate facing him—for the worse. He had heard many stories of Captain Yarbrough and knew him to be a formidable foe.

"I think," he said thoughtfully, "that something better might just have come along."

He outlined his plan to Captain Yarbrough, who nodded
his approval. "You're Devil Ben's son, all right." He turned
to shout at the cabin boy, lurking somewhere outside.
"Bring up the Portagee, lad!"

And Sebastião da Severa was brought to the cabin,
looking elegant and aristocratic despite his cramped days
in the ship's hold.

Tom could not but admire da Severa's calm demeanor,
for from his pallor it was obvious the Portuguese expected
to be forthwith dumped into the sea in a sack.

"Set your mind at rest, Senhor da Severa," he told the
older man warmly. "You'll not feed the fishes tonight. I've
been telling our captain here about you, and he wants to
ask you some questions."

Da Severa's gray head inclined courteously toward the
captain, who slouched back in his chair regarding him, but
the look he shot at Tom was a grateful one, a thank-you for
saving his life.

Southward the great ship fled. Past the rocky cliffs and
winelands of the Portuguese Madeiras, past the spectacular volcanoes of the Spanish Canaries sliding away to lar-
board, south across the Tropic of Cancer. Before the arid
views of the Cape Verde Islands presented themselves, a
decision had been reached aboard the *Douro*, made casually over a three-way handclasp and sealed with wine.

There in the deep-water passages that threaded these
islands, with the hot rainy season drenching the *Douro*'s
decks and canvas, her course was shifted. Instead of following the West African coastline and rounding the Cape
of Good Hope to beat their way north again through the
wild waves and violent monsoons of the hot Indian Ocean
past Durban and drive at last up the Mozambique Chan-
nel to Madagascar, the prow of the *Douro* turned southwest across the equator toward South America and the
lush green rain forests of the vast and rich Portuguese
colony of Brazil.

It would be two years before Tom Westing saw Lisbon
again.

As soon as Charlotte had eaten her breakfast in her new

domain, her feet were untied, the door was discreetly closed, and she was left alone in this strange dim room. She tried to get up, sank back down once, then managed with difficulty to stand on her feet, for she had been several days without using them. It was a barren room, this place they had brought her to. Square and fairly large, with peeling paint of an indeterminate color upon the walls, a bed, two wooden chairs, a washstand with a plain white bowl and pitcher, a cupboard in one corner. And a mirror. Quite a handsome pier glass that stood tall and handsome and out of place. Charlotte recognized it as having come from the house in the Portas del Sol, and wondered why Rowan had had it brought here.

She tottered toward the windows and tried to open the wooden shutters. They were nailed shut.

She turned and tried to run for the door. A swarthy fellow stationed just outside caught her as she came through and pushed her back inside. He turned with a pronounced limp and called "Mae," which Charlotte knew meant "Mother." At that point the sturdy, broad-hipped woman who had called herself Alta Bilbao hurried in, brushing past him. She shook a stubby finger in Charlotte's face and scolded her in rapid Portuguese. From that torrent of words Charlotte was given to understand that madness did not excuse everything—the Senhora was to stay here, *here in this room*, was that understood?

There was another, smaller window in the high-ceilinged room that afforded what light there was, and Charlotte's gaze flew to it when the Bilbao woman left the room. It's shutters were flung wide, but it was high up, far beyond her reach, and heavy with lacy iron grillwork. Peering through a crack in the shutters, she could see that outside her big square room was a small balcony of similar iron grillwork that overhung the street, but the shuttered doors that led to it were nailed as well, and the entire thing was too solid to be beaten down even if she used a chair. Her gaze again sought that heavy—and well-guarded—oak door. Hopeless. She would never get out of here except by trick.

And tricks were difficult with those who did not speak your language—especially if you were clumsy with theirs.

In desperate haste, Charlotte tried to perfect her Portuguese—with the woman who served her, and occasionally with the dark silent man who locked and unlocked the door for the serving woman to get in. What she learned was discouraging enough. The Bilbao family was not local; they were from Coimbra, on the Mondego River to the north. They had once had property but a wagon accident in Coimbra had left Jorge Bilbao lame, and with a crippled son to support, they had become servants. The street they had lived on in Coimbra, Alta told her, was so narrow it was called Quebra Costas, the "rib-cracker." Alta had expected Charlotte to laugh at that, but it had all given Charlotte a sinking feeling as she realized the care with which Rowan must have selected the Bilbao family. They were suitable as servants if she did not transgress, strong and suitable as guards if she did. And she had so easily fallen into his trap. She had underestimated Rowan. . . .

And guard her the Bilbaos did. Charlotte tried bribery, but she had nothing to bribe them with. She promised them rich rewards if only they would let her go. She had money back in England, she told them, lying shamelessly. But Alta and her husband, having lost everything before and been almost reduced to begging in the streets, were cautious. They were being paid richly now, they explained. For every month a messenger—whom Charlotte never saw—brought them a small purse of coins. What more was there?

Desperate, Charlotte tried to throw herself on their mercy. She told them how Rowan had tried to kill her lover long ago and then had tricked her into marriage. It was very tragic, Alta agreed in a soothing voice, but, *senhora*, it was a long time ago and best forgotten. And when the *senhora*'s madness subsided, when she forgot about these stories and was herself again, her husband would come back—himself, he had promised that before he left. And no, he had said she was to have no writing materials. The *senhor* had been very firm about that.

Thus Charlotte was balked at every point, and her bright

spirit slowly sank into a darkness deeper than the semidusk she lived in. Day followed day monotonously in the big square room—windowless so far as her viewing the world was concerned—that had become her prison.

Rage against Rowan tore at her. It distorted her days, skewed them into fury, and she could not eat, but instead paced what now seemed to her a cage, like some trapped animal, nervous and alert for the slightest sound. She sank, shattered, into bed at night to shiver and hate him until sleep mercifully claimed her.

Only to dream savage nightmares, wild dreams in which she managed to kill Rowan—and woke up with her own harsh laughter ringing in her ears. And then she would sleep again and perhaps dream bittersweet dreams of Tom— and wake up sobbing.

One night she waked from such a dream and sat shaking, her head sunk into her hands. When she lifted her head at last she realized that there must be a full moon outside, for a shaft of moonlight from that small high-up window cut through the darkness of the room and illuminated the tall pier glass.

That pool of light seemed somehow to beckon to her, condemned eternally as she was to days of twilight. She left her bed and padded over to the pier glass and stared into the mirror, which gave her back a ghostly reflection. The woman she saw had, she thought, no vestige of her old self. This woman was a haunted vision with a thin haggard face and wild unruly pale hair—for Charlotte had not even been allowed a comb and must needs comb her long locks with her fingers.

She shrank from what she saw.

The mirror, she thought dully; that was why he had left it. So that she might see more vividly her own despair.

The moon waned, and dawn came slowly, but the coming of the new day meant little to Charlotte. Here in the semidarkness of her cell—as she now dubbed her big square bedroom—there was nothing to do but to think about all she had lost. And about Rowan and how much she hated him.

Midnight, the great black stallion, had been shot for

publicly humiliating Rowan. Chase, the hunting dog, had been destroyed for not loving him enough. And she, the erring wife, was to be imprisoned forever and ever.

Rowan would never come back for her, never. She would be kept here until the end of time. Tom was gone from her life, she would never see her children again, what was left for her?

There was the sound of a key turning in the lock, and Alta Bilbao came in, bringing her supper. "You did not eat your breakfast and you have not touched your lunch," she scolded Charlotte.

Charlotte laughed crookedly. Did this woman really believe that food was important? Strange were the ways of fate. . . .

That evening she slashed her left wrist with a knife she had filched from her supper tray. But Alta, who came up looking for the missing knife, found her in time, bound up the wound, and tied her to the bed so that she could not move and injure herself again. After that, all sharp objects were removed from the room. Charlotte was forced to drink from a wineskin and even had to eat with a wooden bowl and a wooden spoon—no knives were allowed. Oh, they were very efficient, she thought sadly, these demons Rowan had set to watch her.

So the interminable half-lit days came and went. Soups and broths and stews—Alta was not a very good cook—followed each other in dreary procession. Since Rowan had left Charlotte with naught but the clothes on her back and thrifty Alta was not about to buy clothes for Charlotte out of her own money, it was necessary for Charlotte to wait naked or wrap herself in a sheet while her own garments were washed downstairs. Her suggestion to Alta that she might make new garments for herself out of those sheets if Alta would bring her scissors, needle, and thread was met with shocked reproof. What, destroy those fine linen sheets? Why, Alta would be held accountable for them by the master when he returned!

Charlotte gave up. She was condemned to wear the same gown forever, it seemed.

All Saints' Day came and went, and Portugal's national

holiday December 8 honoring Our Lady of the Conception. On Christmas Eve the Bilbaos shared with her their traditional boiled codfish and potatoes and rice pudding. But not even the *rabanadas*, that extra treat which Alta had made by frying bread dipped in egg sauce and then simmering it in sugar sauce, could lift Charlotte's spirits.

Back at Aldershot Grange this Christmas her children would be playing in the snow. Or if Rowan had taken them to London, they would be listening bright-eyed to the songs of Christmas carolers. Or perhaps, muffled in woolen scarves and stocking caps, they would be shepherded by Wend through merry, jostling, laughing crowds in the street and stop to eat hot roasted chestnuts or watch a puppet show. Dear God, how she missed them! Her smile was wan as she thanked Alta for including her in this special dinner.

About Tom and his fate, she dared not let herself think, or she would break down completely.

On New Year's Eve, Alta gave Charlotte a slice of the round fruitcake she called "king's cake" and explained that they must lock her in early, as they wished to go out into the town for the New Year's Eve celebration.

Although England had stubbornly refused to follow Europe's lead, and still celebrated the New Year on April 1 as they had for so many centuries, Charlotte—who loved light and life—felt bitter at being cut off from what little gaiety there was. Tears glittered on her lashes as she heard all over the city church bells clanging in the New Year.

The torchlight parade of the Feast of St. Anthony reached her in glimmers through the louvered shutters. And on Twelfth Night there would be the famous battle of flowers at Loule in the Algarve—she remembered hearing Rowan telling someone that if they were still in Portugal in January they would go to Loule to see it. . . .

Charlotte's spirits ebbed even lower when Easter found her still confined to her darkened room. Holidays were always the worst, for Alta loved holidays and never failed to report glowingly about the parades and frivolities— enjoyments Charlotte was never permitted to share. The

Bilbao family knew on which side their bread was buttered. They sympathized with her lot but they had their orders and they were faithful to the coins that reached them monthly, their payment for holding a madwoman captive.

On Whitsunday Charlotte took to her bed and refused to leave it. She turned her face to the wall and refused food.

The Bilbaos hastily held a council of war. If the *senhora* died, their income would cease. Alta explained this carefully to Charlotte and was rewarded by a short bitter laugh.

Alta warned that they would force food down her throat.

"It will not matter." Charlotte shrugged. "For I will surely die if I am allowed no sunshine."

After much debate, Charlotte remaining adamant, her captors were helped in their decision by nature. A great storm visited Lisbon and a flying roof tile broke some of the louvers out of the shutters in Charlotte's room. With this excuse, the Bilbaos, father and son, promptly pulled the nails and unlocked the balcony doors, and Charlotte, blinking at the glare of sunlight after her long confinement, was carried—for she was by now too weak to stand alone—to a cot on her third-floor balcony.

On that balcony Charlotte ate her first solid food in a week. She looked down at the carts and people threading by in the narrow street below and pondered hurling herself headfirst to her death on the cobbles below.

But that was exactly what Rowan wanted—for her to take her own life. He had said so! Her frail resolve strengthened. No matter how desirable death seemed, *she would not do it*.

Besides, the sunshine was working a magic in her feelings. Of a sudden she wanted not to die but to live . . . to live and find her children wherever they were, and, if he had perchance escaped death, to see Tom again, somehow, somewhere, no matter how impossibly long it took.

Once that day she thought she saw someone she knew— florid Lord Claypool, whom Rowan called Ned, striding over the cobbles below in his ginger wig and bottle-green satins. Before she realized that the man below was a stranger, she had risen on one elbow and called down to him—at which point Alta seized her and dragged her back inside and slammed the shuttered doors, blocking out the sun.

Charlotte was too weak to resist, but she wanted to be outdoors in the sunshine. To gain strength. To escape this place.

"If I promise not to call out, will you open the doors?" she asked Alta.

Angry, Alta tightened her lips and shook her head.

"Then I will not eat, I will die, and your money will stop."

Charlotte threw herself facedown on the bed.

Alta stood, biting her lips, considering the mad *senhora*. She stood thus for a long time.

But when Charlotte heard the doors to the balcony creak open and sunshine flooded in, she knew that she had won. She had won the battle but not the war.

26

Summer 1741

Two years after he had been carried off as a prisoner aboard the *Douro*, Tom Westing came back to Lisbon.

For him, all things had changed. Captain Yarbrough, content with a ransom for his wealthy Portuguese prisoner, had sailed away over the horizon, perhaps to Madagascar. But Tom had accompanied Sebastião da Severa deep into the green interior of Brazil to the rich mines that were the major source of da Severa's wealth. And there he had quelled an uprising and once again saved the older man's life. And gotten a poisonous arrow in the leg for his pains. It had been a near thing, and even amid the comforts of Sebastião's handsome plantation house, Tom had been a long time getting well. When he had taken ship at last, Sebastião had clapped him on the shoulder and told him in an emotional voice that if he chose to return to Brazil he could come back as his son and heir. It was a dazzling prospect.

"I've first to find a lady," Tom told him, gripping his friend's hand, his sun-browned face smiling beneath its shock of white-blond hair.

"Find her and bring her back with you," said Sebastião sincerely.

"Aye, that is what I intend," was Tom's hearty response.

His ship had crossed the equator, sailed northwest across the Atlantic's Cape Verde Basin, crossed over the submerged Great Meteor Seamount, with the Canaries and Madeiras off to starboard, and beat its way at last over the dangerous undersea Gorringe Bank, where incredible pressures were building up as deep beneath the sea the European Plate strained against the African. Neither Tom nor the other mariners knew that this vast undersea world existed. To Tom the ocean was made up of soundings that told him they would not come aground, just as the night was made up of stars that guided his way by night, and winds—*winds that were carrying him back to her*! His heart sang with the wail of the winds in the rigging. Charlotte, Charlotte once again!

He trembled that she would be all right—but of course, *of course she would*! Hadn't fate done enough to them? She would be waiting, loving him still, and now he had money, he could sweep her away with her children, he could give them all a good life—in Brazil.

And if Keynes stood in his way . . . Tom's square jaw hardened. If Keynes stood in his way, this time he would kill him.

And so it was that Tom came ashore in Portugal with a springy step.

Only to find the great flat-fronted mansion in the Portas del Sol shuttered and closed.

Eventually he found the owner. Keynes? Yes, he remembered leasing to a man named Keynes. An Englishman. He had let him out of his lease because he wanted to return home to England. His young wife had died and his country was girding for war.

"Died?" asked Tom incredulously. "*Died*, you say?"

The owner looked perplexed. "Yes, something about a fever, I think. I remember there was quite a handsome funeral procession."

That was not good enough for Tom. Charlotte could not be dead! Records were not good enough for him either. He found the doctor who had certified to her death, fully expecting to find there had been some mistake, a wrong name, a servant girl—Wend perhaps.

The old doctor—who for all he had the face of a plaster saint was an inveterate gambler who had squandered three fortunes and would do anything for money—looked uneasily at this square-jawed Englishman. Nervously, he confirmed that Charlotte was indeed dead.

Keynes has murdered her, was Tom's first thought. A rush of blood came to his head. Aghast, he seized the doctor by the throat. "How did he kill her?" he said gratingly. "Tell me, *how?*" For if it was by the sword, he would slash Keynes to pieces. If it was . . . ! He shook the doctor violently. "*How?*" he demanded hoarsely.

The old doctor had seen death in other men's eyes, and he knew he was seeing it now as he looked into Tom's gray face.

"I swear to you," he gasped. "Keynes did not kill her."

"Who then?" Tom shook him so hard his teeth rattled.

"No one! No one!" He was afraid to add, *I know Keynes did not kill her because she was alive and well when I attested to her death!* Instead he gasped out beneath Tom's crushing fingers, "She died of a malady—you are choking me, young sir!—of a sudden fever that carried away many." Best not to mention madness to this dangerous fellow! Out of sheer fright he added, "Her husband was most grieved, I can tell you. He broke down completely."

His gratuitous lie had worked. Tom had guessed Keynes loved his beautiful young wife—he just didn't know the tortuous way that Keynes' mind worked. His fingers relaxed their grip on the doctor's throat. "You were there when she died?"

"Oh, yes, yes!" was the eager response. "A lovely young woman, her death was most tragic."

Lovely indeed. . . . And more than tragic—this confirmation that she was gone had blasted Tom's world apart.

"Where does she lie now?" he asked dully.

"Lie?" Alarm sprang again to the doctor's features. "Oh, you mean where does she lie buried? I was not informed, but I can direct you to the most likely place." He gave Tom directions to a cemetery and quaked in his heart, hoping the Englishman Keynes had raised a stone to her.

The Englishman had. Tom found it, a simple stone giving only her name and the dates. Tom knelt beside that stone and grieved. He felt as if the very heart was being torn from his body.

At last, gray-faced, he rose and hied himself to a stone-cutter. That simple stone was not enough to mark the resting place of his wonderful Charlotte. He commissioned the fashioning of another stone, a footstone of whitest marble, a delicate spire pointing toward heaven, whose gates, he was certain, would have opened wide to receive her. And he ordered carved upon it—no matter what Keynes thought if he viewed it later—a message that came straight from his heart: "Here lies Charlotte, beloved of Thomas, *ate o fim do mundo.*" Until the end of the world. . . .

While that stone was being carved and erected, Tom prowled south through the countryside where he and Char-lotte had been so briefly happy. He slept in the tiny inn where she had lain in his arms beneath a crescent moon—and wept for her. He wandered on to the village of Azeitao and rested beside the stone fountain where they had shared ewe's-milk cheese and drunk muscatel wine, and on to Palmela. There he climbed up toward the battlements of the ancient Knights Templars' Castle that crowned the heights, where he and Charlotte had made their fateful decision to return to Lisbon, and looked out upon the glitter of the Sea of Straw. If only he had taken her away—carried her off by force if necessary—she might be alive today.

Through the drifting sweet scent of the orange groves he made his way back to the Tagus and across it to Lisbon. But for him the lights of the city had dimmed. Moodily he wandered the streets, gazing on sights she too must have seen—as if that would bring him closer to her. His feet carried him through the steep winding ways of the Alfama. Walking in the Alfama made him feel closer to her some-how; he could not imagine why. After all, Charlotte had lived in the handsome Portas del Sol, not in the old Moorish quarter.

Once he lost his bearings, inquired his way, and was told he was on Nowhere Street. A grim smile flickered across his grief-ravaged face. Nowhere Street. . . . Perhaps that was where he belonged.

Halfway along, he paused and for no reason suddenly looked up at a third-floor balcony. He would at that moment have given all that he owned or would ever have and all hope of heaven just to see her once again. . . .

The balcony was empty. Jorge Bilbao had limped home in a hurry and told his wife to get Charlotte off the balcony, for he had just sighted the Messenger at the end of the street. The Messenger's orders had been strict: if the Bilbaos wanted to go on receiving their monthly coins, then the mad *senhora* must get no sight of the Messenger.

Had Tom come by just minutes before—or indeed a few minutes later—he would have seen Charlotte, pensive, on that balcony, and their entire future would have been altered.

As it was, Tom stared at the empty balcony, felt a tug somewhere inside him, and then was jostled by a donkey struggling through with a load of oranges. He moved on.

That afternoon he took ship for Brazil. After a brief but joyful reunion with Sebastião da Severa, who now looked upon him as a son, he plunged deep into the interior. To forget her. He combed the wilds of the Minas Gerais looking for gold.

Instead he found diamonds.

Charlotte had finally given up hope for Tom. He was dead, he *must* be dead or he would somehow have found her. At night she dreamed of him, of course, and by day she longed. Just as she longed for her children and trembled for their welfare.

But now she no longer pinned her hopes on a miracle—that Tom would save her. Instead she pinned her hopes on the Messenger who brought the Bilbaos their money every month—if she could only talk to this man, win him over, make him *understand*! And perhaps the Bilbaos feared she would do just that, for she had overheard their muttered conversations in the hallway when Jorge told Alta that Charlotte must be gotten out of sight—the Messenger was coming.

At last, on the day the Messenger was to arrive, she managed to kick off one of her shoes as Alta hurried her inside, so that the shutters Alta promptly slammed shut before she left the room did not quite close. Alertly Charlotte listened for the front door, heard it open and close behind someone—the Messenger! She dashed to the balcony, closed the shutters behind her, and leaned over the railing, peering down to see who would come out onto the cobbles.

After a while her patience was rewarded. A man—or perhaps a youth—came out of the low front door. Came out stooping, for, though slight, the figure was willowy and tall. Whoever he was, he wore the long black stocking cap traditional to Portuguese fishermen, a shapeless shirt, and baggy trousers over bare sun-browned feet. There was something vaguely familiar about the figure that puzzled Charlotte. Did she know any fishermen?

No matter—she must try!

"Wait!" she called in Portuguese.

Below her the figure looked up. Stocking cap tossed back, the face that peered upward toward the balcony was well known to her.

It was Annette. Annette's mocking face meeting her eyes with a mixture of hatred and glee.

The Arranger had not done it alone. He had commissioned his faithful Annette to select the Bilbao family and pay them their monthly stipend. Annette was the Messenger.

Charlotte knew that she was lost. Between the two of them she would never get away.

Yet that was the very day on which Tom had passed by and paused to look up.

By so short a time had she missed him. . . .

But somehow the sight of Annette had lent steel to Charlotte's resolve. She *would* escape, she would find her way back to the real world, not this half-life of balconies and locked rooms; she would see her children again! Her chance would come, and when it came *she would be ready for it!*

Determined to gain strength and keep her figure, after that she exercised—every day, pacing around and around the big square room. She would wear a path in the floor, she told herself grimly, before she would let herself give up! And she worked desperately to perfect her Portuguese with Alta Bilbao so that when her chance came she could melt into the crowds of Lisbon and disappear. Alta Bilbao was so flattered by Charlotte's sudden interest in her and her language that she was moved to lend Charlotte a wooden comb.

And so the indomitable spirit of the woman lost on Nowhere Street prevailed.

Charlotte waited, waited for The Day.

Annette's was not the last familiar face that Charlotte was to see. For in the fifth year of her imprisonment, Rowan came to Lisbon.

What a battle he had waged with himself in London! On winter nights he would see Charlotte's face in the fire. On summer days the scent of flowers would waft her presence back to him. Whenever he saw that certain shade of blonde hair, his heart leapt. Yet he would not admit to himself that he cared.

Trying to rid himself of Charlotte's witchery, he had plunged into work with a vengeance—and in the increasing furor that swirled about powerful Walpole he at first found ample scope for his talents. Against Walpole's wishes, England had gone to war with Spain—and at first that war had gone well, despite Walpole's cynical comment when the church bells had pealed that declaration of war: "They may ring the bells now—before long they will be wringing their hands."

Nobody listened. After all, had not Admiral Anson sailed round the world, sacked a Spanish port in Peru, and captured the Manila galleon which carried on trade with Acapulco? And on the other side of the Isthmus of Panama, had not Admiral Vernon taken—as the buccaneer Henry Morgan had done long before him—the Spanish fortress town of Porto Bello? And when Admiral Vernon failed in his efforts to storm Cartagena and Santiago, Walpole was blamed, not the admiral. After all, who had let the English navy go to pot during these peacetime years? Walpole!

Amid the furor, in 1742 Walpole was forced to resign. He was given the title of Earl of Orford, which put him into the House of Lords and removed him forever from the great power he had wielded in the Commons. Walpole's power had been divided between two Secretaries of State, and although many—Rowan among them—might deride the incompetent Duke of Newcastle, of whom it was said that every morning he lost half an hour and spent the rest of the day running after it, none could question the competency of that other Secretary of State, Lord Carteret, who was bursting with energy and quickly gained the king's favor.

Walpole's star, which had shone so brightly for so many years, had faded—and with it, Rowan's. From the House of Lords, Walpole still gave the man they called the Arranger an occasional commission, but they were matters of less moment—and far less lucrative.

Still Rowan Keynes was a wealthy man—he could afford this enforced retirement, although it was a bitter pill to see his world breaking up and realize that the world that replaced it would have no place for him. For if he went over to the enemy camp, how could he expect aught but treachery? There were those among them who had said that they would see him hanged. He resolved to give them no opportunity.

For a time he gave himself over to pleasure. Determined to push Charlotte from his mind, he spent his time in gaming hells, and his bed was occupied by a succession of actresses and loose women. But when his long body relaxed and he dreamed, his dreams were of Charlotte, and he woke ashamed and furious that the memory of her bewitching body and clear, unafraid eyes could still torment his dreams.

He knew that Annette would see to it that Charlotte did not escape. Her letters, written in bad French, reassured him on that score. But he was driven by an overpowering urge to see her again, and at last he managed to convince himself that Charlotte had not been punished enough. He would visit Lisbon and—his dark eyes gleamed—he would play a sadistic game with her.

And so in the fifth year of Charlotte's imprisonment in the Alfama, Rowan sailed for Portugal and conferred with Annette, who promptly made her way to the low front door of the house on Nowhere Street, there to give the Bilbaos explicit instructions.

The next day dawned hot, with unrelenting sunshine. And in the hottest part of that hot day, when people stayed indoors to avoid the enervating heat, and even the dogs and cats sought the shade of alleyways and slept, Alta Bilbao carelessly left the door of Charlotte's room ajar.

From her balcony Charlotte had already seen both the Bilbao men, father and son, depart, strolling down the narrow cobbled way toward a tavern they visited almost every afternoon—she knew that because Alta grumbled about it. But when she did not hear the hallway door close or Alta's key turn in the lock, she sprang up from her languid position reclining on the balcony and went inside.

The door to her prison stood invitingly open.

On silent feet Charlotte approached that door. Downstairs in the back of the house she could hear Alta singing and clashing plates about. Charlotte did not know the layout of the downstairs rooms, but it seemed likely that from the back Alta could not view the front hall. Walking softly, almost holding her breath, Charlotte tiptoed downstairs. She winced whenever a step creaked, but always at those points Alta's singing seemed louder than ever. Downstairs she peered toward the back, but Alta was nowhere in sight. The low front door lay just ahead.

Praying that it was not locked, Charlotte stole toward that door. Her heart skipped a beat before it swung open on well-oiled hinges. A moment later she had shut it soundlessly behind her.

For the first time in five years she stood upon the cobbles—free!

The street was empty, baking in the heat. Overhead some laundry flapped lazily. But at the far end of the uphill side was a sight that froze her. Jorge Bilbao lounged there, leaning against a building talking to a stranger. His back was toward her, he had not seen her, but his presence meant that way was barred to her—she would never get past Jorge!

She looked in the other direction. The entire curving narrow street was empty of people. Only a couple of dogs slept in the noonday sun.

Taking a deep breath, she hurried along. At this end Nowhere Street curved and there was a maze of alleys, one of them leading to the main square. She was debating which way to take when suddenly from a shadowed doorway a tall figure stepped forth.

A familiar figure.

"Rowan," she said, looking about her warily to see which way she might run.

His body was blocking her way, and she had the feeling that he would pounce upon her if she even moved. She had been about to take a step, and now she put her foot down gingerly. He was looking her up and down. To her eyes he looked not a day older—fashionably dressed and sporting a cane. But she could not fathom his expression as he stood there. There were shutters over those drooping eyelids.

She could not know how the very sight of her shook him. That was why he had stayed away all this time; some inner voice had warned him that if he saw her again he would forget his vow to punish her and take her in his arms. Fighting that desire made him adopt a harsh, contemptuous manner.

"Your condition seems to have deteriorated, Charlotte," he said negligently, poking at her ragged skirts with his cane.

"I am what you have made me," she said in a colorless voice.

"So you are," He seemed amused. "Well, I am surprised that dress has lasted all this time. I had thought your flesh would have been bared before now." Idly he poked his cane through a recent unmended tear in her worn skirt and brought the cane down neatly through the frayed material, leaving a long rip.

Charlotte fought back a gasp at this further indignity.

"Are you going to strip me here in the public street?" she gasped. "For if you do, I shall shout to all the world that I am your wife and they will look upon you with even more horror than I do now."

A mirthless smile flitted across Rowan's dark countenance. "If you so much as raise your voice to me, I will break your teeth with this." He gave the cane a slight negligent wave.

"I nothing doubt it," she said evenly, giving him a steady look. "Since I stand before you helpless."

Her courage, that slight lift of the head, were both so characteristic of her unbroken spirit that he was taken aback. He had fully expected that after five years of imprisonment she would cower before him. Instead he found himself flinching inwardly before those clear violet eyes, that unrepentant mouth. The witch still had the power to move him, and he hated her the more that it should be so.

"Tell me, Rowan," she said through dry lips, "how are my children? Are they well? Do they miss me?"

"They are well enough," he said shortly. "Or were, when I left them back in England."

"Both of them?" she insisted.

He seemed to consider. Then he smiled. "Phoebe is the delight of everyone," he said.

"And Cassandra?" She was almost afraid to ask. *Suppose Rowan had come to realize that Cassandra was Tom's daughter?* "Does she ask about me?"

"Never."

"Why . . . why not?" She faltered, taken aback.

"She thinks you dead," he told her brutally. "They both do. I arranged a funeral for you, remember? I even let them observe the procession."

Up to now Charlotte had believed that the story about her "funeral" was a lie that Rowan had invented to torment her. Now the enormity of what he had done rocked her. "How could you be so cruel?" She felt herself trembling in revulsion. "They are so small, what have they ever done that you should make them suffer for my sins?"

"Oh, they don't suffer," he said easily.

"They do—they must grieve for their mother!"

"Indeed they are very merry." He gave an indifferent shrug. "It is as if you had never been."

She wanted to strike him, to beat on his chest, to kick those silk-stockinged shins and bring a howl of pain to that handsome cruel mouth. Somehow she managed to keep herself in check. She even kept her voice steady.

"Haven't you done enough to me?" she demanded. "You've locked me up, kept me shut away, made me frantic with worry for my children." Of a sudden all the tears she had shed in her long captivity welled up in her yearning voice. "Oh, Rowan," she choked. "Can't you at least find it in your heart to let me visit them? I would promise never to bother you again, if I could see them just once more. . . ."

Her voice trailed off before the dark blaze of fury that leapt from his eyes. Fury that for a moment he had felt a real compassion for her, alone and friendless, far from home.

"All in England believe you dead, Charlotte. You will stay dead!"

She took a step backward before the fury in that voice. Panic rose in her. "But is there no way—?"

"None!" A door had been slammed in her face. Closed forever. "I told you when last we met that you would never see your children again. Now I tell you that as God is my witness, if ever you manage to get in touch with them or make yourself known to them *in any way*, I will cast them both out into the street with naught but the clothes on their backs. I will cut them from my will. I will turn my back on them and they may live or die as fate pleases, for I will take no notice of what happens to them!"

Charlotte shrank back, trembling. "Oh, God, you would not! Rowan, they are your children too!"

"And as long as they are *solely mine*, they will receive good treatment. But they must have no knowledge that their mother lives—now or ever."

He would do it too. She remembered the great stallion he had loved—and shot dead. A vision of Midnight rose up before her, Midnight, so beautiful and sleek. Charlotte had always felt that in his strange way Rowan loved her. *But he had loved the horse too.*

She could expect no kindness from the implacable man before her. Rowan had not a forgiving nature.

She moistened her dry lips. "Then I have no alternative," she said hopelessly. "I will not try to return to England. I will stay here. I want my daughters to have a future."

He nodded. "Very wise." He sneered. And then, as if he had just this moment thought about it, "How will you live?"

Charlotte was caught short. It seemed he did not plan to continue her imprisonment! "You will give me money enough to exist, I suppose—since you want me kept out of the way."

"You are wrong. I have given you the last coin you will ever receive from me."

"Then . . . Oh, what is it to you?" she burst out. "Stand aside! I will make my own way. You do not care how I live!"

"True." He was very composed, but he made no move to let her pass. "Still, I wish *you* to consider it, and . . . I have a gift for you."

He brought it out from his pocket and she saw the sudden flash of gold. For a wild moment she thought he had changed his mind, that he had been merely baiting her.

"You asked about the children," he said. "I thought you might like to have these portraits of them."

She saw then that he was dangling two locket-size miniatures from a black grosgrain riband. With a cry of joy she snatched them from him, stared down at them greedily. Here was little Phoebe with yellow ribands in her dark curls, looking like Rowan and a little sullen. And here was Cassandra, beautiful Cassandra, with features so like Charlotte's, and Tom's dazzling coloring.

"Those were painted just before I left England," he told her.

Charlotte looked up, her eyes shining with unshed tears. "They are both so beautiful," she said huskily.

Rowan stood looking down at her with a mixture of emotions warring on his intense face. *She* was the beautiful one, he thought. For all her disreputable clothing, she seemed to shimmer before him, a vision of tempting loveliness. He yearned to touch her, to stroke her sweet yielding body, to feel her shiver against him as she once had done. He wanted things to be the way they had been before. *He wanted her back.* For a terrible soul-wrenching moment he struggled with that, fighting the urge to forgive her. He opened his mouth to tell her so, and then his clenched teeth bit back the words, but not before his strangled voice got out her name, *"Charlotte."*

Charlotte caught that sound in his voice, that break that signified indecision, and hope flickered within her. Perhaps after all he would relent and let her see the children. . . .

"Charlotte," he said again more huskily, and he could not believe that he was really saying the words, "can we not find it in our hearts to forgive each other?"

There was a sad mockery in the wan smile that passed over Charlotte's face. "After all that has happened, could I really forgive you, Rowan?"

He had lost the battle with himself. His every nerve was quivering with desire for her. He felt again that old familiar pain in his groin, and all his senses rose up to take her, enfold her, make her his again.

She looked away from him out into the far distance, past the cramped narrow passages of the Alfama, back to other days, other arms. "I might have forgiven you once, Rowan." There was a shiver of grief in her voice. "I might even have forgiven you this long imprisonment. For the sake of the children. But"—her head swung back squarely to face him and her voice rang out hard—*"do you really think I would forgive you Tom's murder?"*

Rowan was breathing hard. His face was white. "So Westing still stands between us?"

"Tell me"—her violet eyes flashed—"that you did not kill him!"

He had humbled himself—he who was not in the wrong! And yet there she stood, this lovely recalcitrant woman

who was his wife, *admitting* that she still loved another
man! It was too much. Pride and vengeance crashed together, blood rushed to his head, the floodgates of his
passion broke.

"*Damn you!*" he said thickly, and the words seemed to
rise out of hell. His hand clamped down on her arm and
he whirled her into a nearby alleyway.

Charlotte would not have gone with him had she had
any choice, but his grip was like steel, threatening to
crush her arm. And if she made any outcry, she guessed
he would snatch back the little miniatures that were now
her only tenuous link with her children—and for those she
would have fought.

The alleyway was deserted, a tiny dead end terminating
in a high-walled courtyard. On either side were blank
shuttered whitewashed buildings. To her left were a pile
of wooden boxes and a crooked stone stair leading upward.
The balcony above was deserted, the wooden door shut.
The heat of the day was blazing down, and those inside
were trying to keep the sun out.

Rowan kicked aside the boxes, and before she knew
what he was doing, he pushed her down into the street
under the stair and fell upon her, jerking her worn skirts
upward.

Charlotte would have screamed, save that she was trying
to recover from being knocked out of breath when she
landed on the cobbles with Rowan atop her. And then she
had no chance to scream, for Rowan's hard mouth sought
hers punishingly. He was sucking the air from her lungs.
She fought him in a terrible panting silence, but he was far
too strong for her. His cruel hands were bruising her
tender flesh, his shoes thoughtlessly bruising her thrash-
ing calves. And then he was entering her and she felt a
revulsion such as she had never known, and tore at him
with her nails, drawing blood from his swarthy cheek. He
did not seem to feel it. Panic rose in her. Rowan was going
to kill her—and make love to her while she died!

But such was not his intent. In his murderous rage and
disappointment, he told himself he was merely assuaging
his passions, using her as he might have used a soothing

lotion to anoint a wound. He told himself he cared nothing
for the woman herself as he drove deep within her. It was
her wonderful body he craved, the delights of her flesh
that he had yearned for—so he told himself as he stormed
her small fortress and tried deliberately to hurt her, as she
had, he thought vengefully, hurt him.

But when it was over, stormily over, to his alarm he
found that she was lying limp in his arms. For a terrified
moment he was afraid that he had killed her. And he
began desperately blowing air into her lungs, now that he
had had his way.

A shiver of relief went through him when she stirred.
But with her revival his anger at the wench washed over
him once again.

"Get up," he commanded.

And when she was so faint that she still could not stand,
he jerked her upward and held her dizzily upon her feet
and lightly slapped her face.

"There," he said callously. "That will restore the color
to those pale cheeks."

"How could you?" she whispered. "Your own wife, and
here in a dirty alley . . . ?" His unspeakable behavior had
left her bereft of words, for she was still trying to gasp in
enough air to keep alive while her limbs trembled.

And now she dared to remonstrate with him, she who
had driven him to this! Well, he would show her a darker
side of the world!

"Oh, I have learned much from you," he drawled.

"Never! The devil taught you!" Her voice was shaky but
her spirit was unbroken.

"You taught me the ways of hell," he said roughly. And
then, looking down at her more calmly as she leaned
trembling against the building wall while he fastened up
his trousers and brushed himself off, "You seem to have
dropped something. Here, I will get it for you."

Charlotte's gaze flashed downward. The miniatures! She
must have dropped them from nerveless fingers as she
struggled with him upon the cobbles! She tried to reach
out for them, but he snatched them away with a nasty
smile, held them tantalizingly just out of reach.

His words were brutal. "I have just shown you how you will earn your living," he said heavily.

"Never!" she gasped.

His cold laughter jarred her. "Here and in worse places than this—and with worse men," he mocked, but he let her snatch the miniatures on their grosgrain riband away from him.

Charlotte looked her tormentor full in the face. "There are no worse men," she said evenly.

His face contorted and he fetched her a light cuffing blow across the face that snapped her head to the side. She almost lost her footing as she reeled to the side, but another cuff brought her upright. Now she stood before him with her back against the whitewashed wall. Her face was very pale and her violet eyes were dark pools of anger and reproach.

He had driven her past the point of no return, but still her rejection of him drove him on. "You will have to grow used to being cuffed," he advised, baiting her. "Street women are often pummeled and beaten by their customers. You must learn to take rough treatment with a smile."

He waited but she made no answer, merely stared at him woodenly.

"You will notice that the backs of the miniatures are made of gold?" he pointed out.

The barest flicker of her lashes told him she had indeed noticed.

"I had the china miniatures affixed in such a way that they will almost certainly be broken should the gold backing be removed," he added conversationally.

"They will remain unbroken," she told him in a toneless voice.

"Oh, I wonder if they will?" He was smiling a terrible smile now. "You have no money, you have not eaten since breakfast, you will soon be growing terribly hungry—and what of tomorrow? If tonight some footpad does not get you and perhaps drive a knife through your ribs for disdaining him, you will find yourself hungrier still. I wonder how long it will take before you are hungry enough to pry the gold from the back of those miniatures?"

Charlotte took a deep breath and her delicate chin lifted. "You can count upon it, Rowan," she said unsteadily. "I will *never* be that hungry!"

His brutal laugh rang out, but there was grudging admiration in his eyes for this woman he had tricked and degraded. Another man, a normal man, would have felt his heart melt at her gallantry in the face of such overwhelming odds, and felt sympathy for her plight. But not Rowan—her humiliation of him demanded vengeance.

He studied her for a long smoldering moment, as if memorizing her features. Then he turned without a good-bye and took himself off. First to walk off his rage, then to find a tavern and there drink himself into forgetfulness.

Charlotte waited, her back stiffened with pride, until Rowan was out of sight. Then her aching body seemed to wilt and she sank down to the cobbles as if she had no strength, leaning against the house wall, eyes shut and body quivering.

She drew a long shuddering breath. Her lawful husband had just had his way with her and she felt dishonored.

In that moment she thanked God that she could no longer bear children. To have carried Rowan's child in memory of these hateful moments in a dirty alley would have been unbearable.

She sat there for a long time while the shadows lengthened. Looking up through her lashes at the sky, she realized that people would soon be coming out of their houses. The evening festivities would be beginning; soon the night would resound with song and the wailing of stringed instruments.

She could not face it, not any of it, not tonight.

There in the shadow of the stairway she pulled the wooden boxes around her in such a way that she was concealed beneath the stairway, and curled up for the night.

Across the city Rowan had found a tavern. He seated himself on a wooden bench and drank steadily into the night until he lay sodden. Realizing him to be a person of quality—such a man as might bring down the law upon a house that let him come to harm—the tavern keeper allowed him to remain, slumped over a table well into the next day, when he lifted his aching head with a groan and demanded more wine.

Fortified by that drink, he lurched out of the place and made his way blindly to the waterfront.

There the brisk salt air, the cries of the *varinas* selling fish, the whole normal scene, restored him to himself. His anger melted and he faced at last his true feelings toward Charlotte:

She had deceived him, she had abused his trust, he told himself, and yet . . . and yet . . .

And yet she was a fire in his blood he now knew would never be quenched.

Pale and haggard now, he turned about. Whatever she had done, he was going to forgive her. Not because she deserved forgiveness but because his desire for her consumed his mind when he was away from her.

He walked faster now, looking for a conveyance to take him back to the alley where he had left her. Finding none, he broke almost into a run. He would sweep her up, he would kiss away her tears, he would take her back to England, he would restore her to her children! Oh, God, anything was better than living without her! He had had enough of that, certainly.

But when he returned to the alley where he had left her among the piled-up boxes, Charlotte was not there. He checked the house on Nowhere Street, thinking she might have retreated to that safe haven, but the Bilbaos had not seen her. He combed the narrow alleys of the Alfama, but turned up no trace of her.

Alarmed now, he began an intensive search for her.

She was not to be found. There were several who said that a blonde woman in peach-colored rags had been seen dancing for coins in the public square. Hearing that, Rowan winced—*he* had brought her to this. His mouth closed in a grim line as he asked what had become of her.

Nobody knew. A crowd had collected, an officer of the law had arrived upon the scene, he had been about to take her away, but a fight had erupted in the crowd and he had turned about to settle it. When the combatants had been separated and he turned back, the woman was gone. Everyone was vague about what had happened to her. One man was of the opinion that she had slipped away during the altercation. Another thought a large woman, a well-known local madam, might have hurried her away. One beggar lad thought she had been whisked into a black-and-gold coach.

Nobody knew for sure.

Half-mad now with fear that something terrible might have happened to Charlotte, Rowan was looking for her. There was not an unsavory place in Lisbon that he did not visit. Yet at the end he came away empty-handed.

Nobody had seen the beautiful blonde woman with the violet eyes and the ragged peach silk gown.

He would have gone to the authorities, but how could he do that? Could he say that he was looking for a woman whose funeral he had arranged five years ago? Dared he admit in this strange land that he had forcibly imprisoned his wife and kept her all that time against her will locked up in a house in the Alfama? The doctor who had signed the death certificate would of a certainty not admit the deed—he was more likely to call Rowan mad and offer to certify him! The Bilbaos would deny it and flee in terror of the law.

He was caught in a trap of his own devising.

Now he spread his search out into the countryside. He was convinced that Charlotte had somehow gotten out of Lisbon—but where could she have gone? North to Oporto he ranged, and into the pine woods and the gorse-covered hills and blue hydrangea hedges. Through the cool reaches of the stream-laced Bucaco forest and into the tall grass country he roamed, and into the wide meadows where the fighting bulls were bred. Southward into the lush Algarve he went, searching for her through Moorish-looking villages until at last he reached Lagos, where the great sixteenth-century caravelles had begun their long voyages to India. Past purplish rock cliffs he made his way to that southernmost tip of Portugal—squall-racked Sagres, where in the wild countryside Prince Henry the Navigator had charted the voyages that had built an empire.

And it was in the wild grandeur of those storm-lashed headlands that Rowan at last gave up. He looked out hopelessly over the forked and rocky promontory that seemed to point an arrow out into the Atlantic, and was chilled by the knowledge that he had combed the length and breadth of Portugal and had not found her.

He, the man who had made a fortune finding the unfindable, who had sniffed out the trail of those who had arranged their escapes and set up their hiding places with gold long months before, had been defeated by a tired, disheveled, penniless wench just free of a five-year imprisonment, loosed suddenly in a city where she had not a single friend. Impossible—but it had happened.

For him it was a nightmare come true.

A chilling thought occurred to him. Charlotte might be dead—and by her own hand. Perhaps, after his last brutal treatment of her—and he now admitted to himself that it had been brutal, and felt remorse—she might have preferred death to letting him find her again, this woman he had mauled and scorned and imprisoned. The thought seared him.

Defeated, he made his way back past almond trees bent by the ever-blowing strong winds, past stunted figs, but the glorious scenery went by him in a blur. Back in Lisbon, he searched for her again, but he no longer believed he would find her. She was gone, gone forever.

Only then, as he stared in desolation at the stars gleaming down over Portugal, did he realize that he loved her. Truly loved her. He had loved her, without realizing it, all the time.

And now she was gone. Vanished forever.

Into the dark alleyways of Lisbon. . . .

BOOK II:

Cassandra

27

London, England,
February 8, 1750

There was the promise of snow in the biting wind that whipped down from the North Sea, rocking the body of the green-painted stagecoach that was lumbering steadily down the Great Essex Road, making the Colchester-to-London run. In Chelmsford, where they had changed horses at a coaching inn while the passengers ate, that promise had become a reality. But despite a sudden flurry of windblown snow that had nearly obscured the square tower of the parish church as the passengers clambered back onto the stage, the cheery red-nosed driver had bellowed out, "We'll be in London on schedule, good sirs and ladies."

"I should hope so," muttered one elderly lady in an aggrieved voice. "I'm black and blue already!"

And indeed she had reason to groan. Devoid of springs, the stagecoach careened down that ancient roadway built by the Romans some sixteen centuries before, lurching and jolting from side to side in a manner that caused the passengers to be thrown in a heap against each other and against the sides of the coach. As they approached London, the snow grew deeper, the road more treacherous, and the driver perforce had to slow his pace in the gray dusk as the horses' hooves fought for purchase on treacherous deep ruts made slippery by hard ice. But inside the coach there was one young passenger who hardly felt the bumps.

Oblivious to the protests of the other passengers, Cassandra Keynes, who would be seventeen in March and should *not*, at her age, the elderly lady's disapproving gaze told her, be traveling alone, lifted the leathern flap designed to keep out the wind. With her other gloved hand holding her hat clapped to her head, she peered out at the big old trees that grew perilously close to the road and the six thundering coach horses.

The dark branches of those massive oak and hornbeam trees seemed to bend down over the road in the whipping wind and to swish menacingly close in the gathering darkness, but she could still make out their sturdy trunks, and in between, the countryside about. Her long green eyes were brooding as she studied them. It had happened about . . . here. Yes, there was the stile over which she had tripped. Head out of the window now, unmindful of the steaming breath of the horses raising a white mist ahead, or of the lurching coach wheels or the iron horseshoes that sometimes struck a bright spark from a rock laid bare of ice by the biting wind, unmindful of the cursing coachman or the crack of the long whip, unmindful of everything until one of the passengers pulled her back inside with a snarl, she was remembering the event that last year had got her exiled to Colchester and the strictest school for young ladies her father could find.

Cassandra's lovely young face was pale as she sat back in her seat, letting the leathern curtain flap against the window until the passenger who had pulled her back in quickly bent over and secured it. She was glad of the dimness inside the coach, for she knew that a tumult of emotions must be pouring over her all-too-expressive features.

She had been afraid of what this strip of road would do to her, for it brought it all back—the accident, everything.

Oh, why couldn't they have stayed at Aldershot Grange, where she and Phoebe had spent most of their childhood? she asked herself, heartsick.

Indeed, it was at Aldershot Grange that Rowan Keynes had brought his small daughters when in 1739 he had left Charlotte imprisoned in the Alfama and sailed back to England. He had left them there in the care of Wend and

gone back to London alone, there alternately to brood and
to carouse.

But England's war with Spain—or "The War of Jenkins'
Ear" as it was popularly called—had begun a conflagration
which had gradually reached out to embroil most of Europe. And when in July of 1745 Charles Edward, the
Young Pretender, had landed in Scotland and in August
raised the royal standard in Glenfinnan, Rowan Keynes
had ridden up from London. He arrived on a lathered
horse and told Wend brusquely that Aldershot Grange
might lie along the route south of an invading Scottish
army and he was taking twelve-year old Cassandra and
eleven-year-old Phoebe with him to Cambridge, there to
enroll them in Mistress Endicott's School for Young Ladies. She was to get them ready at once.

Wend was desolate. Cassandra and Phoebe were like
her own daughters and she bade them a tearful good-bye.
Indeed she and Livesay had had to be surrogate parents
for both children, except on their rare visits to London or
even rarer visits from their father.

It had been a mistake, bringing his daughters to Cambridge. Rowan, thinking only of their safety and need for a
genteel education—and not wanting to enroll them in a
London school where they might drop in unexpectedly at
number forty-three Grosvenor Square and find him engaged in some debauchery unfit for their tender years—
had completely overlooked the fact that Cambridge was a
university town, brimming over with virile young men,
many of them aprowl for whatever skirts seemed to lift
easiest, all of them agog for a pretty girl.

In such a place slim young Cassandra with her moonlight-
blonde hair and emerald eyes and heart-stopping beauty
was hardly likely to be overlooked.

"Boys have been mooning around this school like cats
on a back fence ever since that tow-haired Keynes girl got
here," grumbled Cook. "It's got so every time Maud throws
out the slops I hold my breath waiting to hear a howl as
someone gets spattered in the face!"

Dot, the new and perky seventeen-year-old chambermaid, chimed in: "What with all the little tips I get from

boys who want me to slip notes to her, I'll be able to retire at twenty-three!"

There was general laughter in the school's commodious kitchen.

That Cassandra with her elegant good looks should be the center of all this commotion had made her younger sister restive. For Phoebe, with a wisdom beyond her years, realized full well that she would never be the blazing beauty her sister was. She had inherited her father's looks—and his features fit better on a man than on a woman. Her nose, for instance, she considered too long, too narrow, her dark brows too straight, her lips a trifle thin. Not even in her first bloom would she have Cassandra's heart-stopping loveliness, her wonderful winning smile. "Piquant" was the word they would use for her, never "beautiful" spoken on a long indrawn sigh. Everyone loved serene smiling Cassandra—all but Phoebe. Phoebe loved only herself.

Totally selfish and wrapped up in her own affairs, Phoebe told herself contemptuously that she didn't *need* Cassandra's beauty, she had something better—she was smart.

Cassandra's impression on Cambridge and its students had been very lighthearted at first, just notes and smiles and waves and sometimes tossed kisses. But at Mistress Endicott's the girls were growing up. By the time Cassandra was fifteen, Jim Deveney, a university student whose family lived in the town, managed to wangle an introduction to Cassandra through his mother's long friendship with Mistress Endicott. And Cassandra sometimes on Saturdays found herself having tea with Jim's mother and sisters while Jim sat in the background beaming at her with his irrepressible grin. Jim was bluff and open-hearted. Cassandra was all too aware of his adoration—indeed the whole school tittered when Jim arrived looking like an eager puppy to carry her off to tea—and she idly considered that one day she might marry Jim . . . or someone like him.

There were lots of candidates for that honor, including Jim's wild and handsome distant cousin Tony Dunn, who had descended on Cambridge—having already been sent down from Oxford and two other schools—when Cassandra was fifteen. Tony fell madly in love with her too.

Phoebe, now fourteen and with the school's smartest hairdo—Phoebe was slim and ultra-fashionable even if she'd never be pretty—had grown tired of living in her beautiful sister's shadow. She decided to do something about it. With gifts of pomade and perfume and hair ribands, she managed to corrupt Dot into staying up and letting her in and out of the school's side door by night. Cassandra and Phoebe shared a room, but it was easy enough to wait until Cassandra was asleep and slip away to some tavern and there drink wine with the university students, who were eager enough to buy drinks for any of Mistress Endicott's closely chaperoned young ladies—and especially the sister of beautiful blonde Cassandra.

Cassandra found out about it when she woke to find Phoebe, fully dressed at four in the morning, staggering tipsily into a chair and falling onto the bed.

"Where have you been?" she asked, still half-asleep.

"At the Rose and Thorn."

"The Rose and . . ." Cassandra sat bolt upright in bed, staring at Phoebe in the moonlight. "Phoebe, that's a *tavern!*"

"So it is." Phoebe's voice was slurred. She lay back, making no effort to undress.

"And you're *drunk!*"

"That's possible too," agreed Phoebe cheerfully.

"How did you get out?"

"Why? Want to come along next time?"

"No, I don't. Anything could have happened to you, wandering the dark streets alone by night. Phoebe, you're only fourteen years old!"

Phoebe gazed up at her owlishly. "I'm aging fast."

"Phoebe, have you done this before?" And when Phoebe giggled, "Well, you aren't going to do it again! Do you hear me?" Cassandra was taller, stronger. She grasped her younger sister by the shoulders and shook her for emphasis. "*You aren't going to do it again!*"

"Go to sleep," said Phoebe, her voice still more slurred. "Soon it will be time to get up." Her dark head lolled and she began to snore.

Really alarmed that something might happen to her

little sister, Cassandra sat there studying Phoebe. She had
certainly filled out during this last year, even though boys
still scarcely noticed her. Perhaps if she offered Phoebe a
compromise . . .

"I'll see that Jim's mother invites you to tea and has
some of his friends over, if you'll promise not to slip out
again," she told Phoebe the next day.

Phoebe, who had last night been introduced to gin and
had had to be helped home, was suffering from a hangover, and she groaned. "Don't say it so loud," she pleaded.

"*Phoebe!*"

Phoebe shuddered. "I promise not to visit the taverns. I
promise to take tea—go away!"

All the rest of that week Cassandra tried groggily to stay
awake to make sure Phoebe kept her promise, but the
week after that she found she was getting too sleepy to
stay awake. And the first night she dozed—although
Cassandra never knew it—Phoebe was out on the town
again.

And *this* time she found the man who was to be the love
of her life: Clive Houghton, who had been thrown out of
even more schools than Tony Dunn. Clive was a younger
son of the dowager Marchioness of Greensea and dazzlingly far above Phoebe on the social ladder. He had
gleaming dark hair, a lock of which fell intriguingly over a
dissolute face, and a hot stare which made girls giggle
nervously. His clothes were impeccable—and so were his
manners when he wasn't drunk, which wasn't too often.
Almost from arrival at Cambridge, he was a leader of the pack.

He didn't even notice Phoebe.

But Phoebe was not Rowan's daughter for nothing. She
saw him, she wanted him, and she set about getting him.

First she must get rid of Cassandra. Not only because
Cassandra fully intended to stem the tide of her little
sister's wild ways but also because Cassandra was too
beautiful—she took men's minds off things—other girls for
instance. So reasoned Phoebe.

And it would be remarkably easy to do. All she had to
do was consider Cassandra's independence, her warmhearted
generous nature, and what she would do in time of crisis.

And then create that crisis.

That very night she set about it.

"I'm awfully tired of school," she told Cassandra that night after they had both gone to bed. "I'm tired of being a schoolgirl, I'm tired of Cambridge—we should be in London, Cassandra."

"Well, we will be." Cassandra yawned. "When we have our London season."

"I don't think we'll ever have a London season," scoffed Phoebe. "And anyway, it would be years away!" She laughed mischievously. "I don't mean to wait."

After learning that her fourteen-year-old sister was out by night getting drunk in the taverns, Cassandra found that comment alarming. She lifted her head, rested on one elbow, and peered over at Phoebe. "What is that supposed to mean?"

Phoebe sighed. "I think I'm in love."

"Who is he? Who are you in love with?"

"Oh, you don't know him. He's a university student that I met on one of my nights out."

"Well, go to sleep," said Cassandra ruthlessly. "He'll still be there in the morning."

There was just the slightest ripple of laughter in Phoebe's voice. "But maybe *I* won't be. . . ."

"Oh, Phoebe, you *promised!*" wailed Cassandra.

"Only not to visit the taverns," insisted Phoebe. "I never promised not to become a Fleet Street bride."

"A *Fleet Street bride!*" Cassandra glared at her sister's half-seen form in the almost total darkness of the room. "Don't you know those marriages aren't legal? Do you want to be married by some dirty convict from Fleet Prison? And given some kind of paper that has no meaning to it?"

"Well, it's the wrong season of the year for Gretna," said Phoebe sulkily. "It looks like it may snow anytime."

"Indeed it does! It has a way of snowing in winter! Come now, Phoebe," she coaxed. "The Twelve Days of Christmas aren't far off, and maybe we'll be going down to London then."

"No, Father would have written to us before now. We'll be spending Christmas right here at the school." She sounded bitter.

Charlotte sighed. "Maybe he's waiting till the last moment."

"No." Phoebe was definite about that. "We're stuck here—at least *you're* stuck here. But I've a mind to take the stage to London and get married. Did you know married women have much more . . ." She sought for the word.

" 'License' is the word you're looking for, I presume," said Cassandra grimly. "But while you're contemplating extramarital affairs even before the ceremony, let me remind you that a husband is allowed to beat his wife with a stick no larger than his thumb—and most men have large thumbs."

"Oh, he would never beat me," Phoebe declared confidently. "Not in a thousand years."

"You never can tell," Cassandra warned darkly. "Bridegrooms become husbands awfully fast!"

"Will you miss me when I'm gone, Cassandra?" asked Phoebe.

"If you say one more word, I'm going to pile everything we own against the door and it will all fall down and wake me if you try to open it."

Phoebe was instantly quiet.

She was already up and gone when Cassandra awakened. But that was not unusual—Phoebe's French teacher was an early riser and insisted on starting her classes early, the first one before breakfast.

Groggily, for she had not been getting much sleep, Cassandra pulled on her clothes and prepared to face the day. She was really going to have to do something about Phoebe, she decided. All this talk of Fleet Street weddings and running away to London was getting on her nerves.

Their classes were different, so she did not expect to see Phoebe until lunchtime. Just before the girls went in to lunch, Dot the chambermaid, took Cassandra aside.

"I don't know what to do." Dot was almost wringing her hands. "Mistress Phoebe made me promise not to tell, she warned me if I told anyone she'd tell Mistress Endicott about all those times I let her out at night and I'd be dismissed."

That much was true. Phoebe had warned Dot that if she didn't do exactly as she was told, she, Phoebe, would go to the headmistress and tell all about her nighttime escapades. Blackmail, she had found, worked even better than French perfume and hair ribands. "All that will happen to me is I'll be sent home—where I want to go," she warned Dot. "But *you'll* be dismissed!" Dot had been terrified.

Alarm coursed through Cassandra. "What's Phoebe done now?"

"She made me tell her French teacher that she had a bad headache and wouldn't be down to class. But she didn't stay in her room—I saw her slipping out in the direction of the coaching inn and she was carrying one of her boxes." Dot's voice had risen to a very convincing wail. "Oh, you don't think that she . . . ?"

The Cambridge-to-London stage! It left early. Cassandra looked at the chased gold watch she carried in her pocket. The stage had left two hours ago, to be exact.

"Yes, Dot, I think she may very well have taken the stagecoach," she said soberly. "But don't tell the school just yet. Maybe there's still a chance to overtake it."

Dot looked vastly relieved, but not for the reason Cassandra thought. Dot was merely glad that her part in this charade was over. For Phoebe, she knew very well, was hiding in the cold attic at this very moment, bundled up in shawls and blankets and eating an apple.

"If you're asked, you haven't seen me this morning," Cassandra told Dot. "But do you think you could get a message to Jim Deveney for me? I don't think he has any classes today. He should be at his mother's house, sleeping late."

"Yes, I think I could," said Dot doubtfully. She was wishing she had never seen either of the Keynes sisters.

Hastily Cassandra penned a note. And afterward she counted her money and dressed for travel. If worst came to worst, she had enough money for the coach ride to London. She packed a small bag. After that she stood before the window until she saw Jim striding down the street toward her.

He stopped below the window and she tossed down to

him the bag, and her hat and heavy cloak. Then she tripped down the stairs with great unconcern just as the girls were coming up from lunch. One or two of them stared at her curiously, one whispered she'd be punished, Mistress Endicott had noticed her absence at lunch! Just now a schoolgirl's punishment was the farthest thing from Cassandra's mind. And the least important.

She ran outside, and together she and Jim raced down the street, Cassandra putting on her cloak as she ran. "We've got to stop them," she said. "Phoebe could ruin her life with a Fleet Street marriage!"

Jim Deveney well knew what a Fleet Street marriage was: it put one in limbo, not quite married, not quite single. And although the certificates of such marriages had been used in the courts, everyone knew they weren't legal.

"We could hire horses and try to overtake them," Jim offered.

Cassandra thought of riding wildly down the highway, perhaps in a blast of snow. "They'll have to stop," she said. "At lunch, to change horses, and again for the night. If we take the stage—the next one to London—and then when it stops for the night we hire horses and overtake them at their inn where they're spending the night—"

"Splendid," interrupted Jim exuberantly. He found the thought of a moonlight ride with Cassandra beside him exhilarating.

But the afternoon stage was late. After all, it was an extra stagecoach, put on this time of year when so many people went down to London for the Christmas festivities. Three hours late. Cassandra and Jim looked at each other in consternation.

"We'll catch up with them tomorrow night," said Jim uneasily.

But by then they'd have spent the night in each other's arms. . . . Still, at the moment it seemed the best solution. It wasn't safe to try to ride for long distances on this road by night, with so many highwaymen about!

But the next day the stage broke down in the middle of nowhere and the passengers had to wait until a wheel was procured. At this point Cassandra and Jim held a council of war. They decided that in spite of the time lost, Jim would hire a horse and go on ahead. He would stop the stage, loudly bellowing that there was a trepanner on it! And somehow hold it there until Cassandra caught up.

At the moment it seemed a splendid idea.

The night was clear and cold but the roads were heavily iced.

By the time they reached the outskirts of London, Cassandra was girding herself to meet whatever came. If Jim had not been able to stop the stage, she decided she would go at once to the house on Grosvenor Square. Father adored Phoebe; he would know what to do.

At almost that moment they heard a crash, and the stage had come to a long skidding halt that almost overturned it and caused the passengers opposite Cassandra to scream in unison. Cassandra tore open the leathern flap and peered out.

Up ahead, a heavy dray had come skidding around an icy curve and overturned. The horses were down and kicking and neighing in a tangle of reins; the choleric drayman was cursing his luck and shaking his fist at heaven.

The dray had rounded a turn too fast on the ice. The body of the dray had swayed and swiveled and tilted over and crashed to the roadbed directly on top of a rider who must have found himself trapped between the dray and the thick trunk of an oak tree. He lay quite still beneath the corner of the fallen dray.

It was Jim, and he was very obviously dead. Crushed beneath the dray.

Cassandra heard her own wild scream as she leapt out of the coach and stumbled over the stile to reach him.

It had all been sorted out later. Jim had caught up with the stage as it arrived at the coaching inn in London—and Phoebe had not been aboard. He had been riding back to tell Cassandra that.

To Cassandra's astonishment, her father and Yates had met her when she alighted from the stage, and promptly taken her home, there to receive the shock of her life.

"We must find Phoebe," she protested. "She could ruin her life. She—"

"Enough!" roared Rowan. "Let us have no more lies." He was thinking how like Charlotte to the life Cassandra was—and *she* had lied to him too. "You were trying to cloak your elopement by having this lad from Cambridge ride alongside the stage. 'Tis clear that—"

"It is not clear. Phoebe was running away and Jim and I were following, trying to stop her."

Rowan waved a parchment in Cassandra's face. "I have here a letter from your sister, telling me that you had run away from school on the afternoon stage. She thought you were meeting some lad—she couldn't be sure whether he'd be with you. It was posted with the driver of the morning stage from Colchester."

Cassandra felt the blood drain from her face. Phoebe had tricked her. She knew that whatever she said now, she would not be believed. She lifted her chin.

"So you choose to believe Phoebe and not me," she said bitterly in a tone of, *Do your worst!*

As unrepentant as her mother had been! Rowan took a deep breath. "I have already decided what to do with you," he said pleasantly. "I have found another school for you—the strictest this isle affords!"

Cassandra was not even allowed to stay in London for Christmas. Instead she was promptly bundled up and the very next day sent in a closed coach to Colchester.

Mistress Effingham's school was very different from Mistress Endicott's easygoing establishment in Cambridge. The building was a picturesque wattle-and-daub affair with great blackened timbers and leaded bay windows. It had steep roofs and tall fancy brick chimneys and its second story protruded, medieval-style, perilously over the street. No one had ever been known to enjoy a single day in Mistress Effingham's rigidly austere establishment. Cassandra's room looked out at the towering Norman keep that dominated this ancient Roman city, and she sometimes thought life must be more enjoyable in that grim fortress than it was in the school, where the girls were required to keep their eyes downcast and pray a great deal.

Unabashed by her own treachery—after all, it had all worked out to her advantage!—Phoebe wrote to her:

Jim's family won't believe you weren't running away with Jim; they hold you responsible for his death. I tried to see them and explain, but they wouldn't receive me. And the serving wench brought out word that his mother had burned your letter unread. I haven't told anybody where you are because one of them—Tony Dunn perhaps—might be mad enough to follow you there, and what Father would do with you then, I can't imagine!

He would probably lock her in a dungeon at that point, thought Cassandra with a sigh.

The letter went on to say:

The next time we meet, you must call me Lady Houghton. For Clive's title is Lord Houghton. His mother is the dowager Marchioness of Greensea. She hasn't received me yet—but she will! We were married in Fleet Street. Father doesn't know yet—just as well he doesn't, he'd be furious!

Lady Houghton. Cassandra put the letter aside in amazement. Didn't Phoebe realize that a Fleet Street marriage certificate didn't entitle one to a title? Lady Houghton indeed! And then she reread the part about Jim's mother burning her letter, and the guilt she had felt when she saw Jim's inert body lying there crushed beneath the big dray returned again to haunt her.

Jim's mother had every right to blame her! She had dragged Jim into something that wasn't his affair, and Jim had died of it. It was something she was going to have to live with the rest of her life.

When, in early February 1750, Mistress Effingham suffered a stroke, and died, her assistant and next in command, Mistress Peterson, felt herself unequal to the task of running the school. She simply bundled up everybody, bag and baggage, and sent them home.

And so it was that on February 8, Cassandra Keynes found herself once again entering London in a coach, this time through driving snow. And even though she would never forget what had happened the last time, when the buildings of the city rose up before her, half-seen through the snow, she could not but feel her spirits rise too.

Of a sudden, as the coach negotiated the snowy cobbles, it gave a lurch. Cassandra thought later that she had almost *felt* the horses stagger. Simultaneously there was a muffled rumble that seemed to come from somewhere below. At this point the coach's window flaps were hastily snatched back, letting in not only a shower of snowflakes but also the sight of a nearby chimney toppling and crashing down into the street below.

"It's an earthquake!" shrilled the elderly lady from beneath her thick dark velvet French hood. "It's a judgment on us!" She glared about her at the coach's other occupants—sinners all, she had no doubt—and found them as upset as herself, for earthquakes were popularly believed to be the firm hand of God shaking up sinners and bringing down their houses upon their evil heads.

Atop the coach, the earthquake had even rattled the driver. "Everybody all right?" he roared down.

There had been only that single rippling motion, the earth had settled down, and Cassandra was feeling that someone should call back, "You shook us up worse all the way along the road!" when she realized that the elderly woman was pointing a shaking finger at her.

"I've no doubt you're a young harlot with sins aplenty," she accused. "Young girl like you, traveling alone!"

"I'm a schoolgirl, returning home because the school's headmistress has died and the school disbanded!" was Cassandra's stiff reply.

"Here, here," muttered someone testily. "We're all frightened, but let's not have words. We all know London's a sinful city that's been shaken before—no need to blame one of us for it!"

The elderly lady subsided, but her gaze on Cassandra was still suspicious. And stayed that way through the mild aftershock that shook them before they reached the warmth of the coaching inn.

Perhaps, Cassandra thought uneasily, she deserved that look. For had she not led a man to his death outside

London? And now on her return to the city she was greeted by an earthquake!

It was a great relief to her to hear the gentlemen talking in the common room of the coaching inn where she went to drink hot chocolate before again venturing out into the weather. Their conversation was all about the earthquake. Above somebody's excited cry that her sister's chimney had been brought down by it—and why should it strike her sister, who had always led a blameless life?—Cassandra could hear three well-dressed gentlemen at the next table trying to explain the quake as caused by something in nature.

"I tell you it will turn out to be this electricity in the air that has just been discovered," said one sagely, toying with his wine.

"And do not forget that just before the ground shook, the air pressure was quite low," chimed in one of his companions.

"Nonsense!" The third man struck the table with his fist. " 'Tis the near proximity of the planet Jupiter." He downed his ale as if that settled the matter.

Cassandra was fascinated. So there were those who felt that earthquakes had a *natural* cause! And why not? When frost split open a boulder in winter and sent it rolling down the mountainside, no one suggested that God was punishing sinners, even if the roof of some unfortunate cottage was caved in by the stone!

With more confidence she finished her hot chocolate, called a hackney coach, and headed for Grosvenor Square and the confrontation with her father that she dreaded.

She found he was not at home. Yates let her in and gloomily told her that the master was out on one of his wild-goose chases for young Phoebe, who had been reported seen in Oxford. Cassandra was surprised that her sister had been able to elude her father all this time.

"She hops about like a flea," was Yates' aggrieved explanation.

So Cassandra would be mistress of the house—at least until her father came home. And after that? She winced. She would not consider what might happen then.

Cassandra's bags had not even been brought up before the heavy iron knocker sounded.

"That will be the fellow who's called here every day for a week," predicted Yates, heading for the door.

Curious, Cassandra waited with one foot poised on the stair.

"And would Rowan Keynes have returned from his trip by now?" inquired a courteous voice with a distinct Scottish burr.

"Not yet, sir." Yates was about to close the door in the caller's face when Cassandra said, "Wait. Ask the gentleman to come in, Yates."

Looking surprised, Yates held open the door, and a heavyset graying man stamped the snow off his boots and came into the hall. The candlelight flickered on pink cheeks, bright eyes, and a very merry smile.

"Your servant, lass." He swept her such a lighthearted bow that she judged him to have been a rake in his youth.

"It's very cold out," said Cassandra. "Won't you have a cup of tea—or something stronger—before you venture back into the snow?"

The caller would. While she drank tea and he sipped brandy, she learned that he was Robert Dunlawton, a Lowland Scot from the Cheviot Hills, and that his business with her father was that, having learned that Rowan Keynes was in effect an absentee landlord, he was desirous of purchasing Aldershot Grange.

"Oh, you can ask him, but he won't sell," said Cassandra confidently.

"And why not?" asked the smiling gentleman she was already calling "Robbie."

"Because long ago he promised that Aldershot Grange would be my dowry because I loved it so, while Phoebe should have her dowry in money because she didn't like it there and was always pining for city life."

"D'ye mind if I ask him?"

"No, of course not." Indeed, if Aldershot Grange was not to be hers, she could think of no nicer owner than the man who sat facing her. She said as much.

Across from her Robbie Dunlawton's eyes kindled. "Since

you've just arrived, I take it you did not know that Lady Merryfield's ball is being held tonight despite the snow?"

"No, I didn't know." Cassandra was visibly disappointed, because Lady Merryfield was one of the few people she had met on a previous visit to London and she felt sure she would have been invited. She told Robbie that, sounding crestfallen.

"No need for regrets, lass," he told her staunchly. "Lady Merryfield is one of the few people I know in London too, and she's invited me to her ball this night. Dash upstairs, lass, and change to a ball gown—I'd be honored to squire you."

And why should she not? There was no one here to gainsay her! A smile of such brilliance broke over her face that the Scot was dazzled by it. She set down her teacup and rose.

"Pour yourself another drink—I'll be right down," she told him, and blew him a kiss from the door.

The Scot chuckled.

He stopped chuckling when his lady came down the stairs. Her chaste white velvet ball gown—indeed it was the only ball gown she owned—had been bought in Cambridge so that Jim might squire her to a ball being given by one of his sisters to announce her betrothal. But on the very night she was to wear it, Cassandra had mysteriously slipped on the top step of the school's main stairway and cascaded down the entire flight. She was never to know that Phoebe, bored and annoyed at not being included in the party, had surreptitiously smeared the top step with butter—and even as her gleaming dark eyes watched Cassandra's fall, was leaning down quickly to mop up the evidence with her kerchief. With Phoebe's bright gaze upon her, Cassandra had landed in a heap at the bottom of the stairs. Her high heel had caught in her dress and torn it. The rip was mended, but not the sprained ankle that had accompanied it. Cassandra had missed the ball and lain in bed for a week. But Phoebe had not missed the ball. She had asked Cassandra breathlessly if Jim might not squire her instead, and Cassandra had sent down word asking him please to do so. The dress had never been worn.

But now at last she was wearing it—and to a far more glamorous occasion than the betrothal party in Cambridge. She had struggled into the gown without help, and realized at once that the tier on tier of tiny white lace ruffles with which the Cambridge dressmaker had filled up what should have been a low-cut neckline, "for modesty's sake," was a mistake. A pair of scissors ruthlessly applied took instant care of that and left Cassandra with a dazzlingly low-cut gown. The bodice was too tight—Cassandra was anxious about that, and quite breathless as she struggled with the hooks in the back—but a little push to her breasts brought their temptingly rounded tops above the neckline and gave her a little more room to breathe.

Her hair she could do little about, so she simply combed out its gleaming length and swept it upward, twining in it a cheap necklace of white brilliants she had bought at a fair in Cambridge—in the candlelight they would look like diamonds! She could not make it all stay up, so she let a single lock of it dangle down over one white and almost bare shoulder.

Despite the fact that the velvet was somewhat crushed and the entire gown smelled strongly of lavender, having been laid away so long, her color was high, her emerald eyes sparkling, and the entire effect was such, as she swept down the main stairway with her huge skirts billowing out behind her, that the Scot drew in his breath sharply.

"You're a vision," he said, his voice a bit husky.

"Oh, I do thank you." Cassandra's mind was occupied by other, more important things. "Robbie, would you mind—I don't think I got my top hook fastened properly."

She turned her lovely back. Robbie's strong hands trembled ever so slightly as he fastened the top hook, and again when he bent down to affix the tall pattens, really a kind of platform shoe almost six inches tall, to her white kid dancing slippers. He rose with the scent of lavender wafting through his lungs and gazed down in wonder on this sixteen-year-old beauty who seemed to have changed from charming child to dazzling woman right before his eyes.

"I will go find us a hackney coach," he announced, reaching for his hat.

"Nonsense. Yates will take us in our own coach," said Cassandra recklessly. *In for a penny, in for a pound!* "Yates!" she called. "I desire the coach to be brought round. Robbie and I are attending Lady Merryfield's ball!"

Yates gave her a disapproving look and seemed about to refuse.

"Otherwise we must call a hackney," said Robbie Dunlawton softly.

Perhaps something in the Scot's level gaze decided Yates. He brought the family coach round and it proved much more comfortable than a hackney, as Cassandra pointed out, with deep wine velvet cushions and big fur lap robes to wrap around their legs.

The ball was in full swing when they arrived, the sturdy Scot and the scintillating young girl. Lady Merryfield, who before she had married a viscount had been plain Jane Lane, had once smiled very kindly upon dashing and sinister Rowan Keynes. Now a tolerant and gracious hostess whose cosmopolitan affairs were great events of the London season, she welcomed them both warmly.

"But you've grown up!" she cried, standing back to look at Cassandra. "Lord, it makes me feel old! How nice of you to bring her, Robbie. I had no idea she was in town. You must lead me out for a measure while one of these eager young blades leads out Cassandra." She indicated with a negligent sweep of her arm the five young men who had appeared magically from nowhere at sight of the beautiful blonde in white velvet.

At this command from his hostess, Robbie had no choice but to relinquish Cassandra to the pack. He led stout, bubbly Lady Merryfield out upon the floor.

Cassandra found herself suddenly surrounded by what seemed a sea of smiling masculine faces, all clamoring to lead her out.

"I really have never learned to dance properly," she admitted, blushing.

Not a man there who wouldn't be honored to teach her!

That night the "beautiful blonde in white velvet," as the article about Lady Merryfield's ball in the *Gazette* called her, took London by storm. Another paper called her

"The Fair Maid of Cumberland." Her dance card was filled up instantly. People crowded around to meet her. She met so many people that she couldn't remember their names. She was invited everywhere.

Only one flaw marred the evening. A dark lady in wine velvet, whose beauty, though great, was a little frayed around the edges, stopped and stared at sight of her, then asked to be presented.

"So you are Rowan's daughter," she murmured with a measuring glance. "You look nothing like your father."

"I am said to resemble my mother."

"So indeed you do. Were it not for your coloring, I would have thought you to be Charlotte. I am told you arrived with the earthquake. Tell me, did you bring it with you?"

There was a little chill in the air at that remark, and Cassandra stiffened. But Robbie, standing nearby, eased the tension with a shout of laughter. "If sixteen-year-old lassies are bringing earthquakes to London, I fear mature matrons such as yourself may bring us a tidal wave!"

Katherine Talybont—she was now Lady Scopes, wife of an obscure West Country knight—bit her lip at being called a "mature matron," but she managed a thin smile, for the company was joining Robbie in good-natured laughter.

Robbie took Cassandra swiftly away. Only he saw the menacing expression in Katherine's eyes as they followed the departing Cassandra, and it gave him a deep feeling of unease.

The Talybonts had never accepted their widowed daughter-in-law. Katherine had been forced at last, by mounting debts, into marriage with Sir Wilfred Scopes, who could afford to bring her to London but once a year—and then briefly. All this she laid at Rowan's door. His younger daughter had come to grief—it gave Katherine great satisfaction to hear that he had spent months searching the countryside for Phoebe. But now this older daughter with the dazzling good looks inherited from Charlotte was threatening to eclipse all the "Incomparables" of the season—as the London papers dubbed leading debutantes.

Perhaps Cassandra could be brought down as well.

A frightening smile crossed Katherine's handsome features. All she needed was an opportunity. . . .

Meanwhile, Cassandra asked Robbie in a troubled voice, "Do you think sinners bring earthquakes?"

"Not a bit of it," was his firm response. "I think the earth shakes us about when it chooses, and neither God nor man is likely to do much about it!"

This cynical observation was interrupted by a large lady in a plum gown almost covered with yards of blond lace, who bustled up in the company of Lady Merryfield and introduced herself as Lady Stanhope. Robbie drifted away.

Lady Stanhope, who had five daughters yet to be brought out and whose eldest, Mavis, was currently being overlooked by London's best beaux, descended upon Cassandra with a flurry of motherly clucks. What, her school had closed and she'd journeyed to London alone? And was now without a chaperon on Grosvenor Square? Why, that would never do! Cassandra must come and stay with her, Mavis would love the company! And Cassandra must bring that nice man, the Scotsman who had brought her, along—he wasn't married, was he? Men with wives back home made such tiresome guests. So dreadful that nice people should be reduced to staying at inns during the London season!

Cassandra looked at Lady Merryfield, who nodded imperceptibly, and promptly said she'd be delighted. Indeed she hadn't looked forward to staying in lonely Grosvenor Square with only servants for company. Yates was promptly dispatched to collect her luggage and bring it to Lady Stanhope's.

Robbie was glad to accept too. He'd been a widower these ten years past and his two strapping sons had both died upon the sea. He wanted a pleasant place to retire and raise sheep—or so he had told himself. Now, with this sixteen-year-old pale gold butterfly fluttering into his life, he wasn't so sure what he wanted.

After the ball, Yates, frowning as he maneuvered the coach horses through the icy snow-covered streets to Lady Stanhope's residence in Chelsea, was astonished to hear

Robbie's baritone voice serenading Cassandra with Scottish Lowland songs as the coach wheels crunched over the snow.

The next morning it stopped snowing and Lady Stanhope took Cassandra and her eldest daughter, Mavis, shopping. Having learned that Cassandra had not been shopping for more than a year, she bought her a complete morning outfit and one for afternoon—and charged both, along with a few little items for herself, to Rowan Keynes. "Your father will thank me for it, my dear," she told Cassandra airily. Cassandra, starved for pretty clothes and good times, did not object. Rowan had never been aught but extravagant. If he tolerated her presence at all, he would wish her to be well-gowned.

Robbie met them and took them to tea. It was obvious that Lady Stanhope, herself a widow, had her eye on Robbie. Her laughter trilled at every word he spoke.

Amused, Cassandra cast a quick glance at Mavis, homely and rather silent. Mavis repressed a smile but her pale eyes sparkled. It made the girls into instant friends and they left arm in arm, with Robbie gallantly bringing up the rear alongside Lady Stanhope.

Life at Lady Stanhope's for Cassandra—and for Mavis, now that Cassandra had arrived—was a round of parties. On the second night Tony Dunn turned up at a rout and tried to monopolize Cassandra. At first she flinched away from him, for he brought back memories of Cambridge and Jim. But Tony was quick to dispel that. He told her cheerfully that she and Jim would never have made a match, they weren't suited, Jim was too stodgy for her, she needed a man like himself! He struck a posture that made her laugh, and laughing made her feel better. About Jim. About everything.

That week had been a continual round of parties, balls, routs, and sleigh rides. On one of those sleigh rides, sheltered behind a great overhanging tree, Tony had kissed her, and her young body had responded vibrantly. He had seized her more purposefully then, and might have gone farther—but that the big tree suddenly took a hand by dipping its branches to the wind and cascading a mound of snow upon them.

The incident had left Cassandra shaken.

"You should marry me and make an honest man of me," Tony had said when next they met—for the feel of Cassandra in his arms had roused a hunger within him that would only be quenched by going all the way with her—and he was well aware that with a young lady of fame and fashion such as Cassandra, that would mean marriage.

"Should I, Tony?" She gave him a wistful look. Dark attractive Tony with his vaunted Norman blood and his home in Yorkshire's West Riding. Lighthearted Tony who loved to make jokes, Tony to whom life was one vast playground.

"Yes, you should." He bent over her and she smelled the Virginia tobacco he carried for his fashionable long pipe—Tony hated snuff. "You should indeed."

She laughed and drew away from him, for his warm presence *did* attract her, there was no escaping it. She was half in love with Tony—but only half.

Still, somehow in all the excitement of that first dazzling week—she was never quite sure how it happened—she got herself betrothed to Tony Dunn. At least a halfway sort of betrothal which Tony announced and she did not deny.

For who knew what would happen when her father returned? She didn't want to leave this newfound life of gaiety and good times. And hadn't Tony said they would dash through the snow to Gretna if her father refused his suit?

Two weeks later Rowan returned to London. It was Tony who brought her the news. A friend of his had seen Rowan riding in from the west.

"I have to go home," Cassandra said. *I have to face him.*

Tony wanted to go with her, but she wouldn't let him. "Robbie will take me," she said. "It will be much better that way." And on the hackney ride to Grosvenor Square she told Robbie about Phoebe, about Jim—all of it. "I don't know what my father will do," she said, nervously twisting a glove she'd just removed. "Especially when he hears about Tony. I didn't really *intend* to get myself betrothed, Robbie. Indeed I don't remember saying yes.

But Tony told everyone I did, and when I said I hadn't made up my mind, they all laughed and said Tony would persuade me."

And perhaps he would, and carry her away to Yorkshire, thought Robbie, and already his heart ached for her loss, this wondrous young beauty who had made him feel young again.

"Tell your father about it the way you just told me," he advised. "He'll understand the lad is pressing you. And you don't have to marry Tony just because he tells you to."

"Yes, but I think I want to marry Tony." Cassandra gave Robbie a shadowed look. "I think I'm in love with him. I'm just not sure."

If you aren't sure, it isn't love, thought Robbie with some satisfaction. He was careful not to speak those words aloud.

Rowan Keynes met them in the drawing room, still dressed in his riding clothes and looking tired. He hadn't found Phoebe. No trace of her this time. God's teeth, the girl was like him! Able to hide in plain sight, and move like a will-o'-the-wisp about England! And Phoebe was the daughter he loved. It hurt him to the heart every time he looked at Cassandra, for she wore Charlotte's face. But Phoebe, willful Phoebe, was so like him, she was heart of his heart.

Almost ignoring Cassandra, Rowan shook Robbie Dunlawton's hand. "I understand you've been chaperoning my daughter about, seeing that she doesn't get into trouble," he said bluntly.

A ghost of a smile crossed Robbie's honest face. "Trying to, anyway."

"Very decent of you." Still ignoring Cassandra, Rowan poured some wine. "Madeira?"

Robbie accepted a glass from his host. "Your daughter and I turned out to have a mutual friend—Lady Merryfield."

"So I've heard. She hailed me from her coach just as I was coming into town and told me all about it."

And that meant he'd know about Tony too. Cassandra's hands felt cold. She stripped off her other glove and began to warm her hands at the fire. Her father had not offered her any wine—perhaps he meant to put her on bread and water!

"I'd be honored if you'd consent to be our houseguest—that is, if you can bring yourself to leave Lady Stanhope." Rowan's tone was ironic—everybody knew Lady Stanhope was husband-hunting.

"I think I can tear myself away." Robbie grinned. He drained his glass. "Would you like a word alone with your daughter?"

"No need." Rowan drained his own glass. "Cassandra, what have you got to say for yourself?"

"Well, the school closed and—"

"I know all that. Lady Merryfield tells me that you have managed quite well and are the toast of the town." His voice was dry.

Cassandra's color rose. She was not sure that wasn't ridicule in her father's tone. "Well, I wasn't sure how you'd feel about—"

"About that young man, Tony Dunn? She told me about that too. I have yet to make up my mind on it. When you're ready to consider him, send him to see me. Not until." He was looking at her with grim amusement, seeing her round-eyed amazement. "Well, what did you think I'd do? Have you drawn and quartered?"

All her worry had been for nothing! Whatever Lady Merryfield had told him, it had set well! "I didn't know what you'd do," Cassandra admitted frankly.

Nearby, Robbie laughed. "The young," he commented with a twinkle.

It hit just the right note. Rowan turned to him with a smile.

"I'm dead tired," he said. "I've been riding since morning. Do you think you could get Cassandra's things gathered together and moved over here from Lady Stanhope's? I prefer to have my daughter living under my own roof when I'm in London."

"Delighted." Robbie's eyes shone. "But I'm not sure Lady Stanhope will be. She's grown rather accustomed to all the comings and goings that surround Cassandra."

"She will have to learn to live without that excitement," was Rowan's dry comment. He eyed his daughter again. "I understand from Lady Merryfield that Lady Stanhope has taken you shopping."

"Yes, she has," said Cassandra guiltily. "And bought quite a lot."

"Tell her to send me the bills—and thank her for me."

Cassandra left with Robbie, looking rather dazed. She had not expected her father to take it all so well.

Watching them go, Rowan thought he had behaved rather handsomely too. He was tired, but it was not fatigue that had kept him from accompanying his daughter and the Scot on their mission. It was the sight of Cassandra wearing Charlotte's face. Save for her coloring, she was so like, so like. It tore at him. He wondered if he'd ever be able to look at Cassandra without thinking of Charlotte, longing for her. It occurred to him suddenly that his daughter's departure had been rather speedy.

Cassandra had indeed been eager to take her leave. She had adored her mother, wept for her, grieved for her—but she didn't trust her father. She had early memories that disturbed her. She'd been told they were only nightmares, but she had never really been sure. In any event, Rowan Keynes was a hard man to love. And his daughter had never quite forgiven him for accepting Phoebe's word over her own and forthwith exiling her to Colchester.

It had widened the rift between them.

28

March 8, 1750

On the eighth of March, exactly one month after the earthquake that had welcomed Cassandra to London, another earthquake rocked the city. And this one found Cassandra in a milliner's shop where she had gone with Lady Stanhope and Mavis to buy Mavis a new hat.

There were several other ladies in the shop, but Cassandra's view of them was obscured by the hats, which stood on the counter propped up by little stands or perched high on wig stands as well as sitting in rows upon the shelves that lined the walls.

"Do help us choose, Cassandra." Lady Stanhope's drawing room had declined in popularity since Cassandra had moved back home, and she was determined to bind such a star to her entourage at all costs. "Do you think Mavis would look better in this blue one or—" Her voice broke off in a scream as there was a rumble and the room seemed to sway back and forth, spilling hats from their shelves, causing tall wig stands to dance and overturn, and causing several of the ladies to shriek.

The milliner, whose face was pale with fright, added to the commotion with a hysterical burst of high uncontrollable laughter which seemed to come in waves. Cassandra, unsteady on her feet as the floor rocked, was trying to fight free of Mavis' terrified grasp, for Mavis, who had been just in the act of setting a hat on Cassandra's head to

see how it would look when the quake struck, had knocked
the hat off as she stumbled forward when the room swayed,
and to save herself, had locked her fingers firmly in
Cassandra's blonde coiffure. Lady Stanhope was clutching
the counter, while hats and stands surged past her, and
shrieked anew as a sign outside crashed to the street.

At the far end of the room, one lady had lost her footing
and fallen to the floor in a welter of wig stands and hats
and was emitting a keening wail as her friends tried to
help her to her feet.

And over all, the milliner was moaning and laughing as
she dived about, trying to retrieve her precious merchan-
dise, her inappropriate outbursts caused by a slight case of
mercury poisoning from shaping the hats. Cassandra—who
had heard that all hatters were mad and laughed uncon-
trollably—wished ardently that the milliner would stop
making so much noise so that she could persuade a whim-
pering Mavis to unwind those clutching fingers from her
hair.

And then as quickly as it had happened, it was all over.

The room stopped shaking and they were all left in a sea
of hats and fallen hat stands. The milliner was biting a
quivering lip to choke back her tears and whisking hats
back to the shelves, and Cassandra was remonstrating with
Mavis: "*Mavis*, you're pulling my hair out!"

"Come, Cassandra." Lady Stanhope was trying to retrieve her fallen dignity. "I do not think Mavis would care
to try on hats that have been thrown to the floor and
trampled!" She was about to shepherd the two girls into
the street when Lady Scopes'—the former Katherine
Talybont—malicious voice carried to them through the
shop.

"I have heard that Rowan Keynes is back in town and I
doubt not that it is he who has brought this earth-shaking
upon us. You remember, dear Lady Crispin, that I told
you Rowan caused the death of my former husband in
Portugal. He . . ."

Cassandra was never to hear Katherine's last words, for
Lady Stanhope literally pushed her out the door.

"You are not to listen to such nonsense," she told

Cassandra with a sniff. "Katherine Olney—she is Lady Scopes now—was betrothed to your father before she married Eustace Talybont. Eustace was set upon and killed in Lisbon, and I do think it must have affected Katherine's mind, because she came back swearing that your father had somehow engineered his death—and yet all reports have it that your father was nowhere near Eustace Talybont's inn when he was attacked at the door by some roving cutpurse."

Despite this entirely reasonable explanation, Cassandra felt a little chill stealing over her. It was Lady Scopes who had asked her at Lady Merryfield's ball if she had brought the earthquake with her. Plainly she was an enemy.

A young man erupted from a tobacconist's shop across the street. He had hair as yellow as corn and a satin coat to match over buff-colored trousers. He came to a breathless stop before the ladies, bowed, and said, "Lady Stanhope, are you all right? And the ladies with you? The quake near destroyed the tobacconist's shop. Tins falling off shelves and half of the lids coming off, and the tobacco spilled everywhere! The gentlemen who keep their special blends with him will have some surprises coming, I can tell you!" He sounded very merry; his eyes were on Cassandra and she could see that they were a vivid blue.

"Why, yes, we're all right, thank you," said Lady Stanhope, for once looking confused. "Do I know you, young man?"

His grin was very engaging. "Perhaps you don't remember. We met last year in Bath. At Aunt Abigail's."

"At Aunt . . . Oh, yes, Lady Dorsey. How is she? You'll be . . . ?"

"Her nephew, Lance Riverton. She's fine, thank you. May I get you a chair, Lady Stanhope? You look a bit pale."

"A chair? No, suppose there's another great shaking of the ground. I've no mind to have some wobbly chair carriers spill me out onto the cobbles. But you could call us a hackney coach, young man—that is, if any are to be found in all this!" She gestured down the street, where the bricks of a fallen chimney had raised a dust.

"I must go home," said Cassandra. "I'm sure all this

shaking will have broken the dishes and perhaps knocked some things from my dressing table."

Lance Riverton turned from flagging down a hackney coach, which was even then coming to a smart halt. "I'll be glad to escort you," he said warmly.

Cassandra smiled and waved good-bye to Lady Stanhope, who leaned out the window and called, "You must call upon us soon, perhaps tomorrow for tea?" She pulled her head back from the window and spoke sharply to her daughter. "There was a chance for you, Mavis, and what did you do? You stood there like the green girl that you are and let Cassandra Keynes take him away from you! And I can tell you Lance Riverton is a very good catch!"

Lance Riverton was at that very moment trying to impress that fact on Cassandra, whose beauty had sent him running across the street. He had just arrived in London at the very tail end, as it were, of the season, and he meant to make the most of it.

"My Aunt Abigail has a very elegantly appointed house in Bath," he told Cassandra. "And when she comes to London she insists upon bringing with her a lot of her best china—she will be glad she did not come, when I write and tell her how the ground here has been shaken."

Cassandra was well aware that Lance was making what was called "a dead set" for her. At his urging she let him accompany her into the house "in case a beam has fallen, or a chandelier." They found some books tumbled, fireplace tools knocked over, a picture or two fallen to the floor, and Cook grumbling in the kitchen over a couple of broken crocks, but in the main no damage. Cassandra laughingly refused his earnest offer "to survey every inch of the building" with her.

It occurred to her that Lance was both charming and persuasive and that Tony would be very jealous.

He was indeed. The two of them pursued her relentlessly, and as if to rebuff Tony for trying to rush her into marriage, she decided to show no favoritism between them.

"Which will bring on trouble, mark my words!" her friend Dolly Ellerby warned her when in mid-March

Cassandra celebrated her seventeenth birthday. "For Tony considers you his betrothed."

"Nonsense, I never promised to marry Tony!"

"Nonetheless, he has told everyone that you have." Dolly shook her amber curls. "And if you've noticed a thinning-out of beaux lately, it's because Tony is scaring them off. So watch out!"

Dolly was shrewd and her predictions had a way of coming true, but Cassandra, young and reckless, gaily ignored all warnings. She was up to her ears in social engagements, for as the London season drew to an end, routs and balls and parties sprang up all over the place as hostesses, desperate to repay all their social obligations at once, planned fetes and frolics. Indeed Cassandra threw back her lovely head and laughed when, midway in Lady Haverford's crowded ball three days later, she was first told of the duel to be fought at dawn tomorrow.

"They'll not do it," she scoffed, and the candlelight from the chandeliers sparkled in the brilliants entwined in her blonde hair. "Neither of them cares overmuch for sword-play. Lance's mother had all the swords thrown out of the house after her brother was killed overseas—and Tony can scarce carve a goose! Besides"—she shrugged—"why should they fight over me? I am but half-engaged to Tony and I danced but three dances with Lance at Lady Vanderley's ball last night."

"*And* flirted with him on the terrace," added Dolly Ellerby, who had brought her friend this unwelcome bit of news.

"I was *not* flirting. Well, perhaps I was, but that isn't enough to make Tony and Lance hack away at each other."

"Well, *they* think it was. And this morning at White's, Tony Dunn flung his glove in Lance Riverton's face and Lance chose pistols and they're meeting at dawn tomorrow under the dueling oaks at Lord Cloperton's park just north of town. It's a deep secret, of course, but I wormed it out of Ned," she added with a flirt of her fan and a smug expression that implied she could worm any secret out of her betrothed, Ned Willoughby.

Cassandra smoothed out the white velvet of her ball

gown. It seemed ridiculous that they should even *consider* fighting a duel over her. Still . . .

"Perhaps you can worm out of Ned where the two of them are tonight," she said crisply. "For I have not seen either one of them all evening. Father insists that Robbie take me to parties."

"Oh, I doubt Lady Haverford invited either one," was Dolly's cheerful response. "Her family is at odds with Tony's over a steeplechase or something, and of course she wouldn't have Lance because Lance broke off with her niece last summer. She's cut him dead ever since. Won't speak *to* him or *of* him."

That was no help. Frowning, Cassandra looked around to see where she might turn. No one seemed readily available. "Well, do try to learn from Ned the whereabouts of either one of them."

"Perhaps they are saying their prayers," suggested Dolly composedly.

"Oh, don't be ridiculous, Dolly! They aren't going to *kill* each other over me!"

"Perhaps not." Dolly shrugged. "I'll see what I can find out," she promised.

But Ned did not know, and as the evening wore on, Cassandra, dancing with first one young buck and then another across the shining candlelit floor in Lady Haverford's long double drawing rooms, could learn nothing. They had both, it seemed, disappeared.

She would have left the ball at once and gone seeking them, but Robbie would have insisted on going along. He would have left her waiting in the coach while he searched out White's and other likely places—and how could Robbie persuade them not to fight? No, this was something she must do herself.

Nor could she just go running off, leaving kindly Robbie to worry about her.

No, she would wait until she got home. Then she would slip out and find a hackney coach to take her to Tony's flat in Dorchester Street. It was odd that he had not made some effort to see her this evening, but perhaps he had sent a message and it had been lost along the way.

There was plenty of time, she told herself. She would dissuade Tony. Perhaps by promising to marry him if he called off this duel. She toyed with the idea, her expressive green eyes changing to a deeper emerald as she thought about it. Tony would make a delightful husband—so would Lance!—but of course she was not ready for marriage just yet, she was having too good a time. Still, if worse came to worst and Tony balked, he might be willing to accept a long engagement. . . .

She was thinking about it all the time that Robbie was taking her home. Absently she answered his carefully phrased remarks, never noticing how keenly his blue eyes considered her, or the warmth in a voice that was more used to crisp commands. Robbie was wishing he were in his twenties again and pursuing this delectable girl with her straight glances and her startling beauty. Lord, how she would look running laughing through the heather or standing beside a cairn of stones facing the sea, eyes sparkling, fair hair flying in the wind. She had a Scottish beauty, he told himself—and tried to clamp a rein on his imaginings, for he was fast becoming enamored of the girl he was thought to be "chaperoning."

Her father was not at home when she got back. She never guessed that this was deliberate, for although he could bear to look at her by day, at night when the candlelight turned her hair to a deeper gold and seemed to change the color of her eyes, he felt eerily that it was Charlotte who faced him, and his hands grew damp and regret assailed him. If only he had not left her in the Alfama . . .

Knowing nothing of this, Cassandra hurried inside and was already at the stair landing before she turned to Robbie and said, "I think I'll just go down and fetch a book from the library."

Downstairs she waited until she heard his door close; then she hurried into the library and found a dueling pistol of her father's, made sure it was loaded against footpads or whatever else lurked in the dark streets she must traverse alone—but paused at the front door. The upstairs maid had a habit of leaving doors open after she had cleaned the rooms. It would be unfortunate indeed if her father walked by and saw her door open and her bed unslept in.

She went back upstairs, making plenty of noise in case Robbie should be listening.

Her door was closed.

She would have turned back the way she had come but for a small sound from inside the room. Frowning, and with the pistol concealed in the folds of her wide white velvet skirt, she threw open the door.

Phoebe stood there.

Cassandra drew a deep breath and closed the door behind her.

"Does Father know you're here?"

"No. Cook let me in."

"He's been combing the country, looking for you everywhere."

"I know." Phoebe sounded entirely composed. "But I just wasn't ready for him quite yet."

"And are you ready for him now?" Cassandra's tone was ironic. She noticed that Phoebe no longer looked so young. At sixteen there was a worldliness about her, as if she had seen much.

"Oh, yes," was the lazy answer.

Cassandra blinked at the ease with which this new, older Phoebe had said that. Phoebe was looking very elegant, she saw. Her deep green velvet gown was of the latest cut, trimmed in black grosgrain. And her black hair was topped by a modish little three-cornered hat.

"You're a Fleet Street bride," said Cassandra evenly. "I would think *that* would daunt you."

"Oh, not a bit of it." Phoebe laughed. "I never regarded Fleet Street as anything but a first step."

"You mean his mother will receive you now?" She could not keep the incredulity from her voice.

Phoebe grimaced. "Hardly," she admitted.

"Then what makes Fleet Street a first step?"

Phoebe made a little deprecating gesture. Like Rowan, she had a courtly grace—she moved like a duchess.

"Well, I'll admit Clive never meant to *really* marry me.

Unless of course my claims to wealth turned out to be true."

"Which of course they weren't."

"So in order to get me to be his mistress, he promised me a Fleet Street marriage—and kept his word," she added almost proudly.

"Wasn't that handsome of him?" Cassandra could hardly keep the sarcasm out of her voice. He had debauched a fourteen-year-old girl, and that same misguided wench was actually *proud* that he had handed her a worthless piece of paper as a memento of the event!

"Well . . . we changed our names, of course, and bounced around the country as Lord and Lady Cambridge—for that was where we met. And I kept thinking up marvelous ways that we could spend lots of money and live for nothing, which delighted Clive, of course—and everywhere he claimed me as his wife. Quite proudly, I thought."

Cassandra closed her eyes. They had left a trail of bilked and furious creditors, she had no doubt—debts everywhere. Debtors' prison yawned ahead.

"And time went by while we rushed about, for we didn't dare let Father catch up with us, of course—Clive is very afraid of Father."

He has reason to be, thought Cassandra.

"And now a whole year has passed, living together with Clive claiming me as his wife—by whatever name. So now it's a legal marriage," she added coolly.

Cassandra opened her mouth—and closed it again. Phoebe was right. Although it might be contested in the courts, Cassandra had no doubt that Phoebe and Clive were at this moment legally wed.

"Of course, that hasn't occurred to Clive yet." Phoebe was studying her fingers thoughtfully, one by one. "But Father will explain it to him shortly." She looked up with a smile.

"Father won't like having a daughter who's a common-law wife," warned Cassandra.

Phoebe's wicked smile deepened. "No, I counted on that," she said softly, "when I thought it all out back in Cambridge. Father will now offer Clive a choice: he can marry me in a church or Father will spit his gizzard for him on the field of honor. Clive would *faint* at the thought of a duel with Father!"

"I see you have it all worked out, but suppose Clive prefers to run for it?"

"Oh, he won't." Phoebe was entirely confident. "Because it will also be explained to him that he's tied to me anyway. So Clive will trot nicely along to the church, believing he might as well go all the way."

In for a penny, in for a pound, thought Cassandra grimly.

"And *that*," announced Phoebe with satisfaction, "will open the way for Clive's mother to receive me—at last."

Yes, the dowager Marchioness of Greensea might do just that, Cassandra realized. It would be touch and go, of course, but her devious younger sister might just be able to pull it off.

"That is, if Father is especially generous with my dowry." Phoebe was again airily studying her hands. "And I'll explain the need for *that* to him, of course."

"First you tricked Clive and now you're planning to buy him—with a dowry," murmured Cassandra. "I wish you joy of him—but suppose Father just drags Clive off at gunpoint and makes him marry you in a church. Suppose he won't give you any dowry."

"Why shouldn't he?" demanded Phoebe indignantly. "And if mine isn't enough to impress Clive's mother, why shouldn't he give me *your* dowry too?" And when Cassandra stared at her, speechless, "After all, anyone who ever looked at you would know you didn't *need* a dowry!"

"And why not?" Cassandra was beginning to be angry at Phoebe's high-handed assumptions.

"Your *face* is your dowry!" was Phoebe's instantaneous retort. "I *had* to get you out of Cambridge—Clive might never have looked at me with you around!" And at Cassandra's dazed look, "Oh, I'm sorry, Cassandra." She was instantly placating. "I saw Clive and I wanted him more than anything else in the world—and I still do."

For Phoebe, Cassandra supposed, love was like that. She'd lie, steal, cheat, cause her sister to be locked away, she'd do anything—just to keep Clive beside her. *If I live ten thousand years,* she thought, *I could never be like Phoebe.*

"Oh, do stop looking at me like that!" Phoebe sounded aggrieved. "You should *want* me to have your dowry. After all, everyone always loved you—and they never cared for me."

That argument seemed hardly to merit an answer. It came to Cassandra suddenly that the dueling pistol was growing heavy in her hand. She brought it up.

"*Cassandra!*" Phoebe turned pale and took a step backward.

"Oh, I'm not going to shoot you, Phoebe." Cassandra's voice was ironic. "And as to nobody caring about you, you can hardly have forgotten that you were always Father's favorite—I doubt he can deny you anything."

"Oh, I do hope so," said Phoebe fervently. She had recovered her aplomb, and now she struck a posture. "Do you like this gown?" she asked. "I had it made up in Bath."

And still owe the dressmaker, no doubt.

"You look splendid." Cassandra gave her sister a cynical look. "And I've no doubt it will look even better splashed with your tears as you plead you case with Father." At the door she turned. "I'm off to stop a duel. Don't tell Father I've gone out—let him think I'm asleep."

Phoebe's dark eyes followed her with wonder as she went through the door.

29

The Dueling Oaks, March 19, 1750

A chill morning fog enveloped Lord Cloperton's park and made the shapes of the two smartly dressed young men, with their long dueling pistols in hand, seem somehow unreal against the huge trunks of the ancient oaks and hornbeams, whose spreading branches seemed to disappear into the gray mist. It dimmed the stalwart figures of the seconds, waiting, pistols cocked—for the code of dueling decreed that should either one of those tall determined figures pacing the distance apart before turning to fire should break the rules and try to bring down his opponent before the appointed time, it was the duty of the seconds forthwith to shoot the culprit. Somewhere in the background should have hovered a doctor, but at the last minute the doctor they wanted (a man known to be discreet) had been called away to deliver a baby and—the antagonists being hot to go at it—the seconds after some argument had agreed to forgo the services of medical science. It was the private if unexpressed opinion of both the seconds that neither Lance Riverton nor Tony Dunn really wanted to kill the other; this quarrel was over a lady's wandering affections and would soon blow away. Indeed, it would not have surprised the seconds if both men, having had overnight to think about it, deloped— fired in the air rather than at the opponent. In any case, only one shot would be fired by either party, and at the worst, each man would fire near his opponent—perhaps near enough to wing him in the arm or leg, a little blood would be drawn, honor satisfied, and that would be that. Everyone would be out of this cursed damp and back to an early breakfast at some inn—and soon back to being the best of friends!

Cassandra, viewing this scene as she spilled out of her hackney coach, was not so sanguine. She had tried Tony's flat on Dorchester Street, she had tried the gaming hells, she had searched the town without finding either Tony or Lance. In despair she had ordered her hackney driver to take her to Lord Cloperton's park and had had her head out the window half the time calling to him to hurry. She was already on the verge of exhaustion when the hackney coach turned into the long driveway that wound through the "park," or grounds, of Lord Cloperton's handsome estate, but so keyed up was she that at the first sight of the dueling oaks—and she knew those oaks, for she had attended a party at Lord Cloperton's mansion and they had been pointed out to her—she tumbled out almost before the driver stopped at her breathless command.

She had thought to arrive early, to dissuade Lance and Tony on the spot. And yet there they were, already marching off the fifteen paces before they turned and fired. On the way over here she had nurtured the wild idea of pointing the pistol she still carried at her own breast and warning them both that since *she* was the cause of their quarrel she would do away with herself if they did not desist instantly. Calling out to them at this point, she knew, would do no good. The two young men and both the seconds who stood at right angles facing each other were all far too intent on what they were doing.

With her left hand she scooped up her velvet skirts and ran like a deer across the damp grass beneath the old trees.

The combatants had paced off the distance. In the gray dawn the seconds, young and savoring the drama of the moment, allowed them to stand poised, pistol in hand, still with their backs to each other.

Cassandra was losing her hairpins as she ran, but what

did that matter? She must put a stop to this before it went any further! She raced forward, straining every nerve. Her breath sobbed in her throat.

"Turn and fire!"

At exactly that moment, Cassandra, ignored by the seconds, unseen by the combatants, reached the grassy stretch down which ball and shot would whine as both guns spoke. Reached it at a point midway between.

Tony whirled and saw across the barrel of his gun, not Lance Riverton behind the muzzle of a pistol, but a white-faced Cassandra, who had come to a halt, blonde hair flying. She had appeared like a wraith in her white velvet ball gown.

Tony's nerves were excellent. With an oath he brought up the barrel of his gun. He had not fired a shot.

Lance, on the other hand, was excited. He had never fought a duel before, someone had told him (erroneously) that Tony had fought three, and someone else had told him (maliciously) that Tony had bragged that he would kill not only Lance but also any other man who dared pay court to Cassandra. Although Lance appeared cool and steady, his heart was pounding and he was praying that his hand would not shake as he whirled to face his opponent.

And saw across the barrel of his gun . . . Cassandra.

His jaw dropped and so did the barrel of his pistol. But the shock, combined with his agitated nerves, caused his finger to tighten imperceptibly on the trigger. Dueling pistols being "hair-trigger" devices, the gun went off.

And struck Cassandra.

She was not aware of any pain. She heard the report and she felt as if some great wind was carrying her away. Soundlessly she crumpled to the grass and lay there in a white velvet heap.

One of the seconds, who recounted it later, said that Lance had given a heartbroken cry and run forward to bend over Cassandra's fallen body. He described graphically how still she had lain with her gleaming fair hair spread out like a mermaid's on the lawn and a red stain slowly spreading over the white velvet of her bodice just below her left breast. He said that Lance had crouched there like a hunted thing, moaning as the other three men converged upon him running.

He said that Tony had dashed forward with hell in his eyes and fired point-blank at Lance, shooting him in the head, and that Lance had fallen backward dead.

At that point, in the confusion, one of the seconds, even more horrified at this infraction of the rules than at Cassandra's being struck, for a duelist must fire from where he stands, not march forward to blow out his opponent's brains, raised his gun and shot Tony in the chest.

Tony fell forward across Cassandra's body, and the seconds were left with their own guns leveled at each other, standing tensely over the bodies of all three. The driver of the hackney coach, who had watched this little scene of the gentry in astonishment, reported *that*.

Up to that moment no one had thought to discover whether Cassandra's wound was mortal.

Both combatants died that day, but Cassandra did not. The bullet had only grazed her, although the wound bled copiously. Her wild dash across the grass, her heart-stopping excitement, the sudden shock of the bullet striking her had all conspired together: she had fainted.

The hackney driver, who had run forward too, had the sense to stanch the blood of her wound. All four young men had arrived on horseback, and the seconds now loaded Lance's and Tony's bodies across their respective mounts, and with the hackney coach carrying Cassandra following behind, they made their mournful way back to London.

It was morning now and the third and greatest of the six earthquakes that were to strike London between February and June was about to begin.

Cassandra, sitting in the coach with her head bent and her hands clenched, trying to absorb the shock of this dawn's encounter, felt it first as a violent jerk that seemed to turn the coach sideways and tossed her painfully to the side. Along with it came a deep angry rumble from the earth, a menacing deep growl from the interior. But that rising grumble was promptly eclipsed by the crashing collapse of a nearby shop, the front of which fell into the street, raining bricks on traffic and pedestrians alike. The cascade of bricks caused the horse to rear up, bricks rolled under the wheels, and the coach toppled over on its side. As the coach went over, she could hear people screaming above the rumbling roar.

"Are you all right, young mistress?" The worried driver had wrested the door open and was silhouetted against the sky above her as she lay in a heap below him. He leaned down, extended a hand. "Here, let me help you out. We'll have the coach righted in a minute." He flinched and choked on the dust the fallen storefront had raised. "Give me some help here!" he bellowed.

Cassandra was dragged out into a scene of terror. Up ahead, another building had collapsed and in the melee two carts and a large dray had collided. The horses' lines were snarled, they were neighing and kicking, trying to free themselves, their drivers were howling at each other. People were running about frantically.

And directly in front of her were, now nervous and dancing as the seconds tried to quiet them, the mounts that carried the two young men who had fought and died for her this day. She saw again their bodies.

Cassandra felt a great shudder go through her. Her hand sought the front of her bodice and came away wet. The hackney's overturn had caused her wound to start bleeding again.

"Here!" cried someone. "This poor young girl's been hurt by the earthquake!"

"No," gasped Cassandra. "No."

But it was useless to protest. She was promptly seized by well-meaning hands and taken to lean against the door of a chandler's shop. Through the doorway she could see that the candles were rolling all over the floor, and at her feet an elderly flower vendor was scrabbling about the cobbles trying to retrieve her blooms and wailing as they were stepped on by flying feet.

They got the hackney coach righted and Cassandra back inside and drove on. But chimneys all over town had come tumbling down with the sharp violent shake that had visited London, and here and there houses had collapsed, showering bricks and falling timbers into the street. The driver had to choose his path carefully, and sometimes turn back when he saw the way was blocked.

They were a long time getting home to Grosvenor Square.

From the window where he had been watching for her, Robbie saw Cassandra being helped from the hackney by the solicitous driver. He saw the blood on her dress.

He had never moved so fast. He was downstairs and out into the street, receiving Cassandra from the beleaguered hackney driver, who said in a tired voice, "The young mistress had not enough coins to pay me."

Robbie had enough coins to pay him. He scooped Cassandra up in his arms and carried her, half-fainting, into the house.

"We were wondering what had happened to you," he said. "You were hurt in the earthquake?"

"No," she said. "Oh, Robbie, no!" And as he, without asking whether he might, ripped open the front of her white velvet bodice to see to her wound, Cassandra, having left her modesty somewhere else, choked out the whole terrible story.

" 'Tis not so deep a wound," he said with satisfaction. "And 'twill teach you," he added on a sterner note, "not to step between men who are shooting at each other."

"Oh, Robbie." The woeful face that looked up at him had eyes abrim with tears. "I only wish I could have taken all three shots. And then they'd all be alive."

All but you, thought Robbie, and felt a lump in his throat. He swallowed. "Now to dress that wound," he growled, and bellowed for Cook. She had been hiding beneath the kitchen table in case the house was shaken again, but she came promptly and gaped at the sight of Cassandra leaning back on a velvet sofa in broad daylight wearing a ball gown and with her midriff bare where Robbie had cut away the fabric with his knife—and that midriff displaying a bleeding gash.

" 'Tis not so bad as it looks," Robbie admonished her, for he did not want Cook fainting on his hands. "Bring water and clean linen. I'm an expert at binding wounds," he told Cassandra. "Learned it in battle. Never expected to be binding up a bullet wound for a sixteen-year-old girl, though."

"Seventeen," corrected Cassandra. "Oh, Robbie, what am I going to do? I'm responsible for their deaths!"

"You'll go on as before," he said crisply. " 'Twas the lads who chose to fight. You but attempted to stop them." His gaze on her was pitying. Life had crowded in on her—too fast, too young. She wasn't able to adjust to it yet, all the excitement and triumphs and trouble her extraordinary beauty was going to bring her. She hadn't adjusted yet to the fact that for beauty like hers men would always spatter their blood upon the grass.

He wondered if he should tell her that this morning Rowan Keynes had come to him and said he had need of gold for a dowry and accepted his offer to buy Aldershot Grange. He had given Rowan a draft on his bank and the deed was signed and in his pocket.

He did tell her that Rowan had left the house just before the earthquake to take her sister to the church "to get her married."

"Yes, I knew," she told him. "Phoebe told me last night." But she could not concentrate on Phoebe's problems —not today. "I can't stay here, Robbie, not the way things will be. I am sure to be turned away from both Tony's funeral and Lance's—and yet how in good conscience can I not go? I would wear black for them both, but I have no black clothes and I am sure my father would refuse to let me buy black weeds for a man to whom I was never officially betrothed and another to whom I was nothing at all."

"He would be right. You should not go about in mourning," said Robbie sharply.

Cassandra was not even listening. "And that spiteful Lady Whatever-her-name-is—the one who was Katherine Talybont—asked me if I did not bring the earthquake that struck as I arrived in London. I heard her say my father's arrival brought on the one that struck a month later. She is sure to tell all who will listen that it was my wickedness in bringing on this duel that caused the earth to shake and the houses in London to fall!" Her voice rose to a wail. "And my father shut me up for over a year because he believed I was running away. When he learns of this scandal, he will shut me up in some dark hole forever!"

Robbie had been about to pooh-pooh anything Lady What's-her-name might have to say, but her last remark gave him pause. Rowan was a stern father. Who knew what he might do when he learned of this escapade?

A wonderful new thought occurred to Robbie. He turned and bellowed for Cook, who came running.

"This wound is worse than I thought," he said. "The wench needs a doctor. And she cannot go to him half-dressed. Indeed, she may wish to change her clothes before she returns. Bring me a box, woman, a large one! And then scurry out and find me a hackney coach and bring it here to the front door."

Cook blanched but hurried back with a large box.

"I thought you said—" began Cassandra.

"Hush. Pay no mind to what I say," said Robbie. "Stay where you are and be quiet. I'll be right back." He raced upstairs and began stuffing Cassandra's things into the box. She had a bag, and he swept the contents of her dressing table into it. With her cloak over his arm and lugging the box, the bag and a hat he had found, he reached the downstairs.

By now Cook was back with the hackney coach, and expostulating with Robbie. "But Mistress Cassandra won't need all those things! You aren't taking her to hospital, are you? For her father—"

"Quiet, woman!" roared Robbie. "How do I know what a young wench will want? 'Tis important she not be upset! Now, put these things into the hack." While she did so, he quickly penned a note and left it for Rowan in a conspicuous place on his desk.

Cassandra herself he lifted in, depositing his cherished bundle on the seat beside him, where he could steady her.

As the hackney coach took off, to the accompaniment of a small aftershock of the quake that made the driver up topside curse, Robbie said, "'Tis not your wound that worries me, lass. 'Tis your future."

"I have no future," sighed Cassandra. "Lance would have done me a favor if he'd aimed a little higher and struck my heart." There were tears in her voice. "Oh, if only I could leave London, Robbie. If only I could go home—back to Aldershot Grange, where I belong."

She had unwittingly given him the perfect opening. He took a deep breath.

"And so you can, lass, and 'tis I who will take you there. You need never see any of them again. I will take you home to Aldershot Grange, for I bought it this morning—it now belongs to me."

Cassandra gave him a dazed look. *"You bought Aldershot Grange?"*

"Aye, lass. Your father needed a fat sum of gold for a dowry."

So scheming little Phoebe had got her way. Last night she had said ruthlessly she would have both their dowries, and now it had come to pass. Oh, but what did it matter? Her own life was over. Two good men lay dead on her account.

"But so that your father will not pursue me with powder and shot and lay me out dead on my own hearth, you must marry me, lass. We'll fly away to Scotland and be wed at Gretna Green!"

Cassandra gave him a hopeless look. "Oh, Robbie, dear Robbie, I do love you, but not . . . not in *that* way."

"Nor need you." His voice was husky. "I do not ask you to be a true wife to me, little Cassandra. I only ask that I may take care of you and shelter you from harm."

Aldershot Grange, the home of her childhood. . . . A vision of the silvery Derwent Water with the trees garlanded in mist and the birds singing softly came to Cassandra—a brighter, happier life. The appeal was irresistible.

"Then on those terms I'll marry you, Robbie," she choked.

The Scot's chest expanded and his voice deepened. "I promise you, lass, that you'll never be sorry."

So another man had promised Cassandra's mother in much the same words when he spirited *her* away to Gretna.

But this was different. Robbie Dunlawton, honest Scot that he was, meant every word he said. He wondered for a grim moment what Rowan Keynes would think when he

opened Robbie's letter, written a little prematurely, to be
sure, but now to come true:

I am off with your daughter to Scotland, there to
be wed. And on that day I will settle on her Aldershot Grange. I know I have not your blessing, nor do
I expect it. If you choose to come after me, I will
meet you with swords or pistols at the place of your
choice. In any event, Cassandra will have the home
that she loves.

He had signed it in very large letters: Robert Dunlawton,
Gentleman.

"He might just as well have said, '*In any event, Cassandra
will be free of you,*' " mused Rowan Keynes when he read
the letter. "For once she became a widow—should I follow Dunlawton to Scotland and make her a widow—I
would have small control of her." He grimaced. His vision
had been clouded by Cassandra's myriad of young suitors—
that the graying Scot should be one of them had entirely
escaped him.

He decided not to pursue the fleeing pair to Scotland. It
seemed he had lost two daughters this day—both to men
he would not himself have chosen for them. That, it seemed,
was the way of the world. . . .

But Cassandra and her unlikely suitor did not reach
Gretna unscathed. They had almost reached Kendal when
a wooden bridge over a small tributary stream made into a
roaring torrent by the spring runoff collapsed beneath
them, dumping them and their mounts into the icy waters.
Cassandra's wound was now healed enough that it caused
her no trouble, but her unwieldy skirts did, and she
would have drowned but that Robbie flailed through the
flood to snatch at her skirts just as they would have dragged
her under, and so pulled her to safety.

They were both chilled to the bone as they shook out
their wet clothes and found their mounts, which were
shaking themselves off, having found downstream a bank
up which to clamber. Cassandra bore no scars of the

misadventure, but Robbie developed a hacking cough that deepened as they reached the Scottish border.

Cassandra, looking ever southward, for she feared pursuit by her father, was impatient to be wed and thus removed from his domination.

And so, like her mother before her, she spoke the vows of a loveless marriage before a blacksmith's anvil at Gretna Green.

30

Aldershot Grange

On the pretext that she needed to shop for clothes, Cassandra persuaded Robbie to spend three nights in Carlisle—actually, she hoped the rest would lend him strength, and it did seem to help.

It was night when at last they reached Aldershot Grange and sounded the great iron knocker.

It was Livesay, clad in a long nightshirt with a dishlike candleholder in his hand, who answered the door, peering out at them. At the sight of Cassandra, her hair covered by a large silk scarf against the damp, the color of her eyes made indeterminate by the wavering light, he fell back, pale.

"*Mistress Charlotte!*" he gasped.

"I know, I do look like her, Livesay," the vision greeted him ruefully. "But I'm Cassandra."

"Oh, Mistress Cassandra." Livesay sounded shaken but relieved.

"Robbie, this is Livesay, who has been our butler forever. Livesay, you see before you my new husband and the new owner of Aldershot Grange—Robert Dunlawton."

"No, *you* are the owner," Robbie corrected her in a hoarse voice. "Remember, I have this day made the deed over to you."

Livesay looked stunned. He collected his wits. "Wend

411

is with us again, Mistress Cassandra—but spending the night in Cat Bells at the moment."

"Is she?" Cassandra was overjoyed. "Oh, how is she, Livesay?"

"She's well." He hesitated. "But much has happened to Wend since you've gone. She married and left us, you know."

"No, I didn't know."

"And then *he* left her after the child was born dead. She worked somewhere else for a while, but last month she came back to us."

"Then it's lucky we are. I think we'll need a fire made, Livesay, for I don't like the sound of my husband's cough."

Nor did the doctor, when he was called at the end of the week. He proffered various potions and told Cassandra to apply poultices to Robbie's chest, but nothing did any good. She and Wend both fussed over him, but any fool could see that his condition was worsening. And as time went by, his cheeks were no longer merely pink but quite flushed, although on the whole his skin seemed papery and pale. He lost weight all through that summer and autumn, and it was a mere shadow of his former self who celebrated, with all the heartiness he could muster, the Twelve Days of Christmas at Aldershot Grange.

"He will not make another Christmas," the doctor told Cassandra solemnly.

"Oh, no, don't say it," said Cassandra brokenly. And she thought, *Another death on my conscience. For Robbie wore himself out trying to save me from the torrent and was exhausted and shivering when he pulled me out upon the bank. If he dies, it will be my fault.* She did not tell the doctor that. Instead she went wearily off to plump Robbie's pillows and try to make him eat some of the broth Cook had sent up to him.

Spring came with a shower of blue heather matching the blue of the sky between the clouds, for it was a wet, rainy spring that brought out the blossoms and finished off the ill.

One day Robbie called her to his bedside. "It's sorry I am to leave you, lass," he told her softly. "But leave you I

must—and soon. Send Livesay to me. I'll make my own
arrangements and spare you that, at least."

He died the next Sunday and was buried with the rain
pattering down like tears upon his coffin and upon the old
worn rocks of this ancient land. He had arranged for his
own funeral service, and at the end was sung a Scottish
Lowland song that he had instructed Livesay to say was
"just for her, to tell her what she means to me."

Cassandra listened as a sweet singer from Buttermere
sang out:

And I will love thee still, my dear,
Till all the seas gang dry.

She listened and her tears mingled with the rain that
ran down her face.

In all her life she would never find another man like
Robbie, who had asked nothing of her, nothing. . . .

She grieved for him, deep in her heart, for she had
loved him like a father. And wore for him the widow's
weeds she'd been denied wearing for those she might have
wed.

"Will you go back to London now?" Wend asked her
wistfully when the funeral was over.

She was surprised at Cassandra's shiver, at her harsh,
"I'll never go back, *never!*" Indeed her memories of what
had happened there were all too green.

Men had died of loving her. She would allow no man to
love her—ever again. But only to Wend did she confide
all this.

For a long time Cassandra tried to lose herself in work.
In recent years Rowan had let the house and outbuildings
run down, and Robbie had left her a little money. For
months she concerned herself with repairs to masonry and
stonework and a new roof. But that could not last forever.
Still, Aldershot Grange was a working estate; Robbie had
planned to raise sheep here. Very well, she would raise
sheep. The green-eyed blonde beauty became a familiar
figure at livestock markets and fairs. She hired a shepherd.
But it didn't fill her life.

The big cream-colored Persian cat helped. She found
the cat limping on one of her long restless walks. It had
run a thorn into its paw and was very thin, with burrs
matted into its shabby tangled coat. She coaxed the cat
home, got Wend to hold her while she extricated the
thorn, very carefully removed the burrs and combed and
fed the cat—now named Clover—to purring beauty. Sometimes, Wend thought whimsically, looking at the pair of
them as Cassandra sat in the window seat looking out at
the setting sun with the last rays touching her own pale
blonde hair while she stroked the big cream cat on her
lap, they looked as if they were blood relations—pale
blonde woman and pale blonde cat.

The horse helped too. A cream-colored mare she had
named Meg, who took her on long wild rides through the
low valleys and into the lofty fells up past Fox Elve, and
gallops along the lake down toward Buttermere and Cat
Bells.

Sometimes she rode up past Castle Stroud, which was a
beehive of activity, for the place had been sold and the
new owner's agent had a crew of plasterers and carpenters
and stonemasons busy restoring it to its former beauty.

And sometimes those gallops led her past neighboring
Blade's End, an ancient holding named for a formidable
warrior who was reputed—like Richard the Lion Hearted
—to have hacked men and horses in half with a single
stroke on the field of battle, and which was now dominated by a beautifully proportioned dwelling which had
been built in the Old Queen's time in the last century.
Blade's End was occupied now, after being long vacant.

On one of those rides she met the nephew who had,
after much litigation, inherited the estate. Charlotte had
twice seen him at livestock markets—once he had bid
against her and won—so she knew who he was when he
came striding out of the big stone house and hailed her as
she was riding by. Then as now, she had admired the easy
grace of his tall athletic figure—then as now deplored the
careless condition of his clothing, both the light gray velvet jacket and the darker gray cloth trousers, rent here

and there and casually mended. Plainly there was no woman in his life!

She drew rein, smiling down at him as he approached.

"I've seen you ride by," he said. "And wished my horse had not gone lame, so I could gallop after you! My name's Drew Marsden. And you'll be the beauty of Aldershot Grange, Cassandra Dunlawton. Will you not join me in a stirrup cup? 'Twill give you strength for your journey, I promise, wherever you're bound!"

Cassandra liked him at once. She liked his keen though not handsome countenance. She liked his friendly manner.

" 'Twould be most welcome," she said. She tied her mare to the hitching post and accompanied her genial neighbor in through the two-story stone porch with its colorful Dutch stained glass, making patterns of colored light across the floor. There was more stained glass, medieval and mellow, in the tall windows that lighted the somber great hall into which he brought her. The arms of his mother's family adorned the splendid fireplace before which a pair of white wolfhounds rose at her entrance.

"Cromwell! Ireton! Stay," he commanded in a deep voice, and the dogs obediently settled back. He turned to Cassandra. "I have named the dogs Cromwell and Ireton after the two great bedchambers upstairs," he confided with a grin, "which my grandmother named for our two mighty Civil War generals who are supposed to have sheltered here."

That was typical of the laughing irreverence of his nature, Cassandra was to learn.

"I could lend you a horse," she offered as she sank down upon the tasseled red velvet pillow that covered a long carved bench, and watched him pour the wine, standing before the fireplace.

"Could you indeed?" His gray eyes lit up as he handed her a goblet of ruby port. "I'd be obliged indeed, for the Bishop—that's what I've named my horse because whenever he's mischievous, which is often, he always gives me such a pious, blameless look—must needs rest his leg another two weeks, by my judgment."

"The Bishop?" Cassandra burst into laughter. "And to

think I but named my mare Meg! D'you always use such inventive names?"

"Aye. Naming runs in the family. I've even named you—before I met you, of course. I called you the Wraith of the Derwent Water because you were never in when I called."

Cassandra caught her breath. She had given strict orders to Livesay to turn away all gentlemen callers—but she hadn't meant to include her neighbor just to the south in that order.

"The Wraith will be home next time," she promised penitently.

"Good. Let us drink to that." He lifted his glass and drained it. "You do light up this hall," he murmured, studying her.

After they had chatted for a while, he took her through the house, showing her the renovations he was making, and smiled when she said impulsively, "Oh, don't change either of these," when he showed her the two tapestry-hung bedchambers, "Cromwell" and "Ireton," with their dark oak Jacobean furniture.

"I don't intend to," he said softly, and she knew from the way his gaze caressed those rooms that he felt about them as she did.

They were kindred spirits. And soon Meg and the great dappled gray stallion Drew called the Bishop were galloping across the blue heather and treading their way together through the lofty fells.

Cassandra found it easy to relax with Drew, either at Aldershot Grange or in the paneled drawing room of Blade's End with its portrait heads and gilded allegorical figures. She didn't realize it, but she was falling in love.

How he felt about her was brought home to her the day Meg tripped over a stone and Cassandra went headlong into the bracken. Drew was off his horse instantly and bending over her, white-faced.

"Are you hurt?" he demanded tensely.

"No," Cassandra gasped. "I don't think so."

"Thank God," he said, and cradled her in his arms, burying his face in her thick fair gleaming hair.

It was unexpected and touching and Cassandra forgot for the moment her vow never to let another man love her. She lay back and let Drew kiss her and fondle her, and found life unutterably sweet.

Until she remembered.

Then she scrambled up without ceremony and insisted they ride on. She saw that Drew was puzzled but she did not explain.

After that she tried to draw away from him, to interest herself in other things. She tried to stay away from the great E-shaped stone house to the south, with its steep roofs and dormers and tall chimneys. And especially she tried to stay away from the tall gray-eyed man who lived there.

31

London, England, 1755

In Lady Sotherby's handsome Georgian mansion a great ball was in progress and candles glittered from behind rain-spattered windows as a sudden downpour engulfed London. The ball was the social event of the season and everyone who counted was in attendance. Liveried footmen were all about, attending to the guests' slightest needs. Wine flowed, and in the high-ceilinged mirrored ballroom silken skirts swirled against satin knee breeches and laughter and music drowned out the patter of the rain outside.

Somewhere in that glittering throng was Tom Westing—a man in very different circumstances from when he had last seen his native land. His cynical gaze raked the crowd about him. Who would ever have thought that he—who had seemed more destined to be hanged than anything else—would be standing here today among diplomats and dukes, quaffing wine with the best of them?

Someone jostled his arm, some viscount he had met earlier but whose name he couldn't recall. Travers or something like that.

"Well, Westing," inquired that worthy in a somewhat nasal drawl, "enjoying yourself?"

In point of fact Tom was having only an indifferent time, for to him this was a roomful of strangers all intent on their own pursuits, but he had learned to dissemble. "Very much," he said heartily. "Travers, isn't it?"

The nasal voice cooled a trifle at the vagueness of Tom's mention of his name. "Aye, Travers. Lady Sotherby introduced us early on, before this confounded rain started. We'll all be drenched by it, but then, I suppose that won't bother you—you're used to rain forests, they tell me."

"And other delights of the tropics." Tom's reply was ironic. He was thinking not just of the continuous downpours of the rainy season but about the teeming life that crawled and slipped and slithered over the jungle floor, of the snakes that draped themselves in the dripping trees, of claws and fierce open jaws that lurked in the bush. He wondered if Travers—or any of the rest of them here, for that matter—had any true conception of the Amazon in flood or what it was like to traverse the milky waters of the Orinoco wondering if a poisoned dart was going to pierce your sweating back from one of the dark figures lurking in that high green wall of dense undergrowth onshore. . . .

"There's a lady here who would like to meet you," Travers said.

"A lady?" Tom turned about. "What lady?"

"Lady Scopes." Travers nodded. "She's right over there, the one in the black taffeta gown waving her fan about."

Tom's curious gaze studied the lady. She had luxuriant black hair and high color, and at this distance she appeared to be possessed of considerable beauty. She also appeared to be in mourning, for she was dressed solidly in black. He called Travers' attention to that fact.

"Oh, yes, she is." Travers shrugged. "That is, she was. She's just coming out of it now. She's a friend of Lady Sotherby's, and Blanche—that is, Lady Sotherby—can get the crepe off anyone's sleeve."

Tom doubted it. No one had been able to get the crepe off *his* sleeve, even though he had worn none. The black crepe he wore for Charlotte was twined around his heart too tightly ever to be loosed, he thought.

Had he been a religious man, he could have hoped to find her again in the hereafter. But he was not.

He had only memories, golden and cherished, of a slender, splendid, tantalizing girl he had loved, gone forever. He had only the deepest sense of loss.

At first during those days of despair in Portugal when he had visited Charlotte's grave, Tom had promised himself that he would return to England and seek out Rowan Keynes and hack him to pieces: for having left him to die on Kenlock Crag, for having had him kidnapped aboard ship with orders to sew him in a sack and hurl him overboard. All the while he had waited impatiently for the carving of the great footstone he commissioned for Charlotte's grave, he had been planning to seek out Rowan and finish him off. He had even made inquiries of what ships were leaving, bound for that part of the world.

But then, on the very day the handsome footstone was finished and at last erected, he had stood staring at that stone and asking himself, *What would Charlotte want?* Would she want vengeance or . . . something else?

He had recalled suddenly that Charlotte had two small daughters, children he had never seen, and that she had told him that Rowan loved the children, was good to them.

That day he had felt very close to Charlotte, felt almost that she was watching him from somewhere beyond the clouds, approving of what he did. *But would she approve of his depriving her children of a father, of leaving them orphaned and alone in the world?*

A cold sweat had broken out on his brow at what he had been about to do. True, Keynes had wronged him, had wronged them both. But . . . now at last he put himself in Rowan Keynes' shoes, and tried to see it from Keynes' point of view. Keynes had loved a woman and she had strayed; small wonder he had revenged himself on Tom. But Keynes had not revenged himself on Charlotte, not so far as Tom knew. Charlotte had died of a fever; the doctor in attendance had told him so, indeed had told him how the whole household had grieved, of her lavish funeral. And how Keynes had returned with his small daughters to London. *Should Tom follow them there and forthwith make them orphans?*

He had leaned against the footstone he had erected to Charlotte and felt sick. For fate had been so unkind to Charlotte, and now he, who loved her better than he did his life, had been about to deal her one last hurt—he had been about to orphan her children.

Charlotte would have wanted her children to have a father, a settled home, a happy life. Would he put his yearned-for personal revenge above her wishes?

He would not! Nor would he return to England, where he might one day run across Rowan and be tempted to remove him from the earth.

He went back to Brazil, and there he flung himself into work with renewed effort. Don Sebastião, in failing health, watched him with pride. His gaze upon the tall, powerful Englishman was fond. Tom was the son he had never had, who would one day fill his boots.

He could ask no better.

Save for one thing: he wished Tom would take a wife.

When he brought up the subject, Tom gave a short bitter laugh. "I think I've not much to offer a woman," he said, to Don Sebastião's astonishment. And even though pressed, he refused to discuss the subject. It was not manly to admit that he could not come to a marriage bed with a whole heart. And he would not offer a woman less—not a woman to whom he could give his name.

There were women, of course, for Tom was no celibate. There were bright-eyed native girls who took his attentions lightly, there were brief dangerous liaisons with languorous married women in Rio de Janeiro or São Paulo that entertained him for a time, but nothing lasted, nothing endured. There was always that lovely lost face haunting his dreams.

In Rio, marriageable young ladies sighed behind their fans and whispered that Don Tomas was handsome, yes, but that he had a heart of stone!

And now, in a London ballroom a striking lady gowned in black was asking to meet him.

"Who is she?" he asked Travers curiously.

"Well, she used to be Katherine Olney before she married Talybont. And then that husband died mysteriously in Portugal some years ago and she came back home and married some obscure West Country knight named Scopes that nobody ever heard of, and now she's back in London—

husband-hunting, I believe they call it," Travers told him cheerfully.

But the word "Portugal" had piqued Tom's interest.

"I'd like to meet the lady," he told Travers.

And so it was that Tom found himself in conversation with Charlotte's archenemy, the former Katherine Talybont. And on closer inspection, even by candlelight, which is kind to the complexion, he saw that the bloom was off the rose. Katherine's figure was magnificent but her high color was strictly attributable to cosmetics, and up close her face had a hard look.

"I am told you have been living in Brazil." Katherine flirted her fan. "Tell me, what is it like, living there?"

Brazil was a subject of which Tom never tired. He launched into it, noting that Katherine's interest evaporated whenever the conversation strayed from cities and civilization. No jungle traveler she. . . . He asked her to dance.

Katherine was a splendid dancer, and Tom cut a fine figure. Eyes followed them as they whirled about the floor.

Katherine left the floor, announcing that dancing always made her thirsty. She began to drink wine. Too much wine. Tom suspected her of having to be carried insensible to bed at night by panting servants.

Still, the evening was the better because of her company. Idly he asked her about Portugal. Had she spent much time there?

"I was not there for long, but it was the worst time of my whole life!" Katherine's beautiful dark eyes flashed balefully. "My husband was murdered there."

Died mysteriously, Travers had said. Evidently the widow had a stronger word for it.

"And *there* is the man who killed him!" Katherine's sharp voice rose as she snapped her fan shut.

Tom's gaze followed in the direction that fan was pointing, and a stillness came over him. Not so much as an eyelash moved. There, arguing with an old gentleman who was shaking his head vehemently, and plainly visible through the throng, was Rowan Keynes.

"Rowan Keynes killed your husband?" he asked wonderingly.

"You know Rowan?" cried Katherine, startled.

"I met him once."

"Once is more than enough!" snapped Katherine. "I was fool enough to become betrothed to him, and when I broke it off and married Eustace Talybont, Rowan took a bride and followed me to Portugal and there murdered my husband. Oh, I could never prove it, but Rowan did it all the same."

"You say he had taken a bride when he did this?" Tom asked slowly.

"Yes. Some blonde girl from the Lake Country."

Charlotte. This woman must have known Charlotte!

"Did you know her?" he heard himself ask, his cold eyes never leaving Rowan.

"His bride? Oh, yes, I met her."

"I am told they had two children."

"Two girls. Both turned out badly—but then, that was to be expected with such a father!"

"Turned out badly in what way?"

"The older one caused a rash of duels and amid the scandal ran away and married some Scot and lives on his estate somewhere in the north. The younger one married Lord Houghton and *they* both behave so scandalously that his family won't accept them, I'm told."

Tom discounted duels and scandals. What he got out of Katherine's answer was that one daughter was living on her husband's north-country estate and the other had married a lord. Both Charlotte's daughters had obviously left home and were doing well. *Which left Rowan without his shield. . . .*

Nettled that Tom's interest should stray from herself and focus so fixedly on a man she hated, Katherine added spitefully, "Blanche told me that not long after he married her, Rowan grew very jealous of his bride here in London, and then quite suddenly she disappeared from London. Later we heard that he had taken her to Portugal again and come back without her, telling everybody she was dead. I don't doubt he murdered her as well!"

Tom's green gaze swung round to Katherine with such intensity that she blinked.

"What makes you think Keynes murdered her?" he demanded.

"Because he is a devious man who never forgives anyone. He arranges devious things. He *buys* people, buys their lies."

Buys their lies. The old doctor had been very convincing, but perhaps he was a convincing liar—bought by Rowan Keynes. Tom's jaw hardened. He would have the truth, and he would have it from the one man who knew it best.

Katherine was astonished at the swiftness with which Tom excused himself and left her, crossing the room in long strides after Rowan Keynes, who was already going out the door.

Tom went out into the now slackening rain and saw Rowan just then climbing into a hackney coach and driving off through the puddled street. He hailed another hackney and followed him to a shabby district near the river, for Phoebe's endless pleas for money had pushed Rowan under a sea of mounting debts and he had had to sell the house in Grosvenor Square and move into cheaper lodgings. He had attended Lady Sotherby's ball tonight in the hope of securing a position of some sort through a friend of Walpole's, but the evening had ended in disappointment. He was in a disgruntled mood as he paid off the driver, and paid scant attention to the tall gentleman in gray who had alighted from another hackney nearby.

Both coaches swung off, their wheels turning behind the clip-clop of the horses' hooves, and Rowan was about to insert a key into the door lock when a cold voice stopped him.

"A word with you, Keynes."

Rowan was attuned to men's voices and what some sounds meant. That voice from behind him had death in it. He dropped his key upon the threshold and whirled about, his hand seeking his sword.

It was too dark for Rowan to see who it was, but he had not recognized the voice so he took it to be a stranger.

More important, a sudden flash in the darkness told him that the stranger's sword had already left its scabbard. There was nobody about, the street was deserted. On this rainy night shutters were closed, curtains drawn; everybody had gone to bed.

"What are you, a footpad, to come up behind a man in the dark?" Rowan snarled, snaking out his own blade.

"No," was the imperturbable answer, but the tone was still as deadly. "I am come to ask you about Charlotte. *I want to know how she died.*"

The rain had ceased now, but a sudden flash of lightning illuminated Tom's tall gray-clad figure, that shock of distinctive pale hair. Rowan recognized his adversary.

"Westing!" he growled. "You have more lives than a cat!" He tilted his head upward. "Yates!" he roared. Upstairs a window casement promptly opened and a big head stuck out.

Tom saw that reinforcements were about to arrive.

"You will tell me how she died." Blade outstretched, he advanced upon Rowan.

By now Yates was clattering down the stairs. Rowan was backing warily away over the wet cobbles. Tom had a sudden heartfelt wish for a pistol, but one does not usually feel the need to carry guns at gatherings such as Lady Sotherby's, and he had neglected to wear one upon his person. Hearing Yates' crashing approach, he cast about him for some weapon other than his short dress sword—and the next lightning flash showed him one. A loose brick that had fallen from a nearby chimney. He was edging toward it even as Rowan leapt for him, thrusting.

Tom parried. Both blades slid down each other. They closed, then Tom knocked Rowan away.

"Tell me how she died."

Yates was at the door now, brandishing a pistol. Tom swooped down upon the brick, collecting it in his left hand even as Rowan danced away from him to give Yates a clear shot. But it was very dark now and Yates stood foursquare, carefully drawing a bead upon his victim. His big body was silhouetted against the light in the doorway.

With all the force of his left arm, Tom threw the brick.

It caught Yates full in the forehead and dropped him like a stone. Used to fighting on slippery decks, Tom sprang nimbly over the cobbles to close again with Rowan, who was cursing as he met this sudden assault.

As swordsmen they were well-matched. Both were strong and muscular, both used to street fighting. As they closed again, Rowan tried to knee Tom in the groin and was rewarded by having the hilt of Tom's sword brought upward against his chin hard enough to make his teeth snap together with a crunch. Rowan made an inarticulate sound and Tom guessed grimly that Rowan had bitten off the end of his tongue.

The duelists rebounded from each other again. They circled warily once more, both panting from their violent exertion. Again they clashed, lunge and parry, parry and thrust. Now once again Tom had the advantage as Rowan's foot slipped upon the treacherous slippery cobbles. In a flash he had flicked Rowan's blade from his hand and pinned Rowan's long body against a wet brick house wall with the point of his blade pressed into Rowan's chest.

"*Now* you will tell me how Charlotte died," he said softly.

Rowan glared back at him. This was the man Charlotte had loved, this nine-lives fellow who refused to die, who kept coming back. Would he tell him that Charlotte still lived? He would not!

He was a dead man anyway, Rowan reasoned, with that sword point pricking through his shirt front—but he could still give his enemy one more blow. Contemptuously he stuck out his jaw.

"How do you *think* she died?" he snarled. "*I killed the lying wench!*"

Terribly, slowly, those words sank in on Tom, draining the blood from his face, leaving it gray. And with it drained away any mercy he might have had in him.

"Then accept *this* from Charlotte," he said between his teeth—and drove his blade home. Into Rowan's heart.

For a moment Rowan stood, impaled but sneering, apparently unmoved. Then his long body sagged downward along the wet brick wall.

With his breath rasping in his throat, Tom stood towering over his fallen opponent. *Charlotte had died by this man's hand—had the fellow not said so?* With slow deliberation he drew out his wet blade and wiped Rowan's blood from it on Rowan's cuff. Then abruptly he sheathed his sword and swung away, leaving his fallen foes like carrion to be dealt with by whoever cared to do it.

No one had seen the fight. Tom did not report it. Rowan and his faithful henchmen Yates were pronounced slain by person or persons unknown. And Tom, his business in England at an end, sailed away.

At least he had avenged her, he told himself as he stared from a haggard face over the departing ship's rail.

32

Aldershot Grange

For years now Cassandra had not thought much about her mother, gone like a childhood dream. But now, here at Aldershot Grange where her own earliest childhood had been spent—and especially as she tried to keep her thoughts away from Drew and her attraction to him—she began again to think about her mother and what *her* life must have been like here as a young girl.

Here in these very echoing halls her mother had lived her breathless youth, had fallen in love, had married—and undoubtedly against her guardian's wishes, for had her mother not told her once that she had been married "across the border" at Gretna Green?

Cassandra began to ask questions about her mother, idly at first and then with more interest as she sensed that people were holding something back.

It was Livesay who told her—reluctantly—about the young lovers and Tom's fall from Kenlock Crag, and how, to everybody's surprise, her mother had immediately married Rowan Keynes.

It was a tale Cassandra had not heard before. And having heard it, she found herself somehow unsatisfied. Nagging flickers of memory sparked in her mind, like half-seen shadows flitting through, telling her nothing. But having heard the tale, she could not let it alone.

She found one of the pair of climbers who had guided

Charlotte's guardian and Rowan Keynes up Kenlock Crag that night, and she persuaded him to take her up there.

It was a wild afternoon. A brisk wind blew from the north, and down below stretched a lovely valley—the same valley her mother must have traversed on the way to Scotland and Gretna Green.

Moodily Cassandra walked about the little "alcove" where the lovers had been found embracing.

"And here was where Tom Westing went over the edge," her guide told her tonelessly.

Cassandra looked in the direction he pointed. "And then?" she whispered.

"Then?" His bushy brows elevated. "Why, then the young lady screamed." He could still hear that scream, sometimes in his nightmares. "And fainted."

Cassandra shuddered. Reluctantly she approached that edge, looked down, and saw some twenty feet below her a narrow ledge where a body might have been caught, saving it from a dizzying descent down the sheer rock face to the rushing white water of the cascade far below.

"But if he had fallen here?" She swung about to face the climber, who had now sat down on a rock of the low "terrace wall" over which they had come to reach this place, and was contemplating her steadily. "It was night, you say? And dark? Nobody looked over?"

He frowned. "*I* didn't look over, and neither did Waddy. We were both hanging on to the young lady in case when she came to herself she tried to throw herself over after him."

"But somebody must have looked? You said there was moonlight."

"That fellow we were told she married later, *he* looked over and said Tom Westing was gone." His tone held finality. "That be all I can tell you, young mistress."

Even if he knew more, he would not tell her, Cassandra sensed.

Wordlessly she returned to her silent contemplation of the ledge below. How could a falling body *not* have come to rest there instead of making the long deadly journey down the cliff face? In her mind she could almost hear the rattling stones tumbling downward into the depths. . . .

Her gaze swept upward into the cloudless sky. Overhead, hawks were soaring—or were they vultures? They seemed to be converging on something just beyond the nearest peak.

A terrible certainty surged over her, and with it her forehead and her palms went damp and her breath came shallowly.

Rowan Keynes had wanted her mother. And when she had run away with Tom Westing, Rowan had joined her guardian in pursuing her. And when Tom's body had gone over the edge to presumed certain death, Rowan had come to the edge to make sure—and looked over and seen his rival lying insensible on the ledge below. And he had turned to the others and told them Tom Westing was gone.

And left him there to die! For the cliff face along that first twenty-foot drop was perfectly smooth. She knelt down and peered over to study it. No man could have found a handhold there. Tom Westing, if he had survived the fall, would have found himself trapped in this lonely place where no one would have heard him cry out. She looked up again at the wheeling birds and shuddered, thinking of their sharp beaks and rending talons.

Her damp hands clenched. *Murder had been done here! And by her father, Rowan Keynes!*

And then her mother, doubtless dragged away unconscious, had promptly married Rowan. . . . Why?

Pale and unsatisfied, she turned away and accompanied the guide back down to the base of Kenlock Crag.

But back at Aldershot Grange she found it hard to sleep. Flitting memories flashed through her mind, memories of a night in Portugal when the candlelight had wavered on the stairs and she had heard her mother scream. She had been waked by something, some sound, some cry, something that nagged at her memory. And heard voices in the hall outside. She had pattered to the door barefoot, opened it a crack, and peered out. And seen the wavering candlelight and heard her mother's wild scream, suddenly choked off—and then a scuffling sound and footsteps on the stairs. It had frightened her and she had run back to bed and pulled the covers over her head.

The next morning Wend had told her she must have had a nightmare.

And then they had told her that her mother was dead and never coming back, and she and Phoebe had cried.

Now, remembering, Cassandra sat straight up in bed. That sharp sudden sound that had waked her that night, had it been her mother's voice? And had her mother not called out a name? Was that what lay hidden that she could not quite remember? Yes! Her mother had called out a single word, "Tom!" And then the voices, and then the screams that sounded choked off, and that scuffling on the stairs.

There in the darkness of her bedchamber at Aldershot Grange, with her arms clasped around her knees, Cassandra stared at the truth:

They had told her that it had all been a dream, but it had not been a dream. The night her mother disappeared, she had been calling to her lover!

And that meant . . . that he was still alive. Or at least alive then. And her mother, *how had she died?*

Ever a woman of quick decisions and reckless action, Cassandra threw back the covers and stepped down from her bed in the graying light of dawn. She would go down to London, she would confront her father, she would make him tell her!

Her mare was already saddled and Cassandra was eating her breakfast preparatory to leaving, when the messenger came.

Rowan Keynes was dead.

Shaken but dry-eyed, Cassandra unpacked her saddlebags. The father who had never really loved her—and whom she had been unable to love—was gone with all his secrets. She would never know what had happened to her beautiful young mother. Had she really died of the green sickness, as her father had told her? Or . . . *at her father's hands?*

The thought rocked her. And of a sudden she needed to

have Drew's strong arms around her. She did not even stop to put on a hat or pull on a pair of riding gloves. She did not wait to have Meg saddled. She threw herself on the mare's sleek cream-colored back and rode away like the wind itself to Blade's End.

Drew was outside explaining what he wanted to the men who were repairing a break in the garden wall. He heard the mare's hooves pounding over the turf and came running forward to catch Cassandra in his arms as she slipped from Meg's back.

"Cassandra, what—?"

"Oh, don't ask me any questions, Drew! My father is dead."

His arms closed about her in compassion. She realized that he was comforting her for the wrong reasons—he assumed it was grief for her father's passing that was making her tremble, not fear for what he might have done while he lived. But whatever had happened, it was too late now to change it, she told herself dully. Only Drew's arms were comforting and real. They shut out the world. She could lose herself in them.

"Oh, Drew," she choked. "Drew, hold me, hold me."

And he did, that whole night through. And although he ached to make love to her, he did not. He held himself in check, for he felt it would be taking unfair advantage of Cassandra at a time when she faced him with all her defenses down. He wanted her to come to his arms willingly, deep in love.

And Cassandra, sobbing in his arms, let herself be comforted and finally fell asleep, exhausted, like a child.

The next morning he brought her home to Aldershot Grange and his cold expression dared any of the servants there to so much as blink an eye.

"I will see you tonight, Cassandra." He bent down to kiss her hand, and when he lifted his head the look he gave her was so caressing that she was shaken by it.

Oh, Drew, she thought in panic. *Don't fall in love with me. I can't let you. I couldn't bear it if anything happened to you.* There was an odd little ache in her heart and her throat was dry as she whispered, "Not tonight, Drew, it's too soon. Tomorrow . . ."

"Tomorrow, then." His warm smile flashed and she watched him stride away and mount the Bishop.

He is riding out of my life, she thought, desolate. *Only he doesn't know it . . . not yet.* A veil of tears obscured her vision.

She turned blindly to seek out Wend.

"Wend," she asked in a brooding voice, "I want you to tell me the truth. What happened to my mother? How did she really die?"

Now that Rowan Keynes was dead, Wend was not afraid to answer that question.

"She didn't," Wend said slowly. "At least, I don't think she did. I know there was a hearse and a coffin, but *I* never thought she was dead."

"But I . . . I heard her scream that night, Wend. On the stairs. *You* told me it was just a nightmare."

"And so it may have been." Wend nodded. "But days before that, I saw her ride away in a coach. With *him.*"

"With . . . who did she ride away with Wend?"

"With Tom Westing."

Cassandra drew in her breath sharply.

As if expecting Cassandra to attack that statement, Wend said defensively, "She loved Tom before she even knew Rowan Keynes. He was the man she'd have married if she could. I know Tom was *supposed* to be dead, but the morning Rowan Keynes said he was leaving for Evora, she walked down into the town. She came back riding in a coach and she says to me, 'Wend, I've met some old friends, the Milroyds, and they've asked me to stay with them for a while.' And she packed a bag. And when I looked out the window, I could see Tom Westing in the coach that took her away. I'd know him anywhere. I couldn't be mistaken. And when that coach clattered away, I knew Rowan Keynes had lost her. She'd run away with Tom Westing, that's what. Oh, I know there was a funeral procession and all that, but that was because he was too proud to admit his wife had run away with another man and wasn't coming back!"

"Couldn't you have been mistaken? Perhaps it wasn't Tom Westing." Cassandra's voice was strained.

Wend shook her head vigorously. "I knew I'd made no mistake when we came back from Portugal and Livesay told me Tom Westing wasn't dead, as we'd all thought, that he'd come to Aldershot Grange right after we left, asking to see Mistress Charlotte, and when Livesay told him she'd gone to Lisbon, Tom was off like a shot."

"Why didn't Livesay tell me Tom Westing had come back?" Cassandra was bewildered.

Wend hesitated. Livesay had undoubtedly looked at Cassandra's almost-white-blonde hair and vivid green eyes—so exactly Tom's coloring—and been afraid that she'd worm out of him what both he and Wend had already guessed, that Cassandra was Tom's daughter. But what good to tell her that now? "Livesay was probably afraid for his job," she muttered. "Afraid you'd say something to Rowan Keynes."

"So you think she's still alive?" said Cassandra slowly.

Wend nodded her head vigorously. "I think she's over there somewhere—with him."

It was a marvelously romantic tale and it explained a lot. But somehow Cassandra couldn't quite credit it.

She puzzled over it, but as the day wore on, something more pressing occupied her thoughts.

Drew Marsden had said he would be back tomorrow— and she knew he would keep that promise. Her face grew wistful, thinking of him, wanting him even though she tried to force her thoughts away.

Wend had asked her if she would go back to London now. Perhaps that was the answer, perhaps she *should* go back to London now, today, make a clean break with everything she so ardently desired.

For if she stayed here, she knew that before tomorrow night's moon had waned she would be in Drew's arms, she would forget her fears and know only her dreams. . . . She would be too deeply involved ever to draw back.

She would bring him to disaster!

Her blonde head dropped in defeat and she pressed her

hands against her cheeks, her burning eyes, trying desperately to think.

Wait! There *was* a way, an honorable way, to leave him, to give him time. Time to forget her. . . .

She betook herself downstairs.

"Wend," she said decisively, "come upstairs, we must pack. I'm going to Portugal."

Wend opened her mouth to protest.

"And before you say what you're about to," Cassandra added dryly, quenching the expected outburst from Wend that it was unseemly for a lady to travel alone, "I'll be taking you with me."

She would go to Lisbon. She would find out for herself what had happened to her wayward young mother.

And so the girl whose beauty had caused the London *Gazette* to dub her "the Fair Maid of Cumberland," twenty-two and still a virgin, sailed for Portugal and the city that had been her mother's downfall.

BOOK III

Carlotta

33

Lisbon, Portugal, Autumn, 1755

A brisk wind was blowing up the Tagus, billowing the sails of the merchantman *Pride of Glasgow*, which had carried Cassandra from Carlisle down the Irish Sea, over the great undersea West European Basin, and at last into the mouth of the Tagus. She stood with Wend among the excited chattering passengers on deck, eager to disembark, and her heart quickened at the sight before her.

From here Lisbon was a white city sprawled in a great valley between two hills—crowned on the one side by the mighty fortress of the Castelo de São Jorge and on the other by the Bairro Alto. Other hills rose all about.

Tense now with the thought of what she might find here, Cassandra paid scant heed to the darting lateen-sailed *fragatas*, the tall ships of many countries anchored at the great port. The clamor of the busy waterfront passed by her almost in a dream as she and Wend took a carriage to the Ilho Verde, the Green Island, an inn which one of her fellow passengers had recommended as being both good and reasonable—and one where the landlord spoke English.

All during the voyage she had been nagged by thoughts of Drew Marsden and what *he* must have thought when he found her gone. Had he gone home soberly to stare into the fire and yearn for her? Or had he merely shrugged and turned away? Or ridden off to Carlisle and found himself

439

another girl? That last thought caused her such pain that she was tempted to turn around and take the first ship home, but she held herself in check. And after she got Wend settled at the inn—for Wend had not stood the voyage well, she had come down with some stomach ailment just before they docked, and Cassandra had decreed for her several days of rest in bed—she inquired of the landlord the way to the Portas del Sol, and set out on foot. That was the way to get her mind off Drew Marsden— begin her search!

It was harder to find than she had thought, but she kept bearing upward as the landlord had instructed, making her way through what seemed a dizzying maze of twisting streets and alleys until at last, after she had almost given up, she blundered onto the house her family had so briefly occupied.

It seemed to be closed up and vacant, its windows shuttered.

A pair of interested—and exceedingly cold—eyes had been observing Cassandra's progress almost since her arrival in Lisbon. Their lounging owner had followed her at a discreet distance as she made her determined way to the Portas del Sol and stared up thoughtfully for such a long time at the big flat-fronted mansion, as if somehow its smooth painted face would give her some clue to what she wanted so desperately to learn. He had watched Cassandra bang the heavy iron door knocker and wait, bang again, and eventually give up and turn away.

He had wondered about it, for the house had obviously been vacant for a long time.

Cassandra had been preoccupied and frowning as she made her way back through the labyrinthine ways of the Alfama—getting lost twice and finding her way, bewildered, past slumbering dogs and cats that leapt down from garden walls, past laden donkeys and barefoot *varinas* calling out their wares, and raucous playing children. She wound her way through streets so narrow it seemed to her the walls on either side almost touched, like Holy Spirit Alley. The man who followed her—and he was a remarkably handsome fellow, a tawny figure hardly inconspicuous in apricot silks with a short dress sword chased in silver hanging by his side—made no move to assist her. Instead he paused and lounged in the shadows of various doorways and let her blink into the sunlight, peering past the laundry strung overhead between the buildings, trying to figure out where her directions had gone wrong.

He was assessing her.

He continued to follow her as she made inquiries—difficult since she spoke no Portuguese—of a hackney driver in the main square. He was close enough to hear what she said, and her inquiry astonished him—the lady was off to view a *cemetery?* His own hired carriage ambled along behind at some distance as she searched through several, looking for the one where her mother lay buried, for Wend might have gotten her facts straight enough but not been in possession of all of them. Suppose her mother really had died? She might have run away and suffered an accident, Rowan Keynes might have had nothing to do with it. Or, as Wend believed, Rowan might have ordered a funeral procession to save face, might even have buried an empty coffin. But if he had raised a stone to her, then assuredly her mother was dead, for Cassandra could not believe her father would go *that* far.

She had begun to hope that she would search all of Lisbon's cemeteries and never find it when she was attracted by a grave that seemed backward to the others in its row, with a footstone taller than its headstone. The Watcher gazed upon her from afar, pretending to visit another grave as he did so, and one fine hand, which sported a heavy gold ring set with a ruby, stroked his strong jawline thoughtfully as he saw her bend down to read the inscription. He saw her tense suddenly, then sink to her knees beside the grave and bury her face in her hands, for Cassandra had just read those touching words:

"Here lies Charlotte, beloved of Thomas, *ate o fim do mundo.*"

Wend had been wrong then. . . . Charlotte was dead, she had not run away after all. But her Thomas had found her and raised this stone. Cassandra felt hot tears sting her eyes at the thought that these long-lost lovers could not have found each other again. She knelt there for long moments wishing she could bring her mother back again. . . .

After Cassandra rose and moved away, the Watcher sauntered over, curious, and read that inscription himself. Making nothing of it, he climbed back into his carriage and followed her again, this time back to her green-painted inn, the Ilha Verde—the Green Island.

There he sank back into the crowd, and his hard crystal eyes narrowed when he saw the effect this lady was having on a dark-haired gentleman, just then descending the stairs, who stopped dead at sight of her, peered forward thunderstruck, then turned and bolted back the way he had come.

The lady, thought the Watcher, had proved extremely interesting. He pulled out his handsome gold pocket watch and frowned. Best not be late for his appointment—the prince would not like it. He could resume his surveillance of the English beauty tomorrow.

He moved with the ease and assurance of his kind through the crowd at the Green Island and stood outside, frowning impatiently. A few moments later an ornate vehicle pulled by matched white horses rolled up. New arrivals at the Green Island craned their necks to see who was leaving in a royal coach.

They would have been astonished to learn that the tall gentleman who climbed into the coach with such an air had no visible means of support and no royal blood whatsoever—unless one could count a bit of it that came down through the dalliance of that long-gone and illegitimate wielder of power in England, John of Gaunt. This young man was a swashbuckling adventurer who had been ousted—for gaming with marked cards or the wrong dice, for challenging to duels those who must go unscathed, for sleeping with ladies already committed to men of wealth and power—from half the capitals of Europe. Sent down from Oxford, cashiered from the army, cast out by his family and warned not to return to London, he had traveled under many names. The most recent—and the one he used here—was Leeds Birmingham. Neither name was his own. He had chosen them, with wry humor, from among the names of the many towns he had left on a fast horse with hot pursuit following after.

His face, which might have been too good-looking had it not been for the sinister addition of a couple of dueling scars, was smiling reflectively. He leaned his elbow upon the coach's open window, grateful for the breeze that blew against his tanned forehead and tawny hair as he was carried through Lisbon to a well-known tavern.

The prince would be pleased, he thought, with this day's work.

Cassandra, preoccupied with her search for her mother, and dejected at finding her grave, for she had nourished the hope that her mother was still alive, had not even noticed Leeds Birmingham hovering in the background. Nor had she, on returning to the Green Island, observed the remarkable performance of the dark-haired gentleman who had bolted back up the stairs at sight of her and was at this moment seething with unrest.

He paced the floor. Surely she had not recognized him! No, of course not, that was ridiculous. He had seen *her* when she was going to school back in Cambridge—and no one could forget that face! Indeed, it was that face that had made him show an interest in her little sister, in hopes of wangling an introduction to the Beauty, as the Cambridge students had dubbed Cassandra. But he bit his lip and thought back—she had run away from the school before he had had the opportunity to meet her. Phoebe might well have described him to her in detail, but that description would fit a thousand men. Cassandra would have no way of remembering him unless he had, by some unlucky chance, been pointed out to her.

Still, it was a chance he dared not take. He dashed out and knocked on a door down the hall—the door of a much more resplendent room than his own. The lady's maid answered and showed him in.

A young girl, rather mousy in appearance despite the elegance of her gown, greeted his distraught expression with an anxious, "Clive, what on earth is the matter?"

"I have heard a rumor, Della," muttered Clive, looking

about him as if the walls might have ears, "that there may be a case of plague here at the Green Island."

"What?" Della jumped to her feet. "But we must leave Lisbon at once then! I will hurry next door and tell Mama that we must pack for England!"

"No need of that yet, Della. Indeed, it may not even be true." With a masterful gesture, Clive—Phoebe's Clive, Lord Houghton—barred her rush to the door. "I have a far better solution. There is a place I am told we must visit, and it is some distance from Lisbon, near the fishing village of Cascais. We could pack our things, leave this inn at once, and journey there. We could travel in leisurely style, and if we hear there is plague spreading in Lisbon, we will not return, we will simply journey on to Oporto and take ship for home from there."

"Oh, Clive, all your ideas are so splendid!" Young Della's gaze upon him was adoring. "I will hurry to tell Mama. If there is even a *thought* of plague here at the inn, I am sure she will be eager to leave at once!" She paused in the doorway. "Where did you say we are going?"

Well, he had got out of that one very nicely! Clive grinned. "It is at Estoril and is called the Boca do Inferno— the Mouth of Hell."

Della gave him a doubtful look. Then her trusting smile flashed again. "We will be ready in an hour, Clive."

Back in his own room, Clive mopped his brow. He had been living a lie these past weeks and he had no intention of letting it all crash down on his head. The ladies he was traveling with—Lady Farrington, her daughter Della, and their respective maids—considered him a highly eligible, if slightly tarnished, bachelor.

He intended for them to hold that belief.

Clive had made a career of lying. Blessed with social position, family wealth, a doting mother and a certain stripling grace (his friends told him he had the melancholy air of a poet), young Lord Houghton had cut quite a swath back in England. Then had come an assortment of disgraces—scrapes with women, welched gambling debts, being barred from certain London clubs—which even his tolerant mother, the dowager Marchioness of Greensea, had frowned upon. With the intent of "making a man of him," she had cut off his funds while he was at Cambridge.

Phoebe had heard about that. And she had put out rumors that she was a great heiress. Clive had not entirely taken the bait. He had seduced Phoebe—or rather he thought he had, actually it was the other way around—and had found her both enterprising and ingenious in bed. Such talent at her age surprised him. With that as a lure, he had consented to take her to London and enter into a Fleet Street marriage. He had reasoned that if Phoebe was *not* an heiress, he would be no worse off, for Fleet Street marriages were hardly legal, and if her claims turned out to be true and she actually was heiress to large holdings in the colonies, he would parade the fact that he had debauched her and her father would promptly force him into marriage.

In London, after their Fleet Street ceremony, he had heard about Rowan Keynes' prowess with the sword and that had changed his plans somewhat. He was glad enough to flee with Phoebe into the countryside and await developments. And for a time Phoebe's inventiveness with landlords and tradespeople, her flair for arranging escapes—she was not Rowan's daughter for nothing—had held him in thrall. But no money had been forthcoming, and when they returned to London he had had every intention of abandoning her and trying to make his peace with his mother, who had refused to see him ever since he had taken up with the wayward Phoebe.

He had overlooked but one thing—the passage of time. Rowan Keynes had descended upon him and explained matters at the point of a rapier. Forced into marriage with Phoebe—and he went docilely enough, once it was borne in on him that he was already her husband by common law and that if he satisfied her father with a church wedding there would be a large dowry—he had tried to reconcile with his mother.

But the dowager Marchioness considered Phoebe's behavior scandalous and her son's only a little less so. She wept but she steadfastly refused to receive them. She tore

up his letters unread and so did not learn that her son had
married his paramour in a church.

Cast back upon their own, the pair set themselves up
for a time in Kent, but soon Clive's gaming and Phoebe's
extravagance had eaten away her generous dowry and they
were again on the run from their creditors.

Their next years were stormy ones. When they were in
funds, they had lived high. When they were not, they
quarreled. Sometimes Clive threatened to leave her—and
once or twice he had. Always she had found him again,
and with money—money she had wheedled out of Rowan
Keynes, who found her requests hard to refuse—they had
been reconciled. Eventually Phoebe had reduced her
father to penury and after that lost touch with him.

Clive had brightened at the news of his father-in-law's
death but it seemed Phoebe would receive nothing from
the estate. The house on Grosvenor Square had long since
been sold for debt. Phoebe had no known prospects; she
was estranged from her older sister, who lived at some
unlikely place—Cumberland, he thought.

Their situation, when Clive had assessed it, was hopeless.

He had left Phoebe in Liverpool, telling her that he was
going to make one more effort—this time alone—to get his
mother to accept them. Phoebe had been glad to wait.

But his method of getting in to see the Marchioness
would have caused even Phoebe's stout heart to waver.
He sent in word that his "mistress" had run away with a
sea captain to America and that he was most heartily sorry
for all the trouble he had caused.

He was received as a penitent. And after all, why not,
reasoned his mother. Clive's reputation was a little tarnished, but he might still make a good marriage.

Instantly she set about it. Two of her good friends, Lady
Rhoads and the Countess of Scattersby, were on the brink
of leaving for Portugal in the hope that the more equable
climate of Lisbon might cure the Countess of her painful
rheumatism. *And* they were taking with them Lady
Farrington and her daughter Della, who, though a mousy
girl who had made little impact during her first London
season, would now become heiress to a large estate, for

her half-brother Roger had died in the spring and her elderly grandfather, who had intended to bequeath his fortune to Roger, now intended to leave everything to young Della.

Ah, Della would cut a swath in London *this* season, prophesied Lady Rhoads, for word of her newfound fortune would have got around by then!

No, she would not! silently vowed the Marchioness. *For by then her son Clive—a thoroughly eligible scapegrace—would have plucked the golden apple from the tree!*

"Lady Rhoads has graciously accepted you into her party," she told her son. "I know that Della is not pretty, but she will inherit half of Northumberland." (The Marchioness was given to slight overstatement, but her son got the drift.) "I expect you"—she leaned forward, frowning to emphasize her next words—"to return from Lisbon betrothed to Lady Farrington's daughter!"

And to further that end, she financed Clive's trip and sent him off to his former tailor to make him "presentable."

It had been so wonderful to be back with his own set, spending money again, with not a care in the world other than the fit of his new clothes! And he had made himself so agreeable and paid such ardent court to the susceptible Della all the way to Portugal that when word reached them in Lisbon that Lady Rhoads' husband had died and she and the Countess hastily embarked for England, Lady Farrington had decided to stay on in the Portuguese capital "since Clive and Della were getting along so nicely."

Busy enjoying the delights of Lisbon, Clive had actually forgotten Phoebe for a while, waiting for him back in Liverpool.

But the sight of Cassandra, incredibly strolling into his very inn in Lisbon, had promptly restored Phoebe to his memory. And sent him off with his party to visit the Mouth of Hell. For Cassandra was certain to know that Clive and Phoebe were legally married at last, and she must not meet Lady Farrington or Della. If she did, the truth was sure to come out and his own chances would be ruined.

Cassandra was entirely unaware of the stir she was

causing. Back at the inn, after she imparted to Wend the gloomy news that she had found her mother's grave, her thoughts had drifted back to Cumberland—and Drew, and Aldershot Grange. She wondered wistfully if Meg was getting enough exercise, if Clover was getting enough cream. *Of course they were*, Wend scolded her, for had not Livesay promised to see both himself? And Cassandra sighed and agreed, for like Wend, Livesay was more than a loyal servant—he was an old and trusted friend.

Still, in the morning light, the day after she had visited the cemetery and the house in the Portas del Sol, Cassandra was half-regretting this hasty trip to Portugal. In making her rash decision—and she was a woman given to rash decisions—she had given no thought at all to how difficult it would be to make inquiries in a foreign country where one did not speak the language. Indeed, she had had some difficulty finding out what the words *"Ate o fim do mundo"* inscribed on her mother's footstone had meant. *"Until the end of the world."* It brought a lump to Cassandra's throat. And made her realize anew how hard it was going to be to try to learn more about her mother.

Perhaps she had been wrong to come. . . .

Restless now, after breakfast she took a walk. There was the Rua do Ouro, the Street of Gold—and there the Street of Silver, and there the Gilders' Street, famous for gold leaf. And everywhere the streets were full of carriages and coaches and sedan chairs and horsemen. Cassandra roamed about looking in shop windows and occasionally going inside.

And all the while she was shadowed inconspicuously by Leeds Birmingham, who this day was roaming the shops too, having last night gotten the prince's blessing upon this endeavor.

Strolling along, Cassandra paused at a milliner's. She had actually opened the door and glanced into the interior when she told herself sternly she did not need another hat and closed it again.

Leeds Birmingham had observed this maneuver and was about to stroll on past the milliner's when the door suddenly burst open and a woman dressed all in black arrived into the street with a bound. She was tall and dark and reed slender. She had sharp features and an exceedingly hard face—a face Leeds Birmingham knew all too well. He melted back behind two wrangling gentlemen who were trying to persuade each other to go in different directions, and watched.

The woman in black took a step forward after Cassandra and then suddenly whirled and went back into the shop. A moment later a young lad left the shop running, almost caught up with Cassandra, and then settled into step behind her, pacing her.

So there was more than one watcher following the lovely English girl. Birmingham's hard crystal eyes narrowed. Perhaps the beauteous Cassandra was not such a wise choice after all. For why had Madame de Marceau, Lisbon's most expensive milliner—and a known agent of the Marquês de Pombal—rushed into the street at sight of her and then sent someone hurrying after?

After all, everyone knew that the Marquês de Pombal, who hailed from near Coimbra and five years ago had been appointed Secretary of Foreign Affairs, was fast emerging as Portugal's strongman. A man of enormous energy, Pombal was also a master of intrigue—as Leeds Birmingham had good reason to know. Leeds knew as well—for at Prince Damião's suggestion he had had the place watched—that various of Pombal's agents visited Madame de Marceau's exclusive millinery establishment at odd hours, often arriving or leaving by the back door. It was clear to Leeds that Pombal had recruited—God alone knew how!—this irksome Frenchwoman whose past seemed to defy exploration and was doubtless making good use of her in spying on the aristocratic ladies who frequented the shop and whose thoughtless comments might at the least furnish useful information and at best might implicate their husbands and friends in treasonous plots against the Crown—for Pombal was ever zealous as the king's right hand.

That the English girl had had such a startling effect upon the shadowy Madame de Marceau, he found strange indeed.

It was all very odd—and most intriguing.

Leeds Birmingham decided that it was time to meet the lady. He bent down and held a whispered conversation with a barefoot street urchin. A coin changed hands. The child nodded, tossed the stick he was carrying up the street, and charged after it, crashing into Cassandra from behind so that one of her legs was knocked out from under her—and she staggered back and half-fell into the arms of the gentleman in apricot silks who had sprinted forward to catch her.

"My goodness, that child crashed right into me!" she gasped, trying to right herself. In the confusion of the moment she never noticed that a young lad nearby had stopped and was staring hard at Leeds—but Leeds did. His face bore an amused grin as he saw the lad turn and melt back quickly toward the milliner's—no doubt to report this encounter of the lady he was following with Prince Damião's friend. Leeds turned his attention back to Cassandra, who was smiling up at him. "Thank you for catching me, sir."

Leeds Birmingham had a good grip on the lady. "Below the age of ten," he laughed, "small boys are a menace on the streets!" He set Cassandra carefully upon her feet, peered down at her with sudden interest. "Why, you are the lady I saw yesterday!" he exclaimed. "At the cemetery beside that exceptionally tall footstone with the interesting inscription!"

"Yes." Charlotte was delighted that the man who had set her back upon her feet should speak English. "Do you know it?"

"All in Portugal know that inscription."

She stared at him, fascinated. "How could that be so?"

"Because it is the same inscription as that on the tomb of Ines de Castro. A famous inscription and a tragic story—would you like to hear it, Mistress . . . ?"

"Cassandra Dunlawton. And I would like very much to hear it!"

"Leeds Birmingham, at your service." He bowed. "But since the sun is so hot and the story so long, I would prefer not to tell it in the street. The Royal Cockerel is nearby and they serve an excellent *gazpacho*. Would you join me?" He proffered his arm.

Ordinarily Cassandra would have gone nowhere with someone chance-met on the street. But this was a foreign country and this well-dressed and well-spoken gentleman was obviously English, the sun was shining, and the Royal Cockerel was known to be the finest inn in Lisbon. She took the proffered arm.

In a dim corner of the great dining room, over *gazpacho*, Leeds Birmingham smiled into her eyes and began to talk.

"Ines de Castro was a lady-in-waiting to Crown Prince Pedro's young wife Constanca—and very beautiful. The prince fell head over heels in love with this lady-in-waiting and she became his mistress. After Constanca died in childbirth he married Ines. But Ines had enemies. They persuaded Pedro's father, King Afonso IV, that the prince would be better off without Ines—and then they murdered her."

Cassandra gasped.

A soft heart, Birmingham thought happily. "Prince Pedro was wild with grief. He swore revenge. Two years later he succeeded to the throne—and he avenged her. He followed the courtiers who had murdered her to Castile and . . ." He broke off, smiling. "I do not think you would care to hear what he did to them. Let us just say that among other things he had their hearts cut out—some say he did it himself."

Cassandra shuddered.

"And then"—his pleasant masculine voice grew richer —"he had Ines dug up, dressed in court costume, placed upon a throne, *and crowned as his queen*. All the couriters were forced to kiss her dead hand and swear fealty to her, then to bear her in a litter to a great tomb he had built for her in the Abbey of Alcobaca, a tomb placed foot-to-foot with his own tomb, so that—and these are his words— hers would be the first face he would see on the Day of Resurrection. He had carved upon it, 'Ate o fim do mundo.'"

"*Until the end of the world*," breathed Cassandra, and her eyes were bright with tears.

Leeds Birmingham noted those tears with satisfaction.

Ah, he had made the right choice after all. She had to pass but one more test. . . .

They chatted for a long time over their *gazpacho*, and when she came out she felt she knew all about him. He had a mansion outside Southampton, his fortune came from shipping, he had been jilted by his betrothed, and his sisters had suggested a sea voyage as the best way to get over unrequited love. So she was not the only one running away from a love that could never be. Cassandra felt a rush of sympathy for Leeds Birmingham. His offer of dinner was warmly accepted.

The next morning they met again, seemingly by chance—although Cassandra was secretly sure that chance had nothing to do with it—right outside her inn.

"And where are you bound today?" he wondered. "For Lisbon has many sights and I would be glad to show them all to you—and you to them!" he added gallantly.

"Well, I would love to go sightseeing, but first I must straighten something out." Cassandra waved a piece of paper that had been delivered to her along with breakfast. "I have a note here from Madame de Marceau's millinery establishment that tells me I am to pick up a hat. I know nothing about it but I feel I should go and explain that they have notified the wrong person."

Leeds himself had sent that note—to see whether she would tell him about it or rush secretly to the shop of Pombal's agent, the milliner Madame de Marceau. He gave her a broad smile. "Well, then let us get this hat business over first," he suggested, pleased that Cassandra did not seem to know Madame, and curious to learn why the lady had had Cassandra followed.

Together they went into the shop. The little bell clapper over the door announced them. A smiling clerk stepped forward.

"I am Cassandra Dunlawton," announced Cassandra, "and I have here a note from Madame de Marceau." She waved it airily.

"A note?" The girl looked doubtful. "Ah, here is Madame now."

A tall funereal figure garbed in solid black entered the
room. From the back Madame de Marceau had heard
Cassandra's clear young voice speak her name.

"I am told a hat is being held here for me, Madame.
There must be some mistake. I bought no hat here."

"Let me see the note." Madame studied it. "I did not
write this, Madame Dunlawton."

"Oh?" Cassandra was taken aback.

"But I am glad you brought it." The Frenchwoman's
gaze was measuring. "Does the name Annette mean anything to you, Madame Dunlawton?"

Bewildered, Cassandra searched her memory. "No, it
doesn't—oh, yes, I remember now, I did know an Annette
Farraway in school. But I have not seen her since. She
married and moved to Dorset."

So Rowan had not seen fit to tell his daughter about
her. . . . Annette felt a stab of regret. She had seen Rowan
but once since he last left Lisbon, and that had been
briefly in London. He had told her then that his elder
daughter, Cassandra, had married a Scot named Dunlawton.
Now half-drawn, half-repelled, Annette studied the dazzling blonde before her—*Rowan's daughter with Charlotte's face*.

In truth Annette had run out into the street yesterday in
the belief that it was Charlotte who had opened the door
to her shop. Instantly she had dispatched a lad to follow
her, but had realized even before the lad returned to
report the meeting with Leeds Birmingham that Charlotte
could not be that young, this must be the daughter.

"No, we are not speaking about the same person, Madame Dunlawton, but I am glad you came." Here Annette
gave Leeds a cold look that said, *despite the company you
keep*! Leeds grinned genially back at her. He was well
aware that Pombal's agents would have no liking for any
friend of Prince Damião's! Annette turned back to the
bewildered girl. "I knew your father, Rowan Keynes."

"You did? But how . . . I am sorry, but I thought my
father made only one brief trip to Portugal," Cassandra
confessed.

"I knew him in Paris—and other places." Those sharp

dark eyes were still studying her. "You look nothing like your father, Madame Dunlawton," was Annette's regretful comment.

"So I am told." Cassandra laughed. "Yet my younger sister, Phoebe, is the very image of him."

"Is she indeed? I should like to meet Phoebe."

"Well, I doubt that you will. She is in England." Cassandra sobered. "My father died some time ago in London."

"Yes, I know." It was for Rowan, Annette wore—and would always wear—this mourning garb. To remind her. "I regret your loss, Madame Dunlawton. He was the best friend I ever had—and the finest man I ever knew."

Well, this Frenchwoman was the first person who had ever said *that* about her father. Cassandra was impressed. "Did you know my mother too?"

Something—could it be scorn?—played fitfully behind the dark brooding gaze that was turned upon her. "Yes, I knew her."

"Could you tell me something of her life here in Lisbon?" Cassandra wondered. "Of how she died?"

"We are speaking of the woman with the footstone that is taller than her headstone," put in Leeds conversationally.

Madame favored him with another cold look. "I know nothing about footstones." But she would certainly go and look! "But I know that she had a handsome funeral procession."

"Yes, Phoebe and I watched it from our window." There was a little catch in Cassandra's voice as she remembered that sorrowful day when she had looked down through her tears upon the black-tasseled horses and the casket draped with its handsome black-and-gold funeral pall. "My father rode in the procession, I remember. But there were so many mourners, I thought perhaps you might have been one?"

"They were paid mourners." Some slight roughness in her voice made Leeds look at Madame keenly. There was something here that did not meet the eye.

"I thought perhaps you could tell me how she died."

So that was it! *The wench had come searching.* "I am

sorry." Madame had become politely vague. "I really do not know."

"Thank you." Cassandra felt disheartened. She had hoped that this old friend of her father's might know more about her wayward young mother.

Leeds Birmingham was discovering that he too wanted to know how Cassandra's mother had died. Once they were out on the street, he suggested they try to find records, look up the attending physician.

"Oh, could we?" Cassandra was so grateful it almost made him feel ashamed of himself.

"Indeed we can." He set off down the crowded street beside her, keeping his own tall form well out on the street side to protect her from passing vehicles or riders.

Of a sudden Leeds' hat was flicked from his head and there was a sound like the spitting of a cat.

Cassandra had never seen a man move so fast. With a sudden fluid gesture Leeds Birmingham had whirled, sword bared from its scabbard—to face an imperious dark-haired young lady, magnificently dressed, who sat above him on a sleek black horse, her face shaded by a wide silver-studded black sombrero. Cassandra saw that she was holding a small riding crop in one gloved hand.

It was she who had made that spitting sound, she who had flicked the hat from Leeds Birmingham's head with her whip. And now she sat glaring down at him, sur-rounded by her entourage, two mounted horsemen—not seated upon silver-studded saddles like herself, but look-ing competent enough and ready to fight. And behind her from a carriage an older woman dressed in black waved a handkerchief and entreated, "Constanca! Constanca!" And then a flood of wailing Portuguese which Cassandra did not understand.

Leeds Birmingham's whole demeanor was transformed in an instant. "Dona Constanca!" He swept her a deep bow as he retrieved his hat, and grinned up at her. "How delightful to see you again!"

Dona Constanca jerked her horse's head around and spurred forward, almost riding down a group of pedestri-ans, who leapt out of her way. The carriage rolled forward, her henchmen rode swiftly after her—they were all gone as if they had never been there.

And Leeds was brushing off his hat. "A dangerous lady is Dona Constanca," he mused. "The hot blood of the Alentejo runs in her veins." He turned to Cassandra. "It is a harsh dry land, much like Castile. Desolate country where wild black boars root acorns beneath the cork oaks and fighting bulls are bred."

And fighting ladies as well, thought Cassandra wryly. "Why does she hate you so?" she asked curiously.

Those broad apricot silk shoulders shrugged. "Dona Constanca Varváez, who lives in one of the pink palaces we shall shortly be viewing, is betrothed to one of the king's younger sons, Prince Damião. She resents my influence over him."

Cassandra felt a little thrill go through her—a royal prince! "And do you have this influence over him?" she ventured.

"I hope so." He said that very firmly as he sheathed his sword and clapped his hat back on his head. "This is a day for hats," he declared merrily. "Well, let us be off to view the Tagus River and to sail the Sea of Straw in a *fragata* with a burnished red sail and the Eye of God painted upon its hull!" He took Cassandra's arm jauntily. "And then we will see what we can discover about your mother's death, Cassandra."

It was the first time he had called her that and she did not demur. His shoulders took on an even jauntier stance as he swung forward to show her all that was bright and beautiful in Lisbon.

It was two days later that they learned that the doctor who claimed to have attended Charlotte on her deathbed was dead. That he had been hanged for poisoning a patient was a fact Leeds Birmingham had thought best to withhold —it was something he would look into later himself. Meantime, he was about to spring a golden trap.

He chose to set that trap in what he considered to be the most romantic spot in Lisbon—the storied Tower of Belem.

They stood at one of the openwork stone balconies with

the leaf-green water lapping the stone walls below. "This place has seen much," he said, referring to the turreted tower with its joyous Manueline designs of shells and rope and coral wrought in stone. "Vasco da Gama sailed from here and found the sea route to the Indies. He returned with half his men dead and a hold full of riches—spices, jewels." His voice dreamed. "And became Viceroy of India." He lifted his hand in a silent salute to the great discoverer.

"You would like to become a viceroy?" she guessed.

"I would like to become a kingmaker." His tone was melancholy. "But more than that, I would like to see kings and princes achieve happiness as other men do."

"Whatever do you mean?" Cassandra was puzzled.

He squared around to face her. "You have seen Constanca. The young prince does not love her, yet her family is very powerful. They have enormous holdings on the Alentejo and he will be forced to marry her by his father."

Cassandra sighed. She supposed that was the fate of kings, to make loveless marriages.

"Prince Damião is in desperate trouble." He sighed. "Never did a man have more need of friends," he added gloomily.

Cassandra knew that she should not be prying into the young prince's affairs, but she could not help herself. "What kind of trouble?"

"I tell you this in strictest confidence," he said, and added thoughtfully, "Can I trust you, Cassandra? For it is a woman's life that is at stake here."

The green eyes that met his were steady and fearless. "You can trust me, Leeds."

"Prince Damião has had the misfortune to fall in love with a girl from Nazaré—a fisherman's daughter. Had the prince been like his grandfather, King João V, he might have put her in the nunnery of Odivelas and made merry with her there."

"Made merry *in a nunnery?*" Cassandra was incredulous.

He shrugged. "Why not? It is a place famous for scandals. After all, it was on the convent's patio that King

Afonso VI fought bulls and jousted in honor of Ana de Moura, whom he had promised to make his queen."

A strange world indeed! "But what of poor Prince Damião?" she demanded.

Ah, that note of distress in her tone was exactly what Leeds had been seeking!

"Prince Damião is reckless and a romantic. In secret he has married the fisherman's daughter, and now, as his wedding date with Dona Constanca approaches, he finds himself in a desperate situation. He dares not bring his bride Ines, to Lisbon—lest his father imprison them both, or the agents of his father's chief minister, the Marquês de Pombal, spirit her away somewhere, or Dona Constanca kill her with a stiletto." He sighed again. "It is a terrible time for Prince Damião; he knows not where to turn."

Cassandra's heart went out to the fisherman's daughter of Nazaré. The prince's love even had the same name— Ines—as the tragic woman whose inscription was the same as her mother's. Another Constanca, another Ines. . . . "It is terrible they cannot be together," she said, troubled.

"Yes. Terrible. You see, Prince Damião's father would have countenanced a mistress with good grace. The young prince could have set her up in a handsome establishment of her own and visited her at will—both before and after marriage. But to marry this barefoot maid! Never!"

"He should find some actress or music-hall singer and set *her* up as a blind in some handsome establishment and then bring Ines in as her 'maid' and visit her there any-way!" said Cassandra, on sudden inspiration, for, like her mother before her, Cassandra felt violently that no one should be forced into a loveless marriage.

Those crystal eyes looking down at her lit up. Leeds could not imagine his good fortune that *she* should have suggested it! "Yes, that would be a good solution—at least for now," he said gloomily. "But where to find such a woman?"

"Oh, there must be an endless selection!"

He shook his head. "The agents of the Marquês de Pombal are everywhere, and people are afraid of him— with good reason. If he ever comes to the complete power he seeks, heads will roll in this country. No, it is too dangerous. Who can be trusted? For the woman would have to know the truth, that she was not the prince's real mistress, but that another woman in the house was."

"There must be scads of women he knows who are trustworthy!" argued Cassandra. "Are you telling me there is no female in Lisbon this prince can trust?"

"Oh, there are several." Again that shrug. "But none of a beauty that would make her believable as the young prince's mistress. He is known to prefer beauties. Is he now to take to his bed—apparently, at least—some homely mouse whose only virtue is that she is to be trusted? You see, Cassandra, unless this creature is truly dazzling, Pombal will smell out a plot and set his spies upon her—they would be found out and it would mean disaster for them both."

"There should be *someone*," insisted Cassandra stubbornly.

A sudden light seemed to break over Leeds Birmingham's handsome duel-scarred face. "There *is* someone," he breathed, looking at Cassandra. "You could do it. You are beautiful, you are a foreigner with no family in Lisbon, so you could not be blackmailed on their account, any man who looked at you would believe the prince could fall in love with you—*you could do it, Cassandra!*"

She was backing away, her arm brushing one of the ornate stone pillars. "Oh, no, that's ridiculous—I don't even know the prince!"

"Come, you shall meet him!"

"No, Leeds, I couldn't!"

"Why not?" His crystal eyes sparkled prismlike in the sun. "It would be a wonderful adventure, something to remember all your life! You would live in a palace, ride in a golden coach, heads would crane to look at you, whispering that you were mistress to the prince! Where is your wild blood? Doesn't it appeal to you, Cassandra?"

The trouble was it *did* appeal to her. All the forces of her romantic nature had sprung forward to aid the embattled pair. "No, I—"

"Cassandra." He had caught her arm lightly and she felt anew his compelling masculine presence. Her very skin seemed to ripple at his touch. "The prince did me a great service once. When I first came to Portugal I was very despondent, I wandered listlessly about the country, caring for nothing. In a small village the wench who served me wine learned that I was going to Evora—not so far away—and asked if she might not accompany me, for she was afraid to make the journey alone. She was a pretty little thing and I took her up on my horse with me. We were seen leaving together. Before we reached Evora we were set upon by bandits. We had stopped at a little spring to drink. I was set upon from behind and rendered senseless. When I came to, I saw that the girl was dead—she had been raped and stabbed. I suppose the bandits would have done for me too but that someone approaching had disturbed them and they had run away. No sooner had I staggered up than a cart carrying several people arrived. They knew the dead girl, they were from her village, and they would not believe my story. I had forced myself upon little Conchita, they said, and when she had struck me the blow that was evident upon my head, I had become enraged and killed her. They took me to the nearest town, and there the people became so enraged that I think I would have been promptly hanged had not Prince Damião ridden in at that moment, observed the crowd, questioned the people, heard my story—and believed it. He arranged for my release and brought me with him to Lisbon. The bandits were later found and hanged. But I owe my life to Prince Damião and we have since become good friends and he has confided in me. This is the only way I can repay him. Before you say no, Cassandra, at least come and meet Prince Damião!"

His story had touched her, and Cassandra, still half-unwilling but wanting to help her newfound friend, agreed to meet Prince Damião.

Leeds' eyes gleamed in triumph. She had thus far believed his lies! Now, if only he could take her a little further.

"You can meet him now," he declared. "I know where he is lunching."

So Cassandra was off to meet the prince.

They found him dining alone in the cool loggia of an inn that overlooked the sea. Cassandra had never met a prince before, but she deemed a curtsy sufficient. It was daunting to discover that he spoke no English. During lunch Leeds did almost all the talking—and most of that in Portuguese to the prince—so Cassandra had some time to observe him. He was not very princely, she thought. Dark, slight, elegantly groomed, and foppishly attired in pink silk heavily embroidered in a deep rose. She would have considered his expression sulky had she not understood the reason for his dejection, and as Leeds talked, that dejection seemed to deepen until he looked positively tragic. How could Cassandra know that Leeds was encouraging him in Portuguese to look "doomed"?

After lunch the prince excused himself and left them.

"Well, what did you think of him?" Leeds sighed.

"I don't know," said Cassandra truthfully. "But I do feel sorry for him, Leeds. What will happen when his secret marriage to Ines is discovered?"

Leeds frowned. "Well, I have no doubt what will happen to Ines. She will disappear, the records of the marriage will disappear, and Damião will be free to marry Constanca."

The fate of a barefoot girl who had had the temerity to marry a prince! Cassandra shivered.

"And Prince Damião?" she asked, troubled. "What of him?"

Leeds rose. "Come, you are not to concern yourself," he said. "I was wrong to ask it of you. I don't know what came over me. I have no right to ask you to take such chances. Come, I will take you back to your inn."

"No, I want to know, Leeds. What will happen to him?"

"We have talked it over, Damião and I. He has told me that in the event of discovery, if Ines is wrenched from him—as she most certainly will be—he will end his life. I have tried to dissuade him but he is adamant. I believe he will do it. You can see why I was driven to ask you to undertake this charade, but now that I have had time to think it over—and the prince was of the same opinion, I asked him just now—we cannot ask it of you, Cassandra."

It was all going to end up in disaster, she could see that plainly. Unless she herself took a hand. She, who had been responsible for the deaths of so many men had now a chance to save one.

But the very idea was mad! Imagine posing as a prince's mistress! It seemed preposterous—and yet . . . Her world seemed to whirl about her. Lisbon was nothing like England. This was a fairy-tale place, fabulous, unreal. Here dreams could come true and lost loves reappear.

Common sense reasserted itself. "But even if his marriage to Ines is not discovered, he will still be forced into marriage with Constanca," she pointed out. "He will become a bigamist! What then?"

"It is the prince's hope that he can arrange his escape with Ines long before that. He has been sending funds secretly out of the country, he tells me. But he needs a place where all the arrangements for escape can be made, where Ines can be lodged with no suspicion cast upon her. He needs—"

"He needs someone to pretend she is his mistress," sighed Cassandra. "Someone who can cover for all these mysterious comings and goings."

"And you are not the one to do it," Leeds told her with decision. "I must have been mad to suggest it. After all, why should *you* become mixed up in the prince's affairs?"

Why indeed? But Cassandra's old recklessness overcame her and she made yet another unthought-out decision.

"What . . . what would I have to do?" she asked uncertainly. "If I did decide to do this?"

Leeds knew then that he had won. He seized Cassandra's hand and kissed it. "Very little," he assured her with laughter in his tone.

And that was true. Incredibly, that very afternoon Cassandra found herself—over Wend's astonished protests, for Cassandra had not chosen to confide in Wend about Leeds except to say that she had met a charming Englishman who was squiring her about—whisked from the Green Island to a small pink rococo palace that fronted the main square. And installed in another part of that same palace was Ines, a golden-skinned girl who walked about barefoot wearing the traditional wide skirts of Nazaré, held out by seven layers of pleated petticoats. A girl who spoke only Portuguese and who ducked her head and curtsied every time she saw Cassandra.

"I wish Ines wouldn't do that," Cassandra told Leeds unhappily after she and Wend had been there for a few days. "After all, *she* is the princess and I am only an impostor." She did not add that Wend, who was up and around now and eyeing the Portuguese servants suspiciously, had observed only that morning that barefoot Ines seemed to regard her as a queen.

"Ines knows that even here she may be watched," said Leeds, whose sudden frown had sent Ines scurrying away. "And I would add that even here *we* may be overheard. We must guard our tongues."

"And what of those men who meet here?" demanded Cassandra impatiently. "I am upstairs but I hear their boots clomping in at night. They arrive only in the dark, and I have peered out and seen them disappear into the back of the house. Sometimes I have thought I heard the prince's voice among them. What is going on?"

For a wild moment Leeds yearned to tell her, but he bit back the words. "They are helping to arrange the prince's escape with Ines," he told her imperturbably. "And the less you know about that the better."

Cassandra bit her lip. "I . . . This charade can't go on forever, Leeds."

"Of course not." His sunny smile flashed. "But it can go on until All Hallows' Day—and that is only a week away. You can last till then, can't you?

"And what will happen on All Hallows' Day?" wondered Cassandra. "For I am told the prince is to be married to Constanca the week after."

"On All Hallows' Day the prince will flee the country with his Ines. He would have done it before now, but the arrangements are difficult to make. He must leave no trail that Pombal's agents can follow. And he will leave you weeping, saying you have quarreled and you do not know where he has gone. And you will sink back into obscurity, living here for a while but later going your own way with the fine clothes and jewels he has lavished on you."

"Oh, I don't intend to keep—"

"Nonsense," he interrupted her roughly. "Whatever he gives you is little enough for the service you do him. You will keep *everything*."

His manner was so compelling that Cassandra felt as if a strong wind had blown over her and swept her resolution away.

But despite Leeds' assurances, after he had gone Cassandra still found herself plagued with a sense of foreboding.

Wend noted it and asked her what was wrong.

"Nothing," she assured Wend. "It is just that we will be leaving soon."

"Good!" said Wend with energy. She had never really believed Cassandra's story that she had been offered the house for a song and had found the offer irresistible. Cassandra was mixed up in something. Wend didn't know what, but she wished they were both back home at Aldershot Grange.

Cassandra at that moment was wishing the same thing. For a while she had succumbed to the spell of romantic Lisbon and the glamorous role of aiding a young prince, but of late—and perhaps it was the sound of those booted feet moving about downstairs by night—the shadows in this pink palace had seemed to deepen, and now at last it had come to her what a dangerous game she was playing.

In Estoril, Clive, Lord Houghton, was enjoying his own charade. But unlike Cassandra, he shrank from the idea that it would end. He wished desperately that he were free of Phoebe, free to marry Lady Farrington's mousy daughter, free to enjoy the rich life such a marriage offered. In a weak moment he had already proposed to Della—and been joyously accepted. He had promised her a betrothal ring when they got back to England.

What he would give her instead would be the rude shock of learning that he could not marry her, that he had been lying to her all along. For he hadn't a doubt that the moment the wedding banns were published, Phoebe would hear about it—and be on him like a harpy. And Lady Farrington had absolutely refused to let Della wed him in Portugal. She wanted a big public wedding to show off Della's "catch."

Caught in a trap of his own making, Clive stood staring down into the Boca do Inferno, the Mouth of Hell, as if seeking guidance from somewhere within that awesome chasm.

All that stood between him and this dazzling marriage was Phoebe. His wife. And if that barrier were removed . . .

He thought long and hard about it as he stared down into the frothing milky whirlpool sucked down by the inrushing sea, and he came to what seemed to him an inevitable decision. Phoebe must not be allowed to stand in his way. He must dispose of her. The thought made him wrestle briefly with his conscience—for him that was not too difficult. Although sometimes his misdeeds came back to haunt him, Clive was always able to bend his conscience to his will.

He began to think about how to do it.

It must not be done on English soil. No, that would be too dangerous. Some foreign place perhaps, someplace where Phoebe did not speak the language and where he could set up his story ahead of time. A fall over a cliff, perhaps, into the sea? But not someplace where the body would not be found and so leave a question in people's minds that she might somehow have escaped. No, a place of certain destruction.

Here, for instance.

He looked down at that foaming cauldron and knew that he had found the perfect spot to rid himself of Phoebe. He would lure her to Lisbon. He would set a man to watch for her arrival. And when she arrived, he would slip something into Lady Farrington's food, and Della's. Not something deadly, but something that would make them so sick they would keep to their rooms for two or three days.

And while they were confined to their rooms, he would welcome Phoebe—at another inn, of course. He would appear publicly to be on excellent terms with her. He would bring her here to Estoril. And at the Mouth of Hell, when no one was looking, he would lure her to the edge of the chasm. One little push and he would be rid of her forever! And ready to embark on the new and wonderful life he deserved.

He was suddenly no longer afraid of Cassandra. Indeed he found himself eager to return to Lisbon—they would go back tomorrow! They would stay at another inn far from the Green Island; there was nothing to fear. His waterfront watcher would tell him when Phoebe landed. He would spirit her quickly away to some outlying inn, telling her it was the best he could afford . . . and in Estoril do away with her. No need for the authorities to connect Phoebe with Cassandra—her name was no longer Keynes. Lord, he should have realized that sooner. Phoebe would be gone and Cassandra would be none the wiser.

So buoyed up by the thought of ridding himself of Phoebe was he that he sat down at once to pen a letter to Phoebe back in Liverpool.

"Join me in Lisbon," he wrote. *"I will be staying at the Pico de Ferro—the Iron Crest. I cannot wait to see you."*

He would have been shocked to know that Phoebe already knew he was in Portugal. She had run across a goldsmith with whom she had frequently pawned her jewels—when she had any to pawn. And the goldsmith had been among the crowd at dockside, seeing his daughter off, and had seen Clive board the vessel bound for Lisbon.

Unknown to Clive, Phoebe was already on her way. And although sailing arrivals were always unpredictable, the captain of the *Storm Castle* was at that very moment standing on the swaying deck in bright sunshine telling a group of passengers, including Phoebe, that they should make port in Lisbon in about a week, weather permitting.

Nor was Phoebe the only person of interest to be upon the high seas at that moment.

Back at Aldershot Grange, Drew Marsden had come riding up, and Livesay, who had discussed it all at length with Wend, had told him bluntly the real reason Cassandra had embarked for Portugal.

"She's afraid of *me?*" Drew had been puzzled.

"No, the lass is afraid *for* you," Livesay had corrected him. "Mistress Cassandra believes she's a Death Bringer. And she doesn't want to add you to her list."

"But that's ridiculous!" Drew exploded.

"Nonetheless, 'tis what she believes." Livesay shook his head as if he would never understand women. "She believes she's brought four men to their deaths—and all because of love for her. And she told Wend she loves you too much to watch you die. So that's the *real* reason she ran away to Portugal."

Drew did not look as upset as Livesay had expected. The words "she loves you too much" were the ones that had caught his heart on fire. Lord, he had feared Cassandra did not love him at all, once he found she had run away.

He mounted his horse and favored Livesay with a confident smile.

"Well, I'll just off to Lisbon and bring my lady back!" he told Livesay blithely, and went looking for a ship to carry him there.

As it happened, although Drew had started long before Phoebe, he had been unable to find a ship—they all seemed to be going everywhere else, but not to Portugal. And when he did at last find one, storms blew his wallowing tub off course.

Although Phoebe had embarked much later, her ship was faster and missed the storms that delayed Drew. So actually Drew and Phoebe would arrive in Lisbon only two days apart—and Drew would arrive first.

So matters stood with All Hallows' Day fast approaching. Then . . .

Into Lisbon rolled a black-and-gold coach.

34

The black-and-gold coach, handsome though it was, and bearing the arms of one of Spain's proud families, was dusty and bore scars, for it had traveled overland all the way from Castile. Its two occupants, a man and a woman, were elegant in the extreme.

The man wore black velvet—and a melancholy expression on his pale features. His long fingers, one of them sporting a signet ring bearing the family crest, were curled about a cane of ebony and gold. Whenever the woman spoke, which was seldom, for she spent more time silently staring out the coach windows, he gave her his full attention, and there was a flaring joy in his dark eyes when he looked at her.

The woman—in contrast to the man who lounged at ease beside her—sat stiffly erect. Her magnificent figure was encased in rich black silks which rustled softly when she moved. She wore no jewelry—although the small Moroccan leather case at her feet was filled with necklaces, earrings, and rings of gold and diamonds and several ropes of pearls—unless you could count the delicate gold chain that disappeared into a gold locket somewhere beneath her bodice, or the simple black onyx mourning ring that never left her finger. That ring was a mystery to her maidservant, who traveled behind in the cart which carried this elegant couple's luggage, for to the maid's knowledge, no one had died.

The woman said something in soft slurred Spanish to the man and he laughed. For a moment she gave him a look of deep affection. Then she went back to her gazing. She was, thought a passerby viewing her from the cobbles, the very epitome of Spanish beauty. Her complexion, pale and creamy and tinted ever so slightly with olive, was flawless. Dark winglike brows swept over lightly kohl-accented eyes that looked remarkably light to the passerby— but he assigned that to a trick of the Lisbon sunlight shining down into the coach. A black lace mantilla flowed over her high-backed tortoiseshell comb and down over her dark gleaming curls, as became a Spanish lady.

They alighted at Lisbon's finest inn, the Royal Cockerel. They were expected, and the inn's best rooms had been reserved for Don Carlos and his party. Painfully, with the aid of his cane, Don Carlos made his way up the stairs to his bedchamber, which adjoined that of the lady. He staggered slightly as he reached a chair, and the lady sprang forward to help him, but he waved her away.

"Don't fuss, Carlotta," he said wearily. "Just send José to tell the doctor that I have arrived in Lisbon and will see him now." He bent over in a sudden spasm of pain.

Doña Carlotta bit her lip to see him suffer so, but she went quickly to the door and instructed the footman who waited there silently to find the doctor—who was, after all, the reason for their long difficult journey—at once and bring him here.

The doctor came and there was a low-voiced conversation which Doña Carlotta, waiting tensely in her bedchamber next door, could not hear. She had never been permitted to attend, although Don Carlos had had many sessions with his doctors back in Spain—nor had he allowed her to be present at this one. Don Carlos believed a man must take life's blows alone. His lady, already flying to the door as she heard the doctor's heavy step going down the hall, paused as her maid—a beautiful Englishwoman she had found stranded in Barcelona when Carlos had sought medical help there last year—asked her in English where her jewel case should be put.

"Oh, put it anywhere, Peggy," Doña Carlotta answered her in flawless English—she spoke three languages, did Doña Carlotta.

Peggy's throat tightened with sympathy as she watched her mistress leave. She had a fierce loyalty to the Spanish lady, who had most likely saved her from debtors' prison and who had promised that after this trip to Portugal she would help Peggy return to England. After a moment's hesitation Peggy pushed back her tarnished red-gold hair and put the jewel box in the bottom of a curved-top trunk.

In the next room the doctor was already being shown out. They could hear the door close behind him.

Doña Carlotta, entering, found Don Carlos staring rather fixedly at a golden crucifix that his manservant, Esteban, had hung upon the wall. "What did the doctor say?" she asked.

Don Carlos swung about and smiled at her. "He says there is hope," he told her cheerfully. "He will come every day for treatments."

"They will be painful?" she asked quietly.

Don Carlos shrugged indifferently. "There will be some pain, yes, but he has every hope of improvement."

He was so brave. Her heart bled for him. They had sought the aid of so many doctors, and none of them had helped him. He was a mere shadow of the man she had married in Castile all those years ago.

The treatments were indeed painful. From the next room Doña Carlotta could hear her husband groan—and wept to hear it. This unhappy situation continued day after day, with the doctor coming and Doña Carlotta taking her meals in her room and leaving it only to go next door to cheer her husband. She accepted none of the invitations that—in deference to Don Carlos' position as a man of power and influence in Castile—were brought by messenger to the Royal Cockerel.

And then of a sudden, on the day before All Hallows' Eve, Don Carlo heaved himself unsteadily to his feet and announced cheerfully to his wife that the treatments of this new doctor, who had been credited with working miracles, were working.

Doña Carlotta gave him a worried look. There had been false hopes before.

"No, it is true," he insisted gaily. "I am much better. I will prove it! I will take you to the opera tonight, and tomorrow night there is some reception, is there not?"

"Yes," she said mechanically. "At the Varváez home. For Lord Derwent—whoever *that* may be." She gave Don Carlos a questioning look. "Jorge Varváez sent word that you might remember him from the old days."

"As indeed I do! Jorge and I have enjoyed many a gallop across the parched plains of the Alentejo, where the fighting bulls are bred. That was before I met you, *querida mía*. You will like Jorge. I do not know about his wife—she is his second."

Doña Carlotta winced inwardly. She too was a second wife—and in her own opinion not worthy of such a man as Don Carlos.

"Very well," she said doubtfully. "I have already sent our regrets, but I will send word to the Varváezes that we will be able to attend Lord Derwent's reception after all."

"Good." He smiled at her. For a moment he seemed very like his old self.

There were others who planned to attend the opera that night too:

Clive had quickly become bored with Estoril and Cascais. He told himself that Cassandra might well have moved on to some other town in Portugal by now—and if she had not, they could easily avoid her. So he announced that the plague scare had been a false alarm and brought Lady Farrington and her daughter back to Lisbon—but not to the same inn. This time he chose an inconvenient location higher up, a place called the Sete Cidades, the Seven Cities. His ladies were not too pleased, but they were somewhat mollified when he announced that tonight they would attend the opera.

The opera would have another unexpected patron as well, one who had arrived by ship this morning. Drew Marsden, chafing that the slow tub he had at last managed to board had been beset by storms and thus arrived so late in Lisbon, had hastily put up at the first inn available and gone looking for Cassandra. He had not found her. In his eagerness to find her at once, he had announced to one and all that she was his betrothed and he had come to take her back to England. The Portuguese are a tolerant but compassionate people—he had not found a single one who would tell him that Cassandra Dunlawton was now notorious as Prince Damião's mistress. But at the Green Island, where he had called last, the English-speaking proprietor had taken pity on the tall young fellow with the steady gray eyes. "You should look for her at the opera tonight," he had suggested. "Most of the English hereabouts are fond of it."

Drew, after a long and unsuccessful day's searching, had decided to follow his advice.

Cassandra would indeed be in attendance at the opera that night. Leeds Birmingham himself had made the trek to the pink palace on the square to ensure that.

He found Cassandra walking about a little disconsolately through the enormous, almost square marble-floored area of the first floor that constituted the front "hall" and at the far side of which wound a handsome staircase. At first it had been fun riding about Lisbon in a golden coach with the royal arms emblazoned upon it, spending her days as Leeds had instructed her a royal mistress should, with dressmakers and the like, buying ivory fans and other fripperies—for the prince, especially now that the royal family claimed a monopoly on the diamonds of Brazil, had an almost bottomless purse. But Cassandra had been discouraged from making friends ("Too dangerous," Leeds had warned), and the household servants spoke no English. For that matter, since the prince himself spoke only Portuguese, unless Leeds went along, Cassandra found their evenings—they were few enough!—dull in the extreme. Besides, on closer acquaintance she found it very difficult to like the prince; there was something about him, a shiftiness of the eyes perhaps, a contemptuous set of his slack lips. She had wondered how Ines could have fallen in love with him—indeed she might have asked her, but Ines seemed to fade away at her approach. And anyway, it would have done no good—Ines too spoke only Portuguese.

Cassandra could not know how sharply her life paralleled that of her lovely young mother: both of them brought up on the shores of the glassy Derwent Water, both destined for unhappiness; far from home, each had found herself trapped in a golden cage—Cassandra trapped in a pink palace, just as Charlotte had once been trapped in a flat-fronted mansion in the Portas del Sol.

Actually Cassandra was preoccupied by thinking about those secret meetings that took place in the house by night—and the prince's part in them. How could there possibly be so much to arrange? Or was he trying to move the contents of the national treasury out of Portugal? So that barefoot Ines would actually be "walking on diamonds," as Leeds liked to put it? The thought made her smile.

Leeds Birmingham, greeting her in the great lower hall, was struck forcefully again by Cassandra's startling beauty, but he understood the rebellious expression in her green eyes. Cassandra had a soft heart, she meant to help, but she was growing tired of the monotony and a prince that Leeds himself found difficult to like.

"Greetings!" he said. "Did you know they are writing songs about you and singing them in the taverns?"

"I don't doubt it!" Cassandra grimaced. "And nothing complimentary, either!"

He chuckled. "They call you the fairest of the fair—and indeed they are right!"

Cassandra shrugged. Her beauty was not a subject she cared to waste time discussing. Her *future* would be of more interest.

"I have not gone out all day," she said. "Yesterday a woman hurled a stone at my coach. It went right through the coach window and out the other side. And she screamed something at me and shook her fist. I remember the words." She repeated them to Leeds. "What do they mean?"

Leeds decided to be truthful—after all, Cassandra might very well ask somebody else and find out their real meaning and after that not trust him. "They mean *'You will never be our queen!'* " he told her reluctantly.

"But I don't want to be their queen!" cried Cassandra.

"Obviously the woman didn't know that."

"But it's ridiculous. Damião isn't even the crown prince. He is far down the line—the youngest son! He isn't even *likely* to inherit the throne."

"I know that." Leeds frowned. The rumor that the beautiful English girl Prince Damião had chosen as his mistress would be contented with nothing less than marriage—indeed that she was clawing for the throne itself—was all over town. Leeds couldn't imagine how it had gotten started. When he had tackled Prince Damião on the subject, he had gotten an evasive answer.

"I am trying to put that rumor down by paying more attention to Constanca," the prince had responded vaguely.

When Leeds had frowned at that answer, the prince had been quick to add, "Give the English girl this"—he thrust a box at Leeds—"and tell her to wear it when I take her to the opera tonight."

Leeds had had the strange feeling that the gift had been proffered more to mollify *him* than to delight Cassandra.

Now, as he stood upon the marble floor of the pink palace with Cassandra before him, his voice softened. "I bring you an invitation and a little token from the prince that you may wear tonight when he takes you to the opera." From a crimson velvet case he took out a necklace that sparkled like water and clasped it around her slender neck. "He wishes to show you off, Cassandra. And satisfy the royal curiosity, I may add, for none of the royal family has yet seen you. Tonight they will." He stood back, surveying her. "And they will at least be forced to admit that Prince Damião has good taste in women!"

Cassandra studied the heavy necklace in the mirror with amazement. Its huge stones seemed to cover her entire bosom. "But *I* should not be wearing this," she gasped. "*Ines* should be wearing it!"

"Ines will be walking on diamonds where she is going," Leeds told her indifferently, using his favorite phrase.

"Wear it, Cassandra. But take good care of it," he cautioned, "for it is worth a king's ransom."

He did not have to tell her that.

The corners of his mouth quirked. "Oh, and be sure to look at the prince adoringly. He says that you do not."

Cassandra's brows lifted and she gave Leeds a quizzical look. Somehow, on closer acquaintance, she found the prince difficult to adore. For all his dark good looks, there was something about him she did not trust, something that made her keep her guard up. . . .

Leeds chuckled. "I do not find Damião adorable either, but remember, he is a prince and princelings are brought up as spoiled darlings. Wear the necklace, Cassandra, light up the opera—and remember that I told you you would enjoy this!"

Tonight she would be sitting in a box at the opera beside a royal prince—even if she did not much care for him—and wearing this wonderful necklace. She was living a dream! Cassandra smiled at Leeds and admitted to herself that at the moment she was indeed enjoying this charade. Especially now that she knew it would be ending soon. For tomorrow was All Hallows' Eve, which they would be celebrating in England with bonfires, and the day after that was All Hallows' Day, when Ines would escape with her prince and Cassandra would forget this escapade of being a prince's mistress and go back to being what she had always been.

But for tonight she would play it to the hilt!

Cassandra dressed for the opera with care. Wend helped, albeit disapprovingly. For this occasion Cassandra had chosen to wear her most dramatic gown—this public appearance beside the prince was no time to be shy! The gown was low-cut, of crimson velvet, very lustrous, and clinging subtly to her figure, and the bodice fit her firm young breasts as if she had been poured into it. Her three-quarter sleeves ended at the elbows with a froth of lace encrusted with brilliants. A wide crimson velvet riband cascaded down, along with a waving blonde lock, from her tall headdress, to move lazily across one almost bare shoulder. When she put on the diamond necklace, she could not believe the effect. Wide-skirted, elegant—she had never owned such a dress in England!

She came downstairs beaming, to join the prince and Leeds at the bottom.

Her smile would not have been so bright if she could have heard the conversation that had just taken place between them.

"It would be well if you were to pay more attention to Ana," Leeds Birmingham had been advising the prince. "How much Cassandra observes from her room"—he nodded toward the upstairs—"I do not know, but it must occur to her that you are not here very often. And it would help if you could remember to call Ana 'Ines.'"

"Why the devil did you have to rename the wench? Surely 'Ana' was sufficient!"

"In Cassandra we are dealing with a romantic," grated Leeds, losing patience. "She was awash with the tragedy of Ines de Castro—I played upon it by giving *you* an Ines as well as a Constanca!"

The prince sneered. "Have you unloaded the gunpowder?"

"Yes, it is safe off the ship and in the warehouse."

"Good. There will be more, Pereira tells me, tomorrow."

"Then why the devil does Pereira not unload it? He has men aplenty, you tell me." Leeds' tone was ironic. "And you might tell me if Pereira is holding secret meetings here. I am told there are men stalking about downstairs by night."

The prince bit his lip. So the English girl had ears! "Only once or twice," he hedged. "He asked me if he might."

Frowning, Leeds studied the young prince, noting again his shifty eyes. In point of fact it was chance that had brought Damião and Leeds together. Down and out in Madrid, Leeds had drifted into Portugal, encountered Prince Damião bragging loudly in one of Lisbon's wilder gaming hells—and it had led to this. For Leeds had discovered in the foppish young prince a burning ambition to rule. Cynical Leeds was no stranger to the power plays of princes—in his wanderings he had watched them played out in Europe's brightest capitals. Sensing in this ambitious princeling his own road to wealth and power, the hardened adventurer had cultivated the foppish young man. He had hinted at his prowess, lied about his part in foreign political schemes—and he had impressed Damião. And egged him on.

So young Damião wanted to be king. Well, palace revolts were commonplace, and with enough support—which Damião had always insisted he had—he just might *become* king.

And if Damião became king, Leeds Birmingham saw himself emerging as Portugal's strongman, a replacement for the energetic—and entrenched—Pombal. First he would become Secretary of Foreign Affairs and then Prime Minister, for once ruthless young Damião was on the throne, Leeds believed he would succumb to pomp and extravagant living and carelessly leave the reins of government in other hands—*his* hands.

He, Leeds Birmingham, would be Portugal's true ruler, *he* would wield the power.

Even cynical adventurers have dreams. . . .

It was actually Prince Damião who had insisted that a woman must be brought into the scheme, a woman who would always be around to furnish a ready alibi for Damião's time away from Court so he would be free to meet with his fellow conspirators and make and weigh secret plans. But he had turned down every woman Leeds had suggested. They were Portuguese, he objected, they had families, they could be blackmailed—they were either too old or too young, no one would credit that such a one could be Prince Damião's mistress.

Then Leeds had found the English girl and she had exactly filled the bill. Prince Damião had approved Cassandra's appearance, her lack of knowledge of the country, the fact that she didn't speak the language. And then, to Leeds' surprise, he had frequented the pink palace on the square very little—indeed he had seemed to hew more closely to Constanca. And even a fool like Damião must know that Cassandra must not know that her part was all a sham, a smokescreen hiding the real truth.

It was all very puzzling to Leeds, and irritating as well.

He realized of course that he must deal with seedy aristocrats-gone-turncoat-against-the-crown, such as Pereira, but his own role in all this was begining to chafe.

Perhaps it was time to clear the air. . . . His eyes narrowed.

"I had expected that *I* would be the one having secret meetings here, marshaling my men," he told Prince Damião silkily. "But I have seen no men, although you keep telling me Pereira has hordes of them. My role seems to be to unload gunpowder—and we have enough to blow up all Lisbon already!"

The prince shifted his weight uncomfortably from one daintily shod foot to the other. "It is best that you do it. Pereira says he is being watched."

"A man can scarcely gather an army together without being observed," Leeds said impatiently. "I am probably being watched as well. Has that occurred to you?"

It had indeed. The prince frowned at this upstart. "Pereira wants *you* to do it," he said sullenly.

"Very well, I will keep watch for the ship. But you might tell Pereira that we will need not only gunpowder but also guns if we are to mount a rebellion."

The prince looked around him uneasily. "Guard your tongue—Pombal's agents are everywhere and you know what influence he exercises over my father!"

"I have told you that I would be glad to challenge Pombal to a duel and dispose of him for you. Indeed, it would be a pleasure—he has offended me twice."

"It would do no good for you to challenge him. He would brush aside your challenge and either have you arrested and thrown in a dungeon or banish you from Portugal altogether."

"Your father could put a stop to that."

"Yes, but he would not." Prince Damião sighed. "He is completely under Pombal's domination. No, my friend, we will take care of Pombal later. Pereira says—"

"Hush," muttered Leeds. "She is coming downstairs."

And from the stairs, Cassandra, a vision of loveliness in her low-cut velvet gown, came down happily to greet them.

The opera house was packed and stifling; the performing company was Italian, and the diva onstage singing lustily at the top of her voice was both fat and middle-aged. Nevertheless Cassandra—about to melt in her velvet gown— was enjoying every minute. Seated in a box beside Prince Damião, her bosom ablaze with diamonds, she twirled her crimson ostrich-feather fan and enjoyed her newfound— and undeserved—notoriety.

Clive had not been able to obtain a box for Lady Farrington and her daughter. They sweltered below in the pit, observing the rich and the stately, who sat more comfortably in boxes above them. He was studying that assemblage of wealth and power and wishing he were among them, when suddenly his gaze fell upon Cassandra, looking magnificent, there above him. An expression first of consternation and then of indignant envy crossed his face. Cassandra was, he had been told, a new arrival in Portugal—how had she been able to acquire the favor of a royal prince in this short time? It was most annoying. He slumped down in his seat, fairly certain she would not spot him from above, and was sullen all evening. The ladies with him were mystified by this sudden change in him.

Drew Marsden had made no effort to obtain a box seat. Indeed he did not want one; he had intended to stand up at intervals and study those around him—and look for Cassandra. It was an enormous shock to look up and see her seated above him in a box with a handsomely dressed young fop—and at that very moment looking at the fop with all the adoration she could muster!

About to rise, Drew had sunk back into his seat as if he had been knocked there. Now, bitterly, he understood why people had been so evasive when he asked the where- abouts of Cassandra Dunlawton, pressing home the point by telling them she was his betrothed and describing her! He felt an odd mixture of pain and shame course through him. Cassandra was not his betrothed—she never had been, he had assumed too much. Livesay had been wrong; Cassandra had come across the water seeking a change— and she had found it!

While the diva onstage shrieked out her highest note,

electrifying her perspiring audience, Drew Marsden made his way blindly to the door and out into the cooler night air.

Cassandra, twirling her fan, was aware of neither Drew nor Clive—nor of the attention she had attracted from one other.

In a box across from Cassandra, in the steamy heat of the opera house, Dona Carlotta's mother-of-pearl opera glass swung lazily about the room—and came to rest on Cassandra.

"Who is the girl directly across from us, the one wearing such splendid diamonds?" she inquired of her hostess. "She looks like someone I once knew."

Her hostess laughed. "Ah, that is Prince Damião's mistress, an English girl. You will observe that the royal family can hardly keep their eyes from her!"

"What is her name?" was the next question, asked idly.

"Cassandra something—oh, yes, Cassandra Dunlawton. I am told she is a widow. A merry one, wouldn't you say?"

There was a long silence beside her. Then Doña Carlotta seemed to rouse herself. She beckoned a footman.

"Will you ask Doña Cassandra Dunlawton if I might wait upon her at her home tomorrow morning? Oh, and find out where her home is. Tell her . . . tell her that I knew her mother."

Cassandra was excited at receiving the message, although in the throng she could not locate the sender.

It had seemed to her unfair that she was to have no friends—save Leeds, of course—in Lisbon. Although Prince Damião sat beside her, splendid and bored and so encrusted with gold braid that he seemed made of gold, only the gentlemen present had seen fit to stop by their box— the ladies, although they studied Cassandra with interest through their opera glasses, to a woman shunned her.

Outside the opera house, although Drew Marsden could no longer bear the sight of Cassandra looking so radiant beside another man, he still could not bring himself to leave the vicinity. Warring with himself, he paced up and down. He told himself there might have been some mistake, Cassandra might have been in that box for some other reason—but no, there was no mistaking that look of absolute adoration she had given her companion. So he raged within himself, back and forth.

When the performance ended and the opera patrons poured forth, Drew mingled with the crowd and watched in astonishment as Cassandra and her fop got into a golden coach, unmistakably royal—but to make absolutely certain, he asked and was told it was Prince Damião's coach and that the young lady riding in it was the prince's English mistress.

Feeling that life had dealt him a terrible unwarranted blow, Drew found himself hurrying after the coach on foot, and discovered that it had not far to go. He watched from a distance as Cassandra and her prince alighted at the pink palace on the central plaza and went inside.

Then at last Drew believed it, and such a misery as he had never known swept over him. He swung away, shoulders hunched, and hied himself to the nearest tavern, there to drink moodily far into the night. *She was lost to him, lost forever—she had a prince now*. Deeper into his cups he drank himself until he fell forward sodden upon the table.

35

All Hallows' Eve
October 31, 1755

The morning after the opera, dressed in a new yellow
sarcenet gown which brought out golden highlights in her
pale blonde hair, Cassandra received Doña Carlotta in the
frescoed drawing room of her palace on the square and
eagerly asked the elegant Spanish lady whose lacy black
mantilla practically hid her features, how she had come to
know Charlotte Keynes.

"I met her here in Lisbon," said Doña Carlotta in flawless although slightly accented English. "It was a long time
ago but I have never forgotten her face, and you look
strikingly like her."

"Yes." Cassandra sighed. She was wishing that Wend
were here to hear this elegant lady talk about Charlotte,
but Wend was feeling fine now and had gone out on her
own to investigate the fish market. "I will be grateful for
anything you can tell me about my mother," Charlotte
told Doña Carlotta. "For she died while I was still a child
and all I could find here was her gravestones."

"Gravestones?" The woman in the mantilla started. "You
mean there is more than one?"

"Yes, a headstone and a footstone."

"Oh. Of course." For that was commonplace enough.

"Yes, but in this case the footstone is far taller and
handsomer than the headstone—and I was told they were

erected at different times and by different men. I was hoping you could tell me about it."

"I should like to see these stones," murmured her guest.

"Would you? It is not too far. I will call for my carriage."

Doña Carlotta smiled. The young mistress of the prince came well-equipped, it seemed.

Cassandra was surprised when her newfound Spanish friend asked if they could stop before one of the Alfama's narrow ways, and got out. "There is a place I must see," she told Cassandra. "It is but a short distance from here." As she spoke, she was rearranging her heavy black lace mantilla to drift down entirely over her features.

"Can you really see through that wall of lace?" asked Cassandra doubtfully.

"Oh, yes. In Spain one learns to look out from behind iron lace balconies—or real lace mantillas. And at Court one learns how to mince along by moving one's feet from side to side so that one seems to float." She demonstrated the footwork that made her seem to glide across the cobbles.

"You have been presented at Court?" Cassandra was impressed.

"Oh, yes." And there she had met the English ambassador and had managed during the conversation to ask him if he knew Rowan Keynes, a widower with two daughters. The ambassador had responded without enthusiasm, muttering that he believed Keynes to be one of Walpole's supporters. Undaunted, she had followed that up by telling him that one of her friends had met Keynes' small daughters. At that the ambassador had smiled and told her that Keynes' daughters were both lovely little girls and that for a while they had attended school with his youngest daughter.

She had carried those words close to her heart for years . . . lovely little girls both, and attending a fashionable school.

Now, feeling her heart beat faster as she set her feet firmly upon the cobbles, she moved deeper into the heart of the Alfama.

And paused before a building with a low front door and

a third-floor iron grillwork balcony that she knew only too well.

"What is this place?" wondered Cassandra beside her.

"It is called Nowhere Street," said Charlotte, noting that the place appeared deserted, the shutters were nailed shut. "Your mother"—her voice hardened—"knew it well."

She turned away abruptly and they retraced their steps to the carriage and sought out the cemetery.

The headstone was obviously Rowan's work, Charlotte thought. Very terse. Just her name and the dates. But the footstone . . . She studied that delicate spire of white marble.

"*Here lies Charlotte, beloved of Thomas*," she read in a soft choked voice that had somehow lost its foreign accent. "*Ate o fim do mundo.*"

"It means '*Until the end of the world,*' " supplied Cassandra helpfully.

It means Rowan did not manage to kill Tom after all, thought Charlotte, closing her eyes against the light that was suddenly too blindingly bright. *Oh, Tom, you came back for me, you came back. . . .*

"His name was Thomas Westing." Cassandra was looking at the stone. "And he was her lover."

Tom—alive! There was a glory in Charlotte's eyes. Her voice rang out. "He was indeed my lover Cassandra—*and your father*." With a sudden gesture "Doña Carlotta" swept both the concealing mantilla and the dark wig from her hair and let her golden hair cascade down. "Am I so changed, Cassandra, that you do not recognize me?"

Stunned, Cassandra considered the slender, beautiful woman before her. Like a picture emerging from the past. . . .

"That was why I felt so close to you," she gasped. "Ever since I came downstairs and saw you. But I never guessed, I only thought you reminded me of . . . *Oh, Mother, I have found you at last!*"

And she went blindly into a pair of outstretched arms.

After a long time during which they hugged each other and wept a little, Cassandra stood back and considered her mother critically.

"You look so young—I think that may be partly why I didn't guess you were my mother," she admitted. "But why didn't you tell me at once? I had given up my foolish hope that you might still be alive."

"I was debating whether I should tell you at all," was Charlotte's candid reply. "Life has taught me patience, Cassandra. Now, tell me, what of Phoebe?"

Cassandra thought it best not to tell the whole truth about Phoebe—at least not yet. "Phoebe married Lord Houghton, son of the dowager Marchioness of Greensea —oh, it must be six years now. She and Clive are residing in England." *Unless they have fled to the colonies or somewhere else.* She did not say that, of course. "But what of you, Mother? Where have you been all these years?"

What could Charlotte say to her, this daughter of dreams who had been wrenched from her so long ago? What could she say of those years in Spain?

Now, in this sunlit Lisbon cemetery, she looked into her daughter's green eyes, Tom's eyes looking out at her from Cassandra's beautiful young face, and gave it a desperate try.

"Rowan tricked me into marriage. In his way, he loved me, and I think I loved him too—once. But Tom came back and I could not resist spending several days with him. Rowan's jealous nature could not forgive that. He kept me imprisoned for years in that house on Nowhere Street. When I finally escaped him, I found another life entirely. There was no looking back."

She *had* looked back, but pride would not let her say so.

"My father . . ." Cassandra stopped in confusion. "I mean Rowan Keynes—he is dead, Mother."

"Is he?" Charlotte no longer had any emotions left where Rowan was concerned. "How did he die?"

Cassandra shivered. "He and Yates were found outside his London lodgings one rainy night—victims of footpads, people said."

Victims of their way of life, Charlotte thought bitterly. *Those who live by the sword . . .*

Cassandra moistened her lips. "Didn't you care what

happened to us, Mother? To Phoebe and me?" Her voice was wistful—not accusing, wistful.

Charlotte had been able to hear of Rowan's death with equanimity, but that wistful note in her daughter's voice tore at her heart.

"Of course I cared!" she said huskily. "But Rowan warned me that if I ever tried to get in touch with either of you *in any way*, he would turn you out on the street as beggars! I could not risk it."

"It would have been worth it," said Cassandra impulsively, "if it brought us a mother!"

But would you have thought that when you were hungry and cold, without a roof over your head? Charlotte's eyes filled with tears. "I could not let him destroy you, Cassandra," she choked, "as he destroyed me."

Cassandra studied the elegant woman before her. She did not *look* destroyed. "This Spaniard you have married . . ." she began. ·

"Carlos saved me from the law when I was about to be arrested for dancing on the street for coins. I had been badly treated in Lisbon and I fell ill—I was ill for a long time. Carlos nursed me back to health and we had a brief affair. Then . . ." Her voice drifted off.

She could hear Carlos speaking to her again, not facing her, that day in the Algarve, after the doctor had left him. He had been leaning hunched over the railing of their balcony in the gathering darkness, looking out upon the almond trees, their blossoms like a drift of snow beneath a slender white moon.

He had looked young and defenseless standing there, this man who had brought her back to life with his kindness.

Stirred by sudden unease, she had asked him what was wrong.

He had straightened up suddenly, as if caught at something. He had told her that nothing was wrong, not to concern herself. But there was that in his voice that told her he was lying. She waited, and when he spoke again, his voice was wistful. His words rang in her memory, telling her that he was for Spain tomorrow, and that he wanted her to come with him—as his wife.

Charlotte had caught her breath. It was the first time Carlos had mentioned marriage. Before she could frame an answer, before she could tell him that she had responsibilities back in England, he spoke again, on a note of bitterness—telling her that it would not be for long, the doctor had promised him that.

That had shocked her. She had demanded to know what the doctor had told him. And listened in silence as Carlos coolly explained that the doctor had confirmed what Carlos himself had suspected—that the same malady that had killed his father was now visited upon him. Almost as if he were speaking of some other person, he told her that he would have a while yet. And then there would be a wasting away. And then he would become weaker and weaker, and then—he had grimaced at this point—he would die in great pain.

She had asked him unsteadily how long the doctor had given him.

Carlos had shaken his head and said the doctor could not be sure. But this doctor had attended his father at one time and he had confirmed that Carlos' condition duplicated his father's. That cool voice was grave as he asked her to think, to consider, for as his widow Charlotte would have the law's protection, but as his mistress, once he was dead, she would have none. If she would but marry him, he would know as he lay dying that she would be provided for, not hounded from town to town by his greedy nephews, who would seek to recapture after his death anything that he might give her.

Not long . . . she saw that he had not long. Oh, life was so unfair! Don Carlos was the kindest person she had ever met. And now he was going to die. In great pain, the doctor had said.

She was deeply moved. She told him that he honored her too much and that there was something that she must tell him. What she wanted to tell him was that back in England she had a living husband and two small daughters for whom her heart longed.

But Carlos had refused to listen. He had hushed her, touching her lips with gentle fingers. There had been a dignity in him as he had bidden her to allow him his dreams, to let whatever was in the past stay in the past. Searingly she remembered his words: *We met by chance and we became lovers. God was merciful to a fool, and I could ask no more.* It hurt her heart to remember them.

Still she had felt she must tell him, and he had silenced her again, insisting that before she spoke she must first hear his own story. He had been married in his teens to a girl he scarcely knew. A girl who sat with him in brooding silence with her *dueña* beside her beneath the cork oaks in the sunny courtyard of her family estate, shredding the petals of the blood-red roses he brought her as proof of his love. Although she had seemed to scorn him, her father had assured Carlos that it was just his daughter's wild, high-spirited way, and Carlos had believed it. Her father had assured Carlos that after they were married Jimena would learn to love him. Carlos had believed that too. Oh, he had known that Jimena had had other suitors who serenaded the night away beneath her iron-grilled balcony, but he had never dreamt that Jimena was being forced to marry him.

At the words "forced into marriage," Charlotte's heart had given a lurch. Too well she remembered what it was like, being forced into marriage.

Jimena had been silent and pale throughout the ceremony, and when word came that her older brother had killed one of her former suitors in a duel, she had fainted. By then Carlos was half-drunk—with wine, with life, with the joy of having just been wed to the most beautiful girl in all Castile. His voice in the telling was now so grim that Charlotte leaned forward, hanging on his words. They had told him that Jimena was waiting for him in their bedchamber, and he had stumbled up the stairs joyfully to claim her. How eagerly he had parted the hangings of the canopied four-poster to view by moonlight his wondrous new-won bride!

Behind those hangings he had found instead a woman with a dagger plunged hilt-deep into her chest, a dagger still grasped by her own white hand, a woman whose blood flowed red as the roses across the white lace of her bridal gown. He had learned later that her lover had threatened to disrupt the wedding and abduct her. At that point her brother had challenged him to a duel and killed him. After that Jimena no longer wanted to live. And for a long time Carlos had not wanted to live either.

Listening, Charlotte had drawn a long shuddering breath.

He had looked past her, out into the distance, as he told her that for a long time he had forsworn women, that he had vowed never to marry again. All he could see before him when marriage was mentioned was Jimena lying pale in death, her red blood staining the marriage bed. The years had fled by for him while he played at love and resisted anything deeper, any real involvement, for he had felt cursed by heaven.

And then *she* had come into his life—and wrought a miracle in it. His tone had grown richer, deeper, as he told her that for him she had erased the past. So she would tell him no stories, he would hear no confessions. He had not long to live, and the one thing he asked of life was that she would do him the honor to become his wife.

How could she refuse? A few months more—and her children were being well-cared-for, the painted miniatures had shown her that. Carlos had given her back her life! She would stay with him, she would make his last months happy. He need never know about her past. . . .

She had moistened her lips and told Carlos that she would be *honored* to marry him, told him with such shining sincerity that he had enfolded her in his arms with a groan and held her as if she were the most precious treasure in all God's universe.

Above them a single star had shone down, joining that slim silver scimitar of a moon.

Deeply moved, Carlos had held her, whispering her name.

There. It was done. She had accepted Carlos' offer of marriage, she who had no right to love again. And she had tried not to look back.

But that night, staring up at the cold stars, she had felt her heart weeping. *Oh, Tom, forgive me,* she had whispered to a memory.

Now she looked into the clear green eyes of Tom's daughter, trying to make her understand, hoping she would forgive.

"Carlos took me to Barcelona and there taught me Spanish. He even bought a name for me. A friend of his was in dire straits. For a price, this man was willing to swear a written oath that I was the child of his dead sister, born on shipboard on the way to Cartagena."

"Wasn't that an offense?" wondered Cassandra.

"Beyond doubt. Carlos gave me a new past. He created me Carlotta del Valle—Charlotte of the Valley. I chose the name as nearest my own maiden name of Vayle. With his help I pretended to a religion not my own and he married me in a great vaulted cathedral and took me out into the sunshine. Even then I could see that in the distance, clouds were forming in my life. I was a bigamist and a betrayer and I had walked into a trap of my own making. Carlos had made me promise to tell him nothing—and I kept that promise. But for me there was no going back. If I tried to contact my children—indeed if I so much as showed my face in England—Rowan could declare my present marriage invalid, and he could take me back. The courts would allow that. Worse, he might make good his threat to send my children out into the street to beg their bread. And always I cherished the hope that someday I would see you and Phoebe again."

Her voice was melancholy. "I suppose it is too late to ask you to forgive me for having abandoned you all these years?"

Cassandra had inherited a generous nature from both her parents.

"There is nothing to forgive," she said handsomely. And meant it.

"But what of Prince Damião? Are you in love with him?"

"No, there's someone else—someone back home." Cassandra thought of Drew and her young face saddened.

"Then why . . . ?" began Charlotte, perplexed.

"Oh, it isn't what you think, Mother." It was wonderful

to be able to use that word again—it made her heart sing! "It is all a charade." She told Charlotte about it.

Charlotte listened, frowning. "It is a dangerous game you play," she warned when Cassandra had finished.

"I know, but it is only till All Hallows' Day. Leeds says so. You saw him at the opera. He sat in our box."

"The tawny gentleman?"

"Yes—the attractive one."

"He has led you into mortal danger," observed Charlotte.

"But it is only until day after tomorrow. And besides, I have done my share of leading men into mortal danger," sighed Cassandra. "*And* getting them killed into the bargain." Suddenly she was telling Charlotte about Ned, about the terrible duel in London, about Robbie—and about Drew. "So you see, I should wear a warning emblazoned across my bodice," she finished bitterly. "*Stay away, for it is dangerous to love me!*"

"Nonsense," said Charlotte briskly. "Men have always fought—and gotten hurt riding, and caught colds and fevers that killed them. You cannot take responsibility for the whole world, Cassandra!" It occurred to her that this daughter of hers needed guidance—and that she might attempt it, even at this late date! But *how*?

They rode back together, slowly. Cassandra did not want this afternoon to end; she was greedy for more time with her newfound mother. "Drive around the shops," she called to the driver.

And when they reached Madame de Marceau's exclusive millinery establishment, she called to him to halt and beckoned her mother to alight. "There is someone here who says she knows you," she said as they reached the door of the shop.

Charlotte might have drawn back, but it was too late. Her impetuous daughter had already flung open the shop door and the clapper over the entrance had noisily announced their arrival. From the back room Madame de Marceau suddenly appeared, tall and forbidding in her black garb.

The two women stared at each other in instant recognition. A ghost of a bitter smile crossed Charlotte's lips. "How are you, Annette?" she said.

Charlotte might not seem much moved by the encounter, but the effect on Annette was instantaneous and violent. "So you have come back?" she snarled.

"Obviously." Charlotte studied her. "It would seem you are in mourning," she remarked. And then blandly, "Has someone died?"

"Oh, that you could say it!" Annette's face had gone splotchy red and she was panting with rage. "I mourn for Rowan—which it is clear you do not!"

"No, I do not," said Charlotte coldly. "But then, you were always his creature—it is just that you should mourn him." She turned on her heel. "Come, Cassandra."

With a last bewildered look at Annette, Cassandra followed Charlotte to the carriage and they drove on.

"What was my father's—Rowan's—connection with Madame de Marceau?" she wondered. "And why does she hate you so?"

"She may call herself Madame de Marceau or any other name, but she is Annette Flambord, whom Rowan fished out of the slums of Marseilles and made his accomplice. It was she who kept me imprisoned in the Alfama all those years."

"How *horrible!*" Cassandra swung round in indignation to look back at the shop. "How could anyone do such a thing?"

"Oh, it was quite easy for Annette, I assure you."

Cassandra gave her a puzzled look. "*Why?*"

"Love, I suppose—at least so she claimed."

"She must have loved fath—Rowan very much." Cassandra was awed.

"Enough to kill for him—and more than once I don't doubt she did."

Cassandra shivered. "I didn't like the way she looked at you, Mother. Perhaps we should ask the authorities to—"

"Annette will find it hard to get at me—I am well guarded," Charlotte cut in with a shrug. It occurred to her suddenly that such was not the case with Cassandra. "Forget this charade with the prince," she urged. "Come back to my inn with me. I will explain to Carlos that you are the daughter of my oldest friend—or perhaps my cousin, and that you are in some danger. He will welcome you, Cassandra. I ask only that you remember that he is dying," she added anxiously. "Were it not for that, I would tell him who you are—joyously."

"No, Mother, I cannot do that." Cassandra sighed. "I must play this game out—I gave my word to Leeds. And after all, it is only until day after tomorrow. Then Prince Damião and Ines will have fled the country and it will all be over."

Charlotte wished she thought so, but there had been a malevolence in Annette's gaze that had chilled her. Annette would have no way of prying into her past, she would not know that Charlotte Keynes had been suddenly transformed into Carlotta del Valle, and indeed had papers to prove her new identity! No, she could stand Annette off if need be, but Cassandra was a different matter.

Back in the millinery shop, Annette was thinking much the same thing. The elegant Spanish lady who had been more or less dragged into her shop would not be easy to attack—and indeed might be quickly gone from Lisbon. Annette, from sheer curiosity, had visited Charlotte's "grave" and seen that handsome footstone, which had told her more forcefully than any words that Charlotte had had a lover. And today, looking into fair-skinned Cassandra's green eyes and seeing again that pale moonbeam hair of hers, she had come to the realization that—although Rowan had never told her—Cassandra was not Rowan's daughter. She was Charlotte's daughter—anyone with half an eye could see that—but there was no hint of Rowan's swarthy features there.

Charlotte had borne Cassandra, but her father was someone other than Rowan. Annette was sure of it.

Now she clenched her trembling hands together. How much he had borne in silence all those years, her poor Rowan! she was thinking. And he had never told her, never shared his sorrow with her! Well, she would avenge him now! The mother might be an impossible target, but the daughter was not.

With Annette the thought was mother to the deed. No sooner had she decided to do away with Cassandra than she sent a boy to the waterfront to find a certain unsavory character she made use of from time to time. They held a hurried conversation there in the back of the millinery shop, money changed hands, and Annette sped him on his way with, "And it must be done *tonight!*"

Charlotte and Cassandra were happily unaware of this devil's pact made between Annette and her minion. Charlotte was thinking only of a way to keep Cassandra safe under her wing.

"Cassandra," she said suddenly, "tonight my husband and I are attending a reception in honor of Lord Derwent, who, I understand, is journeying down from Oporto for the occasion. Will I see you there?"

"Hardly!" Cassandra laughed. "Nobody invites a prince's mistress to important functions!"

"Well, this is one reception you will attend," said Charlotte crisply. "As the daughter of my dearest friend, Charlotte Keynes"—her voice grew wry—"I cannot fail to bring you along."

Cassandra's eyes sparkled. "Yes, Mother."

"You will call me 'Doña Carlotta' and you will be very proper, Cassandra."

"Yes, Mother." Cassandra was even more delighted.

"I will call for you in our coach, Cassandra. Be ready."

"Oh, I will be ready, Mother," Cassandra assured her. "But first you must come in, for there is someone you will want to see. I think she is back now—"

Her words were interrupted by a whoop from the house, and Wend, who had been looking out the window, erupted from the door and ran toward the carriage with her arms outspread. Charlotte sprang down from the carriage and the two embraced with all the fervor of old friends.

"Going about in a black wig, are you?" scolded Wend. "And what does Master Tom say about that?"

"Wend—oh, Wend, it is a long story. I can't tell you now. Come back with me to the inn—we will talk while I dress for the reception and you can sleep on a cot in my room. Will that be all right, Cassandra?"

Cassandra nodded. Her eyes were moist at the sight of the two being reunited. She watched the carriage until it turned the corner and was out of sight, and then she went in to get a bite and to dress for the ball herself, and to contemplate how today's events had changed her life. Today she had gained a mother! And tomorrow, when Prince Damião would be out of her life, she could sort everything out.

Cassandra was ready well ahead of time. She was sumptuously gowned in creamy Italian silk aglitter with gold embroidery, a dress that flowed over her round breasts down to her tiny waist and flared out into a wondrously wide skirt—and all of it overlain with ivory tissue alight with brilliants. She wore brilliants in her pale gleaming hair as well—and of course the diamond necklace. She looked stunning.

"I see you are going out," observed Leeds Birmingham, who came into the hall just as Cassandra was descending the stairs.

"Yes. To the reception for the Englishman, Lord Derwent."

Leeds stood stock-still. "The prince is taking you *there?*"

"No." Charlotte hesitated. "A Spanish lady, Doña Carlotta."

Leeds opened his mouth—and then closed it again. When he spoke, it was on a note of amusement. "You are aware of course that the prince will be there?"

"I have *assumed* that he will be there—he has not bothered to tell me," was Cassandra's airy comment. "And after tomorrow he will have no claim on me—*you* have promised me that!"

The amusement left Leeds' face. He frowned. "Yes, I have promised you that." He might have said more, but just then the iron door knocker sounded.

"That will be Doña Carlotta's coach now!"

Leeds watched Cassandra drift like a great glittering moth toward the door. "I wish you a joyous evening," he said grimly.

Cassandra turned. "Will I see you there?"

"I have not been invited." He was tempted to say "either," but she looked so happy that he forebore.

"Well, that will be their loss!"

And she was gone, leaving Leeds to ponder on the ways of fate.

Only Charlotte waited for Cassandra in the coach. Don Carlos had not felt well enough to come after all.

But when Cassandra saw where the coach drew up, she panicked.

"But . . . but this is the Varváez palace!" she protested.

Charlotte gave her daughter a blank look. "Yes, did you not know that?"

"Prince Damião is betrothed to their daughter Constanca. She will hardly welcome me!"

"Oh?" Charlotte frowned. "Well, it is too late to think about that, we are already here." She alighted regally and Cassandra followed with a pounding heart.

"I may decide not to stay, Mother," Cassandra warned under her breath.

"If you wish to leave after we are presented, I will explain that my young friend has been taken ill and that I must leave with her," Charlotte told her daughter calmly—for she had no intention of letting Cassandra leave her side this evening! Indeed she intended to scoop her up and bring her back to the inn, where Wend would look after her and the servants would protect her—let Prince Damião fend for himself! "But," she added sternly, "I must at least make an appearance because I promised Carlos I would attend, since he did not feel up to coming."

Cassandra made no answer because they were being swept along by other guests who were already flooding in. There was a receiving line, with the Varváez family lavishly garbed and their daughter Constanca looking, in her white dress and white lace mantilla, more like a flower than the dangerous woman she was. When her eyes lit on Cassandra they opened wider—and she bared her teeth. Seen at that moment, Constanca looked a little like a tigress, Cassandra thought nervously. Best she melt into the crowd as quickly as possible, before Constanca attacked her!

Her thoughts were interrupted by her mother's voice, for Charlotte was just then being presented. "And by the greatest good luck, I have found the daughter of my oldest, dearest friend here in Lisbon—and of course I brought her along, for I knew you would want to meet her. Cassandra Dunlawton."

Her hosts looked speechless but they rallied and welcomed both newcomers in voices that shook a little. Then, "Do something, Jorge!" muttered his wife, and Varváez turned and whispered something to a young blade in fawn satin, who promptly seized Cassandra's hand, beamed upon her, and led her firmly away through several spacious chambers to a filigreed stone balcony. Cassandra, fully aware that as Prince Damião's "mistress" she had indeed transgressed by invading the house of his betrothed, went willingly enough. She was glad to put distance between herself and that Portuguese wildcat! Here on the balcony the night air cooled her hot face, and her new escort promptly brought her a glass of wine and showered her with all the English he possessed, which consisted mainly of compliments on her beauty.

Charlotte had been following her daughter's progress with her gaze and had not even looked down the receiving line. Noting that Cassandra seemed to have found an interested admirer who had promptly spirited her away, she breathed a sigh of relief.

She moved forward with aplomb, using her floating walk of the Spanish court, her black velvet gown accentuated by a long double rope of pearls and her black lace mantilla drifting back airily from her high-backed tortoiseshell comb. She had not even looked up to see the face of the tall guest of honor, to whom she now extended one graceful black-gloved hand—at the moment he was only a pearl-white waistcoat and a gray coat of handsome cut.

". . . Lord Derwent," her host was just finishing presenting her.

Charlotte looked up and all of the color drained from her face. The guest of honor had gone ashen too.

"*Tom?*" she whispered as if she could not believe it.

"Charlotte," he said hoarsely. "*Is it really you?*"

Their conversation was in English and nobody nearby spoke English. Charlotte had never before faked a faint in her life. This time she did, slumping suddenly, gracefully, toward the polished floor. The guest of honor caught her in his arms, and to the Varváez family's collective discomfiture, promptly bore her away.

"Charlotte," he whispered. *"Charlotte."*

"Stand me upon my feet," commanded his lady. "I will make my excuses and be waiting for you in my coach. Do not be long! I'll send Cassandra a message."

But no sooner had she spoken than a crowd of people drifted in and surrounded the guest of honor, and several of them promptly engaged Charlotte in conversation. They could not get away. Across besatined shoulders they exchanged agonized looks. Her message, to Cassandra, given to a servant, went undelivered. In the crush, it was carelessly thrown away

Time dragged on and at last Charlotte managed to slip away. No sooner was she gone than the guest of honor suddenly developed a migraine from his fatiguing journey down from Oporto—he deeply regretted it, but his host would of course understand—and he was gone as well.

All in all, for the Varváez family, the evening was not a success. They had only one small consolation: Prince Damião, who should have been standing beside them in the receiving line, was very late—he would deal with his impertinent English mistress when he arrived! *And if he did not, Constanca would!* was plainly writ upon the face of the Varváezes' flowerlike wildcat of a daughter!

But Cassandra was considering that in this case perhaps discretion was the better part of valor. She was content to watch the lights of Lisbon from the balcony and sip wine with a young gentleman who seemed never to tire of showering her with compliments. Time was slipping by. She was tempted to stay out here until the party broke up, then find her mother and carry her away home. There was so much catching up to do! She stood there dreaming, scarcely hearing the admiring masculine voice beside her.

After Cassandra had left for the reception, Leeds Birmingham had gone looking for Prince Damião but had not found him in any of his usual haunts. Believing he might have gone to the pink palace for some reason, he ordered his carriage back there, but even as the carriage turned into the square he ordered his driver to stop and let him out—and to wait for him.

For he had seen something that had given him pause. Something not right.

In the darkness a cart had stopped before the small pink palace in the main square. As if at a signal, a door had opened and two men—men who worked harder and faster than the usual day laborer—were swiftly unloading the cart, carrying kegs into the house, and dashing back for yet another and another and . . . *Kegs!*

Leeds, watching from the shadows, was growing angrier by the moment. He had a very good idea what was in those kegs—gunpowder! But what madness was this? Why would Prince Damiao allow the gunpowder to be brought *here*, to a house which he himself often occupied?

Unless, of course, someone was trying to kill the prince?

Leeds sprinted across the square. The unloading was just finished, the driver was already back in place, and another man, a shorter, heavier-set man, was just springing up beside him. The driver swung his whip at Leeds to brush him aside. Leeds ducked, and his sword cut through the air and slashed into the driver's chest. As if the air had been suddenly sucked out of his lungs, the driver collapsed forward and sprawled, tangled into the reins, crashing into the rump of the lead horse. Frightened, the horse reared and then took off, carrying with him, in his rush the horse beside him. With a clatter the cart careened off down the street, by the suddenness of its precipitate start knocking the heavyset man from his almost-gained perch.

He toppled back into the street, and Leeds was upon him. No gallant street fighter was Leeds—he had been assaulted in too many dark alleys. Even as his opponent reached for his sword, Leeds hacked at the arm that would wield it. The blade bit home, and with a moan the other man abandoned his quest for his weapon and reeled backward, sword arm dangling limply and his other upraised to ward off the blow he knew would come.

"No, Birmingham—'tis me, Pereira!"

"Pereira!" In amazement Leeds let his sword drop and peered forward into the darkness. "What are you doing here?"

"I am but following the prince's orders, and I am about to bleed to death from the cut you have given me."

"Come inside." Leeds waved his sword at him. "We will attend your wound."

"No, I would rather go home. I—"

"Inside!" grated Leeds, and seized Pereira by the shoulder of his coat. Roughly he dragged him inside and closed the door behind him with his foot. Its slam resounded through the house.

"Galvão!" he called. "Lopo!"

"It is no use," sighed Pereira. "All the servants have gone."

Leeds frowned about him. In a wall bracket a torch was burning, casting its flickering light upon the great empty hall.

He marched Pereira to the kitchen, observing as he went the small trail of gunpowder that led from the front door, where a keg had leaked the black powder. In the kitchen he tossed Pereira some clean cloths, poured his recent adversary a basin of water, and watched him stanch and bind his wound, which was not very deep after all.

"What were the prince's orders?" he asked Pereira bluntly.

"I think Prince Damião had best tell you himself," sighed Pereira.

Leeds' jaw tightened.

"I will hear it from you."

"I am a fighting man," complained Pereira. "I do not like these intrigues."

"Go on."

"Tonight Prince Damião ordered me to remove all the gunpowder from the warehouse and bring it here. I have done so. You intercepted the last load."

Leeds swore softly. "And the guns? Did you bring them here too?"

"There are no guns."

That brought Leeds up short. *No guns? Mount a rebellion with no guns?* He descended on Pereira with a swoop. "You lie! *Where are the guns?*"

With that fierce face thrust into his own, Pereira felt his heart tremble in his chest. "I swear to you by all that is holy, *there are no guns!*"

In fury, Leeds seized him by the throat.

"Prince Damião said there would be no need of guns!" gasped Pereira.

Slowly the death grip Leeds had on Pereira's throat relaxed. "No need of guns?" he asked blankly.

"He said gunpowder would be all we would need."

So the rebellion had been a sham. The prince meant to blow up something—or someone. Pombal? No, Pombal was an enemy of course, but the prince had rejected the idea of killing him. A terrible suspicion was forming in the back of Leeds' mind.

"Pereira," he said, and now his voice was almost genial, although his eyes were dangerous, "I think you had best tell me the rest of it."

"It is all I know," mumbled Pereira.

"I think not."

Pereira looked into those prismlike eyes and saw death.

"What was I to do?" he burst out. "Pombal has said the Crown would be best rid of me! The royal family ignores me—*me*, with a name as old as Portugal! Only Prince Damião has offered me advancement, and it is from him I take my orders. I do not question them, I obey!"

Pereira knew more than he was telling; Leeds was sure of it. But there was a streak of stubbornness in this seedy aristocrat. It would take a long time to beat it out of him.

"I will take your advice, Pereira," he said softly. "I will ask the prince to explain matters."

"Good." Pereira sounded much relieved.

"And I will leave you here to consider your sins." He grasped Pereira by his good arm and shoved him into a pantry filled with kegs and turned the key in the heavy door.

"No, no, do not leave me here!" Pereira was shouting as he left.

* * *

At the inn where he had staggered in the early dawn hours, Drew Marsden had been suffering through the worst hangover of his life. He had flung himself upon his bed with a groan, and remained there as first the morning and then the afternoon sped by. In the evening he had roused himself and had supper sent up, and after that he had soberly considered his lot.

He could of course take the first ship back to England, and he was tempted to do just that. But that meant leaving Cassandra in the arms of another man—and that cut hard across the grain. Cassandra. . . . Back in England he had filled his world with her. Was he going to let her go without putting up so much as a battle?

The hours wore on, with his lean face growing grimmer by the minute. At last he left his inn. He would have a last word with the wench before he disappeared from her life!

At the Varváez reception, his "wench" was having troubles of her own. Warmed by wine and, undoubtedly, her hot reputation, her new admirer was now making decidedly indelicate advances. Cassandra eluded them, artfully whirling about and waving her fan in his face, but when a servant who spoke a little English happened by, she asked him to tell Doña Carlotta that she had left for home.

Indeed, it was what she intended—she would give one of those waiting coachmen outside a gold coin and he would take her the short distance home and be back before the coach's owner noted it was gone. But before she could do that, a dark gentleman in green velvet almost solidly encrusted with gold embroidery shouldered past her admirer and she found herself looking up into Prince Damião's furious face.

He seized her arm and loosed a storm of Portuguese that Cassandra interpreted to be a rather colorfully worded "What are you doing here?"

She tried to jerk her arm away, but he was already dragging her from the balcony, back the way she had come, and at last into the crowded main reception room, where people paused in their chatter and stood back to watch this lively scene between the prince and his impudent mistress.

His voice was hard, raining words on her like stones. Cassandra felt in her heart that he was cursing her, and indignation sprang to life inside her. "But I did not know you were coming, Damião," she protested in a clear ringing voice that carried across the room and caused Constanca to turn pale. "How thoughtless of you not to have brought me yourself!"

His words poured out even more volubly and his grip on her arm tightened cruelly.

With molten copper fire glowing in her green eyes, Cassandra drew back her other arm and struck the prince with all her strength in the face.

He staggered back; he released his hold. The room was suddenly silent as every breath was held, waiting to see what would happen next.

"I will be out of your life in an hour!" Cassandra shouted, and turning about on her high heels, sprinted for the door, her big skirts held up out of her way.

Constanca had hurried to intercept the prince, who was starting after Cassandra. The prince abandoned his pursuit.

Humiliated, furious, Cassandra found there were tears in her eyes as she blundered through the great front doors. She dashed them away and looked about. The night was very dark indeed, but tall torches burned in front of the Varváez palace. Her mother's coach was long gone, but those torches showed her an unattended open carriage.

Unmindful of whom the carriage might belong to, Cassandra ran toward it, leapt up, and took the reins. She could return the carriage later. Or have it returned, for it was her firm intention, no matter what she had promised Leeds, to drive at once to the palace on the square, gather up her own belongings, leaving everything the prince had bought for her, and find herself a room at an inn. The innkeeper's servants could return this carriage before the reception was over. It might not even be missed.

So her thoughts ran as she drove the short distance home.

She came to a smart halt before the pink palace, leapt

from the carriage, swept up her long skirts, and headed for the front door. She seized the great iron knocker, but before she could sound it, the heavy door gave inward. It occurred to her that the servants must have left it unlocked for the prince.

"Ines!" she called imperiously.

But the wide reaches of the great hall's torchlit interior were empty of life.

"Ines!" She was about to run up the stairs when she came to a stop. There was an *empty* feel to the house. Had she arrived a few moments earlier, she would have heard in the back of the house Pereira shouting and banging on the pantry door, but in his violent efforts to break down the pantry door he had reopened his wound and had fainted momentarily from lack of blood. So the back of the house was as silent as the rest. "Ines!" she called again, more doubtfully. And then she stopped calling. Was that why Prince Damião had been so angry? Had Ines already left, and was he trying to tell her that she was in some way spoiling his plans?

And then on the polished floor she saw what she had not noticed before. Glowing dark red upon the shining marble surface, a little pool of blood. The trail led both ways—out the front door and toward the back of the house.

Blood! she thought. *Had Ines been killed here and carried away?*

She turned instinctively to run back to her carriage.

But that way was now blocked. The front door was swinging silently open.

Annette's messenger had arrived.

And Annette's messenger had a knife.

Cassandra screamed.

After that everything happened very fast. Cassandra turned to run; the wiry dark man who had appeared in the doorway leapt forward to stop her. He had almost reached her, knife upraised, when suddenly there was a shout from the doorway and he crashed down at her feet.

And there, miraculously, was Drew, bounding forward and knocking the fellow down as he tried to rise. This time he stayed down.

Cassandra didn't stop to wonder how Drew could possibly have gotten here. Instead she chose the practical path. "What did you hit him with?" she wondered. "From the door, I mean?"

"With my shoe," said Drew grimly. "I pulled it off and managed to catch him in the back of the neck when I threw it." He was putting his buckled shoe back on as he spoke. "What kind of madhouse do you live in with this prince, Cassandra?"

"I don't live with this prince, Drew. It was all a charade to help . . . Oh, never mind. However did you find me?"

"I looked up and saw you at the opera," he said grimly. "At first I was going to leave Lisbon—then tonight I decided to let you tell me how this all happened. I saw your carriage careening around the corner, and then you jumped out and dashed in. When I saw this fellow lurking there and slipping in after you, I came running."

"Thank God you did!" Cassandra was still shaky.

"You're getting out of here right now."

"Oh, I can't. My things—"

"We'll send for your things. I'm not leaving you anyplace they're trying to kill you!"

Drew was wonderful when he was being masterful, Cassandra thought dreamily. "Where are you taking me?" she asked as he led her outside and lifted her into the carriage.

"To my inn," he said, climbing into the driver's seat. "And then on the first ship back to England."

Cassandra leaned forward, smiling. "I don't own this carriage. I just jumped into it after I struck Prince Damião in the face and left the Narváez reception."

Drew gave her a look. "We'll send it back from the inn, Cassandra. Is there anything else you might have forgotten to tell me?"

Yes. That I love you. But there'd be plenty of time for that later . . . after they'd arrived at the inn! She reminded herself of Charlotte's words: *Men have always fought—and gotten hurt riding, and caught colds and fevers that killed them.* She loved Drew and she knew she would go on loving him. And what could possibly happen to mar that now?

The innkeeper was astonished to see Prince Damião's English mistress accompany her "betrothed" up the stairs to his room—but in his heart he was a romantic, so he chose to look the other way.

"Cassandra," Drew said, when they were alone at last, "Livesay told me how you felt." He drew her into his arms. "I want you to know that I'd take my chances on dying just to keep you beside me forever."

"Oh, I'm not afraid anymore," she told him confidently.

His arms tightened about her. "And whatever this prince has been to you," he said hoarsely, "I want you to know that it doesn't matter. I want you to be my wife."

"Oh, Drew, Prince Damião means nothing to me— nothing." Between laughter and tears she told him about it, and somehow as she talked, her clothes were coming off, until finally, when the last of her story had been told, she found herself in bed with Drew and kissing him and feeling waves of tenderness and heartfelt passion sweeping over her. She who had never given herself to a man—who had indeed been afraid to—abandoned herself to joy and in Drew's strong arms found the true meaning of being a woman.

And afterward, when their passions were spent, Drew stared down at her and murmured as if he could not believe it, "You were a virgin!"

"Yes." She laughed and played with his ear, nibbled at it. "So now you know there wasn't anything between me and Prince Damião!"

The assassin who had tried to kill Cassandra had long since gathered himself up off the floor and gone back with an aching head to tell Annette that he had failed this night.

"Fool!" she raged at him. "*Canaille!* You could not even kill a slip of a girl!"

"I told you, a man appeared—I don't know where he came from, but he struck me down."

"Struck you down indeed!" Annette's teeth grated together. "Well, you can forget her. I will take care of her myself—tomorrow. Oh, get out, get out!" She began to cry stormily.

The hired assassin slunk away feeling abused. He had, after all, done his best.

He might have counted his blessings, for he would have had short shrift if Leeds Birmingham had found him upon the marble floor of the pink palace. Leeds had gone directly to the Narváez mansion and had found his way barred by a servant. "I have strict orders not to let you in," the man explained, frowning.

"I have a message for Prince Damião," said Leeds grimly.

"I will be glad to deliver it, sir."

"That you will not. Ask the prince to come out."

The servant gave him a doubtful look. "I don't think he will come."

"Tell him the message concerns Pereira's activities this night," said Leeds grimly. "He will come!"

Mention of Pereira's name brought the prince out in record time. He stared at Leeds. "I thought the man said Pereira wanted to see me."

"No, it is I who wanted to see you." Leeds lounged forward smiling and leaned over, speaking confidentially into the prince's ear. "There is a knife in your ribs, Damião. And if you so much as blink an eyelash, it will be plunged in to the hilt. You will walk away with me in friendly fashion. You will call over your shoulder that you will be back soon."

Pale and shaken, Prince Damião did as he was bidden.

"Where are we going?" he demanded when they were out of sight of the Narváez mansion.

"Be silent," Leeds said tersely. "I have something to show you."

The prince balked at going inside the pink palace. "We can talk outside," he said sullenly.

"What I have to show you is inside." Leeds prodded him again with the knife.

Prince Damião went inside.

"Do you see that thin line of black powder, Damião?"

"I see blood upon the floor." Prince Damião was beginning to sweat.

"Pereira's blood."

"*Mae de Deus!*" cried the prince. "Have you killed him?"

"Certainly not! I merely used a bit of persuasion to get him to explain your little plot and why you will need no guns tomorrow, only gunpowder!"

"He lies!" cried Damião.

Leeds laughed. It was not a pleasant sound. "And how do you know that, Damião? You do not know what he said!" Of a sudden he struck the prince a hard blow on the side of the head that sent him sprawling to the floor. He stood over the fallen man, breathing hard. "I should kill you now," he said, "for it has all come clear to me. You never meant to have an uprising, the men who met here were never to be part of an army—they were in a plot with you, true, but Pereira's vaunted army was all a dream!"

"No," whispered the prince. "No! It is not true! Pereira will tell you that it is not true!"

There was a sound of hammering and a muffled shouting from the back of the house.

"Get up," said Leeds harshly. "We will let Pereira tell us himself!"

Prince Damião scrambled up and Leeds herded him along toward the kitchen pantry where Pereira was locked in. On their way they walked over the trail of black powder.

"We were to be your dupes, the English girl and I," Leeds said, giving Damião a cuff when he did not walk fast enough. "*How did you plan to lure the royal family here, Damião, so you could blow them up?*"

"I didn't plan it," moaned Prince Damião, now in a state of blind panic. "It was Pereira's idea, I swear it!"

"That is the simple way to become king, is it not? Who needs a rebellion when one has an assassin? Doubtless the king would have been told you were on your deathbed at the house of your English mistress. And it might have worked—they might have rushed here believing you were dying, and you would have killed them all. *What manner*

of man are you who strikes in the dark?" He gave the
unlucky prince another hard cuff.

"It will work, it is bound to work!" The prince was
almost gibbering. "You have only to release me and say
nothing. By tomorrow afternoon I will be king! I can give
you anything then!"

"That is when you would give me my last gift—the gift
of death." Leeds' short laugh was more of a growl. "Your
plot was almost perfect, Damião. You put out the rumor
that Cassandra was ambitious, that she wanted to be queen.
Who would not believe that I helped her arrange it, I the
tarnished adventurer? It would give me pleasure to hack
you to pieces here and now with my sword!" He had
already drawn it, and now he gestured to Damião with it.
With his other hand he was unlocking the pantry door.
"Stand well back, Pereira. Your prince is joining you!"

He flung open the door with force and flung Prince
Damião through it, knocking down Pereira, who had surged
forward as it opened. Even as they both rushed forward
again, the door was slammed and locked.

"Let me out!" wailed Prince Damião. "I will do anything!"

"You have already proved that," said Leeds dryly. "You
are lucky that I give you your life. Eventually you will be
discovered here. By then I will be far away. And I would
suggest that neither of you try to light a candle—it is sure
to blow you sky-high!" His mocking laughter rang out as he
left.

Tom had asked no questions when he joined Charlotte
in her black-and-gold coach outside the Varváez mansion.
Instead he had scooped her up in his arms as if she might
somehow escape him. It was Charlotte, lost in happiness,
who asked the questions, snuggled against his coat.

"Tom, are you really Lord Derwent?" she asked him
wonderingly.

"Yes." His voice was a little muffled, for he had buried
his face in her dark coiffure. "What is this, Charlotte, a
wig?"

"Yes. And the new creaminess of my complexion I owe

to vials and powders, for I was too pink and white to look Spanish! But underneath I am the same woman."

"*My* woman," he said confidently.

Charlotte looked up at that loved face and he knew a rush of exaltation. She was indeed his woman—she had always been, she would always be his woman. And whatever happened, no power on earth would separate them ever again! In her heart of hearts, she vowed it.

But suddenly she remembered Carlos, who did not deserve to be deserted. Oh, no, she could not leave him to die alone, not after all the years he had loved her. . . .

"How did you come by your title?" she asked, trying to cover up her confused thoughts.

"I did some small service for his majesty in Brazil," was Tom's careless answer. " 'Twas no great matter to me, but it meant much to English trade. Perhaps," he said, laughing, "the Crown has chosen to remind me that I am English!"

"Then you live in Brazil now?"

"Aye." He did not choose to tell her that he was the richest man in Brazil, but it was so. Life had hardened him and he had taken many a long chance in South America, for diamonds were supposed to be a royal monopoly—and Tom had found diamonds there. But he had smuggled out the stones and sold them clandestinely in Amsterdam, where they had since been cut, and he had put his newfound fortune into land. Last year Sebastião da Severa had died and left his estate to Tom. Combined with his own land, that had made him Brazil's largest landowner. "I will take you home with me," he told her caressingly.

Home with Tom—it was a heady thought!

"My home estate had another name, but now that I have found you again I will rechristen it 'World's End.' "

Through the coach window the night and Lisbon were rushing by.

Charlotte closed her eyes.

"By the way," he asked conversationally, "where is this coach taking us?"

Charlotte roused herself. She had been afraid to take Tom to any of the well-known Lisbon inns—she was too conspicuous and he was too well-known. She did not want stories getting back to Carlos. Whatever Carlos was told, she would tell him herself—and she could not face that just now. All she could think of was that she would never let Tom leave her, never!

But as to where to instruct the driver to take them tonight, she had remembered suddenly that when she had asked Cassandra what she had planned to do should things go wrong, Cassandra had told her that Leeds had instructed her, in case of trouble, to meet him at a tiny ruined chapel just below the frowning Castelo de São Jorge—and if he did not come speedily, she was to put up at the tiny inn nearby in the medieval village that sheltered just below the mighty fortress. The inn was—perhaps mockingly, perhaps in admiration—also called the Castelo.

"To an out-of-the-way inn," she said. "One where we will not be found."

He sat straighter at that. "You have married again," he guessed.

"Oh, Tom." Charlotte's voice held a note of wild entreaty. "Rowan kept me imprisoned for *years*, and when I escaped it was Carlos who saved me and took me to Spain. Yes, I did marry him—he gave me a whole new life, I would have died had it not been for him. Oh, Tom, please try to understand!"

Tom looked away. Charlotte was his only love, and it seemed to him that all his life other men had held her. His strong hands clenched but he managed to keep control of his voice.

"We will take what the gods give, Charlotte. How long do you have to spend with me?"

She wanted to say, *All my life, Tom!* Carlos had been feeling too ill to attend the Varváez reception and had insisted that she go on alone. He had told her not to disturb him when she came back and that he would let her sleep late, he would lunch with her after he had attended Mass, for tomorrow was All Hallows' Day. She moistened her lips. "We have until ten o'clock tomorrow, Tom."

"Then it is until ten o'clock, Charlotte." There was a

tinge of bitterness in his voice. "For I have no real hold on you."

Oh, but you do, you do! "I never stopped loving you, Tom," she said with a break in her voice. "Not for a single moment. . . ."

And tomorrow, he told himself, *I will find a way to take you with me no matter who stands in the way!* He did not say that. Instead he said, "I have bought a place in England, Charlotte. It is the most beautiful house in the world—or so a girl once told me."

Charlotte caught her breath. "You have bought Castle Stroud?" she asked unevenly. "Why did you do that?"

"Memories," he told her, touching his hand to her cheek. "I remembered a girl who loved it, a girl I thought long dead, and I told myself if I could go there sometimes it would bring her closer to me. I could stare into the fire and imagine her beside me."

Charlotte seized his hand and rubbed it against her cheek. Her eyes were luminous indeed as she looked up at the tall man beside her. "Tom," she whispered, "I don't deserve you."

They had reached their destination now, and the driver ("I can trust him, Tom, he is devoted to me") was pounding on the door of the small one-story building. The sleepy innkeeper finally opened it and their coachman arranged for a room.

In silence, with Charlotte's black lace mantilla concealing her features, she and Tom went inside and found their tiny room, which overlooked the city, was surprisingly cozy. Reluctantly, common sense had returned.

Charlotte scarcely glanced at the room, revealed in the light of a single candle. She tossed aside her mantilla, removed her wig, and let her golden hair cascade down over her shoulders. Her voice was wistful.

"Life is a trap, Tom," she said slowly. "Its jaws close down upon us, and before we realize it, the trap has sprung. I will not leave Carlos and I will not hurt him—no matter where my wayward heart would take me. We have only tonight. . . ."

Tom's gaze was wistful too. He had always thought of

his beautiful Charlotte as pliant, swaying like a flower in the wind. He had never thought of her as made of steel.

"I will do nothing to endanger you," he said hoarsely.

"So when the coach calls for me tomorrow morning, that will be the end of us, Tom." Her voice was uneven.

"So be it."

What happened then was inevitable. He blew out the candle and they moved into each other's arms as if they had never been apart. Tom's lips traveled over hers like a song, like a prayer, and he held her as if she were the most valuable treasure a man could ever possess.

Charlotte melted against him in a torrent of emotion. A miracle had happened. Tom was back, he was snatched from the dead, he was hers again. . . . She was scarcely aware when he carried her to the bed. She felt her clothes leave her, felt his bare skin, and she was back again, young again, and outside was no foreign city but the silvery sheen of the Derwent Water and the snows of Cumberland. She had thought her body grown cold, for it had been more than two years since Carlos had been able to make love to her, but now abruptly every sense had come alive, awake and tingling beneath Tom's gentle insistent caresses. Her whole being vibrated like a drum to the beat of his heart, to the rhythmic swaying of his hips as, like a drowning man seeking rescue, he plunged deep and tenderly within her. *He had come back, he had come back, her world was right again.* . . . Her senses sang and she quivered as his strong masculinity moved vibrantly within her, promising, promising. . . . *Oh, let this never end,* she found herself wishing as she felt her body pulsing to an age-old rhythm, creating a storm of desire that surged through her whole being, making her very senses swim.

"Tom," she whispered brokenly. *"Oh, Tom, how I have missed you. . . ."*

And the world slipped away as the lovers gave—and received—endless delights.

For them the magic was still there, wreathing them, when Tom at last slipped away and they lay touching, fondly stroking each other's naked bodies in the golden afterglow of passion.

There were no words to express how they felt—and they needed none. Theirs was a silent communion of the heart, a depth of compassion and a yearning that would know no end.

They were made for each other, these two, and they knew it. And for the moment they had both pushed away the nagging truth—that this too would end.

They made love again. And then again.

At last, exhausted, they slipped into sleep, and slept until the sun was shining.

And were awakened violently to a great roar, a sound like the end of the world.

36

All Hallows' Day
9:30 A.M.
November 1, 1755

The terrible rumbling roar brought Tom and Charlotte to their feet and to the window. They looked out on an unbelievable sight.

Although on their hilltop they were barely shaking, the buildings in the city below were dancing and teetering and collapsing. Steeples and chimneys were cracking and falling over into the streets, red tile roofs were breaking up, walls were collapsing. That first terrible jar had brought Lisbon to her knees.

There was a sudden pause as if the earth itself was taking a deep breath—and in that pause there was suddenly, all over town, the licking of flames.

The earthquake had struck during First Mass, and in the crowded churches thousands of candles had been overturned—not to mention the braziers over which the poor cooked their food in the open in winding streets and alleys. Hundreds of fires were kindled in an instant. The city had begun to burn.

Abruptly the shaking began again. But this time it was no great single shock—this time it was a violent whipsawing motion that tore buildings apart, seesawing them back and forth as the ground beneath heaved and shimmied and buckled and rose again, bringing down palaces and churches and modest homes alike in a deafening, terrifying din.

Again there was a pause during which the earth seemed to hold its very breath.

"Oh, God!" whispered Charlotte. "Carlos . . . Cassandra . . . Wend!" She plunged for her clothes.

But before she could get into them, the violent shaking had begun again, along with a deep growling fearsome roar that rumbled from what must surely be the very center of the earth. And now Lisbon's very face was changing. So many great buildings had collapsed, and such a storm of dust was rising from the ruins, that an unreal night had settled over the city—a darkness pierced by jagged flashes of lightning that lit the scene briefly with a ghastly glare.

Transfixed for a moment, Charlotte and Tom stared out into this gathering blackness and heard all the sounds of hell erupting from the dying city below: falling buildings, breaking glass, human screams, collapsing walls, crumbling masonry. And rumbling through it, drowning it, that hideous inhuman tormented din rising from deep within the earth as the bedrock cracked and tore and twisted. All of it combined into a single terrifying torrent of sound that froze the blood and stunned the senses.

What they were hearing was the agonized jolt as continents collided.

Nerveless they stood, staring awed at the blackness swirling toward them.

And suddenly out of that blackness careened a riderless horse. It came up the hill at full tilt, and from one empty stirrup dangled an empty boot.

Charlotte stared in horror at that boot. Boots did not easily depart their owners. Had this one's owner been knocked from his mount by the quake and pinned under falling masonry that held him firm while his terrified horse jerked free, tearing off the boot as he went?

"Oh, God," she whispered again, and then Rowan was leading her out of the inn "lest the building crash down upon our heads" and she saw the horse again. It stood trembling and exhausted, then at sight of them rolled its eyes wildly and galloped away.

A lifetime seemed to have gone by since that first great

jolt. In all, this violent upheaval had lasted no more than ten minutes—but it had brought the city down.

The great earthshock which had torn into Lisbon from the southwest when the undersea Gorringe Bank had shifted had brought Lisbon down like a jigsaw puzzle. Beneath the city's visible loose sands and gravel stretched other, deeper layers—of blue clay, of hippurite limestone, and of basalt. Those parts of the city that rested deep down on blue clay—and that was most of the central city and the waterfront—were totally destroyed, while those parts that rested on basalt or hippurite limestone—like the crowning hilltop of the Castelo de São Jorge—were, miraculously it seemed, undamaged.

The Sete Cidades, the Seven Cities Inn, where Clive had brought Lady Farrington and her daughter, was on such a location—it survived, and so did the ladies. But Clive had gone into the city that morning. They never saw him again.

The pink palace on the square miraculously held during the first violent shock. And when the pause in the shaking came, Prince Damião and Pereira, bellowing at the top of their lungs and pounding against the heavy door with their fists, felt sure they would be rescued. But the shaking had knocked the still-burning torch from its bracket on the wall and the torch had rolled across the long line of black powder, setting it alight. Black powder was scattered all about under the howling pair's feet as they had stumbled about, knocking over some of the kegs of gunpowder that were stored in the dark pantry. They saw the licking flames fizzing toward them underneath the door but they were powerless to stop them.

The pink palace blew up like a powder magazine, taking the prince and Pereira with it. But its spectacular disintegration went unnoticed in the general debacle, for it blew up just as the violent whipsawing began that brought the neighboring buildings crashing down in a choking cloud of dust.

The prince had sought a throne—and might have reached it. His macabre death was but one of many ironies to be visited upon Lisbon that day.

And one of those ironies came to Don Carlos—and came

to him in church. And it had been a long time since he had attended Mass.

Sitting there in the vast dimness of the lofty church, with the light of the candles winking before him and the sonorous voice of the priest intoning, brought Don Carlos back to his childhood—and the faith of his childhood, so long forgotten.

He had sinned. Before God, he had sinned—and not until he had returned to Lisbon on this last difficult journey, in hopes of restoring his health, had he ever been sorry. He had loved a woman, and although she did not know it, would never know it, he had found out all about her. About her husband, her children. And he had tricked her into a bigamous marriage with him by telling her he was soon to die. Which was certainly not the case then: he had known he had many years to live. He could have helped Charlotte, he could have restored to her the daughters she loved, he could have told her the fate of the lover she had lost—for he had found that out too. But to have done those things would have been to lose her, and more than anything else in this world he had wanted to keep her beside him.

Don Carlos' hands clenched with a fraction of what had been his old strength, and for a moment his eyes flashed with their old amber fire. He could feel death stealing upon him, although God alone knew how long it would take before he was laid finally to rest, but for the moment his thoughts were all for his beloved Carlotta.

She was honest and true and he had used her ill. God would punish him for that. Indeed—his lips curled in a mirthless smile—God had already punished him for that: rather than visiting on him some merciful "accident" that would carry his soul away, God had made him suffer the torment of the damned—just as his father had. And he was even now fast wasting away, just as so long ago he had predicted to Charlotte that he would.

It was just. He admitted it. And he—so long away from the Church and from grace, how long was it since he had been to Mass?—had been content just to keep her beside him.

But then they had come to Lisbon, seeking a cure for him. Then her lover, the man of whom he had heard so much in her delirium back in the days when he had first known her, the days when her life had hung by a slender thread, had returned.

Tom Westing, now a titled gentleman, Lord Derwent, and the richest man in Brazil. . . .

Don Carlos had had no need to see them together. Just knowing that Tom was in town had sent a chill through his heart. But he could imagine them together as they would be if they met, for he had had a very full description of Tom. A magnificent pair, they would be, their faces full of splendor as they looked into each other's eyes, made for each other.

He had known then that he could keep up the charade no longer.

Nor could he bring himself to tell her. He could not bear to watch that warm expression he so treasured change and chill. He could not endure her scorn, her hatred.

So he had chosen another way. He had sent Charlotte off to the Varváez reception for Lord Derwent, knowing full well she could not escape meeting the guest of honor. And he had told Charlotte not to disturb him, that he would go to early Mass, that he would not be back until after ten.

He had given her a night with her lover. And even now, jealousy was grinding in his heart.

He had meant to do it differently. He had meant to linger with her as long as he could, to confess and be given last rites, he had intended to make his peace with the God of his fathers and to depart this life cherishing the hope of an uneasy heaven where perhaps he would see her again someday.

Now, sitting in this great drafty church, listening to the priest's voice droning on, he knew that it was not to be. He had kept Charlotte apart from her lover all these years. Now, in a last handsome gesture, he would restore him to her—and in a way that would leave her without shame.

He would forget confession, he who had so much to confess, for upon leaving this church he meant to go home and lock his door and cry out loudly that the pain was too much to bear—and then he would fall upon his sword and die a suicide.

And Charlotte could go back to the man she had never stopped loving.

It would be his gift to her. Perhaps the best thing he had ever done in a wasted life. And all it would cost him would be his immortal soul, for from his early rigid upbringing in Holy Mother Church he knew in the depths of him that to die by his own hand an unconfessed sinner and be buried in unconsecrated ground would cast him into a burning hell forever.

For her, he would endure the flames.

Don Carlos' face was very set on this All Hallows' Day, and suddenly through his dark thoughts penetrated a terrible rumbling noise that might have come from the very hell he had been envisioning. And simultaneously the floor beneath him dipped and swayed. About him people were lurching to their feet, shouting, screaming, running over each other in frenzy, trying to escape as the walls cracked and the holy statues toppled.

Don Carlos looked up. The ceiling above him bore a long crack, a crack which fanned out into a hundred others. The lofty roof of the church was collapsing upon those within.

Don Carlos' gaze remained fixed upward during those moments when, wrenched loose by the fury of the quake, roof and ceiling came hurtling down upon the packed multitude below. The air was filled with screams—but among the screams there was one who laughed.

God had been good to him—he would not have to take his own life after all. And perhaps in some merciful heaven he would find her once again—someday.

It was the last thought Don Carlos was ever to have, as the heavy roof caved in, crushing the faithful below.

For Clive, Lord Houghton, who had gone down into the town, the situation was different. He had been standing near the Cays Depreda, the new stone quay that had been erected on the riverfront, when the first tremor struck. It had not even occurred to him to go back into the town to look for Lady Farrington or her daughter. He had cowered back onto the quay, joined by thousands of others who had sought its safety as well, and watched in fear as the ruined city now became a raging inferno, its hundreds of fires whipped into one vast conflagration by the high winds that fanned it. It was a fearful sight indeed, the new-made ruins evilly lit up by licking wind-driven flames beneath an overhanging blackness made up of smoke and dust and laced by lightning bolts. To the frightened thousands who jostled each other upon the stone quay, that was a far more electrifying spectacle than the view upon their other side, where the waters of the Tagus River seemed to be draining fast away.

They never learned what that would mean.

Just as the second great earthquake struck, the foundations were jolted from beneath the Cays Depreda and the entire stone quay plunged into the river, carrying Clive and screaming thousands of men, women, and children with it. What happened in those dark churning waters, no one ever knew, but none of them were ever found.

Not all who died in Lisbon that day were on land. Some were on the river, some upon the sea.

And one of the many tall ships caught irresistibly in the holocaust was the *Storm Castle*—the white-sailed merchantman that carried Phoebe.

Beneath the blue Atlantic over which the *Storm Castle* had sailed so placidly, the great continental plates bearing Africa and Europe were locked in titanic struggle. Unseen, that mighty undersea escarpment southwest of Lisbon that would come to be known as the Gorringe Bank, racked and stretched by unbearable strains that reached down and down to depths unimaginable, was reaching the breaking point as the *Storm Castle* sailed over it.

Many ships were unlucky that day, but none unluckier than the *Storm Castle*. She was just in position to feel the main force of the catastrophic shift below as the fault broke open beneath the strain and Africa lurched against Europe, sending a violent shudder through the planet Earth.

At sea they had heard a sound like a distant rumbling thunder coming from the east. The passengers, crowded on deck with their possessions, for they were soon to disembark, had looked at each other uneasily. A heavy storm, no doubt.

Phoebe, watching that distant dark cloud rising from the earth, had been, like the others, unaware of the water's first imperceptible rising. She watched that low dark cloud raptly, for beneath it was where she had been told she would have her first glimpse of Lisbon's distant skyline. She leaned upon the rail at the prow, uncaring that the salt spray might mar the lustrous dark green velvet of her gown, which—like everything else in her life now—had not been paid for.

Phoebe had never looked better. Her high cheekbones were flushed beneath the rouge she always wore these days to heighten her own slightly sallow color. Her dark hair shone in its fashionable coiffure beneath a three-cornered hat of dark green felt that became her rather witchlike features enormously.

Oh, it would be so good to find Clive again! His love was worth all the humiliation, all the bailiffs. In her desperation to join him, Phoebe had sunk lower than ever before. In Liverpool she had wangled a job as chambermaid to a wealthy family, and on her first night there she had passed all the family plate out the window to an accomplice—and used her share of the money they got from the fence to purchase her passage on board the *Storm Castle*. But she had been suspected, and now it would be chancy for her to return to England. No matter, she and Clive could wander about Europe as expatriates, making new debts!

Her dreaming face broke into a sudden frown and she leaned forward, peering ahead. Something was wrong up there! That sullen dark cloud laced by lightning seemed to lie on glowing coals—no, it was flames, the city was ablaze!

Even as that fact was borne in on her, a terrible torrent of sound engulfed her, a deep growling roar that seemed to her in her fright to come out of that distant burning city—an enormous and terrifying blast of sound that roared in her ears with no beginning and no end.

Her green-gloved hands seized the rail.

To Phoebe it was as if the ship were being lifted by giant hands, up and up, and being flung forward.

The wind blew her hair, and her hat was gone. Phoebe

clung to the rail with all her strength, suddenly aware of being caught up by mighty forces beyond her understanding.

Around her men shouted and women screamed, their voices lost in the general tumult.

It was not the sail-billowing wind that carried them forward now. It was a force from below that swept them inexorably up the mouth of the Tagus, rising higher and higher as millions of tons of raging water bursting in from the ocean flooded up a narrowing river that had now become a bottleneck. The *Storm Castle*—and Phoebe with it—was riding the crest of a giant wave that would break over Lisbon.

Before that wave, helpless and doomed, the city waited.

Those flung ashore by that first great wave that broke over Lisbon would never live to tell it. But for Phoebe the mighty "tidal wave" had done something else—it had saved her from being dishonored one more time.

Indeed fate dealt out a strange kind of mercy that day—at least to Phoebe. She died never knowing that the man she loved so desperately had intended to kill her.

Wend had waited in Charlotte's bedroom at the Royal Cockerel for Charlotte to return from the reception. Exhausted from the excitement of the day, she had fallen asleep and had not waked until morning. Although it seemed logical that Charlotte had returned and slept the night, then dressed without waking her and gone off with Don Carlos, who had already left for church, the sight of that unslept-in bed disturbed Wend and she went outside and wandered about, hoping to catch sight of Charlotte.

And so it was that that terrible first shock that reduced the Royal Cockerel to a rubbish heap, killed everyone inside, and shuddered through the entire street, showering stones and roof tiles and debris onto the cobbles in a deadly downpour, found Wend in the center of the street staring into the distance at a well-dressed woman she hoped might be Charlotte. The shock was so great that it knocked her feet out from under her and sent her, feeling nauseated and dizzy, onto the cobbles in a choking cloud of dust.

Coughing and battered from—luckily—small stones rather

than the huge ones piled all about, Wend scrambled to
her feet in terror and stumbled through that dusty
smokescreen in she knew not what direction. But when,
choking, she broke through the dust enough to see ahead,
she realized that she was heading for the high ground and
forthwith broke into a run, with the frowning castle on the
heights as a beckoning lodestar.

Her instinct to seek the high ground was correct, and as
she stumbled over fallen debris, she was calling out, moaning actually, that none of them should ever have left
England—nothing like this ever happened there!

Annette had only just been able to crawl out of the ruins
of her millinery shop when that first great wave, approaching at incredible speed, roared up the Tagus. She had
heard the distant roar of it and had with difficulty struggled to her feet from a welter of fallen masonry that had
left her bruised and bleeding.

Her one thought, as she fought free of the debris, had
been, *Let this earthquake have finished off both of them—
Charlotte and her daughter by that other man!*

She gained her feet in time to see the great wave
coming, towering, it seemed to her, a hundred feet into
the air above her. Always a survivor, Annette turned to
run, but she was too late. The wave smashed into the city
and a wall of water crashed through the smoldering ruins,
carrying ships and small boats and the debris of the streets
and buildings far inland and then retreating to sea with all
the broken bits of a civilization—and blanketing the sea
nearby with the dead.

The waters of that wave had not even subsided before a
second great convulsion struck Lisbon, breaking up what
had not been broken before, collapsing what had been
only cracked, churning the earth beneath the waters and
leaving a destroyed, gutted area in its wake.

In the inn, with his arm cradled around Cassandra,
Drew had waked early that morning. And lain there worrying. The tale Cassandra had told him last night was a
wild one, but one thing was certain: she was not safe here.
The feeling that the prince's enemies would seek her out
was so strong that he leapt up and told Cassandra that they

were leaving Lisbon. At once. No, they would not stop for breakfast, they would secure that on the road. They would not attempt to leave Lisbon by ship—the prince or someone else might reach out long arms to stop them. They would travel north overland to Oporto and take ship from there.

Cassandra would have liked to say good-bye to her mother, but Drew told her roughly that there was no time.

He was right, but not for the reasons he thought. They were making their way out of town and were passing a pretty house with a long veranda when the first great earthquake struck. Cassandra, just taking a step, caught her foot in the cobbles and staggered against Drew who, not expecting it and thrown off balance himself, gave ground. Around them the world was crashing down. The long veranda collapsed immediately and the rest of the house came tumbling after it, scattering stones and pillars and roof tiles in the street about them. All the streets around them were instantly clogged with rubble and made dangerous as well by the instant fires that sprang up to lick the ruins.

"My Mother's inn!" cried Cassandra. "She and Wend are there! It lies that way." She waved her hand in the direction of the Royal Cockerel. "We must go there and try to save them."

Drew looked about him grimly at the impassable streets, the great piles of dust-choked debris. "We'll be lucky to clamber over this rubble to safety before the fires reach us," he warned—and even as he spoke, flames spurted out of the fallen structure beside them. "And how we escaped that first rain of stones as those walls collapsed, I cannot understand. Oh, yes—you had just lurched against me. The stones are heavy where we were standing. Had you not flung yourself against me, we would both be dead." He gave her a sardonic look, this woman who had run away for fear she would bring him disaster. "So it seems you have brought me luck!"

Cassandra's green eyes widened. When the earthquake struck, she had for a terrible moment thought, *I have lured Drew to Lisbon and now I have brought him death!* But now he was telling her that she had *saved* him, that she had brought him luck!

Despite the horror of their situation, despite all that she must do, a reckless feeling of joy welled up in Cassandra. She was free to love him, free to love him at last! But even with the thought, reality crowded back and she was plucking at Drew's arm.

"I can't just run away, Drew. I've only just found my mother. I can't leave her here to die—and there's Wend as well."

"Perhaps we can strike up toward that castle on the hill." Drew cast a narrow glance upward. "I cannot see much through all this murky dust, but the streets do look a bit clearer up there. Come, we will circle around and work our way up. Perhaps we will be able to see a way to reach the Royal Cockerel from there."

Midway up the hill they encountered Wend, struggling toward them, dirty and bruised and wailing Cassandra's name as she hobbled quickly toward them.

"Oh, Wend, where is my mother?" cried Cassandra. "Why isn't she with you?"

"I don't think she came home last night," said Wend, who now that she had found friends was recovering her aplomb. "Leastways her bed wasn't slept in."

"I remember that her coach was already gone when I left last night," Cassandra recalled. "Oh, Wend, I mustn't have found her only to lose her again!"

"We'll find her," said Wend sturdily but she looked frightened.

"Let's keep going toward the castle," Drew's voice prodded them as a wave of acrid smoke billowed over them, making them choke. "We could be cut off where we stand."

Obediently they moved off, stopping now and then to help people struggle out of the ruins of houses they had lived in all their lives. It suddenly came to them, the reason why so few cries for help were coming out of the inferno below. It was All Hallows' Day, and almost everyone had gone to church.

And died there.

Even as they moved up the hill, Charlotte and Tom were hurrying down it, fighting their way through the rubble of walls and houses toward the church. But a wall of flame pushed them back and they were forced to retreat up the hill crowned by the Castelo de São Jorge, knowing it was no use. Through dancing orange flames and waves of sooty smoke they could see that the church was but a mound of rubble in which nothing could live.

Beside Tom, Charlotte was weeping softly for a man who, until the very day he died, had loved her.

But Tom, who had not known Don Carlos, for all his gravity and sympathy, was walking with a jauntier gait as he led Charlotte around and over small mountains of rubble that had once been houses and wells and garden walls. By a stroke of fate his lady would be his again! He would never know that Don Carlos, from the inferno of the city below, had planned it that way.

It was as they stopped to rest in their struggle upward toward the great frowning castle and looked back in awe upon the doomed city that they saw Cassandra and Drew and Wend climbing up toward them—and Charlotte's tears turned to tears of joy that her daughter had been spared.

She called out to Cassandra, beckoning her forward, but her voice was lost in a new thunder of sound from the seaward side as the second of the three huge "tidal waves" that were to inundate Lisbon that day raced in to further devastate the stricken city, where, among the thousands of houses destroyed, more than fifty palaces and more than thirty magnificent churches had already come crashing down. But even though they had not heard her calling, Cassandra had seen her, and presently she and Drew and Wend toiled up and joined them.

"Tom." Charlotte waved her arm airily. "Allow me to present to you your daughter, Cassandra!"

Tom, who had just straightened up from lifting a heavy beam to free a dog trapped in what was left of a house with broken shutters, was so startled that he missed a step on the cobbles and nearly fell on the dog, who ran yapping away.

"My *daughter?*" he said almost in disbelief. But his gaze had only to flick over Cassandra's coloring, so exactly like his own. "Charlotte," he murmured, "you are a wonder." And then he was embracing Cassandra and meeting Drew.

"You will come with us to Brazil, of course, Cassandra." Tom was very much the father figure now.

"Oh, yes, do!" cried Charlotte.

Drew Marsden shifted his feet restlessly. Cassandra could guess what he was thinking: *Leave Blade's End? Never!* And as for herself, the lands of perpetual sunshine were not for her. She loved the wild high crags and silvered skies of the north of England, she loved to see the sudden bursting of spring and to drink from her cupped hands the cold clear water that cascaded down from snow-capped peaks. Back in England her cream-colored mare, Meg, waited, eager to take her on wild rides among the lofty fells beside Drew's dappled stallion, the Bishop. Back at Aldershot Grange a long-haired cat with knowing green eyes was even now licking her paws and waiting for the day Cassandra would return so that she could leap into her lap and have her creamy fur stroked. Indeed Clover must have had her kittens by now—she would be eager to introduce them. And there would be long nights by the winter fire while the wind tore at the chimneys. . . .

"Drew and I want to be married in England," she told them.

Tom put a proprietary arm around Charlotte. "I will marry this lady anywhere she will have me," he said. "But I had hoped to have my daughter in attendance."

"No—I can't go to Brazil," said Cassandra. "Drew and I have spent too much time away from home already. We must go back and resume our lives."

Charlotte's face clouded with disappointment. "Perhaps," she said uncertainly, "we should not go to Brazil just yet, Tom. I have not yet seen Phoebe."

"She and Clive were busy escaping the bailiffs when last I heard," Cassandra warned her mother ruefully. "Phoebe will be hard to find!"

"I must go back," said Tom quietly.

"Well, then perhaps . . ." Charlotte gave Tom a look of yearning. She wanted so much to accompany him, to go where he was going, wherever that was—forever. And the sunny lands of the south were *her* lands, where she was meant to be. The daughter of the sunny Scillies would be at home amid the brilliantly colored flowers and rustling palms of faraway Brazil. She pictured herself there in the long-galleried house Tom had described, walking through its cool high-ceilinged rooms, hearing its fountain tinkle—indeed she could almost feel the hot sunlit tiles of the great courtyard beneath her feet at this moment. She cast a last look back at the fiery hell of the great doomed city, smoldering like a great funeral pyre. Carlos would be there forever now, his pain at last departed; she could leave him with a clear conscience, knowing she had done what she could. And—for a moment a look of slight distaste crossed her beautiful face—Don Carlos' greedy nephews would be delighted to believe that she too had perished in the holocaust of Lisbon. It would be a clean break. Carlotta del Valle would disappear forever and Charlotte Keynes would be reborn. As Charlotte Westing, at long last wife to the man who had won her heart so many years ago. "Perhaps we should not insist, Tom," she said softly. "After all we will be visiting Castle Stroud—"

"World's End," Tom corrected her, smiling.

"And they can come to Brazil to visit us—perhaps next year?"

"Oh, yes." Cassandra's voice was warm. "I'd like that so much!"

Tom was looking discomfited. Having discovered he had a daughter, he wanted to bring her home with him at once, show her the wealth and grandeur he now possessed, display her beauty and her charm to all the leading families of Rio de Janeiro.

"I had hoped to cover you with jewels." He laughed ruefully. "And show the world my daughter."

"You can send Cassandra presents," said Charlotte quickly. "And cover *me* with jewels!" She was laughing because no gems in all this world would ever mean so much to her as Tom's emerald eyes looking down upon her with so much love and trust.

"That I will do," sighed Tom.

Cassandra cast a look back at the smoldering city, and wondered what had happened to Leeds Birmingham. She felt a little chill pervade her. He had seemed so indestructible, she had felt he would go his laughing way forever. Could he too be lying, like so many others, crushed beneath the fallen stones of Lisbon's palaces with the flames licking at his bones?

Her somber gaze combed the billowing clouds of smoke. And as if in answer to her silent call, a figure was coming out of that smoke, a figure with soot-blackened face and clothes, with one cuff charred and all of him well-begrimed.

"Leeds!" she cried.

He came sauntering toward them with all of his old aplomb. "I came up here to see if you made it," he told Cassandra, nodding toward the little ruined church above them. "I remembered telling you to go there if anything happened. I had no idea you would have your own entourage." He glanced around him.

Cassandra was quick to introduce him.

"How fares the city?" asked Tom, knowing Leeds had just come from there.

"As you can see." Leeds shrugged and gestured toward the billowing smoke that rose threateningly even higher. "The king has turned everything over to Pombal and he'll be mopping up what's there before he sets loose the firing squads." As if to emphasize his words, there was a sporadic volley of gunfire from the great conflagration below.

"Then the royal family is safe?"

"All save Prince Damião," said Leeds blandly. "They cannot seem to find him. The rest of them were on the road to the Tower of Belem when the earthquake struck, and so were unharmed. If any of you are thinking of going down into the city to help out, abandon the idea. They will not let you through. Pombal has already stationed men to search out looters and shoot them. On a nervous day like today they are as like to shoot you as not."

"We were not thinking of going down," said Tom, frowning down at the holocaust.

"Pombal has also closed the ports," added Leeds.

At that moment the third of the three great earthquakes that were to hammer Lisbon that day jarred the city again. The group watched it shudder beneath the flames. The terrible ear-splitting sound washed over them, leaving them stunned.

"I have my own ship in Oporto," Tom volunteered. "I had left her there to have her keel scraped, but if she has not been too damaged by these great waves that have visited this coast, you may all voyage with me—to England or Brazil or anywhere along the way."

"Thank you. I may join you in Oporto." Having satisfied himself that Cassandra was all right, Leeds stretched and took a step back the way he had come.

"Oh, you aren't going back into *that?*" cried Cassandra unhappily.

He looked surprised. "But of course I'm going back. Who knows what may be found there on a day like today?"

"You'll be shot as a looter," Tom warned.

"Not I." Leeds grinned genially at him.

Tom recognized freebooter's blood when he saw it. He did not insist.

"But one last word." Leeds paused and smiled appraisingly at Cassandra. There was something very warm in that smile. "If you should find yourself tiring of this great fellow"—he nodded toward Drew—"you have only to let me know where you are, anywhere in the world. I will find you and take you away with me!" He was laughing as he strode back down the hill.

Cassandra's gaze followed him wistfully. He was the kind of man who would always go back into the fire—in search of what he might find there. And like as not he would come out of it with a whole hide. She wished him well.

They dined together at the little inn called the Castelo and looked out the window at a murky red sunset that turned the sky to blood except where the dark smoke swirled over Lisbon.

Cassandra smiled at Drew. Despite all that had befallen, tomorrow's sunset would be laced with gold. Perhaps she and Drew would not wait until they reached England to marry. Perhaps they would do as Charlotte and Tom proposed to do—let the captain of Tom's ship say the words over them that would bind them together lawfully, though with no bonds stronger than the love they already bore each other.

Tonight she would sleep in Drew's arms, tonight and all the nights to come. Ten thousand future sunsets would shower their golden radiance upon them and they would ride the wild crags forever!

The Gorringe Bank had done its deadly work. Africa and Europe had collided beneath the sea, crunching up parts of the outer shell of two gigantic continental plates.

And Lisbon, glorious Lisbon in its Golden Age, would never be the same.

But for those wayfarers beset by so many storms, for Drew and Cassandra, the pair of lovers who had found each other anew, and for Tom and Charlotte, the lovers who had found each other again, this time of peril and holocaust marked a new beginning, and love that would last, in the words of that Lowland Scottish song: *Till all the seas run dry.*

In the same room where they had embraced last night, Tom took Charlotte into his arms again.

"And so the wheel of fate turns full circle, Charlotte," he murmured against the sweet fragrance of her lemon-scented golden hair. "And we are together again, for we have survived everything."

And there above the burning tormented ruins of Lisbon it was so. For them, just as for young Cassandra and her Drew, the sea air would blow fresh and free, it would take them to worlds beyond the horizon, ever happy, ever young. . . .

Author's Note

The destruction of Lisbon on All Hallows' Day, 1755—by earthquake, fire, and "tidal wave"—was the greatest catastrophe of the eighteenth century. Three great earthquakes struck the city that day—the last two mainly stirred the rubble left by the first. These great shocks fanned out in all directions for a thousand miles. They jolted a third of Europe.

Scotland's fabled Loch Lomond on a windless day abruptly rose more than two feet and as suddenly fell back four. In Holland ships and buoys were torn free from their moorings as canals and rivers were beset by turbulence. In England plaster fell and a fissure opened in a field. Sweden's lakes sloshed ominously. All over Europe chandeliers swung and jangled, wells and springs were disturbed —some rose, some stopped flowing, some gushed red water or spewed out mud, as far away as Czechoslovakia, fourteen hundred miles away from the epicenter.

Nor did Africa escape. The great waves engendered by the collision of the continental plates and the shift of the undersea Gorringe Bank swept down toward North Africa and broke across the coast, washing some ten thousand people into the sea from the Moroccan coast alone. Those same waves reached England five hours later, the West Indies by evening, but by then their fury was largely spent. The Earth had spoken. . . .

At least fifty thousand died in Lisbon. The earthquake changed the face of Portugal and was felt over a million square miles, caused in England the sudden abandonment

533

of masquerades, inspired a rush of church attendance all over Europe for a year, began the study of seismology, and prompted the cynical Voltaire to write *Candide*.

London's earthquakes of 1750 took place on the dates I have described—indeed the strong quake on March 19 of that year was the strongest of six earthquakes that shook London between February and June; it panicked animals and fish, collapsed some houses, and knocked down numerous chimneys, as well as jarring stones from Westminster Abbey's new spire.

Although the characters and plot of this story are entirely of my own invention and there was no Prince Damião, most of the settings are real and readers will doubtless recognize many of them.

Grosvenor Square was developed just as I have shown it, and George I's exceedingly tall German mistress, "The Maypole," did actually reside at number forty-three.

The building in which I have set Mistress Effingham's school in Colchester will of course be recognized as Colchester's famous Old Siege House.

The Legend of Fox Elve with its Golden Maiden is a fanciful tale of my own devising, as is the great peak of Kenlock Crag, where Tom is thrust over; but Buttermere and Cat Bells, Friar's Crag, the Jaws of Borrowdale and Castlerigg Stone Circle are all as real as the silvery Derwent Water.

Castle Stroud is lovely Haddon Hall, almost to the life, although I have spirited it away, complete with terraced gardens, from Derbyshire and deposited it along the east bank of the Derwent Water in Cumberland. I chose Haddon not only because of its beauty but also because of its parallels to my story—the romantic elopement of Dorothy Vernon with her lover John Manners in 1558, as well as the fact that Haddon, like the Castle Stroud of my story, was abandoned by its owners in 1700 and left to molder—in Haddon's case for more than two centuries. I was kinder; I allowed Castle Stroud to molder only slightly more than half a hundred years!

Blade's End, where Cassandra's lover lives, although more ruined, is based closely upon Elizabethan Chavenage in Gloucestershire—I have even transported some of its furniture and its interesting tapestries named "Cromwell" and "Ireton" to the banks of the Derwent Water.

Although Gretna Green did not become a popular marrying spot for English runaway lovers until after London's half-accepted Fleet Street marriage mart was closed to them, it was still the law in Scotland that anyone could perform a marriage ceremony before witnesses, and at least in England's North Country it was common enough for runaway lovers to flee across the border and there be married, like as not by some village blacksmith with an anvil for an altar.

The Lisbon that we see today is not the Lisbon of Charlotte's time. It was largely rebuilt by Pombal (for brevity's sake I have referred to Sebastião José de Carvalho e Mello as the Marquês de Pombal throughout).

In all, three enormous waves, looking higher than mountains from the streets of the doomed city, rushed up the Tagus from the Atlantic and broke over Lisbon that day. Sweeping back seaward, they took with them the debris of a civilization—jewels and plate, destroyed paintings by masters like Rubens and Titian, broken gilt furniture, crosses and goblets, silks and tapestries, coaches and horses and broken ships—and the dead. Always the dead.

And with the destruction of fabulous Lisbon, Portugal's Golden Age—born of diamonds and gold and sailing ships and the spices of the Indies—ended forever.

We shall not know its like again.

The Devil's hand shook Lisbon town
And brought the houses crashing down,
Sent great waves roaring from the sea,
Fulfilling her doomed destiny. . . .
The Devil took his choice that day
Of human pawns with which to play,
Chose who should live and who should die
Beneath a thunderous smoke-filled sky. . . .
           —Valerie Sherwood